Forever in Time

Also available from
BARBARA BRETTON
and MIRA Books

GUILTY PLEASURES
STARFIRE
SHOOTING STAR
NO SAFE PLACE

BARBARA BRETTON

Forever in Time

ISBN 0-7783-2136-3

FOREVER IN TIME

www.MIRABooks.com

Printed in U.S.A.

CONTENTS

SOMEWHERE IN TIME

In memory of John and Abigail Adams,
who continue to show me what true love is all about

With special thanks to the following friends
who made the impossible possible:
Lass Small, who worried;
Susan C. Feldhake, who advised;
Sandra Marton, who understood;
Dallas Schulze, who gave me the most valuable
commodity a writer has—her time.

"She was what a woman ought to be."

—tombstone of one
Woman of Trenton,
late eighteenth century

Prologue

Zane Grey Rutledge downshifted into second as he guided the black Porsche up the curving driveway toward Rutledge House. Gravel crunched beneath the tires, sending a fine spray across the lacquered surface of the hood and fenders. He swore softly as a pebble pinged against the windshield, leaving behind a spiderweb crack in the glass. He stopped the car behind a huge moving van and let out the clutch. The bricks had faded and the stones were worn smooth, but still the house stood, proud home to more generations of Rutledges than Zane had desire to count.

"One day it will matter to you," his grandmother Sara Jane had said to him not long before she died. "There's nothing more important than family."

Sara Jane had been dead now for three months and finally he was about to put the last of her estate to rights. Lately he'd had the feeling that she was watching him from somewhere in the shadows, shaking her head the way she used to when he was a boy and he'd been caught drinking beer with his friends from the wrong side of town.

He leaned back in his contoured leather seat and watched as the treasures of a lifetime were carried from the house by a parade of moving men. Winterhalter portraits of long-dead Rutledges, books and mementos that cataloged a nation's history as well as a family's.

His fingers drummed the steering wheel in a nervous rhythm. He'd done the right thing. Damn it, it was the *only* thing he could have done, given the circumstances. Playing curator to a museum masquerading as a house held little appeal for him. He wasn't about to change his way of life to suit a collection of inanimate objects just because they came with a pedigree as long as his. So far he'd done a pretty good job of escaping responsibility and he wasn't about to blow his reputation as the black sheep of the family at this late date.

Not that there was any family left to speak of. Sara Jane's death had seen to that. With her passing, the once-mighty Rutledges of Pennsylvania had only Zane to carry on the tradition of pride and patriotism that had begun back in the time of the revolutionary war. Too bad there was no one else around to appreciate the joke.

"Mr. Rutledge? Oh, Mr. Rutledge, it *is* you. I was so afraid I'd missed you."

He started at the sound of a woman's voice floating through the open window of the car.

"Olivia McRae," she said, smiling coyly. "We met last week."

He opened the door and unfolded himself from the sleek sports car. "I remember," he said, shaking the woman's birdlike hand. "Eastern Pennsylvania Preservation Society."

She dimpled, and Zane was struck by the fact that in her day Olivia McRae had probably been a looker.

"We have much to thank you for. I must tell you we feel as if Christmas has come early this year!"

He cast her a quizzical look. She was thanking him? In the past few days he had come to think of her as his own personal savior for taking Rutledge House and its contents off his hands.

"A pleasure," he said, relying on charm to cover his surprise.

"Oh, it's a fine day for Rutledge House," she said her tone upbeat. "I know your dear departed grandmother Sara Jane would heartily approve of your decision."

"'Approve' might be too strong a word," he said with a wry grin.

"Accept is more like it." Bloodlines had been everything to Sara Jane Rutledge. No matter that the venerable old house had been tumbling down around her ears, in need of more help than even the family fortune could provide. So long as a Rutledge was in residence, all had been right with the world.

"Just you wait," said Olivia McRae, patting him on the forearm in a decidedly maternal gesture. "Next time you see it, this wonderful old house will be on its way to regaining its former glory."

"It's your business now, Olivia. Yours and the state of Pennsylvania." He'd never been one to bow down before the grandeur of history, family or otherwise. He didn't give a damn if he never saw Rutledge House again.

"We would welcome your input," the older woman said. "And we would most certainly like to have a Rutledge on the board of directors at the museum."

"Sorry," he said, perhaps a beat too quickly. "I think a clean break is better all around."

The woman's warm brown eyes misted over with tears. "How thoughtless of me! This must be dreadfully difficult, coming so soon after the loss of your beloved grandmother."

Zane looked away. Little in life unnerved him. Talk of his late grandmother did. "I have a plane to catch," he said gruffly. No matter that the plane didn't take off until tomorrow afternoon. As far as he was concerned, emotions were more dangerous than skydiving without a chute. "I'd better be on my way."

Olivia McRae peered into the car. "You do have the package, don't you?"

"Package?" His brows knotted. "I don't know anything about a package."

"Oh, Mr. Rutledge, you *must* have the package I set out for you." She looked at him curiously. "The uniform."

"Damn," he muttered under his breath. "I'd forgotten." *The oldest male child in each generation is entrusted with the uniform,* his grandmother had told him on his twelfth birthday when she'd handed him the carefully wrapped package. *Someday you'll hand it down to your son.*

Not if he could help it.

He hadn't forgotten about the uniform. He knew exactly where it was: in the attic under a thick layer of dust, as forgotten as the past should be—and usually was.

"You wait right here," said Mrs. McRae, turning back toward the house. "I'll fetch it for you."

He was tempted to get behind the wheel of the Porsche and be halfway to Manhattan before the woman crossed the threshold. For as long as he could remember, that damn uniform had been at the heart of Rutledge family lore. His grandmother had woven endless stories of derring-do and bravery and laid every single one of them at the feet of some long-dead relative who'd probably never done anything more courageous than shoot himself a duck for dinner.

Moments later Olivia McRae was back by his side.

"Here you are," she said, pressing a large, neatly wrapped package into his arms with the tenderness a mother would display toward her firstborn. "To think you almost left without it."

Zane looked at the package curiously. "Heavier than I thought it would be," he said. "You sure there isn't a musket in there with the uniform?"

Mrs. McRae's lined cheeks dimpled. "Oh, you! You always *were* a tease. Why, you must have seen this uniform a million times."

"Afraid I never paid much attention."

"That can't be true."

"I've never been much for antiques."

"This is more than an antique," said Mrs. McRae, obviously appalled. "This is a piece of American history... *your* history." She patted the parcel. "Open it, Mr. Rutledge. I'd love to see your face when you—"

"I will," he said, edging toward the Porsche, "but right now I have a plane to catch."

"Of course," she said, her smile fading. "I understand."

She looked at him and in her eyes Zane saw disappointment. But why should Mrs. McRae be any different? Disappointing people was what he did best. He tossed the package into the back seat and with a nod toward Olivia McRae roared back down the driveway and away from Rutledge House.

As always, Manhattan welcomed him with open arms. The anonymity of the crowded city soothed his restless nature in a way the security of hearth and home never could. Nobody expected anything of him in Manhattan, and he'd managed to live down to the lowest expectations.

Not even the dense traffic coming through the Lincoln Tunnel was enough to deter him, or the stop-and-go progress he made as he traveled from the west side to his co-op east of Fifth Avenue.

His apartment was on the thirtieth floor of a faceless high rise not far from UN Plaza. He'd bought it a few years earlier, flush from a great run at the baccarat table in Monte Carlo. *You can't put down roots in midair,* his grandmother had said, shaking her head in dismay. He'd smiled and told her that was exactly why he'd bought the place.

He didn't want a home, not in the way Sara Jane had meant it. That was one of the reasons for the failure of his marriage. The apartment was base camp, the place where he stowed his supplies and picked up his mail and made plans to move on to somewhere else. Running the bulls at Pamplona. Parasailing off the Kona coast. It didn't matter. The point was to keep moving.

He'd learned that lesson as a child and it was one lesson he never forgot. As soon as you grew attached to a place, you were in trouble. There was no gain to be found in getting comfortable.

"Afternoon, Mr. Rutledge." The liveried doorman tipped his hat to Zane. "Thought you were on your way to Australia."

"Tahiti," said Zane as he entered the gilt-and-marble lobby. "Tomorrow afternoon."

The doorman, a retired mechanic from Bensonhurst, sighed loudly. "Boy, that's the life," he said, massaging the small of his back. "You musta seen just about everything this world has to offer."

"Just about," said Zane. And a few things the gods would envy. Why it no longer seemed to be enough was a good question.

"Sorry to hear about your grandma. Hope her passing was easy."

"It was," said Zane, heading for the elevator. "Thanks for asking."

The elevator rose swiftly to the thirtieth floor, and moments later Zane let himself into his apartment. Cool, silvery-gray walls. An endless expanse of polished, bare wood floors. So relentlessly geared for function over style that it became stylish by default.

Not that he gave a damn, he thought, as he tossed the package containing the uniform onto an off-white leather-and-chrome chair. To be stylish you had to care and there were few things in his thirty-four years that Zane had cared much about.

Sara Jane, however, was one of them.

He yanked off his tie, slipped out of his jacket, then headed for the bottle of Scotch waiting for him atop the bar. Modern life had its benefits, but not even the wonders of the twentieth century could hold a candle to the sweet oblivion to be found in a bottle of good Scotch. He poured three fingers of the potent liquid into a heavy tumbler, paused, then poured some more.

Sara Jane Rutledge had lived ninety-three years, all but one of them in robust good health. When she'd found out she was dying, she had approached the inevitable with the same grace and fortitude for which she was known. He doubted if he would have been able to summon up as much courage as that tiny, white-haired woman had managed to do. "A new adventure," she'd told him during their last conversation. "In a strange way I'm looking forward to it."

He shook his head at the memory, then downed a long swallow of Scotch. There were people who said he courted death with his exploits. Race cars...cigarette boats with keels made to slice through the water...planes that climbed high and fast, then flung open their doors for him to challenge the wind. It wasn't death he was courting, not really. He had simply learned early on that if he kept moving he had at least a fighting chance to stay ahead of the loneliness.

Things came easily for him. They always had. Good grades when he'd needed them. Women when he wanted them. He'd been blessed with acute powers of observation and a damn good memory. He even walked away from car wrecks without a scratch. The only thing he'd failed at had been his marriage and he liked to think even that hadn't left a scar.

His gaze wandered to the package resting on the far edge of the bar. "I almost got out of there without you," he said, glaring at it. He'd noticed it the other day when he was up in the attic at Rutledge House, showing the moving men what to pack, and had assumed it would have been on its way to the museum by now with all the rest of the stuff.

So why hadn't he handed it right back to nice little Olivia McRae and been done with it? There wasn't a law against giving away family heirlooms. If there was, he wouldn't have been able to unload the portraits or the jewelry or the contents of Sara Jane's library, either.

You didn't think I was going to let you get away without a fight, did you, boy?

He started, spilling Scotch on the front of his shirt. Two gulps of booze and he was hearing Sara Jane's voice? Ridiculous. Probably his guilty conscience speaking. He would have given his grandmother anything, except the one thing she really wanted: a family to continue the Rutledge name.

It's not too late, Zane. Open your eyes to what's around you and your heart will soon follow....

He wasn't entirely certain he had one.

He put down his glass and stalked toward the other end of the bar and the wrapped package containing the uniform. Experience had taught him the best way to handle anything, from a hangover to a guilty conscience, was the hair of the dog that bit you.

"Okay," he said, unknotting the string, then folding back the brown paper. There was nothing scary about a moth-eaten hunk of cloth. "Let's take a look."

He pushed aside the buff-colored breeches and inspected the navy blue coat. Dark beige cuffs and lapels. A line of tarnished metal buttons. The only unusual thing about the garment was the decorative stitching inside the left cuff and under the collar. He looked again. He was surprised to note that the shoulders of the jacket seemed broad enough to fit him, and he was a man of above-average size. He didn't know all that much about history, but he vividly remembered diving off the Florida coast around the wreck of the Atocha some years back and noting the almost lilliputian scale.

What are you going to do, Zane, toss it in your closet and forget it the way you forgot everything else? You owe my memory more than that....

"This is getting weird," he said out loud. Next thing he knew he'd find himself breaking bread with a six-foot rabbit named Harvey. "I'm on my way to Tahiti. I don't have time for this."

Make time, boy! Wasn't I the only one who ever made time for you?

The truth hurt. Sara Jane was the one person he'd been able to count on when he was growing up, the only one who'd never let him down. This was the least he could do for her—even if it was too late to really matter.

Two hours later he climbed back behind the wheel of the Porsche. It wasn't possible. The odds were just too damn unbelievable.

Yet time and again he'd heard the same thing: "Emilie Crosse is the one for you." A Rutgers professor and two museum curators had all sung the praises of this woman with the old-fashioned name and outdated occupation. The woman who just happened to be his ex-wife.

"You play dirty, Sara Jane," he said as he headed across town toward the Lincoln Tunnel, "but it's not going to work. I'm dropping off the uniform and getting the hell out of there, understand?"

It's a start, boy. It's a start.

Chapter One

1

At the moment her life changed forever, Emilie was standing on a stepladder on her front porch watering a flowering begonia plant that had seen better days. She was considering whether or not to put the poor thing out of its misery when the roar of a car engine brought her up short.

She wasn't expecting anyone. The most traffic her street usually saw was the appearance of the red-white-and-blue U.S. mail jeep every morning, and the jeep's engine sputtered rather than roared.

She climbed down from the ladder and, wiping her hands on the sides of her pants, glanced toward the street. The sound grew closer. Then, to her amazement, a shiny black foreign car turned into her driveway. She didn't know too much about foreign cars, but it didn't take an automotive genius to figure out you could run the Crosse Harbor school system on what the driver had paid for that sleek beauty.

It roared up her driveway as if it were the home stretch of the Indianapolis 500, and she bristled with indignation when it screeched to a stop near her own sedate sedan.

She hated people who drove fancy cars as if they owned the road and everyone on it. As far as she was concerned, a car was nothing more than a hunk of metal, four rubber wheels and a lot of extra parts that broke down when you could least afford it.

A Porsche, she noted. Flashy, sexy, impossible to ignore.

She'd known only one person in her life who wouldn't be overshadowed by a car like that and she'd been crazy enough to marry him—and sane enough to divorce him six months later.

"It couldn't be," she said as she stood on the top step, doing her best to ignore the sudden jolt of excitement that urged her to fly down the porch steps and tear open the car door. Tinted windows should be outlawed, she thought wildly. It wasn't fair that the driver could see her while she—

The car door swung open and the driver of the Porsche climbed out.

She leaned against the railing for support, feeling as if she'd looked into the heart of the sun. Real men didn't look like that. He looked like the pirate hero on the cover of a romance novel, dangerous and compelling and totally out of this world.

She pinched herself sharply on the inside of her arm then looked again, but he didn't disappear the way dreams always did. Instead he started toward her, his long legs eating up the distance between them with powerful strides. She wanted to run. She wanted to hide. She wanted a crash course in 101 Reasons Why Divorce Was The Only Solution.

Hiding her trembling hands behind her back, she offered up an easy smile.

He didn't smile back. Why was it gorgeous men never smiled? She wondered if it was some code of honor or a congenital incapability.

He had a small cleft in his chin, a stubborn jaw and the most unabashedly sensual mouth she'd ever seen. She remembered how that mouth had felt pressed against—

"Been a long time, Emilie," he said in a voice so rich with testosterone that it made her knees buckle. "You look great."

"Don't tell me," she said. "Let me guess. You were in the neighborhood and decided to drop by." She snapped her fingers. "So what if it's been five years?"

"Still the feisty redhead. I'm glad some things never change."

"Did it ever occur to you to call first?"

"Why?" he countered. "You're here, aren't you?"

She glanced pointedly toward the watch on her left wrist then back at him. "Is there something I can do for you?"

"You're not going to ask me in?"

"I hadn't planned on it."

He flashed his movie-star grin. "You used to be a lot friendlier."

"And a lot dumber. You're here for a reason, Zane, and it isn't to talk about old times." She sounded cool and collected. He'd never in a million years suspect the way her heart was thundering inside her chest.

"I have a package in the car," he said. "I'd like you to take a look at it."

"I'd be happy to," she said, "but you'll have to make an appointment."

"But I'm leaving for Tahiti tomorrow afternoon."

"Then you can make an appointment for when you return." He'd always been on his way to Tahiti or the Hamptons or the Côte d'Azur, too busy looking for a good time to see that happiness had been right there for the asking.

And he'd always been able to do this to her, turn a sensible, intelligent woman into a hopeless romantic with a soft spot for happily ever after....

Don't give up so easily, boy. Convince her. Zane started at the sound of Sara Jane's voice in his ear. He hoped his grandmother was enjoying this encounter more than he was.

Sara Jane had to be enjoying it more than Emilie was. His ex-wife was glaring up at him with that redhead's intensity that had always been part of her appeal. The other part of her appeal was obvious. She was a beautiful woman—difficult, but beautiful. Their brief marriage had been a wild blend of sexual chemistry, romantic love and the absolute certainty that it could never last.

Still, the sight of her stirred something inside him, something he hadn't felt in a very long time.

Unfortunately she didn't seem to be feeling anything but impatient, and he pushed aside nostalgia in favor of the business at hand.

All it usually took was a sincere smile or two to win fair maiden. He had an address book filled with the names of women who enjoyed his company. How hard could it be to convince his ex-wife to look at a uniform?

"Look," he said, leaning forward, all charm and persistence, "this is important."

She started to protest, but he held up his hand to stop her.

"I made a promise to someone I care about and you're the only one who can help me."

"How do you know I'm the only one who can help you? If I remember right, you thought my career was a lot of nonsense."

"You've built yourself quite a reputation out there, Em. I called two museums and a professor at Rutgers and they all came back with the same name: yours." He upped the wattage on his smile. "I'm impressed."

"Don't be," she said. "It has nothing to do with you."

"I know," he said honestly. "And I'm still impressed."

"Well," she said, offering up her first smile of the encounter, "that's very flattering."

"It's meant to be." He gestured toward the car. "Will you take a look?"

"Five minutes," she said. "If I think I can help you, we'll work something out after you get back from your vacation."

Emilie waited on the top step while he jogged over to the car and retrieved a brown paper-wrapped parcel from the passenger seat. He cut a dashing figure in his tailored gray pants and white shirt of silky Egyptian cotton. Broad shoulders. Narrow hips. Powerful legs. Definitely the poster boy for pirate fantasies.

Too bad her idea of marriage had entailed more than great sex and a well-worn passport.

"Okay," he said, thrusting the parcel at her as he mounted the porch steps. "Here it is. When do we start?"

She eyed the package. "What is it?"

"A uniform."

"How old?"

"Two hundred plus a decade or two."

She whistled low. "Bring it inside. We don't want to expose the uniform to any more light than necessary."

"Don't tell me you're one of those ozone-layer crazies."

She shot him a look. "Don't tell me you're one of those idiots who think all's well with the world."

"You can't turn back the clock," he said as she led him inside the house. "Technology's given us a hell of a lot more than it's taken away."

"Right," said Emilie, ushering him into her studio at the side of the house. "Acid rain...smog...shall I go on?"

"I should've known you'd become an Earth Day groupie," he said as he tossed the package down on the worktable. "Can't see the trees for the rain forest."

"Spare me your list of technological wonders," she snapped. "We could live without microwaves and computers. We can't live without clean water and fresh air."

"No wonder you're good with antiques," he shot back. "You always did think like one."

"Okay," said Emilie, folding her arms across her chest. *I don't care how gorgeous you are.* "That does it. Goodbye, Rutledge. It's been interesting, if not enjoyable."

He stared at her blankly. How anyone so good-looking could be so dense struck Emilie as a terrible waste of natural resources.

"What about the uniform?"

"That's your problem," she said with a dismissive look. *A uniform, Emilie! A two-hundred-year-old uniform. My God....* It took every ounce of willpower at her command to keep from ripping into the package. The last revolutionary-war-era uniform she'd actually worked on had come her way over four years ago and, unfortunately, it had proved to be a lost cause. Time and the elements had done damage not even Emilie could undo.

He glared at her from across the room. "You promised me five minutes."

"And I've already given you eight."

"You said you'd examine the uniform."

"Why bother? I know you, Zane. You've probably had it dry-cleaned three times and lined it with mink."

"Wrong again. Original equipment from collar to cuffs."

The temptation was more than she could bear. "All right," she said in her most businesslike tone of voice. "Let's take a look."

She approached the workbench with the edgy excitement of a high roller at a no-limits table. Except no high roller worth her weight in chips would have hands that trembled the way Emilie Crosse's trembled as she began to untie the string.

He would have liked to think it was his overwhelming male presence that brought about that reaction, but he had the feeling she really found this stuff exciting.

"Damn," she muttered under her breath as her slender fingers worked at the knot. He'd already noticed she didn't wear a wedding ring and cursed himself roundly for looking.

"Need some help?"

"Scissors," she said, gnawing at her full lower lip. "The red ones on the pegboard."

"Real authentic," he drawled as he handed her the scissors. "Didn't I see Made in Taiwan on the blade?"

"Very funny," she said, not looking at him. The string fell away at the first touch of the implement, then she moved to fold back the thick brown paper.

An odd sensation moved its way up his spine, raising the hairs on the back of his neck. *See, Zane! I told you so. It's starting to matter!* Sweat broke out at his temples. He felt as if he was standing at the end of a long pier and Circe herself was beckoning him into the floodwaters rushing past.

There was no reason for hearing voices—or for the almost unbearable sense of anticipation that gripped him by the throat and refused to let go.

Emilie's sharp exhalation of breath echoed throughout the room as the centuries came to life beneath her fingertips. *It's your imag-*

ination. You've read too many books.... Still, there was no explaining the sound of drums beating cadence in her ears or the icy winds of Valley Forge raising goose bumps on her arms and legs.

I know this uniform, she thought. Each decision made by that long-ago tailor was one she would have made herself. The alterations had been skillfully rendered, made even more unusual by the fact that the sleeves had been altered to fit a shorter man.

Zane broke the silence. "So what do you think?"

She swung around to look at him, her eyes flashing fury. "If this is some kind of joke, so help me, I'll—"

"It's not a joke."

She traced the collar with her fingertips. She'd always favored that method of rolling a collar, although she'd never seen it used in colonial-era garments. "It's a reproduction—it has to be. The color is too rich...the weave is still tight...."

"It's not a reproduction," he said. "It's the real thing."

"Believe me, two hundred years leave their mark on a garment. I've made a career out of undoing the damage time can cause."

"Okay, then prove it's a reproduction." She didn't expect him to leave so soon, did she? Damn it, he wanted to watch her breathe just a little while longer....

She turned the uniform over and held the back seam up to the light. "Look at this," she ordered. "The fibers are long and supple. Very little stress on any of the stitches. This wasn't worn more than a handful of times."

"I suppose you're going to tell me the fabric is polyester?"

She shook her head. Okay, so she still didn't have a sense of humor. She was still beautiful.

"It's wool, all right. Tight weave...." The texture and weight and smell of the wool used in colonial army uniforms. The drum beat louder inside her head. "I just don't see how—"

"But it's possible?"

"Logically, no." She pressed the uniform to her nose, inhaling the heavy smell of wool and vegetable dye. It couldn't be...it simply couldn't.

"But?"

"There's one way to find out," she said, looking up at him. "If you could give me an hour, we'll know for sure."

"I don't have an hour. I have a long drive back to New York."

"And a plane to catch."

He looked at her sharply. "And a plane to catch."

"Then I can't give you an answer." She sounded cool and self-possessed, but inside, her stomach was twisted in sailor's knots. *Oh, God,* she thought. *You can't leave now. There's something happening here...something I don't understand.* Everything about the uniform seemed strangely familiar, from the braid of stitches that formed the buttonhole to the hand-finished seams.

He reached for the uniform and their fingers brushed. A brief spark flashed between them. She pulled her hand away as if burned.

"Static electricity," she said, ducking her head to hide her embarrassment. She still felt his touch reverberating through her body.

"Right," he said, totally unconvinced.

There was enough sexual electricity in that room to light Atlantic City and he found it impossible to believe she wasn't aware of it. She was close enough for him to catch the scent of spring flowers in her hair, and his blood quickened.

No way was he about to make that mistake again.

He glanced at his watch. "An hour's pushing it," he said. "Thirty minutes would be better."

"It's a deal. Just let me run a few tests on a fabric sample and see what we come up with." She pointed toward a wooden stool to the left of an enormous spinning wheel. "You can sit over there while I get started."

He took his first real look around him. The studio was a dizzying blend of color and texture and style. Colonial samplers vied for wall space with Erte prints and a Renoir poster of an extremely healthy female nude. Despite the twentieth-century intrusions, however, there was no mistaking the fact that the love of Emilie's life was the colonial era in American history. Back when they were first married he had teased her mercilessly about living in the past. Little did he know she'd end up doing it professionally.

"Do you really use this thing?" he asked, inclining his head in the direction of the spinning wheel.

"Of course I do," she said, casting a curious glance at him.

He spun the wheel, listening to the creak of wood. "Seems like a lot of work to make a piece of thread." He'd always believed if you couldn't find it in a store, you didn't really need it.

"It is a lot of work." She filled a basin with liquid from a brown bottle then stirred the mixture with a wooden spoon. "It's also a lot of fun."

He looked skeptical but Emilie ignored him. He hadn't understood her when they were married and there was no reason to assume he'd understand her now. He was a fast-food, fast-car type of man, while she longed for the days of butter churns and coaches-and-fours.

She worked quickly, easing open a seam and snipping a tiny swatch of fabric. She was painfully conscious of every detail in the room, from the scratchiness of the wool to the sound of his breathing to the way she couldn't quite shake the feeling that the adventure of a lifetime was about to begin.

Zane had no idea what the hell she was doing over there at the worktable and he didn't particularly care. He liked watching the way she moved, studying the graceful line of her shoulders and back, remembering how she had felt beneath him, all warm and open and ready….

He shifted position on the stool, grateful she had her back to him.

She wasn't particularly friendly, and she'd been anything but flirtatious; still, he found himself content to sit there and watch her fiddle around with inanimate objects as if she was a first-run movie and he was her captive audience.

But she'd always had that effect on him. The only thing they'd ever had in common was a major physical attraction, and they'd leaped headfirst into marriage, refusing to believe they'd ever need anything else.

The marriage was over.

He couldn't say the same thing about the physical attraction.

Maybe it was the fact that she seemed totally immune to his masculine charms that made her more alluring by the second. Was she in love with somebody? Not that it mattered to him, but he glanced around the workroom looking for clues. No photographs hanging on the walls. No men's clothes or shoes anywhere. He considered excusing himself to use the john and taking a quick look through the rest of the house for any telltale signs of an active love life, but, all things taken into account, he'd rather just sit there and watch her breathe.

Why on earth was he watching her so closely? Emilie could feel the heat of his gaze burning through the thin fabric of her shirt. For a man who seemed uninterested in the uniform she was examining, he hadn't taken his eyes from the proceedings…or from her.

"It's getting terribly hot in here." Emilie tossed her hair over her shoulder as she positioned a tiny scrap of fabric on a glass slide. She tried to sound matter-of-fact, but had the feeling she'd failed miserably. "Would you raise the air conditioning, please?"

She heard the scrape of the step stool against the tile floor, followed by Rutledge's footsteps as he walked across the room to the thermostat on the far wall.

"Thanks," she mumbled, not looking up. "Strange the way it got hotter after dusk, isn't it?"

"No," he said, his voice a rough caress. "Doesn't seem strange to me at all."

She waited for the sound of the stool scraping against the floor again as he sat back down, but it didn't come.

"I'll be a while longer," she said, struggling to sound casual and unconcerned. "Make yourself comfortable."

"I'm comfortable."

She jumped at the sound of his voice so close to her ear. "Don't stand over me like that, Zane. This is very precise work."

"I won't get in your way."

"You *are* in my way." She gestured toward the overhead fixtures. "You're blocking the light."

"I thought you were using the microscope."

"Would you please sit down?" she persisted, her voice unnaturally high. "This is serious business." And she was having a terrible time remembering that fact with him standing there next to her, close enough for her to breathe in the smell of his skin.

He retreated to the wooden stool. "Is this good enough?"

"It's fine."

"I don't want to get in your way."

"You're not in my way any longer."

"I'll just sit here and watch you."

"Great."

Not great. There was no way on earth the air-conditioning system could keep pace with the heat building inside her body. Damn it. They'd been divorced for five years. Wouldn't you think she'd be immune to him by now?

She cleared her throat. "I have a TV in the front room."

"I'll pass."

"You could catch the end of local news."

"Not interested." He glanced up at the clock. "You going to be much longer?"

"Just...another...minute." She bent over the uniform, squinting against the harsh glare of a high-intensity light clamped to the side of the worktable.

There was something happening in that room, something he didn't understand, but apparently he was the only one aware of it. He didn't like the way she made him feel, off balance and hungry for something he couldn't put a name to.

The hunger was soul deep and it scared the living hell out of him. It had always been like this. From the first moment he'd seen her, pinning a satin dress to a skin-and-bones model in a Hollywood costume studio, he'd known Emilie represented the one thing in the world he could never have.

That hadn't stopped him, however. Their courtship had been as swift and wild as a summer storm, and their impulsive wedding had been more the act of a desperate man, hell-bent on hanging on to something he really didn't understand.

She'd always managed to elude him. He'd known her body intimately but he'd never quite managed to touch her soul.

He brought himself up short. Introspection had never been his strong suit. This whole escapade had been a lousy idea and the sooner he escaped, the better he would feel.

"Look," he said, approaching the worktable, "I've run out of minutes. I've got a long drive ahead of me."

"What about the uniform?"

"I trust you," he said. "I'll pick it up when I get back."

"Don't trust me." She turned to face him. "I think it's the real thing."

He arched a brow. "I thought you said that was impossible."

"Lots of things are impossible. That doesn't mean they don't happen anyway." She smoothed her hands over the chest of the uniform jacket, palms tingling from the scratch of wool. "Try it on."

"Forget it."

"I need to see how it drapes."

He gestured toward a mannequin in the far corner of the room. This whole damn night was getting out of hand. "Let your pal try it on."

She shook her head. "Not good enough. I need some motion."

What are you afraid of, Zane? It's only a uniform.

"Shut up, Sara Jane," he mumbled.

"What was that?" asked Emilie.

"Nothing," he said, vaguely embarrassed. He reached for the uniform. "Let me try the damn thing on, then I'm out of here."

She held up the jacket for him to slip his arms into the sleeves. "I know it's none of my business anymore, but you really should do something about that attitude of yours."

"There's nothing wrong with my attitude." He rotated his shoulders, settling the regimental jacket into place, then changed the subject. "It fits."

Emilie's eyes widened. "Like it was made for you." She tugged at the cuffs, settling them over his wrist bones. The fit was perfect. "The odds of finding a uniform large enough for a man your size are—"

"A million to one?"

"Just about."

Of course it fits you, boy. You're a Rutledge, aren't you?

Emilie tilted her head and looked at him curiously. "Did you say something?"

He shook his head.

"I'm sure I heard something." Her brow furrowed and she looked at him even more closely. "Are you okay?"

"I'm fine."

"You don't look fine."

"I will once I get out of this thing."

"But I wanted you to try on the breeches."

"I don't wear tights." He yanked off the coat and handed it to her.

"They're not tights," she said, a grin tugging at her lush and beautiful mouth. "Spandex is a new invention."

"I don't give a damn if George Washington wore them. I don't."

"You'd probably look great in them. You always did have terrific legs."

"Forget it."

"Okay," she said. "I give up. I'll wrap the uniform back up and you can be on your way." She should have known better. She'd made this same mistake the first time they'd met, only she'd been younger and naive enough to believe in happy endings. That's why they were called fantasies; no woman in her right mind expected them to come true.

"You can keep the uniform."

"No," said Emilie. "This is a piece of history."

"History means nothing to me," he said bluntly. "You might as well keep the uniform for all the good it'll do me." *This isn't going the way I'd hoped, Zane....*

"If it doesn't matter to you," she shot back, "why did you come here?"

Again that odd sizzle of electricity in his veins, a rush of adrenaline with no place to go. How did you tell your ex-wife that your dead grandmother's voice had told you to come? She'd be dialing

911 before he reached the hallway. "It seemed like a good idea at the time."

"Remind me to tell Professor Attleman at Rutgers to recommend someone else next time around." She reached for the brown paper the uniform had been wrapped in.

"I wasn't kidding about the uniform. You can have it. It already means more to you than it ever will to me."

"If sentiment doesn't carry any weight with you, how about money? It's worth a small fortune."

"I'm rich. I won't miss it."

"Don't you care about anything?"

"Not if I can help it."

"You haven't changed a bit," she said with a shake of her head. "I feel sorry for you."

"Don't. I do what I want, go where I want, whenever I want. Most people would kill to have my life."

"You can't run forever," she said, not understanding why she cared. "Sooner or later you'll have to slow down long enough to figure out why you're so lonely."

He laughed out loud. "Lonely? Give me a break. You don't know a damn thing about my life anymore."

She looked at him as if she could see into his soul. "I'm right, aren't I?"

He bent down and kissed her hard and fast on the mouth, a kiss of anger and need and lost possibilities.

"Have a nice life, Emilie. I'm out of here."

Chapter Two

2

One moment he was kissing her with more hunger and heat than she'd ever longed for.

The next moment he was walking out of her life as if nothing had happened.

Emilie stared out the window as Zane Grey Rutledge leaped into his fancy sports car, then vanished up the street the way all good fantasies were supposed to do.

She shook her head, trying to banish the memory of his mouth on hers. The last time he'd kissed her had been on the steps of the L.A. County Courthouse after they'd signed their divorce papers.

"I'm on my way to Australia," he'd said with that cocky grin of his. "Why don't you come with me?"

She'd barely restrained herself from kicking him in the shins. Their marriage had been an unqualified mistake, but there he was suggesting they fly off together to the other side of the world as if they were lovers.

And the truly awful thing was, deep down inside she was tempted. *Very* tempted.

Obviously nothing had changed.

Not his reckless attitude or, to her dismay, the way he made her feel. She'd been alive to his touch, filled with a sweet longing that seemed to promise something wonderful that was just beyond reach.

Five of the best seconds of her life....

A full moon hung poised in the sky beyond her window, splashing silver on the turbulent waters. She should have known there'd be a full moon tonight. She'd felt crazy, out of control. With any encouragement she would have thrown her arms around his neck and begged him to make love to her right there on the floor in her workroom with the ghosts of the past all around them and only the stars to see.

The way he'd looked at her. The tone of his voice when he'd said her name. The signs had all been there, but she'd let the opportunity slip through her fingers and now she felt empty and very alone.

She turned away from the window, furious with herself for letting sexual chemistry cloud good, old-fashioned common sense.

If it wasn't for the uniform on the worktable, she might have believed she'd imagined the whole encounter. She crossed the room and picked up the jacket, holding it close to her chest. He'd worn it for only a few minutes but his scent, a blend of wind and rain and sea air, was everywhere.

He was everything she didn't want in a man, yet when she'd seen him striding up the driveway toward the house, she'd known the same sense of reckless excitement she'd experienced the very first time.

She'd been living in Hollywood at the time, working for a movie studio that specialized in big-budget films grounded in historical detail—especially when it came to the authenticity of the costumes.

Zane had been on the set visiting a stuntman pal of his who earned his salary by risking his neck. Zane, of course, was nothing like the stuntman.

Her ex-husband had been more than happy to risk his neck for nothing.

"Zane Grey Rutledge?" she'd said when he told her his name.

He'd shrugged with the casual ease of someone who'd never had to struggle for anything in his life. "My parents had a sense of humor," he'd said. "They were reading *Riders of the Purple Sage* in the labor room the night I was born."

Everything about him had been larger than life, from his movie-star looks to his relentless search for adventure. It had taken her a while to realize that his endless quest for the next thrill was a mask for a loneliness that went deeper than he'd ever admit.

He'd never been one to talk about the past, but she'd learned about his adventure-loving parents who had placed their five-year-old son in a fancy boarding school, then jetted off in search of their latest thrill. When they died on a mountain in Nepal, it took six months before Zane even realized they were gone. Only his grandmother, a Philadelphia mainline matron, had ever been there for him, but by then it had been a case of too little, too late.

Emilie had longed to fill the empty parts of his soul with her love but, like a shooting star, he was impossible to catch. He'd spent too many years alone to believe in happy endings.

They had nothing in common. She loved the past. He worshipped the future. He liked fast sports cars and trips to exotic locales, while she liked old quilts and museums. This miraculous wonder of a uniform meant less to him than a pair of sweat socks or a worn-out jockstrap.

He should have stayed in Tahiti or Manhattan or wherever it was he called home these days. She didn't need him in her life again, making her long for the impossible.

Lately she'd found herself pushing against the boundaries of the lazy town where she'd grown up. The kindhearted concern of her neighbors grated against her nerves. The cry of the gulls, the smell of salt air, the familiar routines of daily life all seemed alien to her, as if they belonged to someone else.

Just yesterday she'd raised her voice to Mrs. Willis at the market and told John Parker that no, she *didn't* like the way he'd wallpapered her powder room. She could still see the look of astonishment on the faces of those two nice people when she'd stormed out the door of the Stop'n'Shop with her quart of milk and half-dozen eggs.

"Poor Emilie," she'd heard Mrs. Willis say. "A girl so pretty shouldn't be alone."

Amazing how Mrs. Willis understood more about Emilie than Emilie did herself. She craved an adventure, a walk on the wild side of life. A jolt of electricity called excitement before she grew too old to care.

None of which was likely to be found in sleepy Crosse Harbor, New Jersey.

The one thing she hadn't needed, however, was her ex-husband roaring back into her life, reminding her that once upon a time she'd been naive enough to believe she could find adventure and security in his arms.

She turned, about to head for the kitchen, then stopped in her tracks. She tilted her head to the side, listening. The doorbell? It was almost eight o'clock at night. She had to be hearing things. The doorbell buzzed again, louder this time and more insistent.

She hurried through thc house toward the front hall. "Who is it?" she called through the heavy wooden door.

"Zane."

The uniform...he's come back for the uniform....

She swung open the door.

"Took you long enough." He stood there in all his piratical glory, dark hair gleaming in the glow of the porch light. "Did I interrupt something?"

"What are you doing here?"

"Ask me in and I'll tell you."

"You're on your way to Tahiti," she said as her heart slammed into her rib cage.

He placed his hand on the door frame and grinned down at her. "I don't leave until tomorrow."

"Go home and pack."

"I will," he said, then paused a beat. "Will you?"

She couldn't breathe. His presence surrounded her, drawing her closer to the flame. *He's a game player, Emilie. Sophisticated, adult games with rules you never understood.* "I can't answer that," she managed finally.

"It would make it a lot easier on me if you could."

"Sorry. I've never been good at making life easy for men I used to be married to."

She sensed, rather than saw, the change in him, but the effect it had on her was profound. Behind his bravado hid the loneliness she'd recognized earlier, and it reached inside her heart and wouldn't let go.

"I got as far as the parkway," he said, "then I turned around."

"You came back for your uniform," she said, feeling terrified and thrilled and hopeful.

"No," he said, pushing past her into the dimly lit foyer. "I came back for you."

"There's no future in it," she said, devouring him with her eyes. "Nothing's changed. We're still the same people. Still—"

"There's no future in anything," he said. "There's only the moment...."

She was in his arms in a heartbeat. No questions. No second thoughts. *No promises.* Tilting her chin upward with his finger, he lowered his head and claimed the sweetness of her mouth with his. The kiss was gentle at first, a sweet melding of softness and strength, then just as she found herself wanting more, he slipped his tongue into her mouth and a fierce hunger rose up from the center of her soul.

Her hands rested against the hard wall of his chest and she felt the violent thudding of his heart against her palm. How could she have forgotten the feel of him and the smell, this explosion of pure sensation.

He swept her off her feet with one swift and unexpected motion. Instinctively she looped her arms around his neck, dizzy with longing. The amazing planes of his face...the high, almost cruel cheekbones, the proud nose of a warrior-prince. Those deep blue eyes shadowed by lashes as dark as the night. She could get lost in those eyes.

"The door," she whispered against his shoulder.

He kicked the door closed, shutting out the world and enclosing them in their own private world.

"Where?" he asked, his voice a husky, sensual growl.

"Through the hallway."

Her bedroom was the last door on the right.

He would have known it in the dark. The smell of her perfume, faint and evocative, was everywhere. For years he'd told himself he'd imagined that scent, but he hadn't. It was as real, as exciting, as the woman in his arms.

He remembered it all. The texture of her mouth. The silky flow of her hair against his cheek. The coiled female strength.

The thick feather mattress cradled them as they fell together into its softness.

"I can't believe this is happening," she said, touching his face with her fingertips.

"I couldn't leave," he said, running his hand along the proud curve of her hip. "I did my damnedest but I just couldn't leave you."

"I know," she whispered. "When I saw your car backing out of the driveway—" She shook her head. "I wanted you to come back." More than anything. More than air or sun or safety.

"No second thoughts?"

"No second thoughts." Did he have any idea how overwhelming he was? How beautiful?

He drew his hand across her flat belly, easing his fingertips under the soft fabric of her shirt, across her rib cage, to the lacy band of her bra. In an instant he undid the front hook, parting the wisps of lace, then cupping her breasts in the palms of his hands.

She felt his touch everywhere. In the fire that suddenly blazed to life in her belly and at the spot between her thighs. Slowly he drew the pads of his thumbs across her nipples until they grew hard and taut. She wanted his mouth on her, that hungry and sensual mouth, his lips hot and wet as he sucked on her nipples, drawing them into his mouth—

"That's it," he said, stripping her of her bra and shirt. "Let me hear you. Scream if you want to, Emilie. I want it all…everything you have to give."

A groan of pleasure, pagan and unbridled, broke free. The sound terrified her with its urgency even as it destroyed the last of her inhibitions with its pure, female power. It was all so strange yet so familiar, as if she'd been waiting for his touch to bring her back to life.

He lowered his mouth to her breasts, then slipped inside her heart and absorbed her fantasies. His mouth was hotter than flame against her skin. He captured one nipple between his teeth and she cried out again, not from pain but from a feeling so primitive and fierce that she wondered if she would survive another onslaught of sensation.

She was weightless, floating in the clouds, suspended in the throbbing darkness of an erotic dream. A rhythm, insistent and old as time, began to move inside her as her back arched, offering herself up to him on the altar of sensuality.

She'd waited forever for this moment. Dreamed about it. Longed for the only man who could take her on this journey.

And now she wanted more.

She wanted him to brand every part of her body with his mouth. She reached for the waistband on her white pants but he pushed her hands away and accomplished the task with a caress that brought her even closer to the edge of madness.

She was more beautiful than he'd remembered. Long slender legs, rounded hips, the dark red curls, wet with desire, that begged the touch of his tongue. The sounds she made as he touched her inflamed his soul.

She wanted to touch him, to reach out and place her hand against him and know that his power and heat belonged to her and her alone, if only for the night.

Again he seemed to understand what she wanted before she could translate desire into words. Rising from the bed, he stripped off his clothing. He didn't need the trappings of style to impress. His body was lean, powerfully muscled. A thick mat of dark hair furred his chest, narrowing down over his flat belly to—

He didn't disappoint. He'd never disappointed.

He was everything she'd remembered and more.

Tears sprang to her eyes and she blinked and looked away so he wouldn't notice.

But he did.

He dropped down onto the bed next to her and curled her body against his. "I want you," he said bluntly, "but as much as I want to make love to you, I've never taken an unwilling woman." He moved away so their bodies were no longer touching. "It's your choice, Emilie. Your decision."

She felt no shame. No guilt. This was a moment out of time. Her chance to taste life at its sweetest with no regrets to shadow her memories later on. She could be whoever she wanted to be tonight, captive or conqueror or both.

What she felt, what she wanted, went beyond words. She nodded, meeting his eyes, letting him touch her soul the way he'd touched her body.

He gathered her in his arms. They lay together on the bed, bodies pressed together, savoring the primitive feel of skin against skin. The pure, animal pleasure of it tumbled the last of her defenses.

She began to move against him, small, silken movements designed to tempt and tease. She felt as if she were spinning out of control and he was her anchor, the one real thing in a world she no longer recognized.

She was ready. He knew it by the sounds she made deep in her throat, by the moist heat of her when he cupped her with his hand, by the wild and hungry look in her green eyes when he parted her thighs and knelt between them.

He stroked her slowly at first, letting the need build between them to a fever pitch, then he deepened the motion until she cried out and he knew he could wait no longer.

"Now," she whispered against his mouth. "Now...now...now...."

Her words were all he needed.

She was softness and warmth, hesitant and passionate both. So small, so tight, that for a moment he feared he might hurt her with his power, but she urged him on, shuddering beneath him as she finally opened for him, sheathing him inside her welcoming body as if they had been made for each other by a benevolent god.

He had been the first man to know her body, to teach her the rites of lovemaking, and the thought that she had been with anyone else in the intervening years made him long to wipe their memory from her mind and brand her as his and his alone.

It was a fierce and primal call of the blood. She was all that he wanted—and more than he'd dreamed. He was a physical man and he knew a moment of pleasure with the woman he'd loved that ripped him apart then made him whole again.

And very soon he would come to understand that nothing about his life would ever be the same.

In the dark all things were possible.

That night she explored the wilder shores of sensuality with a man who understood her secrets before she gave them voice. As long as the moon cast its light upon them, the magic was theirs alone.

They napped briefly, then she brought a bottle of champagne to the bed, an old and dusty bottle she'd saved for a celebration that had never materialized.

"Cristal," he said, with an appreciative whistle. "I'm impressed."

"You should be," she said, climbing into the feather bed with him.

She eased the cork from the bottle and laughed as the resounding pop shattered the stillness of the bedroom. "I love that sound," she said, pouring the bubbly golden liquid into the cups. She placed the bottle down on the night table then raised her cup. "To unexpected guests."

He met her eyes. "To you."

She took a sip of champagne. "I suppose this is where we catch up on old times."

"I was hoping we'd talk about new times ahead."

She lay back against the pillows, eyes twinkling. "Suppose I tell you all about the Patriots' Day celebration the town's having tomorrow."

He groaned and she swatted him with a pillow sham.

"Laugh all you want," she said in mock outrage, "but it's big stuff here in Crosse Harbor. I'm sure you'll find this hilarious, but we all dress up in eighteenth-century costumes and drink cider and pretend the British are coming. Mayor Gold is playing Andrew McVie." McVie was Crosse Harbor's claim to fame, their one bona fide revolutionary war hero. Emilie had spent much of her childhood daydreaming about his daring rescue of General Washington not long before the Battle of Princeton.

She told him of the legend of the mysterious hero who had been cloaked all in black. Before a group of terrified onlookers, he'd vaulted onto Washington's horse and knocked the general to the ground, just as a musket ball split the air instead of the general's heart.

Emilie's family had always laid claim to the identity of the masked hero. Who else but a Crosse, they'd said, would have the fortitude to execute such a daring rescue? Everyone else credited Andrew McVie.

"Unfortunately, most of them were at a wedding celebration that day," she said with a laugh. "So much for family history."

"So who do you dress up as tomorrow?" he asked. "Betsy Ross?"

"No, smart guy, but I am the star of the show." Tomorrow morning, she told him, she would arrive at the village square for the festivities in a hot-air balloon.

"You're kidding!"

She crossed her heart. "Scout's honor. The research is faulty but it's great publicity for the historical society. How could I say no?"

"I wouldn't have had trouble."

"That's because you don't understand history and you never will."

"There are a few other things I do understand," he said, taking her champagne and placing it on the nightstand. "Why don't I tell you about them. . . ."

They polished off the champagne afterward. Emilie padded back out to the kitchen, positive she had some more tucked away in the pantry.

"It's not Cristal," she apologized, "but I always say there's no such thing as bad champagne."

Zane, who had followed her into the kitchen, took the bottle from her.

Emilie disappeared back into the pantry and returned with a box of crackers, some peanut butter and a gift-sized jar of raspberry jelly. She arranged the items on an old lacquered tray she'd found at a yard sale the previous summer, then added two plates and a beautiful silver knife.

Back in her bed, she made a show of spreading the peanut butter and jelly on the tiny crackers, then presented each one to Zane with a flourish. He watched as she arranged the crackers along the edge of the plate in a semicircle. She'd always had the gift of turning straw into gold, he thought. Somehow she'd made the peanut butter and jelly taste like nectar of the gods.

"I haven't been to the market in ages," she said, refilling their cups, "or I would have made something wonderful for you. I *can* cook, in case you don't remember."

He grinned at her over his cup of champagne. "Don't mean to upset you, Emilie, but I never did give a damn if you could boil water."

Her eyes widened at first in dismay, then she laughed. "I guess it really doesn't matter, does it?"

"Not one damn bit." He pushed the plate aside. "Lie down."

"What?"

"Lie down," he repeated, more forcefully this time.

This was part of the fantasy. In that secret world, for just this one night, a man could command and a woman would obey.

The sheets felt cool and silky against her back. The champagne had softened the edges of her perception. It was difficult to tell where her body ended and the feather bed began. She was floating on a cloud, drifting along in a wonderful erotic haze—

"Zane!" She propped herself up on her elbows and stared at him. "What on earth—?"

"Trust me," he said with a piratical smile.

Her belly was warm. The champagne wasn't. She gasped at the sensation as it trickled toward her navel.

"You're crazy!" she said, laughing. "The sheets…"

The sheets, however, were in no danger. Drop by drop, inch by tantalizing inch, he licked the golden wine from her skin. Her navel...the slope of her belly...the juncture of her thighs...the sweet, sweet center of her being.

She threaded her fingers through his hair, holding him close to her, wanting this dark splendor to go on until she exploded into a thousand glittering pieces of gold.

But more than anything, she didn't want it to end.

Emilie sat up against the headboard the next morning and stared down at the man sleeping next to her. She'd been lying there for ages, eyes pressed tightly closed, listening to the slow and even ticking of the clock on her nightstand, praying she would wake up to discover she was all alone in her four-poster bed, same as she'd been every single night for the past five years.

She reached over and touched his shoulder. Hard muscle. Warm flesh. A living, breathing man.

Her ex-husband!

The gentle ache between her thighs...the delicious feeling of having been loved often and well...the sensation of standing at the edge of a high cliff and stepping out into space.

Vivid images of his mouth against her belly, his hands against the small of her back...she couldn't have imagined the deep, almost primal pleasures, no matter how hard she tried.

"Oh, God." She pulled the covers over her head and scooted to the edge of the mattress. She'd gone insane, that was it. Totally, completely mad.

Zane mumbled something and punched at his pillow. Emilie held her breath. He turned over and flung a hard, muscular leg across her hip, pressing up against her. She found herself leaning back into his warmth, wanting his strength....

"No!" she said out loud. Not again. She wasn't going to give in to the urge to throw caution to the winds again. Last night was last night. It was over, and if she had her way it would be forgotten as quickly as possible.

He wasn't her type of man and he never had been. He had no

sense of history or continuity and he didn't feel the loss. Giving her heart to a man like Zane Rutledge was the romantic equivalent of tying herself to the railroad tracks and waiting for the next train to arrive. She'd escaped once with her heart intact. She'd be crazy to think she could escape a second time.

The magic that had existed between them yesterday couldn't possibly exist in the light of day. The sense of destiny, of being at the mercy of the fates—she'd blame it all on the full moon.

If you asked her, he seemed too darn comfortable sprawled out on her pale peach sheets with the satin duvet barely covering the essentials. He was tall and inordinately broad shouldered with powerful muscles that had felt like warm marble beneath her hands and—

Thinking like that would only get her in trouble.

Taking a deep breath, she took another look at him, determined to see only his shortcomings. Unfortunately, his shortcomings were not the first thing you noticed about Zane Rutledge. The packaging had always been impressive.

Wouldn't you think he'd have the decency to look out of place in such a frankly feminine setting? Instead, he looked as if he'd conquered her bedroom the same way he'd conquered her body.

The thought annoyed her and she poked his shoulder. "Zane." He stirred but he didn't awaken. "Zane, I have to leave in an hour."

"Mmph." He rolled over on his stomach and scrunched his face more deeply into the pillow.

She debated the wisdom of yanking at the corner of the duvet but the thought of all that naked male splendor was more than she could bear. She fled for the bathroom as if the hounds of hell were nipping at her heels, then closed the door behind her.

It was almost enough to make her laugh. Wasn't it the man who was supposed to be counting the seconds until he could make his escape? She read the women's magazines: she should be in the kitchen whipping up a delectable post-tryst breakfast of French roast coffee, fresh strawberries and cream while he calculated the distance between the bedroom and freedom.

Instead she found herself hiding in the bathroom, wondering if she could squeeze through the tiny window and vanish into the woods behind her house.

Quietly she padded into the dressing room off the bathroom, then slipped into a pair of leggings and an intricately laced bodice with ribbon ties that was part of her costume. It was too darned hot to wear the entire ensemble. She'd slip into the skirt and sash on the balloon.

She caught a glimpse of herself in the full-length mirror and stifled a laugh. She looked like *Mad Magazine*'s idea of an eighteenth-century streetwalker. An embroidered purse, faded with age, rested on the window ledge. She added a few dollar bills, two quarters, her driver's license and American Express card to the sewing kit inside, then tucked it into the waistband of her leggings. Sliding her feet into a pair of ballerina flats, she gathered up the flower-sprigged muslin skirt and draped it over her arm.

She glanced into the bedroom as she headed toward the kitchen. He was still asleep, sprawled diagonally across her bed as if he intended to stay awhile. It took a certain kind of person to get that comfortable that quickly. Emilie shook her head in dismay. Some things never changed.

A pad of hot pink Post-It notes rested atop the microwave. She scribbled a quick note with a bright green felt-tip pen, then stuck the note to the sugar bowl in the center of the scarred maple breakfast table. Her car keys hung from a hook near the door and she grabbed them on her way out.

Backing her car out of the driveway she absolutely refused to look at the sexy black Porsche parked there or think about its incredibly sexy owner.

She'd made a dreadful mistake. It was over.

She didn't intend to think about it again as long as she lived.

Langley Park was a good half-hour drive from her house. The morning was cool for late July and surprisingly clear. Although it was barely past dawn, the low-lying fog had already burned off. If it wasn't for the smell of auto exhaust mingling with the scent of salt air and summer flowers, it would be a perfect day.

She switched on the car radio, tapping her fingers on the wheel as an old Beach Boys' song came on. At twenty-nine she was too young to remember them in their prime, but there was something wonderful about their music that made it absolutely perfect for driving down a country lane on a beautiful summer morning.

Glancing in the rearview mirror she saw a jazzy black sports car making the left onto the main road. Impossible. The last she saw of him, he'd been sprawled across her bed sound asleep. She pressed down harder on the gas pedal but the sports car still trailed behind.

Gunning the engine, she made a sharp right onto a side road, only to see the black car follow suit a few moments later. Her heart lurched. Unless his Porsche had cloned a twin overnight, it was Zane. Maybe he'd lost his wallet or misplaced his watch. She slowed down, expecting him to pull even with her, but he maintained his distance. He looked grimly determined.

She turned back to the main road. He did the same. She considered trying to lose him, but the huge crimson balloon in which she'd soon be riding was a destination you couldn't hide. It hovered over the trees, gleaming bright red in the morning light, impossible to ignore.

"Stop tailgating," she muttered as she turned into the parking lot and swung into a spot. He'd always driven as if he had a death wish. She had half a mind to slam on the brakes then sue him for rear-ending her old sedan. It would serve him right.

He screeched to a stop behind her.

The Porsche's door swung open so fast it nearly popped its hinges. She considered locking her door and waiting out the storm but had the feeling he would peel the door open with his bare hands. He climbed from the sports car and stormed over to where she sat.

"Get out," he said through clenched teeth.

Some things an ex-wife never forgot. That tone of voice was one of them. Arguing with him seemed unwise.

She took a deep breath and swung her legs out of the sedan. He didn't offer any help. Not that she needed any, but it would have been a nice gesture.

In for a penny, in for a pound. She'd die rather than let him know the effect he had upon her.

"You made a wrong turn," she said airily, gesturing back toward the main road. "Manhattan's thataway."

At that moment he could cheerfully have wrung her neck. He'd been close to homicide a few other times in his life—most of them with Emilie—but this was the one time he could have legitimately labeled it a crime of passion.

"What the hell do you think you're doing?" he demanded.

She looked up at him, her grass-green eyes wide and innocent. "I'm afraid I don't know what you're talking about."

"The hell you don't."

Her gaze darted toward the crimson balloon, looming large in the open field. He grabbed her by the shoulders.

"A note on the kitchen table? You can do better than that, Em."

"Don't make such a big deal out of it." She looked up at him, the expression in her eyes all fire and heat. "I had to leave. I told you about Patriots' Day."

She pulled away and started toward the balloon.

He blocked her way. She tried to duck around him but failed. "Breakfast would've been a nice touch."

"Sorry if I'm not as experienced as the other women you've been with."

"You're out of milk," he said, "and you're real low on OJ. A man could starve to death."

"Thanks so much for the grocery update," she said, an edge to her voice. "I'll add them to my list."

"If I'd walked out on you like that, you'd call me a son of a bitch."

"I didn't walk out on you. I had an appointment."

"Bull. You ran for your life."

"Don't flatter yourself, Rutledge. I tried to wake you up but you were dead to the world." She ducked under his outstretched arm but he grabbed her again by the shoulder. "Don't you have a plane to catch?"

"This afternoon," he said. "That's why I'm here."

"Hey, Em!" Dan Walsh's voice carried across the parking lot. "Better get it in gear. We're ready to let 'er rip."

"I have to go," she said to Zane. "They rent those contraptions by the hour."

She started toward the balloon.

Rutledge was hard on her heels.

The roar of the propane gas tank sounded loud in the quiet morning air. Two young men sat in a yellow minivan, sipping coffee and stifling yawns.

"There's the rescue squad," said Rutledge, lifting his hand in greeting.

She winced. "What do you mean, rescue squad?"

"Spotters," he said. "The ground crew. They keep you in eyeshot in case you run into trouble."

"Don't say that! I've never been up in one of those things before."

"Nothing to it. You go where the winds take you."

"We're supposed to land near the village green."

"You will if nature cooperates."

"I suppose you've been up in a balloon before?"

He nodded, grinning broadly. "Balloons, gliders, ultralights."

"Have you ever considered gainful employment?" she drawled.

"Hey, Em," said Dan, looking from Emilie to Zane with open curiosity. "Baxter's ready to go." He pointed toward an overweight man in a red satin bomber jacket that had the logo Soul Man embroidered across the back. "He's grabbing a last cup of coffee before you take off."

Emilie took a good look at the cane gondola. It was about six feet wide with a large tank of propane secured to a support anchored to the centerpiece. "That's it?" she asked, swallowing.

"That's it," said Dan. "Just glad it's you and not me that's going up in that contraption. I told the missus you wouldn't get me going up in anything smaller than a DC-9."

Wise man. "How do I get in there?"

Zane grabbed her by the waist and swung her into the basket.

"Oh," she said, feeling very alone and very nervous. "My skirt," she said, pointing toward her car. "I'll need it when we land." The colonial hooker look wouldn't be appreciated at the Patriots' Day celebration.

"Do you mind?" Zane asked the older man. "We have a few things to settle."

Dan hesitated.

"It's okay," said Zane with a friendly smile. "Emilie and I are engaged."

"Well, whaddya know," said Dan as he turned to retrieve the skirt from Emilie's car.

"I could kill you!" Emilie leaned out of the basket and landed a punch on Zane's shoulder. "Why did you say something so stupid?"

"I didn't think you'd like it if I told him we were lovers."

"Why didn't you tell him the truth?"

"I told him the truth," he said with maddening male logic. "We were engaged...once."

"Now the whole town will be buzzing about it by the time we land."

"That we're engaged or that we're lovers?"

He was enjoying this altogether too much for her taste. "That I'm a total idiot."

"A touch of scandal never hurt anyone."

"You don't know Crosse Harbor."

"The hell with Crosse Harbor. Come with me today, Emilie." His smile was piratical, seductive. "We'll explore Tahiti, then I'll show you moonlight in Cairo and sunrise in Spain. We can breakfast in Paris and dine in Hawaii and make love in every city, port and country in between before we say goodbye."

Her heart thundered inside her chest as a fierce longing sprang to life. When she was old and gray and sitting on her front porch counting down the days, she'd have something to warm her soul besides an afghan and a pot of tea. The notion of walking away from reality and into a dream was extremely compelling.

"Absolutely not," she said over the insistent noise of the pilot burner.

"Last chance," he said, eyes narrowing.

"Forget it," she said. "I'm not going anywhere with you."

"Then I'll come with you."

She froze in place, shocked beyond description as he pulled up the two stakes anchoring the balloon to the ground then leaped into the gondola just as it started to rise.

"Hey!" Dan Walsh came running back from the parking lot, Emilie's skirt waving behind him like a muslin banner. "You come back here!"

"Do something!" Emilie shrieked. "Grab the ropes, Dan! Stop this thing!"

"Relax," said Zane, adjusting the flow of gas. "I'll get you to your celebration in one piece."

"Are you *crazy?*" she screamed over the roar of the propane tank that was propelling the balloon upward into the sky. "What do you think you're doing?"

"Taking you for a ride."

"You *are* crazy!" She backed away toward the edge of the basket. "Do you know how to fly this thing?"

"We'll find out soon enough." He fiddled with the control on the propane tank. "I've flown in hot-air balloons before."

"And I've flown in a 747. That doesn't mean I think I could fly one."

"That's the difference between us. I'm willing to give it a try." And the problem was he usually succeeded.

The flame shot upward while Emilie entertained visions of tangled power lines, and giant birds with very sharp beaks. The crimson silk balloon carried them higher and higher, leaving the safety of earth far below.

"I hope they arrest you for this," she said, struggling with a combination of fear and elation. He'd always been one for grand gestures and, fool that she was, she'd always been a sucker for them.

"Would you press charges?"

"Damn right. How dare you risk my life because you feel like pulling some crazy stunt!"

"Playing it safe has killed more people than craziness ever could."

"You think you can move mountains, don't you?"

Again that pirate's grin. "If there was something I wanted on the other side."

His meaning was unmistakable. She closed her eyes for a second against a flood of longing that went beyond sex to a place she'd thought existed only in her dreams. "I wish you hadn't done this," she whispered. "There's no point to it. Last night was last night. We both know there can't be a future for us." He was so perfectly gorgeous. Why couldn't he have the soul of a poet besides the face of a god? "I want more from a man than great sex. I want a man I can love."

"Most people would settle for great sex."

She shook her head and looked out at the panorama drifting by below them. If that had been enough they would still be married. "You never did understand."

"Are you sure *you* do?"

"What's that supposed to mean?"

"I get the feeling you're not as connected to that little town of yours as you'd like me to believe."

"I wish you wouldn't say things like that." She suppressed a shiver. He'd come too close to exposing her own fears. "Crosse Harbor is my home...my family helped build that town after the war was over."

"We're a lot alike," he said over her objections. "We're both looking for something we may never find."

"I'm not looking for anything." How false her words sounded. How empty. "I like my life the way it is."

"Like hell. You're an adventurer, Emilie. Admit it. You want more." His words, taunting and too close to home, broke the last of her control. She lurched across the swaying gondola and tried to land a punch. He grabbed her by the wrist then pinned her arm behind her, a wicked glint of amusement in his eye. She tried to pull away but each time she did, the gondola swayed alarmingly, sending her stomach into a roller-coaster dive.

"You got away with it once," he said, his tone holding a hint of steel. "I wouldn't push my luck."

Dangerous or not, she went to kick him in the shins but he pulled her up against his body and held her fast.

"Take a look, lady," he warned. "It's a long way down to earth."

She peered over the edge of the basket and gasped. They were sailing over the treetops, and into the clouds.

He saw the look of wonderment pass across her face, and his grip eased. "Impressive, isn't it?"

She nodded, unable to pull her gaze away from the panorama beneath her. "There's the main road into town," she said, pointing to a dark ribbon winding its way through the lush green countryside. "I never thought of it as beautiful before."

"Perspective is everything."

She shot him a sideways glance. "How cynical."

"Realistic."

"Isn't there anything in life that matters to you?"

"I thought you figured out the answer to that question last night."

"There's more to life than sex."

"Maybe," he said, "but there are few things that are better."

"I have to hand it to you," she said. "You always did know how to make the morning after as memorable as the night before. I wish—" She stopped. "My God, it's freezing." She wrapped her arms across her chest against the sudden drop in temperature. The sensation of movement had ceased. She felt as if the balloon was suspended in an icy, silver-gray cocoon. "Is this normal? It *is* normal, isn't it?"

The words were no sooner out of her mouth than the balloon and gondola dropped like an elevator shimmying between floors.

"It's okay," Zane said, raising the pilot flame to combat the sudden descent of the balloon. "Don't worry. Nothing's going to happen to us."

"There's something wrong, isn't there?"

"Those clouds." He pointed to the east. "A second ago it was dead clear. They blew in out of nowhere."

She started toward him as he worked with the sputtering tank of propane. The balloon shook like a platter of Jell-O, then dropped again.

"There's nothing to worry about," he said. "If I can just stabilize her, we can regain altitude once we clear this cloud cover."

He sounded so sure, so confident. One of the chosen few who could face down a tornado and live to tell about it. She wanted to believe him, but wicked crosswinds rocked the gondola and she was thrown against him as they plunged even deeper into the icy gray clouds.

He pushed her toward the floor. “Lie down,” he barked. “I don’t like—” His words were lost in the vicious gust of wind that roared in from the west.

The gondola tilted to the left like an amusement-park ride gone crazy, followed by the horrifying sound of the silk balloon ripping apart.

“Hold on, Emilie!” he shouted, as tatters of bright red silk drifted down from the sky. “We’re going down!”

Chapter Three

3

Emilie was alive—or at least she thought she was.

If she was dead she was fairly certain she wouldn't hurt as if someone had dragged her across five miles of bad road.

Her eyelids stung. Her shoulders ached. Knees, hands, face... every single part of her body, including the appendix she'd lost when she was three years old.

Champagne, she thought groggily. She had a vague recollection of a bottle of Cristal and—

And what?

She didn't know.

There must have been a good reason for polishing off a bottle of fancy French champagne but for the life of her she couldn't imagine what it was. If she'd had any idea what torture lay ahead of her, she would have reached for the diet soda instead.

She tried to pry open her eyelids but the sunlight was so intense that she just groaned and buried her face in the sand.

Wait just a minute. *The sand?* Spreading her fingers wide, she felt the area around her. Small pebbles, sharp pieces of shell, silky grains of beach sand—

"Dear God!" She pulled herself upright and opened her eyes. The sky overhead was an amazing, picture-postcard shade of blue, streaked with one or two snowy-white clouds. She found herself wishing she had a pair of sunglasses with her to shield her eyes from the glare bouncing up off the sand.

Gingerly she touched her face, her shoulders, wiggled her arms and legs. Nothing was broken, thank God. Her knees and hands were badly scraped, stinging each time the salt water lapped against the shore. She supposed she should be greatly relieved to be in such good shape, but she'd be even more relieved if she only knew how it was she'd come to be there on the beach.

With a groan she rose to her feet and looked about in an attempt to regain her bearings. The lighthouse rose from a rugged outcropping of rocks not thirty feet away from where she stood. She shuddered as she looked at the jagged boulders with the sharp edges and imagined what might have happened. Many a man had met his Maker along the shores of Eagle Island, the tiny spit of land across the harbor from her house.

"Think, Emilie," she said out loud, searching for a clue. "It's morning. You're near the lighthouse." She glanced down at her bizarre attire: an eighteenth-century bodice worn with black leggings and ballet flats. She was all in favor of mix-and-match but usually she tried to limit her choices to the same century.

A costume party, maybe?

If only she could think straight. Her brain felt as if it were filled with those Styrofoam peanuts that came tumbling out of packing boxes when you opened the lid. Not even the worst case of jet lag had made her feel so goofy and disoriented. She squinted down at her watch. The crystal was cracked but the second hand was still ticking. Nine in the morning on July twenty-fifth.

Suddenly the images came at her in a dizzying blur.

The sleek black foreign car with the lion's roar of an engine.

The uniform from a distant time.

A man with eyes the color of the deepest sapphire blue who'd held her close as the earth rushed up toward them and—

Zane!

She swayed on her feet as her center of gravity realigned itself. A mounting sense of panic gripped her by the chest, making it hard to breathe. Where was the gondola? The crimson silk of the balloon itself? Even the beach looked oddly different, as if all signs of life had been airbrushed away. No soda cans tossed into the dune grass. No bottles bobbing up and down at the water's edge. Not even a McDonald's wrapper or a Burger King bag, two of the most ubiquitous signs of human life.

But, worst of all, no sign of her ex-husband.

"Okay," she said out loud. "There has to be an answer to all of this." The sound of her own voice steadied her. "Just use your head, Emilie. You can figure it out."

Maybe it wasn't so confusing after all.

They'd drifted into some pretty weird cloud formations. She wasn't an expert in aeronautics, but everyone had heard stories about wind shear and crosscurrents and weird thermal down drafts that had vexed better pilots than Zane Grey Rutledge.

She remembered the stomach-churning sensation of vertigo as the gondola tumbled end-over-end after the balloon itself collapsed. She'd probably tumbled from the basket as they drifted past the beach, while Zane continued to struggle with the gas tank and the sputtering flame.

"The rowboat," she said, brightening. If she remembered right, the rowboat was tucked away near the east side of the lighthouse. All she had to do was jump into the boat, grab the oars, and she could be back on the mainland in fifteen minutes flat. She patted her waistband, amazed to discover that the embroidered purse with her car keys, American Express card and spare change was still there. A quick phone call to Crosse Harbor Taxi and she could make it to the celebration before they sent out the rescue squad to find her.

She turned, about to head toward the lighthouse and the rowboat, when something caught her attention. Shielding her eyes against the sun's glare, she scanned the shoreline. Everything seemed okay, but she could have sworn she'd seen a flash of crimson in the water.

"Yes!" she said, focusing all her attention on that point of color. There it was, something bobbing in the water about one hundred yards out. "Oh, my God! Zane!" He was struggling against the current and from the looks of it he was losing the battle.

She kicked off her shoes and raced for the water, trying desperately to keep him in sight, but he kept disappearing beneath the swells. *Hang on, Zane,* she pleaded silently as she plunged into the water. She was a strong swimmer, but the current presented a daunting challenge and each time he disappeared she thought her heart would stop beating.

"Zane!" she managed as she reached him. "Grab on to me!"

No response. A feeling of dread washed over her as she realized he had lost consciousness.

Working frantically, she rolled him onto his back, making sure his nose and mouth were clear of water. "You can do it," she urged. "Hang on to me."

Her words were as much for herself as they were for him. He was a big man, large boned and heavily muscled. She thanked God for the buoyancy of the salt water. Without it, they wouldn't have had a prayer.

The shoreline was growing closer and she rejoiced when her knees scraped against the sand. She stumbled to her feet in the calf-deep water, then continued pulling him toward safety. His eyes were closed. An ugly gash ran from the end of his right eyebrow down to his cheek. Blood mingled with salt water, leaving an ominous trail behind them.

"You can't be dead," she said as she struggled to haul him onto the sand. "You wouldn't dare do that to me." She tried to ignore the trail of blood, deeper and more frightening, that he'd left behind on the sand. He had to live, if only so she could tell him that he was the most arrogant, irresponsible, crazy excuse for a grown man she'd ever met.

She placed her ear to his chest but couldn't hear a thing. His color was dreadful. She pried open one lid, but he didn't stir. Her own breathing was rapid, ragged, and she willed herself to calm down before she hyperventilated, something that would do neither of them the slightest bit of good.

There was only one thing she could think of that might help and, straddling his chest, she began to administer CPR, praying the class she'd taken last year at the fire department had covered all the necessary bases.

"Breathe, damn you!" she ordered as she pounded his chest. "Breathe!"

It was like being trapped in a bad dream, the kind where you were running and running through an endless tunnel with no end in sight. But she couldn't stop, she couldn't just let him slip away, no matter how hopeless it seemed.

And then she heard it. Faint at first, then louder, stronger. He was coughing, spitting up seawater. And then the wonderful, miraculous sound of him breathing!

"I could kill you for this," she said, brushing away tears of relief. "You scared the living hell out of me."

When he came to, she intended to give him a piece of her mind, enough so that he felt guilty all the way to Tahiti. Her relief was short-lived, however, as her eyes were drawn again to the blood seeping into the sand. A man didn't bleed like that for no reason. She'd saved him from drowning, but what if there was something more serious wrong with him?

She was no doctor, but it occurred to her that the worst thing she could do was leave him lying on wet sand. He could go into shock or take some water into his lungs and end up with pneumonia. The thing to do was get him dry and warm, then call for help.

She glanced toward the lighthouse. She'd manage somehow to drag him through the sand but she wasn't entirely certain she'd be able to get him up the wooden stairs that led inside.

"You won't know unless you try," she said. The only thing she knew for sure was she couldn't leave him lying there on the sand. She retrieved her shoes, then approached him.

Gingerly she bent down and gripped him under the arms. He groaned loudly and she backed away, horrified that she'd obviously hurt him. She looked closely and noticed that his right arm was bent at an odd angle, one that made her insides twist into a knot.

She tried to favor his right side, but with his weight balanced unequally she felt as if she were dragging him around in circles.

"I know this hurts," she said apologetically, "but it's the only way."

Gripping him beneath both arms, she moved as quickly as her burden would allow, dragging him across the damp sand toward the bottom of the lighthouse steps.

She paused to catch her breath while she tried to figure out the best way to get Zane Rutledge up the stairs and into the lighthouse. She'd always believed wit and ingenuity could see a woman through any difficulty, but this time she had to admit that brute strength would have been a welcome addition.

"Zane." She touched his shoulder. "I need your help."

He mumbled something but didn't open his eyes.

"I have to get you inside," she persisted, "and I can't do it if you don't help me."

He opened his eyes and struggled to a sitting position.

"Do you know what I'm saying, Zane? I have to get you up those stairs."

He nodded. It was obvious even so small a motion as that caused him excruciating pain. Her heart ached for him but this wasn't the time for sympathy.

She moved to his left side. "Put your arm around me," she ordered in her most businesslike voice. "I'm going to help you stand."

His hold on consciousness was tenuous at best, but she managed to get his arm around her so she could use leverage to bring him to his feet. He tried to help. She could feel it in the way his weight shifted and in the sight of the beads of sweat breaking out across his handsome face.

"Too heavy," he said, "…forget—"

"Shut up," she ordered, not unkindly. "Keep your mouth shut and don't fight me. We'll get you up these stairs."

She'd spoken the words with great assurance, confident that her adrenaline would kick in and give her that little extra strength she'd need, and to her everlasting gratitude it did. They made it to the landing and she reached for the doorknob, overjoyed to discover that someone obligingly had left it unlocked.

That extra second might have spelled disaster.

They staggered together into the lighthouse as he once again lost consciousness. She tried to cushion his fall with her own body, wincing as his elbow caught her behind the ear.

What was one more bruise, she thought as she rolled him onto his back. She'd managed to get him up the stairs and into the lighthouse and now all she had to do was see to it that he was dry and warm. Then she could figure out a way to call for help.

"Now don't take this personally," she said with a wry smile as she reached for his belt. "This is all in your best interest."

He was as gorgeous today as he'd been last night. She felt like a pervert for even noticing. The poor man was in agony and she was admiring his pecs and abs. Still, you'd have to be blind not to notice.

Quickly she stripped him of his wet pants and shirt. She debated the wisdom of leaving his shorts on him, but decided that was ridiculous. A beautiful quilt rested on a ladder-back chair near the fireplace, along with a pale blue coverlet. She dried Zane with the coverlet, then used the quilt to wrap around his body for warmth.

She glanced around the front room of the lighthouse for a blanket or another quilt. It struck her as odd that these two beautiful specimens had been waiting for them here in the lighthouse. The place had been empty for more years than she could remember, and quilts as fine as these were collectibles that fetched impressive sums.

Sam Talmadge, one of the members of the Crosse Harbor Historical Society, was in charge of the light show that would be staged later tonight from the harbor. Could he have brought over the quilts to keep his grandkids warm while they watched the spectacle from the tower?

She'd never been inside the lighthouse before and she noted with interest that it looked anything but abandoned. The walls had obviously received a recent coat of whitewash. The wooden staircase that led up to the tower seemed sturdy and solid. The dilapidated radar equipment was gone and in its place were a compass, a telescope and a copy of *Poor Richard's Almanack*.

"Good for you, Sam," she murmured as she helped Zane to the trundle bed beneath the leaded-glass window. She'd always known

Sam Talmadge was a great believer in period detail during these revolutionary war re-creations that Crosse Harbor was so fond of, but there was something about this that made the hairs on the back of her neck rise.

Maybe it was the silence. She tilted her head to one side, listening. Eagle Island was small, but it was never quiet. This morning all she could hear were the faint sounds of gulls circling overhead as they hunted for food.

Where were the sounds bouncing across the water from Crosse Harbor? Lawn mowers, the laughter of kids playing stickball, the putt-putt engines of the motorboat that cruised the waters in search of the ultimate fishing spot. Even the gnatlike buzz of small planes en route to the glitzier pleasures of the Atlantic City casinos was absent.

Apparently *everyone* was at the village green enjoying the celebration.

Or were they?

"Now you've really gone crazy," she said as she went back into the front room to check on Zane. Her imagination was running riot.

Her body had weathered the accident in good form; she was no longer so sure about her brain cells.

From the trundle bed Zane moaned loudly, bringing her back to the situation at hand.

"Oh, God," she murmured as she bent down to look at him. A huge purple bruise had blossomed over his right eye, which was almost swollen shut. She was positive his arm was broken and she wouldn't be at all surprised if he'd broken a rib or two in the bargain.

She sat next to him for a while as he drifted in and out of consciousness. It was almost noon. Her own clothes clung to her damply and her hair cascaded over her shoulders in a wild mane of wet curls and waves. Obviously no one had gone out looking for her. She had to do something. That broken arm wasn't going to set itself, and she knew that even a simple fractured rib could lead to complications.

There was only one thing she could do. She had to grab the small boat Sam Talmadge kept stashed behind the lighthouse and row back to the mainland for help.

"I'll be as fast as I possibly can," she said to Zane, who looked up at her with glassy eyes. "You have to stay in bed. Please, whatever you do, don't get up."

He nodded but she wasn't sure exactly how much he comprehended. He seemed to be in some kind of twilight zone, and it made her very apprehensive to see the self-confident Zane Grey Rutledge so vulnerable. She had visions of him tumbling down the stairs or something equally dreadful. If she had some rope she would even consider tying him in place, but there was nothing handy.

She made her way around to the back of the lighthouse. Funny thing, but she'd always thought there were beach roses on this side of the structure. Instead she found herself fighting her way through a veritable thicket of brush and untended shrubbery. She followed a stone path down toward the waterline where Sam kept his boat.

Only that wasn't Sam's boat bobbing gently in the water. Sam's boat was a small but jaunty metal vessel with a hot-pink heart painted along the starboard side and the name *Janine* emblazoned in throbbing Day-Glo purple. The rowboat bobbing in the water was enormous and built of wood with oars of a size to match.

Again that odd prickling sensation overtook Emilie, but she swallowed hard against it. Boats like that one hadn't been seen around Crosse Harbor for a very long time.

It's for the Patriots' Day celebration, she thought as she untied the boat then climbed into it. Sam Talmadge loved everything to do with holidays and he obviously was just making certain that all the revolutionary war re-creation details were right on the money.

She didn't know Sam all that well. For all she knew, he even raised his own turkeys for his Thanksgiving feast.

She hadn't rowed more than three feet before she found herself sorely regretting letting her membership at the health club lapse. The wooden oars were as heavy as they were huge and a few weeks of pumping iron would have been a welcome rehearsal for the enterprise.

"Think positive," she admonished herself as she struggled to move the oars through the water with firm, even strokes. She'd already done the impossible twice today when she'd saved Zane from drowning, then dragged him upstairs and into the lighthouse. Certainly she could manage to row a measly boat across the harbor and get help.

Lowering her head, she channeled all her concentration into the job at hand. Under normal circumstances a person could row across the harbor in fifteen minutes.

After a half hour, even Emilie had to admit that she was getting nowhere fast. Her arms trembled from the effort and she was starting to feel light-headed. At the rate she was going, she could row all day and all night and not see one of the usual landmarks.

But that was ridiculous. Still, there had to be some reason she was having so much trouble getting her bearings.

She stopped rowing and stared across at the shoreline she had known and loved all her life. Where was Brower's Dockside Restaurant? The marina with the brightly colored flags waving overhead in the sea breeze? The fishermen who should have been plying their trade for hours by now?

"Don't panic," she told herself. "There has to be a simple explanation."

Maybe this wasn't Eagle Island after all, and that wasn't Crosse Harbor.

Maybe she and Zane had floated down toward Cape May or up toward Long Branch.

Or maybe—

Her breath caught in her throat as she wondered why it had taken her so long to see what was right there in front of her very eyes. The water was crystalline, the sky a blue so pure and deep that it reminded her of a Disney movie. The air had the sweet, fresh smell of a mountaintop. Where were the signs of modern life in the mid-twentieth century, the sludge and pollution and ever-present noise?

Her entire body jerked with the shock of realization. It couldn't be. Things like that didn't happen in real life. Peggy Sue and Marty McFly might travel through time but real people were bound by the laws of nature, not the whims of some Hollywood scriptwriter.

New strength filled her arms as she rowed back to the lighthouse, determined to unravel the mystery. She brought the rowboat into the dock, then tied it to a post.

The first thing she noticed when she reached the front door was the absence of a lock. In 1992? Not very likely. The hinges were new and free from rust. She burst into the front room and headed straight toward the window seat where she'd found the dog-eared copy of *Poor Richard's Almanack* that she had laughed at earlier.

Her hands trembled as she opened to the first page. *Printed in the year of Our Lord 1776.* No copyright. No reprint information. No mention of Doubleday or Simon & Schuster or McGraw-Hill.

Exhilaration rocketed through her.

It was a first edition.

And it wasn't very old.

Chapter Four

4

This couldn't be happening. There was no rational explanation for any of it, but Emilie couldn't deny the evidence right there before her eyes.

She'd seen enough reproductions in her day to know the difference, and this copy of *Poor Richard's Almanack* was the real thing.

She sank to the floor, her legs trembling too violently to support her weight.

No wonder Crosse Harbor had looked so different. The signs of progress had been erased as if they'd never happened.

At least, not *yet*.

A wave of dizziness spiraled through her body and she lowered her head, breathing in the clean salt air. The Industrial Revolution was yet to be born. Clean air, clear water—everything the citizens of the late twentieth century were struggling desperately to regain—were standard issue here.

Why on earth hadn't she realized it sooner? She lifted her head, then looked slowly around the cabin, trying to absorb the enormity of it all. No telephones. No electrical wiring anywhere to be seen. Amenities like indoor plumbing and refrigeration were still the stuff of dreams. She'd sensed something was different, but her eye had seen only what it was accustomed to seeing while her imagination had filled in the blanks.

Any reasonable woman would have been downright terrified to find herself catapulted back through the centuries. Fear of the unknown was one of the most basic human responses. Emilie, however, was galvanized with an almost supernatural energy that rocketed through her veins and flooded her mind with wonder.

Could it be that fate had had something planned for her, something more dangerous and exciting than even the adventure-loving Zane Rutledge had ever known?

"Oh, God," she murmured, glancing toward the man sleeping fitfully on the trundle bed by the window. He'd never believe it. No matter what evidence she paraded before him, he wasn't going to relinquish the world he knew.

Not without a fight.

Zane was a man comfortable in his own skin—and in his own time. The uncertainties and longings that had shadowed Emilie from the day she was born were alien to him. He took from life what he wanted and moved on when he'd had enough. How would he react when he found himself stripped of everything he knew and understood?

There had to be a logical answer, some combination of elements that would explain what had happened. She thought about that shimmering sense of destiny she'd experienced the first moment she saw Zane striding up the driveway.

How they had managed to end up back in the eighteenth century mattered less to her than *why,* but she knew he would never rest until he understood.

"What the—?" He opened his eyes and tried to prop himself on his right arm. "Jesus Christ!"

She was at his side in an instant. "Easy. Lie back down, Zane. You broke your arm."

He fell back on the bed, breathing heavily. "I'm either seeing two of you or you're the Doublemint twins."

His normally ruddy complexion seemed dangerously pale and she remembered the bloodstains on the sand. "There's only one of me," she said, struggling to keep her voice light and optimistic. "I'm right here." He tried to sit up but she placed a hand against his chest. "Don't."

"What happened?"

"Remember that stunt you pulled with the hot-air balloon?"

He nodded.

"Looks like we didn't make it to Langley Park in one piece." Or in the same century, but she'd save that nugget of information for another time.

"You...how are—?"

"A few bumps and bruises, but I'm okay. I'm afraid you took the worst of it."

"Good." Her heart turned over at that simple word. *He's in bad shape. You've got to do something!* The thought of setting his broken arm herself made her feel faint, but who else was there? She'd always prided herself on her knowledge of Crosse Harbor during this time period, but her mind was a blank. Until she gained her own bearings, she didn't dare risk searching for a doctor.

"How are you feeling?" she asked, leaning over him.

"Stupid," he said, wincing as he tried to shift position on the trundle bed. "Where are we?"

"The lighthouse," she said, truthfully enough.

"Where's the balloon?"

"I don't know. I woke up on the beach. You were in the water." And the balloon and gondola had both vanished without a trace.

"You saved my life?"

"I did what needed to be done."

"Remind me to thank you," he said, closing his eyes. "After I wake up...."

"Don't thank me yet, Zane," she whispered as he drifted back into sleep. Once he discovered where they were, he might not feel particularly grateful.

She'd survived the first round of questions, but the second round was bound to be her undoing. Wait until he asked her to dial 911 or arrange for an X ray or call his travel agent to change his flight to another day.

First things first. Survival was the order of the day. They needed water and they needed food. And if she could find some clean bedding and a smooth piece of wood to use as a splint she'd consider herself a very lucky woman.

She'd noticed a cellar door hidden beneath some wild strawberry vines when she was tying the rowboat to the dock after her aborted trip to the mainland. Hurrying outside, she elbowed her way past the thicket of vines and dune grass then breathed a sigh of relief.

There it was! The door was painted a dusty grayish blue, weathered only slightly by the salt air and water, and she was struck anew with the knowledge that the lighthouse was in its prime, not dilapidated and forgotten as it is—*was?*—now.

These hinges also were free of rust and she easily threw open the heavy door and made her way down the stone steps into the cool darkness of the cellar where, if her knowledge of colonial ways was half as good as she'd always believed, there was a better-than-even chance she'd locate a cache of preserved foods.

Ceramic pots of jams and preserved vegetables were lined neatly on wooden shelving, rough and unfinished, while a smoked ham hung from a hook suspended from the ceiling. It was far from an impressive display of goods but she couldn't have been happier if she'd been let loose in her local supermarket with a blank check.

"I hope you don't have a blood-pressure problem, Zane," she murmured as she made her selections. Without refrigeration, most people of the late eighteenth century relied upon salt as a preservative. It was bound to be a shock to their modern palates, but beggars couldn't be choosers.

"We'll learn to adapt," she said, wishing she had a basket to carry her bounty. "We can—" She gasped as the food went flying and she found herself pinned face first against the damp stone wall of the cellar.

"State your business fast, lass," a man hissed as he held her against the wall, "or I'll slit your pretty throat from ear to ear." He was about her height and triple her strength and she wondered if she'd survived a lightning trip through the centuries only to meet her Maker in a musty root cellar.

She considered her options, her situation, the incredible happenings of the past twenty-four hours, then she did exactly what a proper eighteenth century woman would have done in her position: she fainted dead away.

Andrew McVie was many things, but a fool was not among them.

Ofttimes the enemy appeared in a comely package, designed to cloud a man's vision and lead him astray from the road he was sworn to travel.

These were dangerous times in which they lived. A wise man withheld his trust until a reason for that trust was offered.

But when the beautiful lass with the flaming red hair swooned at his feet, caution took second place to gentlemanly concern and he dropped his blade to the ground and sprang to her aid.

"Aye, you're a tall one," he said as he placed her on the stone bench near the door. Her shoulders were broad, her breasts rounded and full. She was a strapping woman, one a man could easily imagine warming his bed on a cold winter's night, but he started in surprise as he realized she wore not the usual maidenly array of skirts but a pair of black breeches much like his own.

If he'd seen a donkey walk like a man, he would not have been more surprised.

What manner of female was this? The cellar was bathed in shadows and he bent down to look more closely at her. No demure mobcap held back her fiery tresses; they cascaded freely about her face.

His eye was drawn to the hand at her throat and to the king's ransom he found there. On the middle finger of her right hand she wore a heavy ring of braided silver and gold and at her neck, on a fine golden chain, was a most amazing glass globe that seemed to have captured all the colors of the rainbow within its depths.

His gaze moved from the rise and fall of her breasts to the amazing display of wealth she carried on her person. He was uncertain which intrigued him more. He frowned as he followed the line of her limbs with his gaze. The black breeches were an affront to her womanliness. Surely she could afford to garb herself in clothing more pleasing to the eye.

He wondered if this lass might be part of the spy ring, but the notion was so absurd he laughed aloud. Who would believe such nonsense? No, this was probably the wife of one of the local fishermen, who had rowed across the inlet looking to steal a few potatoes for her children's supper. Times were difficult and the good woman could not be held accountable for doing what was necessary to keep their bellies filled. Yet, this woman looked as if she'd ne'er known hard times.

He remembered the early days of his marriage to Elspeth when he was struggling with his commitments to family and to his law practice in Boston and how, time after time, Elspeth and their son had suffered for his ambition. He had wanted so many things for them: a fine house and servants so Elspeth could sit by the leaded-glass windows and dream away the hours, a farm filled with produce instead of problems, a library stacked with the books necessary for the classical education he was determined his only son would enjoy.

Cinders now, all of it. Gone in the instant it took an ember from the hearth to ignite the blaze that had destroyed everything Andrew held dear while he pursued the almighty shilling.

Strange that the sight of this strapping woman should call to mind memories of his wife. Elspeth had been as delicate as a budding rose, but that fragile beauty had hidden a strength he had come to rely upon.

Mayhap too much, for Elspeth's strength had freed him to pursue the fleeting pleasures of life that had seemed so important at the time. That beautiful little boy they had created on a warm summer night had been more important than the accumulation of wealth. If only he had come to that realization while there was still time....

Today there was only the rebellion to give reason to his hours upon this earth and he intended to offer up his heart and spirit in the pursuit of independence, even if it ultimately meant nothing at all.

His last foray into English-held land on Manhattan Island had been for naught. He had come away with little but a sense of despair that grew stronger with each day that passed.

He had returned to the lighthouse, unlighted since the advent of war, hoping to find Josiah Blakelee awaiting him, but only silence had greeted his return. Blakelee, who owned a farm near Princeton, believed strongly in the cause of liberty and had offered his services in the pursuit of those blessings that flowed from independence.

Blakelee was one of those rare men whose demeanor and affability made him instantly welcome wherever he went. He also was possessed of a courage that took him many times into danger—perhaps for the last time some two months ago when he vanished north of Manhattan Island.

Andrew had intended to inflict upon Blakelee a sermon whose purpose was to impress upon the man the fleeting happiness to be found with family. Blakelee's disappearance tore at Andrew's soul, for it seemed to point out the ultimate hopeless nature of the struggle.

Family was all. Without it, even independence from the Crown meant little.

But Josiah Blakelee burned with the fires of liberty. For the past few months he had liberally quoted from Thomas Paine's *Common Sense,* and he understood what Sam Adams said better than Sam Adams did himself.

Last year, not long after Concord and Lexington, Andrew and Josiah had dined at Braintree with Samuel's redoubtable cousin John and John's wife, Abigail, and John Adams had given a vigorous discourse on the necessity to separate the colonies from the mother country.

Josiah had fair to boiled with the righteousness of the cause. There had been a time when Andrew, too, had known the same passionate commitment as shared by these two fine men, but that night he had only sat and listened, his mind on a time and place lost to him forever.

Mrs. Adams, a small and handsome woman whose powers of intellect were a match for those of her husband, seemed to sense that Andrew gave but lip service to the cause.

"There is a comfort to be found in a commitment to a cause," she'd said to Andrew over a pot of chicory-laced coffee. She and her husband had lost a child in infancy, and they took much solace in diverting their sorrows into pursuing a greater good.

And so it was that Andrew had joined forces with those who cared deeply about the pursuit of liberty.

Now he faced the unpleasant task of telling Blakelee's wife that her husband was still among the missing. A score of patriots had been rounded up near the Harlem Heights, and rumor had it they were on their way to one of the prison ships moored in Wallabout Bay in New York Harbor. A worse punishment could not be imagined, and it was Andrew's fond hope that Blakelee had been spared that fate.

The red-haired woman stirred, and his thoughts returned to the moment. The first order of business after she came around was to discover why the auburn-tressed woman had come to the root cellar—and what, if anything, she knew about his business.

If Emilie had fainted back home she would have found herself in the emergency room trying to explain her reaction to a pimply-faced intern with a fistful of forms and very little in the way of concern.

Instead she opened her eyes to find herself lying flat on a stone bench to the right of the cellar door. A man knelt on the floor next to her, a knife protruding from the waistband of his breeches. It took her less than a second to remember that, like Dorothy in *The Wizard of Oz,* she wasn't in Kansas anymore.

Sitting bolt upright she fixed him with her deadliest look. "Touch me once and you'll find yourself without a hand."

He rose to his feet. He was approximately her height, but much broader of chest and shoulders. He had the look of a solitary man, one who cared little for fancy clothing or grooming. His light brown hair was shaggy, drawn back into a ponytail and tied with a length of black fabric. His shirt was made of a rough cambric material in a natural color while his breeches were a faded tobacco brown. He looked oddly stylish to her modern eyes, yet totally in keeping with the time period.

"What brings you to this place, lass?" His accent was part Scottish brogue, part flat New England.

Would you believe a big red balloon? Withholding that particular nugget of information seemed the better part of valor. "Begging your pardon, sir, but I—I find myself in most difficult circumstances." She was horrified to find legitimate tears welling up in her eyes.

And elated to see the effect those tears had on this rough-looking man.

"Aye, now none of that," he said, his voice gruff.

"Begging your pardon, sir," she said, dabbing at her eyes. He handed her a rough square of cambric with the initial *A* in the corner. "Thanks."

Instantly she wished she had chosen her words with more care.

He looked at her, his thick, bushy eyebrows rising. "Thanks," he repeated. "What manner of speech is that?"

"It's—it's a family word," she said, stumbling badly over her white lie. "How foolish of me to use it with a stranger."

He nodded, outwardly accepting her explanation, but she had the feeling the warning bells were going off inside his head. *Watch yourself, Crosse! This isn't a man easily tricked.* She blessed her lifelong interest in the methods and mores of colonial America and prayed they'd be sufficient to see her through.

"Your most difficult circumstances—" he prodded.

I knew you'd come back to that. "My...my companion and I were partaking of a leisurely boating ride when a most unexpected storm swept us decidedly off course and onto your shores."

That flinty look reappeared in his hazel eyes. "And when did this aberration of nature occur?"

His word choice belied his rough-hewn appearance. The man was educated. This would be even more challenging than she had feared. "Before the noon hour," she said, praying her own word choice wouldn't give her away.

He nodded. That would explain why he had seen nothing untoward when he'd reached the lighthouse late last night. He had devoured a few slices of ham then dropped into a dreamless sleep, only to be roused by the sight of this redheaded woman helping herself to his cache of food.

"I see no evidence of a companion," he said, reminding himself that beauty and veracity did not always walk hand in hand.

"Inside the lighthouse," she said. "I fear he has a broken arm among other injuries."

He looked more closely at her. "Have you taken a full accounting of your own?"

She waved her hand and his eye was caught again by the glitter of gold and silver. "They do not matter."

Her gaze was as direct as a man's and Andrew found himself taken aback. "Would this man be your husband, then?"

"My friend," she said simply. "He has lost a great deal of blood, sir, and I—" Her voice caught and she lowered her gaze, but not before he saw the shimmer of tears.

"Take me to your friend, lass. I have not the skills of a doctor, but I can offer some assistance." He smiled, and his rawboned face was transformed. "'Twould be useful if I knew your Christian name."

"Emilie," she said, returning his smile. "Emilie Crosse." The name meant nothing to him, but it would be a few years yet before her family helped to build the town that would one day bear their name.

"'Tis odd circumstances under which we meet, mistress Emilie."

"You have me at a disadvantage, sir." *This is fun,* she thought. Like dancing a minuet with words instead of steps.

"Andrew," he said. "Andrew McVie." He reached for her. "Mistress Emilie, are you feeling faint?"

Mistress Emilie was just plain blown away.

Andrew McVie!

The man whose name had been on the lips of every Crosse Harbor schoolkid for the past two hundred years—the most wanted rebel of them all—was standing right here in front of her! Was it only last night that she had recounted McVie's story to Zane, glorying in the tale of courage and patriotism?

"It has been a long and difficult morning," she said at last, accepting McVie's hand as she rose to her feet. "I pray you will disregard my momentary weakness."

"Weakness in the fair sex is a most agreeable trait."

"Strength is more agreeable, no matter the sex," she returned. How disappointing it would be to discover her childhood hero was a male chauvinist pig. "Don't you agree?"

The woman was sharp-tongued and swift to voice her opinions. That would explain how it was that she remained unwed. "Take me to your companion," he said, ushering her toward the stairs that led out from the root cellar. "A broken arm left untended can rob a man of his ability to earn a living."

You don't know the half of it, thought Emilie as she climbed the steps, wincing at the assault of late-afternoon sunlight. Zane was a physical man. He was accustomed to pushing himself to the limit, then beyond. Being restricted in any way would drive him right up the wall.

Unfortunately, that was the least of their worries.

Andrew followed the redheaded woman along the stone pathway toward the front door of the lighthouse. Her abundant tresses seemed to capture the sun, then send its fire shooting back toward the sky. He wondered how she would look with her auburn waves piled neatly atop her head in the style the good women of his acquaintance favored.

Of course, her style of hairdress was not the only unusual thing about the woman. He allowed that her strange attire must be the result of the accident. Perhaps her skirt had been torn on the rocks or she had used the fabric to bind her companion's wounds.

She had no womanly embarrassment about her attire. She was neither coy nor modest. She walked before him with her head held high, unmindful of the shocking way her limbs were outlined for the world to see. The breeches fit her like a second skin. He wondered how or why she had knitted a pair designed to cling to her curves in quite so indecent a fashion. He could plainly see the shape and fullness of her buttocks, the slender shape of her thighs, the—

She stopped abruptly and turned to meet his eyes. He felt as if he had been caught stealing apples from an unsuspecting farmer's orchard.

"My companion isn't—he is not. . . thinking as himself since our boating accident."

McVie looked back toward the dock where the rowboat was tethered.

"That's not our boat," Emilie said quickly.

"Where is your boat?"

"I don't—I do not know."

"I see no sign of it anywhere."

"Of course you don't," she said, prepared to weave a tale of misfortune. "We found ourselves dashed against the rocks, torn apart by fearsome waves, then tossed into the ocean with naught but our wits to save us." She hadn't had this much fun since her honeymoon, and that was six years ago.

Or was it two hundred and ten years ahead? She wasn't entirely sure.

She would have continued spinning her tale of adventure and derring-do, but McVie threw back his head and started to laugh.

"That is unconscionably rude of you, Mr. McVie."

"I do not know what the truth is, lass, but this story of yours is most enjoyable."

"It's not a story," she protested. Well, maybe the part about the boat was, but that was picking nits. "I saved his life."

Were it any other but the strapping lass before him, Andrew would have had grievous doubts. He had never known a woman who was tall enough to look him straight in the eye before and the sensation was unsettling. However, it did explain her ability to save a grown man from drowning.

His Elspeth had been a tiny creature, barely reaching his shoulder even in her best shoes. She had made him feel strong and protective. Everything a man should feel about the woman he had taken to wife. Sometimes late at night when sleep danced just beyond reach, she came to him in the shadowy world of his imagination, and he could smell the scent of vanilla on her skin and hear the sweet sound of her laughter as she said, "Put aside the ledger, Andrew. The hour is late and our bed is warm."

No, this Emilie Crosse was a different type of woman and he found himself wondering what type of man would be a suitable companion.

Emilie approached the front door with trepidation. This wasn't going to work. She was crazy to think she had a chance of pulling it off. Here she was bringing a revolutionary war hero inside to talk to a man who thought he was still back home in the twentieth century.

Talk about a worst-case scenario.

She cast a glance over her shoulder at Andrew McVie. He was justly suspicious of her. The wonder of it was that he hadn't carted her off to the nearest representative of the law.

But wait until he met Zane. The minute Zane opened his mouth, McVie would know beyond a shadow of a doubt that something was amiss. She supposed she could explain Zane's "eccentricities" away by saying he'd suffered a blow to the head in their fictitious boating accident, but McVie wasn't likely to buy that for long.

Let Zane be asleep, she prayed silently as she reached for the doorknob. Maybe just a tad unconscious. She needed time to explain the situation—and he would need time to accept it.

What happened after that would be anybody's guess.

Zane paced the length of the front room, waiting for Emilie to return. His arm hurt like hell, he was sure he had the mother of all shiners over his right eye and he was hungry enough to eat sand.

He'd looked all over for a telephone, but to his surprise he couldn't find one anywhere. As a matter of fact, he hadn't been able to find a jack or wires or any other signs of human habitation. The place looked new. Rustic, but basically new. Emilie had mentioned something last night about renovations to the lighthouse. Maybe they just hadn't gotten around to rewiring the place.

He glanced at his watch. The damn thing must've taken as much of a beating as he had when the balloon collapsed on them. Too bad he hadn't bought a Timex. At least then he'd know if he had a prayer of getting to the airport on time. Let alone to a doctor for his arm.

Since Emilie had told him about the balloon accident, he'd racked his brain in an attempt to figure out what had gone wrong, but all he could come up with was a cloudy memory of watching the earth coming at him like a runaway train, and then nothing. The relief he'd felt when he saw Emilie had weathered the accident with nothing worse than a few bumps and bruises was still enough to make him consider a return to religion.

She'd said no when he'd asked her to throw caution to the wind and join him on his trip to Tahiti, but that was before they'd faced the grim reaper together. She'd always wondered what he found so seductive about courting disaster. Now that she'd experienced the ultimate thrill, maybe she'd understand.

He'd learned a long time ago that you were never more alive than you were when death was staring you in the eye. That adrenaline pumping through your veins...the white-hot certainty that you were running at top speed...the rush of pure elation when you met the challenge and emerged victorious.

Last night with Emilie in his arms he'd known the same sense of danger and renewal. He didn't believe in happy endings and he never would, but he couldn't help but wonder if maybe they should have fought harder to make it work—at least a little while longer.

Sara Jane used to say—

He stopped.

"That's it," he said out loud. That's what was different. For the past hour he'd been trying to figure out what had changed, and now he knew.

He wasn't hearing Sara Jane's voice any longer.

He didn't know exactly when it had happened, but sometime last night he'd stopped feeling as if his grandmother was inside his head, trying to tell him something.

But he knew when it was: when he'd taken Emilie in his arms and—

No way was he about to pursue that thought. What he and Emilie had found last night had been both real and powerful. He'd be the last person to deny that. She'd stirred something in his soul, a sense of wonder and yearning that he'd forgotten was even possible.

But to read anything more into it than a wonderful case of chemical attraction was to fall prey to the same romantic babble that had led to disappointment the first time around.

The rasp of the doorknob being turned brought him up short. Maybe she'd reconsidered Tahiti....

"He might be sleeping," Emilie said to Andrew McVie as the door to the lighthouse swung open. "We should—"

"What the hell took you so long?" Zane demanded as they entered the room. "If we're going to make that plane, we'd better—"

Poor Andrew stopped dead in his tracks and stared at Zane as if he'd encountered a hungry bear in his den. A hungry bear with a brightly colored quilt knotted at his waist. She could only imagine what Andrew must be thinking. Nervous laughter tugged at her, but she swallowed hard in an attempt to control it.

"This is Andrew McVie," said Emilie, forcing a pleasant smile and praying Zane would see the plea in her eyes. "I am afraid this is his home in which we have sought refuge."

Zane glanced around the room. "Monastic, isn't it?"

Andrew stepped forward. He seemed unconcerned at the difference in their heights and Emilie had the feeling that, appearances notwithstanding, the two men were more evenly matched than either might care to admit. "I have yet to learn your name, sir."

Emilie sensed rather than saw Zane's hesitation as he extended his left hand. Did he remember her stories about Andrew McVie's heroic exploits? *Please, God, let him forget....*

"Zane Grey Rutledge."

"What manner of name is Zane Grey?" asked Andrew, obviously puzzled. "Are you German?"

Zane met Emilie's eyes. "Is this guy kidding?"

She could only shake her head miserably.

Zane turned back to McVie. "I'm named after Zane Grey."

Andrew looked at him blankly.

"The writer," Zane persisted, apparently enjoying the other man's confusion. "He wrote Westerns. Cowboys…Indians…the last frontier."

McVie had yet to take Zane's outstretched hand. "Cowboys?"

"Okay, I give up." Zane backed away, shaking his head. He looked again toward Emilie. "What the hell's going on here?"

McVie glared at the taller man. "I must ask you to refrain from such language in front of mistress Emilie."

Zane's lips twitched as if he was about to laugh, but apparently he thought better of it. "Isn't this carrying the whole revolutionary war thing too far, McVie?"

Both men turned to Emilie, who wished quite fervently that she had disappeared along with the crimson balloon and the basket.

"I do not know what you mean, Zane," she said demurely, then turned toward Andrew. "I am afraid Mr. Rutledge hit his head upon the rocks when we ran aground. He is still discombobulated."

Andrew visibly relaxed.

Zane, however, was beyond understanding. Discombobulated? What the hell kind of word was *discombobulated?* He was one step away from going ballistic. "I don't know what in hell's going on around here, but if somebody doesn't give me some answers soon, I—"

"Leave the room, mistress Emilie," said Andrew, not taking his eyes from Zane. "Mr. Rutledge and I have a most pressing matter to discuss."

"The only thing I want to talk about is getting to the airport on time to make my plane."

"Airport?" Andrew looked toward Emilie. "His injury may be more grave than you figured. He speaks nonsense."

Zane approached the smaller man, bristling with righteous male indignation. "Why don't you try saying that to my face, pal?"

Emilie stepped between the two men. "Please! We forget why we're here, gentlemen. Zane's arm needs tending and the hour grows late even as we stand here."

Zane looked down at her, his handsome features creased in puzzlement. "You sound weird."

"It must be your imagination."

"The hell it is."

McVie stepped forward. "Rutledge, I fear your manner is insulting to mistress Emilie."

Zane's mood slid from bad to worse. "If 'mistress Emilie' has a problem with my manner, she'll tell me."

"Your arm," said Emilie. "Please. . . ."

"Lie down on the bed," McVie ordered Zane. "Mistress Emilie, bring me a thick branch from the stack of kindling near the cellar door."

"That guy's not laying a hand on me," Zane snapped, barring Emilie's departure. "Don't you have an emergency room in this town?"

"We will have," said Emilie.

"Emergency room?" said McVie. "Is this a new language he speaks or is it the blow to his head?"

"I'm going to land a blow to your head, if you don't butt out," Zane said to McVie.

McVie reached for his knife, wrapping his fingers around the hilt in a threatening gesture. Zane grabbed an andiron from the hearth and stared menacingly at the other man.

Emilie, at the end of her rope, knew there was only one option left to her.

"Gentlemen," she said, stepping between them, "we have to talk."

5

"I've got a plane to catch," Zane said. "The only thing I want to talk about is whether or not you're coming with me." It was time to move on and he wanted Emilie with him.

"Sit down," she said, gesturing toward the trundle bed. "This is going to take some time."

Andrew McVie, still clutching the knife, glanced from Zane to Emilie. At first glance he had mistaken Rutledge for his compatriot Josiah Blakelee, and the similarity in size and physique still had him shaking his head in wonderment. It occurred to him that this could be part of an elaborately concocted scheme whose ultimate goal was the defeat of the thirteen united colonies.

"You can sit over there," said Emilie, pointing to the straight-back chair near the hearth.

He shook his head. "Nay, mistress. I think not." He took a position near the door. There was nothing about the situation that could be deemed normal and it was his intention to be prepared for any happenstance.

"Oh, God...." Her words were exhaled on a sigh. She looked from one man to the other. "This is going to be tougher than I thought."

"Just spit it out," said Rutledge. "If we're going to make it to JFK, we'd better—"

"We're not going to JFK."

"You mean *you're* not going?"

She shook her head. "Nobody's going to JFK because there *is* no JFK." She laughed, but there was the sound of panic in her voice. "In fact, there are no airplanes, no automobiles, no computers. You name it and you won't find it here."

"What manner of object is a com-pu-turr?" asked Andrew.

Zane whirled toward the other man. "What's with you, McVie? You been living in a cave for the past twenty years?" *McVie...Andrew McVie...why does that name sound so damn familiar?*

"Don't you understand?" Emilie's expression was as intense as her tone of voice. "This isn't Crosse Harbor and it isn't 1992. We've gone back in time."

Zane's gut twisted. It was worse than he thought. She'd obviously lost her mind. He stood. "Listen, it's been a lousy morning. Why don't you lie down on the bed and get some rest. McVie can take me into town to the doctor. A broken arm's no big deal. I'll be back before you wake up from your nap—"

"Listen to me, Zane!" Her voice filled the room. "Look around you! This isn't the world you knew." She gestured toward McVie, who was standing, eyes watchful, near the door. "This is *his* world!"

Zane met McVie's eyes. "Do you know what she's talking about?"

McVie shook his head. He tapped the side of his head with his forefinger in a gesture Zane recognized.

Unfortunately so did Emilie, and she let out a shriek of exasperation.

"Where are the electrical outlets?" she demanded, poking Zane in the chest. "The telephone? Refrigerator? Have you heard a car go by or seen an airplane or motorboat? Where's the bathroom, for God's sake, Zane?"

Sweat broke out on the back of his neck. "You told me last night that they were restoring the lighthouse," he said, evading the issue. "They just haven't gotten around to everything yet."

"That's right," she said, meeting his eyes. "It will take another century or two to finish the job."

He stormed through the lighthouse as a dark cloud of fear settled itself around him. "You're wrong," he said, overturning tables and kicking open doors as he searched for proof. "You don't go to sleep in one century then wake up in another." There had to be another explanation, some simple answer that they were overlooking.

Emilie was hard on his heels as he made his way up the winding staircase toward the lookout tower. "Remember the cloud cover that blew in on us? You said you'd never seen anything like it before."

"Shut up!" he roared. "I don't want to hear it. This whole thing is nuts. *You're* nuts!"

She laid a hand on his forearm. "I'm scared, too," she said, her voice soft. "It's normal to be—"

"It's bullshit," he said, pulling away from her.

"No, it isn't, Zane. You know it isn't."

"I'll prove it to you." He pulled himself up into the lookout tower, trying to ignore the sharp waves of pain radiating from his forearm to his shoulder and across his chest. "Most of the lighthouses today are automated."

"Not this one," said Emilie, popping up at his side.

"Bet me."

Emilie's heart ached for him. He was a man accustomed to being in control and this was a situation over which neither had anything resembling control. Beads of sweat poised over his upper lip and he held his arm at an odd angle, almost as if the appendage belonged to somebody else. Under normal circumstances Zane's arm would be set by now and he'd have access to the painkillers almost everyone took for granted.

"This is a trick," he said, staring at the oil and wick that served as a beacon. "Some kind of practical joke."

"Look toward the west," she said quietly. "Toward the harbor. That's not the Crosse Harbor we left behind."

He didn't want to look. There was something in her tone of voice, some deeper note of truth, that was scaring the hell out of him.

He turned slowly, bracing himself, then looked around.

Maple trees, heavy with leaves, crowded the shore. The sky was a rich, deep blue streaked with a few high cirrus clouds. The water was clear, the air was fresh, the whole thing was impossible, but in his gut he knew Emilie was right.

"Beautiful, isn't it?" she whispered, coming up behind him.

He nodded. There was a certain wild magnificence to the sight before him but he refused to acknowledge it. Still, he found it impossible to turn away from the sight. "What year?"

"I'm not certain." She paused for a moment. "Around 1776, as near as I can tell."

His body jerked as if struck a blow. "How do you know?"

"*Poor Richard's Almanack.* I found it near the trundle bed."

Her face seemed lit from within, almost incandescent with the thrill of discovery, and it occurred to him that this woman wasn't like anyone he'd ever known. She wasn't afraid or angry or any of the hundred other emotions anyone else in their position would be feeling. The notion of being torn from the life she knew and thrust back in time seemed to fill her with excitement, as if she'd been waiting all her life for this moment.

Last night with her in his arms he'd felt they were on the brink of a new relationship, but he'd never imagined it would be anything like this.

"Zane." She moved into his line of vision. "Are you—"

"I'm okay," he said, not entirely convinced of that fact. "I just wish I'd paid more attention to high school history classes."

"I may not remember all the dates, but I paid close enough attention to everything else." Again she touched his arm and images from the night before seemed to shimmer in the air between them. "Think of it, Zane. The revolutionary war is going on and we're the only people on earth who know how it's going to end."

Andrew McVie had heard more than enough and he stepped from the shadows.

"Aye, 'tis talk like that that has led many a man to an early grave."

Emilie and Zane turned to see him standing at the top of the stairs, brandishing a wicked-looking knife.

"Oh, not again." Emilie motioned toward the weapon. "Come to your senses, Andrew. We're on your side."

He narrowed his eyes and looked from one to the other. "Lass, your countenance is most agreeable but I fear there is still much about you and your companion to cause me great affliction."

"You heard what I said, didn't you?" The mistress Emilie fixed him with a look from those huge green eyes of hers and it was almost his undoing.

"You spoke of war," he said, knife at the ready should they try to make an untoward escape. "What is it you know about the engagement?"

Mistress Emilie met her companion's eyes, then looked back toward Andrew. In television and movies there were rules that went hand in hand with time travel. Too bad she couldn't remember any of them at the moment. "I know that your cause will be victorious."

"And how is it you know to which cause I pledge my allegiance?" He'd been right to hold the couple in suspicion, and now the redheaded woman was about to betray her true convictions.

She hesitated.

"Aye, lass, it's as I thought. A noble ruse, I must admit, but one that will know an unhappy resolution."

"Wait a minute!" said the man with the inexplicable name. "What did you say your name was?"

It occurred to Andrew that he'd been a fool and more to have given his rightful name to these strangers. "McVie," he said with reluctance.

"That's it!" Zane Grey Rutledge looked unconscionably pleased with himself. "You're the one who saved George Washington from an assassination plot."

It took Andrew but an instant to react. He put the knife between his teeth, grabbed the redheaded woman, then held the knife to the softest part of her throat. "How is it you know anything about me?" he asked in a tone that brooked no argument. "Anything less than the truth and the lass will know the sting of my blade."

Zane lurched forward, ready to do battle, only to have the full fury of his broken arm drop him to his knees at the first swing of his fist.

"Touch her, McVie, and I'll kill you."

If Emilie felt anything more than surprise at the situation, she hid it well.

"I know this is difficult for you to believe, Andrew, but we're from the future."

Andrew's laugh echoed in the empty tower. "Witches no longer cast their spell in the colonies, mistress Emilie. Not even in Massachusetts."

"This isn't witchcraft or fortune-telling," she persisted in that oddly accented voice of hers. "We had an accident—"

"I know," he broke in. "On your boat."

"Well, not exactly." He released his hold on her, then spun her around by the shoulders so he could see her face. "It was a balloon accident."

He knew he must resemble the village idiot with his mouth agape, but her words were so preposterous that he could do naught but laugh. "You speak nonsense."

But she was not to be deterred. "I speak the truth. Zane and I were floating in a hot-air balloon. We sailed into bad weather and crashed to the ground." Her laugh was uneasy and it made him suddenly uncomfortable. "Only thing is, we misjudged our destination by about two hundred years."

He felt the way he had the last time he attempted to drown his prodigious sorrows in a tankard of ale at the Bunch of Grapes. "So you say you come from the future—from the year nineteen hundred and seventy-six?"

Emilie's mouth turned up in a smile. "Well, nineteen hundred and ninety-two, but who's counting?"

Andrew was. Every single unbelievable year. "I suppose you have proof of this phenomenon?"

She looked toward Zane. "Do you have anything?"

He shrugged. "I'm naked under this blanket, Emilie. How about you?"

"I don't—" She stopped. "Wait a minute. I think I *do* have something. . . ."

Andrew watched with great caution as she reached into the waistband of her breeches and withdrew a heavily embroidered purse much like the ones the good women of his acquaintance carried on their person.

Emilie looked at the purse and tears of wonder sprang to her eyes. The faded silk threads were vibrant, pulsing with rich color. The worn spots on the outer edges were plush with texture. If she'd required more proof of their situation, this was it. She felt Zane's eyes on her as she untied the ribbon then withdrew a one-dollar bill.

She handed the single to McVie. "This should do it."

McVie took the bill from the redheaded woman. There was a linenlike texture to the note that felt substantial to his work-roughened fingers.

"Take a close look," she urged.

"Federal Reserve Note," he read from the top of the currency. "The United—" He blinked. Surely his eyes were playing tricks upon his brain.

"The United States of America," said Emilie. "And that's George Washington right there looking back at you."

It was more than Andrew could comprehend. "General Washington?"

Emilie smiled wide. "*President* Washington. The first president of the United States of America."

"This is— I cannot. . . ." His words trailed off as he stared again at the currency in his hand. Indeed, the portrait of the white-haired man did seem to bear more than a passing resemblance to the likenesses he'd seen of His Excellency, the general. He read off a string of letters and numbers near the upper right-hand corner, then looked twice at the words beneath. "Washington Dee Cee. What does that mean?"

"District of Columbia," said Rutledge. "The capital of the fifty states."

"It's on the Potomac River," offered Emilie. "Near your Maryland and Virginia."

Her words were lost on Andrew. "*Fifty* states?"

"Thirteen colonies became fifty states," said Emilie, eyes shining. "From the Atlantic Ocean to the Pacific."

A green seal was positioned beneath the name of the nation's capital and within that seal were the words *Department of the Treasury 1789*.

Andrew dropped the bill as if it had suddenly caught fire. His chest felt tight, making it hard to draw sufficient breath into his lungs. He looked again at the redheaded woman and her tall companion. It would explain so much about them. Her strange attire, the king's ransom in precious metal that bedecked her person, the odd manner of speech they both affected.

There was no denying Rutledge's fury when the mistress Emilie related the story. The man had had the look about him of a wild animal caught in a trap. Andrew knew the feeling of being caught in circumstances not of his own design and, despite his better judgment, he well understood Rutledge's agitation.

But what then was he to make of mistress Emilie? Andrew recognized something of himself in the redheaded woman, as well, and that threw his mind into a whirlpool of confusion.

The patriots had been engaged in the battle against British tyranny for more than a year and still had not achieved a victory. His Excellency, General Washington, had sent numerous missives to the Continental Congress in Philadelphia, begging the good men of conscience to provide more troops, more food, more weapons to aid in their cause.

Andrew had seen the swift horror of Lexington and Concord. Little had happened since to raise the spirits of the patriots.

"You spoke of the general," he said, choosing his words with great deliberation. "Of some danger—?"

"A plot to assassinate him," said mistress Emilie. "In my day you are thought of as a hero."

He was many things, but a hero was not among them. "And what is it that I have done to deserve such praise?"

She told him quickly of a man, garbed all in black, who had risked his own life to save the commander of the Continental army.

"When did this happen?"

"In the summer of 1776."

Andrew grew quiet. July was all but gone. "Can you put a date and place to this event, mistress Emilie?"

"I wish I could, but there has always been a degree of uncertainty attached to the event." She hesitated, dropping her gaze in a most uncharacteristic fashion.

"Mark me well, mistress. I am not a man afraid of harsh news."

"The truth is that I have no news, Andrew. From that moment forward, you exist only in speculation." Her smile was gentle and for a moment he was reminded of his Elspeth. "I have always imagined that you retired to a life in the country with a wife and children and lived to be a very old man."

Her words struck a chord deep inside him, hidden away in that place where love had gone to die. For the past few years he had not felt himself long for the world. When Elspeth and their son had died, they had taken with them all that was fine and good in the world, leaving him behind to mark the days until he met his Maker.

Some men joined the militia because the fires of independence burned hot in their breasts. Those men became generals, leaders of men. Andrew had joined because he had nothing of value to lose. They made him a spy.

He looked at Emilie, who was standing near her companion. "How is it you come to know the ways of this time to such a degree?" Were he to find himself in Plimouth colony at the time of its beginnings, he would be without a clue as to proper behavior. "Sorcery, perhaps?"

"Nothing so exotic. I earn my living—Zane!"

Rutledge suddenly doubled over, clutching his right arm against his chest.

"He's in pain," she said, eyes wide as she looked at Andrew. "Can we fetch a doctor?"

"I cannot risk such an enterprise," he said. "My presence here cannot be revealed."

"I can risk it," said Emilie. "Tell me the best place to moor the rowboat and I can find my way into town."

"Over my dead body," said Zane, gritting his teeth. "I'm fine."

McVie slid his knife back into the waistband of his breeches and approached. "You are a fortunate man," he said, looking at Zane's right forearm, which had sustained a fracture. "If the bone had broken the skin, the cause would be lost."

"You're the local hero," Zane growled, "not the doctor."

"A physician would tell you same as I, Rutledge. You and your arm would be parting company."

Zane gestured toward McVie. "Keep him the hell away from me."

"We have to set that arm, Zane."

"I'll do it myself."

"You're talking like a fool."

"Hey, I'm not the one who says a balloon dropped us into the middle of the Revolution."

Emilie started to laugh. She couldn't help it. Maybe it was lack of food or the jet lag to end all jet lag. She didn't know. But whatever it was, the whole thing struck her as so absurd, so funny, that the laughter bubbled up and it wouldn't stop.

It took Zane all of about five seconds to catch the wave. He laughed until his sides hurt as much as his broken arm.

Emilie was draped over the bench, tears of mirth rolling down her cheeks, while Zane leaned against the wall and roared. McVie stood in the doorway, his expression perfectly deadpan. Each time they looked at him they laughed all the harder.

"I'm starving," said Emilie, holding her sides. "Let's call out for a pizza."

"Great idea," Zane managed. "Think it'll get here in thirty minutes?"

"Oh, no!" cried Emilie, wiping her eyes. "I left the water running in the kitchen."

"I can go you one better," said Zane. "I left the Porsche running."

Andrew watched them patiently from the doorway. He knew the words they spoke were English, but the meaning behind them was impossible for him to comprehend. All this talk about por-shuh and peet-zah—what manner of world did they come from?

He glanced out the window, then cleared his throat. "It grows dark soon. We should tend to business while we can."

Both Emilie and Zane grew abruptly silent as reality once again rushed in on them.

"We have to do something about your arm," Emilie said at last. "The longer we wait..."

"I am no physician," said Andrew, "but I am skilled in certain basic remedies."

"I don't have a choice, do I?" asked Zane.

No one argued with him.

In silence they filed down the winding staircase to the front room where the blue light of dusk had begun to soften the stark simplicity of their surroundings.

Emilie borrowed McVie's knife and proceeded to rip into one of the beautiful quilts. They would need lengths of fabric to serve as a sling, as well as to bind the makeshift splint to Zane's forearm.

Andrew found a sturdy branch outside that he quickly broke down to a more manageable size.

Zane watched the proceedings with detached curiosity. The whole thing was beginning to take on an almost Kafkaesque quality and he half expected the alarm to ring and wake him up from the strangest dream he'd had in his entire life.

The two men locked eyes.

"The pain might be considerable," said Andrew, taking the other man's measure.

"Do it," was all Zane said.

McVie motioned for Emilie to stand at the head of the trundle bed. "Keep his shoulders down, mistress Emilie."

She nodded, biting her lip nervously. McVie placed one hand on Zane's wrist and another at his elbow. It was she and not Zane who cried out at the sound of bone against bone as McVie urged the broken pieces into the proper position.

Quickly he laid the splint along Zane's forearm, then instructed Emilie to bind the splint tightly in place. Zane's face was pale and his eyes were closed. A small muscle in his jaw worked furiously, but that was the only sign he gave that all was not right.

"You're very good at this," she observed as McVie finished his task.

McVie nodded. "I have always been so."

They listened to the sound of Zane's rapid breathing as he dozed on the trundle bed.

"I know I should be worrying about all sorts of dreadful things," said Emilie, "but right now all I can think about is food."

Andrew started for the door. "Come with me and I'll cut some ham for you and Rutledge."

He wasn't entirely certain what he was going to do with the two travelers through time, but he did know he wasn't about to let them out of his sight.

Chapter Six

6

The ham was salty and tasted of wood smoke and the rum was potent, but Emilie polished off each with gusto. Zane awoke once in considerable pain and McVie pushed the bottle toward him. Zane didn't hesitate, and soon slept peacefully once again.

"The pain will ease by the morrow," said McVie from his spot near the door.

"I hope so," said Emilie, smoothing Zane's dark hair off his forehead with a gentle touch. McVie had helped her to dress the cuts on Zane's forehead and back and together they had used the rest of the quilt to bind his rib cage. She had thanked God that his ribs had been bruised and not broken. "I appreciate all you're doing for us, Andrew. I know this must seem more unbelievable to you than it does to us."

He tossed the quarter she'd given him into the air then caught it in his palm. "You have shown me some things that not even logic can disprove."

It was hard to see his expression clearly in the gathering darkness, but Emilie thought she caught a look of concern in his eyes.

"Is something wrong? Is there something about Zane's condition that I should know about?"

So that was the way the wind blew, thought Andrew. Her concern for Rutledge went deeper than perhaps even she realized.

"Nay, madam, I have kept nothing about Rutledge's infirmities from you. It is another, more distressing, matter that concerns me."

She nodded as if she knew. "You have to leave us," she said, in that oddly accented voice of hers. "I understand."

Andrew arched a brow in question. "That notion does not cause you alarm?"

"It doesn't thrill me," said Emilie, "but I know that you have a life of your own." *And a destiny to be met.* "I believe I can make a life for myself here."

Andrew gestured toward Rutledge, sleeping deeply on the trundle bed, his broken arm propped upon a pillow at his side.

"What of Rutledge?" he asked. "He does not strike me as a man willing to forego the world he left behind."

"Has he a choice? We're alive and we're here. The sooner we make our peace with that truth, the happier we'll be."

Andrew considered his words carefully. "And what of you, madam? Do you not feel the pull of friends and loved ones left behind?"

"There's no one," she said. "Not a soul."

He wondered about the bond between her and Rutledge but he refrained from asking. She obviously had affection for the giant of a man, but how deep that affection ran was beyond his knowing.

As for Rutledge, he had about him the look of a man who had made claim to a woman. A vivid image, shockingly explicit in its attention to detail, came to life and he closed his eyes against it. The mistress Emilie had said she and Rutledge were unwed, but Andrew was worldly enough to know that meant little when the blood ran hot.

He cast a curious glance toward her as she sat by Rutledge's side. She sat stitching the plain blue fabric from the coverlet into a skirt. She had an air of industry about her and he wondered if there was any goal she could not attain if she put her mind to it. She was a woman of bountiful charms, not the least of which was a most intriguing demeanor that was at once both fierce and agreeable.

He cleared his throat. "About your manner of dress," he began. "It appears to my eyes to be most...unusual attire."

For a moment she forgot what she'd been wearing when this whole thing began and she looked down to find herself clad in a demure eighteenth-century bodice and twentieth-century leggings. She quickly explained to him about the celebration and the outfit she'd intended to finish sewing while on the balloon ride to Langley Park.

Andrew gestured toward the apparel on her lower body. "Do others garb themselves in such fashion?"

"And worse!" she said, laughing at the expression on his face. "You would be scandalized if you could see the outfits, Andrew." She held aloft a cambric handkerchief she'd had tucked in her embroidered purse. "There are some women who wear as little as this."

Andrew's face flamed and he rose to his feet. "It grows dark," he announced unnecessarily. "You should sleep."

"I doubt if I'll ever sleep again," she said. "There's so much to do...so many things to think about."

"I bid you good night, mistress Emilie. Rest well."

"And you," she said.

With that he climbed the stairs to the lookout tower while Emilie laughed softly to herself, wondering how he would react when she told him about *Playboy.*

Zane awoke the next morning with the sun. His arm ached, as did his ribs, but all things considered he felt remarkably clear-headed and filled with resolve.

He climbed from the trundle bed, careful not to disturb Emilie, who slept on the smaller of the two mattresses. During the night he had come to terms with the reality of their situation. Although it went against all logic, he accepted the fact that he and Emilie had somehow tumbled through a rip in the fabric of time.

However, he was not about to accept the fact that the world he'd left behind was lost to him forever. If he did that he'd be saying that his entire life up until now hadn't been worth a damn, and that admission was too close to the bone for him to contemplate.

Besides, this world held little appeal. He liked everything modern life had to offer and was willing to accept the drawbacks as well as the benefits. Where was the challenge, living within boundaries that had been set by history long before he was born?

But there was one challenge on the horizon and it was probably the most important one he'd ever face.

He was going to find a way back to his own time.

And he was going to convince Emilie to come with him.

For years Emilie had prided herself on her love of the colonial era, but when she awoke that morning she realized how little she'd really known about the time. She could live without her electric sewing machine and her microwave oven, but indoor plumbing was another story entirely.

What on earth was she going to do?

Peering out the window she saw McVie and Zane engaged in animated conversation near the well. They looked as if they would be there for some time. Now if only she could find a chamber pot, maybe she could convince herself that the situation wasn't as dire as it was beginning to seem.

She scowled as she searched the lighthouse for the object. Did men have any idea how lucky they were? She doubted it. As a sex, they seemed to take for granted the ease with which they could perform necessary bodily functions. The thought of squatting down behind some prickly rosebush filled her with dismay, but the other alternative was even more appalling to consider.

Flinging open the front door, she stormed down the steps. "If either one of you comes anywhere near the rosebushes in the back, I will single-handedly see to it that neither of you reaches his next birthday."

With that she marched around the corner of the lighthouse and disappeared from view.

"Is she always thus?" McVie asked after Emilie had vanished from sight.

"She has a temper," said Zane. "No doubt about that."

McVie nodded. "She has the look of the Irish about her."

Zane knew McVie wanted to ask about the exact nature of Zane's relationship to Emilie, but his eighteenth-century caution kept him silent.

They had spent an interesting hour discussing the options open to both him and Emilie, and it was agreed that throwing in their lot with McVie—at least for the time being—was the wisest course of action.

Besides, there was the issue of McVie's obvious distrust. Emilie's eyes had shone bright with admiration each time she talked with McVie, and Zane had found his gut twisting with a jolt of white-hot jealousy, the likes of which he'd never experienced.

Only this time the jealousy wasn't directed toward a name in a dusty old history book, but a living, breathing man. Emilie's lifelong hero was more competition than he'd counted on bumping up against.

She saw McVie as a hero, the kind of man who would risk everything for the higher good. Funny thing, though: Zane had the distinct feeling that he and McVie had more in common than anyone, including Emilie, would think.

McVie was a risk taker, but it wasn't the higher good that concerned the man. McVie was running away from something, sure as hell, and Zane intended to find out what it was.

He looked at McVie. "So what's next?"

"We leave for the Blakelee farm when mistress Emilie returns," said McVie. "If luck is with us, we'll be at the edge of Milltown before night falls again."

The first thing Zane noticed on the mainland was the absence of sound. Back when he was in high school he'd read *Atlas Shrugged*. The mysterious John Galt had managed to stop the engine of the world and Zane finally understood what that was all about. It was gone, all of it. No planes, no cars, no computers, no machines, no constant low-level sizzle of electricity keeping the world on-line.

McVie tied the rowboat to a tree stump a few feet away from the waterline, then plunged into a thicket of branches and bushes, with Emilie and Zane bringing up the rear.

"Milltown lies some miles to the northwest," said McVie. "We'll make camp on the outskirts of town for tonight."

"We can't stay in the town itself?" asked Emilie. She had been thinking of a wonderful colonial inn, rich in atmosphere.

"Not Milltown," said McVie, glancing over his shoulder. "'Tis said the Britishers have made considerable inroads, and with your unusual attire we should draw too much untoward attention."

There was no arguing with his reasoning. McVie planned to make contact with his cohorts in the spy ring and obtain proper clothing for both Emilie and Zane before daybreak so they would blend in with the populace once they reached Princeton.

"How do we know you're not going to turn us in?" Zane asked.

"You do not," said McVie. "As I do not know with certainty if you intend to thwart my plans."

"You have our word," said Emilie.

"As you have mine," said McVie, "and I do not believe that is enough for any one of us."

They walked in silence for what seemed like hours. Emilie had feared McVie would plot a course through the swamplands that dotted the boundaries of modern-day Crosse Harbor, but he led them instead into a forest of maples and pine trees that towered so high overhead that she felt as if she'd entered a cathedral. Outside the forest the summer sun was blisteringly hot, but inside it was dark and cool. The forest floor was softly cushioned by fallen pine needles and dropped leaves and she found herself struck by the toll industrialization would soon take on the natural order of things.

They stopped by a stream to rest for a few minutes. McVie knelt down on the bank and leaned forward, cupping his hands to fill them with water.

"Don't do that!" Emilie said. "The water's probably—"

She stopped, glancing down at the crystal-clear reflections in the glassy surface.

"The water's clean," said Zane, sounding as amazed as she felt.

McVie looked at them both with curiosity. "You act as if clean water is an oddity."

"It is in our time," said Emilie. She told him about medical waste and acid rain, and the absurdity of designer bars where people paid good money for a cup of clean water.

McVie looked at Zane. "Why is it you wish to return to such a place?"

"Freedom," said Zane. "We can go anywhere we want, do anything we want. Hell, we've even been to the moon."

McVie turned toward Emilie. "He speaks nonsense."

"He speaks the truth," said Emilie, sipping the cool, fresh water. "The American flag flies on the surface of the moon."

McVie sat down on a mossy rock and looked up at the sky. "And how did the American flag reach the moon, mistress Emilie? A high-flying bird, perhaps, or an act of God?"

She shook her head. "Hard work, brain power and a dream."

Zane, however, understood what McVie was really asking. In broad terms he described the principles behind jet propulsion and outlined the development of the space program.

"I was a little girl when the Eagle landed, but I remember it as if it were yesterday," Emilie said.

"Neil Armstrong," said Zane. "For a while he was every boy's hero."

It sounded like a world of wondrous possibilities. Andrew's head swam with the notion of mortal men hurtling through the sky in a ball of flame, only to set foot upon the silvery surface of the moon. "And how is it you go about your daily business? In those...rockets you tell of?"

"All different ways," said Emilie, perching on a rock near him. "Some people walk to work, but most people drive."

"Horses?"

"Cars," said Zane.

McVie listened, eyes widening with surprise, as Rutledge described metal vehicles with wheels that were powered by controlled gas explosions. "I believe you are making sport at my expense."

Emilie shook her head. "He tells the truth, Andrew. The country is paved with roads and you can drive anywhere you want, any time you want." She reached into her waistband for her embroidered purse, then removed a hard and shiny piece of paper. "This is a driver's license," she said, handing it to him. "You take a test to prove your skill, then the state grants you the right to drive a car."

"What manner of substance is this?" McVie asked, tapping the license with his thumbnail.

"Plastic," said Zane with a grin. "It's everywhere."

McVie looked closely at the card. "'Tis your image, mistress Emilie. The artist was quite proficient."

"There was no artist," Emilie said. "That's what we call a photograph."

Zane started to explain the principles of photography, but McVie stood up abruptly. "Time passes. We must continue."

"So much for your lectures, Professor Rutledge," Emilie commented with a laugh.

"He kept your driver's license," Zane said as they fell into position behind McVie once again.

"I don't think I'll be needing it. Besides, if it helps him to believe us, he's welcome to it."

"We're going back one day," Zane said with great determination.

"I don't think so."

"We don't belong here."

"Speak for yourself."

"Come on, Emilie. I saw your face when you headed for the bushes this morning. You wanted porcelain, tile and running water."

"Too bad for me. I'll get used to it."

"Wait until December," he said. "You'll be praying for indoor plumbing."

"And so what if I do? That still doesn't change things. We're here and we're staying here."

"Not if I can help it."

"I don't think you can, Zane."

"It happened once," he said. "It can happen a second time."

"If you're planning to hijack another hot-air balloon, you'll have another seven years to wait until they're invented."

"We can build one."

"Why don't we build a spaceship while we're at it and go to Mars?"

"If it would get us the hell out of here, I'm all in favor of it."

He strode ahead, ostensibly to talk to McVie. Emilie bridled at his stubborn refusal to accept the fact that their lives had been changed irrevocably. He couldn't control this situation any more than he'd been able to control the hot-air balloon. For a man like Zane, that would be a difficult admission. Old rules no longer applied and the sooner he accepted that, the easier things would be for everyone.

"This is it?" asked Emilie two hours later when Andrew stopped for the night near an outcropping of rocks that overlooked a stream. "We're staying here?"

"There is a small cave beyond the lilac bushes where you may take shelter for the night."

"A cave?" Somehow her imagination hadn't taken her this far. "Bats sleep in caves."

It was Zane's turn to laugh. "You were expecting the Holiday Inn?"

"Oh, be quiet!" she snapped. "I'm only thinking of you."

Even McVie recognized the humor in that statement, and he barely knew her.

"The woods abound in game," McVie said. "Hunger should not be a problem."

Emilie determined that a shift to vegetarianism was in order.

"I'll need a pistol," Zane said to McVie, "unless you expect me to strangle something."

McVie retained his pistol but handed over his knife.

"You're leaving us?" Emilie asked as Zane carefully slid the knife into the waistband of his trousers.

"I'll return before dawn," he said.

"You won't let us down, will you?" Emilie implored.

McVie shook his head. "Nay, mistress. I will not."

The look on Emilie's face hit Zane like a slap. She followed McVie with her eyes until he disappeared, then turned back to Zane with obvious reluctance. She'd come to rely upon the rough-hewn patriot for a sense of security and that realization stung more than he cared to admit. He found himself wanting to reassure her that she was in good hands.

"If you're worried about starving out here, don't be. The broken arm'll slow me down, but it won't stop me." He'd done his share of roughing it up in Alaska and down in Peru. Central New Jersey shouldn't pose too much of a problem, no matter what the year.

"Don't kill anything on my account," Emilie said, gesturing toward the berry bushes and wildflowers growing everywhere. "These woods have a better selection of produce than my local supermarket."

He was just as glad she felt that way. Killing for sport had never done it for him. He knew he could kill if his life depended on it, but right now berries sounded fine to him, too.

Still, as he watched Emilie inspecting the berries and picking ripe specimens, he found himself wishing she was a little less self-sufficient. When he'd said he didn't belong, he'd only scratched the surface. Neither one of them belonged in that time and place, but he had the feeling he was the only one who realized it.

"Okay," said Zane as he stuck another branch on the stack. "All we need now is a match."

"Very funny," said Emilie. "I hope you have a lighter in your back pocket."

"You don't have any matches on you?"

"I don't smoke," she reminded him. "Don't you know how to start a fire without matches?"

"I was never the Boy Scout type," he drawled, "but I'd pay good money to see you rub two sticks together."

"Do you have any better ideas?"

"Different," he said, "but not better."

"It's a darned good thing you have me around," she said, metaphorically rolling up her sleeves. "You'd be lost here without me."

She'd tossed him a perfect straight line but the requisite wisecrack wouldn't come. She was right. Although it killed him to admit it even to himself, she was his guide in the strange new world in which they found themselves and he wondered how he would have managed without her.

They ate berries and picked at the dandelion grass, drank their fill of the stream's cold, clear water, then returned to the campfire.

"I don't know about you," said Zane, "but I'd kill for a Big Mac."

"I thought the berries were delicious," said Emilie with a prim set to her mouth.

"Pizza," he continued. "Pepperoni with onions."

"The dandelion grass had a certain tang to it." She struggled to suppress a smile.

"Szechuan shrimp, hot and sour soup, all thirty-one flavors for dessert."

"You win," said Emilie, stifling a groan. "I'd give anything for a bowl of chili and a diet Coke."

"What the hell do they eat around here?" he asked, genuinely puzzled. "How did—how *do* they cook?"

"In the hearth, mostly. Beef roasts, game, lots of eggs and butter." She grinned. "The cardiac blue plate special."

"Great," he said, reaching for another handful of berries. "That gives me something to look forward to."

"It's not so bad, Zane," she said. "Not really."

"Tell me how it could be worse."

"We could be dead."

"In a way, we are," he said, his voice uncharacteristically flat. "And so is everything we knew."

"Maybe not," she said softly. Once again she sensed that deep chord of loneliness that she'd always suspected was part of his soul. "Maybe we're exactly where we're meant to be."

"That's a crock."

"I don't think so," she said, warming to the notion. "Haven't you wondered—even for a minute—if we aren't exactly where we're meant to be?"

"I know where I'm meant to be," he said grimly, "and it sure as hell isn't here."

* * *

When night came, it fell with a swiftness and finality that surprised them both. The temperature dropped, as well, and Emilie found herself drawing closer to the fire for warmth. They'd been inordinately proud of themselves when they'd coaxed fire from dry tinder by using a rock to strike a spark off the blade of McVie's knife.

If only she had a metal pot, she could have boiled water for herb tea. Indoor plumbing and a cup of tea, and she'd be a very happy woman. She was contemplating the inequities of life when Zane rose to his feet.

"Get inside," he commanded in a tone of voice she'd never heard before.

"Why?" She held her hands over the fire. "If you need privacy, go find yourself a spot behind the trees."

He grabbed her by the arm and yanked her to her feet. "Now!"

She stumbled toward the cave. What on earth had gotten into him? She crouched inside the mouth, listening. An owl hooted softly in the night breeze and from somewhere close by she heard the sound of leaves crunching.

Footsteps?

Maybe it's Andrew, she thought, wrapping her arms tightly around her chest. *Or maybe it's a bear.* They had bears in New Jersey in 1992. She could only imagine how many had lumbered through the woods before turnpikes and subdivisions.

All Zane had was a knife and a broken arm. He wouldn't stand a chance. She searched around the dark interior for something—anything—to help him. She grabbed a rock the size of a large cantaloupe and made her way carefully from the cave.

The fire was nothing but a pile of embers. Without the flames casting their light, she felt as if she were walking through a black hole in space. Her heart pounded loudly in her ears as she tried to decide which way Zane had headed.

It was quiet.

Too quiet.

Not even the owl was hooting.

She was so tense she could scarcely draw breath into her lungs. *Where are you, Zane?* She'd been in the cave only a minute or two. He couldn't have gone far in such a short period of time. Unless—

She screamed as a hand clamped down on her shoulder.

"What the hell are you doing here?" Zane growled in her ear. "I told you to stay put."

"I thought you might need help."

He tapped the rock with the hilt of the knife. "You were going to hit a bear in the head with that thing?"

"That was the idea."

"Next time do what I tell you."

"The hell I will," she said, bristling. "I suppose going *mano a mano* with a black bear makes more sense—especially with your broken arm?"

He dragged her back to the cave. "If I need help, I'll ask for it."

"For heaven's sake," she grumbled, dropping the rock to the floor of the cave, "I didn't mean to impugn your masculinity."

"You didn't." She heard the scuffle of dirt as he sat down. "But you did act like a jerk."

She glared into the darkness. "If I could find you, I'd kick you for that remark."

"You always were an original, Em. Another woman would be crying into her embroidered hanky, but you're out there looking for bear."

She found herself a spot to sit in his general vicinity. "Is that a compliment?"

"What do you think?"

"I'm not sure."

"It's a compliment," he said.

"Thank you." A pause. "So what *did* make the noise?"

He mumbled something.

"What was that?" she repeated.

"A skunk," he said. "It was a close call, but I was faster than he was."

"There is a God," she said wryly.

Again the rumbling laughter that had stirred her blood two

nights ago. "You know, you never did answer my question," he said. "Would you have gone to Tahiti with me?"

She smiled into the darkness. "You'll never know."

"Come on," he said. "I won't hold you to it when we get back home."

"This is home, Zane," she said softly.

"Not for me."

"It doesn't seem as if you have a choice."

"There's always a choice, Emilie. Don't think otherwise."

His last remark brought her up short. The circumstances might change but the essence of the man remained the same. He'd never been a man for the long haul, not by any stretch of the imagination, and she'd be a total fool to think otherwise. As soon as he got his bearings, he'd be off in search of the eighteenth-century equivalent of Tahiti.

He shifted position and slid over closer to where she sat.

"Cold in here," he observed.

"Mmph." Late July and she was shivering.

"What happens if McVie doesn't come back for us?" Zane asked.

"He'll come back," she said. "He gave us his word."

Zane refrained from pointing out that many men gave their word but damn few managed to keep it. She was almost thirty years old. If she didn't know that by now, it was time she learned.

"McVie said something interesting this morning," he went on. "He thinks we should pose as husband and wife."

A wave of heat rose up from the soles of her feet. "He may be right," she said after a long moment. "Women always traveled with a companion." And a man traveling alone would be viewed with suspicion, especially with the war raging. "Does he—did you tell him?"

"That we were married? Sure."

"Oh, God." She buried her face in her hands. "What on earth must Andrew be thinking? Divorce is practically unheard of."

"Who cares what he thinks? It's none of his business."

She knew McVie's opinion of her shouldn't matter, but it did. "I suppose you had to tell him."

"Glad you agree," Zane drawled, a definite edge to his voice.

"I wonder what he'll think we should do if we stay at an inn."

"If we're supposed to be married," Zane pointed out, "he'll expect us to share a room."

She narrowed her eyes and looked in his direction. "Did you put him up to this?"

"You've got to be kidding." He sounded sincere. She wished she could see if the expression on his face matched the sound of his voice.

"We need some ground rules," she said, doing her best to ignore the memory of the night they'd shared. "We'll share a room, but we won't share a bed."

He said nothing.

"Zane? Did you hear me?"

"I heard you."

"You didn't say anything."

"What do you want me to say?"

"That you understand what I'm talking about."

"I don't understand."

"We're not meant to be together," she explained. "If we were back home, we would have gone our separate ways. I refuse to be manipulated by circumstances."

"Don't worry," he snapped, visions of seduction vanishing before his eyes. "Your virtue's safe with me."

"Good," said Emilie.

"Great," said Zane.

She lay down and pillowed her head with her arms.

He leaned against the wall of the cave and closed his eyes.

It was a long time before either one slept.

Chapter Seven

7

"Godspeed, Andrew," said the buxom, dark-haired wench as she handed him the package. "Don't you be makin' yourself a stranger to us, now."

Andrew thanked the kindly woman with a kiss. "Mark me well, Prudence. You will be rewarded for your generosity."

Prudence made clucking noises with her teeth. "Keep your good self safe and well and that be all the generosity a body could wish for." She opened the front door. "Out with you. I'm a workin' lass, m'boy, and you cannot afford my favors."

"Treat those Redcoats kindly, Pru, for happy men are ofttimes careless."

Prudence kissed him on the mouth. "Maybe next time?"

He kissed her back. "With all certainty."

Thus far it had been a most profitable night. Prudence had performed a miracle and conjured up clothing for mistress Emilie. She had also filled a pillow slip with all manner of things that Prudence said a woman would love.

He had been too preoccupied to enjoy Pru's charms. He'd found himself thinking about the strange and wonderful inventions his new companions had told him about. Over a supper of mutton and ale, he'd asked Prudence if she believed man could ever fly through the sky like a bird. Prudence had laughed so hard she developed the hiccups.

He stepped to his right as a man on horseback galloped by, the animal's hooves kicking up a cloud of dust.

Rutledge had said that in his time men traveled by harnessing small explosions. He had drawn a picture in the dirt of a rectangular metal container on four wheels and Andrew had stared at it, trying to imagine thousands of those contraptions racing about at speeds he couldn't even begin to comprehend.

The word pictures Rutledge and mistress Emilie had painted for him were of such a fantastical nature that it was a wonder he did not commit them to the lunatic asylum on Manhattan Island.

Mayhap you are the one in need of the asylum, he thought as he neared the tavern. He had no reason to believe Rutledge and Emilie. As yet, he had not uncovered even a whisper of a plot against His Excellency, General Washington. In truth, he believed the general was in residence on Long Island with his troops, some one hundred miles from central New Jersey.

One thing distressed him, however. Rather than being pleased to know his life would merit even a sentence of mention in the books of the future, he found himself vaguely uneasy. Mistress Emilie said that he had vanished from the history books after the rescue of General Washington. Did he sink back into obscurity or had something more untoward happened to him?

The unforeseen always brought with it a healthy dose of apprehension. Living in the shadows, as he did, he tended to view every surprise as a possible calamity, which was why his acceptance of the two strangers amazed him.

The Black Dragon was crowded when he pushed through the door. Smoke from pipes and cigars filled the room, while the pungent smell of burning tobacco mingled with the smells of whiskey and ale and unwashed flesh. Tavern girls in tantalizing costumes swayed about the room dispensing tankards of ale and promising smiles. He glanced about the room for the man he'd been instructed to find, made eye contact, then claimed a table some ten feet away.

"Evenin', sir," said a spritely lass with big blue eyes and a plump bosom. "What would you be needin'?"

"A tankard of ale and some cheese," he said, his attention on the man he was to meet. "And a loaf of dark bread."

With a flip of her skirts the lass vanished toward the back room. Andrew rose from his chair to enter into a game of darts being played at the far side of the room. He passed close to his contact's table and the rotund man never missed a bite. He hefted his bread and cheese, took an enormous mouthful, then casually plucked the message from Andrew's hand in a movement so perfectly planned that it took Andrew a moment to realize the transfer had even occurred.

Two hours later Andrew approached the edge of the forest. He had gone out of his way to seek mention of a plot against the life of General Washington, but had heard nary a whisper. The thought occurred to him that his two mysterious traveling companions might have concocted the story from whole cloth, but again he found himself wanting to believe they spoke only the truth.

The forest enveloped him in its embrace as he left the town behind. His mind leaped with the images mistress Emilie and Rutledge had conjured of men who walked on the moon, of fire-breathing contraptions that raced across the wilderness on roads that people paid money to use. He'd spent a goodly amount of time staring at the green currency with the general's countenance set upon it, and he'd known a hunger for knowledge that defied place and time.

Ever since losing Elspeth and their child, he had been courting danger at every turn, all in the name of patriotic fervor, caring little for the outcome of the battle. In truth, it was well and good that his work with the spy ring was beneficial to the patriots, but he went where others dared not because he had nothing of value left to lose.

He had no trouble finding the spot where he had left them. The embers from their fire had long since been extinguished but the pile of ashes gave it away. He wondered if Emilie had merely snapped her fingers and called forth a flame from the accumulated branches and twigs. Little would surprise him. They had come from a time of great wonderment and he understood full well how it was that Rutledge fought against the boundaries of the world Andrew was part of.

He slipped beside the cave as the first light of dawn limned the tops of the trees. It took a moment for his eyes to adjust to the absolute darkness inside. The sight that revealed itself to him caused him a sharp stab of pain. Emilie lay curled against Rutledge, her head resting on his chest. The skirt she had wrought from the lighthouse coverlet was draped over their sleeping forms. Rutledge sat with his back against the wall of the cave, his broken arm resting across his stomach.

There was no denying the way they fit together. They had the look of contentment about them as if— He had no wish to pursue the thought.

Apparently Rutledge slept lightly. His eyes opened and he met Andrew's gaze across the dim light of the cave.

"How goes it?" Rutledge asked, his voice husky with sleep.

Andrew tossed down a sack. "I cannot vouch for the fit of the garments, but I believe mistress Emilie will be well pleased." He found his gaze drawn again and again to the rise and fall of her breasts against the other man's chest. Since Elspeth, he had not wanted for the companionship of a woman, and he wondered why it was this strapping lass had such an uncommon effect upon him, body and soul. "We leave for Princeton after daybreak."

Zane watched as McVie left the cave. There had been no mistaking the tension between them, and he was certain he knew the cause.

Zane had sensed the other man's fascination with Emilie from the start. What man wouldn't react to a beautiful redhead with a body to match? What bothered Zane was her reaction to McVie.

Back on his own turf Zane could've given the guy a run for his money, but here in the middle of nowhere he was stumped. How did you compete with a woman's hero? Zane had money, freedom and entrée to the best of everything the world had to offer, and none of it mattered a damn.

This wasn't his world, it was McVie's.

For thirty-four years he'd charted his singular course through life, needing nothing and no one but himself.

Stripped of all the trappings of modern life, he felt naked. He had dodged bombs and bar stools and more bad tempers than a man twice his age, but he had never faced his own limitations, in the way he was doing now.

He hated feeling anything less than in total control of himself and his situation. The broken arm was an unpleasant reminder that he was only human. The way Emilie made him feel went even deeper.

Is this what you wanted, Sara Jane? he asked, wondering if his grandmother was somewhere laughing at the predicament in which he found himself. *You told me there was more to life.... Is this what you had in mind?*

He waited, but there was no answer.

As they followed Andrew on their journey north to Princeton, both Emilie and Zane were moved to stunned silence by the beauty of the land. The dense forests gently gave way to rolling meadows dotted with wildflowers, peach orchards and small springs that sparkled with water as sweet and clear as liquid diamonds.

"You went to school in Princeton," Emilie said as they crested a small hill. "I wonder if you'll recognize anything."

Zane looked at her as if she were crazy. "I don't think Marita's Cantina's been around that long." Then a thought struck him. "You know, Nassau Hall's pretty damn old."

"And the old governor's mansion on Stockton Street—"

"Morven," he said, shaking his head. Buildings he'd walked by every day for four years and never noticed were taking on monumental importance in his life. The whole thing was enough to make him think longingly of a bottle of Scotch and sweet oblivion.

"At least we're dressed for it," Emilie said, gesturing toward her mint green outfit with the snugly laced bodice.

Zane looked down at her, taking careful note of the deep valley between her breasts. "Can you breathe in that thing?"

"Barely," she said with a groan. "I suppose I should thank my lucky stars Andrew was able to find anything at all."

Zane scowled. "I feel like a jerk."

"You look great." Andrew had been unable to find clothes that would fit a man of Zane's size, but they had managed to cobble together a passable imitation of period clothing by combining Zane's twentieth-century garments with a dark gold cape. Emilie had combed his hair back and tied it with a length of black ribbon. If they could change his attitude, she'd be very happy.

"It's hot as hell under this damn thing."

"You'll survive."

"Right."

"It's a different world, Zane," she reminded him. "I'm wearing more layers of clothing than the flying nun and you don't hear me complaining."

"That's because you like this kind of thing."

"No," she said, "it's because I can accept it."

"I don't see the difference."

"I know," said Emilie, "and that's always been our problem."

The Post Road, formerly known as the King's Highway, led into the heart of town.

"This can't be real," said Emilie as she stared at the horses and livestock, the peddlers and merchants, the crowds of people choking the thoroughfare. Men in white powdered wigs and silk brocade jackets in vibrant oranges and reds strolled up the road, rubbing elbows with milkmaids wearing homespun skirts and plain bodices and street porters whose laced shoes bespoke their lowly station in life. "I feel like I'm on a movie set."

A blacksmith shop sat next to a printing establishment. There was a silversmith's shop across the street, and that was adjacent to a wigmaker, which was near the barber's storefront.

A woman carrying a basket of lemons approached, a hopeful look upon her face. "Fine lemons to cool you on a summer day," she said, extending the basket. "Brought up from Jamaica by my very own husband this Saturday past."

Emilie reached for a lemon, savoring the smoothness. "Oh, I'd love some."

"Two pence the half dozen," said the woman, her smile revealing two missing front teeth.

Emilie looked to Zane, who shook his head. Andrew stared at her, his expression impassive.

"I'm sorry," Emilie said to the woman, replacing the lemon in the basket. "I cannot, after all."

The woman's eyes flashed fire. "'Tis a dreadful thing, wasting a good wife's time with idle promises."

"I should truly love to buy one," said Emilie, trying to match the woman's speech patterns, "but I fear I am not able."

The woman's gaze took in Emilie's braided ring and crystal pendant. "A basket of lemons for one of those trinkets would be a fair trade."

Andrew took Emilie by the arm and propelled her up the street to where Zane stood near the door of the Plumed Rooster.

"Engage in no idle talk with tradespeople, mistress Emilie, or you will find your pockets picked before you reach the other side of the street."

"It's the same way back home," Emilie marveled as they caught up with Zane. "Only we call them flea markets."

"Fleas?" The expression on Andrew's face made both Emilie and Zane laugh out loud.

"It's a long story," said Zane. "We'll explain it to you some day."

Andrew gestured toward the Plumed Rooster. "I have business to attend inside and then on to the Blakelee farm."

"Fine," said Emilie. "We'll come with you." She started for the door to the pub.

"Nay," said Andrew, barring her way.

"Don't be ridiculous," said Emilie. "Move away, Andrew."

"'Tis not proper."

"What isn't?"

"You would not be welcome in the Plumed Rooster."

"Because I'm a stranger?"

"No," said Zane. "Because you're a woman."

For a moment she'd forgotten the inequality of the eighteenth century. She turned to Andrew. "Surely I can—"

Andrew shook his head. He'd never seen such fire before on a woman's countenance. It both intrigued and alarmed him. "'Tis but one kind of woman who frequents the Rooster," he said, trusting she would infer his meaning from his words.

"Oh, God," she groaned, shaking her head in dismay.

Andrew glanced toward Zane. "Do you understand the cause of her distress?"

"Equal rights," said Zane.

Andrew looked relieved. "A notion put forth by the Continental Congress in Philadelphia a few short weeks ago. It is one with which I am familiar."

"Of course you are," said Emilie, still smarting. "All *men* are created equal."

"I do not understand your dismay, mistress Emilie. Certainly the notion of equality is one appreciated in your time."

Zane snickered audibly and Emilie whirled about. "Stop that!" she ordered. "You know exactly what I'm talking about."

"Women's liberation," Zane said to a wide-eyed McVie. "Equal pay for equal work."

"A major consideration for a man," Andrew acknowledged, "but surely a wife does not expect recompense for her services."

Emilie strangled on a scream of frustration. "Women do more than cook and clean for a man in the future," she snapped. "We fly planes and own companies and even rule countries."

Andrew laughed. "For a moment I did not realize you were jesting."

Emilie's hand clenched into a fist and Zane stepped between his ex-wife and her girlhood hero. "I'd shut up if I were you, McVie. She's got a great left hook."

Emilie, however, had more to say on the subject. "In our time, a woman ruled Great Britain."

"That is not difficult to believe," said Andrew, "for Good Queen

Bess inherited the throne two centuries ago upon the death of her father."

"Well, there is another Queen Elizabeth on the throne of England," said Emilie, "but her power is only ceremonial. I speak of someone else."

Andrew's rugged face was split by a wide and knowing grin. "Aye, it's a cunning lass you are, mistress. Her powers are ceremonial for it is her husband the king who rules, is it not?"

"Wrong again," said Emilie, beginning to wonder if this whole discussion had been such a great idea after all. She would have been much happier not knowing Andrew McVie was a male chauvinist—a term she had no intention explaining to him. "England is governed by a parliament presided over by a prime minister." She paused. "For many years that job belonged to a woman."

"Nay," said Andrew, "that cannot be." How could she expect him, an intelligent and worldly man, to believe such nonsense?

"It's true," Emilie persisted.

Andrew again looked toward Zane.

Zane almost felt sorry for the guy. He himself still had trouble with the notion of women's equality and all it entailed, and he'd lived through that particular revolution. McVie had to be completely dumbfounded.

"It's true," Zane said. "One day a woman will probably be president of the United States."

"I have heard enough," said Andrew. "I will finish my business and meet you at this spot shortly." He disappeared inside the Plumed Rooster.

"Poor guy," said Zane as the door swung closed behind McVie. "He couldn't wait to get away. We'll be lucky if we ever see him again."

"Was I that bad?"

"He didn't know what hit him."

"I just couldn't believe his attitude," Emilie said. "It was Neanderthal."

"Take a look around, Em. You won't find a copy of *Ms.* magazine anywhere. If you're looking for equality you're about two hundred years too soon."

His words hit Emilie hard. Women had played an important part in the war for independence. She could recite tales of wives who had followed their husbands into battle, mothers who'd risked their lives to further the cause of freedom for their fighting sons.

To hear McVie talk, they'd done nothing but sit by the fire and dream.

"Serpent in paradise?" Zane asked, grinning.

"Oh, shut up." She started off down the street, picking her way through the crowd of fishmongers, vegetable grocers and assorted livestock.

"Careful where you walk," Zane said, catching up with her. "Pooper scoopers haven't been invented yet."

She was about to snap out a sharp retort when a hen raced across the road, followed by a yipping dog. She stopped abruptly, almost tumbling into Zane's waiting grasp.

"Told you to be careful where you walked."

"Am I crazy," said Emilie, regaining her balance, "or is it as busy here now as it is in the future?"

"You won't get an argument from me." He glanced across the street, then cupped her elbow with his left hand in a protective gesture. "Keep looking at me, Em," he ordered.

Her eyes widened. She made to turn toward the street but he gripped her more tightly and propelled her back toward the Plumed Rooster. "What's wrong?" she asked.

"Soldiers," he said, "and I don't think they're on our side."

The urge to stop and stare was almost irresistible. If Zane hadn't looked so stern, she was sure she would have made a show of herself.

"They're watching us," Zane said as they waited for Andrew to come out.

"We're not doing anything wrong," she said indignantly. "What can they do to us?"

"Anything they want," said Zane, struck by that knowledge. "Isn't that what the war was about?"

Chapter Eight

8

The Blakelee farm was situated a mile north of town. Cows grazed in the meadow near the weathered red barn, while a flock of sheep wandered about the front yard in the waning light of late afternoon.

At fifty acres the farm wasn't overly large, but it did afford the Blakelees a comfortable living—or at least it had before the advent of war.

The farmhouse itself was a two-story clapboard structure, unadorned by shutters or flower boxes. The only decorative touch was the red roses blooming to the right of the front door.

As they walked up the lane toward the house, Emilie's heartbeat accelerated and her hands began to tremble.

Andrew had explained little of his involvement with the Blakelees but both Emilie and Zane had deduced that they were somehow linked to the spy ring of which McVie was a part. They did know that the man, Josiah, was missing, but beyond that they were in the dark.

Andrew stopped a few yards from the front door and turned to them. "'Twould be best if the Blakelees think of you as a wedded couple."

"We've already covered that," said Zane. He knew all about eighteeth-century sensibilities and was more than willing to play along. He glanced at Emilie standing beside him. At least, in this instance he was.

McVie had more to say. "You should be average in every way possible."

Emilie nodded. "Don't worry. We'll be careful."

"I don't know if I can pull it off," Zane said to Emilie as McVie climbed the steps to the front door.

"I can," said Emilie, switching her silver-and-gold ring from her right hand to her left. "Just pretend you're the strong, silent type and follow my lead. You can—" She stopped abruptly as the door to the farmhouse swung open and a tiny brown-haired woman appeared in the doorway. She wore a simple dress in a dark beige color. A white mobcap sat atop her head.

Mrs. Blakelee looked at Andrew then her gaze slid past him and landed on Zane, whose back was turned to her.

"Oh, sweet merciful heavens!" the woman exclaimed, hurrying down the steps. "Josiah!"

Andrew grabbed the woman by the shoulder. "Nay, Rebekah. It is not Josiah."

Zane turned to see what had caused the commotion, and the good woman's narrow face lost the glow of happiness.

The woman looked back at Andrew. "I had so hoped Josiah would be with you."

"As I had hoped to find him safe at home. I fear we are both doomed to disappointment."

"Nine weeks and nary a word," said Rebekah Blakelee, wiping her eyes with the edge of her apron.

"He lives," said Andrew, comforting the woman with awkward pats on the back. "It cannot be otherwise." The specter of the dreaded British prison ships in Wallabout Bay rose before him, but he steadfastly refused to acknowledge its presence.

A child of about three years appeared at Rebekah's side. He held a small wooden hoop in his plump hand. Rebekah was too distraught to acknowledge his presence, even as he tugged at her skirts. From the front window came the sound of an infant crying. Emilie could only imagine how trapped and alone the woman must feel with so much responsibility on her slender shoulders.

Andrew spoke low to the farm woman. She nodded, then glanced toward Emilie and Zane.

"These are the Rutledges," Andrew said. "I discovered mistress Emilie in a most dreadful situation and have endeavored to lend aid until such time as her spouse is mended."

Zane shot McVie a deadly look. *Spouse* was bad enough. *Mended* made him sound like a canary with a broken wing. He started to say something to that effect, but a subtle poke in his ribs, courtesy of his ex-wife, made him reconsider.

Emilie stepped forward. "We shall endeavor to be a help and not a burden to your good family."

The woman's narrow face was transformed by her smile. "My Christian name is Rebekah."

"And I am Emilie." She gestured toward Zane. "This is my hus—" She stumbled over the word. "This is Zane."

He inclined his head toward the good woman and smiled. Emilie watched, both amused and somewhat piqued, as high color rose to Rebekah's cheeks and her smile deepened, making her plain face almost pretty.

"Zane," Rebekah said. "What manner of name is that?"

"It's a family name," he said easily.

Emilie breathed a sigh of relief that he had bypassed his *Riders of the Purple Sage* explanation.

Rebekah ran a hand across her forehead, smoothing the wispy strands of hair that had fallen toward her eyes. "I am sorry that you see my home in a time of turmoil." Her brown eyes filled with tears but she did not acknowledge their presence. "Without Josiah the farm has suffered greatly."

Twice her farmhouse had been commandeered, once by British officers and once by the Continental army, neither group exhibiting any concern for her well-being or that of her family.

"We are in need of lodging," Andrew said simply. "Rutledge has a broken arm and mistress Emilie—"

“Not another word,” said Rebekah. “My husband holds you in high esteem. It is an honor to have you in my home.”

Rebekah Blakelee was a practical woman. No sooner had she extended her generous invitation than she put Andrew and Zane to work bringing in more wood for the kitchen hearth and extra buckets of water.

Emilie followed the woman into a cool and spacious sitting room that ran from the front of the house to the back. Emilie instantly gravitated toward the spinning wheel situated near the stone fireplace. A basket of knitting rested next to a comfortable-looking wing chair by the window, while another basket, this one piled high with mending, sat atop the ledge. Military uniforms, in various states of completion, were stacked on a gateleg table in the corner.

“I am proficient at the wheel,” Emilie said, turning to face Rebekah. “I would be honored to be of assistance.”

“My daughter will be delighted to hear of your generous offer,” said Rebekah, “for Charity is a most unwilling participant.”

As if on cue, a pretty, dark-haired girl of about sixteen swayed into the room in a flurry of flowered skirts. “How can I embroider my wedding linens, Mother, if I am forever enslaved to that dreaded wheel?”

“This is Charity,” said Rebekah with a rueful shake of her head. “My outspoken oldest child.” She turned to her daughter. “Mistress Emilie and her spouse, Mr. Rutledge, will be spending some time with us.”

Charity did not receive the news with any particular degree of interest. *A typical teenager,* thought Emilie. It was comforting to know that some things never changed.

“Charity is to be married a few weeks hence,” said Rebekah as Charity sat down by the window with a child’s shirt she’d been working on. “A most agreeable young man from a fine family north of here. I had so hoped Josiah…” Her words trailed off and she glanced away.

Impulsively Emilie reached for the woman’s hand and took it in her own. "Everything will work out," she said earnestly. "I am certain of it." She tilted her head at the sound of a baby crying. "Have you an infant?"

Rebekah nodded. "A hungry one. Let me pour a pitcher of cider for you and your husband and then I shall tend to Aaron."

"Let me," said Emilie, then caught herself with a laugh. No bottles and formula here. "Not with Aaron, of course, but with the cider."

Rebekah was not accustomed to accepting help from guests in her home, but Emilie insisted. She wanted to see and experience everything she possibly could. For years she'd been insufferably proud of her knowledge of colonial ways. It would be interesting to see if her conceit was merited.

The kitchen was situated in the rear of the house. It was a large room with a high, beamed ceiling, dominated by an enormous hearth, some ten feet wide and over five feet high. As was the custom, the main meal had been served at midday and the fire was banked now. Emilie peered curiously at the two keeping ovens built into the bricks on the sides of the hearth and at the assortment of iron pots and copper pans that hung from hooks overhead.

It was all so perfect—and so perfectly wonderful—that she threw back her head and laughed with joy.

Zane looked out at the farmland from the bedroom window on the second floor. Acre after acre of pastoral tranquillity luminous in the fierce light of the setting sun. Throughout history men had lived and died to hang on to the land, bound to it through mysterious ties of blood and dreams.

No matter how hard he tried to understand that longing for roots and stability, the secret eluded him. Things that had been impossible for him to understand in 1992 were just as impossible in 1776.

He wasn't entirely sure what that said about him, but for the first time in his life he felt a sense of lost possibilities that had nothing to do with fast cars and exotic cities.

Downstairs Emilie sat in the front room, cradling Rebekah

Blakelee's infant son. He and McVie had just come in from inspecting the barn and root cellar for any indications of foul play that Rebekah might have missed, when the sound of a baby's laughter had caught the men's attention.

McVie had stood in the entranceway, transfixed at the sight of Emilie with the laughing infant cradled in her arms. There was something so intimate, so ethereal about the scene that Zane had found it difficult to look at the expression of wonder on his ex-wife's beautiful face, and he'd turned away.

For all he knew McVie was still down there, staring at Emilie as if she held the secrets of the universe in her arms.

"So what's it to you, Rutledge?" he mumbled as he looked out at the bucolic scene. None of this mattered. All he had to do was bide his time and stay alert to possibilities and he was certain he'd find a way to get back to the world he'd left behind.

The image of Emilie gazing down at the infant cradled against her chest rose up again before his eyes, more vivid than the sight beyond the window. She'd always wanted a child. Even though their courtship had been brief and their marriage short-lived, that one fact had been painfully clear. She'd longed to cast her lot in with the future, while Zane had wanted to live for the moment with no regard for the past.

Children deserved more than biological parents. They deserved all the time and love and energy a mother and father could give. He knew firsthand what happened when parents cared more for their own happiness than for the new life they had created. If you couldn't make that kind of wholehearted commitment, you had no damn business bringing a kid into the world.

Even if the thought of a baby with her eyes and her smile made something strange happen inside his chest.

He turned away from the window, his gaze resting briefly on the wooden rocking chair in the corner, the highboy near the door...the narrow bed pushed up against the wall.

They'd never had any trouble in bed. If they'd been half as good at talking as they were at making love, they'd be celebrating their sixth anniversary. It struck him as a damn shame that two people who'd had so much going for them had let it all slip through their fingers without so much as putting up a fight.

Rebekah served a hearty supper of cold meat, bread and cheese with cider. The rest of her family joined them at the table and Emilie was amazed that the slender woman had borne Josiah Blakelee five sons and a daughter. The eldest son, Isaac, was fifteen and eager to throw in his lot with the patriots. The boy listened with rapt attention to Andrew's description of the situation at the Harlem Heights and Long Island.

"General Washington has but ten thousand troops against the hordes of British regulars and Hessians." He took a drink of cider. "The Harbor is choked with British vessels."

"The cause seems lost," said Rebekah with a sigh. "Such a miracle as independency has never been done in the history of civilization. We were foolish to believe it could be done now by sheer power of will alone."

Isaac leaped from his seat, his face alight with determination. "I'm going, Mother! I'll join the general's troops like Sam'l Pearce did. We'll drive those Redcoats into the ocean!"

"Sit down, you fool!" snapped his sister, Charity. "Pa may never come back. You have to stay here and run the farm."

"Half the army has broken rank and gone home," Andrew observed. "'Tis hard to leave fields that need ploughing and crops that need tending when circumstances ahead may require much in the way of supplies."

Emilie noted the look of gratitude on Rebekah's drawn face. Before today she would have imagined that every mother's dream was to have her son serve the cause with distinction. But these were a practical people, their forebears, as concerned with growing crops as with securing independence from the Crown.

"The soldiers are a dreadful lot," Charity said, casting a look toward Zane, who was eating in silence. "Just last month they tore down our fences and commandeered our horses without so much as a by-your-leave."

"The British soldiers have been here?" asked Emilie.

"Our soldiers," the girl replied. "Five officers moved into the old Whittaker place and stole sugar and flour and all the silverware."

Zane looked up from his plate. "Is that true?" he asked Rebekah.

"That and more," said the good woman. "Dreadful things have happened from Trenton to New York. We buried our silverware and pewter in the herb garden. Without Josiah, I fear for our safety."

The Blakelees were held under a cloud of suspicion by the Tories, who speculated, correctly, that Josiah was a spy, while the patriots claimed the man had been too friendly with the enemy.

First thing tomorrow Andrew would head back into Princeton and begin his search anew. He'd learned much this afternoon at the Plumed Rooster. New intrigues were afoot. The British were planning mischief in Trenton to the south, while Hessian troops waited to cross the Hudson to the north. He found himself weary of the endless speculation and the absence of resolution.

Time and again his mind wandered to the stories Rutledge and mistress Emilie had told him and he wished with all his heart he could leave this place and find that other world that existed somewhere in the future.

Emilie excused herself immediately after supper, claiming dreadful fatigue.

"After your ordeal you must long for a hot bath," said Rebekah, who had been told the same story about a boating accident that Emilie originally had told Andrew.

"I must admit the notion holds considerable charm," said Emilie, holding back a yawn.

"Then a bath you will have," Rebekah declared. "There are few luxuries left to us. A hot bath is one I shall not forsake without a fight."

Amen to that, thought Emilie a half hour later as she sank blissfully into the warm water.

Rebekah had commandeered her children into setting up the copper tub in Emilie's room, then seeing that it was filled with plenty of warm, scented water. Rebekah hoarded attar of roses, which she doled out in minuscule portions for her weekly soak. Emilie had been touched that the woman would share her bounty with a stranger.

The copper tub was meant for soaking, not reclining, and try as she might Emilie could not submerge her knees or shoulders beneath the water at the same time. It was a small quibble. A marble bath the size of a swimming pool couldn't have been more appreciated.

She closed her eyes, letting her head fall back against the edge of the tub. She ached from toes to eyelids. In the past two days she'd walked more than in the past twenty years. Funny how you could know so much about a time period, understand the customs and the history, and still be surprised by the most basic differences.

All the Jazzercise classes and StairMaster sessions in the world hadn't prepared her for life without a car. No wonder the average life expectancy had been lower. People were just plain exhausted.

How did Rebekah manage, she wondered, with a home to take care of and a farm to run, not to mention six children of varying temperaments and needs. Large families had always held a certain appeal for Emilie and she had been charmed by them all, from about-to-be-wed Charity right down to six-month-old Aaron with the big brown eyes and tufts of blond hair.

She could still feel him cuddled against her chest, his plump baby hands pressing into her breasts. And that smell—was anyone immune to that sweetly seductive smell? She knew it was all part of a plot engineered by Mother Nature, designed to ensure the survival of the species, but that didn't matter.

Once again, Mother Nature was successful. The fierce yearning for a child that she had experienced during her brief marriage to Zane swooped in on her with the primal force of the tides.

She took a deep breath, then tried to think of something else. The red roses in the front yard, for example. Charity's wedding plans.

Or the beautiful sapphire blue of Zane's eyes.

As if on cue, the door swung open and Zane strode into the room.

"Zane!" She crossed her arms over her breasts and tried to slide lower in the tub. "You should have knocked."

"I tried to call," he said, sitting down on the edge of the bed, "but the phone's out of order."

"Very funny." She gave him a fierce look. "I was here first."

His gaze swept over her like a hot breeze. "So I see."

"Hand me a towel," she said, gesturing toward the stack resting next to him. "And stop looking at me like that." She was struggling to maintain a detached composure and the struggle grew more difficult with each second that passed.

"Don't get out on my account," he said, grinning. "I'm enjoying the view." More than she could imagine.

"That's exactly what we have to talk about." She tried to look authoritative but found it difficult given the circumstances. "Just because we—I mean, we made a mistake the other night and I don't intend to compound it."

He leaned back on the mattress, looking as comfortable as you please. "I couldn't agree more. Pretending to be married was McVie's idea, not mine."

"You agreed to it."

"Why not? You'd already stripped me down to the skin. He probably figured there weren't many surprises left."

Emilie cringed at the thought. "Between that and the divorce I can just imagine what he must be thinking."

Zane sat up straighter. "Who gives a damn what he thinks?"

"We should if we expect his help."

"You sure there isn't more to it than that?"

"I don't know what you mean."

Zane leaned forward. "The guy's your childhood hero and he's about fifty years younger than a childhood hero should be. Think about it."

"Really, Zane," she said, feigning nonchalance. "You sound like an idiot."

"I think you're falling for him."

"Ridiculous!"

"Is it?"

"Absolutely." She rose from the tub and reached for one of the towels stacked on the bed next to Zane. For an instant, as she leaned forward for the towel, she stood naked before him and the air seemed to shimmer between them. The towel didn't cover much, she noted with dismay, but it did manage to shield the essentials.

"McVie is serious and patriotic," Zane said, "just the kind of guy you always wanted."

"You don't know anything about what kind of man I want."

"I know you're looking at the kind of man you don't want."

His words stung, and she didn't know exactly why. She stepped from the tub. "This is a ridiculous conversation. There are more important things to think about." She reached for a cotton wrapper Rebekah had been kind enough to supply. "Like what we're going to do after we wear out our welcome with the Blakelees."

"Ask McVie. He seems to be the answer man around here."

There it was again, thought Emilie. The sound of jealousy. She couldn't believe her ears. "We're the ones with the answers," she pointed out, "and we have to decide which ones we're going to provide."

"You can't change history."

"I don't intend to," said Emilie. "Just give it a push in the right direction."

"If it's already happened, why would it need our help?"

"Did it ever occur to you that maybe we're part of the bigger picture?"

"No," he said. "Not for a second."

She stood by the window, brushing her hair with a large tortoiseshell comb. "There's a reason for everything that happens," she said, "and I can't help thinking we've been sent here for a purpose."

"Where's Shirley MacLaine when you need her?"

She sighed and put down the comb. "I didn't think you'd understand."

"There's no reason, Em," he said, walking toward her. "It just happened and now we have to find a way to get back where we belong."

Her gaze was drawn to the bed pushed up against the far wall.

"You should be in Tahiti," she said, meeting his eyes. "You would have been if you hadn't hijacked that balloon."

"Would you call it fate?"

"I call it temporary insanity."

He drew her close, draping his left arm around her shoulders. "You shouldn't have taken off the way you did."

She tried to move away, but he held her fast. "I made a mistake," she said softly. "There was no point to pretending otherwise."

"It didn't feel like a mistake."

"No," she said, "but that doesn't change things. We want different things from life, Zane. We need different things. Not even traveling two hundred years through time can change that."

He understood her meaning. "I'd sleep on the couch," he said, "but they don't have one."

"You don't have to sleep on the couch. We'll manage."

He looked at the narrow bed. "I doubt it."

"It is kind of small, isn't it?"

"Turn over once and we're talking conjugal rights." He reached for the closure on his trousers.

"What are you doing?"

"What do you think I'm doing?"

"I think you're taking your pants off." Hadn't he understood a single word she'd said?

"Best way to take a bath." He gestured toward the tub in the middle of the room. "Is the water still warm?"

She nodded.

"Great." Even with his broken arm he managed to divest himself of his clothing in record time. He placed his gold watch on the window ledge. "You'll scrub my back, won't you, Em?"

"Zane, you really don't want to get into that tub."

"Look," he said, "I'm tired and hot and grubby. If we're going to share a bed, I need the tub."

"But the water—"

"Is just right," he said, lowering his impressive body into the small tub. He frowned, sniffing the air. "What the hell is that smell?"

"Roses," said Emilie.

"From the front yard?"

"From the bathwater," she said, starting to giggle.

"You're kidding me."

"Afraid not. Rebekah gave me some attar of roses to put in the water."

"Why the hell didn't you tell me?"

"I was trying to. You were too fast for me."

"I'm going to smell like a damn bridal bouquet."

"Nobody'll notice."

The look on his face spoke volumes.

She approached the tub, clutching a flannel washrag. "Would you like your back scrubbed?" she asked sweetly.

He grunted.

"Once for yes, twice for no."

"Don't push it, Emilie," he warned.

She knelt down behind him then leaned forward, dipping the washrag into the scented water. "Keep your arm out of the water," she advised. "You don't want to get the splint wet."

"I don't give a damn about the splint."

"You will if it ends up smelling like rosewater."

She noticed with a smile that he made a point of keeping his right arm well out of the reach of the bathwater. The only light in the room came from a candle set upon the nightstand. Its light sent shadows flickering across the wooden floor. Slowly she drew the wet, warm cloth over the muscles of his back and shoulders, watching the drops of water glisten in the candlelight.

The feel of his skin beneath her hands was both strange and familiar, and once again she felt that dark need building inside her. It had always been like this. The sound of his voice, the touch of his hand, the way his hair always smelled of sunshine and sea breezes—any one of those things was enough to send her foolish heart into a spin.

If only she didn't want him. This whole ridiculous mess would be so much easier if she didn't yearn for him. She hated feeling so open, so vulnerable, wanting the one thing on earth she shouldn't have.

Thank God she wasn't still in love with him, that what she felt was nothing more than lust.

"That's great," Zane murmured, letting his head drop forward as she kneaded the muscles of his neck and upper back. "Down there...yeah, that's it...."

She watched, mesmerized, as a bead of water inched its way down his spine, fighting the urge to follow its trail with her tongue.

This was the life, thought Zane as Emilie ministered to him. A warm bath—even if the water did stink of roses. Candlelight. A beautiful woman and a waiting bed. He had the feeling all of the elements were about to come together.

For the first time since he'd hijacked that damn balloon, he felt hopeful.

"Well," said Emilie, rising and moving away from the tub. "Your back is as clean as it's going to get. I think I'll go to bed."

Zane's thoughts exactly. The feel of her hands against him had focused all his attention on the same idea.

She threw back the covers and climbed into the narrow bed. He noticed she was still wearing the pale blue robe, and he grinned. He'd always liked helping her undress.

He watched, amazed, as she yawned, scooted down beneath the covers and closed her eyes.

"You're going to sleep?"

She nodded, eyes still closed. "Of course."

That's what he got for having an overactive imagination. She'd told him she wasn't interested in continuing where they'd left off two hundred years from now. He'd have to remember his ex-wife was one of the few women in the world who meant exactly what she said.

Not that it made the situation any easier. Climbing into that narrow bed and staying on his own side of the mattress would be a major-league test of willpower, and where Emilie was concerned he'd never had much of that commodity.

"A deal's a deal," he muttered as he climbed out of the tub.

Emilie peered at him through the flickering candlelight. "Did you say something?"

"Not me," he said, grabbing for the scratchy tissues that passed for early-American towels. "You must have heard me yawn."

"Mmm," said Emilie, not sounding terribly convinced. "That must have been it." She turned on her side and closed her eyes. "Last one in bed blows out the candle."

It was going to be a very long night.

Chapter Nine

9

From sunup until sundown the Blakelee farm was a hotbed of activity. Andrew and the boys set out for the fields soon after dawn, returning to the farmhouse only for food and drink.

Emilie was swept up into the household routine that was uniquely the province of females. She swept the bare wood floors, beat the rugs when necessary, mended stockings and repaired worn trousers. She helped Rebekah with kitchen chores, shuddering at the sight of an unplucked chicken lying on the table, and she was again struck by the realization that knowing about a way of life and actually experiencing that way of life were two totally different things.

Still, there was something exhilarating about being tested to the limits of your knowledge and ability, and as they began their second week in this strange new world, Emilie found herself more confident that she could find a way to make a life for herself.

Unfortunately Zane was finding it difficult to carve a place for himself. Day after day he watched McVie and the Blakelee boys working in the fields while he sat on the top porch step and waited for some sign, some indication that he'd find a way back to the world where he belonged.

He was a coiled mass of energy, a taut mainspring ready to snap. The damn broken arm kept him from burning off his tensions with hard work. His usual diversions of fast cars and bright lights were unavailable. Pretending he and Emilie were married was easy enough during the day but at night, when she was only a heartbeat away, he burned for her.

In desperation he had taken to sleeping on the floor and, he noted wryly, she had offered no protest. He had only his thoughts for company and as the days passed those thoughts grew increasingly dark.

All around him the talk was of independence, but to Zane independence would begin only when he regained financial freedom. Back in his time he'd never had to worry about things like earning a living. He'd been born into money and all that entailed, and the pursuits of lesser mortals had always seemed murky at best. McVie had said that once Zane's arm healed he would be an asset in the fields. "Josiah was a large man such as you," Andrew said, "capable of lifting his weight and more."

Pumping iron was one thing. Baling hay was something else again.

He supposed he could get work as a fortune-teller, but that was probably the best way to insure his place as first in line at the gallows. In his pocket his hand rested on the wristwatch he'd refused to hide with Emilie's twentieth century booty. You could probably feed the Continental army for a year on what he'd paid for the damn thing—and on top of everything else, it no longer worked.

"Wait a minute," he said out loud as he slipped the watch off his wrist. Times may have changed but gold remained constant. If he removed the watch face and separated the band into segments, independence might no longer be as far away as it seemed.

Money could make the difference. He could repay Rebekah Blakelee for her generosity, then purchase a horse and carriage so he and Emilie could return to the lighthouse. He had the feeling that if they were to have any chance at all of returning to the future, they would have to be waiting for that chance at the place where the future began.

* * *

As for Andrew, he was faring no better than his counterpart from the future.

Each day he worked the farm with vigor.

Each night he slipped from the quiet house to meet with the other members of the spy ring. A spy ring whose numbers were dwindling away faster than the coins in his pocket. First Blakelee. Now Fleming. Arrest warrants had been issued for Miller and Quick.

Papers had fallen into the wrong hands and, to everyone's dismay, invisible ink had proven to be less than reliable. There must be a better means of achieving the desired end, but neither Andrew nor the other members of the spy ring could discover what it might be.

Rumors abounded about British troop movements on Long Island and anarchy in the Hudson River valley. Militiamen in Pennsylvania and New Jersey had laid down their arms and returned home to farms and families in desperate need, with promises to return to the front once the harvest was past.

Andrew listened with a keen ear for any mention of a new plot against the life of General Washington, but there was none.

To his puzzlement, he found himself both relieved and disappointed. He wished no danger upon the head of His Excellency, but he wanted to believe that all mistress Emilie and Rutledge had told him was true. If the general faced no threat to his life, did that mean that the other stories his companions had told him were so much whole cloth?

He had spent much time considering the curious bond between the beautiful red-haired lass and Rutledge. They had once been wed, had stood before man and God and repeated those sacred vows that he and Elspeth had repeated on that long-ago summer's day. *Until death*... They had promised, and only death's finality could have torn Elspeth from his side.

He had little experience or knowledge of divorce. He knew that it existed, but beyond that the notion was as foreign as it was distasteful. Doubtless it had been Rutledge who instigated the separation. There was much of the rogue about the man. He had not the aspect of stability that a woman found important in the man she would wed.

Of course, he reminded himself, they came from a time and place unknown to him where men watched moving images on giant screens and made a fortune in gold tossing a leather ball through a hoop. Perhaps in that world divorce was an everyday occurrence, but still he found that impossible to believe. He wondered what manner of difficulties he had visited upon the lass by forcing her to share a room with the man who had turned away from their conjugal vows.

And he wondered how it was that any man could turn away from such a beautiful woman....

One morning, in the third week of their stay with the Blakelees, Emilie was in the kitchen kneading a batch of bread. Rebekah stood at the open hearth, stirring the stewpot, while Aaron slept soundly in his cradle beneath the window.

Isaac and two of his younger brothers had gone into the fields to work with Andrew. Charity was in the sitting room working diligently on the pillow slips she would take to her marriage bed two weeks from now.

Zane had been gone when Emilie woke up, and she found herself vaguely disturbed that no one had seen him yet today. Not that his whereabouts were any of her concern. They lived in edgy proximity in the small second-floor bedroom, married in name but not in fact. That would have been hard enough for any man and woman but, given their volatile history, it was rapidly becoming impossible.

That first night alone in the second-floor bedroom had been the turning point. The urge to give in to temptation once again had been strong, but she had been stronger. Strange how little pleasure that fact afforded her.

They were polite to each other, and considerate, but that was where it ended. Passion still simmered beneath the surface, and she was determined that was where the passion would remain. It would be too easy to make the same mistake over again, settling for lust when what she wanted was the whole, incredible, wonderful package: lust and love and a future that included a home and family.

All the things Zane had never wanted—and probably never would.

She glanced toward baby Aaron asleep in his cradle.

"You're a lucky woman," she said to Rebekah as she divided the bread dough into four portions.

Rebekah looked at Emilie, then at her infant son. "I thank the Almighty every day," she said simply. "Josiah and I lost two daughters to the pox three springs past. A day does not go by where I do not think of their beloved faces."

Emilie spoke without thinking. "Surely you had your children inoculated?"

"'Tis a dangerous and painful process," Rebekah said, looking at Emilie's obvious curiosity. "We would have had to uproot the children and spend many uneasy days in Philadelphia while we waited to see if the pox would come."

"I'm sorry," Emilie said, flustered by her own thoughtlessness. What miracles they took for granted in the twentieth century. "You owe me no explanation."

"Nor do you, Emilie, but there is a question that has plagued me now for days."

Emilie directed her attention to the bread dough. "You may ask me anything."

Rebekah wiped her hands on her apron, then walked over to the table where Emilie was working. "This is a most delicate matter but one to which I must address myself."

Oh, God, thought Emilie, heart pounding inside her chest. Could Rebekah possibly suspect that Emilie and Zane were not what they seemed to be? She had cut the zipper from Zane's trousers and buried it behind the barn with her American Express card. To her knowledge, Andrew still had her driver's license. She prayed he hadn't decided to share their secret with Rebekah Blakelee.

"Speak your mind," Emilie said with more serenity than she was feeling.

Rebekah's cheeks were flushed with high color. Emilie watched, unnerved, as the small-boned woman squared her shoulders, then met her eyes. "'Tis about Andrew McVie I speak. He is a fine man, you will agree."

"I agree," said Emilie, puzzled. "He is a man of honor and principle and I—"

Rebekah raised her hand. "He is also a man in love."

The tension rushed from Emilie's body and she laughed. "How wonderful!" she said. "Who is the object of his affections?"

Rebekah's brows slid together in a frown. "You are."

"Rebekah! That is ridiculous. I am—I am a married woman."

"That may be so, but I have seen the way he looks at you when he believes no one is about, and I fear the signs are clear."

Emilie abandoned all pretense. "He scarcely knows me," she said. "Love does not grow in such a short span of time."

"Love does not set its pace by the clock, Emilie. I am a woman and I know what I see. Andrew loves you."

"This is dreadful," she said. "Certainly I have done nothing to encourage such a thing." She wiped her hands on her apron. "I must find Andrew and settle this matter immediately."

"No!" Rebekah grabbed her by the arm and held her fast. "You mustn't! It has been a very long time since I have seen Andrew smile. He would be much embarrassed if he knew we read his thoughts."

Andrew McVie—*her childhood hero!*—in love with her? "Surely it is a temporary thing," Emilie said, twisting the gold-and-silver ring on her left hand. "He—he knows that Zane and I..." Her words trailed off. Andrew knew the truth. The entire truth. If he had fallen in love with her as Rebekah believed, it was with the full knowledge that a future between them was within the realm of possibility.

"He has known great sorrow these few years past," Rebekah was saying. "Since losing his wife—"

Emilie's head snapped up. "His wife?"

"I did not know Elspeth," Rebekah said, "but I believe he loved her and their son with his heart and soul."

"Is his son—?"

Rebekah nodded, her brown eyes glistening with tears. "A terrible fire," she said, shaking her head. "He lost them both…he lost everything."

A cold chill rose up Emilie's spine. She shivered and wrapped her arms around her chest. "I'd always wondered," she murmured. "There'd never been any mention of a family."

Rebekah looked at her. "I thought your acquaintanceship was of a short duration."

For one crazy moment she considered telling Rebekah the truth, that she and Zane were not only divorced, but from the future. Then reason returned and she caught herself before she made a dreadful mistake.

"What should I do?" she asked the brown-eyed woman, who was watching her closely. "How shall I handle him?"

"Gently," said Rebekah. "Without harshness or idle encouragement." There was the faintest reproach in her tone, almost as if she'd felt Emilie had been leading him on.

"I—I would never do anything to hurt him."

"He is a good man," said Rebekah once again.

Emilie gazed out the window toward the fields. In the distance she could just make out Andrew's wiry figure and she looked away, her chest tight.

"Your husband is a fine-looking man," Rebekah said. "How long have you been wed?"

"Five—no, six years," Emilie said. "Yes. Six years."

Rebekah smiled. "The years pass swiftly."

"Faster than you could ever imagine," said Emilie.

"You have been blessed with children?"

Emilie shook her head. "Not yet."

Rebekah's smile faded and she reached out to pat Emilie's hand in a sympathetic gesture. "You are young. I am certain you will be blessed."

"I'm afraid I'm not *that* young," Emilie said with a small laugh. "Thirty years old my next birthday."

"You jest," said Rebekah.

"I haven't been sleeping well," said Emilie, gesturing toward the circles beneath her eyes, "but in truth I will turn thirty in December."

"That cannot be."

"Rebekah!" Emilie's voice rose in indignation. "Do I look that unwell?"

"It's just—I mean to say, you look so young. I did not think it possible that you were—" She shook her head. "I hesitate to stand next to you, for I appear old enough to be your mother and I am but three years your senior."

Emilie made polite noises of disagreement but, in truth, the difference in their appearance was startling. "I have had a gentle life," Emilie said.

Rebekah sighed deeply. "I cannot say the same."

Childbirth and toil aged a woman in ways the years could not. Emilie experienced a moment of fear, primal and inarticulate, as she thought of the life she'd left behind. Why had she never realized the depth of ease, of privilege, that the most average of women enjoyed as a matter of course? She wondered what Rebekah would think if she told the woman about microwaves and washing machines, about face-lifts and birth control pills.

It won't always be so hard to be a woman, she thought, but that knowledge wouldn't help Rebekah—or herself. The realization was sudden and overwhelming.

Retin-A, cosmetic surgery, the wonders to be found in Estée Lauder and Elizabeth Arden—gone, all of it. This was a rougher world, harsh and unyielding. A woman's beauty was as short-lived as a rose in winter. She had always talked a good show about superficiality and the cult of youth but, when push came to shove, would she be able to face the uncompromising truths that her mirror would soon reveal?

By two o'clock Zane had still not returned. Neither Emilie nor Rebekah had any idea where he had disappeared to. Emilie briefly considered walking out into the fields to ask Andrew or Isaac if they knew where Zane had gone, but Rebekah's words lingered in her ears and she stayed away.

Andrew did not come in for dinner, but continued working.

The two women shared the meal of slaw, hot rolls and mutton with the Blakelee children, except for Isaac who remained in the fields with Andrew. Charity and her mother had much to consider as the day of the wedding celebration swiftly approached, and Emilie found herself drifting along on a wave of bittersweet longing.

Baby Aaron slept contentedly in his cradle near his mother's chair. Benjamin and Stephen, eight-year-old twins, teased each other mercilessly, while the toddler, Ethan, entertained Emilie with tales of his imaginary friend, John the Flying Dog.

It was a simple meal, served in a simple way and shared with people she barely knew, yet Emilie experienced a sharp stab of envy. It seemed so little to ask for: a home of her own, a husband to love, children to care for. Somehow that most basic of dreams had always managed to elude her. Leave it to her to find the man of her dreams, only to discover her husband had no interest in any of it.

He loves you, Emilie, Rebekah had said about Andrew. *I see the way he looks at you....*

She couldn't imagine the despair Andrew had felt when he lost his wife and child. It explained so much about him. That haunted look in his hazel eyes. The sense of restlessness. The depth of his commitment to the cause of independence. He was the kind of man a woman could admire: strong and loyal and—

She stopped, shocked by the direction her thoughts were taking her. What on earth had come over her? Surely she wasn't attracted to him—not in the fiery way she was attracted to Zane.

But how would it feel to cast your lot with a man who wanted the same things you wanted, home and family and happy endings? Maybe that type of wild and passionate love was, by its very nature, doomed to failure. Certainly it had been with her marriage to Zane. She'd had such high and shining hopes for their future, only to discover he cared more for adventure than he ever could for her.

After the meal, Emilie helped Rebekah with cleaning up.

"You are looking pale," Rebekah observed, placing her palm against Emilie's forehead. "Are you unwell?"

"Tired," Emilie said.

"You should rest."

Emilie shook her head. The last thing she wanted was to be trapped in a room with her tangled thoughts. "I think I'll sit outside and work on the mending."

Rebekah grew thoughtful. "Is there a chance that perhaps you are with child?"

"No!" Emilie took a deep breath. She laughed nervously as vivid images of that one magical night heated her blood. "I mean, I don't believe so."

"It will happen," Rebekah said with a gentle smile as she took Aaron from his cradle and prepared to nurse him.

Emilie fled before the woman could say any more.

Emilie found a shady spot beneath an old maple tree and settled down with the mending a few minutes later. Her fingers shook as she unfolded the man's shirt and searched for the worn spots in need of repair. Rebekah was a practical woman and she was seeing to it that her husband's garments were in perfect shape for his return.

This had to be the strangest day she'd had since this whole adventure began. First Rebekah told her that Andrew loved her and now Rebekah asked if she might be pregnant. It was enough to make Emilie throw her hands in the air and flee.

Which, it occurred to her, was exactly what it seemed Zane had done.

There was no telling where his thirst for adventure might take him. This was probably the longest period of time he'd ever spent in one place since he was in diapers. In another week or two his arm would be healed, and she wouldn't hazard a guess what course of action he would take after that.

He still talked about finding his way back to their old lives. She'd caught him once, drawing designs in the dirt with a stick. "Our escape hatch," he'd said when she asked what he was doing.

A hot-air balloon. "Great," she'd said, shaking her head. "Now all you have to do is manufacture a propane tank and you're all set."

Obviously he was still unable to accept the reality of their situation. For all she knew he was out scouring the countryside in search of a wicker gondola and a few thousand square yards of silk.

"Rebekah told me I would find you here."

Emilie jumped, pricking herself with the steel needle. "Andrew!" She popped her finger into her mouth, and looked up at him. "You snuck up on me."

He squatted down next to her. "I have not heard that expression before."

She grinned. "Consider yourself lucky. We've done terrible things to the language in my time. You would be appalled."

"Yesterday you told Rutledge that his socks would be knocked off by Rebekah's apple betty. I spent much time trying to envision that occurrence but came up wanting."

"It's slang," she said, noting the touch of green in his hazel eyes.

"What does it mean?"

She thought for a moment. "Overwhelmed, but in the best possible way."

"And if the situation was dire?"

"You'd be bummed out," said Emilie. "Of course, that only applies if you're a surfer—or from California."

He looked at her blankly. "Those words mean nothing to me."

"California is the state that curves along the western coast. They found gold there in 1848 and that really put it on the map." She told him about the perfect climate, the perfect beaches and the perfect specimens who rode the waves.

"I don't believe I understand it correctly," Andrew said, considering her words. "A man stands on a wooden board and sails through the waves?"

"Women do it, as well."

"This world of yours," he said, sitting down a few feet away from her. "Rutledge would sell his soul to Beelzebub to return, but you—" He stopped abruptly.

"I don't seem to care if I go back. You're right. I don't." There.

She'd said it. She hadn't intended to, but now that she'd given voice to the words she felt as if she'd crossed into alien territory.

"I do not understand. All the wonder you've left behind." He shook his head in bewilderment.

"We've told you only about the wonders, Andrew. There is much wrong in our time. Many people fear that the earth will not survive."

The world he knew was one of bounty, of clear skies and clean water. She tried to explain the differences to him, but when she came to garbage dumps the size of mountains he started to laugh.

"Forget it," she said, laughing too. "What difference does it make? Maybe it'll never happen."

"But you have seen them with your own eyes, have you not?"

"I've also seen myself pulled back two centuries through time. Who knows what else is possible?"

"You are unlike any woman I have ever known, lass."

"Given the circumstances, I'd have to agree." She tried to sound bright and breezy, the opposite of the way she felt.

"You are so full of life, so strong and—"

"Andrew." She placed a hand on his forearm. "Please don't."

He placed a hand over hers. "I cannot stop, lass. There is so much I have to say and I fear that time is my enemy."

She made to withdraw her hand but he would not allow it. "Andrew, you must believe it is just the circumstances that make you feel this way. It has nothing to do with me."

"It has everything to do with you."

"We shouldn't be talking like this."

"Do you love him still?"

"Andrew!"

"'Tis a logical question."

"We're divorced," she said. "Whatever existed between us is long gone." It was less than the truth but not quite a lie.

It was also the best she could do.

"He abandoned you and still you are friends. I find it easier to comprehend a man walking on the moon."

"So do I. The truth is a little more complicated than that." She hesitated. "Actually, I walked out on Zane, not the other way around."

"Do not try to shield him."

"Andrew, I'm not trying to shield him. I'm telling you the truth. We wanted different things from marriage. I was very unhappy, and so I left him."

"And he allowed this?"

"It's a free country," she said. "Or at least it will be in a few years."

"Did he beat you?"

"If he'd tried it he'd be walking funny today."

Andrew's face turned beet red. "Then why was it that you left him?"

Emilie sighed deeply. "I wanted a home. He didn't. I wanted a family. He didn't."

"You speak as if there are choices to be made. Only the Almighty can decide when a couple will start a family."

She wasn't up to a discussion on birth control. She cleared her throat and changed the subject. "Have you uncovered anything about the assassination plot?"

It took Andrew a moment to regain his emotional balance. "Nay, I have not. Our troubles have been of a more personal nature."

"Tell me." Emilie moved her needle and thread through the fabric of Josiah's shirt as Andrew told her of Fleming's disappearance, and of the arrest warrants issued against two more members of the spy ring. "And what of the messages you've been passing through to General Mercer?"

"It grows more difficult with each day." An important dispatch of a very sensitive nature had fallen into British hands two nights ago and Andrew feared the Jersey spy ring might be coming to the end of its usefulness.

Emilie watched the rhythmic motion of the sewing needle as she pushed then pulled it through the fabric of Josiah's shirt. "Maybe you're going about it wrong," she said thoughtfully. "Letters can be stolen."

"And what alternative is there, lass?"

Sunlight glittered off the silvery needle. "Embroidery," she said, meeting his eyes. “A message could be embroidered onto a garment then handed over to a courier without arousing undue interest.”

Andrew frowned. “No man would wear a schoolgirl’s sampler on his back.”

“Not a sampler,” she said. “What I’m thinking about would be tiny.” Quickly she rethreaded her needle, then stitched her name along the seam of the shirt.

“’Tis no bigger than a grain of rice.”

“Exactly. An entire message could be embroidered beneath a collar or inside a cuff.”

“Not many are skilled enough to do such work.”

“I am,” she said without hesitation.

His heart felt light inside his chest. Surely there was more to her eagerness than patriotic fervor.

“The thinnest floss of tan or gray will disappear…”

Her voice carried the sound of angels.

“Inside seams or on the underside of a lining…”

Her eyes flashed with the fire of priceless emeralds.

“…work clothes or uniforms or even a baby’s blanket…”

Her skin smelled sweeter than the roses blooming by the front door.

She looked up at him and smiled. “I think it will be wonderful, don’t you?”

“Aye, lass,” he said, his heart soaring. “Wonderful.”

Chapter Ten

10

"Are you going to tell Ma?"

Zane looked down at the lanky youth. "I don't know, Isaac. What do you think I should do?"

Isaac Blakelee, carrying a parcel of muslin fabric for his mother, considered the question with almost comical deliberation. "I think it should remain a secret between men."

Zane had to bite his lip to keep from laughing. The boy was still wet behind the ears. Barely fifteen years old and already burning with the righteous fires of independence, both personal and patriotic. Rebekah had sent the boy into town for fabric with strict orders to return home without delay. Isaac, however, had been unable to pass the Plumed Rooster without paying a visit.

He cleared his throat and struggled to look stern. "Next time I would avoid rum, Isaac, and stick with ale."

Zane felt better than he had in weeks. Money might not be able to buy you happiness but it went a long way toward buying a man his freedom. Those chunks of gold from his watchband had translated into a considerable stack of notes, like the New Jersey three-shilling with the warning To Counterfeit is Death printed on the front. His pockets bulged with coins, most of which bore the likeness of King George II and dates in the 1740s.

If he had had any doubts as to the reality of his situation, they were gone now.

He and Isaac walked together in silence for a while. Zane had been enjoying a tankard of ale in the Plumed Rooster, with the mixed clientele of farmers and Continental soldiers, when he noticed Isaac engaged in an altercation with the proprietor. The boy had been vigorously defending his father's honor, but the owner of the pub had been having none of it.

"Out with you, boy. I'll not be servin' a traitor's son."

Zane had stepped in, settled Isaac's tab, then dragged the hot-tempered teenager out into the sunshine and pointed him in the direction of home.

"Feel like talking?" he said as they waited for a coach and driver to rumble past.

Isaac shrugged his narrow shoulders. "They think my pa's a traitor but I know that ain't so."

"People say a lot of lousy things," Zane said. "Sometimes you have to forget them."

"I can't forget my pa," the boy snapped. "Old man Carpenter's a Tory and he says my pa and the others are in jail by Little Rocky Hill and next week they're going t'be moving the lot of them up to the Hell Ship."

Zane's interest was piqued. "What's the Hell Ship?"

"Floating prisons," said Isaac. "They say Wallabout Bay's fillin' up with bodies of dead prisoners." The boy's eyes glistened with tears but he fiercely blinked them away. "We ain't got enough soldiers to stand against the Lobsterbacks. My ma's got to—"

"Forget it," said Zane. "She needs you with her, Isaac. At least until your father comes back."

"What if my pa don't come back?" the boy asked, voice trembling. "What then?"

There was, of course, no answer for a question like that, and there never would be an answer for it, at least not in either of Zane's lifetimes.

Isaac looked up at him with curiosity. "The army'd be needing lots of help. I know my pa will join sooner or later. How about you?"

"I don't think I'm military material."

"Neither's my pa, but he says you do what you can to help."

"It's something to think about." And he'd been thinking about it a lot lately as he watched McVie and the Blakelees and Emilie strive toward a goal they couldn't see or hear or touch but knew was as necessary as air and water.

He draped an arm around the kid's shoulders and they walked the rest of the way home in companionable silence.

"One of the cows has been feelin' poorly," Isaac said as they started up the lane that led to the farmhouse. "Would you give this to Ma so I can go straightaway t'the barn?"

Zane motioned for the parcel and Isaac tossed it to him.

"Much obliged," the boy said, then dashed off in the direction of the barn.

Isaac was a good kid, filled with energy and loyalty and high ideals. Zane couldn't help but wonder how life would treat him. Sooner or later Isaac would make good his threat to join the Continental army, and he found himself hoping that fate would treat the boy with kindness.

He climbed the front steps and was about to go inside when the sound of Emilie's laughter, sweet and high, drifted toward him on the heavy summer air. He glanced across the front yard, expecting to see her walking toward him.

Instead he found her sitting in the shade of an enormous maple tree, smiling at that damn McVie as if they shared a secret.

He placed the parcel of muslin on the porch railing, then headed over to where Emilie and Andrew sat.

"Zane!" Her eyes widened as he approached. "We've been wondering where you were." She motioned for him, to join them beneath the tree.

"I had some business to take care of." He looked from Emilie to Andrew and didn't like what he saw. Not one damn bit.

"Business?" Her eyes widened some more. "What business could you possibly have?"

"I'll tell you later." No way was he going to let McVie know he had a king's ransom stuffed in his pockets. He didn't trust the guy as far as he could throw him.

"Where did you go?" asked McVie.

"Princeton."

McVie looked surprised. "How was it you were able to find the town without a guide?"

Zane started to say something both profane and right on target, but Emilie leaped into the fray.

"Zane has the most amazing memory," she said brightly. "People, places, conversations—" She laughed. "It's almost scary."

No, thought Zane, what was scary was the way she looked. Edgy with excitement. Soft and beautiful and female.

"So what's going on here?" he asked. "You two looked thick as thieves."

Emilie's face reddened and she looked down at the sewing in her lap.

McVie, however, met his eyes. "Mistress Emilie has provided a way to transport messages that will greatly aid our cause."

Great, thought Zane. Next thing he knew she'd be leading a protest march at Independence Hall.

"Yeah," he said, "she's another Betsy Ross."

"I'll explain it to you later," Emilie said to Andrew, who'd been about to ask.

"So what's the big idea, or is it a state secret?"

She looked toward Andrew who nodded. "I'm going to embroider the messages right on the messengers' clothing."

"That's it?" he asked. "Why don't you have them carrying billboards while you're at it?"

"We're not stupid," she snapped. She handed him a shirt. "Take a look at this and tell me what you see."

He glanced at the garment. "Other than a hole on the elbow, nothing."

She crossed her arms over her chest. "I rest my case."

"Take careful note of the underside of the collar," McVie said. "Mistress Emilie has embroidered her name."

"I'll be damned," said Zane as he held the garment up for closer examination. "That's microscopic."

"Mi-kro-scoppik?" McVie repeated.

"Tiny," said Emilie. "And that's the point, Zane. If I use the right shade of floss, you'd only know it was there if you were looking for it."

"Great idea," he said, "but what happens once they figure it out?"

"Then we'll come up with something else," she said.

McVie was watching them both with avid interest.

"Built-in obsolescence," Zane drawled. "It's what made America great. Why not throw a few roadblocks in their way from the outset?"

"I suppose you have a brilliant suggestion."

"Damn right. Use a secret code."

Both Emilie and McVie burst into laughter.

"What's so funny?"

They told him that secret codes were far from a revolutionary idea.

"Sorry," said Emilie. "It just proves there's nothing new under the sun."

"Depends on the code," he said, not cracking a smile.

McVie leaned forward. "Explain."

Zane grinned. McVie was a lot of things, but stupid wasn't one of them. "What if the key to the code was unbreakable?"

"Such a thing does not exist," said McVie.

"It does if the key comes from 1992."

Emilie's sharp intake of breath was audible. McVie's attention was directed solely on Zane.

"It doesn't matter what you use," Zane continued. "The Gettysburg Address, an old Beach Boys song. There's an endless supply and, unless I miss my bet, Emilie and I are the only people around who could break it."

"My God," said Emilie, heart pounding. "It's perfect!"

"I know," said Zane. "I thought the same thing when I first came up with the idea back in grade school."

"What song did you use?" she asked.

He grinned. "'Twist and Shout.' The Beatles' version."

Emilie launched into a rousing version of the old rock-and-roll hit that had McVie staring at her as if she'd grown a second head.

"Sorry," said Emilie after two verses. "I always loved that song."

"Are there many such songs?" McVie asked.

Emilie and Zane looked at each other and laughed.

"Don't worry," said Emilie. "Plenty to last until the end of the war."

"You have told me the resolution will be favorable to our cause," said McVie, "but will that resolution be a long time in coming?"

How did you tell a man that another five bloody years would pass before Lord Cornwallis and the British troops surrendered at Yorktown?

Emilie finally broke the awkward silence. "It will be a long time coming," was all she said.

Emilie was too excited to eat supper. Her stomach felt shaky, as if she'd taken one ride too many on an amusement-park roller coaster. She excused herself and sat down by the window in the front room, embroidering a message into the underside of McVie's collar.

It was a simple message and a simple code. She and Zane had decided "Jingle Bells" was a good way to start. Zane wrote out the words for Andrew on a piece of foolscap, muttering loudly about the quill pen.

As it turned out he needn't have bothered, for Andrew quickly memorized the song, and they determined that each of the next three nights would key into a different stanza of the old Christmas carol.

She wondered if the day would come when she and Zane taught a group of colonial spies the lyrics to "Doo Wah Diddy." Apparently there were a lot of things that didn't make it into the history books.

Two hours later she said goodbye to McVie in the doorway. She had worked diligently to embroider the message into the underside of his collar with stitches as fine as the web of a spider, and she was pleased with her accomplishment.

"I wish I could come with you," she said, admiring her handiwork as she smoothed down his collar. "This is incredibly exciting."

The look in his eyes made her step back, flustered. He'd made his feelings clear this afternoon beneath the maple tree. Apparently he had spoken the truth. Be kind to him, Rebekah had warned, for he'd known his own brand of heartbreak.

"Wish me Godspeed," he said, his voice both rough and caressing.

"Godspeed," she said. "And be careful."

He turned and left the farmhouse.

She stood in the doorway for a long while, staring out into the darkness. Her thoughts were scattered, as if she were caught in one of those crazy dreams where people changed shape and nothing was quite the way it seemed.

"You're tired," she told herself, turning away from the door. That's all it was. After a good night's sleep, everything would seem normal once more—or whatever passed for normal these days.

As she climbed the stairs to the bedroom, it occurred to her that this was why television had been invented: for nights like these when being alone with your thoughts was too awful to contemplate.

Zane was standing by the window when she entered the room. He was naked from the waist up, his torso illuminated only by the starlight twinkling above. His hair had grown longer. She'd come to love that ponytail, but Zane swore he never would.

"Did McVie leave?" he asked.

She nodded, sidestepping the enormous tub set up in the middle of the room. "I'll come back after you've taken your bath."

"I'm finished," he said.

She sniffed the air. "Roses?"

He didn't meet her eyes. "This tub's for you."

She chuckled softly at the reference as her heart slid into her rib cage. "Thank you, Zane."

He nodded, then turned away from the window. "I'll sit on the porch until you're done."

"Zane." She touched his arm. "You look exhausted. Haven't you been sleeping?"

He shrugged. "It's too damn quiet around here. I miss noise."

She took a deep breath. "I'm going to take a *very* long bath," she said, gesturing toward the bed. "Why don't you sleep?"

He didn't need to be convinced. "Thanks," he said, stretching out on the narrow bed. "Kick me out when you're done."

"I will."

He closed his eyes, and conversation ended. She stood there watching him, wondering if she should admonish him to *keep* his eyes closed while she bathed, but he didn't show the slightest degree of interest in her activities.

She considered forgoing the pleasure of a warm bath, but the temptation was more than she could stand. A candle flickered on the highboy and she quietly crossed the room to blow it out. The room abruptly plunged into darkness. She wondered if she'd ever grow accustomed to this total and complete absence of light, so different from the nights she'd known in that other, faraway world.

Zane's breathing was the only sound in the room. She fumbled with the laces on her bodice, acutely aware of the enforced intimacy of the situation. She took off the pale green dress, the petticoats and her cotton hose, then laid them over the back of the rocking chair.

The scent of roses enveloped her senses as she slipped into the tub. Sighing, she leaned back and closed her eyes, willing herself to clear her mind of everything but the blissful sensation of warm, silky water caressing her body.

If only her mind would cooperate. Not even the seductive pleasures of the warm tub could compete with the tangled thoughts vying for her attention. Why couldn't life be easy, she wondered. You met someone, you fell in love. You married and built a life together. Case closed. Maybe there was something to be said for the days when you expected nothing more from marriage than a united front to present to the world and children to move that world into the future.

Sex only confused things. Andrew McVie seemed to be everything she'd ever wanted in a husband, yet she didn't feel that inexplicable jolt of electricity that she experienced every time she looked at Zane. Her heart ached for Andrew and the family he'd lost. How empty his world must seem without his wife and son. You could see the yearning in his eyes each time he looked at baby Aaron or little Stephen, and she could only imagine how he must long for a home and family of his own.

Isn't that what marriage should be, a union of like minds with a single goal? Wouldn't that be enough for one lifetime....

"You can do it," he said, supporting her shoulders. "Just a little longer...."

"No!" She bit her lip as another wave of pain tore through her midsection. "I can't...I just can't do it anymore."

"Push, Emilie!" urged the midwife positioned at the foot of the bed. "The head's crowning."

"C'mon, Em," he urged. "We're almost there."

Her scream ricocheted off the walls then lodged itself between her legs. Pain...more pain than she'd imagined existed in the world...then the overwhelming, irresistible urge to push and then that sound...that incredible sound of life beginning right there before their very eyes.

"Oh, God!" she cried out. "We did it. We have a son!"

She touched his cheek, feeling his tears against her skin.

"I love you," she said, her words mingling with her own tears. "More than you'll ever know...."

"I love you...." The voice came toward him from a great distance. "More than you'll ever know."

Zane woke up, completely alert to his surroundings. The nightstand to his left. The window open wide to the night air.

Emilie asleep in the copper tub.

He rose from the bed and walked toward her.

"Wake up, Em. You're dreaming."

She murmured something he couldn't understand and sank more deeply into the tub.

"C'mon. That water's getting cold."

Her breathing was slow and regular. Trying to wake her up

seemed cruel. He leaned forward and scooped her into his arms. His movements, hampered by the splint on his right arm, were clumsy. She barely noticed.

Zane, however, couldn't say the same.

Her naked body was warm and supple as he held her against his bare chest. He scarcely noticed the water dripping from her hair and skin onto his, except to register a deep sensual thrill that stirred his blood.

Slowly he carried her to the bed, laying her down gently on the horsehair mattress. He wanted to light a candle against the dark so he could see the splendor of her naked form, but the truth was he knew exactly how she looked, every spectacular inch of her.

She shivered slightly and he remembered that she was wet from her bath. Two towels rested on the seat of the rocking chair and he brought them back to the bed. Kneeling down, he took her right foot in his hands and pressed a towel to the instep and arch, the elegant toes. Her ankle was narrow, delicately made. The muscles of her calf were strong and firm, yet still extremely feminine.

He shifted position, aware of the way his blood was pounding inside his head. She managed to combine delicacy with strength, the most beguiling combination imaginable. He drew the towel over her knee, then slowly dried his way up the length of her thigh. Her performed the same actions on the other leg.

She moaned low in her throat.

He waited.

She sank again into sleep.

The curls between her thighs were damp, fragrant with roses and the smell of a woman. Her smell. He leaned forward and pressed his mouth against her for an instant, branding her.

Branding himself.

It would be easy to lose himself in her, to take her before she awakened enough to protest, and prove that whatever problems they'd had, this powerful physical desire wasn't one of them. This was the best thing life had to offer, the one chance human beings got to walk with the gods.

But, damn it, there were some things you didn't do no matter how much you—

She shivered again, despite the warm summer air drifting through the open window. He took a deep, steadying breath and drew the cloth over her hips and belly. He relished the female softness of her flesh.

Her waist was narrow and he could feel the flare of her rib cage. He sensed the fullness and warmth of her breasts before he touched them. He cupped them in his palms, savoring their weight.

He was enjoying this too much.

Swiftly he dried her chest and throat. He tried to gather her hair together in a makeshift ponytail, but failed.

The coverlet was folded at the foot of the bed. He opened it, then placed it over her body.

"I love you...." Her voice was low, that faraway voice of someone deep in a dream.

"Who do you love, Emilie?" he asked as he lay down on the bed next to her and gathered her gently into his arms.

He was almost glad when she didn't answer.

Chapter Eleven

11

When Emilie awoke the next morning she was alone in the second-floor bedroom.

She was also naked.

She sat up, holding the coverlet to her breasts, then glanced around. Everything looked normal. The tub was pushed against the far wall, same as it had been last night. She smelled like roses, so she must have finished her bath, but she didn't remember anything beyond settling into the warm water and closing her eyes.

Either she was the world's only sleepwalking bather or Zane had plucked her from the tub and deposited her beneath the covers.

A long, slow heat slid along the insides of her thighs. Surely she'd know if something had happened. But she remembered nothing save an odd series of dreams that had left her feeling sad and hopeful and everything in between.

Last night she'd given birth to a baby. At least, she had in her dreams. If she closed her eyes she could still feel the crushing pain that was followed by a wave of pure joy that made all that had come before it seem meaningless.

And he'd been there with her. Holding her hand. Whispering encouragement. Sharing that miraculous moment when the visible proof of their love entered the world.

She felt empty now. Her arms ached for her child.

Her heart yearned for the man who had helped create the child.

If only she had seen his face.

The next few days passed in a blur of activity. The embroidery method of transmitting messages was a rousing success, and Andrew grew more daring. Zane, watching from the sidelines, found himself growing restless. His life seemed to be at an impasse and he knew the time was approaching when he would have to make some difficult decisions.

As for Emilie, her confusion manifested itself in a fatigue that seemed to sap the energy from her very bones. She'd fall asleep instantly at night, then awaken in the morning feeling as if she'd barely slept at all. She'd never mustered up the nerve to ask Zane what had happened the night he'd lifted her from the bath. In truth, she didn't really want to know. Either way, she had the feeling she would lose.

Why couldn't life be as simple and clear-cut as one of those TV dating games that she'd left behind?

Two men.

Two choices.

They were as different as night and day. Choosing between them shouldn't be difficult.

But then, who said they both wanted her? She knew in her heart that Andrew cared and she had little doubt he would welcome a chance to build a life with her. She wasn't vain enough to believe it was her beauty that held his interest; she brought with her the secrets of the future, and that had to be a potent attraction.

And then there was Zane. He'd been so distant lately, so preoccupied that some nights he hadn't bothered to come to bed. She tried not to imagine where he might be spending his time, but heated visions of him making love to some tavern wench from town made her stomach knot in jealousy.

It occurred to her that he no longer needed her the way he had when they'd first discovered themselves in this strange new world. He might not like eighteenth-century living, but he was a survivor and he'd adapted to it better, in some ways, than Emilie had.

Now that he had traded the gold from his watchband for usable currency, he didn't need her to help him find his way. He was fully capable of charting a course for himself. After all, she had made it clear that she refused to allow circumstance to dictate her future.

Who'd expected him to suddenly take her at her word?

Things were changing quickly and Emilie only wished she had the energy to change along with them.

For the first time in days, everyone was gathered at the Blakelees' pine trestle table for the main meal. Andrew and Isaac were caught up on the work in the fields and, for a change, they came in to join everyone else. Even Zane, who had taken to keeping himself distant from the others, took his chair opposite Emilie.

The house was beginning to take on a festive air as the final preparations for Charity's wedding were being completed. The simple dark pine furniture gleamed after being rubbed with oil and polished to a high sheen. The curtains were freshly washed and hung smartly at the windows. Rebekah was putting the finishing touches on her daughter's wedding dress, while Emilie worked on the soldiers' uniforms in the morning and work for the spy ring in the afternoon.

The only thing missing was Josiah Blakelee himself and, unfortunately, hope was fading quickly that he would be home in time for the wedding. Each day brought a different rumor as to his whereabouts. The most ridiculous was that he had joined the Tory cause; the most frightening, that he was imprisoned aboard the *Jersey* in New York Harbor.

Rebekah, however, was determined that their daughter's marriage not be postponed. Life was short and the sooner you embraced the future, the better. It was a lesson not lost on anyone at the table that August afternoon.

Indeed, the air in the room was charged, the same way it was before a storm.

Andrew thought it was his own dissatisfactions making themselves evident.

Zane was sure it was the power he'd gained with the acquisition of money.

Emilie was positive it was her own state of confusion.

None of the Blakelees noticed a thing amiss. They were too busy running a house, tending a farm and planning a wedding.

"The sugarloaf!" Charity exclaimed, leaping from her chair. "We must have a sugarloaf or Timothy's parents will think we're poor as church mice."

"Would I forget such an important item?" said Rebekah with a laugh.

"And the sugar-scissors?" the bride-to-be asked.

"Don't worry," her mother said. "Things are well in hand. Why don't you—"

Her words were interrupted by the sound of horses' hooves in the distance.

The four adults at the table looked at one another.

"Are you expecting visitors?" Andrew asked Rebekah.

Rebekah shook her head.

Andrew pushed back his chair and stood up. "Behave naturally. I will wait in the pantry." He collected his plate, utensils and cup, then disappeared.

Emilie's heart lodged in her throat and she found it difficult to draw a full breath into her lungs. Rebekah's face went pale, and the children grew ominously silent. It was Zane who took charge of the situation.

"Do as McVie said," he ordered, resuming his meal.

The fricassee of chicken tasted like straw but Emilie forced down a bite. The others at the table did the same.

The hoofbeats drew closer and the drinking glass at Emilie's place trembled with the vibrations.

"I can't stand it," Emilie mumbled.

"Shut up," Zane snapped. "This isn't a game."

Emilie's cheeks flamed. Rebekah had heard every word.

Moments later someone pounded on the door.

Rebekah rose to her feet to answer it.

The dining room was cloaked in silence.

"Talk," Zane said.

"What about?" asked Isaac.

"It doesn't matter. Just do it."

Small conversations broke out like random brushfires. Nobody paid any attention to the words because everyone's attention was focused on the front door and the unexpected guest.

Rebekah returned to the room with a stocky, red-haired man dressed in the uniform of a Continental soldier. He introduced himself as Benjamin Fellowes. His manner was affable, but Emilie saw the way he seemed to notice every inconsequential detail in the room.

Rebekah's face was composed, but she fingered the ties on her apron with a nervous gesture. "You will see for yourself, Lieutenant Fellowes, that we are a simple family eating a simple meal."

"So it would seem," said Fellowes. His glance swept the table. "And you are certain you have not seen Andrew McVie?"

Rebekah did not so much as blink. "As I told you, Lieutenant, I have not seen the man since my beloved Josiah disappeared and if this Andrew McVie were to show his face I would give him a piece of my mind for leading my poor husband—" She stopped abruptly, tears welling in her soft brown eyes.

Charity leaped to her feet and faced the soldier. "Go away! Isn't it enough that my pa won't be here for my own wedding?"

"'Twasn't my wish to upset the lot of you, folks. We just need to talk to the man."

"You won't find him here," said Zane, rising to his feet.

The shorter man looked up at Zane. "Lieutenant Benjamin Fellowes, sir."

Zane paused a moment. "Captain Rutledge."

The wonder was that nobody at the table fell over in shock.

"An honor, sir." Fellowes stepped back. "Sorry to be bothering you. I'll be on my way."

Zane motioned for conversation to resume as Rebekah saw the soldier to the door. They continued to talk and eat until the sound of horses' hooves faded away.

"I can't believe you did that," Emilie said after Zane flashed the all-clear sign. "What if he'd asked for some proof?"

"He didn't," Zane said.

"What do you think that was all about?"

"Trouble," said Andrew, reentering the room. He turned toward Rebekah. "'Twould be best if you knew nothing of the plans."

Rebekah nodded and shooed the children out of the room. She lingered for a moment in the doorway, casting curious glances at Zane and Emilie, then disappeared.

Andrew summed up the situation with an economy of words. The code system worked well. Unfortunately it would soon be of no use, for the spy ring had all but ceased to exist. Miller and Quick had been arrested, leaving Andrew as the only courier in the area between Princeton and the lighthouse where Emilie and Zane had met him.

"We are being thwarted at every turn," he said, his voice heavy with disappointment. "We had cause to believe we were near to discovering where Blakelee is being held, and now even that is but a dream." He met Emilie's eyes. "You tell me that we will win this bloody war, but I find no sign of it. Tonight I was to make an important contact and now I am imprisoned in this house with no hope in sight."

"There will be another night," Emilie said soothingly, trying to dispel the smell of desperation in the air.

"There are some things that cannot wait for the time to be right." A thousand shadings colored his words.

"I'll do it," said Emilie. "Who on earth would ever suspect a woman?"

Andrew started to protest, but Zane broke in.

"I'll go," he said.

Both Emilie and McVie turned to stare at him.

"This isn't the time for jokes," she said.

"I'm not joking."

McVie didn't think he was joking. But neither did he jump at the offer.

"'Tis a dangerous mission," he said.

Zane nodded. "Now tell me something I don't know."

Hope, crazy and improbable, sprang to life inside Emilie's chest. Maybe he was changing, she thought, looking at Zane's beautiful face. An experience like the one they'd shared had to have an effect on a person. Certainly she was vastly different from the woman she'd been back in twentieth-century Crosse Harbor.

Besides, it wasn't every day you got to be in at the birth of a nation. Maybe he really *was* beginning to care about the bigger picture.

She listened as Andrew explained the situation to Zane in blunt detail, not minimizing the risks involved. Her heart thundered wildly inside her chest as she watched Zane's expression. He looked so strong, so brave, so—

"Hell, yes, I'll go," Zane said. "It's not like I have something better to do, is it?"

Zane knew he'd made a mistake the second the words slipped out. The words were true, but that didn't mean they had any business becoming public knowledge.

Unfortunately there was no taking them back.

They were out there, hovering in the air between him and Emilie, and she looked as if she'd never forget them. He felt like a stupid teenager who'd gone out of his way to annoy the one girl he really cared about.

Trouble was, he wasn't a teenager. He was a thirty-four-year-old man who was throwing away his last chance for happiness with both hands.

McVie, however, didn't give a damn about his motives. All he apparently cared about was the fact that Zane was willing to put his ass on the line. They both knew Zane's memory would be an asset. People, places, conversations—he'd be able to commit everything he saw and heard to memory and add an extra dimension to a simple delivery.

"So what's the deal?" Zane continued. "I could use a blast of excitement." *Great going. Now she'll really think you're worthless.* He couldn't bring himself to look at Emilie and see the disappointment on her lovely face.

McVie had managed to gain a copy of the layout to one of the prison ships currently moored in New York Harbor. "A man will be waiting for this at—" He hesitated, growing obviously uncomfortable. His eyes rested on Emilie. "Perhaps you would leave, mistress Emilie. This is of a delicate nature."

She lifted her chin and glared at him. Of all the outdated, sexist notions. "I'm not going anywhere. I'm in this as deep as any of you now. I don't need your protection."

"'Tis not your safety I speak of," said Andrew. "It's something…a subject not usually—"

"Just say it," Zane broke in. "She'll find out anyway."

Andrew turned to Zane. "You will meet your contact at a…house south of Princeton, not far west from the cave where you spent the night."

"A house?" Emilie asked. "What's the big deal about a house?"

A grin twitched the corners of Zane's mouth. "I don't think he means a two-story Colonial."

Her jaw dropped. "You mean—"

Zane nodded, then met McVie's eyes. "A whorehouse. Am I right?"

Andrew couldn't bring himself to look at Emilie. "Officers from both armies congregate there."

"I'd heard this was a gentlemen's war," Emilie drawled, "but that's ridiculous."

"'Tis the nature of man," said Andrew simply.

Emilie snorted in disgust. "'Tis the nature of a beast," she mimicked.

"Knock it off, Em," said Zane. "This has nothing to do with you."

She glared at them. Two pigheaded, hormone-saturated examples of American manhood, separated by two hundred years but connected by testosterone. Why was it men accepted the most insulting institutions as both logical and natural? She could just imagine the screaming that would go on if some enterprising Yankee wife gathered together a score of handsome men and opened a bordello that catered to women.

Of course, neither one of them cared a fig for what she had to say about this situation. They continued making their plans for Zane's James-Bond-meet-George-Washington adventure while she continued to burn.

* * *

"You're wearing *that* tonight?" Emilie stared, eyes wide, as Zane walked into their shared bedroom with a Continental army uniform slung over his arm.

"McVie's idea," he said, tossing the uniform down on the bed. "Rebekah was making this with Josiah in mind and she said we're about the same size. McVie said you'd finish up the collar and cuffs."

"How nice of him to volunteer me for the job."

"Rebekah's busy with the wedding preparations." He shot her a sidelong look. "I thought you said you were in this with the rest of us."

"I am," she said. "It's just—" She stopped abruptly. She didn't want to think of what this bad mood of hers was really about.

He gestured toward the uniform. "Are you going to take care of it, or not?"

"Dusk is still hours away. What's the rush?"

"I'm not waiting for dusk. I'm leaving as soon as the uniform's ready."

"Such a patriot," she drawled, her tone etched with sarcasm. "Can't wait to give your all for your country."

"Give it a rest."

"No, I won't give it a rest. All this is to you is another excuse to risk your damn stupid neck."

"I suppose you think it's all flag-waving and moral outrage on McVie's part."

"He cares what happens to this country," she snapped. "He understands what's important."

"Grow up, Emilie," Zane growled. "He's running away from something and if you can't see that, you're not as smart as you think."

She bit her lip in dismay as she thought of Andrew's late wife and child. Andrew was running away from something but not in the way Zane thought. At least Andrew had managed to channel his pain and anger into a positive course of action, while Zane—

"You don't understand," she said after a moment. "Why don't we just forget it?"

"Are you going to finish the uniform?"

She nodded. "I'll finish the uniform."

"I'll be back for it in a half hour."

"Great," said Emilie dully. "It'll be ready."

For Zane, gold was the most valuable commodity he'd brought with him to the past.

For Emilie, it was pins.

The thought was laughable but true. Now that the war was raging, colonial women were at a loss for the basics of their existence. Items like sewing pins and needles were in short supply and Emilie found herself frequently thanking God that she had stumbled backward through time with her sewing kit intact.

She spread the uniform jacket out on the bed and took a good look at it. There really wasn't much left to be done, she noted. Josiah Blakelee was obviously a big man, taller even than Zane. She would have to hem the cuffs an inch or two. The edges of the collar were unfinished and the pewter buttons needed to be sewn on, but it wouldn't take her long to handle either job.

Her embroidered purse rested on the window ledge. She retrieved it, pulled out the sewing kit, then chose a needle. Threading it with a length of navy floss, she settled down to work.

As always, the rhythmic motion of the silver needle soothed her, linking her in time and space with all the women who had come before and all who would one day follow. She was rolling the edge of the collar between thumb and forefinger and placing a stitch when a feeling of déjà vu washed over her like a soft rain.

For a moment she felt as if the barriers of time and space were melting away.

Then, as suddenly as the feeling had appeared, it vanished.

"Strange," she murmured, continuing her work. She couldn't imagine what had brought about that odd sensation. She'd been working on uniforms intermittently for the past few weeks and she'd never felt anything remotely like that.

Zane returned just as she was snipping the last threads.

"Good timing," she said, determined to keep her emotions under tight control.

"Finished?"

She nodded, glancing up at him. Her breath caught in her throat. He wore a pair of buff-colored breeches that cupped his buttocks and molded themselves to his powerful legs, and his old white shirt of silky Egyptian cotton. His hair was freshly washed, slicked back into a ponytail, tied with a length of black ribbon.

He reached for the jacket, but she rose from the chair where she'd been working and approached him. Would she never get used to the sight and sound of him? He was like a drug to her and every bit as dangerous.

She held up the jacket.

"Where's your splint?" she asked as he slipped his arms into the sleeves.

"I took it off."

"Do you think that was a smart thing to do?"

"Why not?" he answered. "It's been a while."

"Only a month."

"Sounds long enough to me."

Of course it did. Zane did what he wanted whenever he wanted to do it. Nothing ever stood in his way. Not a broken arm. Not his marriage. Not the mission he was about to undertake for Andrew.

"I know this is a lark to you," she said, her voice fierce, "but it's vitally important to a lot of other people."

"Right," said Zane. "Like McVie. I'll keep that in mind."

She reached up to smooth the collar of his coat and a wave of dizziness overtook her. "My God," she whispered. "That's why..."

He turned to face her, a look of curiosity on his face. "What's wrong?"

"Remember?" she said, gesturing toward his outfit. "The uniform. The one you brought to me." The odd stitching on the collar, the hemmed sleeves...

She watched as the realization dawned on him.

"Jesus," he said, his voice low. "You don't think—?"

"You have to admit it's a possibility."

He found it hard to wrap his mind around the knotted puzzle that was the concept of time. “You telling me I’m my own ancestor?”

“I don’t know what I’m telling you.” All she knew was that she had the strangest feeling of having come full circle.

Andrew was waiting for them downstairs. He handed Zane a folded piece of paper that contained the detailed deck plan of the prison ship in Wallabout Bay, New York Harbor.

“Mark me well, Rutledge,” he said, his manner stern. “One slip and all is lost.”

Zane slid the deck plan into his coat pocket. “I won’t slip.”

Emilie met Andrew eyes. “What do you mean, all will be lost?”

“Each morning dead prisoners are buried in the mud flats. Those who survive live crowded together in the dark below deck with no light and little air and rancid food.”

His eyes strayed toward the Blakelees, who were standing near the entrance to the front room.

“Josiah?” asked Zane.

Andrew nodded. “’Tis feared he has been sent to the Hell Ship.”

“Wait a minute,” said Emilie, struck by a dreadful thought. “I understand what will happen to other people if that map falls into the wrong hands, but what about Zane?”

The silence from the two men spoke volumes. She looked down at her hands, focusing on the gold-and-silver ring. The ring that was serving as her imitation wedding band. She covered it with her right hand.

“You are there to see Maggie,” Andrew said. “She knows what you are about and will see to it that you connect with the necessary people.”

Emilie was proud of herself. He’d handed her a perfect straight line and she’d resisted the urge. She didn’t know anything about this Maggie, but she had a pretty good idea she wouldn’t like her.

“Can you ride?” Andrew asked Zane.

Zane nodded. “Won’t that draw more attention?”

“You’re an officer,” Andrew said. “It’s in keeping with your position.”

And then it was time for Emilie and Zane to say goodbye.

Andrew stepped aside to allow them a moment of privacy, but he didn't look away. Emilie glanced over her shoulder and saw the entire Blakelee family, from Rebekah all the way down to Aaron, watching them with rapt attention.

A handshake just wouldn't do it. Rebekah was already curious enough about the two of them.

Zane met her eyes. "Come on, Em," he said, his voice low. "Let's give it our best shot."

He took her in his arms. The smell of soap and wool enveloped her as he held her close. Tilting her chin with his forefinger, he lowered his head and brought his mouth down on hers.

His kiss was bittersweet. Her tears were hot.

"Be careful," she whispered.

He smiled at her and, with a nod toward the others, he was off.

Chapter Twelve

12

Emilie tried to throw herself into the frenzied preparations going on at the Blakelee house, but not even the excitement surrounding Charity's wedding could ease the feeling of disaster settling itself around her.

Saying goodbye to Zane, she'd wanted to throw herself into his arms and never let him go. But when she'd turned away from the door and met Andrew's eyes she'd felt embarrassed and confused and altogether positive that she was losing her mind. There was a connection between herself and Andrew, a deep and important connection, but she found it difficult to understand exactly what it was.

As it was, Andrew seemed restless. He'd wanted to go out into the fields and work off his energy, but he knew the farm was being watched and he dare not risk being seen.

And so he paced from one end of the farmhouse to the other, muttering to himself. Finally Rebekah could stand it no longer and she put him to work polishing the pewter service she'd dug up from the backyard where she'd had it hidden.

It was obvious he'd give anything to be in Zane's place, facing danger head-on, and Emilie found her own feelings on that subject surprisingly tangled.

* * *

At dusk Rebekah served a light supper of beans and brown bread with tankards of cider. Emilie found it hard to concentrate on her meal, and she ended up moving the food around on her plate with her fork. Afterward, she helped Rebekah and Charity tidy the kitchen, grateful to have something to occupy her mind.

Isaac had wanted help with something he was building for his sister's new home and Andrew had climbed up to the boy's attic room to help him. Emilie, Rebekah and Charity settled down in the front room to finish work on the girl's wedding linens by candlelight.

"Are you getting nervous, Charity?" Emilie asked as she put the finishing touches on a table runner embroidered with daisies and forget-me-nots. "Your wedding is less than forty-eight hours away."

"Charity is much like her father," said Rebekah fondly. "There is little in this world that can sway her from her course."

"Timothy's folks arrive tomorrow evening," Charity said. "I find myself wondering if I'll like them half as much as I love him."

Rebekah laughed out loud. "How like my girl to care not what they think of her but to worry if she will like them."

"I'd always wished for in-laws," Emilie said, more to herself than to Rebekah or Charity. "Zane's parents died years before I met him." She'd had but one chance to meet his grandmother Sara Jane during their brief marriage, and had longed to get to know the woman who'd meant so much to Zane.

"Poor man," said Rebekah. "'Tis no wonder he hurts as he does. He told me that he was sent away from home long before they met their untimely end."

Emilie's head shot up from her needlework. "He told you about his parents?"

Rebekah nodded. "The morning before last when he helped me hang the wash."

Zane Rutledge helped Rebekah hang the wash? Emilie found she could only stare at the woman in surprise.

"He is a good man," Rebekah continued, her needle dipping in and out of the open-weave fabric of the nightdress she worked on. "And he loves you very much."

Emilie looked back down at her own work again. If Rebekah only knew the truth: that Emilie and Zane had been married and divorced and were living a lie.

"You can always tell when a man loves a woman," Rebekah was saying. "'Tis the little things that give it away."

Charity smiled smugly. "Timothy gave me a tortoiseshell comb for my birthday."

"I don't think that's exactly what your mother meant," Emilie said. She looked at Rebekah. "Is it?"

Rebekah shook her head. "I always said I realized Josiah truly loved me the night he sat up with Charity when the girl was cutting her teeth." Rebekah, about to give birth to Isaac, had appreciated that unbroken night's sleep the way another woman might have appreciated a flawless emerald. "A man gives what he can," she said, meeting Emilie's eyes, "and he gives it in his own way."

Her thoughts went back to the warm tub of bathwater, scented with roses, that had awaited her in their room the other night. "Perhaps a woman ought not read more into a simple gesture than actually exists."

Rebekah smiled. "And perhaps a woman ought not read less into a man because he does not conform to the ideal."

"If I didn't know better, Rebekah, I would believe you spoke of me."

"Your husband is a good man, Emilie, and a kind one. I fear you do not always see that."

"He does not often allow that to be seen."

From the other room, baby Aaron started to cry and Rebekah motioned for her daughter to check on the infant. She waited until Charity was beyond earshot.

"When I spoke of Andrew some days ago, I spoke from concern for his well-being."

"I know that, Rebekah. I—"

Rebekah raised her hand to silence Emilie. "When I speak of Andrew now, it is from concern for all."

"I believe you see trouble where none exists."

"And I believe you do not see what stands before you."

"Rebekah—" Emilie stopped. What could she say? Anything she told the woman would sound either like a lie or a bad excuse. The truth was inconceivable.

She would more than likely find herself sentenced to an asylum somewhere.

The good housewife leaned back in her chair and considered Emilie, her soft brown eyes holding a subtle challenge. "Some would say you are a fortunate woman, Emilie Rutledge, to have two such men in love with you."

"Oh, Rebekah," she said on a sigh. "There are so many things you don't understand. . . ." *So many things I can tell no one.* She met the woman's eyes. "Zane—" She paused to collect her thoughts. "Zane is not a man like Josiah. Home and family are not uppermost in his heart."

Rebekah made a dismissing motion with her hand. "Nor were they in Josiah's heart. It takes time for a man to learn what is truly important in this world."

"That may be so," said Emilie, "but at least you have been given the luxury of a permanent home." She gestured toward the farmhouse and the land beyond. "A place to put down roots."

Rebekah's laugh was loud and full-bodied. "'Tis but a year that we have been back on our land. Josiah has led me on a merry chase these eighteen years past."

Emilie listened in shocked silence as Rebekah told of her vagabond marriage. Josiah was a crusader against injustice, a lawyer as well as a farmer, and he had combed the land from New Hampshire down to the Carolinas in search of a cause.

"I do not mean to make light of the grievous situation in which we find ourselves, but 'twas the first volley at Bunker Hill that gave me back my beloved home."

"Are you happy?" Emilie asked.

"What is happiness?" Rebekah parried. "I am content. I ask no more than that."

"I want more than that," Emilie said, unable to stop herself. "I want to be happy."

"And how will you accomplish that end?" Rebekah asked.

"Had I that answer, I should be at General Washington's side, conducting the war."

Rebekah laughed. "You must love your husband for who and what he is, Emilie, not for what you wish him to be."

The good woman had zeroed in on the root of her problem. "And what if that is not possible?" she asked, her voice little more than a whisper.

"Then you adjust," Rebekah said. "When you love, there is no other way."

Andrew stood to the left of the doorway and listened. When Emilie and Rutledge had embraced, he'd thought his heart would stop beating, so intense had been his anguish. Now he felt his spirits soaring upward like an eagle, freed from the bonds of a cruel captor.

Hope, elusive and wondrous, took root inside his heart. There was a chance to win her heart! That fact was undeniable. If she loved Rutledge, she would have stated thus to Rebekah.

He wondered how it was that only he saw how different, how amazing, Emilie was. How could Rebekah and the others not sense that she was as unlike the other good women of his acquaintance as night was unlike day? Her accent held a blend of the colonies and her voice, the melodious tones of music. The way she walked with her head held high, the strength in her voice, the youthful appearance of her skin—surely there was no other woman like her in this world.

He moved away from the door. It wouldn't do to be found there listening. Turning, he started for the attic stairs and Issac's project. His mind, however, remained with Emilie.

Was it possible all women were like her in the twentieth century? She'd spoken of strength and independence, and at first those notions had seemed unappealing when applied to the fairer sex. But as he watched and listened to Emilie and noted the way she rushed headlong into life, he felt a yearning for another time and place—a time and place he knew only through her eyes.

Rutledge spoke often of finding his way back to the world he'd left behind. Andrew had thought it a fool's errand. But now he wondered. Could it be possible that the same mysterious forces that had propelled them backward through the centuries could be waiting to shoot them forward once again?

What a miracle it would be if he could one day share her world with her....

"Did you hear a noise?" Emilie asked, tilting her head toward the doorway.

Rebekah shook her head. "Only the mice."

Emilie shivered. "There's a wonderful thought."

Rebekah looked at her curiously. "Surely you are accustomed to mice. I know not of a single house that hasn't known their company."

"That doesn't mean I enjoy their company."

"Most farm wives take little heed," said Rebekah. "You are an unusual woman, Emilie. Each time I believe I have come to understand you, I realize I have but scratched the surface."

More than anything, Emilie wanted to confide in Rebekah. Lately she'd been feeling puzzled and confused and more worn-out than she'd been at any other time in her life. The notion of having a woman friend was very tempting and she couldn't think of anyone more understanding or compassionate than Rebekah.

Unfortunately, the secrets Emilie had to confide were so unbelievable that she knew she could not open her heart. Besides, now that she and Zane were involved in the spy ring, she would do nothing that might compromise the Blakelees' already-shaky sense of security.

Emilie put down her sewing and stood, in order to stretch her aching back muscles. A wave of dizziness, unexpected and quite surprising, washed over her and she slumped back into her chair.

Rebekah was by her side in an instant, offering her a cup of water and a shoulder to lean on.

"As I figured it was," said Rebekah with a knowing smile. "You *are* with child."

"No," said Emilie, struggling to overcome the vertigo. "I'm not. Honestly."

Rebekah's gaze strayed toward the bodice of Emilie's gown. "The signs are there."

Emilie shook her head. "I'm retaining water," she said.

Rebekah looked puzzled. "Your monthly flow," she said with great delicacy. "Have you—"

"I'm fine," said Emilie. "Don't worry." They said travel could cause a woman's cycle to become irregular. God only knew what *time* travel could do....

The two women worked in companionable silence for a while longer, then Emilie again put down her sewing.

"Where is he?" she said, rising to her feet and walking toward the window that looked out across the moonswept farmland. "Shouldn't he be back by now?"

As if on cue, Andrew strode into the room.

Nodding politely toward Rebekah, he addressed himself to Emilie. "I would not expect him tonight, mistress Emilie. These matters develop at their own pace."

Her cheeks flamed as she considered exactly where these matters were developing. "I hope he is safe."

Andrew chuckled. "As a babe against his mother's breast."

She whirled to face him. "I'm glad you find this matter amusing, Andrew. Zane is unfamiliar with the ways. Anything could happen—*anything!*"

"Hush, lass," he said, his voice low. "Rebekah listens intently." In truth he was experiencing his own measure of apprehension about Rutledge's safety, but to his chagrin, his feelings were not entirely unselfish. If Rutledge were to find comfort in the arms of a willing wench, he doubted if Emilie would look upon the man with fondness.

Aaron's cry pierced the air and Rebekah put aside her sewing and rose to her feet. "I must see to my son." She held out her arms to Emilie, who crossed the room for her embrace. "'Twill work out," Rebekah whispered against her ear. "I promise you."

"What was that about?" Andrew asked as Rebekah left the room.

"A personal matter," said Emilie, surprised that the circumspect McVie would ask.

"Rebekah Blakelee is a good woman," Andrew said. "Josiah is a lucky man."

Emilie sighed and sank wearily into her chair. "And you, Andrew?" she asked. "Were you a lucky man?"

Her question shocked him with its lack of delicacy.

"Elspeth was all a wife should be," he said after a moment. "Would that I could say such about myself."

She eyed him with curiosity. "I'm sure you were a wonderful husband."

"Nay, lass. I was many things, but I fear 'wonderful' was not among the lot."

"I know what the problem was," she said with a chuckle. "You always forgot to take out the garbage."

"Lass?"

"Pay no attention to me," she said, waving her hand in the air. "I'm overtired. That's an old twentieth-century joke. You wouldn't understand."

He walked over toward her. "I should like to understand."

She leaned forward, eyes glowing with intensity. "So what was it you did wrong, Andrew? How were you less than wonderful as a husband?"

Years of memories crashed over him and for an instant he found it difficult to speak. "I thought not of Elspeth and David," he said slowly. "I thought only of my business."

"What was your business?"

"I am a lawyer."

"Like Josiah?"

"Like Josiah."

She shook her head in bemusement. "A colonial yuppie." Who would have imagined.

"A yup-pee?"

"Young urban professional," she said. "It was a disease in the 1980s. I had no idea it had started so early."

She listened to the familiar story of a man who sacrificed family and friends on the altar of career, knowing that the problem would only increase with time and grow to include women, as well.

"I rode the circuit," he told her, his mind far away. "For many months at a time, Elspeth was left alone with David to cope with a myriad of troubles."

"Did she complain?" Emilie asked.

He shook his head. "'Twas not in her nature." But he would never forget the terrible pain in her beautiful eyes each time he packed his satchel and walked out the door in search of the shilling.

"She should have," said Emilie. "People who accept mistreatment get what they deserve."

"Is that how it is in your time?"

She nodded. "The pursuit of happiness," she said. "That's a big part of what you're fighting for."

"I have never considered happiness a possibility in this world."

"You're wrong, Andrew. This world may be all we have. If you cannot find happiness here, then what is the purpose to life?"

Her intent was clear. Her words found their mark inside his soul.

He knelt down next to her chair and took her hands in his.

"Andrew!" Her voice went high with surprise. "What on earth—?"

"The pursuit of happiness," he said, heart beating loudly in his ears. "I have found it with you."

"Don't say that. I'm a—" She stopped. She had been going to say she was a married woman, but Andrew knew full well the lie to that statement.

"You are a free woman," he said. "There is no impediment to our happiness."

She leaped to her feet, almost knocking him down in the process. "You don't know what you're saying. I'm nothing like your Elspeth or the other women you know. I would fight you every step of the way on every issue imaginable."

"And I should welcome the challenge." He stood up next to her. "It is all the things you are that endear you to my heart."

She wanted to tell him that it wasn't Emilie Crosse whom he

loved, it was some romantic image of the future. But something stopped her. Was this her destiny, she wondered. Could it be that Zane would never return and she would be left alone to chart a course through life?

"From the first moment, I have sensed that you hold my destiny in your hands," he said, his voice low and urgent.

"I know nothing of your destiny," she said, "beyond what I have told you." Once General Washington's life was spared, Andrew McVie's life—or death—was never mentioned again.

"Mayhap my destiny is yet to be written," he said. "Could it not be that you are the key to my future?"

"No," she said, suddenly terrified of what might lie ahead. "That cannot be! Your destiny and the country's are intertwined."

"I cannot lose you," he said, drawing her into his arms. "I have searched so long for the likes of you that we cannot be parted."

He was going to kiss her. She knew it by the questioning look in his eyes, the way his head dipped forward, and she stood there waiting for it to happen.

His mouth slanted across hers. There was wonder in his kiss and a hunger for something she knew she could never provide.

Turning her head she broke the kiss, but not before he saw the tears glistening in her eyes.

"Next time you will think twice before dallying with a whore," said the man as he opened the door to the jail and shoved Zane inside. "Some of the wenches prefer English swords to American sabers."

The door swung closed behind the English soldier and Zane found himself plunged in darkness. He sensed rather than saw the presence of other prisoners.

"Speak up, man," a voice called out. "Tell us who goes there."

"Rutledge," he said. "Who are you?"

"Fleming from Little Rocky Hill."

The name was familiar. "Who else is here?"

Names came fast through the darkness.

Miller...Quick...Hughes.

"Blakelee," he said. "Is Josiah Blakelee here?"

There was a moment's silence. Waves of distrust emanated from the other side of the cell. The only sound was his blood pounding in his ears.

"And how do you come to ask of Josiah?" asked one of the men.

"McVie," he said. "He asked me to—"

He never finished the sentence.

Chapter Thirteen

13

Daybreak came and with it no sign of Zane.

"Something terrible has happened," Emilie said to Andrew as the first light of dawn appeared beyond the trees. "He should have been back hours ago."

"There may be another explanation," said Andrew, "one you will not care to hear."

"I know all about sex," she snapped, scarcely registering the blush staining his cheeks. "That's not why he hasn't returned."

"How can you know with certainty?" They had married and divorced. Both were free to do with their lives as they wished without reproach.

"I know Zane and I know he wouldn't have left us." Certainly he wouldn't have left her alone with Andrew. Of that she was sure. "I have to find him, Andrew."

"You cannot do that."

"I *must*."

"The hour is still early. He may yet return."

The noon hour arrived, followed by the main meal of the day. Neither Emilie nor Andrew could swallow a bite of beef stew.

"Aye, lass," he said after the dishes had been cleared from the table. "I fear Rutledge may be in trouble." Even the good wenches at Maggie's needed their sleep.

"Tell me where you sent him," she pleaded. "If you won't go for him, then I will." A wave of nausea, the result of fatigue, came, then blessedly went.

Andrew knew when he had met his match. Despite the precarious nature of his situation, he promised he would search for Zane. "I make no guarantees."

He dressed in the garb of a farmer, complete with concealing hat.

"I will return as soon as I am able."

He started for the door. Emilie was right behind him. "No," he said. "I cannot be responsible for your safety. 'Tis too dangerous an undertaking."

"You can't stop me," she said flatly. "I will go whether or not you allow it."

They stared at each other.

Andrew was the one who blinked.

"We go," he said. "I pray that I am not making a mistake."

They skirted Princeton proper, keeping to the paths worn smooth by tradesmen and Indians. The lush woodland scenery that had delighted her was all but invisible to her now. Keeping a steady pace, they reached the clearing at dusk.

"You can go no farther," Andrew said as the whorehouse came into view. There was no sign of the Blakelees' horse, a magnificent roan that Zane had ridden off the farm yesterday, but that meant nothing. "Your presence would draw suspicion."

She couldn't argue with his logic. "You won't be long?"

"As long as it takes to obtain the information."

She nodded, feeling as fragile and brittle as blown glass. "Please hurry," she said. She promised to wait beneath the towering pine tree that had lost a limb to a bolt of lightning.

She could stand anything more easily than she could stand not knowing.

* * *

Andrew had been gone no more than ten minutes when darkness fell. Each time she thought she'd grown accustomed to the swift finality of nightfall, she was again struck by the differences between the world where she'd grown up and the world she lived in now. The only light came from the three-story house where Zane had met his fate.

She shivered, although the night was warm. She had to stop thinking in these melodramatic terms. There would be a simple answer to Zane's absence. Perhaps he'd drunk too much wine. Or, now that he had money, he might have found the temptation of a game of chance to be more than he could resist.

Of course, there were other more exciting temptations to be found in that gabled house. Temptations that only money could buy.

It's not as if you have any rights over him, she thought, keeping her gaze trained upon the establishment. Except for that one incredible interlude the night before the balloon accident, she had kept him an arm's length away, emotionally and physically.

Would it be so terrible if he decided to find comfort in the arms of another, more willing woman?

Yes.

She started toward the house. She had no idea what she would do once she got there, but there was no way on earth she could just stand there in the woods, waiting for Andrew to return. If something had happened to Zane, she needed to know.

And if he was happily ensconced in some upstairs bedroom with a brunette—well, she'd cross that strumpet when she got to her.

Good or bad. Right or wrong. Smart or crazy.

They belonged together. It seemed so clear to her now that she wondered how it was she'd fought so hard against the inevitable. They were two people with absolutely nothing in common except the fact that fate had destined them to be together.

How wrong she'd been when she'd said she wouldn't allow herself to be ruled by circumstances. She and Zane had shared an experience that few people, if any, had ever known. It was impossible to travel through time and not be changed in the process. And sharing that incredible event with the man with whom you'd once shared your life—how could she have thought that wouldn't make a difference?

Of course, that was only one of the mistakes she'd made along the way. Strange that Rebekah had been able to see so clearly the things that Emilie couldn't see at all. She had been so busy sympathizing with Andrew that she'd been blind to all that Zane must be feeling.

You accepted your spouse for what he was, Rebekah had said, and then you learned to adjust. A few months ago Emilie would have argued the point. Now she wondered if there wasn't a touch of eighteenth-century wisdom at work in the woman's simple words. She'd been so busy trying to change Zane into her image of the perfect man that she had overlooked all the things about him that were wonderful. His strength. His love of life. His fearlessness.

The way he'd loved her....

Laughter spilled from the open windows as Emilie approached the house. She heard the deep rumble of men's voices and the high-pitched trill of women being coy. Her stomach knotted as a painfully clear image of Zane in bed with another woman rose up before her.

But, dear God, even that was preferable to the dark fear sending chills up her spine. Zane had to be safe. She refused to accept the idea that they had come so far only to let it slip through their fingers now.

"Why are you taking so long, Andrew?" she whispered as she knelt behind a hydrangea bush. Certainly he wouldn't dally with one of the women while she waited out here with bated breath.

A strangled laugh broke free and she covered her mouth with her hands to muffle the sound. She was losing it, that's what was happening. Her nerves were frayed to the breaking point. She'd been running on pure adrenaline. Too little sleep. Too little food. Too much excitement. Any moment now she'd march right up the steps, kick in the door and demand to see her ex-husband.

The front door creaked open and she ducked down into the

shadows. The stairboards groaned as a man wearing heavy boots hurried from the house. Cautiously she lifted her head to see who it was.

"Andrew!" Her voice was an urgent whisper. "Over here."

He spun around, his expression hard to read in the darkness. "Who goes there?"

"Emilie."

He strode toward the bushes. She didn't need to see his face to know he was less than pleased. "You were to wait near the tree."

"I couldn't stand it. Zane—where is he?"

He grabbed her by the wrist and yanked her from her hiding place. They headed down the pathway at a fast clip. Although they were close in height, Emilie had difficulty keeping up with him.

"Say something, damn it!" she snapped as they reached the shelter of the woods. "If you don't tell me where Zane is, I'll—"

He spun her around to face him. "A score of prisoners were rounded up soon after midnight last night," he said, his voice tense.

"Zane?" The word was little more than a whisper.

McVie's expression was tender and infinitely sad. "He was one of them." The whore, Maggie, had turned Loyalist and, as luck would have it, Zane was the last member to join the spy ring and the first to be betrayed.

She sagged against Andrew as her knees gave way. "Oh, God." All the dreadful things she'd heard about the British prison ships in New York Harbor came back to her. "The *Jersey?*"

He shook his head. "Tomorrow morning they will transport the prisoners from a temporary jail to one of the prison ships."

"Then we have to do something tonight."

"I will take you back to the Blakelee farm, then consider the next step."

"The hell you will!"

He stared at her as if she'd grabbed the devil himself by the tail.

"Stop looking at me like that, Andrew. We have no time to spare."

He struggled to ignore her unladylike language. "This is a dangerous business, mistress Emilie. I cannot allow you to risk your person in a venture with little hope of success."

"I make my own decisions," she said, lifting her chin. "And I say we must do something now."

He raised his hand. "Quiet," he said, his voice low. "Someone approaches."

They crouched behind the wide trunk of a maple tree as two portly gentlemen, obviously in their cups, stumbled down the road.

"I would sell my soul for an hour of that lass's time," said the taller of the two.

"Aye," said the other. "There's little a man won't do for a willing wench...."

She turned to Andrew when the two men disappeared down the lane. "How big is the jail?"

"'Tis a small one," said Andrew, looking at her curiously. "A stone building with but one room."

"And many soldiers guarding it?"

"One soldier," said Andrew slowly. "There is a party tonight south of Morristown for the regiment."

"We could do it," she said, gripping his forearm tightly. "You have your pistol with you and I know you are never without your knife."

He said nothing.

"Think of it, Andrew. If you don't care about Zane's safety, think about the other men...think of Josiah Blakelee and his family."

"The chances of victory are slight."

"But if we do not try," reasoned Emilie, "they have no chance at all."

The prison ships were a death sentence as surely as a trip to the gallows.

He touched her cheek with his forefinger, as if commending her visage to memory against the day when they would ultimately be parted. If they succeeded in rescuing Rutledge, he would lose the red-haired lass forever.

But, looking at the expression in her eyes, the sound of her voice as she pleaded Rutledge's case, he feared in his heart that he had already lost.

"Over there," said Andrew, pointing toward a structure on the north side of the trail.

Emilie's spirits soared. "It *is* small," she said. "We should have no trouble at all."

Andrew shook his head in dismay. "You speak as if we have accomplished the task and, in truth, we have yet to begin."

"It's called a positive attitude," she said. Or Dutch courage. "If you believe you can do it, you can."

"Is that how men think in your time?"

"Some men and *women* make a lot of money teaching others to think that way."

"Then teach me those ways quickly, mistress Emilie, for what we attempt might lead to disaster."

She refused to believe failure was even a possibility. Zane was in mortal danger. Nothing else mattered.

"The moon is full," said Andrew. "We will not have the benefit of darkness to conceal our actions."

Emilie took a deep breath and loosened the top two laces of her bodice. "That will be no problem for me." Her heart was pounding so wildly that she was surprised only she was aware of it. "I will keep the guard occupied. The rest is up to you."

"I fear that you are in the more dangerous position," he said. "I cannot guarantee how long I will allow you to be at risk."

"That's my business, Andrew, not yours," she said. "If you're so worried, then give me a weapon."

To his credit, he didn't hesitate. He handed over his pistol and told her how to use it.

Emilie nodded, then tucked the weapon into the garter that held up her cotton hose. Obviously no one would be able to call her Quick-Draw Crosse, but there was a measure of comfort to be gained in knowing that the gun was there.

The plan was simple. Emilie was to distract the guard long

enough for Andrew to speak to the prisoners through the barred window they'd noticed on the side of the small building. When he gave her the signal, Emilie would step aside, Andrew would leap forward and knock the guard unconscious. Once they had the key to the jail, they were home free.

"'Tis time," said Andrew as a cloud drifted across the face of the moon.

Emilie squared her shoulders and met Andrew's eyes. "You have been a good friend," she said. "I could not have asked for a better one."

It wasn't enough and he could not pretend otherwise. "Godspeed," he said, kissing her hand in a gesture of luck and farewell.

"Godspeed," she said, then whispered a prayer that the end would be a happy one for them all.

The guard, a ruddy-complexioned man in his fifties, was dozing when Emilie first approached. A musket lay across his lap. A jug of Jamaican rum rested at the ground near his booted feet and it was obvious by the way he was snoring that he had enjoyed every drop. Her hopes soared. *Let him be drunk,* she thought. Then she could heft the musket and render him unconscious and not have to go through with part of her plan.

But that wasn't meant to be. On a loud snore the guard roused and turned his bloodshot eyes on her. "Who goes there?" he called.

Not answering, Emilie resignedly sashayed over to him, swishing her skirts the way heroines did in old costume-drama movies. He eyed her appreciatively. Lustily.

She stopped a few feet away from him, her eyes drawn to his nasty-looking beard with God knew what disgusting substance clinging to it. She prayed her roiling stomach would settle down long enough for her to act seductively.

She stepped closer. She'd never been much of a flirt. All of that simpering and eyelash batting had seemed an incredible waste of time and effort. Now she wished she'd paid more attention.

"'Tis a fine night," she said, summoning up a saucy smile.

He nodded and sat up straight on the wooden bench.

She leaned forward, allowing him a view of her cleavage. "Poor man," she said, tapping him on the top of his head with her forefinger. "Left all alone while the others dance and make merry. 'Tis a shame to let a full moon go to waste."

His hot gaze trailed across her bodice, lingering along her shadowy cleavage. It took all her self-control to keep from shuddering.

"You're a fine-looking wench," he said. "Has Maggie taken to sending her girls in search of work?"

"Nay," she said with a toss of her head. "But our hearts go out to a man who isn't free to search for his own pleasures."

He licked his lips and bared his teeth in a leering smile. "And do you have a name, mistress?"

She gave him what she hoped was a sultry look. "Bonnie."

"Aye," he said, "and it's a bonny girl you are." He removed the musket from his lap and leaned it against the bench. "Sit with me."

She dimpled prettily. "There is no room for me on that bench."

He patted his lap. "I have a spot for you."

Casually she glanced about to see if Andrew was anywhere in sight. "You presume much, sir," she said coyly. *Where are you, Andrew?*

The guard reached out and clasped his fingers around her wrist. "Give us a kiss," he said, pulling her down onto his lap.

Her skin crawled as he toyed with the laces on her bodice. *Think of Zane,* she ordered herself. *Anything is worth his life. Even this.*

She leaned over and retrieved the jug. "How ungenerous you are, sir. Fine Jamaican rum and you do not offer me a drop."

"There are better things to do than drink rum, lass." His fingers traced the swell of her breasts. "We can drink after."

What she wouldn't give for a scalding tub of water and a bar of lye soap. "You're a randy one," she noted, striving for lusty enthusiasm. "I hope you won't be in too much of a rush."

He threw back his head and laughed heartily. "You need not worry," he said, placing a hand on her thigh, "for there is plenty more to be had."

A slight motion caught her eye, and to her relief she saw Andrew crouched at the corner of the building. He met her eyes and flashed the signal.

She made to stand but the guard held her fast.

"Patience," she said, trying to get free. "I promise it will be worth your wait."

He leaned forward and she gasped as his hand slid under her skirts. His rough fingers snagged the fine cotton of her stockings as his hands roamed unerringly up her legs. She could only imagine how they would feel against her skin. She struggled against him, praying he wouldn't find the pistol.

He groaned with pleasure. "You're a fine piece," he said. "Jack knows how to pleasure the women—" Suddenly he stopped. His hand had no doubt found the gun. "What the hell—"

There was no time to think. If he grabbed Andrew's pistol, it would be all over. For all of them. Andrew was still several yards away. Emilie grabbed for the musket leaning against the bench and brought it down sharply on the back of the guard's neck.

He yelped in pain. "You bloody bitch!" He reared back and struck a blow to her cheek. She fell to the ground at his feet. "I'll teach you to—"

Andrew was on him like a mountain lion. Emilie, cheek throbbing with pain, lifted her skirts and pulled out the pistol. With trembling hands she aimed it at the guard as Andrew's next blow sent the man tumbling into unconsciousness.

"Thank God you showed up when you did," she said to Andrew as he threw the guard to the ground.

"The keys," he snapped. "Hand them to me quickly."

She did as he asked, her stomach twisting at the sour smell of the guard's flesh.

"Do not let him go," Andrew warned. "If he awakens, do what is necessary."

The next few minutes were the longest of her life. Voices emanated from inside the jail, but none of them were Zane's. Beads of sweat trickled down her back. He had to be there. *But what if he's sick,* a small voice worried, *or injured?*

"Just let him be alive," she whispered. They could handle any other eventuality together.

Two men stumbled from the jail, stiff legged as if they hadn't walked in a long while.

Neither one was Zane.

Her mouth went dry with fear. *Dear God, please let him be in there. If he is, I'll never ask you for another thing....*

A tall man with a head of red hair even brighter than her own staggered out.

She bit her lip as tears stung her eyelids.

And then she heard his voice, that low and thrilling voice that had first captivated her years ago, and she felt as if someone had handed her future back to her, all golden and shining and wonderful.

"Emilie."

She turned, unable to control the tears that fell freely down her cheeks. So tall, so strong—the one man she'd ever loved.

The only one.

Somehow she was in his arms. There was no other reality beyond the sight and sound and feel of him.

"I thought I'd lost you," she murmured against his lips.

"McVie told me what you did. If you ever try a stunt like that again, I'll—"

His words were lost in the kiss they shared, and when he broke the kiss she felt bereft.

"Emilie was right," he said as McVie approached. "There's a plot against Washington."

McVie looked puzzled. "I have talked to the others. They mention no such intrigue."

"They don't know about it," said Zane. "I found out about it at the whorehouse. They thought they'd knocked me out cold, but I heard every damn word they said." Sometime in the next ten days an attempt would be made on the general's life and it would be made at close range.

"Who is behind it?" asked McVie, still skeptical.

"Talmadge," said Zane. "Does that name mean anything to you?"

McVie paled visibly. "Talmadge is one of the general's closest advisors."

"We have to move fast," said Zane. "These guys mean business."

McVie called two of the other prisoners over. "Where is the general?"

"Long Island," said the man with the red hair.

"And Talmadge?"

"With the general," said the man.

McVie began barking orders at the assembled men. "Spread out into the countryside," he said. "Alert the others to the imminent danger."

"What about Washington?" asked Zane. "He has to be told."

"I am most familiar with the territory of Long Island," said McVie. "'Tis a dangerous trip and I have the least to lose." The other men had sweethearts and families. Andrew had nothing but regrets.

"I left the Blakelees' horse with a blacksmith at the edge of town," said Zane. Ten shillings and the man had been ready to adopt the roan. "Tell him Captain Rutledge granted his permission."

Emilie listened to the exchange with a growing sense of bewilderment. The trip to Long Island was everything Zane loved: long, difficult and extremely dangerous. Yet there he was, literally handing the reins over to another man.

The guard began to stir and Andrew motioned for the other men to scatter.

"Wait until first light, then return to the Blakelee farm," said Andrew. "I will see you there again."

"Take care, Andrew," said Emilie, "and come back safely."

He nodded. There was a world of sadness in his eyes and it tore at her heart that once again life had seen fit to deny him the happiness he deserved.

Zane, too, noticed the darkness in his countenance as he extended his hand to Andrew.

"Mark me well, Rutledge," he said, taking the hand and meeting Zane's eyes with fierce determination. "I would fight you if I believed there was a chance of victory."

With that, McVie vanished into the darkness.

Chapter Fourteen

14

For the second time in as many days, Zane found himself a prisoner. This time, however, it was not the British army who held him captive; it was Emilie.

The woman he loved.

All around them the members of the spy ring were vanishing into the night. Their movements barely registered on Zane. There was only Emilie. Once again he was struck by her beauty, but for the first time he saw her soul, as well.

A bruise, purple and angry, was blossoming along her temple near her hairline, and a murderous rage filled him as her gaze strayed toward the guard slumped on the ground by the door.

"Don't," she said, reading his mind. "It doesn't matter."

Gently he cupped her chin and tilted her face until it was bathed in moonlight.

"Why the hell did McVie let you pull a stunt like this?"

"He couldn't stop me," she said, cradling his face in her hands. "I had to find you."

She had risked her life to save his. The enormity of what she'd done hit him full force in the middle of the chest. There was so much to say, so many things to tell her, and no time to say any of it.

The guard was coming to and they had to escape.

"We're near the cave," Zane said, grabbing Emilie's hand. "Come on."

Swiftly they blended into the forest, away from the revealing moonlight. Zane cleared his mind of everything but the location of the cave where they'd spent the night many weeks ago. A small stream, a stand of towering pine trees, and a fifteeen-degree slope to the land, give or take a degree or two. It wasn't much to go on, but he'd worked with less before.

Faint shafts of moonlight penetrated the canopy of trees, casting an eerie glow. From somewhere an owl hooted and it seemed as if the Christmassy smell of pine was all around. He let instinct and memory guide him and, to his amazement, Emilie never hesitated.

She was with him every step of the way, his partner, his soul.

His wife.

"Over there," he said, pointing to an outcropping of rocks to their right.

"Your memory is amazing," Emilie said as they found shelter inside the velvety darkness of the cave. "Rand McNally couldn't have done better."

"I remember a lot of things, Em." He drew her into his arms. "Everything about you." The little freckle on her left shoulder. The sound of her delighted laughter when he kissed her unexpectedly. Her strength and goodness and absolute certainty that happiness was theirs for the taking.

She rested her head against his shoulder. He could feel her heart thundering inside her chest, its wild pulse beat matching his own.

"You were wonderful," she whispered, her lips brushing the side of his throat. "Brave and selfless. I was so proud of you."

"You sound surprised."

She chuckled softly. "I was."

"I don't think anyone's ever been proud of me before."

"How does it feel?"

"Good." He found her mouth with his. "But not as good as this."

Their kisses held another dimension, a sweetness that transcended the purely sexual. He felt as if he'd been living behind a wall of glass and now that glass was shattering before the force of something greater—and more dangerous—than anything he'd ever imagined.

"It's so dark in here," she said, laughing softly. "I can't see your face."

"I can see yours," he said.

"That's impossible."

He traced the contours of her chin, her mouth, her cheekbones with his fingertips. She was part of him, burned into his heart, half of his soul. "I know every inch of you."

A voluptuous shiver rose up from the center of her being. There was nothing beyond this moment. No one except this man. Everything that had come before, every dream, every fantasy, all of the endless days and nights of wanting something that danced just beyond reach—all of it vanished before the feeling of destiny that held them in its embrace.

He used their clothes to cushion the ground where they lay together, limbs tangled, hearts beating wildly. There was no hesitation. There were no missteps. They moved together as if they had spent their lives waiting for this night.

She gloried in his strength. He took comfort from her softness. The act of love became a sacrament.

This was the secret that had always eluded him, the secret that was at the heart of a marriage, at the center of life.

"All those years," he murmured against the curve of her breast. "All that time wasted...."

"We're together now." She arched against him, all softness and strength. "That's all that matters."

"This is forever," he said, moving slowly inside her. "Nothing can tear us apart."

"Don't say that." She kissed his mouth as if to erase his words.

His laugh rumbled against her lips. "Don't tell me you're superstitious."

"Why tempt fate?" she said. "We have so much. If I lost you I would die."

"To hell with fate," said Zane fiercely. "This is forever."

* * *

It was a night of wonder, of promises made and pledges given.

"We're getting married again," Zane said, holding her close to his heart as dawn broke beyond the cave.

"How on earth will we explain that to the Blakelees?" she asked, listening to his heart beating beneath her ear. "They'll be scandalized."

He looked at her, his blue eyes twinkling with a wicked light. "Are you suggesting we live in sin?"

Emilie traced the line of his muscular calf with her bare toe. "I'm suggesting we use some discretion."

"You mean no Elvis impersonator officiating?"

She laughed out loud at the memory. "I haven't thought about that in years." She shook her head in amazement. "I can't believe we were married by the King."

"Bet nobody around today can make that statement."

"Unless it's King George," she said dryly.

"You haven't given me an answer."

"I haven't heard a real proposal."

"You'll marry me."

"That's not a question."

"Damn right," said Zane, rolling her onto her back and straddling her hips. "There's only one answer I'll accept."

"I love it when you're macho."

He moved against her and her back arched in response.

"I also love it when you do that."

He leaned forward, drew one nipple into his mouth and sucked deeply.

Her eyes closed as a slow wet heat suffused her body.

He shifted position, parting her thighs and positioning himself between her legs. He cupped her with his hand and she moved against him as the need built inside her.

"You're ready for me." He brought his hand to her lips, letting her taste herself on his skin. "Hot and sweet."

"Oh, God...Zane—" She wrapped her legs around his waist and

fiercely drew him into her body, demanding all that he had to give and more.

And neither was disappointed.

The sounds of laughter and music reached them as they crested the hill near the Blakelee farm a few hours later.

"The wedding!" said Emilie. "It must be today."

The events of the past few days were all jumbled together in a crazy quilt of fear and joy, and it came as a surprise to see that the regular patterns of life were exactly as they'd left them.

"There must be a hundred people down there," Zane said, whistling low. "I guess big weddings were always in style."

It was something out of a dream, Emilie thought, as they made their way down the gentle slope then headed toward the revelers milling about. The harshness of their life and the realities of war were not visible today as friends and family gathered together to celebrate the marriage of Charity Blakelee and her Timothy. A fiddler sat atop the porch railing, his spirited music perfectly capturing the mood of the crowd. Long tables had been set up in the front yard, and they groaned with the weight of smoked hams and hearth-roasted chickens and bowls of salads and fresh vegetables.

She gestured toward the scene below them of family and friends, little children and tiny babies. The whole spectrum of life in all of its aspects and all of its beauty.

A life without the walk-on-the-highwire intensity Zane thrived on.

"Look, Zane," she said softly. "That's all there is. Will that be enough for you?"

"I have you," he said, ruffling her hair with a gentle hand. "And one day we'll find our way back where we belong."

"That's not going to happen."

"I think it will."

"And in the meantime?"

"Hell," said Zane, looking young and filled with hope, "there's a whole world out there for us to discover."

"There's a war going on," she reminded him.

"That's the best part," he said. "We've helped save George Washington's life. Who knows what else is in store for us before we leave."

"We haven't exactly saved George's life," Emilie corrected him. "That's Andrew's job."

"We made it possible," said Zane with a snap of his fingers. "We'll clear up the confusion in the history books when we get back where we belong."

Why argue the point? If he needed to believe they'd return to the future one day, it was no worse than believing in Santa Claus or thinking that calories really didn't count.

So what if they had no home, no family and no steady source of income? Things would work out for the best. She had to believe that. After all, this was everything she'd ever wanted. The man she'd always loved had become part of the world she'd always longed for. The puzzle pieces that had been her life had finally joined into a beautiful picture.

So why did she have the feeling that one piece of that beautiful puzzle was still missing—and that that one piece might change everything?'

It wasn't as if he could click his heels together three times and wake up in the future. Things didn't work that way. The best they could do was build a life for themselves in the here and now. It was all that anyone could do, no matter what century he lived in.

Zane took her hand and they walked across the meadow to mingle with the wedding guests.

"Look over there," Emilie said, gesturing toward Charity, who was dancing with a handsome young man. "The bridal couple."

"They look awfully young," Zane said after a moment. "Do you think he's old enough to shave yet?"

"It's a different world now," Emilie said. "Real life starts a lot earlier. Let's go over and wish them well."

"Emilie!" Rebekah's sweet voice rang out across the yard. "Zane!" The woman, dressed in a pretty pink muslin gown with flowered trim, hurried toward them. She embraced Emilie warmly, then her brown eyes widened as she noticed the bruise near Emilie's hairline. "What on earth—?"

"I am fine," said Emilie, returning her hug. "Truly."

"You cannot know how worried I was for your safety. When you did not return the next morning I feared the worst." Rebekah glanced about. "Andrew...?"

"He is well," Emilie said quickly, "but he has been called away."

"And—and Josiah?"

"We discovered nothing," said Emilie. "I am sorry."

Rebekah whispered a quick prayer for both her husband's safety and Andrew's, then her narrow face lit up with a smile. She linked one arm through Emilie's and the other through Zane's. "Come and join the merriment," she said, leading them toward the tables laden with food and drink. "We are here to celebrate!" She lowered her voice conspiratorially. "Rumor has it we are to be honored with a most welcome guest."

"Anybody we know?" asked Zane.

"Of that I'm certain," said Rebekah.

Emilie gestured toward her wrinkled dress. "I must change into something more presentable."

"Hurry," said Rebekah, "for the dancing is about to begin!"

Zane followed Emilie into the farmhouse and upstairs to the second-floor bedroom.

"Oh, no, you don't," Emilie said, laughing as she eluded Zane's embrace. "Rebekah's waiting for us downstairs."

"She won't mind if we take our time."

"Patience, Mr. Rutledge," she said, reaching for her favorite mint green dress. "We have the rest of our lives ahead of us."

She changed quickly, then drew the comb through her tangled hair in an attempt to tame the fiery waves. She then gathered up the mane and twisted it into a loose Gibson-girl knot atop her head, securing it with a pair of ivory pins. She loosened a few tendrils around her hairline to hide the bruise and hoped for the best.

Turning, she saw that Zane had changed from the uniform and was dressed in black breeches and a black shirt.

"Very piratical," she said with an approving nod. "A nice blend of centuries."

"Everything else has to go to the cleaners."

"Remind me to explain the eighteenth century to you later on."

He pulled her into his arms and kissed her soundly. "Remind me to explain a few other things to you after that."

"Don't worry, Mr. Rutledge," she said. "You have my word."

Zane helped himself to several slices of ham and chicken, but Emilie found the mixture of smells off-putting and she instead accepted a pewter cup of sangaree. The sun blazed overhead and the cool blend of wine and fruit provided welcome refreshment.

"What's going on over there?" Zane asked, gesturing toward a crowd over near the barn.

"Maybe Rebekah's special guest has arrived. Is it me or did you think she was being awfully secretive about it?" She tilted her head as a thought struck her. "You don't suppose Josiah has returned?"

"Who knows," said Zane. "Let's check it out."

Zane put down his empty plate and Emilie was looking for a place to leave her cup of sangaree when Charity and her new husband, Timothy, approached.

Charity, looking lovely in a white silk dress with embroidered roses along the curve of the bodice, smiled up at Zane. "'Tis our custom that each married man dance with the bride before the cake is cut."

Zane winked at Emilie, then cut a dashing bow. "And who am I to break with tradition? May I have the honor, mistress?"

Smiling, Charity stepped into his arms.

Her husband, a pleasant-looking fellow with dark auburn hair, bowed toward Emilie. "It would please me greatly, mistress, if you would honor me with a dance."

"I would very much enjoy that—" She paused. "Timothy, isn't it?"

His smile was as sunny as the day. "Timothy Crosse," he said, offering his hand.

She gasped, feeling as if the breath had been knocked from her body. "What did you say?"

"Timothy Crosse," he repeated, looking at her curiously.

She couldn't breathe. The heat of the day seemed to press upon her chest, making it impossible for her to draw breath into her lungs.

"Mistress Emilie..." Timothy's voice seemed to come toward her through an airless tunnel. "You look unwell. Let me see you to a chair."

She sank onto the porch step and closed her eyes against a wave of dizziness. "Please," she managed as the young man peered at her worriedly. "I—I am fine. It's only the heat."

He waved his arm in the air, motioning for Zane and Charity to stop dancing and join them.

"I do not know what happened," Timothy said to Zane when he approached. "One moment she was fine and the next—"

He shrugged his shoulders.

"I could use some water," she said. "If you would—"

Timothy and his bride went off to fetch a cup.

Zane helped her to a chair inside the cool darkness of the house. "You look like you've seen a ghost."

"I did," she said, a wild laugh breaking free. "And his name is Timothy Crosse."

Zane stared at her. "You've got to be kidding."

She shook her head. "That why I've been so comfortable here, so at ease." She gestured broadly. "In a way, they're family."

"We're getting into weird territory here. How can you meet your own ancestors?"

"I don't know," she said. "How can you travel back in time?"

"Don't look at me," he said. "You're the one with all the answers."

She thought of the other wedding guests for the first time. The laughing woman in the yellow brocade dress...the portly gentleman in the snuff-colored waistcoat...that beautiful towheaded baby who sat playing in the grass. She was related to half of these people by blood and to the other half by marriage.

A lifetime of familial history rushed in on her, making her dizzy. She heard her mother's voice and her grandmother's, each story forging a link in the chain that wound through the centuries.

Sweat broke out on her brow. "I can't think." She struggled to find the words, but they eluded her. "There's something...something, but I can't seem to remember what."

"Don't worry about it," he said, his gaze drawn to the bruise near her temple. "Whatever it is, it can't be too important."

"I know it sounds crazy," she said, shaking her head, "but I can't stop thinking about George Washington."

"Okay," he said carefully, "that's not too hard to figure out." McVie was on his way to Long Island to warn the general of the assassination plot. It had to be on her mind. "You're concerned."

"It's more than concern." She looked up at him, green eyes wide and puzzled. "I'm afraid something terrible is about to happen."

"Even if that's true, there's nothing you can do about it," Zane said with one of those displays of logic men pride themselves on. "You're in New Jersey. General Washington is in New York."

"But all those family stories—" she persisted.

"You did your best," Zane said. "Don't worry. History will bear you out."

Isaac burst through the front door, his narrow face bright with excitement. "My ma says to come on outside fast as you can! He's about to leave."

Zane and Emilie looked at each other.

"Who's about to leave?" Zane asked.

"General Washington," said Isaac, heading for the door. "He came to the wedding to deliver a letter from my pa. My pa's a hero! He—"

His words faded as it all came into terrifying focus for Emilie. The answers had been right there in front of her all the time. Her family. The wedding celebration with the fiddle music and laughter. She looked at Zane. *The man dressed in black who saved the general's life....*

"Oh, my God!" She started for the door, fighting down a wave of nausea. "This is it!"

Zane grabbed her by the arm. "Are you sure?"

"Yes!" Her voice was high and tight. "Andrew's not the hero. It's—"

He bolted for the door, knocking Isaac onto his behind. There'd be time enough for apologies.

Rebekah stood on the front porch, clutching a letter to her

heart. "Zane!" Her smile was radiant. "We tried to find you. I so wanted to introduce you to His Excellency."

He grabbed the woman by the arm. "Where is he?"

She pointed toward the barn, where he saw a man in uniform astride a horse. "He leaves now for Philadelphia."

"Is he alone?"

Rebekah shook her head. "He travels with his aide." She frowned. "Now, what is his name? Ah, yes...Talmadge."

Zane vaulted the porch railing and hit the ground hard. A sharp pain shot through his right arm and it occurred to him that he'd probably broken it again. It didn't matter. Scrambling to his feet he headed full speed toward the barn.

One hundred yards...fifty...faster...he had to run faster....

The assassin could be anywhere. The musket could be trained on Washington right now.

He kept running. Somewhere behind him he heard Emilie's voice. Whatever happened, however it ended, he wanted her to be proud.

"Get off that horse!" he roared at the general. "Now!"

Washington turned slowly and looked toward Zane. The man was a dollar bill come to life, the face on a thousand President's Day circulars. The impact stopped Zane in his tracks.

But not for long. If he didn't do something in the next ten seconds, the future he and Emilie took for granted wouldn't stand a chance, and that dollar bill would be a pound note instead.

The general's hand moved toward the hilt of his sword.

Behind him, he heard Emilie scream.

Sorry, George. This is gonna hurt me more than it hurts you.

And with that thought, Zane Grey Rutledge threw himself headlong into history.

Chapter Fifteen

15

Rebekah stood in the doorway, watching as Emilie collected the last of her things from the second-floor bedroom that had been their home. "Are you feeling better?"

"I'm fine," Emilie said with a smile. "Truly."

"The nausea?"

"Gone," said Emilie. "The lemon crackers did the trick." She could no longer deny the symptoms. She had tried to attribute the dizziness and nausea and skipped period to everything but the truth: she was pregnant with Zane's baby, this miracle child conceived in the future on that moonlit night when she'd thrown caution to the winds and followed her heart.

"'Tis a good sign. Misery now means a healthy babe when your time comes."

"From your mouth to God's ear."

Rebekah looked at her curiously. "I have not heard that expression before."

Emilie folded Zane's black shirt and added it to the small pile of clothing. "It's a very popular expression in New York."

"So you say. Still, there is something about you and your husband that sets you apart."

"Our accents?" asked Emilie.

"How I wish I could pinpoint it with precision. I have never known a friend such as you."

Emilie gave the other woman an impulsive hug. "I'm going to miss you, Rebekah. Especially now."

Rebekah nodded, her brown eyes wet with tears. "I am afraid I do not know how I will manage without your friendship."

"The friendship will not end," said Emilie, meaning it. "Only the proximity."

They heard the sound of Zane's footsteps on the staircase.

"Not a word about the baby," Emilie warned.

"You still have not told him?"

Emilie shook her head. "He has had enough to think of this week."

Zane had rebroken his arm during his heroic rescue of General Washington. Between that and all the excitement the rescue generated, there had been little time to break news of such a delicate nature. As soon as they were settled in their new home near Philadelphia, she would tell him.

It wasn't that she was nervous about telling him. Not really. Just because they hadn't gotten around to talking about children didn't mean he didn't want any. Sure, during their first marriage he'd made it clear that reproduction was near the bottom of his list of priorities. But that was a long time ago—and this was a different Zane.

As if on cue, Zane appeared in the doorway. "It's time, Emilie. We have a long trip ahead of us."

As always, the sight of him tugged at her heartstrings. "Is the wagon loaded?"

Zane nodded, then turned to Rebekah, a stern look on his handsome face. "You've given us enough food to last a year."

"'Twas the general's orders," Rebekah said with a saucy grin.

"How will you feed your family?"

"His Excellency said that will no longer be a problem for us."

"You must be so proud of Josiah," Emilie said. "Working behind British lines the way he has been doing must take a great deal of courage."

For the past three months Josiah Blakelee had been collecting valuable information for the patriots' spy ring that General Washington devoutly prayed would lead them to their first decisive victory of the war.

It was all Emilie could do to keep from telling them that the victory they so desired was in sight. In just a few short months, on a cold winter's day in January, the Battle of Princeton would be fought and won, setting the Continental army on the road to glory.

Zane turned to Emilie. "I'll meet you downstairs."

Emilie's eyes filled with tears. "Will we see each other again?" she asked Rebekah. "Now that Zane and I are both part of the spy ring—"

"Life is filled with surprises," Rebekah said. "That is one thing that eighteen years of marriage to Josiah Blakelee has taught me."

Emilie glanced about the room, suppressing a smile as her gaze fell upon the copper tub. "It appears that I have everything."

"You came with so little," Rebekah said. "I have often wondered how it was you and your husband came upon Andrew."

Emilie sighed. "It seems a lifetime ago, Rebekah. So much has happened since." She gathered up the satchel of clothing from the bed.

"Do you have the letter of protection from General Washington?" Rebekah asked.

Emilie patted the pocket of her gown. "The most valuable item in our possession." She had placed it in the embroidered purse, along with the items she'd retrieved from their hiding place near the barn. She could just imagine the uproar if Rebekah had discovered the money with the general's picture on it.

Washington's gratitude had been sincere and overwhelming in its generosity. In addition to the letter granting them safe passage, he had procured for them a wagon and horse, the eighteenth century equivalent of a BMW and free gasoline for life. They had been asked to join the Philadelphia branch of the spy ring, where Zane's powers of observation and Emilie's skills with a needle and floss would be put to their best use.

What Washington had done, in effect, was to hand them their

future—the one thing they'd been unable to do for themselves. And now, with their baby growing beneath her heart, that future took on new importance.

Zane waited near the wagon with Rebekah's children. Even Charity and Timothy, home from their wedding trip to a cousin's house in Delaware, had returned to say goodbye. Emilie was deeply touched, and she hugged the two young people warmly. The thought that her life would be forever intertwined with the lives of these good people made her feel part of that invisible chain that linked her still with the world she'd left behind.

"The post runs well between Philadelphia and Princeton," said Rebekah. "You must write and tell me how you fare in your new home."

"No sister has ever been more kind," said Emilie as the two women hugged one last time. "We'll never forget you—not any of you."

Isaac, looking terribly adult, offered his hand, which Zane shook with great solemnity. Emilie detected a certain mistiness in Zane's eyes, which only made her love him more.

Finally they could delay no longer. Emilie took her seat next to Zane on the wagon as he took the reins in his left hand.

"Do you know how to drive this thing?" she whispered.

"How hard can it be? The horse does all the work."

"Godspeed!" cried Rebekah and her children as Zane urged the horse forward.

Emilie sniffled loudly for the first hour as they skirted the town of Princeton and headed south.

"We'll see them again," Zane said. "Our paths are bound to cross."

"How can you be sure?" she asked, her green eyes brimming with tears. "It's not like we can jump in the car and zip over for coffee."

He started to laugh. "What's that I hear? The sound of a woman longing for modern conveniences?"

"Don't make fun of me," she said, glaring over at him. "I miss Rebekah."

"You haven't been gone long enough to miss anybody."

"I don't care. I miss her and that's that."

Zane shot her a quizzical look. Apparently her familiar red-head's temperament had a few variations he'd yet to discover.

He'd seen Emilie furious, he'd seen her jealous, he'd seen her indifferent. But the one way he'd never seen her was weepy.

"Don't look at me like that!" she snapped. "I hate it when you look at me like that."

"I'd tell you to count license plates, but I don't think we're going to see any."

"I don't think you're funny."

They rode on in silence for a while, stopping once so an aggrieved Emilie could disappear behind a large bush only to return moments later complaining loudly of brambles.

Andrew had envisioned himself a hero.

In his mind, his return to New Jersey was as the hero Emilie had claimed he would be. But, instead, he was returning once again in anonymity.

When he'd reached Long Island he'd discovered that George Washington had left suddenly for New Jersey, leaving Andrew feeling like a fool as he spoke of assassination plots and daring rescues.

The men had looked at him as if he were crazy.

But then maybe he was.

The torch had been passed. Even he could see it. There were new men to take his place. Younger men. More impassioned men. Men with brains and vision who could do things for the cause that Andrew hadn't dreamed. Rutledge, for one. Even Emilie had more fire in her belly for independence than he had today.

He had stayed on Long Island only long enough to visit with Elspeth's mother. Then he had set out on the journey back to New Jersey. Back to what, he did not know.

Lately he had found it difficult to concentrate on the matters at hand when his mind was drawn again and again to the world that Emilie had described to him.

He could imagine the riotous cacophony of noise on a city street. When he closed his eyes he conjured up a gigantic silver bird that streaked through the sky like a shooting star. Nothing was more real to him now than those images Emilie and Rutledge had painted for him.

He had made up his mind that when he saw them again at the Blakelee house, he would tell them that he wanted to see their world. At least, that was, if they ever figured out a way to return.

Of course, that didn't seem very likely, but then neither did anything to do with the whole amazing enterprise.

Why he had bypassed Princeton and continued southeast until he reached the lighthouse puzzled him. Strange, but the need to see the lighthouse again had been too strong for him to resist. Like some unrelenting call of nature, he'd found himself going miles out of his way just so he could row across the harbor and spend the night listening to the waves crashing against the shore.

Just one night, he thought as he gazed out at the harbor. Just one night and then he'd move on.

After a few more miles of silence, Emilie leaned over and placed her hand on Zane's leg.

"Sorry I've been so disagreeable."

"I'd rather have you cranky than crying." He met her eyes. "You'll see Rebekah again. I promise you."

That brought about another few minutes of sniffling.

"You're not acting like yourself," he observed.

"Yes, I am." Her tone of voice brooked no discussion.

They approached a fork in the road and he guided the horse to the path on the right.

"I think you're making a mistake," Emilie said.

He gritted his teeth. Why hadn't someone told him this was going to be the ride from hell? "The directions said to bear right."

"I think you're wrong."

"I'm the one with the photographic memory."

"And the lousy sense of direction."

Zane bristled. "I seem to recall *I*'m the one that found that cave not so long ago. I didn't hear a sound from you then about my so-called lousy sense of direction."

Emilie flushed at the memory of that night—the daring rescue...the passion that followed. No, the only sounds Zane had heard then were her sighs of pleasure.

Still, she said, "Well, that only proves you can find places the *second* time around, Zane. The first time is the problem."

He just shook his head.

But after a few more miles even Zane had to admit things were looking a little bleak. He was supposed to be watching for an ancient weeping willow tree adjacent to an abandoned well. Unfortunately, there was nothing even remotely like that on the horizon.

They'd been on the road for hours. They were tired, hungry, and their butts were sore from bumping around on the wooden bench.

"I thought we were supposed to stay at an inn tonight," said Emilie.

"We are," he said, his teeth still clenched.

"So where is it?"

"We're getting there."

"I don't see it."

"If you tell me to pull in to a gas station and ask for directions, I'll—"

He never finished the sentence. He and Emilie took one look at each other and burst into laughter.

"We're gonna be okay," he said, ruffling her hair in an affectionate gesture.

"I know," she said. But even as she said the words, she felt a pang of guilt. This was the man she loved, the man who loved her. If they were going to build a life together, he should know about the tiny life growing inside her. Waiting until they reached Philadelphia suddenly seemed ridiculous. "Zane," she began slowly, "there's something I have to tell you."

No response.

"Zane?"

She followed his line of vision. "What is it?" she asked, straining to see over the trees.

"Over there." He directed her to the right. "Do you see it?"

Suddenly she felt dizzy, chilled as if by a gust of icy wind. "My God," she murmured. "The lighthouse."

"How the hell did I screw up like this?" he asked, jumping down from the wagon. "Only a moron could mistake east for west."

"I don't think it was a mistake."

He looked up at her. "What was that?"

She couldn't control her trembling. "Let's go," she said, her voice thin. "Let's get out of here."

"What's the matter, Em? This is as good a place as any to spend the night."

A sense of dread gripped her and would not be denied. "This could be dangerous."

He made a face. "No one expects us to be here. If anyone sees us, we're just another couple."

But they weren't just another couple. They were a couple from the twentieth century.

"Come on," he said. "Let's take a look around. We didn't have time to check it out when McVie found us."

She wanted to grab the reins and speed away as fast as she could, but she couldn't do it. Not without Zane. Reluctantly she allowed him to help her from the wagon.

"This is old hat," she said as they strolled toward the water. "There are so many new things to explore. Why should we bother with reruns?"

A rowboat bobbed at the water's edge, loosely tied to a post. Goose bumps danced over her flesh. If you asked her, it was all too damned convenient.

She tugged at Zane's sleeve. "Have you seen enough?"

He headed toward the boat. "Let's row over to the lighthouse."

"We can't do that, Zane. You have a broken arm."

"So what? I'll use the left oar, you use the right."

"I don't want to row across to thc lighthouse."

"Then you wait here."

"Why are you so interested in checking out the lighthouse? You already know what it looks like."

He stopped, considering her words. "I don't know why I'm so interested," he said slowly. "I feel—I feel drawn to it somehow."

"I don't like this," she said. "I'm getting really bad feelings about this whole thing."

Nothing she could say, however, was enough to dissuade him. She climbed into the rowboat next to him.

"Let's get it over with quickly," she said, manning her oar. The wind was picking up. Unless he intended to sleep in the wagon, they still had to find a place to spend the night.

When they reached the island Zane helped her from the rowboat and she tied it to the dock.

"Look," she said, pointing to her left. "Another boat. Do you think they're manning the lighthouse again?"

"No," said a familiar voice from behind them. "We're all alone here."

Both Zane and Emilie spun around to see Andrew McVie looking at them.

"Andrew!" she exclaimed. "What on earth—?"

"I was on my way to the Blakelees'," he said.

Zane met his gaze. "We were on our way to Philadelphia."

Neither man commented on the obvious, that they had both gone considerably out of their way to get there.

"We look like a local meeting of the New Jersey spy ring," Emilie observed, struggling to sound calm and unconcerned. "Perhaps we shouldn't be seen like this. It would only—"

She stopped. Both men were looking off toward the horizon. She followed their line of vision. Spirals of icy gray cloud cover moved swiftly toward them. She gripped Zane's arm. "I know that cloud cover," she said urgently. "I knew I should've tried to put together a balloon. Anything that would give us a chance to—"

"Look over there!" Andrew broke in. "Down on the beach."

"That's it!" Zane yelled over the roar of the wind. "The balloon!"

Emilie knew without looking that the balloon and the gondola were in perfect shape. How could this be happening?

"This is our chance, Em!" Zane grabbed her by the waist and swung her around lamely with his one good arm. "We've done whatever it was we were supposed to do. Our job is done and we can go home."

"It's an illusion," Emilie said, grasping at straws. "This isn't really happening."

Zane started toward the balloon with a reluctant Emilie close behind. "I was beginning to think it wasn't going to happen, that I'd missed the chance somehow. This is a miracle, Em!"

No, she thought. *The miracle is that I ever thought you and I had a chance.*

That icy silver-gray cloud cover blanketed the entire island. The clouds were so low they obscured the top of the crimson hot-air balloon.

"Come on, Em. We don't have much time."

"I—I can't go." She felt paralyzed by a feeling she could not even identify.

He stared at her as if she were a stranger. "We're not going to get any second chances, Emilie," he pleaded.

"It might be a trick. What if something happens?"

"Then at least we know we gave it a shot."

She shook her head. "I can't do it."

"Sure you can."

She stepped back. "Not this time." Earlier, she'd vowed she would follow Zane to the ends of the earth and beyond, but now… Now there was another life to protect. She couldn't risk the safety of their unborn child. Her heart ached with pain. She knew if she told him about the baby he would let that balloon fly off without him. But she wanted more than that for him.

"I love you," she said softly through the tears that constricted her throat, "but I just can't do this."

He felt as if he were trapped in the middle of a nightmare with no beginning and no end. She couldn't be saying no.

"You can't stay here, Emilie," he said frantically. How would he convince her of that when the clock was ticking away those precious few moments they had to reach the balloon? He grabbed her shoulders. "Emilie, please, we belong together."

"Go," she said, breaking his hold and gesturing toward the balloon. "Don't lose your chance at happiness because of me."

This way of life was harsh. Without his crutches of money and power, Zane Grey Rutledge was just another man. He wasn't entirely sure he could make a living at that.

"The balloon is beginning to rise," Andrew shouted. "It's now or never!"

Zane realized he couldn't convince her. This had to be her choice. "What is it, Em?" he asked her. "Are you coming or aren't you?"

"I can't, Zane," she whispered on a sob. "Dear God, how I wish I could…."

Tossing him her embroidered purse with the money and credit card, she ran toward the lighthouse. She threw herself down across the bed and did the only thing she could—she cried as if her heart would break.

You did the right thing, her heart consoled her. *You let him make his choice without telling him about the baby.* He had the right to return to the world he knew and loved, the same as she had the right to opt in favor of their child. The thought did little to comfort her.

A few minutes later she heard the front door creak open.

Andrew, she thought dully. Zane must be gone now.

She lay there listening to the sounds of the lighthouse. Then she heard a voice.

"Emilie."

How cruel, she thought, for the Almighty to fill her heart and mind with the sound of Zane's voice when he was so far away from her.

But then the bed dipped low on the right and a strong arm pulled her close until her cheek rested against a broad chest that could belong to only one man. The steady beat of his heart was a benediction to her soul.

She looked up into his eyes. "It didn't work?"

"I didn't try."

Her breath caught in her throat. "I—I don't understand." *Please let this be real…please let him stay here with us….*

"This is home," said Zane Grey Rutledge, the man who had never understood the meaning of the word. "It doesn't matter a damn if it's the twentieth century or the eighteenth. The only place I want to be is with you."

They were the words she'd always longed to hear, but she had to be sure. "It's not too late," she said. "I want you to be happy. I—"

The thought struck them simultaneously and they raced for the window.

"Oh, my God!" she whispered. "Andrew!"

There, in the wicker gondola suspended from the crimson balloon, was Andrew McVie.

"I'll be damned," said Zane as they watched the clouds wrap the balloon and gondola in their icy embrace. "He's going for it."

Tears filled her eyes. "There's so much he doesn't know…so many things he'll need to learn."

"He'll manage," said Zane, putting his arm around her as the balloon vanished from sight. "McVie's a survivor."

She shivered at the words. "I hope he makes it."

"So do I." He kissed the top of her head. "Is that why you wouldn't go?"

"It's a little more complicated than that."

"You like the eighteenth century better than the one we left behind."

"That's only part of it." She took a deep breath, then met his eyes. "There's someone else to consider."

And then he wondered how it was he hadn't known. The easy tears, the secret smile, the way she looked at him as if he'd helped create a miracle. "A baby," he said, his voice filled with wonder.

"A baby," she said, her hands resting protectively across her belly.

"That first night," he said, struck by the enormity of it all. Not only was this child the visible proof of their love, but he was also the product of two centuries.

"Do you need to sit down?" Emilie asked with a soft laugh.

He shook his head. "I think I'm supposed to say that to you." He drew her into his arms. "How long have you known?"

"I had my suspicions, but I've only been sure for a week."

"You should have told me."

"I— To tell the truth, I wasn't sure how you'd feel about the whole thing."

"I can't think of anything I'd like more than a little girl with your eyes and your zest for life."

Those beautiful green eyes shimmered with tears. "I have my heart set on a little boy who's as adorable as his daddy."

Blinking rapidly, he glanced away for an instant. "We're going to do this right, Em. We're going to be there for our kid…let him know he's loved."

"And we have to get married."

"We'll make it legal as soon as we get to Philadelphia, but no piece of paper could make us any more married than I feel right now." The kiss he gave her was one of communion and she felt it all the way through to her soul. "This time it's forever."

Epilogue

Eight months later
Somewhere near Philadelphia

"Sit down, Rutledge," Josiah Blakelee ordered. "You're wearing out the floorboards."

Another groan issued from the birthing room next to the kitchen and Zane shuddered.

He stopped pacing and looked at Josiah. "You have six children," he said. "Is it always like that?"

"Sometimes it is worse," said Josiah. "'Tis a woman's lot."

"Why do they do it?" Zane asked as his wife's pain ripped into his heart.

"For love," said Josiah. "Rebekah claims not to remember the pain once the babe suckles against her breast."

"Never again," said Zane, resuming his pacing. "I won't put her through this again."

Josiah simply smiled. The entire Blakelee family had been uprooted by the cause from their home in Princeton to begin again on a small plot of Pennsylvania land not far from where Emilie and Zane had settled. The two men had become close friends through their shared work in the spy ring, while their wives had simply picked up their friendship where they'd left off.

Right now Zane didn't know what he'd do without them.

Every time Emilie groaned he felt waves of pain tearing at his gut. When she was silent, beads of sweat broke out on his brow until he heard the sound of her voice again.

Josiah rose from his seat and handed Zane a bottle of rum. "Drink up," he ordered the younger man. "'Twill be a long day."

Morning became night and still she labored.

He might as well have been drinking water for all the good the rum did. His wife's agony was his own.

Zane wanted to be with Emilie the way he would have been in the future, but the shocked look on Josiah's face each time he broached the topic held him back.

Finally, he could take it no longer.

"She's my wife, damn it," he said. "This whole damn thing is barbaric. I'm going in."

He strode toward the birthing room and pushed open the door.

"Zane!" Rebekah was horrified. "This is no place for a man."

"Let him in." Emilie's voice was weak. She looked small and pale and exhausted against the plain white bed sheets. Suddenly her back arched and she reached for his hand, gripping with a strength that threatened to break his bones.

"The baby's crowning," said Rebekah. "Push, Emilie! Push!"

The room echoed with his wife's pain as she strained to deliver their child. He found himself horrified, scared, elated and every emotion in between.

"A little more," Rebekah urged. "Just...one...more...push!"

"Come on, Em," he pleaded.

"I can't...I'm tired.... It's too much...I—"

"You can do it, Em. You can do anything."

From some hidden wellspring she summoned the strength to try one more time. Her face contorted from the effort. "It's coming...I can feel it. The baby's coming!"

And then their child's first cry rang out, strong and lusty and miraculous.

"It's a girl!" Rebekah shouted joyously. "A beautiful baby girl!"

"Oh, God—Zane!" Emilie turned her face toward him, tears sliding down her cheeks and mingling with his own.

He thought he had known what love was about. He thought he had learned the secret to it all, thanks to this woman in his arms and their incredible journey through time. But when he saw that beautiful squalling infant placed in her mother's arms, he realized he'd known nothing at all.

Suddenly Emilie's back arched again and she cried out.

"'Tis the afterbirth," said Rebekah, still positioned between Emilie's legs. Rebekah placed her hand on Emilie's distended abdomen and an odd look passed across her features.

"What is it?" asked Zane, fear striking his heart. They couldn't have come this far for something to happen to Emilie. "Is something wrong?"

"Take the baby," she ordered in a clipped voice. "It seems Emilie's labors are not yet over."

Take the baby? He stared at the tiny, fragile infant in Emilie's arms. He couldn't take the baby. He didn't know the first thing about—

"Take the baby!" Rebekah's voice brooked no argument.

Long ago he'd heard someone say you scooped up a baby the way you scooped up a football. Since no one was offering any new suggestions, that's what he did, and to his relief it worked. She was so little, so perfect, so—

"Push!" Rebekah barked, sounding like a twentieth-century drill sergeant.

"I can't," said Emilie, gripping the bedpost with white-knuckled hands.

"You must."

Emilie's back arched.

"Push...push...sweet Jesus!" Rebekah's tears were mixed with laughter. "You have a son."

"A son?" Zane stared down at the child in his arms. "I thought we had a daughter."

"Twins?" asked Emilie, sounding both exhausted and triumphant. "We have twins?"

"'Tis a wonderful day," said Rebekah, wrapping the second newborn in a receiving blanket and handing him to his mother. "The Almighty has seen fit to bless you twice."

She turned, tears of joy running down her cheeks, and left the room to announce the exciting turn of events.

"We're a family," Emilie whispered, meeting Zane's eyes. "A real, live family."

He looked at his wife and their children and knew that he would lay down his life for them. Their way would be rocky in this new world, this new century, but Zane knew he'd do whatever it took to keep them safe from harm.

For the first time since he'd slipped through time—what seemed like a lifetime ago—his future seemed clear. He threw back his head and laughed with joy.

"I love you," he said, wishing the words didn't seem so inadequate when it came to describing the wondrous feelings that lived inside his heart. "I couldn't live without you."

"Poor Zane," she said as he bent to kiss her lips. "This isn't the life you planned on, is it?"

"No," he said without hesitation. "I got lucky."

"No regrets?"

"Not a one."

It's about time you realized it.

Emilie's eyes widened. "Did you hear something?"

He grinned. "I was wondering when she'd come back."

"Who?"

"Sara Jane."

"Your grandmother?"

He nodded. "In a way, she's responsible for this whole thing."

"I don't understand."

"You will," he said. "One day I'll explain the whole thing."

I'm proud of you, Zane. You've become a fine man—a true Rutledge.

"I heard her again," said Emilie, glancing around the room, "but I couldn't make out the words."

He smiled as a feeling of peace settled itself inside his heart. "I think she just said goodbye."

The door to the room swung open and in burst Rebekah and Josiah, Charity and her husband, Timothy, Isaac and Stephen and Benjamin and Ethan and even baby Aaron, who was beginning to walk.

The babies were proclaimed absolutely beautiful and as clever and brilliant as their besotted parents.

"But they don't have names yet," said Rebekah. "What are you going to call them?"

Zane met Emilie's eyes and she nodded.

"His name is Andrew," said Emilie as their newborn son yawned. For their friend, wherever he might be.

Zane smiled as their daughter waved her tiny fist in the air. "Sara," he said. "We'll call her Sara Jane."

And so it began....

TOMORROW & ALWAYS

For my husband, Roy, with love and gratitude, for twenty-five years of showing me what the word *hero* really means. I love you more than I can say, Bretton. Thanks for giving me your summer. This one's for you!

With special thanks to Karin Stoecker, whose enthusiasm and daring made this book possible. Your kindness in Chicago meant more to me than I can ever say.

I am almost ashamed to be living in such peace while all the rest struggle and suffer. But, after all, it is still best to concern oneself with eternals, for from them alone flows that spirit that can restore peace and serenity to the world of humans.

—Albert Einstein
Princeton, N.J.

Prologue

Late August, 1776

Andrew McVie sat on the slope behind the lighthouse and waited. He wasn't certain what it was he waited for, but the need in him was so great it could not be denied.

He had awakened near Milltown before dawn that morning, as sharp of eye and clear of head as if he had slept a full night and more. The innkeeper, a good woman named Annie Willis with two sons serving under General Washington, had offered him fresh coffee and bread still warm from the ovens but he found himself unwilling to spend the time.

"A body cannot subsist on patriotism alone." She wrapped a loaf of bread in a clean white cloth then handed it to him. "Think of mistress Willis when you sup, and pray her boys come home to her again."

Patriotism. The very word that had filled his soul with fire not so many years ago held no meaning for him now. Indeed, there were times when he felt as if he'd never known what it truly meant to sacrifice everything on the altar of revolution.

They called him a hero. They said he risked his life to go where others feared to tread because he understood that the need of the colonies far outweighed his own pitiful need for comfort. But they were wrong. All of them. Since he'd lost Elspeth and David he had been moving through the days both blind and deaf to anything but the pain inside his heart. It was easy to risk everything when you had nothing of value left to lose.

But now even his effectiveness as a spy had been taken from him.

He shifted position on the rock and rested his head in his hands. His journey to Long Island to warn General Washington of a plot against his life had resulted in naught save embarrassment. Not only was General Washington not there but the soldiers he'd spoken with had looked at Andrew as if he was daft.

"Surely you have spent too much time in the sun," one had said, laughing at Andrew's expense. "His Excellency is safely ensconced in Trenton now as we speak."

Later he had sought solace in a tankard of ale but there was no solace to be found anywhere on God's green earth. The truth was as plain as his own face in the glass each morning. His time was past. He could see that now. The torch had been passed while he dreamed, passed to men who were younger and stronger than Andrew. Men who were willing to fight the battles Andrew no longer understood.

A bitter laugh rose from the darkness of his soul. Indeed, it would be better if he lay dead on the sandy soil of Long Island. He had nothing left to give, nothing left to offer save a lifetime of regrets. Words he should have said, actions left untaken, the sad procession of mistakes made by a man who should have known better.

The ambitious young lawyer from Boston had been replaced by a patriot who no longer believed in the rebellion other men gave their life's blood to pursue.

None of it mattered any longer. He knew how it would all end. The patriots would be victorious. The Crown would become an ally. The sun and the moon and the stars would all remain in the heavens. And Andrew McVie would be alone.

He looked up at the lighthouse and shook his head at the absurdity of it all.

He'd never thought to set eyes upon the place again. Indeed, he had no understanding how it was he'd come to this particular spot on the New Jersey shore when he had been traveling toward Princeton. All he knew was that the need to be here had overtaken him, driving reason from his brain.

In truth, he should be sitting at Rebekah Blakelee's table at this very moment, eating her fine food and considering how it was his life had amounted to so little.

He had neither wife nor child, no home where he could lay down his head and rest his weary heart. The loneliness he had accepted as his punishment ofttimes rose up from the depths of his soul and threatened to choke off the very air he breathed.

Other men had friends to share a summer's night or warm a cold winter's afternoon. Andrew had nothing but regrets, and those regrets had grown sharp as a razor's edge these few weeks past, cutting him to the center of his being. For a little while this summer he'd rediscovered his heart and believed that happiness could be possible for him in this lifetime.

Emilie Crosse had come to him on a morning such as this, in this very spot, spinning a story about a big red balloon that had carried her through the centuries. At first he had thought her mad and vowed to grant her a wide berth but he soon found it impossible to turn a blind eye to her considerable charms.

She intrigued him with her fierce intelligence. She delighted him with her saucy wit. At times her independence enraged him and he found himself longing for the more docile women of his acquaintance but again and again he found himself drawn back to her side.

Andrew was not a man given to flights of fancy. He did not believe in ghosts or portents or a world beyond the one in which he lived. But on the day he had met Emilie Crosse in the cellar of the lighthouse he had had the unyielding sense that his life would never again be the same.

She was taller and stronger than the good women of his acquaintance and she carried herself with a sense of purpose he envied, but still it was more than those traits that had captured his imagination. It was the world she'd left behind. A world of wonders so miraculous his mortal mind could scarcely comprehend their scope.

She talked of flying through the air inside a shiny metal bird, of men leaving their footprints on the surface of the moon. In her time existed contraptions that could outthink a man of Jefferson's intellect or Franklin's invention. Music could be captured on a shiny brown ribbon and listened to whenever you wished. Indeed, entire libraries could be contained on an object the size of a saucer. The poorest of citizens possessed riches beyond Andrew's wildest dreams. Not even Fat George on his English throne could fathom the wonders of which Emilie spoke.

And still she talked of these things as if they were of little value, as if she cared not if she returned to her own time and place.

Not so the man she'd traveled through time with. Zane Grey Rutledge had no use for Andrew's world. He was a man of his own time and Andrew knew Zane would move heaven and earth to return there again with Emilie, to the world where they belonged.

And there was the rub.

To Andrew's everlasting dismay, Emilie had traveled backward through time with the man she'd once been married to. Andrew had watched helplessly as the couple had found their way back to each other, wishing with his entire being that he could be the man she loved. That she could somehow make him whole again in a way that neither rum nor revolution could accomplish.

But it wasn't to be. Emilie and Zane belonged together. In truth,

Andrew had known it from the start, known it deep in the part of his heart that had died with his wife and child so many years ago. A man might say Emilie and Zane were bound by the past they shared, the world they'd left behind, but Andrew believed a force more powerful than commonality linked their souls together.

Had it been that way with his Elspeth? Andrew could not remember. Late at night, in those moments before sleep claimed him, he saw her beloved face, heard the sound of her voice, felt the satin of her skin beneath his hand, but what she had thought and wished for and needed still danced somewhere beyond his ken.

"Aye," he muttered, wishing for rum or whiskey to blunt the edges of his pain. He had made so many mistakes, directed so little attention to matters of true importance that now he was doomed to go to sleep each night and wake up each morning in a world that held nothing for him but the shadows of what could have been.

His wife and child were dead and buried. The woman who'd captured his imagination loved another man. Not even the battle for independence that raged all around him was enough to ignite the fires of passion inside his cold and weary heart. It seemed he existed to do naught but take up space, counting down the days until he breathed his last.

Mayhap that was his destiny, he thought as he rose to his feet and walked to the edge of the outcropping of rocks that overlooked the water. To live alone there on the rugged island with only his own despair for company, as useless as the lighthouse was without a flame burning from the tower windows to guide the way for other lost and lonely souls.

If the Almighty had other plans for him, Andrew couldn't fathom what they might be.

He stood there at the edge of land for a long time, scanning the horizon for a sign, something—anything—that would show him the wrongness of his thinking, prove to him that there was still a purpose to his existence. But he saw nothing, save an odd cloud cover drifting in from the Atlantic, vertical bands in shades of pewter that moved steadily toward him, casting shadows across the harbor and whipping the still waters into a froth.

The hairs on the back of his neck rose.

"'Tis naught but a storm gathering force," he said into the wind over the mournful call of the gulls. The Jersey coast was known for the unpredictability of its weather. A fortnight ago he'd heard a sailor at the Plumed Rooster weave a tail of a towering waterspout that had toppled his frigate and drowned half the crew. Surely a band of gray clouds was no cause for alarm.

Still the sight tugged hard at his memory, as if it held some significance he had forgotten. *Enough,* he thought, turning away. He had felt the need to see the lighthouse again and he had done so. Surely there was no reason for him to linger, not with a storm threatening. He would row back to the mainland, mount his horse, then reach Princeton before nightfall. Rebekah, the good wife of Josiah Blakelee, would provide a roof over his head and food for his rumbling belly. Tomorrow morning he would see Emilie and Zane, tell them about this foolish trip to the lighthouse and—

A spot of crimson caught his eye. He narrowed his eyes, focusing in on the billowy fabric floating atop the choppy waters.

A big red balloon, Andrew...that's how it happened....

Beads of sweat formed at his temples and across his forehead. He could hear Emilie's voice as clearly as he had on that first day.

Where is that red balloon, mistress Emilie? he had asked, disbelief dripping from every syllable. *Where is the basket?*

I don't know, she had answered him simply. *We crashed into the water. I assume all was lost.*

He looked again but this time he saw nothing but the choppy water. Had the scrap of crimson been his imagination playing tricks upon his addled brain?

"No," he said aloud, gaining strength from the sound of his own voice. "'Tis there. It exists."

Thc cloud cover was settling itself around the island, obscuring the top of the lighthouse. A damp wind, too chilly for late August, stung his face with salt as a sense of destiny began to build inside his chest.

The sight of Emilie and Rutledge rowing toward the island from the mainland came as no surprise. They would help him find his way in their world as he had helped them in his.

A few minutes later Emilie embraced him. "Andrew! What on earth—?" Her face was taut with anxiety.

"I was on my way to the Blakelees'," he said.

"We were on our way to Philadelphia," said Zane.

Andrew and Rutledge clasped hands in the awkward way of men who shared more than either would admit.

"The cloud cover," Andrew said, pointing. "It seems most familiar to me but I cannot say why."

"Oh, God...." Emilie's face went pale and she sagged against Rutledge. "Please not now—"

"Why are you here?" Rutledge asked him.

Suddenly he knew beyond doubt. "Because there is no other place for me in this world."

"Let's leave," Emilie said, her voice holding a touch of panic. "We don't have to be here at all, none of us do. We can row back to the mainland before the storm hits." She started for the rowboats but Rutledge grabbed her by the wrist.

"Look," he said, pointing beyond the lighthouse.

Andrew turned slowly. His breath caught sharply in his throat as he saw the magnificent sight before him. A large basket danced lightly across the rocks, suspended by ropes attached to a crimson balloon so large it dwarfed even the lighthouse. "Sweet God in heaven," he whispered in awe. Despite its size the vessel seemed so fragile, so insubstantial, that he wondered how it was it had survived its amazing journey.

Rutledge swept Emilie into his arms. For the first time Andrew felt not the smallest pang of envy. She belonged to Rutledge and she always would. "This is our chance, Em!" Rutledge spun her around. "You said it wouldn't happen but it did. This is our chance to go back home where we belong."

Andrew heard the squeak of rope against wicker. "It's beginning to rise!"

Emilie pulled away from Rutledge. "This can't be," she murmured. "You just don't understand."

"We don't belong here, Em," Rutledge pleaded. "Let's—"

"Zane—" Her voice broke. "I can't...there are reasons I—" She tossed her embroidered purse to Zane but it fell to the ground at her husband's feet. Gathering up her skirts, she ran toward the lighthouse.

"Stay or go, man!" Andrew bellowed as the winds howled around them. That glittering world they had described was calling to him. "The chance may ne'er come again."

"You're right, McVie." Suddenly Zane smiled, a smile that could mean but one thing. "Damn right." With that Zane turned and went to join his wife.

The basket shuddered then rose higher. Somehow Andrew had never imagined braving the mysteries of time without his friends from the twentieth century. But there was no hope for it. He was sick unto death of struggle. The happiness others took for granted was not part of the Almighty's plan for him, but this grand adventure was and he'd be more than a fool to let this opportunity slip through his fingers. In the glittering world Zane and Emilie described he could lose himself in the wonder of it all and maybe—just maybe—forget that there'd been a time when he'd wanted more.

He reached down and scooped up Emilie's fabric purse and tucked it into the cuff of his leather boot.

"Stay or go," he said again. If only someone could prove that his existence here mattered, that one small thing he said or did lived on. But he was asking for the impossible. Hadn't Emilie said his name vanished from the history books, never to reappear?

Maybe the reason he vanished from the history books was that he vanished from the eighteenth century entirely. Maybe he had accomplished all he was meant to accomplish in this world and it was time to seek newer worlds to conquer.

And maybe he was as crazy as a mad dog baying at the full moon. Did any of it matter a whit in the greater scheme of things? When you'd already lost everything, not even death seemed too much to risk.

The world Andrew McVie had known since birth no longer seemed familiar. This was the reason he'd been drawn to this place, at this moment in time. Moments ago his future had seemed as bleak as the skies overhead. Now, in the blink of an eye, he found himself filled with hope for the first time in years. His life here was over and his new life in the future was about to begin. He prayed to God there would be a place for him there.

His dreams were of other times, and to deny them would be to consign himself to an early grave, and so he climbed into the basket just before it floated free of the earth's shackles and headed into the unknown.

The last thing he saw as the balloon rose into the clouds was Emilie and Zane silhouetted in the window. They were waving goodbye.

Chapter One

1

Somewhere over New Jersey

"Yo, man! Lookin' good!" The dark-haired wench in the basket of the green dragon balloon waved at Andrew as she drifted by.

Andrew wasn't certain what manner of address she used, but he nodded politely and lifted his hand to salute in kind.

Was that the sixth person to address him thus, or the hundredth? He no longer remembered. Indeed, it seemed he had scarcely ascended above the clouds before he was joined by balloons in the shapes of houses and half-moons and oddities for which he had no name. And to make matters even more perplexing, each balloon held a basket and each basket held a passenger bound for the same adventure.

Emilie and Zane might believe they had lived a miracle, but they were wrong. Traveling through time was as commonplace as riding the Post Road between Trenton and Princeton. They had said what happened to them was an act of fate, a once in a lifetime occurrence, but the evidence to the contrary was there right in front of his very eyes.

A balloon in the shape of an elongated dog drifted close. A man and woman waved to him from the bright yellow basket. "Party at the Forbes mansion at nine," the woman called out. "Champagne supper."

The man cupped his hands around his mouth. "Great costume! I have one like it at home."

No one had ever seen fit to comment upon his attire before. Andrew glanced down at his faded brown breeches and tobacco-colored waistcoat and found it to be a most ordinary outfit.

"What century would ye be from?" he called out, but the flames beneath his balloon roared, and with it the basket rose up and away. They had the look of the future about them, but for all Andrew knew they were farmers from the commonwealth of Pennsylvania.

All things seemed possible.

He peered over the side but the clouds obscured his view of the ground below. Save for one heart-stopping view of the lighthouse growing smaller beneath him, he had seen naught but clouds and more clouds. And now to discover that he did not make the journey alone… It was enough to make him wonder if he would find himself back at the point from which he had begun, an hour older and much wiser.

A huge striped balloon of green and white crossed his path but the occupants were too engrossed in conversation to pay him any heed. It would appear he was the only one on God's earth who found it unusual to sail above the clouds with nothing but the wind beneath him.

He wondered how it was that he would be returned to the ground below. Zane had suffered a broken arm when he and Emilie had come down from the sky. All that stood between Andrew and a painful death was the fragile basket that shuddered beneath him.

The magic fire propelling the balloon sputtered, hissed, then finally died. Andrew, heart thundering inside his chest, gripped the edge of the basket as it began to drop. As a child he'd imagined clouds to be soft pillows of down suspended in the air, but that was far from the truth. Each cloud hid an unpleasant surprise, rocking the basket to and fro, rattling him to his bones. He considered the wisdom of leaping to the ground but he had no idea how far away the ground might be or how many broken limbs such a feat might entail.

Gritting his teeth, he prepared to find out.

Shannon Whitney believed in three absolutes: the necessity for clean air, clean water and the Sunday *New York Times.* Or, more specifically, the crossword puzzle from hell that was tucked away in the magazine section each week and whose sole purpose was to drive sane people to madness.

Of course, there were those who would say doing the puzzle in ink was the first sign of incipient lunacy, and Shannon was among them. Still, that didn't stop her from uncapping her favorite pen every Sunday morning and spending more time than she would care to admit wrestling with six-letter words for crustaceans and eight-letter words for undergarments worn by seventeenth-century courtesans.

"Pantaloons...too long," she muttered, gnawing on the cap of her Bic. "Bloomers...too practical." She tossed the pen across the backyard and watched as it skittered along the flagstone path and rolled toward the pool. What was the point in trying to exercise her intellect when she could scarcely hear herself think over the rumble of propane tanks overhead?

Every year members of the blasted Central New Jersey Hot Air Enthusiasts club pleaded with her to allow them to use her land for their festival, and every year she refused. "We won't hurt a thing," their president claimed. "You have our word we'll leave your land exactly as we found it."

That, of course, wasn't the point but she didn't expect a man who spent the better part of his life flying around in a hot-air balloon to understand.

That was one of the many things wrong with the rich, she thought. The more money a man had at his disposal, the more ridiculous his toys. And what could be more ridiculous than flying over central New Jersey in a wicker basket suspended from a balloon filled with nothing but hot air.

She'd grown up in a world of privilege where polo ponies and private tennis courts were as common as guest rooms and finished basements, where grown men who should know better bet fortunes on the outcome of a chukker or the spin of a roulette wheel. People said that money couldn't buy happiness but Shannon wasn't convinced. Delinquent mortgages, bankrupt businesses, parents unable to pay their children's medical bills—money could do a lot more than gather interest in a Swiss bank account.

She tilted her head and listened as the rumble came closer. Whether or not the members of the club understood her reasons, she'd made her stand perfectly clear. She valued her privacy and wasn't about to compromise her stand on the issue just because some idiots liked to take to the air like Dorothy in *The Wizard of Oz*. If the wizard could give them brains she might rethink the position, but until then her land was off-limits.

Disappointment clogged Andrew's senses as he brushed dirt and twigs from his hair and clothing. The adventure of a lifetime had turned out to be another folly in a lifetime of abundant folly.

There was nothing exciting about falling through the branches of a silver maple tree and landing with a thud on the ground. In truth, he was fortunate to have escaped with his limbs intact but he took little consolation from that fact.

When the clouds had finally given way he'd been granted a clear view of the Raritan River and of a landscape most familiar to him, even from his peculiar vantage point. He sailed over the roof of a house identical in form and size to the houses he'd left behind. The only unusual sight was the rectangular pond behind the dwelling. He'd heard sailors speak of the turquoise waters of the Caribbean but he had never thought to encounter such a thing.

He wasn't in the glittering world of the future Emilie and Zane had beguiled him with. He wasn't even in another colony. He was still in New Jersey, perhaps no more than a few miles from where his journey had begun.

The basket had come to rest upside down in a thicket, while the deflated balloon dangled from the branches of a towering silver maple. There was no sign of the contraption that fired the mechanism that kept the balloon aloft. Whatever it was, it had been lost in the plummet to earth.

"'Tis of no consequence," he said, heading for the footpath that led to the house. His chance to leap forward through the centuries had passed him by. He tried to tell himself it was not meant to be, but the words held cold comfort.

He would inquire of his whereabouts, partake of a cool cup of water, then be on his way. If he put a good foot under him, he might be able to reach the lighthouse before nightfall. He had much he wished to discuss with Emilie and Zane.

There was an odd smell to the air, he noted as he made his way along the path. The wet, rich smell of rotting leaves and earth mingled with something heavy and sharp, something he'd never smelled before. Smoke? The tang of pine teased his nostrils but not the sting of burning wood. This was something different, something that made his eyes feel scratchy and his throat ache.

He glanced up through the canopy of trees. Indeed, the sky held a yellowish tinge that was unfamiliar to him. He was not a man who spent time contemplating the wonders of the natural world, yet even he could see that all was not as he knew it should be.

The balloons, he thought. Fires had propelled them into the air.

Surely those fires were responsible for the strange yellow haze that blanketed the sky. He felt a surge of relief that a logical answer could be found to explain the occurrence.

The path narrowed as he neared the house. The hedgerows were neatly trimmed along this section of the path and he noted bundles of firewood stacked equal distances apart. Only a person of great personal wealth would lavish such care on the back end of his property. Andrew found his gut twisting with suspicion. Persons of great wealth invariably found themselves on the side of the British, and he prepared himself for a confrontation.

He had no doubt that the owner would greet him with questions he couldn't answer...and a loaded musket.

Shannon dangled her feet in the swimming pool and waited. The balloon had gone down somewhere on her property and she knew it was simply a matter of time before the hapless pilot made his way to the house in search of something cold to drink, a trip to the john and a comfortable place to wait for the spotters to show up. She knew the drill as well as she knew her own name and she dreaded it.

The fact that she was alone at the house didn't disturb her, although she supposed it should. Mildred and Karl, the couple who took care of things, had the summer off and, for a welcome change, the safe houses Shannon maintained for battered women and their children were vacant. Of course, that was a temporary condition. In the next day or two another terrified woman would stare down her fears and take that first step toward an independent life, same as Shannon had more than three years ago.

Walking out the door and leaving the violence behind was how it had begun for Shannon. Facing her husband across that crowded courtroom and speaking the truth for all to hear had freed her from the last of her fears and she would let no one and nothing intimidate her ever again. Not even the fact that Bryant had been paroled six months ago was enough to rob her of her independence.

If only it was that easy to conquer the aching loneliness deep inside her heart.

Every now and again she managed to convince herself that she'd grown accustomed to being alone, to being satisfied that what she had was all she'd ever need. But then she would see a man and woman walking hand in hand or hear the soft laughter of lovers and she'd be struck anew by how the best part of life continued to elude her.

And probably always would.

A difficult truth but one she could no longer deny. She was almost thirty. She had been married and divorced. She had learned firsthand that when it came to the rest of your life you didn't settle for anything less than the man of your dreams.

The fact that the man of her dreams existed only in her imagination was proof positive that she'd end her days alone. She wanted a man of strength and character. A man who could take charge of a situation without losing sight of her needs and desires. A man who would love her above all else and recognize the gift she gave when she loved him in return.

All in all, she might as well pray for Aladdin's lamp and three wishes because that was the only way she could ever conjure up such a paragon of masculinity.

She heard a rustle of branches, then turned toward her right. A man stood in the shadow of the silver maple tree.

"Took you long enough," she commented as he moved into the waning sunshine. "I was about to give up on you."

He strode across the lawn toward her as if he owned the property and everything on it. He was clad in a scruffy version of some old outfit from the Revolutionary War period: faded brown breeches, a rough shirt of tan cloth, a leather waistcoat and worn boots. As costumes went it was almost painfully authentic. She found herself wishing for a touch less realism and a bit more theatricality.

He stopped some ten feet away from her and stared down as if he'd never seen a woman before.

"Doesn't anyone in that blasted balloon club of yours understand the concept of private property?"

His gaze moved from her face to her breasts and belly and for an instant she wished she was wearing a sedate maillot. She rose to her feet and threw back her shoulders, daring him to challenge her right to make the rules for her own land.

The lass was nearly naked. She stood there with the stance of a warrior, almost daring him to look at her. Had she no modesty? The sight of her body, barely covered by the narrow strips of yellow fabric, enflamed him with desire unlike anything he had ever known. Heat, dark and dangerous, threatened to overcome years of civilized behavior and turn him into a rutting stallion.

May the good Lord forgive him, but he wanted nothing more than to strip the lass of her garments and have her right there in full view of God and man.

Where Emilie had been tall and strapping, this woman was small and finely made, but he sensed that she was not a woman easily bested in any way. This was a woman a man courted, not one you lay down with then forgot come the morrow.

With great difficulty he tore his eyes away from the splendor of her ripely curved body and glanced at his surroundings, and what he saw made his heart beat even faster. That wasn't a pond as he knew ponds to be. Not only was it a perfect rectangle filled with bright blue water, but a long wooden board extended out over one end. White stripes were faintly visible beneath the water.

"Haven't you heard a single thing I've said?" the almost-naked lass snapped. He looked back at her and felt a new rush of desire that rattled him to his bones. "Will your spotters be able to find you?"

Spotters? What in bloody hell was a spotter? "Nay, mistress," he said with deliberate caution. "I come alone."

She tilted her head to the right at the sound of his voice. "A Scotsman, is it?" A long and lovely sigh floated on the air toward him. "I suppose no one told you this property was off-limits."

He nodded. Agreeing with her seemed the wisest course of action until he knew what she was about.

Something was obviously wrong with the poor man. He seemed incapable of stringing more than a handful of words together at any one time and, truth to tell, he was beginning to look a bit the worse for the wear.

"You're pale as a ghost," she said. "Did you hit your head when you landed?"

"I have no wish to cause you alarm, mistress. If you would show me the direction to town I will bid you a good night."

He rolled his *r*'s like a refugee from an old Hollywood costume drama. She'd known a Scotsman or two in her life and they certainly didn't sound like him. Or look like him, for that matter.

"I'm nowhere near town," she said carefully. "You just flew over my house. You should know that."

"A post road, then," he persisted. He looked up at the sky. "Enough daylight remains to cover considerable ground once I find my way."

The poor man *must* have struck his head. He might even have a concussion. She hated to think he was merely dense. "I think you'd better come inside," she said. She'd give him something cold to drink while they waited for his pals to track him down.

No response from him. Why on earth should that surprise her? The man was silent as the tomb. She turned around to find him squatting next to the chaise longue. He was staring at the sections of the Sunday *Times* scattered about the way primitive man must have stared at fire.

She started to say something flip and funny but the words died in her throat. Dear God, but he was magnificent in his own way.

His thick brown hair was pulled back into a ponytail and tied with a strip of leather. His face was craggy, his features rough-hewn. It was the face of a man who had braved the elements and more than one man's wrath. He wasn't handsome by anyone's standards. Still, he was the most compelling male she'd ever seen. His eyes were hazel with flecks of gold, unspectacular as eyes went, but there was something else at work, some indefinable something that stole her breath. He was of no more than medium height but he had about him an aura of such solidity, such strength, that deep inside her heart an ache began that felt much like yearning.

My life will never be the same after today. The thought came to her full-blown, as clear as if she'd spoken the words aloud, and she didn't know whether to laugh or cry. *This is the man you've dreamed about. There is no one else like him in the world.*

She pushed aside the ridiculous thought, the same way she'd learned to push aside her fears. What an overblown, ridiculously romantic notion. The man had fallen out of a hot-air balloon—and gracelessly, at that. He wasn't a knight on a white charger come to rescue her from her lonely life. Obviously she'd watched *Ghost* and *Sleepless in Seattle* one time too many.

It was time for a dose of reality.

They'd go inside, he'd make a phone call, drink some cold water, then he'd be on his way.

And Shannon's life would go on same as it had before he walked out of the woods and made her remember how it felt to want something she could never have.

Chapter Two

2

The evidence was there in front of Andrew's eyes. Printed across the top of each page of the newspaper were the words Sunday, August 29, 1993.

He was not a man given to great emotion, but his hands trembled as he put the paper back down. *Done,* he thought. *The deed has been done.*

The world he knew was naught but a memory, a relic consigned to a chapter or two in a dusty history book. General Washington. Thomas Jefferson. He paused as a huge lump formed in his throat. *Emilie and Zane.*

Gone, all of them, vanished into the mists of time.

For one powerful moment the enormity of what he'd done swept over him, filling him with a sense of loss that threatened to be his undoing. But then his eye was caught by a picture in the lower left-hand corner of the first page of the newspaper. The words beneath the picture made no sense to him: Shuttle Blast Success. Astronauts Eager. But the picture...good God in heaven, what artist had imagined such a sight? A towering structure that proudly angled toward the skies, leaving a trail of fire in its wake.

It was indeed a world of wonders even more heart-stopping than those Emilie and Zane had described. And now he was part of it all.

The last of his doubts vanished in a surge of elation that sent his spirits soaring higher than the balloon that had carried him through two centuries to this place and this time. It mattered little that he had seen other time travelers making similar journeys. All that mattered was that he had accomplished the impossible. He had seized opportunity with both hands and wrought a miracle, and his life would never again be the same.

He sensed the dark-haired woman's gaze intent upon him and looked up. Indeed, she watched him openly, her aqua eyes wide, her expression most curious. Suddenly he felt the need to keep his method of travel to himself, although he could not say why. Despite the evidence to the contrary, Emilie and Zane had been of the opinion that traveling through time in a balloon was an uncommon occurrence. Better to keep his own counsel until he knew the situation in which he found himself.

Would you believe me, lass, he wondered, *or would you mark me for a fool?*

"Did you say something?" Shannon asked.

"Nay, mistress."

"I'm sure you did."

"Nay," he said. "'Tis your imagination."

"No," she replied. "You said something. I heard you."

He said nothing.

You're losing your mind, Shannon thought. *Look at the way he's watching you, as if you were certifiable.* She slipped into her terry robe and pulled it close to her body, though she didn't know why she bothered. The Scotsman made her feel exposed in a way that had little to do with bare skin. There was no accounting for the odd sensation that had gripped her at the first sight of him striding across the lawn as if it was his name on the mortgage instead of hers.

The accent, she thought. *If he didn't have that accent I would've sent him packing.* She'd always been a sucker for a man with a burr.

"You can bring the paper inside with you," she said in a dry tone of voice, meant to hide the rapid thudding of her heart. "I don't mind."

"'Tis most interesting," he said, straightening up.

"Apparently so." She noted the way he clutched it close to his chest. "I don't suppose they have anything like the *Times* where you come from."

"Nay, mistress. We have naught to compare."

"What on earth is with this 'mistress' bit, anyway?" She felt suddenly contentious. "A bit archaic, don't you think?"

Again that look of uncertainty, which was so much at odds with the aura of raw masculinity that he projected with so little effort. "I have no knowledge of your Christian name."

She couldn't hold back a soft laugh of surprise. "Shannon Whitney."

"Andrew McVie." He inclined his head. "Would you be married, lass?"

"I have to hand it to you Scotsmen. You certainly don't waste any time."

He looked at her blankly.

She felt her cheeks flush with color. "I was married. I'm not any longer."

"A widow."

"No," she said, "a divorcée."

"'Tis an epidemic."

"What is?"

"Divorce," he said, shaking his head. "Mistress Emilie and Rutledge were torn asunder by the malady. How is it that marriage has fallen into such disfavor?"

"Welcome to the nineties," she said, again struck by the feeling he was unlike any man she would ever know. "Half the marriages in this country end in divorce."

"Such a thing is not possible."

"Good grief, McVie. What rock have you been hiding under? I can't believe it's that different in Scotland."

"How is it you believe I know of life in Scotland?"

"You're certainly not from New Jersey."

"I was born north of Boston."

"I know Boston accents and that isn't one of them."

"I speak the truth."

She sighed. "I'm sure you do, but why is it I have the feeling we're having two separate conversations here?"

"Mistress?"

She waved her hand in the air between them. "Never mind." The man had crashed into the trees a few minutes ago. Was it any wonder his conversation didn't quite track? "Let's get you a chair and something cold to drink." With a little luck his people would spot the balloon and come to fetch him before nightfall.

"Aye," he said. "'Twould be most agreeable."

The man was a bundle of opposing forces. One second she was certain he was coming on to her and the next he was bemoaning the prevalence of divorce in America. He was as solidly built as an oak tree, yet she sensed a vulnerability in him that touched her in a way little else ever could have.

All of which was patently absurd. She didn't know the slightest thing about him, save for the fact that he was one of those hot-air balloon enthusiasts who drove her nuts every summer like clockwork. So what if he had a delectable accent? So what if he was built like a powerful oak tree? If anyone knew the utter unimportance of externals it was Shannon, and she'd be doing herself a favor if she kept that fact uppermost in her mind.

"The necessary," he said. "Where would it be?"

"The necessary?"

"The privy, mistress."

"The bathroom. Why didn't you just say so? There's one down the hall near the kitchen."

A privy inside the house, near the kitchen? Andrew's stomach roiled at the thought.

Surely the lass had misunderstood him. He followed her along the stone path to the door at the side of the house. A wooden structure that looked a great deal like a privy stood not far from the striped pond with the bright blue water. He started to say something to mistress Shannon, then remembered the wonders Emilie and Zane had told him about and he held his tongue. Mayhap there were more miracles to be discovered.

The dark-haired woman's hips swayed in a most agreeable fashion as she walked and Andrew didn't find it difficult to remember how she looked beneath the short white robe. Her fingernails were painted a soft shade of pink and to his amazement he saw that her toenails were painted thus, as well.

Was this how it was in the future, then, where even something as unimportant as a woman's toenails received an artist's attention? And, even more astonishing, he wondered if there were people in this world who made their living providing that attention. He tried to imagine himself kneeling before a woman, paintbrush in hand, but the concept was more lustful than practical and one best put from his mind.

"The back door is broken," she said over her shoulder, "so we'll have to go in through the kitchen. The bathroom's right there."

He was surprised that such a big house didn't have a separate building for the kitchen. No man of wealth would welcome the stench of singed chicken feathers wafting through the parlor. Indeed, it was a most average house, no more or less imposing than the ones he had known in Boston and New Jersey. Made of stone and brick, the house stood two stories high. Three chimneys graced the roofline and a pair of dormer windows looked out toward the woods beyond the pond. The windows were six-over-six, the sashes painted white and in need of some repair.

Andrew felt it difficult to contain his disappointment.

Thus far, except for the rectangular pond and the newspaper tucked under his arm, his surroundings were much as he remembered them. The house he'd shared with Elspeth had boasted a large backyard with a stone wall blocking off the vegetable garden, same as mistress Shannon's.

Mistress Shannon opened the side door then pressed her hand against the wall. Instantly the room was flooded with the light of a dozen suns and Andrew stepped back in alarm.

"Sweet Jesus!"

The woman looked at him. "Are you okay?"

"'Tis bright as midday."

She gestured toward the ceiling. "Recessed lighting."

He leapt onto a ledge and placed a hand against the ceiling. It felt cool against his palm. "Where would the candles be placed?"

"Get down from there, you colossal idiot!" Her voice rose in agitation. "Get your filthy feet off my counter *now.*"

He ignored her. "'Tis a most clever device, but I am of a mind to find the candles."

"And I'm of a mind to call the police if you don't come down from there." She looked around the room as if searching for something to beat him with.

He did as the lass bid. His boots left clods of dirt behind and he brushed at them with his arm. The reddish brown dirt fell to the shiny white floor. She looked angry enough to strike him, and by all that was holy he could not fathom why.

She pushed a chair toward him and motioned for him to sit down. "If you didn't look so dreadful I'd throw you out on your ear," she said. "Sit down while I pour you some iced tea."

The chair was a shiny silver metal, bent into a curving shape that pleased the eye but baffled the mind. He wondered what silversmith had accomplished such an enormous job, for there were five more chairs exactly like it surrounding the matching table. Attached somehow to the metal was a cushion covered in a fabric he'd never seen before. It was slippery to the touch and shiny yellow in look, and when he sat upon it the squeaking noise it made was most astonishing.

She crossed the room and swung open a white door, revealing a closet, also bright as day, that held all manner of foodstuff.

"O.J., milk, there's the iced tea." She removed a big green pitcher then poured the liquid into a tall glass. "Drink this," she said, handing it to him.

He gulped some down then drank some more. "A pallid brew," he observed, "but cold." He wondered how that state had been achieved.

"A simple thank-you is sufficient."

He studied the glass, then the half-filled pitcher. "I see no evidence of tea leaves. Perhaps that is the problem."

"Awfully picky for a trespasser, wouldn't you say? If I were you, I'd drink the tea and keep the opinions to myself."

"'Twas not my intent to criticize, mistress."

The look she gave him brooked no argument. "If you need the john, now might be a good time."

"John?" Thus far he had seen no evidence of a man.

"The bathroom," she said, sounding exasperated. "The privy, as you called it."

He brightened. At last, something he understood. They both spoke English but the variations within the language were extraordinary. He refused to believe she had an indoor privy and pointed out the window. "The wooden structure beyond the blue pond?"

"Very funny, Mr. McVie. That's the cabana." She pointed down the hallway. "Second door on your right."

* * *

"You are one very strange man," Shannon murmured as Andrew disappeared down the hallway. You'd almost think he didn't know what a bathroom was. She'd been to Scotland twice. They had bathrooms over there and overhead lighting and everything else the twentieth century had to offer. Her unexpected visitor acted as if these things were brand-new inventions.

She heard the bathroom door open then close behind him. At least he understood the concept of privacy. When he had leapt up on top of the counter she hadn't been sure civilization had quite reached his rung on the evolutionary ladder.

She looked out the window in the direction from which he'd first appeared. Dusk was washing over the tops of the trees and there wasn't a sign of life except for a blue jay squawking his loud displeasure. You'd think McVie's spotters would have found him by now. In the past it hadn't taken more than ten minutes for wayward balloonists to be retrieved. *Cheer up,* she told herself. Maybe they were collecting his gear at this very moment and would come traipsing across her backyard any minute in search of their cohort.

Of course, there was also the possibility that he'd been fool enough to go up without any backup system at all, in which case she'd just call him a cab and he could worry about his blasted balloon and gondola in the morning. It wasn't like her to let a stranger into her home, especially not when she was alone. From the moment she'd heard him land in her trees her reactions had been completely skewed, as if she were being ruled by her emotions rather than her brain.

Her eyes strayed toward the telephone. Maybe she should call Dakota and let her friend know what was going on.

The idea had some merit and she was about to reach for the receiver when the telephone rang.

"I should've known it would be you," she said as Dakota's familiar voice greeted her. "You do this all the time."

"It's one of the problems with being psychic. My phone bill takes a beating." Dakota laughed. "Is everything okay? I was meditating and kept hearing your mantra."

Shannon, who was not a believer in mantras and things that went bump in the night, cut to the chase. "There's a man here."

"I know," said Dakota. "I could feel it in my bones. Is he friend or foe?"

"Neither. He's a weird Scotsman. If I didn't know better, I'd say he's not part of this century."

"Maybe he's not," said Dakota, who believed in just about everything. "Where did he come from?"

"My backyard," Shannon said with a slight laugh.

"I mean, how did he get there?"

"His hot-air balloon went down in the woods."

Dakota sounded almost disappointed. "One of those guys from the festival?"

"I suppose so." She wished she sounded more certain. The man was in her house, for God's sake, and she hadn't had the brains to ask for identification. What on earth was the matter with her? She was usually a hell of a lot smarter than that.

"Do you want company?" Dakota asked. "I could drive over."

"I'm fine," Shannon said. "But thanks for—" She tilted her head to the side and listened.

"Shannon? What's going on? Are you still there? I'm picking up some very strange vibes."

"He's flushing the toilet. What on earth is the matter with the man?"

"Flushing the toilet is a *good* thing," Dakota said. "It's leaving the seat up that drives me crazy."

"Nobody flushes five times in a row."

"Maybe he's sick."

"Again! That makes *six* times! I don't care if he did hit his head. He can wait for his damn friends in the woods."

"Shannon, maybe—"

"I'll call you later."

She hung up the telephone, her heart pounding double-time. Colorful was one thing. Crazy was another. Normal people didn't flush toilets as if they were playing a Las Vegas slot machine.

Quietly she stepped into the hallway and listened. It sounded as if a plumbers' convention was going on in the guest bathroom. Water ran full blast. The toilet flushed continuously. And above the racket came McVie's exuberant "Bloody hell!"

"Enjoy it while you can, buster," she said, marching toward the drawer where she kept her gun, "because you've flushed your last commode."

It was a miracle, that's what it was. A bloody miracle. Water everywhere and on command! Andrew crouched on his hands and knees and peered into the white marble bowl. A veritable whirlpool of icy cold water swirled about then vanished, to be followed by another whirlpool at the tug of the brass handle.

Then there was the waist-level basin that provided an endless stream of water so hot it caused mist to form on the looking glass behind it. And there wasn't a fire anywhere to be seen. To make matters even more fantastical, the entire wall was a giant looking glass where he saw himself grinning like a jackanapes as he watched the water swirl about the marble bowl.

Nothing Emilie and Zane had told him had prepared him for this surprise. He felt beneath the bowl and touched the cold tubes of metal that disappeared into the wall. Did the water come through those tubes or did it make its exit thusly? And why was it necessary to force water into a room from so many places? What went on in here that required so much water of so many different degrees of heat?

She'd called it a privy but it was not like any privy he'd seen or imagined. There was a seat attached to the white marble bowl and its purpose was obvious, but that splashing water and the loud noise it made had him reluctant to put it to use.

Besides, there was the question of the waist-level basin. There were only so many things a man could do in a privy and none of them had anything to do with looking glasses or fresh flowers displayed in glass bowls.

He opened the doors beneath the basin and stuck his head inside the small cabinet. It smelled of cedar and more roses and he sneezed at the combination. His hand fell upon a container and he withdrew it, holding it up to the fading sunlight at the window. Air Freshener, it read in bold type. The words held no meaning for him. He turned the receptacle over in his hand. Make Your House Smell Like An English Garden. Most peculiar. He sniffed at the container and caught the scent of roses again. He tapped the metal cylinder against the floor but nothing happened. Then he spied the words Press Here on a ridged button at the top.

He did so, sending a cloud of sickeningly sweet flower scent into the room. "Great God in heaven!" he roared. "'Tis a stink unlike any I've known."

His eyes watered as a mist of scent settled across his head and shoulders, and he stood and plunged his head into the warm water flooding the basin. At that moment the door swung open and, through the water streaming down his face, he saw the mistress Shannon standing before him with a pistol pointed straight at his heart.

Chapter Three

3

"'Tis a small gun," Andrew McVie mused, "but I fear it is more deadly than the firearms I knew."

Shannon gripped the pistol with both hands. "Over there," she said, motioning toward the wall. "Put your hands against it and spread 'em."

"A strange request to make of an innocent traveler."

"I'll show you strange. Now spread 'em."

"The words are familiar but the usage is not."

"Oh, for God's sake. Don't you watch cop shows in Scotland?" It had always worked for Angie Dickinson in *Police Woman*.

He looked at her with the blank expression she was coming to know.

"Put your hands against the wall and spread your legs so I can frisk you."

A broad smile spread across his craggy face, making him almost handsome. "Mistress, I am your humble servant."

He did as told. There was something intimidating about all of that raw maleness that was hers for the taking. Not that she wanted to take anything, but still, the whole situation was exciting in a bizarre way.

She stood there, gun in hand, staring at his bold, extremely masculine form. She'd seen Crockett and Tubbs frisk suspects a thousand times on "Miami Vice" reruns, but the thought of doing so herself was daunting.

You have to do something, idiot. Pat him down, at the very least.

Holding the gun in her right hand, she quickly patted him across his shoulders and down his back. She doubted her nerves could take much more. His musculature was impressive, to say the least, and she knew without asking that those muscles weren't the result of pumping iron in front of mirrors in some fancy health club. He'd got them the old-fashioned way—through hard work.

The question was, what kind of hard work?

"Empty your pockets," she commanded. Not terribly original but it was a start.

"Is that part of frisking, mistress? Thus far it has been a pleasurable interlude."

"Just do it!"

"I have nothing of consequence to show."

"That's absurd. You must have something."

He reached into the pocket of his waistcoat and removed a quarter, a cambric kerchief and something he quickly slipped into the waistband of his breeches.

"What was that?"

"'Tis nothing of importance."

"I'll be the judge of that."

He handed her a laminated card. She turned it over. A photo of a pretty, red-haired woman looked up at her. Emilie Crosse, it read, followed by a New Jersey driver's license number.

"What on earth are you doing with this?" she asked, almost afraid of the answer. Maybe he was a carjacker and this was the only piece of evidence that could link him to his hapless victim.

"Return that to me," he ordered.

"I want an explanation."

"I have none I wish to offer."

"Where is Emilie Crosse?"

He said nothing.

She aimed the gun. "I want some answers, McVie, and I want them now."

"You are a comely lass," he observed, "but most unwomanly in demeanor."

She didn't know whether to laugh or shoot him. "I'm standing here with Emilie Crosse's driver's license and it's pretty damn obvious you're not Emilie, so either you start talking now or I'm calling the police."

"You have a sharp tongue, mistress. 'Tis no wonder you and your husband are no longer wed."

"You're really pushing it, mister."

He took a step toward her.

She held her ground.

He took another step.

"I'm an expert marksman," she said. "I hit what I aim for."

"'Twould be a sorry thing were you to miss at such close range."

"You're not funny."

"It is not my intention to be so."

"I'd like to give you the benefit of the doubt but you're making it impossible."

He lunged for the pistol, knocking her right hand to her side. Her fingers flexed open and the gun clattered to the floor. They both dove for it but Shannon threw herself on top of the pistol, trying to ignore the way it dug into her ribs when McVie landed on top of her.

He was strong. Too strong. She felt the sharp teeth of panic as memories crowded against her, but she refused to acknowledge their power. *Take a deep breath,* she commanded herself. *You can han-*

dle this. Three years of self-defense training had to be good for something.

She forced herself to go limp.

He hesitated.

She bucked her pelvis sharply, knocking him off balance, then flipped him onto his back and straddled him, pressing the gun against his Adam's apple.

"This is my home," she said, her voice taut. "I will not let you or anyone else take that away from me. Tell me what you're doing here or I swear to God I'll shoot you from here to kingdom come."

Andrew had no wish to meet his Maker at the hands of mistress Shannon, but neither did he wish the moment to end. The white robe had fallen from her shoulders, exposing her golden body to his roving eyes. Her breasts, covered only by that strip of yellow fabric, rose and fell to the rapid tempo of her breathing.

The delectable curve of her waist was plainly visible, as were her flat belly and womanly hips. Her most secret self was shielded by naught but a band of cloth. And—sweet Jesus!—her naked thighs grasped his hips, so tightly he could feel her muscles straining with the effort.

'Twould take naught but the slightest movement to topple her and regain mastery of the situation, but no man worth his mettle would willingly forgo such a glimpse of paradise.

But there was the look in her wide aqua eyes to consider. This was her home, her land. She deserved the truth even if in the telling he put himself at risk.

"Emilie Crosse was a friend, mistress, and a good wife to the man she loved."

"What are you doing with her driver's license?"

"She has no need of it." *Do not ask more, mistress, for I do not know what that driver's license is about.*

"That's what I was afraid of."

"Nay, mistress, 'tis not a cause for worry."

"Is she dead?" Her voice cracked on the last word.

He considered the question for a moment. In truth, he could but say that Emilie no longer walked this earth, but following that line of reasoning, it should not be possible for him to be drawing a breath in the year of our Lord nineteen hundred and ninety-three. "She was well and contented the last time I laid my eyes upon her."

The lass's relief was obvious. "I don't want to think the worst of you, McVie, but you're making it difficult to get to the bottom of this. All I know is that there was a hot-air balloon festival today and you dropped onto my property. If there's anything else, I'd like to hear about it."

A festival? Was it possible the balloons were used for more than traveling through time? "'Tis a simple explanation," he began slowly, "but I am uncertain if you will accept it with ease."

"Try me." How was it a woman so finely made could sound as forbidding as a man twice her size?

"I am not part of your world."

"Tell me something I don't know."

He frowned, unable to discern her meaning. "I detect a note of irony but fail to understand its source."

This from the man who flushed toilets for entertainment? If he'd spouted Kierkegaard, Shannon couldn't have been more surprised.

"You already told me you're not from Scotland." She swallowed hard. "So where are you from?"

His hazel-gold eyes met hers. "My last home was in New Jersey."

"This is New Jersey."

"I passed much of the summer on a farm near Princeton."

"Princeton isn't far from here."

"Nay, mistress, the Princeton I know is long gone."

Let him talk...you know he's telling you the truth, Shannon.... Don't be afraid....

His expression darkened, yet still she felt no fear. Strangely enough, her courage did not come from the gun but from some inexplicable sense of connection she felt with this stranger.

"When I awoke this morning, it was the year of our Lord seventeen hundred and seventy-six."

A buzzing began in her ears and she shook her head to dispel it. "I must be going crazy," she said with a short laugh. "I thought you said 1776."

"Aye, mistress, 'tis what I said."

The buzzing grew louder and she started to tremble, as well. "That's not possible."

"I am proof that it is."

"You're not proof of anything. You don't look more than thirty-five."

He winced. "Thirty-three the fifth of May last."

"No," she said, beginning to laugh. "If what you're telling me is true, you're two hundred and fifty years old."

"That does not bear closer consideration."

She stopped laughing as abruptly as she'd begun. "Are you telling me you found Emilie Crosse's New Jersey driver's license in eighteenth-century Princeton?"

"Aye."

"Do I really look that gullible?"

"I have no knowledge of that word nor do I wish to upset you, but in truth, mistress Emilie and her husband came back to my time in a hot-air balloon."

"Right," she said, beginning to think of things like rubber rooms and straitjackets. "And you jumped into the same balloon and flew it right into my backyard?"

His face was transformed by his smile. "'Tis the way it happened."

"Give me a break." She stood, making certain to keep the gun pointed in his general direction. "You expect me to believe you used a hot air balloon like some kind of time-traveling cab service?" *He's telling the truth...the unvarnished, unbelievable, undeniable truth....*

"Believe as you will, mistress. I can do naught to convince you, save present the story as it is."

She considered him for a long moment. "Why would anyone in his right mind come to our time?"

"Mistress Emilie's husband described a world of wonder and riches."

"For the fortunate few."

"He said man has walked on the surface of the moon and traveled toward the stars."

"Did he tell you about homeless families sleeping on the streets or old people living alone and in squalor?"

"In the United States of America any man can amass a fortune if he is willing to work hard for it."

He said it with such conviction that her heart seemed to turn over inside her chest. The last time she'd heard such starry-eyed optimism it had been from the Korean grocer in town, who still believed in the American dream. "True in theory but the reality is less rosy."

"You live in splendor," he said, gesturing toward the artwork on the walls, the soft carpet on the floors.

"But I'm not happy."

The words hung in the air between them. To Andrew it seemed as if they had not only sound but form and substance, as well.

"Why not, mistress?" he asked softly. "'Twould seem you have all a lass would need for happiness." If a woman needed more gifts than beauty and wealth and intellect he could not imagine what they might be.

"I don't know why I said that." She turned away from him. "Forget you heard it." The robe she'd used to cover her form dipped low on her shoulders and as she moved to pull it back up he saw a crescent-shaped scar.

He moved toward her. "A knife wound," he said. "How is it you suffered such an injury?"

She adjusted the collar on her robe but kept her face averted. "An old story and a boring one. I'd rather hear more about you."

"Someone hurt you."

"I don't want to talk about this."

"I wish to know."

She turned to face him, a defiant glare in her eyes. "Why don't you call someone? It's time you were on your way."

"'Tis no one to call to, mistress, but I will take my leave if that is your wish."

She felt his words pulsing through her body.

She was wary and he had no stomach for being the cause of her discomfort.

"Tell me," she said, voice low and urgent. "Level with me just once and I'll help you. Don't tell me this nonsense about traveling through time—"

"I can tell you no story but the truth and you must choose what it is you wish to believe."

"It's not that I don't want to believe you," she said. "It's just that I'm finding it difficult."

"I cannot believe man has walked on the moon, yet I am willing to accept it as fact."

"It's not the same thing."

"Mayhap it is."

She shook her head. "'Mayhap.' I really wish you'd stop saying things like that. Nobody talks like that."

"As you wish." He started for the door. *I would not hurt you, Shannon. Not in this life or any other.*

His words pulsed their way through her body, leaving a trail of fire behind. She'd heard his thoughts as clearly as if he'd spoken them out loud. *I would not hurt you...not in this life....* She refused to acknowledge them. Trust and danger lived side by side.

Instead she stood perfectly still, arms wrapped across her chest, and listened to the sound of his heavy footsteps as he headed for the door. *Don't go,* she thought, surprising even herself.

He stopped, hand on the doorknob. "Mistress?"

She looked up and met his eyes. "I didn't say anything."

"I heard your voice most clearly."

"I don't think so."

He swung open the door.

Please stay.

He hesitated. Her heart slammed into her rib cage.

"Damn it," she said finally. "You can sleep in the cabana." She noticed the expression on his face. "The structure beyond the pool."

"You have nothing to fear, mistress. I will not harm you in any way."

"Don't go reading anything into this," she warned in that fierce, warriorlike tone of hers. "It's getting dark, you fell into the trees, I'm just being a Good Samaritan. If you try anything funny, you'll find yourself staring at my gun."

"I have no wish to be funny," he said, confused by her choice of words to describe what was happening between them. "I will take my leave at daybreak."

Too soon.

"Nay," said Andrew. "Not too soon at all. The early morning is the best time to feel the road beneath you."

She stared at him, her face white as a sheet. He'd heard her words but she hadn't spoken them out loud.

Or had she?

"Have it your way," she said, turning away. "Good night."

Chapter Four

4

"Everything's fine," Shannon told Dakota for the third time in as many minutes. *Except for the fact that McVie and I are hearing voices.* "The crisis is over."

"I've been sitting here by the phone for an hour. I ate a pint of ice cream. You should've called."

"I *did* call," Shannon pointed out. "Besides, you should've known I was fine. You know everything else before I do."

"That's what had me worried. The vibes were skewed."

"I beg your pardon?"

"I don't know how else to put it. Every time I tried to concentrate on you, I came up blank."

There is a God, Shannon thought. She was having enough trouble sorting out her own emotions. She didn't need her best friend inside her head, sorting them out for her. "You're not picking up anything at all?"

"Zip," said Dakota.

"Nothing about Mr. McVie?"

"Not since we last talked. Total blank."

A weird sensation rippled up Shannon's spine and she shivered. "Has that ever happened before?"

"Just once," said Dakota after a moment. She hesitated, then she added, "Maybe I should come over there and check this guy out. Something's weird. I can feel it in my bones."

"No!" Shannon realized she'd overreacted and tried to step back from it. "I mean, there's nothing to check out. He's gone."

"His spotters came for him?"

"Not exactly."

"What exactly?"

"He's out in the cabana."

"The cabana?"

"There's nothing wrong with the cabana. Running water, a toilet, a chaise to sleep on."

"Why didn't you call him a taxi?"

"You're the psychic librarian. You tell me."

"Very funny," Dakota said, sounding huffy. "I'm worried about you. So shoot me."

"Look," Shannon said, "I appreciate your concern, but I'm fine."

"Right," Dakota said. "I'll call you in the morning."

Shannon hung up the telephone, feeling a weird combination of affection and annoyance. Dakota meant well but she had to realize Shannon was perfectly capable of dealing with whatever life threw her way.

She'd proved that the day she filed charges against Bryant and didn't back down, not even when it grew as ugly as their marriage had been. Not that she'd realized how ugly their marriage was. It took months before she understood that what he passed off as loving attention was really a dangerous obsession. One that had left its marks on her body and on her soul.

She went upstairs and stripped off her bathing suit then slipped into an old pair of jeans and an oversize T-shirt. She wandered back down to the kitchen, moving through the room in a daze, running her hand along the bleached wood countertops and across the shiny lip of the stainless steel sink.

This is a good life, she thought as if trying to convince herself. She had security, solitude and the satisfaction that came from helping other women discover that being alone wasn't the worst thing that could happen to you.

It should be enough.

So why was it she felt a gaping emptiness in her chest where her heart used to be each time she thought about the future and came up blank?

She stood in the solarium and looked out the still-broken French doors at the backyard. It was dark outside now and the temple lights that lined the perimeter of the pool glowed softly against the blackness of the summer night.

He was out there. She couldn't see him but she knew he was there. Maybe Dakota couldn't sense his presence, but Shannon registered it in every nerve and fiber of her body. She carried the sense memory of him in her thighs, the way his powerful body had felt beneath hers, the strange smell of him as they'd rolled together on the floor of the hallway, locked in strange and exciting combat.

Maybe she was going insane. Maybe the reason Dakota couldn't sense his presence was that he didn't really exist. Maybe she'd conjured him up out of her own loneliness and need, created him to fill an empty summer's night.

She caught the slightest movement next to the pool. He stood there, legs apart, hands on hips, looking back at her as she stood in the doorway, watching her watching him. It was like those endless reflections in a series of mirrors where reality and fantasy flash by so quickly that you can't tell where you begin or end.

A crack of lightning illuminated the sky, followed moments later by a clap of thunder. A soft rain spit against the glass.

He doesn't even know enough to come in out of the rain, she thought.

He could go into the cabana and be safe and dry. He didn't have to stand there staring at her as if she was the Super Bowl or something. *So what are you going to do? Make him stay out there like a German shepherd that isn't quite housebroken yet?*

She opened the door and motioned for him to go around to the front and come inside.

"Were you going to stand out there in the rain all night?" she asked as he stepped into the house. "You could have gone into the cabana."

"'Tis different from the rains I know."

"Rain is rain."

"As I would have said but twenty-four hours ago."

"How is it different?"

"The taste," he said. "The smell of it. Indeed, the way it falls upon the skin."

"God help me, but I almost believe you."

"I have no wish to deceive."

"Who are you?" she asked, voice rising in agitation. "One last chance to tell me the truth."

"I am Andrew McVie," he said, his voice echoing in the quiet sun room, "and I have told you the events as I know them to be."

"I don't know why I should believe you."

"Nor do I, mistress."

"You can sleep in here," she said, pointing toward a chaise longue in the far corner. "You already know where the bathroom is."

"Aye." His solemn face split once again in a wide grin and, despite her misgivings, she found herself smiling back at him. "You possess all of your teeth," he observed with a nod of his head.

She started to laugh. "What did you say?"

"Your teeth," he said, gesturing. "They are white and symmetrical and you still possess them all."

"You're serious, aren't you?"

"Mistress Emilie possessed all of her teeth and she was one score and ten. A most wondrous thing in a woman."

"Well, I am almost one score and ten as well, and I not only have all of my teeth but most of them have no cavities."

"And to what magic do you attribute such a thing?"

"Good genes," she said with a shrug. "That and Pepsodent."

"Pepsodent?"

"Toothpaste." She groaned. "I hate it when you give me that blank stare." Was she really going to explain toothpaste to a man who might be pulling the biggest stunt since "Candid Camera"? "Stay here. I'll be right back."

She grew more beautiful with familiarity. Andrew could detect no signs of artifice about her person, simply a most pleasing combination of face and form, designed to delight a man's eye. Although he had been disappointed to see she no longer wore the skin-baring yellow costume, she looked most appealing in men's trousers and a billowy shirt.

The first time he had seen Emilie she had been wearing tight-fitting black trousers that hugged her in a most indecent fashion. Walking behind her had been an enlightening experience. She had explained to him the freedom of dress available to women in her century but Andrew had found it impossible to believe such outfits existed...until now.

He paced the huge and airy room, taking note of the spare white furniture and the way it seemed to hold the faint smell of her skin at its heart. He had believed that knowing Emilie Crosse Rutledge would prepare him for the twentieth-century woman, but he had been wrong.

Mistress Shannon had the delicacy of form with which he was familiar, but she also possessed a strength of body that astounded him. And, as if those opposing traits were not puzzling enough, she spoke with Emilie's disturbing bluntness yet he sensed shadows lurking behind her beautiful aqua eyes that had not clouded Emilie's vision.

"A mistake in the offing," he muttered as he picked up a silky coverlet from the back of the long chair. He had not come forward in time to find love or companionship. The coverlet also carried with it the scent of mistress Shannon's perfume, and he quickly replaced it atop the long chair. He was not a foolish man. He recognized danger when danger was about and he would do well to keep temptation at bay.

Loneliness made a man think with his heart and not his head. For a brief time last summer he had believed himself in love with Emilie when, in truth, he had fallen under the spell of the world she'd left behind.

He would not make that mistake again.

The dark-haired woman glided back into the room. "A toothbrush and some toothpaste." She handed him a flexible metal tube and a long-handled brush with tiny bristles.

He unscrewed the white top of the tube and watched, fascinated, as a roll of some sweet-smelling white substance oozed slowly out as he applied pressure.

"You put that on the bristles," mistress Shannon said, "then use the brush to clean your teeth." She frowned. "You do know how to clean your teeth, don't you?"

"Aye," he said indignantly. "Soft twigs and a good washrag achieve much the same results."

"Apparently not," she said. "If it did you wouldn't be so surprised to see that I have all my teeth." She stepped back toward the door. "I'll leave you to get some sleep."

"I will see you to your chamber."

She smiled briefly. "That won't be necessary."

"Aye, mistress, 'tis the proper thing to do."

"Now I know you're not from this century," she said, her smile reappearing. "There isn't a man on this continent who'd do that without an ulterior motive." She narrowed her eyes. "You don't have an ulterior motive, do you?"

"Naught but the desire to give you safe passage through the house."

He means it, Shannon thought as he followed her through the hallway and into the kitchen. He was determined to see her safely to her bedroom. She was charmed, despite herself.

She checked to make certain the kitchen door was locked then fastened the chain, aware all the while of his intense scrutiny. "I'm going to set the alarm," she told him as she punched in the code. "You'll hear a loud—"

A high-pitched wail filled the room and McVie swore in surprise.

"A loud noise," Shannon finished.

"What in bloody hell is that?" he demanded.

"A security alarm."

"I do not understand."

She pointed to the device, wondering why she was explaining the system to a man who might—just might—be as much a product of the twentieth century as she was. "There are units at all of the windows and all of the doors. If someone tries to break in, an alarm sounds and the police are called automatically."

"There is danger abroad? A war in progress?"

"Not the way you would think," Shannon said, "but most home owners take special care these days."

He grew silent. She could see the consternation in his eyes.

"You need a man's protection," he said at last.

"No," said Shannon. "That is the one thing I don't need at all."

He followed her into the living room and watched as she checked the alarm at the window. "No child's toy can provide safety."

She marched into the foyer and set the alarm at the front door. "I don't expect it to provide safety. I expect it to alert me to trouble." She met his eyes. "My gun will do the rest."

"And what if a man wrested the pistol away from you?"

"I doubt if that could happen."

"It can and will happen, mistress. You are strong but slight of frame. You can be overpowered."

"Like hell," she snapped. "You couldn't do it before."

"I did not try."

"Right," she drawled. "You just like having pistols jammed into your Adam's apple."

"Trust me in this regard, mistress Shannon."

"I'm a brown belt in karate."

"I have no knowledge of belts. I only know that you are at a natural disadvantage."

"If I felt like it, I could throw you to the ground before you drew your next breath."

He laughed in a most infuriatingly male fashion. "A most unlikely possibility."

She darted toward him, off balance in her eagerness to show him exactly who was boss. Three years of training went right out the window as she tried to topple him to the ground without the proper leverage, concentration or control.

Basically it was like trying to topple an oak tree with her bare hands.

"Damn you!" she panted in frustration. "Fall down."

He gripped her by the forearms and forced her to meet his eyes. *I can best you,* his look said, *but I choose not to.* There was no denying his strength or his mastery of the situation, yet she felt no fear.

He held her tightly enough to make his point but at no time did he cause her even the slightest pain. For those few moments she was completely under his control and he was man enough not to take advantage of the situation.

A sense of elation gathered inside her chest as she felt the tension and anger drain from her body.

"Your actions were untoward, mistress," he said, releasing her.

She nodded. "I know that now."

The expression in his eyes shifted and she found herself drawn to him against her better judgment.

"You will have no need of screaming boxes this night," he stated as if it were any of his business.

"I don't understand."

"I will protect you against danger."

She stopped breathing. Literally stopped. Her heart pounded so violently at his words that it hurt to draw air into her lungs.

"Mistress?"

She struggled to regain her composure. "Th-thank you," she finally managed to say.

He followed her through the quiet house, up the staircase, then down the hallway to her bedroom. "Good night," she said, stepping inside.

"I bid you a good night." He inclined his head toward her.

She had the insane urge to curtsy in return, but nodded instead, then closed the door behind her.

Andrew stood in the hallway in front of mistress Shannon's closed door, listening to the sound of her soft footsteps as she moved about the room.

What manner of world was it when women lived alone in fear, forced to rely upon a screaming box for protection? Had she no family or friends to see to her safety and well-being, no one with whom to break bread?

He paced the narrow hall, considering his options. He could go back downstairs and explore this strangely familiar modern house. There was all manner of oddities to discover. He was certain he could pass the night uncovering one miracle after another, until his brain spun with new sights and sounds and possibilities.

But he had made a promise and he was, above all things, a man of his word.

Who hurt you, mistress? he wondered, leaning against her door and closing his eyes. *And why are you alone in this world?*

Chapter Five

5

Dakota Wylie worked as a librarian at the New Jersey Historical Society in Princeton. The library itself was tucked into a corner of the campus near McCarter Theatre. On Monday mornings she usually performed as a tour guide, leading Girl Scout troops and senior citizen clubs through the restored Colonial mansion on Stockton Street that housed the museum.

She wasn't sure if it was serendipity or part of a larger plan, but on that particular Monday morning the museum was closed for repairs and nobody expected her at the library until noon.

Not that anything as insignificant as her job would have stopped Dakota. She'd tossed and turned all night, thinking about Shannon and the unexpected visitor and wondering why on earth she couldn't get a fix on the situation.

Bits and pieces of conversation…the spine-tingling sense of the unknown…the certainty that destinies were being played out right that very minute and Dakota couldn't quite figure out who and where and why. Once she even flashed on a lighthouse and George Washington, two peculiar thoughts that didn't bear contemplation.

By the time the sun finally came up she was a frazzled mass of nerve endings.

Something wasn't right. She couldn't put her finger on exactly what it was, but she'd learned a long time ago to trust her instincts and follow her hunches, no matter how outlandish they might be. Shannon needed her. You didn't pick up vibes about a person one minute then lose them the next, and that was exactly what had happened last night. One minute the whole thing had been as clear as the quartz crystal she wore around her neck, then the next minute her mind screen went blank.

The last time that happened had been with Cyrus Warren from Lawrenceville. She'd been doing a reading for him behind the stacks in the library when his aura had disappeared just like that. That night Cyrus choked on a chicken bone in T.G.I. Friday's right under the placard describing the Heimlich maneuver.

So of course she'd read Shannon's cards over morning coffee then checked the runes just to be sure. Each time all seemed as it should be. Long life. Good health. Wonderful family. But the one thing that didn't quite make sense was when and where this was going to happen.

Try as she might she couldn't pick up a time frame or a setting for the events that would transpire, and she had the strongest sense that it had something to do with the man who had dropped into Shannon's life from a hot-air balloon.

Shannon woke up with a start. Dakota was leaning over her bed, eyes wide with excitement.

"It's about time!" Dakota tossed her the robe that had been draped over the rocking chair. "I was beginning to think he'd slipped you a mickey."

"What on earth—?" Shannon twisted around to get a glimpse of the clock on her nightstand. Somehow the notion that Andrew McVie stood guard on the other side of her door had been as exciting as it was comforting, and dawn was on the horizon by the time she'd finally fallen asleep. "It's not even seven o'clock. Have you lost your mind?"

Dakota, psychic but not subtle, paid no attention. "Get up! I want to meet him."

Shannon stifled a yawn and swung her legs from the bed. "He was right outside the door all night."

Dakota gestured toward the hallway. "Well, he isn't there now."

"What about the alarm? Why didn't it go off?"

"Don't ask me," Dakota said with a shrug. "I came in through the French doors in the back."

"Those doors are broken."

"They aren't anymore."

Andrew.

Shannon darted toward the window and looked out toward the backyard. The surface of the pool was calm. The lounge chairs were undisturbed. There was no sign of life anywhere. A sudden sense of despair threatened to overwhelm her and she could do nothing to keep it at bay.

"He's gone," she whispered, pressing her cheek against the glass. Somehow she'd believed he would be there, seeing her safely into the new day.

"Where did he go?" Dakota asked.

She aimed a sharp look in her friend's direction. "I was hoping you'd be able to answer that."

"Not me," said Dakota. "I can't get a bead on that man, no matter how hard I try." She tilted her head slightly to the right. "He was in this room, though. I can feel him."

"You must be wrong," Shannon said. "He never came inside."

"Yes, he did," Dakota persisted. "I'm picking up some very definite vibes."

"Then you're picking them up from me because he never crossed the threshold."

The look on Dakota's face said otherwise, but Shannon chose not to pursue the issue. Had he watched her sleep? Instead of annoying her, the thought sent a charge of excitement up her spine. There was something unbearably intimate about the image, something both erotic and tender and too tempting for her own good.

"You look different," Dakota said. "Are you okay?"

"Tired." She'd been reluctant to give herself over to sleep. Knowing he was a heartbeat away from her had felt so intoxicating, so *right,* that she'd wanted to savor the moment as long as she could.

"It's more than that. You look...enthralled."

"Good word," Shannon said dryly. "I don't think I've ever been enthralled in my life."

Dakota peered out the window. "Maybe he's in the woods looking for his balloon."

"Or maybe he's gone."

Dakota shook her head. "He's not gone. Not yet."

She looked at her friend. "You don't think so?"

"Absolutely not. His business here is far from complete."

"You make him sound terribly mysterious," she said, forcing an awkward laugh. "He's just some guy from one of those hot-air balloon clubs."

"I don't think so."

Shannon's heartbeat accelerated. "Don't let your imagination run away with you, Dakota. He veered off course and his spotters lost the trail. There's nothing more to it than that."

"You don't believe that any more than I do."

"Gimme a break," Shannon muttered, forcing herself away from the window. "I'm going to go downstairs and start the coffee."

"I'll start the coffee. You get dressed."

"No!" With great difficulty Shannon tried to modulate her tone. She felt a strong and illogical need to protect Andrew McVie, even from her closest friend. "I've tasted your coffee," she said with a quick smile. "I'll do it."

Dakota followed her downstairs, chatting the whole while about auras and vibes and whether or not the New York Yankees would go all the way. Typical Dakota Wylie conversation, and Shannon found herself relaxing. *He's still here,* she told herself as she started the coffee. Dakota had picked up his vibes and, despite her general distrust of all things psychic, she had a grudging and mystified respect for Dakota's abilities. Besides, didn't most people believe exactly what they wanted to believe, no matter what common sense had to say about it?

"Your countertop is filthy," Dakota remarked, drawing her index finger through a layer of reddish brown dust. "What did you do, repot your geraniums in here?"

"It's a long story," Shannon said, pouring them each a glass of orange juice.

"I'm not going anywhere."

She handed Dakota a glass. "He jumped up on the countertop last night."

Dakota's big brown eyes widened behind her granny glasses. "Any particular reason?"

"He—there was something wrong with the recessed lighting."

"So he's a balloonist and an electrician, too? What a guy."

Shannon glared at her friend. "Will you stop it?" she snapped. "The man's weird, okay? Case closed."

She busied herself taking the milk from the refrigerator and finding two clean cups in the cabinet. Dakota wandered over to the back door and looked out toward the pool.

"We have company," Dakota drawled after a moment.

Shannon raced to the door in time to see Andrew McVie dragging a gondola and a deflated crimson balloon from the woods.

"Stay here," she said, wiping her hands along the sides of her robe. "I'll go help him."

She darted out the door, hoping against hope that Dakota would stay where she was.

"Good day, mistress Shannon!" Andrew called when he saw the beautiful dark-haired woman hurrying across the yard to greet him. She wore a filmy, flowing gown and cloak and looked much like the women of his acquaintance...except for the fact that her limbs were plainly visible through the sheer fabric. "'Tis a fine summer morning, is it not?"

"Go away!" she said, her words at distinct odds with the friendly smile upon her lovely face. "Go back into the woods and wait for me to call you."

"I am in need of a place to store these objects," he continued, assuming her greeting was perfectly normal for the year 1993. "It would be most unlikely that I should need them again, but they may help another one day hence."

"I don't give a damn about that blasted balloon," she said in a tone of voice more heated than before. "Just go *now!*"

He looked over her shoulder and saw a woman of medium size running toward them, and he felt his mouth gape open in surprise. She wore a long, flowing skirt in a brightly colored print, a frilly white blouse, heavy black boots that were better suited to a shipbuilder, and a tiny pair of spectacles that Ben Franklin would have favored. Huge earbobs of shiny silver dangled from her lobes, and around her neck and wrists she wore clanking chains of silver and gold. Each of her fingers was encircled with a ring of varying style. Her black hair, what there was of it, was cut close to her head, framing her face in soft curls that were short as a child's. Yet it wasn't the strange hairstyle or the display of jewelry that most amazed him; it was the tattoo of a heart on her right shoulder.

He turned to mistress Shannon. "A tavern wench?"

Shannon groaned out loud. Not even seven-thirty in the morning and already the day had the makings of a disaster. "That's my friend Dakota. She's going to ask you a lot of questions. Don't answer them, McVie, not if you know what's good for you. If people find out, your life won't be worth a plug—"

"Introduce us, Shannon!" Dakota stopped right in front of Andrew. "I'm dying to meet your new friend."

Shannon grimaced. "Andrew McVie. Dakota Wylie." She turned to Dakota. "Don't you have to go to work?"

Dakota smiled guilelessly. "Not until noon."

"Damn it," Shannon murmured under her breath.

Dakota extended her right hand. "A pleasure."

McVie looked skeptically at Dakota's hand, then at Shannon, who nodded.

"An honor, mistress Wylie."

Dakota's eyebrows lifted toward the sky.

Oh, God, thought Shannon. She could almost see Dakota's psychic antennae going up.

McVie clasped Dakota's hand in greeting and Shannon watched in horror as Dakota crumpled to the ground in a heap.

Andrew reacted more swiftly than Shannon. He scooped Dakota up into his strong arms and carried her into the house, while Shannon brought up the rear. *This is a nightmare,* she thought. He had no idea what his life would be like if news of his two-century balloon ride got out.

The tabloids thought they had a gold mine with Charles and Di. Shannon could only imagine what they'd do with a real live Early American with a grudge against the Crown.

Not that Dakota would ever deliberately do anything to harm another living soul. It was just that Dakota was a slave to her emotions, prone to outbursts of psychic gossiping that left mere mortals gasping for air.

"She is unwell?" Andrew asked as he set her down on the living room sofa.

"It's the heat," Shannon offered. "Would you bring me a glass of cold water?" He stood there unmoving. She turned and saw the look of puzzlement on his face and her heart went out to him. "The glasses are in the cabinet to the right of the window—" She stopped abruptly. This was all well and good but it didn't explain how to find the cold water. There wasn't time to detail the inner workings of the refrigerator. "The sink in the bathroom," she said at last. "Turn the handle to the right and pull up for cold water."

He vanished down the hall. Shannon looked down at her friend and wondered what it would take to make Dakota vanish that easily.

A lighthouse with its tower dark...a tall, red-haired woman and a man of size and stature...a sense of danger everywhere, but that danger was mingled with a deeper sense of commitment to a cause...but what cause?

Dakota felt herself pulled back into her body. She fought it the best she could but the force was stronger than her will to resist and her eyes flew open as she struggled to sit up.

"You're not pregnant, are you?" Shannon asked, handing her the glass of cold water.

Dakota took a long sip. "No, I'm not pregnant. You need a man to get pregnant." She met Shannon's eyes. "It was him. His touch."

Andrew McVie stepped into her line of vision. "I am not always aware of my own strength, mistress. I offer my most humble apology."

She glanced at Shannon. "He's not joking, is he?"

Shannon looked decidedly uncomfortable. "We're not accustomed to good manners here," she said to McVie by way of explanation.

Dakota finished the glass of water, then wiped her mouth with the back of her hand. She glared at Shannon. "You know darn well what I'm talking about. It's him. Something isn't right."

McVie tapped his temple with a forefinger, then turned toward Shannon, who looked as if she was barely suppressing laughter.

"She's not crazy," Shannon said. "She just has an overactive imagination."

McVie nodded, and Dakota had the overwhelming urge to knock their heads together just to hear the sound their skulls made.

"I'd like to know what the two of you are up to," she said, bristling with indignation.

"You know I'm only teasing," Shannon said with a smile.

"I don't know anything," Dakota shot back, "except the fact that there are some damn strange vibes around here."

"Vibes?" McVie came closer. "Say again. I am not familiar with such a word."

"I know you're not," Dakota said, "and I intend to find out why."

Chapter Six

6

"Friend or foe?" Andrew asked as Dakota slammed the front door behind her.

"Friend," Shannon said with a sigh. "Strange, psychic friend."

"Physick?"

"No, no. Psychic. She can see the future."

"My mother had second sight," Andrew said in a matter-of-fact tone of voice.

"Dakota has more than second sight," Shannon continued. "Sometimes I'd swear she can read minds."

He fixed her with a steady gaze. She tried not to notice the burnished gold flecks in his hazel eyes. "You chose not to reveal the details of our acquaintance. If she can read thoughts, that should not have deterred her from obtaining the truth."

"I know," said Shannon ruefully. "I'm still working on that one." And thanking her lucky stars for the reprieve.

"Why is it you wish to keep such knowledge for yourself?"

"Because it's a cold, cruel world out there, McVie, and they'd eat you alive."

"I do not understand your meaning."

"People today thrive on gossip," she went on, pacing the living room. "If it got out that you were from another century, you'd be pulled apart by television producers, movie directors, reporters from all around the world. You'd end up a prisoner of your own miracle." And why any of this should matter to her was beyond her.

A smile broke across his craggy face. "You believe I am of my own time, mistress?"

She sighed. "I believe, Mr. McVie. God help me, but I believe."

The fact that she believed him should not have mattered to Andrew. Her belief in his story altered nothing. Yet he knew deep in his soul that with her words "I believe," everything between them had changed.

"Mark me well, I have no wish to be a burden upon you, mistress Shannon. I need only to be pointed toward the town of Princeton."

"You need more than that."

His brow lifted. "Explain yourself."

"Look at you." She pointed toward his garments. "If you went out on the street dressed like that, you'd be arrested for vagrancy."

"In my time the mistress Wylie would be pilloried for her attire." He dared not discuss the wanton yellow outfit mistress Shannon had worn the previous day.

"Then you understand what I'm saying."

He looked down at his clothing. "There is nothing wrong with my choice of garments."

"They're two hundred years old."

"They provide warmth and coverage."

"They're beyond shabby."

His brow lifted higher.

"They are," Shannon continued, spots of color staining her cheeks. "And they don't smell that great, either."

"Mistress, 'tis a difficult task to remain spotless in the woods."

"I understand, but if you intend to make a life in my time, you're going to have to make a few changes." She wrinkled her nose in a comic fashion. "Preferably beginning with your wardrobe."

She was a most disarming lass, even when she was criticizing his person. "I know only one way of dress."

"What about your friend who came from the future? What kind of clothes did he wear?"

"I do not recall in detail, mistress, but that tells me the difference between us was not great."

She squared her shoulders. "And that tells me it's time we begin introducing you to the twentieth century."

"I am most eager to learn."

"There's no time like the present."

"Aye," he said. "Wherever the present leads you."

Thirty minutes later they sat down to breakfast on the patio, and the first lesson began.

"Your table manners are atrocious," Shannon said bluntly. "Don't shovel your food into your mouth."

He looked up from his plate of eggs and ham. "I eat with dispatch and efficiency."

"You eat like a pig."

"This is not Fat George's table laden with silver and china," he observed. "'Tis a common table and I eat like a common man."

"Well, not here you don't. We don't hold our forks that way any longer. You look like you're mining for gold."

He leaned back in his chair and folded brawny arms across his chest. "Show me then how it is, since you hold the key to such wisdom."

"You're right," she said, dabbing at the corner of her mouth with her linen napkin. "I will." She speared a tiny piece of egg with her fork and raised it to her mouth, then made certain to chew at least thirty times. She swallowed, then offered him a dazzling smile. "That, Andrew McVie, is how it's done."

"A man's meal would be cold as ice before it passed his lips."

"A gentleman wouldn't comment on such a thing."

"Hot food should be eaten hot," he observed.

"Agreed," said Shannon, "but you don't have to look like a slob when you're eating it."

"A slob?"

"A pig," she explained. "An untidy person."

He lifted another forkful of eggs and ham. "Do all people comment thusly upon the dining practices of others?"

She thought of Miss Manners and laughed. "Some people even make their living doing so."

"'Tis a strange world," he said.

"Stranger than you know." She rested her fork on the side of her plate. "I think a trip to the mall is in order."

He frowned. "A mall is a public promenade in the center of town."

"It's more than that today." She told him about the collection of enclosed stores and restaurants that comprised Bridgewater Commons.

"Such an enterprise is beyond my ken."

"Mine, too," said Shannon, who had given up power shopping with her marriage. "But there's no hope for it. We're going shopping."

After their morning meal Andrew watched as Shannon stacked dishes in a kitchen cabinet, poured liquid soap into the same cabinet, then closed the door. He was about to ask why she didn't put the dishes to soak in the big sink beneath the window, but she pressed a few buttons and a horrific grinding noise and the sound of rushing water filled the room.

"What in bloody hell—?"

"A dishwasher," she said. "It automatically washes the dirty dishes."

He nodded as if a dishwashing cabinet were an everyday occurrence. A dishrag, hung from a peg, caught his eye. "And then you dry them with a rag."

"No," said Shannon. "The dishwasher dries them for me."

"That cannot be." He crouched in front of the infernally loud dishwashing cabinet. "There are rags inside the cabinet?"

"Hot air."

"Say again, mistress."

"I'm not a mechanical genius but I think hot air circulates through the dishwasher and that dries the dishes after they've been cleaned."

"'Tis a miracle."

"No," she said, "'tis everyday life."

"You mock my speech, mistress?"

"Never that." Her lovely face seemed lit from within by her smile. "Your speech is delightful."

"You have no wish to change it?"

"I thought you were a Scotsman," she said, still smiling. "I imagine others will make the same mistake. Besides, there's great diversity in this country. You'll blend right in."

"You need not be so solicitous of my needs, mistress. I am most resourceful and will make my way through your world."

"Your friends who traveled back to your world," she said, smile fading. "Didn't they need your help?"

"A revolution is being waged," he said. "Danger is afoot everywhere. I did only what I deemed necessary to afford them safe passage."

"I can do the same for you. We're not in revolution, but I guarantee my world is more dangerous than yours could ever be."

He thought of smallpox and influenza, of childbed fever and the losses of wartime. Nothing Emilie and Zane had described to him could surpass those horrors, and he strongly doubted that mistress Shannon could show him anything that would alter his thinking.

"You can open your eyes," Shannon said. "The worst is over."

"Nay, mistress." Andrew's eyes were still tightly closed. "I think not."

"I merged onto thc highway and we're going along in our own lane now." He had accepted the existence of her car with remarkable aplomb. Merging onto Route 287 with an eighteen wheeler jockeying with her for position was another story entirely. "There's nothing to be afraid of."

The poor man looked positively green. Her heart went out to him as he slowly opened his eyes and looked around. *You're incredible,* she thought, drawing her own gaze back to the road. She wondered if she would exhibit one-tenth McVie's courage if the situation was reversed.

"We move with great speed," he observed, color returning to his face. "Is such rapid movement the norm?"

She gazed at the speedometer. The needle rested firmly on fifty miles per hour. "Actually, we're in the slow lane. That guy in the red Porsche's probably doing seventy."

"I have no understanding of porshuhz or doing seventy."

She checked her side mirror and moved into the center lanc. "I can go faster if you want to see what doing seventy is all about." What was a speeding ticket compared to showing off for a spectacular man?

He shook his head. "I see no benefit to moving faster."

"Most men would tell me to go for it."

He met her eyes. "I am not most men."

Oh, God, she thought as her heart seemed to slide into her breastbone. *He has no idea how true that is.* Not in appearance or demeanor or the overpowering sense of strength that seemed to emanate from every pore.

"I find myself wondering how it is you begged me stay."

"I didn't beg you to do anything."

"I heard the words clearly, mistress, from your own lips. *Don't go. Please stay.* Said in a tone of entreaty."

Was it truly possible that he'd heard her thoughts as clearly as she believed she'd heard his?

"Maybe we should forget the mall and take you to a doctor." She tried for a light and breezy tone of voice, but failed miserably.

"I am not in need of a doctor's care."

She moved back into the right-hand lane as they neared the exit to Bridgewater Commons. "Suggesting you stay on a little longer and begging are two vastly different concepts."

"There was deep emotion in your tone."

"What about you?" she asked, tires squealing as she took the exit faster than normal. "It's not like I tied you to a chair to keep you prisoner."

"There was logic to your reasoning. Common sense told me to heed your suggestions."

"Hah!"

"You mark me a liar?"

"You mark me for a fool if you think I'm going to believe that."

"You are a suspicious woman, Shannon Whitney. A most undesirable trait in a female."

"Now there's something that needs work," she said as she stopped for a red light in front of the mall. "That patronizing, paternalistic attitude of yours stinks."

"I am a man," he said. "And I treat women as women."

"In this century men treat women as equals."

"Women are not equal to men."

"The hell they're not."

"Your strength is inferior to mine."

"And my brain is superior to yours," she shot back. "It all evens out."

"We have not tested our intellects to know such a thing."

"Simple logic would bear me out," she said, falling back on male tactics. "My world is more advanced than your world. I am a product of my world. Therefore I am more advanced than you."

"I am a graduate of Harvard," he said.

"Sure you are," said Shannon, heading toward the parking lot.

"And I practiced law in Boston."

She drove the car up onto the curb then dropped down again with a thud. "Right," she said. "And I'm a nuclear physicist."

"You do not believe me."

"A lawyer?" She swung into a parking spot, then looked him full in the face. "Do all lawyers dress the way you do?"

"I have not practiced law since my—" He stopped abruptly.

"Go on," Shannon urged. "You can't drop a bomb like that and not give me the details."

"The details do not matter any longer," he said, his voice gruff.

"I'd like to know."

"My past is dead. I look to build a new life here, in this time and place."

She thought of her own past, the painful details of her marriage, and something inside her gave way. *I've been there,* she thought. *I know how you feel.*

She checked her lipstick in the rearview mirror, then summoned up her best smile. "If you're looking to build a new life, you've come to the right place, Andrew McVie. There's nothing more American than the mall."

Andrew had the profound sense that he had just managed to elude danger. Not the type of danger that broke bones or drew blood, but danger of a more subtle and deadly kind. How close he had come to unburdening himself upon mistress Shannon, telling her of Elspeth and David, letting the endless parade of his mistakes march past her until she knew his soul the way she knew her own face in the glass.

Nay, he thought, casting a glance at her lovely profile. To reveal himself to her would be a mistake of colossal proportions. One he did not intend to make.

He managed to unsnap the bonds that held him in his seat, then pulled the silver handle that opened the door. Zane had done an admirable job of describing an automobile. He remembered the night Rutledge had drawn a picture in the dirt of a square box that rested atop inflatable wheels. Accepting that as a possibility had not been difficult, but then Rutledge had gone on to tell him that the box, called a car, was not drawn by a team of horses but powered by a series of sustained explosions deep within its own self.

"Does everyone own one of these cars?" he asked, taking in the endless rows of such things lined up in the open field behind the enormous building called a mall.

"Almost everyone." Shannon shut her own door.

"How can you find your own amidst the crowd?"

"It's not always easy."

"There are no horses?"

"Sure there are." She started walking toward the mall and he fell into step with her. "But it's expensive to keep a horse."

"And it is not expensive to drive a car?"

"Depends on the car and the driver and the insurance."

"Insurance?"

"Against accidents."

He thought of the thing she had called a truck and the damage it could have inflicted upon his person had they collided. "I do not wish to hear any more, mistress Shannon. I have seen many a serious carriage accident in my time. I can but imagine the result among cars."

He heard a sound behind them and turned to see a group of children of perhaps sixteen laughing and looking in his direction.

"See what I mean?" said Shannon, glancing sternly in their direction. "Those clothes have got to go."

Andrew stopped in his tracks and watched the children pass. "Surely such attire as theirs is not commonplace in this world."

"Biker pants, tank tops, Doc Martens," said Shannon. "Just your average everyday teenagers."

He was not familiar with the word *teenagers,* but its meaning was clear. The only thing about their attire that made him feel comfortable was that the boys wore their hair in much the same fashion as Andrew himself.

"I will not wear those trousers," he said, walking again toward the mall.

"I promise I won't ask you to." They approached the wall of glass doors leading into the mall itself. "You're going to see a lot of strange things, Andrew. I'll do my best to explain them all to you, but it would serve us both well if you let me do most of the talking."

"'Tis not natural for a man to let a woman lead the way."

"And it's not natural to sail through the centuries in a balloon. You're in my world now. Let me help you."

Her words were based on good common sense but they went against the grain. She had seen him in a way no woman should see a man, needful and uncertain. He was accustomed to dominating situations, not looking to others for direction. He was a man, and as a man it was his lot in life to lead.

But thus far not in this world.

And not with this woman.

Which were two of the many reasons he must get about the business of establishing a new life in this new world in which he found himself.

Chapter Seven

7

Andrew made to push open the door, then leapt back, astonished, as it swung open of its own accord.

"Electronic eyes," Shannon said with a groan. "I forgot to tell you about them." She pointed up toward the red light overhead. "It senses your approach and signals for the door to open."

"How?"

"Don't ask me," she said as they stepped inside. "Some of it amazes me as much as it amazes you."

Good grief, what other everyday wonders did she take for granted that could throw McVie for a loop?

Like the crush of people lined up in front of the movie theater to see *Jurassic Park* for the umpteenth time.

"What is it they wait for?" Andrew asked.

"You're not ready for movies yet," Shannon said briskly. Especially not movies about man-eating dinosaurs with major attitude. "Let's get you dressed first."

"Nay, mistress." He walked toward the railing and leaned against it to stare at the skylights overhead. "'Tis an amazing sight, trees growing within a building and reaching for the sky."

"I suppose it is amazing," she said, glancing down at the tiny grove of trees planted in the rock garden. "I never really gave it much thought."

"These are the things Emilie and Zane told me about." He was like a kid let loose in a toy store. He wanted to see and touch and understand everything he saw. "Everywhere I look I see abundance."

They paused in front of a pricey jewelry shop and looked at the diamond rings and Rolex watches.

"You adorn your person with jewels," he commented, looking at her diamond studs and tennis bracelet. "And Emilie arrayed herself in gold and silver. The king of England could not ask for more."

"The *queen* of England," she corrected with a smile. "And, trust me, she can put us all to shame."

"'Tis beyond my ken," he said as they strolled past a card shop, toy store and two more jeweler's establishments. He gestured toward two older women chatting in front of Sam Goody's. "They glitter like foreign princesses. How can it be the average citizen can have such wonders at her command?"

"Now I know why you came forward in time," she said dryly. "You're an eighteenth-century yuppie."

"Emilie had called me thus but I do not remember its meaning." He frowned. "I believe it was not a good thing."

"A yuppie is a thirty-something consumer whose greed outstrips his income."

"You offend me, mistress."

"I didn't mean to." She tried to steer him toward one of the men's stores but he seemed transfixed by the display of maternity bras at one of the women's shops. "It's just if you're looking to understand what we're about, you have to look past the glitter and get to the heart of it."

She started for the escalator then decided that was asking for trouble.

"We can take the stairs," she said, "or—" She stopped. Where was he? A second ago he'd been right next to her, staring at nursing bras. *Think,* she told herself. Where would a man go?

The combined smells of pizza and hot dogs and chow mein wafted down toward her. The food court, she thought, dashing across the corridor. Chinese, Italian, Greek and all-American deli foods, stall after stall of them, there for the asking. How could he possibly resist?

She checked from one end of the food court to the other. She asked counter clerks, customers and the security guard. Nobody had seen an oddly dressed man of medium height who looked as if he'd never seen a mall before in his life.

"Go downstairs to mall information," the security guard suggested. "They'll make an announcement through the P.A. system."

Great idea, Shannon thought as she raced for the down escalator. Great idea for anyone except Andrew McVie, who didn't know a P.A. system from a hole in the ground and might think he was hearing the voice of God at the Bridgewater Commons mall.

Andrew watched as three women with babies walked through an open door, then disappeared. Once a long time ago at a tavern near Boston he'd seen a magician make various items disappear in an amazing display of legerdemain. A lady's kerchief. A half-crown piece. A pack of cards. He had been suitably impressed by the man's talents, but not even that had prepared him for this.

He approached the door. An older woman, arms laden with parcels, waited by the door, as well. Her eyes widened as she took in his apparel, then she looked away. In truth, she looked quite peculiar to his eyes. He had never seen such a display of naked flesh on a woman of such advanced years. Her legs were bare and he could see each and every vein as they coursed up and down her muscular calves. She wore a short pair of men's trousers, a top garment without sleeves or collar, and enough paint on her face to cover the side of a barn.

Madam, he thought with a shake of his head, *wouldn't you be better served at home, tending to your grandchildren?*

Tearing his gaze away from the painted woman, he noticed the numbers above the door and the way they seemed lit from within. The highest number lit up and the doors slid open. A gaggle of children burst forth, followed by their mothers, and two men in strange dark garments that were almost mirror images, each of the other. If Shannon intended for him to dress in such ridiculous attire he would tell her in no uncertain terms how he felt about the matter.

He motioned for the older woman to cross the threshold before him. She seemed surprised but did as he bid her. Two girls of perhaps sixteen entered, as well. Their lanky bodies were clad in tight-fitting trousers of faded blue and half-sleeve shirts that bore the messages U2 and Virginia Is For Lovers. Neither girl had been blessed with bosoms that merited notice but one was slightly more endowed than the other. Beyond that they were as twins, even down to the tiny earrings that glittered at their lobes.

So when the doors closed and the two girls fell upon each other in a heated embrace Andrew was so shocked by their actions that it took him a moment to realize the room he stood in was dropping down in space while music blared from some unknown source.

"Sweet Jesus!" Andrew exploded. "What in bloody hell is happening?"

"Vulgar display," sniffed the older woman next to him, gesturing toward the kissing couple. "Necking in public...dreadful. Simply dreadful."

"Why don't you both chill?" said one of the girls, whose deep voice proved her not a girl at all. "All you old people got a problem with sex."

His companion giggled. "Maybe it's because they're not gettin' any."

"Yeah," said the boy, moving toward the older woman. His arm shot out and some of her parcels tumbled to the floor of the moving room. "Don't think this chick's gettin' any, do you?"

Rage filled Andrew's gut. He stepped forward, wedging himself between the boy and the woman. "You will tender an apology to this good woman," he said in a voice that brooked no argument.

"You and who else're gonna make me?"

Andrew grabbed the child by the scruff of his neck and lifted him off his feet. "You will apologize *now,*" he roared, "or you will have breathed your last."

"Don't let him threaten you, Mike!" the girl cried out. "If he hurts you, you can sue him for every penny he's got."

The boy's eyes flashed fire.

Andrew's grip upon him grew stronger. "Say it," Andrew commanded in a low voice. "Say it now before us or say it before God at heaven's gate."

"S-sorry," the boy managed. "J-just havin' some fun."

The moving room came to a stop, the doors opened, and Andrew fairly tossed the boy from him. The pair vanished into a crowd of people.

"You are a brave man," said the painted lady as he bent to retrieve her parcels. "He could've had a knife. Not many people would have come to my aid the way you did."

"That is difficult to believe," said Andrew, helping her from the moving room. "There was naught to do but offer my assistance."

"Such a lovely accent," the woman said with a smile. Her teeth were white and straight and all there. Another miracle. "Are you from Scotland?"

"Aye," said Andrew with an answering smile. "I am."

A loud voice seemed to fill the mall. "Will Andrew McVie please return to the information booth. Andrew McVie, please return to the information booth now."

His eyes widened. "Sweet Jesus."

The painted woman looked up at him curiously. "Are you Andrew McVie?"

"Aye."

"And you don't know where the information booth is, do you?"

He shook his head. "'Tis a fact I do not." *Nay, madam, and in truth I do not know* what *it is.*

She linked a bony arm through his. "Then let me have the honor of escorting you. It's the least I can do after what you did for me."

"It's only been three minutes, ma'am," said the woman manning the information booth. "It's a big mall. I'm sure your friend will be here any time now."

"I'm not," said Shannon, turning away. Andrew McVie was a strong and independent man, but even he was no match for what the late twentieth century could throw at him. The sheer size of the mall itself must seem daunting to him. He could have fallen down an escalator and broken a leg. He might have wandered outside and been hit by a car.

She buried her face in her hands and groaned as another awful thought presented itself. What if he'd strolled into Lord & Taylor, seen something he wanted and tried to stroll right out again with it tucked under his burly arm? Not only didn't he have any money, the only identification he had was a driver's license belonging to Emilie Crosse who, as far as Shannon could tell, was alive and well in 1776.

A familiar voice caught her attention and she peered between her fingers. Andrew was striding toward her. A sixtyish woman strode right along with him, chattering up a storm. Relief came close to buckling her knees.

"Well, here's your missing friend," said the woman, obviously reluctant to part company with Andrew. "You make sure he tells you what he did back there on that elevator." She reached up and pinched his rugged cheek. "You hang on to him, miss. They don't make men like this anymore."

The woman bustled away and Shannon met Andrew's eyes.

"So, what did you do back there on that elevator?" she asked.

"'Twas nothing another man wouldn't have done in similar circumstances."

"A few more details would be appreciated."

A frown pleated his forehead. "A simple thing. I reminded a boy that elders are deserving of respect."

"How strongly did you remind him?"

"I struck no blows."

"I'm glad to hear that," she said dryly. "I don't know how it is back in your time, but this is a litigious society. Sneeze wrong and you'll find yourself on the receiving end of a lawsuit."

"The girl threatened to pursue such an avenue."

"This is a less...physical world in some respects," she said, trying to ignore the rampant violence that was part of everyday life in so much of the country. "We handle our disagreements with words, not blows."

"You may wish to make that speech to the boy who threatened harm to the elderly woman." He wheeled right, then started walking away.

"McVie!" Shannon tried to catch up with him but he managed to stay a few lengths ahead of her. On purpose, no doubt. "Where are you going?"

He continued walking.

"McVie!" she shouted. "Stop!" *Have you gone mad, Shannon? Don't run after the man. It's his life...and he'll only complicate yours. Let him go.*

But he was alone in the world and lonely. You didn't give up everything you knew and travel to a distant world if you were happy with your life. He didn't realize it, but he was a babe in the woods here. One wrong step and he'd be gobbled up by the twentieth century and forgotten.

She couldn't let that happen.

He was heading toward the exit near First Place. She broke into a run and grabbed him a few yards from the door.

He shook her off and kept walking.

"Andrew!" She darted in front of him, almost daring him to stomp right over her. "Please."

He stopped. "I have no wish to argue with you, mistress."

She prided herself on the fact that she never cried, yet found herself blinking back hot tears of frustration that confused as much as they embarrassed her. "What's wrong? Why are you so angry?"

She looked up at him with aqua eyes wide with emotion and he wondered how it was those emotions had grown so strong, so quickly.

"Andrew?" She rested her hand on his forearm. "Tell me."

"I do not know what to tell," he said, struggling to control the battle of opposing forces inside his chest. "I am a stranger here."

A quick smile lifted the corners of her mouth. "You just realized that?"

"Yes," he said slowly. That moment of near violence in the moving room made it all real to him in a way nothing thus far had.

"You won't be a stranger for long," she said, drawing her index finger beneath her right eye in a quick motion. Was it for him she cried?

"I believed it to be a difference in language and ease," he said, "but there is more to understand than that."

"Poor Andrew McVie," Shannon whispered, meeting his eyes. "Are you wondering if you made a mistake when you came forward to our brave new world?"

"Nay, mistress—" He caught himself. "No, Shannon," he said, pushing the eighteenth century into the shadows. "This is not a mistake. This is where I am meant to be."

She smiled but remained silent and in her silence he read something akin to sadness.

Chapter Eight

8

Dressed in his eighteenth-century attire, Andrew had been an intriguing figure.

Garbed in upscale twentieth-century clothing, he was devastating.

While he would never be a handsome man in the classic tradition, his strong-boned face and powerful form commanded attention, and Shannon experienced a jolt of pure jealousy as the register clerk at the pricey men's store turned on the charm for Andrew, who was now wearing soft brown trousers, a cream-colored silk shirt and Italian loafers. He had expressed serious misgivings about the loafers, convinced they would flop off with the first few steps he took.

The clerk's eyebrows lifted when Shannon whipped out her American Express gold card to cover the purchases, and Shannon's elation was overshadowed only by the look of discomfort in Andrew's eyes.

"You'll get used to it," she told him as they exited the store with their purchases. "I promise you the shoes will stay on. Indians got along fine in their moccasins, didn't they?"

"'Tis not the shoes," he said in a gruff tone of voice. "My indebtedness to you increases each hour."

"Believe me, I have more money than I can spend in a lifetime," she said with a careless wave of her hand. "Don't give it a second thought." Surely her ex-husband never had.

"This is not what I am about," said Andrew, apparently unwilling to let the subject drop. "I have always made my own way in the world."

"But this isn't your world," Shannon countered gently as they walked toward the restaurant. "This is *my* world and until you understand the rules, you'll need someone to help you."

Andrew said nothing until they were seated in a booth. He seemed not to notice the half dozen TV screens that broadcast different sporting events day and night.

"I will pay for the meal," he stated after she ordered hamburgers, fries and Cokes for them.

"With what?"

He reached for the bag that held his old clothing. "This." He withdrew an old pocket watch from within and pushed it across the table.

Shannon held it in the palm of her hand. "It's gold, isn't it?"

He nodded. She noted the way a muscle on the left side of his jaw tightened. She turned it over and squinted to make out the tiny, faded script etched into the case.

"From Elspeth." She looked at him curiously.

"My wife." Such simple words, but the sadness in his eyes was anything but. "On the occasion of the birth of our son."

"Gold?" she said again, her voice rising on the word.

"There was a time when I need not beg for money, Shannon."

"Oh, God," she whispered handing back the watch. No man should have to sacrifice his past in order to obtain a future. "Have I made you feel that way?"

His expression softened. "'Tis the situation that makes me feel this way. I did not intend to be a burden to others in this world. I thought—"

"You're not a burden. You're my—" She stopped. What on earth had she been about to say? *You're my destiny.* Pathetic. Truly pathetic.

"I will leave you tonight."

"No!" The word exploded with the force of years of loneliness behind it. "You can't."

"I must."

She felt angry. She knew it was unfair but the emotion overwhelmed her. "If you believe you have a debt to repay, then repay it." A thought struck her and she seized it eagerly. "You repaired the back doors this morning, didn't you?"

He nodded. "A simple thing. I am surprised you did not see fit to have it done a long time ago. You are not a poor woman, as you told me yourself."

"I have many other things to do with my money," she said. More important things. "But the windows do need to be repaired and painted and the cabana needs a new floor. You could work off your debt and—"

"Done. I will stay until all is completed."

The waitress served the hamburgers, openly eyeing Andrew as she did so, and Shannon barely resisted the urge to kick her hard in the shins.

"There is fire in your eyes," Andrew noted over the French fries.

"It's your imagination."

"Nay, Shannon, I see it quite clearly."

She leaned back in her seat. "I think that waitress likes you."

He followed Shannon's gaze. "She was most attentive," he said with a wicked grin. "Back home a wench such as she would do well."

"Don't get any ideas," Shannon snapped, appalled by her jealousy. She'd never felt that way about Bryant. "Sexual harassment doesn't go over very well these days."

"Men and women draw their own battle lines and those lines are never the same twice."

Again she felt that strong stirring of the blood, a deep yearning toward him that defied her understanding. She took a sip of soda then leaned across the table. "I suppose this is as good a time as any to set some battle lines, as you put it, for us. I mean, since we'll be living under the same roof we should—"

"You have nothing to fear from me, mistress. I have never taken by force something that should be freely given in trust."

She looked down at her hands, clasped on the tabletop, and took a deep breath. "I wish my ex-husband had felt as you feel."

Andrew's gut knotted at her words. All along he'd sensed a deep sorrow about her, a wariness that belied the generosity she had thus far shown him. She was strong and brave, it was true, but those virtues had been won in battle.

"He was harsh with you, mistress?"

"Harsh?" Her laugh held no mirth as she touched the side of her face. "He broke my jaw on our wedding night. Said I had spent too much time dancing with my brother-in-law." She laughed again. "Can you imagine that? My brother-in-law."

Bile filled his throat and he reached for the sweet-tasting brown liquid to wash it away. "No sign of such treatment remains."

"Ah, the wonders of modern surgery," she said lightly. "One thousand and one ways to keep a family's secrets a secret."

"There is more?"

"More than you need to know."

"I wish to hear it."

Her look held a challenge. "Nobody wishes to hear it, Andrew. Not my mother, not my father, not any of my brothers or sisters."

"I do," he said. "I will listen."

"There's nothing much to tell," she said in a flat tone of voice. "I wanted a husband. He wanted another possession to put on a shelf." She moved her hair off her forehead in an impatient gesture.

He noted the diamonds and rubies glittering on her slender hand. "I tried to walk out on our wedding night but he told me he was sorry...he swore he would never do it again...that he'd had too much to drink." Again that impatient gesture. "I loved him," she said simply. "And I wanted to believe him."

"Your family," Andrew said, aware of the way his heart beat fiercely inside his chest. "Why did they not intercede on your behalf?"

"Because Bryant came from a good family. Because he was powerful." She glanced away toward the window. "Because they figured he was the best thing to ever happen to my family, and my little problem was a small enough price to pay for all he would do for us. We had money but he had connections."

"Bloody bastards," he said, slamming his fist down on the wooden tabletop.

"Yeah," said Shannon with a quick smile. "Bloody bastards about says it all."

"Did you never try to escape?"

She nodded. "Once I made it to the check-in counter at the airport." She held her thumb and index finger a hairbreadth apart. "I was that close to freedom when Bryant burst through the doors and swept me out of there."

He couldn't bring himself to ask how she had paid for her attempt at escape but she told him anyway and he knew her words would stay with him until he breathed his last.

"He beat me in the back of the limousine," she said, a faraway look in her aqua eyes. "Punched me again and again.... He was careful not to hurt my face this time...punched me in the shoulders, the breasts, my belly.... The driver kept looking in the rearview mirror but he didn't do a thing. He just kept watching."

His gaze strayed to her shoulder.

"Yes," she said, voice strong. "The knife wound you saw was from Bryant."

A red mist of rage threatened to devour Andrew as he imagined an ugly death for the man who had caused her such untoward pain.

"But you are divorced," he said when he could again speak. "How is it you came to break free?"

"The last time I tried to leave Bryant hired a hit man—someone who hurts people for money—and the police got involved." Her voice gathered power as she spoke, as if in the telling, the story was losing its hold upon her soul. "The hit man was an undercover cop—policeman—and they offered me a deal. They would help me to fake my death, then lead Bryant into a trap.

"It was dicey, but it worked. I found out they weren't as interested in helping me as they were in arresting Bryant for his involvement in some drug-smuggling scheme out of the Bahamas. They needed to get him out of circulation so they could break down the chain and put them all out of business. He plea-bargained it down to five years and was paroled the beginning of this year."

"He walks free? I would have consigned him to a cold and lonely grave."

"It doesn't much matter," she said. "I'm safe now."

"How is it that you can say with certainty neither he nor another in his employ will threaten your person?"

She hesitated. "I became a different woman."

"I do not understand."

"I did what you did, Andrew. My old life no longer fit and so I found a new one."

"You left your home?"

"I left everything. My home. My family. My friends. I even left my old identity."

"You are not Shannon Whitney?"

"I am," she said, her voice strong with certainty. "I am more Shannon Whitney than I ever was the woman I used to be. Katharine Morgan doesn't exist any longer and I'm not certain she ever did."

He felt himself wishing he could find the man who had hurt her and rip the man's lungs from his body. His own body ached with her pain. The image of her laid low by a man's hand was enough to drive all reason from his brain and send him out in search of blood.

"I hear all that you have told me and yet, despite all, you opened your home to me. It is beyond my understanding that you would find it in yourself to trust a stranger."

She met his gaze full on. "It's beyond mine, too, yet I feel that we are…connected in some way."

"Aye," he said slowly. "'Tis nothing I want or need, yet I cannot bring myself to leave."

Her hands rested together on the tabletop. His right hand lay mere inches away.

"You don't have to leave," she said in a soft voice. "Not until you're ready."

He covered her hands with his and for a moment he felt whole again and hopeful, the way he had when the world was young and his whole life stretched out before him, all shiny and new.

No one in the restaurant thought it strange when Shannon paid the bill for their lunch. Andrew had felt most uncomfortable when she reached into her purse and produced the same shiny gold rectangle she had used to pay for his clothing. The serving wench took it and the bill and disappeared into the back.

"I believe that rectangle is some form of currency," he said, "yet it is returned to you unaltered each time you give it away."

Shannon smiled, and it was good to see the light of humor in her sad eyes. "It is a form of currency," she said, "but not in the way you think." She went on to explain a system of credit that seemed to put a great store on faith among strangers.

"And all of this is accomplished using the post?"

"Sounds unbelievable, doesn't it?"

"The post in my time was most unreliable. A letter might take seven days to travel from Philadelphia to New York."

"Still does." Her eyes twinkled. "Some things never change."

Her good humor should be of no consequence to him. She was neither wife nor lover. Their acquaintance was too new to call her friend. Yet the sight of Shannon, face aglow with laughter, lit a fire deep inside his soul that would not be extinguished. He wondered what it would take to keep her thus all the days of her life.

More than you could ever provide, he told himself as they walked outside to her car. She was from a world of ease and wealth, a world he wished to call his own one day. But until the time came when he could walk through that world as an equal in privilege she could be naught but a dream.

He began to cough as they made their way toward the place where they had left the car to rest.

"'Tis something most disagreeable," he said, rubbing at his scratchy eyes. "Never have I encountered air with such characteristics."

"Pollution," said Shannon, jingling the keys she held in her right hand. "I never notice it here, but when I go up to Manhattan I can't breathe without coughing."

"What is the origin of this pollution?"

"Something called the Industrial Revolution."

"I have not heard of that particular uprising."

She laughed, but not unkindly. "It isn't an uprising, Andrew. It's more of a result than anything else. When we get home I'll sit you down at the computer and let you do some exploring."

"Emilie remarked once about a cum-pyoo-turr. It is an object that thinks like a man but has not emotion nor intellect."

Her eyes widened. "I'm impressed. What else did Emilie tell you?"

"About metal birds that carry men through the skies and talking boxes and pictures that move and have sound and music."

"She covered a lot of territory, didn't she?" Shannon muttered. For a moment he thought he saw a flash of jealousy and his heart soared, but that was absurd.

Shannon opened the doors to her car and Andrew was about to climb inside when she motioned for him to stop.

"Look!" She pointed toward the sky. "You're about to see one of those metal birds your pals told you about."

He craned his neck and looked up, squinting into the bright sunlight. He saw muted blue sky and some cloud cover and little else.

"Do you hear that noise?" Shannon asked. "That's the plane. It'll probably break through the clouds any minute."

He watched and waited, heart pounding in anticipation, and then when he was about to give up he was rewarded with a glimpse of something silvery and sleek, moving majestically across the heavens. It seemed a thing apart from man, as if it had sprung wholly from imagination and needed no help to stay aloft.

"Probably heading for Newark," Shannon said, watching him. "It's a 747."

"What is that?"

"A huge plane that became popular in the late sixties, early seventies. It carries three hundred people."

"That cannot be."

"I should take you to the airport," she said. "Hundreds of planes take off and land every day of the week."

"Such an adventure must be only for the wealthy."

"Not at all," said Shannon. "I'd bet most men and women in this country have flown at least once."

That statement was beyond his comprehension, and when the plane vanished into the clouds he climbed into the car feeling acutely aware of how little he knew about this world.

It was devilishly hot in the car and he grimaced as the metal buckles on the seat strap burned his fingers. He wondered how a strap could save his life in the event of catastrophe but decided to cast his lot with the future and hope for the best.

"It's a beautiful day outside." She inserted a key beneath the wheel and the car came to life. "We could go home if you like, but I thought there might be some place you'd like to see." She hid her eyes behind shadowed spectacles. The urge to pull them from her face was strong but he resisted. "The airport, maybe, or Philadelphia."

He considered her suggestion. "I believe you said Princeton is not far."

"Ten miles or so."

"I would like to see it." So much had happened near Princeton. In his mind he could see the Blakelee farm, the spot in Milltown where he and Emilie and Zane had spent a night. So much of his life was tied into that small parcel of New Jersey land.

"Sure," said Emilie. "I'll show you Nassau Hall and Morven and Bainbridge House—"

"I'd like to see Princeton," he said again, "but not today."

She lifted the glasses and rested them atop her head. "Why not?"

"There are windows to be repaired and other chores to do," he said, "and if I am ever to be free of debt 'tis time I started."

He needed to remind himself that he had come forward in time to find purpose for his life.

And not to fall in love.

Chapter Nine

9

Dakota smiled at the young girl with the green-and-white-striped socks and triceratops T-shirt. "You'll find everything you ever wanted to know about the New Jersey Devil in our folklore section in the east wing." She handed the girl a flyer. "Our map will help you find the right section."

The girl scurried off with her mother, a woman who was obviously at the end of her summer-with-kids rope. It happened every year like clockwork. Only the most dedicated researchers visited the historical society from June to August 15, then bam! Parent after parent trooped their offspring through the society's hallowed halls in an attempt to amuse children who had overdosed on summer fun.

As far as Dakota was concerned, you didn't need to be psychic to recognize a lost cause when you saw it.

You either loved history or you didn't. For some people the sweep and romance of the past was as dead as yesterday's newspapers. They didn't hear the music or feel the passion or understand the fluid nature of time itself.

Dakota did. For her the past, especially the revolutionary war past, lived side by side with the present, turning her days into a rich blend of what was and what had been.

Which was why she'd spent most of the afternoon up to her elbows in documents dating back to the summer of 1776.

Not 1775.

Not 1777.

Seventeen hundred and seventy-six.

And she wasn't reading about the Declaration of Independence or any of the things most people associated with that time period.

She was looking for anything she could find on Andrew McVie.

"You're losing it," she muttered, reaching for another huge volume of town records from the time. *You meet a perfectly normal man—if you don't count the way he talked—and suddenly you're convinced he's a time traveler.*

Dakota believed in the energy of crystals, the power of runes, and that being a Gemini gave you license to change your mind as often as you liked. She saw auras. She read minds. And now and again she had the unshakable feeling that just because she was born in the latter half of the twentieth century, that was no reason to believe she belonged there.

But real, live time travel? That was pushing the edge of the envelope, even for her. When you started playing around with the laws of physics, the logical side of her brain—underappreciated though it was—kicked in and yanked her back to reality with a thud.

She was too much her parents' child. Her father was a professor of physics, cursed with a brain that saw the inherent logic in everything from mathematics to MTV, while her mother adhered to the chaos theory of existence: sooner or later something incredible was going to happen and she intended to be ready to enjoy it when it did.

The four Wylie children were an odd mix of 4.0 grade point averages and enough ESP to turn the world on its ear. Frederick

Wylie had been telling his children to plan for the future since they were old enough to understand the words *bank balance* and *career.* Ginny Wylie had just smiled and told them bedtime stories about Atlantis and spaceships to Mars. "Life is short!" Ginny had exhorted. "When adventure comes knocking, fling open the door."

So what was Dakota doing searching for McVie's name in every yellowed, mildewy old book she could find?

"Because I've lost my mind, that's why," she said out loud.

"Ms. Wylie!" Dr. Forsythe, head of the museum, glared at her from across the room. "Shh!"

Shh? I'm twenty-six years old and you're telling me to shh?

She hadn't been shushed since seventh-grade study hall. No wonder Forsythe's aura was so gray and forbidding. The man had the soul of a bureaucrat. Auras were funny things. Most people didn't believe they existed, but they did. And they were as individual and precise as fingerprints. All Dakota had to do was see an aura once and—

That's it, she thought as her heart rate doubled. *Auras.* Or the lack of them. That's what had been bothering her since she'd first seen McVie dragging that red balloon across Shannon's backyard.

She closed her eyes tightly and reconstructed their morning encounter. She conjured up the rugged face of Andrew McVie and studied his features one by one. Nope. No aura. Not even a glimmer of one. She would have settled for a faint hint of gold, a touch of pale blue, the slightest wash of red, but there was nothing.

Her heartbeat speeded up yet again. And that wasn't the half of it. The man had a force field around him that wasn't to be believed. Talk about the thunderbolt. He'd clasped her hand and she had felt as if she'd been hooked up to a major source of electricity and all of that power was zapping its way through her.

You'd think power like that was sexual but it wasn't—at least, not with her. It was something different, something harder to define, as if the entire chain of history had followed him to this time and place.

"Ms. Wylie!"

She started at the sound of Dr. Forsythe's nasal voice next to her left ear.

"Good grief," she said, hand to her throat. "Did you have to sneak up on me like that?"

"I asked you the same question three times, Ms. Wylie. Have you located the master directory of casualties under General Mercer during the Battle of Princeton?"

"No—I mean, yes." She shook her head to brush away the cobwebs. "I mean, I'll find them for you."

His bushy gray brows knotted together in a disapproving frown. "We don't pay you to daydream, young lady."

She scowled back at him. *And you don't pay me enough to live on, either.* If it wasn't for working the psychic fairs on the weekends and private parties on Monday nights, she'd be living in Shannon's cabana along with Balloon Boy.

She rummaged through the tower of papers on her desk and found the information Forsythe was looking for. Being psychic helped a lot when you thrived on disorganization, chaos and a deep-rooted love of the unexpected. She tucked the papers under her arm, then marched into his office.

"Here you go," she said, tossing them down on his meticulously clean blotter. "I'm going home for the night."

He glanced at the eight-day clock on his credenza. "It's only four forty-six."

"I have a headache," said Dakota, which wasn't that far from the truth. "I want to go home and take care of it."

Ten minutes alone with Andrew McVie—without Shannon hovering around like a too-protective mother hen—should do it.

"I thought you'd be more surprised by the radio," Shannon said, vaguely disappointed, as the last strains of "Surfin' USA" by the Beach Boys faded away.

"Emilie told me about such things."

Shannon made a face. “And I suppose she taught you the words to ‘Doo Wah Diddy’ in her spare time?”

“In truth, she did. ’Twas part of the plan to save General Washington.”

She looked over at him. He wasn’t smiling. “Are you pulling my leg?”

“Nay, mistress. My hands are nowhere near you.”

“I mean, are you…making sport of me?” A phrase directly out of an old costume drama on cable television. *Okay, Hollywood, let’s see how good your research is.*

“I tell the truth.” He started to sing the words to the old sixties rock song and Shannon slammed on the brakes. All around her on the highway horns blared and tempers flared.

“Sweet Jesus!” Andrew roared. “Is it death you’re courting?”

Embarrassed, she signaled then moved over to the slow lane. “Warn me the next time you decide to do something like that.” She wondered if her heartbeat would ever return to normal. “Do you have any more surprises like that up your sleeve?”

He launched into a rousing version of “Jingle Bells” that soon had her laughing out loud.

“You’re a man of many talents, Andrew McVie.”

“Aye,” he said with that grin she was coming to know, “but those talents did naught for the cause. His Excellency was already departed when I reached Long Island.”

“His Excellency?” She signaled again to exit the parkway.

“General Washington.”

“You called him ‘His Excellency’? Good grief, I thought the whole idea of the Revolution was to get rid of royal titles and everything that came with them.”

“I can say naught that will explain such a thing to you.”

She rolled to a stop at a red light. “I can’t believe I’m having this conversation, but what happened when you got to Long Island and found Washington had already left?”

"I went to the Grapes and Ale and downed three tankards."

She started to laugh. "Really?"

He nodded. "Aye."

The more things change... "So what happened with Washington? Did someone really try to kill him?"

"You have little knowledge of history," he observed.

"Guilty. It was never my favorite subject." Although it was beginning to take on dimensions she'd never dreamed.

"The people of Crosse Harbor believed me a hero for saving His Excellency's life but 'twas Zane who did the deed."

"Well, so what?" she said with a snap of her fingers. "Who cares what it says in some stuffy old history book? Nobody pays any attention to them, anyway."

"You do not worry about your place in history?"

She laughed as she turned onto the street that led to her house. "My place in history? I won't even be a footnote, Andrew. This world's a much bigger place than the world you left behind. Most of us will live and die and the world won't even know we were here."

A harsh observation, perhaps, but better he knew what he was dealing with.

For some reason Andrew seemed surprised to find the balloon and gondola still on the lawn in Shannon's backyard.

"Did you think it was going to reinflate and fly away?" she asked, casting him a curious look. "That's where you left it this morning."

"This is not the way it was for Emilie and Zane." He began gathering up the balloon into a manageable parcel. "It vanished when they crashed into the water."

"Obviously it didn't vanish permanently," she said, "or you wouldn't be here."

"There is something different about it," he said, staring down at the billowing crimson fabric. "It seems...paler. Faded."

"Wouldn't you look faded if you'd traveled across two hundred years?"

"'Tis more than that," he said, obviously disturbed. "We were gone but part of the day and the change is noticeable."

She inspected what she could see of the balloon and shrugged. "I don't see any difference."

"Aye," he said. "The difference is there, Shannon, but the meaning is beyond my ken."

Without the balloon he was trapped there forever. Her elation made her feel almost guilty. "Nothing about this entire situation makes any sense. Why should this be any different?"

"Because it is," came a third voice.

They both turned around to find Dakota leaning against the weeping willow tree.

"Don't you ever knock?" Shannon asked in exasperation.

Dakota rapped three times against the trunk of the tree. "So, are you guys going to come clean or do I have to get down on my knees and beg?"

"You're not going to start again, are you?" Shannon's hands itched to wrap around Dakota's throat.

Andrew continued to calmly fold the balloon into a neat package as if the end of life as they knew it wasn't rapidly approaching.

Dakota moved closer to Andrew. She was openly staring at him, her psychic antennae all but flapping in the breeze.

"Dakota." Shannon's voice sounded a warning.

"You don't have an aura," Dakota said to Andrew. "It took me a while to figure it out, but that's what bothered me when we first met. It isn't every day you meet someone without an aura."

"I do not know what an aura is, mis—"

"You must excuse Andrew," Shannon said, feeling like a guilty rat for holding out on her closest friend. "He's not from around here."

"I picked that up pretty quickly," Dakota said with a short laugh.

She leveled a sharp look at Shannon. "If you tell me he's from France, I'll brain you."

"He's from Scotland," Shannon said, once again realizing just how easy it was to lie.

"I don't believe you," said Dakota. She turned back to Andrew. "Okay, so you don't know about auras. I can handle that. Half the people I work with-don't know about auras. But the way you talk, this faded balloon—"

"You see the difference?" Andrew asked. His intensity was almost visible. "You see that the color has faded?"

"Of course I see the difference," Dakota said with an impatient gesture. "How can you *not* see the difference? It was a lot darker this morning."

Andrew looked as if he wanted to sweep Dakota into his arms and kiss her. "It is not a product of my imagination," he said to Shannon.

"I never said it was your imagination." She glanced uncomfortably in Dakota's direction. "The sun was strong today. It faded the fabric. Things like that happen."

Dakota ignored her and focused on Andrew. "Take my hand," she ordered him.

"Don't," Shannon said to Andrew in a clipped tone of voice. "Pay no attention to her."

Dakota held out her hand. The multitude of silver and gold rings on her slender fingers glittered in the sunshine.

"Please, Andrew," Dakota said. "I need to know."

Shannon stepped between the two of them. "There's plenty of room in the garage for the balloon and the gondola," she told Andrew. "Put it wherever you like."

He looked relieved to escape Dakota's intense scrutiny and quickly vanished.

"What on earth is wrong with you?" Shannon snapped as soon as he was out of earshot. "Have you lost what's left of your mind?"

"You're hiding something," Dakota persisted, not in the least bit cowed by Shannon's rising anger. "This is your funky, embarrassing, New Age-psychic-librarian best friend you're talking to. I can't help you with trust funds or charity galas, and now that there's finally something I *can* help you with, what do you do but push me away with both hands. I know he's not from this time. I know—" Dakota drew in a deep, shuddering breath and began to sway on her feet.

Again? Shannon thought. *How can it be happening again? She didn't even touch him!* She grabbed Dakota by the shoulders and steadied her.

"I need a diet Coke," Dakota managed.

Shannon started to laugh. "Diet Cokes stave off fainting spells?"

"I didn't faint," Dakota protested. "I swooned. There's a difference."

"Nobody swoons," Shannon said, leading her friend off toward the house. "I don't think anybody has actually swooned since hoop skirts went out of style after the Civil War."

"Bingo," said Dakota with an evil grin, "although it's an earlier war I have in mind. So, tell me, why am I swooning now?"

"Because you're a nut."

"I resent that."

"Okay," said Shannon. "You're an eccentric."

"A visionary," Dakota amended. "I come from a whole line of visionaries on my mother's side and I know visionaries are always misunderstood. Trust me when I tell you I'm picking up definite vibes from another time and place."

Shannon motioned her through the French doors.

"He did a good job with these," Dakota said, glancing about.

They'd been broken all summer. But the doors weren't the only things to change since Andrew McVie arrived, Shannon thought.

"You were born under a generous star," Dakota said as they entered the kitchen. "With my luck a plumber would drop out of the skies into my backyard and he'd tell me he didn't work on Sundays."

Shannon opened the refrigerator and pulled out two cans of soda. "Still having trouble with the kitchen sink?"

Dakota rolled her eyes. "The kitchen sink. The bathroom sink. The bathtub. The heating system." She popped the top on the soda can. "That's what happens when you live in an old house."

Shannon sat down at the kitchen table. "My offer still holds," she said, meeting her friend's eyes as Dakota sat down opposite her.

"I'm not going to let you pay for repairs to my house."

"Why not? I have more money than I know what to do with. Why can't I spend it on my friends?"

Dakota took a sip of soda. "You're spending it on him, aren't you?"

Shannon's brows lifted. "The clothes?"

"Don't look so surprised. Did you really think I wasn't going to notice? Suddenly the guy looks like he stepped out of the pages of *GQ.*"

Shannon smiled innocently. "I did think that shirt was particularly attractive."

"You paid for all of it."

"What makes you say that?" *Don't flirt with danger, Shannon. You know she'll catch you every time.*

"How could he pay for it?" Dakota countered. "He doesn't have any money."

"He has money."

"Yeah, but it's not from this century."

"You really do have a one-track mind, Wylie."

Dakota put her can of soda down and met Shannon's eyes. "This isn't going to last."

Shannon felt as if someone had her stomach in a vise grip. "What isn't?"

Dakota's gesture encompassed the house and beyond. Her eyes were dreamy behind the tinted lenses of her granny glasses. "Him. You. All of this. I just don't see him here for long."

"You're not making any sense."

Dakota leaned forward and placed a hand on Shannon's forearm. "Sooner or later he's going to have to make a decision, and when that time comes you'll have to let him go."

"Let him go? He's not an indentured servant, Dakota. He could leave right now if he wanted to."

"But you don't want him to, do you?"

That vise grip on her stomach tightened. "It doesn't much matter to me either way."

"Baloney it doesn't. You've fallen in love with him."

Shannon leapt to her feet, overturning the soda can. "Oh, damn it! See what you made me do."

Dakota pushed a napkin across the table to mop up the spill. "Falling in love is nothing to be ashamed of."

"The man's a stranger, Dakota. He dropped into my backyard less than twenty-four hours ago. I'd have to be insane to fall in love with someone I don't even know."

"Maybe so," said Dakota with maddening calm, "but the fact is you're in love with him and he's not going to stay around. You know it. I know it. And sooner or later he's going to know it, too."

Shannon felt her control begin to crack. She thrust her shaking hands into the pockets of her linen trousers and met her friend's eyes. "Stay out of this, Dakota. I love you dearly, but this time I'm asking you to butt out."

"I'd do anything in the world for you," Dakota said with a sad smile, "but that's the one thing I don't think I can do. Like it or not, we're in this together."

Chapter Ten

10

The garage was a large enclosure with room enough for at least three cars such as the one Shannon drove.

Andrew quickly found a place for the balloon and wicker basket in a stall to the left of Shannon's car. A sense of unease tugged at him as he pushed the entire contraption up against the back wall and covered it with a large white cloth he found on a shelf. Why had the balloon not vanished from his life the way it had with Emilie and Zane? Shannon's friend seemed to believe there was meaning to all of these events and he was not above wondering if that might not be so.

In truth, it had thus far been a most disturbing day. The glittering world he'd imagined did indeed exist, but there was a darkness at its heart that threw a shadow across the landscape. He had been surrounded by splendor that all else took for granted and yet in the midst of that splendor he had encountered the sharp blade of violence, as senseless as it was unexpected.

And still no one seemed surprised. Not the painted lady at the mall to whom it had been directed, nor Shannon who had suffered the effects of such violence within the sacred bonds of her marriage.

The world he came from lacked much in the way of luxury but

at least a man knew who his enemies were and where they might be found.

There was a sense of defeat about everything and everyone, a curious lack of the commitment that propelled a man or woman to right the wrongs of the world. They took the wonders of their time for granted, as if flying through the air or owning a king's ransom in jewels was their right and not the miracle it truly was. It was as if the endless string of wars had extinguished the flames of righteousness and left only bitter spoils.

Shannon had said it to him in plain and simple words—that the average man stood little chance of making his mark on the world, and no chance at all of influencing history. How had such a thing happened in two short centuries?

Their trip to the mall had taught Andrew that the time had come for him to take charge of the situation and adapt himself to this new century with as much dispatch as he could muster. He had always been master of his own fate, willing to rely on no man for direction.

How difficult it must have been for Zane to be thrust back in time to a world that did not easily recognize his worth. Not only was his currency worthless, so were his credentials. And that was a bitter pill to swallow.

During his time at Harvard Andrew had learned that knowledge was power. He was an intelligent man. He had chosen to travel forward in time of his own free will. Now he must make it his business to learn to function in this world as swiftly and efficiently as possible or resign himself to being a leech upon others for the rest of his days.

At first he had not understood Shannon's insistence that his story remain a secret between them, but today at the mall her fears suddenly made sense. There was a hunger in this world that he'd not seen or felt anywhere before, a need that he could not define but felt as a persistent vibration in the very air he breathed. What could they want, he wondered, when miracles were the stuff of everyday life?

He spent much of the afternoon at work repairing the windows of the structure Shannon called a garage. He wielded the hammer like a weapon. With every nail he pounded into place he pictured the supercilious clerks he'd encountered at the mall, all of whom had found great amusement in his dependence upon Shannon.

Apparently even in the year 1993 it was the man's place to provide clothing and sustenance for the woman. He'd felt a fool and worse each time she reached for that shiny rectangle she used to obtain credit from the shopkeepers.

A gold card, Shannon had called it. A most apt name for an object that served as gold's equivalent. If only other objects were so aptly named. The room that moved up and down was called an elevator, while the silver stairs that carried you up of their own volition went by the odd name escalator. Men's trousers were called pants or slacks. Shoes no longer came with buckles. Hair could be long or short or anywhere in between and there was not a powdered wig in sight.

In general, people seemed to wear as few items of clothing as they could, and Andrew doubted he would ever grow accustomed to seeing a woman's nipples looking back at him through the sheer fabric of her bodice. And then there were cars and trucks and the flying metal birds called airplanes.

He knew he must make an effort to adapt to his new situation. He would no longer say "mistress." When he did not understand a reference he would wait and cobble together its meaning with bits and pieces of other information and clues. He would find a way to make a place for himself in this world, even if it was bigger and faster and more dangerous than he'd ever imagined possible.

"What manner of food is this?" He looked askance at the triangle of dough covered in a red sauce and melted white cheese.

"Pizza," said Shannon, eating it with her hands in a most disconcerting—yet appealing—fashion. "It's Italian."

"Italian? Is such foreign fare common?"

She wiped the side of her mouth with a square of soft paper. "As common as hot dogs."

"Sweet Jesus!" He stared at her in alarm. "Has it come to that?"

She looked at him and burst into laughter. "I don't mean the four-legged kind, Andrew. It's—" She stopped. "Actually, it sounds pretty disgusting, but it's ground-up meat pushed into a casing and boiled. We serve it with mustard and sauerkraut."

"Aye," he said. "'Tis a vile concoction you describe." He took a bite of the pizza, struggling with a long, stretchy string of the mild white cheese. "This, however, is most agreeable." He took another bite then looked across the table. "This came in a box?"

"That's how they deliver it," Shannon explained. "I called in my order and thirty minutes later they brought the pizza here to me." She reached for a strange-looking object, roughly the size of a woman's shoe, then pulled a long rod from its depths.

He watched, mouth agape, as she touched her finger to the center of the object in quick movements much like playing the piano. Grinning, she handed it to him.

"Put it to your ear," she ordered, then laughed. "No, not that way. Turn it around."

He did as told and heard an odd ringing noise, then a human voice, clear as day, talking right into his ear. "Good afternoon, everybody. At 6:05 the temperature at Newark Airport is eighty-five degrees and—"

Andrew dropped the object to the tabletop. "There is something unnatural about such a thing."

"It's a telephone," Shannon said, obviously amused by his reaction. "Probably one of the most important inventions the world has ever seen."

"'Tis a foolish invention," he said. "How can you judge the worth of a man if you cannot look him in the eye?"

"You wouldn't think it a foolish invention if you were talking to someone in England, would you?"

He picked up the telephone and turned it over in his hand. "How can this object make conversation possible across the ocean?"

"I know it has something to do with fiber-optic cables and satellites and all sorts of things."

"All of that so a man can have strange food delivered in a box."

"If you want to put it that way, yes," said Shannon.

"People make a living that way?"

"A good living," Shannon said. "Fast foods are big business."

"Does no one sit down at the family table and partake of a normal supper?"

"This is a normal supper these days, Andrew. Families are on the run during the week. It's a rare clan that has the opportunity to sit down for a meal at the same time."

"Where do they run?"

"They work late, they go to night school, soccer practice, Little League, Girl Scouts, Pop Warner, you name it, they're out there doing it." She sprinkled red flakes on top of her pizza. "And when they're not out there, they're at home watching TV."

"The moving pictures on the small glass window?"

She nodded. "If you don't feel like going out to see the world, TV brings the world into your home." She considered him for a moment. "If you want to learn about this strange place you're in, TV is one of the best ways to start."

"Have you no books?"

"Thousands of them," she said. "Finish your pizza and I'll show you the library."

He's like a kid in a candy shop, Shannon thought as Andrew devoured *Timetables of American History.* He hadn't moved from his spot near the window. His torso was curved over the book, almost as if he were protecting it from harm.

Her heart went out to him. Talk about culture shock. The poor man was racing through the pages, flying from the minuet to the Virginia reel to rap without a parachute.

She recognized in him a need to know all there was to know, to absorb as much information as he possibly could in order to arm himself against the unknown. Dakota's warning repeated in her brain. *Temporary...this is only temporary.*

Shannon wasn't a fool. She knew the time would come when he moved on. You didn't travel through more than two hundred years of time and space to content yourself with a small town in central New Jersey. *Or with one very lonely woman.*

Where on earth did that thought come from? She was alone but she wasn't lonely. Not really. She had Dakota and the people who ran her shelters, not to mention the women and children who passed through them on their way to happier, better lives. And, God knew, she had a social life other people would envy. An endless array of society functions and charity balls and luncheons that would gobble up as much of her time as she would allow. Her picture was a staple in local society columns.

She wasn't looking for a relationship with a man. She didn't need a man to make herself complete. *Are you sure of that?* the same small voice asked. Wasn't there one small part of her heart that still yearned for home and family, for someone to share her days and warm her nights? She'd trained herself not to wish for the impossible and it annoyed her to fall prey again to those old longings.

Dakota is right, she thought, struggling to shake off the melancholy mood she'd fallen under. There was nothing permanent about any of this. As soon as he grew comfortable with twentieth-century ways, he would be gone. Men like Andrew McVie weren't meant to spend their days lounging by the side of a swimming pool, sipping margaritas and listening to baseball on the radio.

He was a dynamic man from a dynamic time and sooner or later he'd be looking to make his mark on the world in which he found himself.

And she would be left behind, sitting alone in her fortress, safe from anything that could cause her harm...including love.

Valley Forge. The terrible winter at Morristown. The War of 1812. Abraham Lincoln and the unimaginable horrors of the War Between the States. The pain of Reconstruction. The Spanish-American War.

As he read on, Andrew felt as if he were being pummeled from all sides, battered and bruised by decades of struggle. Aye, there were triumphs along the way—the westward expansion, the Industrial Revolution—but it seemed to him that each of those triumphs was offset by strife.

World War I and its legacy of shell-shocked veterans whose nerves were permanently damaged by something called mustard gas. His gut knotted as he read on, unbelievably to World War II where millions of people were slaughtered cold-bloodedly for their religion or nationality or choice of friends. Try as he might he could not comprehend an entire world engulfed in the flames of warfare.

In 1950 warfare had erupted again in Korea, an island on the other side of the world, and then in Viet Nam, and the Holy Land, and Arabia and—

He flung the book at the far wall and rose from his chair.

"The wonder of it all is that the world still exists," he roared as he paced the empty library.

Shannon appeared in the doorway. "It's a bit much to digest in one sitting." She handed him a cold drink.

He gulped it down and wished for rum. "How is it that life continues?" he asked, knowing there could be no answer. "The weapons of destruction are everywhere. How does a man build a life knowing it can be destroyed in the blink of an eye?"

"Optimism," she said with a shrug of her slender shoulders. "Stubbornness. Wasn't it the same in your day? Life has always been an uncertain proposition. We just make the best of it while we're here."

"'Tis not the way I thought it would be," he muttered.

"And isn't that just too bad," she snapped with a harsh edge to her lovely voice. "If you were looking for something easy, McVie, then you've come to the wrong time and place."

"Aye," he said. "I am quickly learning that."

"What did you want?" she asked, moving toward him. "What on earth did you think you could find here that you couldn't find where you were?"

The word leapt forth of its own accord. "Purpose," he said. He had meant to say both wealth and ease, and the truth of his statement surprised him.

Her expression softened and he had the sense that she understood his meaning in a way few others of this time or any other ever could.

"I hope you find it, Andrew McVie." Her voice caressed him. "Life isn't worth a damn without it."

"You have purpose?"

She considered his question. "I do," she said at last, "but purpose and happiness don't always go hand in hand."

"Happiness is a fool's errand. A man is more well served by a sense of purpose."

"Said by a man who once held happiness in his hand."

"You have no knowledge of that, mistress Shannon."

Her eyebrows lifted. "Mistress? I thought you had put that aside."

He ignored her comment. "How is it you believe you know so much about me? Have you skills like your friend Dakota?"

She shook her head. "I'm not psychic, if that's what you mean. I simply remember the way you looked when you showed me the watch Elspeth gave to you."

Emotion gripped him by the throat, making it difficult to speak. "As a husband I was a grave disappointment."

She said nothing, simply leaned against the doorjamb and watched him with those big aqua eyes.

"I had but one goal," he continued. "The pursuit of the almighty shilling. All else paled by comparison."

"You'll find little has changed. Many men and women make the same mistake each and every day."

"'Tis a sorrow to hear that. I would wish no man the grief I knew when Elspeth and David were lowered into the ground." *They're in the arms of Jesus,* the good Reverend Samuels had said as Andrew stood silently next to the grave, cold as the December winds blowing across the cemetery. *They'll never hurt again.* If only someone had been able to say that about him.

She moved closer, so close that he caught the sweet scent of her skin, felt the warmth of her body near his. "I'm sure they knew you loved them."

"Love is not always enough for a good woman to warm herself with on a winter's night."

"Your wife was unfaithful?"

"Nay," said Andrew, "although I gave her just reason to seek comfort with another. The law was wife and mistress and child and all else walked behind. Elspeth lived a life of loneliness in a town that was not her home and she did it to help serve my own purpose."

"What happened to Elspeth and David? How did they—?"

"Fire," he said bluntly. "I was on my way back from Philadelphia. They died just hours before I reached them." His voice broke and he looked down at his feet, strange to him in the low-slung leather shoes. "That was when I left the practice of law and took up the cause of rebellion."

The words tumbled from his mouth like so many marbles through a child's fingers. He told her of the spy ring, of the chances he took, the praise he received for risking his life. "I had no right to such praise," he said, wishing for the sweet oblivion to be found in a bottle of rum. "A man who risks his life when his life is a thing of value does a praiseful thing. A man who risks his life when death holds strong appeal deserves naught but scorn."

She placed her hand on his forearm and for a moment he thought his battered and weary heart felt whole again. *'Tis your imagination. What you feel is but a man's need for release.*

Her cheeks flushed and he looked at her sharply. Had she somehow heard his innermost thoughts? The notion both pleased and alarmed him in equal measure. He'd always held his emotions on a tight rein in the belief that a man did not acknowledge anything that spoke of weakness.

Yet this woman had seen him stripped of all wealth and power and knowledge—reduced to learning how to survive in a strange new world—and still she viewed him as a man of worth.

"I am not what you think, Shannon," he said, his voice gruff with emotion.

"And you are not what *you* think, either," she whispered. "Let it go, Andrew. Get on with your life."

He looked down at her hand resting against his forearm. Seeing where his gaze lingered, she gave him a brief smile and made to deprive him of her touch, but he placed his hand over hers.

She met his eyes.

He reached out with his other hand and let her dark hair drift through his fingertips. So soft...so silky...so sweetly perfumed. A man could grow drunk on such sweetness.

Dame Fortune did me an honor when she brought me to this place, mistress.

"I am pleased you think so, Andrew."

He jerked back in surprise. "I said nothing to warrant a reply."

"You did. I heard you quite clearly."

"I did not speak aloud."

"Still," said Shannon, "I heard your voice and it's not the first time...."

"The world is a strange place," he said. "There are many things we are not given to understand."

"I don't want to understand this. Magic doesn't need to be understood."

The urge to draw her close against his body was growing more difficult to ignore. "From the first moment I have felt a sense of destiny, as if all things in my life have led me to you."

"Oh, God," she whispered, resting her forehead against his chest. "When you stepped out of the woods I felt as if my life was just beginning."

He cradled her head between his hands and lifted her face to his. Her eyes were wide. Her lips parted slightly on a sigh. He knew if the Almighty called him home at that very second he would have died already knowing the face of paradise, for he could wish for no greater reward than the taste of her mouth against his.

Chapter Eleven

11

This can't be happening, Shannon thought, even as her eyes closed for his kiss. *Things like this don't happen in real life.*

"They do happen," he said, his breath warm against her skin. "We are the proof of it."

He knew her thoughts before she gave them voice, the same way she knew his. There was a connection between them, inexplicable though it was, and she was powerless before it. But not frightened. This was surrender of a sensual kind, the kind of giving over of control that promised even greater rewards. Something deep and real and forever.

He brushed his lips across hers, lightly at first, as if taking her measure. She inhaled the scent of his skin, reveled in the delicious sensations awakening within her body. His fingers were callused and rough against her face but his touch was so gentle, so tender that she wondered if you could die from feeling cherished. She'd never felt cherished before, never felt as if her pleasure mattered. And it would with Andrew. She knew it instinctively, the same way she knew that they were moving toward something that would change her forever and in ways she couldn't imagine.

She wanted to crawl inside his heart and ease his pain. She wanted to slip into his mind and know his secrets. But, dear God, more than anything she wanted to hold him deep inside her body and spend the night in his arms.

And a night would be enough. She would make it be enough. Nothing lasted forever. Not youth or beauty or riches. Certainly not happiness. But she would rather grow old knowing that she'd followed her heart this once than knowing she'd let a chance for happiness slip through her fingers like so many grains of sand.

He deepened the kiss, drawing her breath from her body on a shuddering sigh of longing. She felt drunk with it, so intoxicated with the smell and touch and sight of him that she thought she was hearing bells.

Unfortunately she *was* hearing bells.

"Someone's at the door," she murmured against his mouth.

He kissed her again—thoroughly—and it took a great display of willpower on her part to leave his embrace.

"You are expecting visitors?" he asked, smoothing back her hair with a gesture of such affection that her knees threatened to buckle beneath her.

She shook her head. "Whoever it is, I'll tell them to come back tomorrow."

"That is a sound idea."

She grinned, feeling young and flirtatious and filled with hope. "I thought you'd like it. I'll be right back."

She floated down the hallway toward the front door in a romantic haze. The doorbell rang again just as she unfastened the dead bolt.

"I was beginning to wonder if you were home," said the attractive African-American woman who waited on the doorstep. "I rang twice."

"I was in the library." She hugged the woman and ushered her into the foyer. Karen Naylor was an attorney, an advocate for battered wives, and one of Shannon's favorite people in the world. "Business or pleasure, Karen?"

"Business, unfortunately. We're going to have a full house tonight in the old building."

Shannon reached for the notebook she kept in the basket by the door. "How many?"

"Six," said Karen. "Mother, grandmother and four children. The mother is being seen by the doctor right now and then Jules will bring them over in the van."

"How old are the children?"

"Eleven, eight, five and eighteen months."

"Do we need the crib?"

"Not a bad idea. The little one has some sleeping disorders."

"Why doesn't that surprise me?" Shannon muttered. So many women stayed in an abusive marriage for the sake of the children, only to find the children scarred by the endless cycle of physical and emotional abuse. "Did you call Dakota? She'll want to stop by tomorrow after work and see to the kids." Dakota's crusade was literacy and she'd taught many a young mother and child about the joys of reading.

"I left a message," Karen said, "but I think Monday is psychic party night. You might want to try her again in the morning."

"I'd better check the guest houses and make sure everything's in order," Shannon said, her mind shifting into high gear. "I have a stack of new magazines, some videotapes and some really terrific kids' clothes." She looked up at Karen. "Are any of the kids girls?"

"Three of them," said Karen. "You'll be in your glory."

Shannon scribbled a few hasty notes then glanced at her watch. "What on earth are you doing out so late? You could've called to tell me this."

"I know," said Karen, "but I have some papers I wanted to drop off for you to read, so I figured why not do everything at once?"

Shannon's interest was immediately piqued. "My updated will?"

Karen nodded. "That and the new modules for the trusts."

Shannon rolled her eyes comically. "Both will make wonderful bedtime reading, I'm sure."

"Just make sure you *do* read them," Karen warned. "This is important stuff. I need to make certain you know what you're signing."

"I told you what I wanted, you say you've delivered it. What more can I ask? I trust you."

"Don't trust me," Karen said, rolling her eyes. "Double-check everybody."

"Words to live by," said Shannon with a wicked grin.

Karen considered her carefully. "You look like the cat that ate the canary."

"Do I? I can't imagine why."

Karen gestured toward the doorway. "Could he be the reason?"

Shannon spun around to see Andrew, arms folded across his chest, watching them.

"So, introduce us, girl." Karen beamed a smile in Andrew's direction. Then, sotto voce to Shannon, "Where have you been hiding him? He's adorable."

"He's an old friend," she said, motioning for Andrew to join them. "He, ah, he just dropped in the other day and I've asked him to stay awhile."

He's not smiling, Shannon noticed as he walked toward them. If anything, he looked annoyed.

Karen thrust out her right hand. "Karen Naylor," she said, hanging on to her smile.

Andrew ignored the outstretched hand, and Shannon groaned inwardly. Darn Dakota and her swooning spells. The poor man would probably be afraid to shake hands for the rest of his life. She considered the wisdom of giving him a poke in the ribs to urge him forward but decided against it. With her luck Karen would tumble over in a dead faint and they'd have someone else to worry about. Karen was a literal, intellectual type. If Shannon told her Andrew had dropped in from the eighteenth century, Karen would arrange to have them both committed.

She cleared her throat.

Karen's smile faltered but her hand remained outstretched.

Shake her hand, she thought. *You're embarrassing the daylights out of me.*

Andrew looked down at her, a puzzled expression on his raw-boned face. With obvious reluctance he reached out and clasped Karen's hand for a nanosecond then backed away.

"Andrew McVie," he said.

"What a wonderful accent," Karen said, a flicker of embarrassment in her chocolate brown eyes. "Where are you from?"

"Boston," said Andrew.

"Scotland," said Shannon at the same time. "I mean, first Scotland, then Boston."

"Ahh," said Karen, her gaze darting from Andrew to Shannon then back again to Andrew. "So what brings you to New Jersey?"

"He's taking a sabbatical," said Shannon.

Andrew's brows lifted.

So did Karen's.

You're making a mess of this, Shannon, she berated herself. *Let the man answer for himself.*

"I'm taking a sabbatical," said Andrew.

Karen's mouth twitched as if she was holding back a laugh. Who could blame her? This was worse than Abbott and Costello's *Who's on First?*

"What is he taking a sabbatical from?" Karen asked Shannon.

"Very funny," Shannon said, then fell silent so Andrew could answer for himself.

"The law," Andrew said.

Karen's eyes widened. Shannon wished the floor would open up and swallow her whole.

"You're an attorney?" Karen asked.

"I am," said Andrew.

"I've always wanted to meet an attorney from the U.K.," Karen said, zeroing in on him. "Now, are you a barrister or a solicitor or a lawyer?" She laughed. "Or have I totally botched it all up?"

"I am a lawyer," he said in a tone of voice Shannon hadn't heard before.

"So how is that different from a barrister?"

"I do not know."

"Well," said Karen, turning back toward Shannon, "I have to get home." She reached into her leather tote and removed a large white envelope. "Read the papers and we'll set up a time for you to come into the office and sign everything."

Karen gave Shannon a quick embrace, then, with a nod for Andrew, she said good-night and left.

Shannon turned on him in a fury unlike any he'd seen before.

"What in hell is wrong with you?" she roared. "How dare you be so rude to Karen."

"I did nothing untoward," he said, bristling.

"You treated her abysmally."

"I answered her questions."

"You had no intention of shaking her hand."

"Aye," he said. "'Twas not my intention at all."

"Why in hell not?" she continued, her anger increasing. "You shook Dakota's hand."

"And you are aware of the results."

"But that's not it, is it?" she persisted. "It's because she's black."

He could not deny it.

"Bigot!"

He glared at her. "I come from a different world. Black slaves do not embrace their owners."

"You jerk! Slavery's been dead for over one hundred years. For your information, Karen's a lawyer, same as you."

The notion was so preposterous he laughed out loud. "You speak nonsense."

"I speak the truth, Andrew. Karen is a lawyer."

"I do not believe you."

"She graduated Harvard law."

"You make that up to goad me into an argument."

"What bothers you more—that the lawyer's a woman or that she's black?"

"In truth, I find both impossible to believe."

"You're honest," she said. "I'll grant you that. But that doesn't make your opinions acceptable."

"Is there but one way to think in 1993?"

"No, there are many ways to think, but when it comes to the basic rights of others, there is only one way that is acceptable to decent, caring human beings."

"You believe me to be uncaring."

She lifted her chin. "In this regard, yes I do."

"Elspeth and I did not hold slaves."

"How wonderful for you," she drawled. "But did you do anything to convince others to release theirs?"

"'Twas not my business to tell others how to live their lives."

"Even if the way they lived their lives kept other lives in bondage?"

"Most slaves were well cared for."

"Oh, please!" She raised her hands in disgust. "Care to explain the Civil War to me, or didn't you get that far in your reading?"

"There were reasons beyond the existence of slavery for the War Between the States." He had read the story that very evening and the facts were clear in his mind.

"But none more important."

"You act as if I bear the weight of slavery upon my shoulders."

"You do," she said with righteous fury. "All of you who allowed such a system to continue. You had the chance to eradicate it with the Declaration of Independence and you let it slip right through your greedy fingers."

"There is little time to debate such things when you are fighting for the future of your country. I know of this declaration and I know of how it was wrought. There would be no United States of America had Jefferson and Adams not bowed to the needs of the Southern gentlemen present."

"An easy answer," Shannon said, "but I don't buy it. There had to be another way."

"Much of life is compromise," he said. "Have you not learned that yet?"

"Of course I have, but I find myself wondering if you've mastered the art."

"Do not hide your meaning, Shannon. Tell me straight."

"You still don't get it, do you? Think of me, Andrew. Those same attitudes toward blacks carried over toward the treatment of women. How did you view Elspeth? Was she your property? Your partner? Your slave?"

"She was my wife and all that entailed." The words sounded apologetic. He didn't mean them to be. Why was she asking him to defend something that needed no defense?

"I'll tell you what that entailed. Up until this century being a man's wife meant being his property. And up until a very few years ago a man could do anything he wanted to his property, including destroy it. A man could beat his wife, rape her, even kill her and nobody—nobody!—would say a word."

He wanted to pull her into his arms and soothe her fears but knew that would be the wrong thing to do. It wasn't his touch she needed, it was something much harder for him to give.

"On God's oath, I never struck Elspeth nor wished to cause her harm of any kind," he said. "Nor would I harm another woman in any way."

"I know," she said, her voice a whisper. "I believe that."

He felt the need of her touch and took her hand in his. "Then what still troubles you that you look at me in such a manner?"

"Many women come through my life, Andrew, and they all are in need of help."

"I understand you feel a kinship with the other good wives who have suffered unjustly."

"I do," she said, squeezing his hand. "And those wives and women and children come in all shapes and sizes and religions and races. If—if you are to be here…with me…then you must accept them as your equal and mine."

"'Tis a great deal you ask of me."

"I know it is," she said, "but you are a good man."

His mouth quirked upward in a smile. "You presume a great deal upon limited acquaintance."

"I know what I know." She touched his face with a gentle hand and he felt as if he'd been blessed by God. "You are a better man than you realize, Andrew McVie, and I believe you can learn to accept Karen and others like her."

"I cannot say with certainty if that will prove true."

"I can."

"It is not possible for you to know things that I do not know about myself."

"I've learned to rely on my gut instincts." She faced him full on, that warrior-woman stance he'd been taken by on first acquaintance. She saw in him something that he'd thought long gone, a finer self he would sell his soul to believe still existed. "You will try, won't you?"

He nodded. "I will try."

Her smile was brighter than the sun and it warmed him to the marrow. "It's a start."

"Aye," he said. "'Tis a start."

Where it would end he could not say, but he hoped with all his heart that the end would be a long time coming.

Chapter Twelve

12

The shelters were a short distance away, located at the other side of the woods that were part of her property. Originally they'd been intended as guest cottages by the privacy-loving first owner of the estate, but the second Shannon saw them she knew they were destined to serve a much more important purpose.

With Andrew's help she loaded the trunk of her car with supplies and magazines and baby gear. She hadn't asked for his help. The fact that he thought to lend a hand touched her deeply. Their discussion had been painfully frank—for both of them, she would imagine. She'd half expected him to turn and walk away from her, and the fact that he didn't, that he stayed to help, meant more than she could say.

When she climbed behind the wheel he took his place in the passenger's seat. "We won't be back for a while," she said as she started the engine. "Sometimes it takes a few hours to get everyone settled in."

"Aye."

She backed out of the driveway, then turned onto the dirt road that led to the cottages. Minutes later she pulled up in front of the tiny house that served as one of the shelters.

"They're not here yet," she said. "That'll give us a chance to open the windows and put the food away."

Andrew inspected the front door with a critical eye. "'Tis in need of repair."

"Karl isn't much for repair work," Shannon said with a shake of her head.

"Karl?"

"Karl's my handyman. He and Mildred take care of things for me."

"I have seen naught of Mildred and Karl."

"Vacation," she said. "They've gone to visit relatives in Sweden."

"The window sashes are in sad condition." He looked at Shannon. "How is it you continue to employ a man who does so little to earn his salary?"

Shannon hoisted two bags of groceries and headed for the kitchen. "I'm what's known as a soft touch," she said over her shoulder as Andrew followed her through the tiny hallway. "Karl and Mildred worked for the previous owner. They're practically at retirement age. I doubt if anyone could've let them go."

They barely had time to unload the trunk before Jules's van rattled its way up the dirt road and rolled to a stop behind Shannon's car.

You never get used to it, Shannon thought as they watched the two women help the children from the van. If you did, you were a poor excuse for a human being.

"Gonna have a full house," Jules said as the grandmother gathered up the baby blankets from the back seat. "I've got two more pickups."

"Two more? What on earth's going on?"

"Full moon. Hot weekend. Your guess is as good as mine."

"Any more babies?"

"Teenagers this time. Two in one family, one in the other."

"We'll need more food," she said. "As soon as I get everyone settled in, I'll go home and raid the pantry."

"I will go for you," said Andrew as Jules set off to collect the next two families.

"I admit you've adapted amazingly well but I'm not about to let you drive."

"I have no need of your car," he said. "I will walk."

"It's pitch-black outside. You'll never find your way there and back."

"Tell me what you require and I will see you get it."

She named a few staple items, told him how to bypass the alarm system and where to find the pantry. Then she crossed her fingers that he'd manage to find the house before another two hundred years had passed.

In truth Andrew would have walked from there to kingdom come if it meant escaping the sorrowful eyes of the women and children.

He had seen terrible things in his lifetime. He'd held a young boy's hand as he lay dying on the village green near Lexington, victim of a Redcoat's musket. And he'd carried home the boy's meager belongings to his mother, who had already buried two sons before him.

But nothing had prepared Andrew for the sight of the two women who had come to Shannon for help. The older had the look of defeat about her person, visible in the slumped shoulders and fearful expression, as if she expected danger to leap from behind the trees or drop from the skies. It was the younger woman, however, who had borne the burden of some man's anger. Heavy bandages hid her left eye from view, while purple-and-black bruises ringed the right. A stepladder of what appeared to be tailor's stitches angled across one cheek, each stitch a testament to the horror she had sustained at the hands of the man to whom she'd pledged her life.

He made his way through the woods swiftly, relying on skills he'd thought would be unimportant in this world. A man did not need a road to find his way. A formation of trees, the stars overhead, all could be used to guide a man if he understood how to use them. There were differences, however, that made the exercise difficult in a way he hadn't foreseen.

Darkness did not fall with the same finality in Shannon's century as it did in his. He was accustomed to an all-encompassing blackness, a blackness so dark and deep the stars shining above seemed close enough to touch. But here there was a grayness to the night, as if a scrim separated him from the sky itself.

And the quality of the silence continued to confound him. Even now, alone in the woods, there was a constant noise he could not identify. Instinct told him it was not the noise of the wind or some strange insects or animals but something unnatural.

The back of Shannon's property was brightly lit, almost as if the afternoon sun shone down upon the land and reflected in the blue depths of the rectangular pond. Electricity made these miracles possible, harnessing the same power that split the skies during a summer storm. Was that the source of the ever-present hum that hovered at the edges of his mind day and night? In truth, he wished for just an hour of the deep silence he had taken for granted.

He followed Shannon's instructions and entered the house without causing the box on the wall to scream.

"A small triumph," he muttered as he headed toward the pantry. He wondered if the rest of his life would consist of small triumphs that amounted to nothing at all.

Fifteen years ago, on the day after their college graduation, Pat Conner married Jack Delaney. Everyone said they were the perfect couple. Jack was poised at the starting line, about to enter an executive training program, while Pat was eager to start a family, something they accomplished with dispatch on their honeymoon.

They bought into the whole American dream: kids and career,

the beautiful home in a trendy suburb, station wagon and golden retriever, the endless parade of expectations that could never be met.

Not by them.

Not by anyone.

"He'll find us," Pat said as she sipped warm broth through a straw in the kitchen while the kids wolfed down hot dogs. "He said if I ever tried to run, he'd find me and he'd find the kids and he'd kill us."

Pat's mother, Terri, looked up from her cup of coffee. "He was killing us anyway, honey, day by day." She met Shannon's eyes and Shannon tried not to notice the bruises along the older woman's jaw. "Tell her this was the right thing to do, miss. Tell her he can't find us here."

"You're safe," Shannon said, reaching across the table to squeeze Pat's trembling hand. "Nothing can happen to you here."

"You don't know Jack," Pat said, glancing nervously toward her children. "He's a powerful man. He has friends everywhere."

"So had my husband," Shannon said.

Pat looked up in surprise. "You?"

"Me," said Shannon with a small smile. "I've been there, Pat. I know how it feels."

"But you— I mean—" Pat gestured broadly to encompass the estate. "I didn't think it could happen to someone like you."

"You thought wrong," Shannon said. "Abuse cuts across all social classes and all economic backgrounds."

"I pushed her into this," Terri said, looking down at her cup of coffee. "Last night when he— If he lays a hand on my baby or my grandbabies one more time, I'll kill him."

"Don't say that, Mom!" Pat's voice quavered with emotion. "He's my husband."

"He's a no-good bastard."

"You don't understand." Pat looked toward Shannon for support but Shannon kept still. "He doesn't mean to hurt us.... It's just—he's under so much stress at work. His job is shaky and..." Her voice faded and she took another sip of soup.

"See?" said the mother. "First she says he wants to kill her, then she's feeling sorry for him. I didn't know what to do. I figured this was our only hope."

"You live with them?"

"Since February. My—my husband died and Pat took me in."

"You made the right choice," Shannon reassured her. "The important thing is that you got her out of that house before it got any worse."

"I can make my own decisions." Pat spoke up. "I just want to give Jack a chance to rest." She looked toward her kids as they polished off the hot dogs and moved onto the ice cream. "It's hard for him. The kids make a lot of noise and they need so many things—" Her voice broke as she started to cry.

"It's okay," Shannon crooned, putting a comforting arm around the woman's shoulders. "Nothing can happen to you here. You're safe."

"I'm s-so scared," Pat said through her sobs. "I don't know what I'm going to do, where I'll go—"

"First things first," Shannon said. "The six of you need a good night's sleep. Tomorrow morning is soon enough to start planning your future."

Andrew moved deeper into the shadows. He'd seen the look on her face, heard the infinite tenderness in her voice, and it occurred to him that she was the finest person he'd ever known.

In times of war ordinary men and women rose to greatness with acts of heroism that were the stuff of history. But in truth it was easy to be heroic when the situation demanded it.

Heroism in the face of everyday trials was a rare thing indeed. Something Shannon possessed in great measure. She saw pain and she tried to ease it. She saw inequity and she tried to remedy it. He could not imagine many men or women who would open wide the doors of their home and take in strangers in need.

Take heed, a voice inside his head warned. *'Tis her way to lend comfort.* To read anything but human kindness into her behavior was to mark himself a fool.

"You were great with those kids," Shannon said a few hours later as they rode the short distance back to her house.

"They are angry," Andrew said.

"Is it any wonder? Their father beat the hell out of their mother and turned a gun on the two of them. That's enough to make anybody angry."

"'Tis more than that. Much of their anger is aimed at their mother."

Shannon glanced at him as she pulled into the driveway and hit the garage door opener. "Did they tell you that?"

"It was not necessary for them to tell me. It was there for all to see."

"I didn't see it."

Andrew shrugged his powerful shoulders. "There are things you see about women that are invisible to me."

She shut off the engine and turned to face him. "So what you're saying is it's a guy thing."

His forehead wrinkled. "A guy thing?"

"You know." She gestured broadly. "Male bonding, all that sort of stuff."

His frown deepened. "Male bonding?"

"I'd give you a copy of Robert Bly but I have the feeling you'd grab your balloon and go back home if I did."

"Speak plain, Shannon. Your words make no sense."

She sighed, struggling to find a way to explain self-help books, television talk shows and making peace with your inner child.

"Many Americans spend a lot of time thinking about their lives," she said, "and a few very clever Americans make a lot of money writing books that help the others think better." He was looking at her so strangely that she had to laugh. "Of course, if you don't like self-help books you can always go to a therapist."

"I do not know that word, *therapist*."

"A world without Freud? It sounds like heaven." She searched about for a definition. "A therapist is someone you pay to listen to your problems."

His mouth literally opened in surprise. "You pay someone to listen to your problems?"

"Well, yes," said Shannon. "And then the therapist offers solutions."

A funny smile lifted the corners of his mouth. "A few tankards of ale shared with friends at the Plumed Rooster accomplished much the same."

"I suppose it would," said Shannon as they got out of the car and walked across the side yard to the house. "The only problem is we don't have time for friends these days. We're too busy working three jobs in order to pay the mortgage, the baby-sitter, taxes—"

"Aye," said Andrew with a groan. "A man could work half his life in payment to the Crown."

"Well, we don't have to worry about the Crown these days, but Uncle Sam is more than happy to take his share."

"I thought you were not in communication with any of your family."

"Uncle Sam isn't really my family. He's everybody's family." She explained how it was a quasi-affectionate name for the American government. "He's a tall man with white hair and a beard and he wears very strange red, white and blue clothing that looks suspiciously like our flag."

"The same colors as the flag of England," he said, sounding quite indignant about the choice.

She unlocked the door and they stepped into the kitchen. "I don't know how to tell you this, Andrew," she said, turning on the lights, "but England is our staunchest ally and closest friend."

"And is she still the most powerful nation on earth?"

"No," she said. "Actually, we are."

"In truth?"

"In truth."

"'Tis been a most enlightening day."

"Yes," she said, thinking about the remarkable happenings of the past twenty-four hours. "'Enlightening' just about says it all."

Their eyes met and a fine tingle of anticipation began to buzz against her breastbone and move up the length of her spine.

"Well," she said, straightening her shoulders, "it's late and I have so much to do tomorrow at the shelters." She flipped on the door alarm, then started toward the hall. "I'll see you in the morning."

He fell into step beside her. "I will see you safely to your room."

She nodded. It felt good and right and she loved him for thinking it necessary.

They climbed the stairs together, not speaking. It was only the second time they'd climbed those stairs, yet she felt as if it were part of a shimmering chain of events that bound them to each other. Which, of course, was romantic nonsense, but still…

"This house has seven bedrooms," she said when they reached her door. "Feel free to use whatever one you like."

"I will be here, as I was last night."

She felt heat rush to her cheeks. "You don't have to do that, Andrew. I'm perfectly safe. Please sleep in comfort."

He didn't answer, just watched her with those beautiful hazel eyes of his, watched her until she thought she would dissolve into a pool of longing.

"Well, good night," she said, hand on the doorknob. Her heart thundered so loudly she could barely hear the sound of her voice. "I'll see you in the morning."

Still he said nothing, and the heat building inside her body rose another degree. *Why are you looking at me like that? Are you going to kiss me?*

"Aye," he said, drawing her close. "I am."

She inhaled the smell of his skin.

He cupped her face in his hands.

She thought she would die of anticipation.

He wondered if pleasure could kill a man.

It was a simple kiss, as kisses went.

Their lips met.

Their breaths mingled.

It wasn't enough…yet it was everything.

And the miracle of it all was that they both knew it.

Chapter Thirteen

13

Andrew was repairing the window of the guest bathroom the next morning when the Negress lawyer arrived.

"Good day," the woman said, not extending her hand to Andrew. "Is Shannon around?"

"She is at the house with the women," he said, not looking up from his work. He felt uncomfortable and did not like feeling thus.

She ran her dark hand along the sash. "Nice work you're doing." He sensed that she was smiling at him in a most friendly fashion, but chose not to acknowledge it. "Is carpentry your hobby?"

He nodded, wielding the scraping implement across the peeling layer of paint.

"I'm into running," she said.

An odd statement and one for which he had no reply.

"You don't like me very much, do you?" she asked.

"I did not say that."

"You didn't have to, Mr. McVie. Your silence pretty much says it all. I'm going to go find Shannon. Have a good day."

Andrew waited until the sound of her car died away, then tossed the tool to the ground. There was nothing deferential about the woman. She neither courted him nor treated him as her inferior.

In truth, she spoke to him as if they were equals before both man and God, and that unsettled him more than anything she could have done.

He thought of his days at Harvard, then tried to imagine a woman walking those hallowed halls in search of knowledge. The image simply would not come clear for him. The fact that the woman in question was a Negress made it all the more impossible for him to comprehend.

Shannon believed him a bigot in matters of race. He chose not to label himself that way. It was understood in his time that the division between slave and master was absolute. Even when a slave was released into freedom, that freedom bore a great similarity to all that had come before.

Such was not the case today. The descendants of slaves—men and women alike—were lawyers and doctors. Successful in their own right and on their own terms.

And in a world that Andrew had once considered his for the asking.

He wondered if there could be room enough for every man and woman to find power and success or if some fell by the wayside and were forgotten.

Nothing was as he'd imagined it would be. His dreams had been of a world where men lived like kings, where women stayed beautiful into their fourth decade and beyond, where he would instantly find meaning to a life that had long ago lost its sense of purpose.

"And where are you now, Andrew McVie?" he muttered. Repairing doors and scraping paint from windows. A common laborer performing menial chores for a woman with a cloud of soft dark hair and eyes the color of the sea.

A woman whose beautiful face was matched only by the beauty of her soul.

Back in his own time he would have known how to woo such a

woman. There had been a time when he'd held a position of respect in the world, when the good people of Boston had hailed him in friendship when he passed.

A time when he might have deserved a woman like Shannon.

But that time was no more and he wondered if it would ever come again.

Three more families had arrived during the night. Each woman had a story to tell of abuse and fear and the loss of self-respect. Their stories cut across all economic and social barriers, and each story reminded Shannon anew of how important these shelters were.

By nine in the morning, Shannon spent thirty minutes on the phone with a vocational school in Bridgewater, called for a repairman to fix the air-conditioning in both guest houses and refereed a loud fight between two of Pat Delaney's kids. Karen Naylor stopped by on her way to court to see if any of the women were interested in obtaining restraining orders against their husbands, but she met with resistance all around. The young lawyer did a great deal of *pro bono* work for the shelter and was often as frustrated as Shannon at the reluctance many battered women showed when it came to prosecuting the men who'd beaten them.

"I saw your friend Andrew," Karen said over a cup of coffee back at Shannon's house. "He was scraping paint off your windows."

"He enjoys working with his hands," Shannon said smoothly.

"An attorney who works with his hands? Not very likely."

Shannon offered up a bland smile. "What can I say? He's a Renaissance man."

"So, is it serious?"

Shannon arched a brow. "What's with all the questions?"

Karen pushed her coffee cup away from her and sighed. "It's been a while since I've come across something like this. I guess I'd forgotten how it felt."

"I don't think he meant to be rude."

"Maybe not," said Karen, "but he succeeded admirably."

"I wish there was something I could say to make you feel better."

Karen patted her on the forearm in an easy, affectionate gesture. "Not your responsibility, Shannon. Believe it or not, you can't change the entire world."

"I'm doing my damnedest," Shannon said with a smile.

"Speaking of which," Karen said, checking her Filofax, "I have an opening at one o'clock, if you'd like to come in and take care of the paperwork for the foundation." She looked back up at Shannon. "You did read everything, didn't you?"

"I'll get around to it."

"By one o'clock?"

"I promise."

"Ms. Wylie, we need to talk."

Dakota peered around the side of the huge stack of books she'd been hiding behind since lunchtime. "What's up, Dr. Forsythe?"

"You were fifteen minutes late. You know how we feel about lateness."

"My alarm clock didn't work."

"And you went home early yesterday."

She thought for a second. "I had a headache." *Didn't I?* She couldn't remember exactly what she'd said, only that she couldn't wait to get to Shannon's and grab a minute alone with Andrew McVie.

Dr. Forsythe tapped one loafered foot impatiently. "I can't talk to you with you hiding behind that stack of books."

She forced a bright, lighthearted laugh and rose to her feet, brushing decades of dust from her flowing paisley skirt. "Whatever gave you the idea I was hiding? I'm cataloging, for heaven's sake. That's all." *Right, Dakota. Just pray your nose doesn't start to grow....*

"Mrs. Payton will be in to make her bequest this afternoon. I'd like you to join us in my office to witness her signature."

Her brows knit in a frown. "What time is she coming?"

He frowned right back at her. Not a good sign. "Three o'clock. I hope that doesn't interfere with your schedule, Ms. Wylie."

It did, but she didn't think Dr. Forsythe would care to hear about it. "I have a luncheon appointment but I should be back by three o'clock."

His frown degenerated into a scowl. "Your work ethic is deplorable, Ms. Wylie. I would give great thought to my attitude, were I you. You're up for review in November. It would pain me to have to put you on probation."

What else could you expect from a man with an aura the color of a faded puce bedspread? He stormed off down the hallway and Dakota dived back behind the stack of books. Of course, none of this should have surprised her. Last night she'd dreamed Dr. Forsythe would try to throw a monkey wrench into the works and he had, just like clockwork.

Which also meant she was about to find what she'd been looking for. Closing her eyes, she visualized the book. It was a small, slender volume with a navy cover, no dust jacket and a chip in the bottom right corner. The frontispiece was missing and half of page eleven, but the name "Andrew McVie" was in the second sentence of the first paragraph on page 127.

She could see it all. She could almost smell it. But, damnation, where was the book hiding? It wasn't every day a psychic got her hands on proof that her best pal's new boyfriend was a time traveler. She flipped through the titles. *Apothecaries in Colonial New Jersey...Artists of the Revolution...Declaration of Independence: Call to Arms...Forgotten Heroes.*

"Forgotten Heroes," she whispered, grabbing the book from the shelf. Her hand tingled as she cradled the volume to her chest. This was it. She didn't even need to turn to page 127 to make sure. She

felt as if she'd been plugged in to a giant source of electricity and all of that electricity was zapping through her body right that very minute.

Though why Andrew McVie should have such an uncommon effect on her was beyond Dakota. He was an average man in every way. Average looks. Average height. Average coloring. Nobody she'd look twice at on a given day. And yet when she'd clasped his hand she'd felt the same sensation of pure electricity that she felt right now as she held the book.

She took a deep breath and flipped to page 127. First paragraph. Second sentence. *Pay dirt.*

> In an act of courage unequaled at that time in the War for Independence, Boston lawyer-turned-spy Andrew McVie staged a daring raid on British troops near Jockey Hollow during the winter of 1779-1780 and single-handedly saved two of the most important members of the Spy Ring from certain death when—

"Darn," she muttered. The bottom of the page was torn but it didn't matter. She had seen enough to know the truth.

Shannon reached Karen's office at one o'clock on the nose, and by one-thirty the papers had been signed, sealed and notarized.

"Okay," she said as she placed the cap back on her pen, "now let me get this straight. If I decided to pack a sarong and move to Borneo and live on coconuts, the shelters would survive."

"Not just survive," said Karen, handing the documents to her secretary to photocopy, "but thrive. You've done an extraordinary thing, Shannon. I don't know if you realize how extraordinary."

"It's only money," Shannon said with a shrug. "There's a limit to how many diamonds one woman can wear."

Karen shook her head. "No, kiddo, trust me when I say there's no limit. You're exceptional."

Shannon brushed away the compliment with a wave of her hand.

"So how are we doing with the overflow facilities? Last month's fund-raiser brought in plenty of promises, but how many followed through with satellite shelters?" She had new facilities under construction in Gloucester, Monmouth, Middlesex and Warren counties, but more were needed. It was exciting to see her brainchild grow, but the need for her brainchild was a constant source of sorrow.

Karen recited a list of names, only a few of which were regulars in the society pages. "See what I mean?" the attorney said, leaning back in her chair. "The ones with money and empty houses can't be bothered."

"We'll see about that at the gala this weekend."

Karen grinned. "You're going to hit them hard?"

"Like a sledgehammer," Shannon said, grinning back. "A sophisticated, well-dressed sledgehammer."

"You realize you don't have to do any of this, don't you? That's what the foundation is for."

"It's easy to say no to a foundation," Shannon said. "It's a lot harder to say no to me."

"The question, of course, is *why* do you do it? I was thinking about this the other day and I realized how little I actually know about you."

"I do it because it needs to be done."

"But there's more to it, isn't there?" Karen persisted. "Something personal."

Shannon just smiled. "You've been reading too many mysteries, Karen. Some things are exactly as you think they are."

"Not you," said Karen. "There's a lot more to you than meets the eye."

Shannon grinned and stood. "I'd better head home."

An odd expression flitted across Karen's face. "So how serious is it with you and Andrew McVie?"

"What makes you think there's anything between us, serious or otherwise?"

"He's living with you. That's a first to my knowledge."

"He needed a roof over his head."

"So now you're running a shelter for displaced Scotsmen?"

Shannon sighed. There was no avoiding this particular issue. "I know he has his problems, but Andrew is a decent man."

"I'm sure he is," Karen said, not sounding convinced.

"He just has a few things to learn about race relations."

"Don't we all?" Karen said in a dry tone of voice. "Every time I think we're making real progress, I run into someone like your friend and realize how far we still have to go."

Shannon gathered up her purse and portfolio. "I'll work on it."

Karen rose from her desk and showed Shannon to the door. "Take care of yourself," Karen said, giving her a warm hug. "You give me hope."

Andrew swung open the door to the white closet in the kitchen and stared at the array of foodstuff arranged within. Cold milk in a tall blue box, sticks of butter wrapped in shiny paper, chicken eggs nestled in a receptacle with depressions made to cup them like a nest. Two large beefsteaks rested on a glass shelf. Each was wrapped in pliable material that he could see right through. He bent and pulled out a bin marked Vegetables and saw an assortment that could have fed the Continental army.

Shannon had told him to help himself to anything he desired but he found that with such bounty to choose from he was unable to choose anything at all. In truth, he would gladly trade the contents of the white closet she called a refrigerator for a tankard of ale, a loaf of bread and a leg of mutton.

Surely there must be some bread in the house. In his world even the poorest families had bread in the cupboard. In the back of the refrigerator, behind a large metal cylinder marked V-8, he found a package.

The bread was mushy and sweet and not at all what he was accustomed to, but it filled his stomach. He ate five slices and took a few gulps of cold, thin milk and was about to return to his work outside when the telephone shrieked.

He tried to remember what it was Shannon had done to make it work, but before he had a chance to do so, it stopped shrieking and the sound of Shannon's voice filled the room.

"Sorry I can't come to the phone right now," she said, "but if you leave your name and number at the tone, I'll get back to you as soon as I can. Thanks."

He had started to say something when a peeping noise sounded, followed by a voice he didn't recognize. "This is Terri from the cottage. The kids went for a walk in the woods over an hour ago and th-they're not back yet. Do you think maybe you could drive over and help us? Sorry to bother you but we don't know what to do. Thanks a lot."

"I can find them," he said out loud to the empty room. He had walked those woods just the night before. It would not be a difficult task to find the children in the full light of day.

A few minutes later he crossed the yard behind the house, walked past the rectangular pond, then headed into the woods near the silver maple trees. He recalled a grove of pines a few hundred paces away, and a lightning-struck sassafras tree at a diagonal from the grove. The spot where the hot-air balloon had landed was some distance from there but Andrew found it without any difficulty, then stood perfectly still for a few moments, gaining his bearings.

He turned in the direction of the shelters, narrowed his eyes and slowly scanned each inch of leaf-strewn ground for signs of the children. It didn't take long. The leaves were disturbed near the shelter side of the woods, and he found a thumb-sized piece of bright orange paper with the strange words Peanut Butter Cups printed across it. It smelled sweet, like a candy, and Andrew reasoned one of the children had discarded it along the way.

In truth, it was a simple task to follow their path. It surprised him that the mothers were unable to do so. Footsteps in the dirt, crushed blades of grass, a copper coin glinting in the filtered sunlight.

Up ahead he heard the high-pitched sound of young voices and he picked up his pace. Moments later he stepped into a clearing and found the four children sitting on a log, morose expressions upon their faces.

"Oh, great," said one, looking up at him with disgust. "They sent the guy who talks funny."

"'Twould seem to me you would welcome my appearance," Andrew said, maintaining his temper in the face of such disrespect.

"Are you a cop?" the only girl in the group asked.

"I am a lawyer," Andrew said.

The children looked at each other and burst into merry laughter. Andrew did not much care for the sound of that laughter, for it seemed to hold an unpleasant edge within it.

The oldest boy met his eyes. "So what do you call a lawyer at the bottom of the ocean?" he asked.

"A good start!" the Negro boy next to him called out as the two slapped hands together.

"You find the death of a lawyer a topic of amusement?" Andrew asked, wondering about the nature of children.

"Lighten up," said the girl. "It's only a joke."

"I thought humor was the object of joke telling."

The Negro boy frowned. "You didn't think that was funny?"

"No," said Andrew, "'twas nothing funny about it." He could feel his spine growing rigid in true Boston fashion.

"But I got it from a book," said the first joke-teller. "They got about a hundred lawyer jokes."

Andrew's brows knit together in a scowl. "What is it about lawyers that creates such mirth?"

The children looked at each other, then at Andrew.

"Lawyers are greedy," said the girl.

"They're bad people," one of the boys said.

"My uncle is a lawyer," said the oldest boy, who was then treated to a series of rude noises and much laughter from the others.

Andrew crouched down near where they sat on a fallen log. "The function of a good lawyer is to maintain order in a civilized world."

"Tom Cruise was a lawyer in *The Firm,*" said the girl.

"Tom Cruise is a weenie," said the Negro boy, to cheers from the other boys.

"He is not," said the girl.

Andrew, thoroughly confused by this conversation, rose to his feet. "Your mothers are worried. 'Tis time you returned and put their minds at ease."

"It's boring back there," said the oldest boy. "There's only one TV."

"They don't even have Nintendo," said the Negro boy.

"I wanted to bring my Barbies," said the girl they called Angela, "but my mom was in too big a hurry to let me pack them."

They started walking back toward the shelters with Andrew in the lead. He did not know the nature of Barbie or Nintendo but he did know bone-deep fear when he saw it. The children hid that fear behind a cloak of rudeness and hilarity but it was still visible for those who looked beneath the surface.

He thought of his own David and wondered how the boy would have felt if violence between his parents had been part of his daily life. His imagination could not conceive of such a burden on so frail a pair of shoulders.

"How did you find us?" Angela asked, hurrying to keep up with him. "Derek and Charlie got us lost in the woods so deep we didn't think we'd ever get out."

"'Tis no great feat," Andrew said. "You need only know how and where to look."

Derek, the Negro boy, fell into step. "Everything looks the same in here. It's just a bunch of trees."

Andrew chuckled. "Pine, fir, sassafras, silver maple, holly—"

"I see Christmas trees," Derek said, "but the others still look the same."

Christmas trees? Andrew wondered what a tree and Christ's birthday could have in common.

Charlie, the oldest of the four, lagged behind with Scott, the youngest. "Who cares about this, anyway?" he asked in a belligerent tone of voice. "Only Boy Scouts know that stuff."

Andrew looked back at him. "You would not have been fearful had you known your way about."

"I wasn't scared."

"You were," said Andrew in an easy tone of voice.

"They're babies," Charlie said. "They were scared, but I wasn't."

"You were, too," said Scott.

"Yeah," said Angela. "You wanted your mommy."

"'Tis normal to feel afraid in a strange place," Andrew said, "but the more you understand about the things around you, the less afraid you will be."

Angela looked up at him and smiled. "I'm afraid of the dark," she confided. "Daddy took out the belt last night 'cause he caught me sleeping with the light on."

Andrew caught sight of a deep purple bruise peering out from beneath the half sleeve of her bodice. In his mind's eye he saw the little girl, crouched in fear, as her father made to hit her. What kind of world was this that a child should bear the marks of violence upon her person? He could not help but wonder if the seeds for this violence had been sown in his own time.

And if there was something that could have been done to save little girls like Angie—or women like Shannon—from knowing a man's rage.

The little girl looked up at him, considering, then took his hand. They didn't speak, which was just as well, because the lump in Andrew's throat made words impossible.

Chapter Fourteen

14

Shannon arrived home from Karen's office feeling tired and vaguely depressed. Not that she regretted signing the papers that secured the future for the shelters. Knowing that her fortune would be put to good use was a deep and abiding source of happiness.

But it was something else, something more elemental, that had triggered the sense of time passing quickly. Too quickly for her taste. She felt as if she'd lived a lifetime in the past forty-eight hours, as if everything she said and did and felt had more meaning now than at any other time in her life.

From the start she'd felt connected to Andrew in a way that defied logic, almost as if their souls were linked together in some strange form of communication. Then, in the space of a heartbeat, she'd stopped hearing his voice within her heart. Was this how it would be then, she wondered, a gradual pulling away until he left her behind to start a new life on his own?

Sighing, she walked up the driveway and around the corner of the house toward the French doors in the back. She had her hand on the doorknob, about to go inside, when something caught her eye and she turned. Andrew was hard at work at the far corner of the yard beyond the pool, and at a distance behind him sat four of the kids from the shelter. Not that she saw the children. All she saw was Andrew.

He was magnificent.

She stood stock-still, car keys dangling from her fingers, unable to draw a breath.

Utterly magnificent.

There were no other words for the sight of him, stripped to the waist as he split firewood in the backyard. She stepped beneath the shade of the silver maple trees and watched as the muscles in his back and shoulders flexed with each powerful swing of his ax.

This was the real thing, she thought as hunger sprang to life deep in her belly. Bone-melting, heart-stopping desire. She closed her eyes against a wave of pure heat radiating outward from the center of her being.

This was nothing she'd sought, nothing she'd expected to be part of her existence, but there it was in all of its elemental glory. The magical, life-affirming need to join with another human being and cast your lot with the future. She smiled to herself. Or with the past, as the case may be.

There has to be a way to make this work, she thought, watching him. She had wealth and position and influence. She could create for him a life that would surpass his wildest dreams if he would only let her.

The squeal of brakes brought her out of her reverie. *Please, not another emergency,* she thought as she hurried back toward the driveway to see who'd arrived. Sometimes they went weeks without seeing a soul, then all hell would break loose, the way it had last night.

She rounded the corner of the house in time to see Dakota leap from her battered '72 Mustang, holding a book aloft.

"Where is he?" Dakota called out as Shannon approached.

"In the backyard."

"Good," said Dakota. "This is important. I don't have time to faint right now."

"Very funny," Shannon said as prickles of apprehension nipped at the back of her neck.

Dakota glanced around. "Let's talk inside. This isn't the kind of thing you want anyone to overhear."

Shannon led the way into the kitchen, then leaned against the counter and looked at her friend. "So, what's with the book?"

"Page 127," Dakota said, handing the volume to Shannon. "First paragraph, second sentence."

Shannon checked the title. *"Forgotten Heroes."* Her hands began to tremble and she prayed Dakota wouldn't notice.

"Open it," Dakota urged, her voice high with excitement. "There's something I think you should know."

"This isn't another one of those New Age books about a man who saved the world with squash blossoms or something, is it?" *You know what it is, Shannon. This has something to do with Andrew....*

Dakota looked wounded. "I come to you with news that can change your life and you make a joke."

Shannon started to open the book, then handed it back to Dakota. "I don't think I want to look at this."

"He's from the past," Dakota said, pushing the book back to Shannon.

"That's ridiculous." She pushed the book back toward Dakota.

"Page 127," Dakota said, practically leaping around the room with excitement. "It's all right there."

"I don't know how to break this to you, Dakota, but people don't time travel. That only happens in the movies."

"It happens," Dakota said sagely. "We just don't hear about it."

"Uh-huh," said Shannon, striving for nonchalance. "And Martians are working at K mart."

"What you know about K mart could fit on the head of a pin." Dakota wagged a stern finger under Shannon's nose. "Just because you don't understand something is no reason to make fun of it."

"Sit down," Shannon said, gesturing toward a chair. When in

doubt, fall back on hospitality. "It's hot as blazes outside. I'll pour us some iced tea."

"Nice try," said Dakota, "but no dice."

"You're not going to let up on me, are you?"

"Absolutely not."

"I know what this is going to be," Shannon said as she grabbed the book back from Dakota and thumbed through the first few pages. "Some kind of crazy allusion to a guy with a Scots accent who—" She stopped, looked up, drew a deep breath, then looked down again at the torn page.

> In an act of courage unequaled at that time in the War for Independence, Boston lawyer-turned-spy Andrew McVie staged a daring raid on British troops near Jockey Hollow during the winter of 1779-1780 and single-handedly saved—

"Shannon?" Dakota touched her arm. "Are you okay?"

"No," said Shannon, sinking to the floor, "I don't think I am." Knowing Andrew was from the past was one thing. Seeing that fact right there in black and white was something else altogether.

"Are you going to faint?" Dakota asked.

"I never faint. You're the one who faints."

Dakota crouched next to her. "Your aura's looking a little pale."

"Leave my aura out of this."

"You knew, didn't you?"

"About my aura?"

"About McVie. He told you, didn't he?"

Shannon struggled to regain her wits. "Andrew McVie is hardly an uncommon name. There must have been hundreds of Andrew McVies alive back then."

"Check out the painting on the next page. If that's not McVie I'll turn in my crystal ball."

With great trepidation Shannon turned the page and found a reproduction of an eighteenth-century painting that depicted the Battle of Princeton. "I don't see anything."

Dakota leaned over her shoulder. "Right there," she said, pointing toward a figure in the lower left-hand corner. "That's him."

Shannon looked. No doubt about it. That was Andrew right down to the stubborn jaw and muscular torso. "They say everybody has a twin."

"Did you see the caption?" Dakota asked. "It says his identity was kept secret until the end of the war so he could continue sneaking around, doing all sorts of heroic things."

Shannon was beyond coherent thought. Her brain felt as if it had suddenly turned to mush. Dakota's got you dead to rights.

"That's why I fainted, you know," Dakota went on. "The guy has a force field you wouldn't believe. It's like he's carrying two centuries of baggage along with him."

She grabbed Dakota's hand, all pretense abandoned. "You can't tell anyone about this," she begged.

"Of course not," Dakota said with indignation. "What kind of person do you think I am?"

"And you won't tell any of your psychic pals, or your mentor, or Dr. Forsythe."

"What about the National Enquirer while you're at it? I might be able to get a few thousand for the story." Dakota lifted her chin. "You insult me, Shannon. I'm not an opportunist."

Shannon rested her head in her hands. "I know you're not, but this is important. If it got out that Andrew's a time traveler, we'd be signing his death warrant. The media would eat him alive."

"I agree," said Dakota. She leaned closer to Shannon and lowered her voice. "So, how did he get here?"

"Remember that hot-air balloon you saw him dragging across the backyard yesterday morning?"

Dakota nodded.

"That's how."

"You're kidding."

"No, I'm not kidding. He landed in the woods during the balloon festival, just like I told you."

Dakota frowned. "But that's not possible. The first hot-air balloon flight wasn't until 1783...and it was in France or some place like that."

"I can't explain it. I can only tell you what happened." She hesitated, then decided to go for broke. "He—he said he made friends with a couple who time-traveled back last summer."

"What were his friends' names?"

"I don't know," Shannon said. "Radcliffe, Rutledge. I think her name was Emilie."

"This is so exciting!" Dakota grabbed Shannon's hand and tried to pull her to her feet. "Let's go tell him about the book. I'm dying to see his reaction. I mean, the man is living history—"

"No!"

"No?You have to tell him about it. Wouldn't you like to see your name in some history book and know you influenced the course of events?"

Shannon held firm.

"Oh," said Dakota, the light dawning. "He can't read, is that it? Don't worry, I'll teach him. What's one more student?"

"He was— I mean, he is a lawyer, Dakota. He can read."

"So what's the problem?"

"This." Shannon pointed to the date.

"The winter of 1779-1780," read Dakota. "So?"

She met Dakota's eyes. "Andrew left his world in August 1776."

"Time is fluid," said Dakota after a moment. "It might've happened."

"Time isn't that fluid," Shannon shot back. "Besides, wouldn't he remember doing something heroic in the middle of a blizzard in the middle of a war?"

"But it's here in black and white," Dakota said. "How do you ex plain it?"

"You're the psychic. I was hoping you could explain it."

"Maybe he goes back in time again."

Shannon felt a sharp stab of pain deep inside her chest. "Give me that book." She grabbed it from her friend and headed for the library.

"What are you doing?" Dakota ran after her. "That's museum property."

"Not anymore it isn't."

"Shannon! I'm in enough trouble with Dr. Forsythe. It's bad enough I took the book out of the building. He already thinks I'm a flake. If he finds out the book's missing, I'm out of a job."

"I'll pay for it." Shannon strode across the library and climbed the rolling ladder in the far corner of the room. "*Plutarch's Lives.* That's the ticket." She dropped *Forgotten Heroes* behind the tome. From the looks of the dust, *Plutarch's Lives* hadn't been touched in aeons. For once she was glad her cleaning service wasn't as thorough as they claimed they were.

She climbed back down the ladder, feeling quite pleased with herself until she saw the look on Dakota's face.

"I can't believe you did that," Dakota said.

"I'll write you a check," Shannon said defiantly. "I'll write you two checks. I'll buy you a house in Bermuda. Whatever it takes to keep you quiet."

"You don't look like yourself."

"I don't feel like myself."

Dakota narrowed her eyes and peered at Shannon. "Your aura's changing again. I swear it's Day-Glo orange now."

Because I'm doing something for me, Shannon thought. Because I've waited all my life to find someone like Andrew and I can't let him go. "You're not going to tell Andrew, are you?"

"I won't have to," Dakota said, placing a hand on Shannon's forearm. "This can't last, Shannon. This isn't his destiny. His future is somewhere else."

"You're wrong." Shannon backed away from her friend. "We make our own destinies, and this is where he wants to be. It was his choice, Dakota. Not mine."

"That ain't gonna work." Scott looked up at Andrew. "You need a power screwdriver."

"It will work," said Andrew, considering the eaves of Shannon's house. He had not the slightest notion as to what a power screwdriver was, nor would he ask any of the children who had been watching his every movement since he found them in the woods. There was something unseemly about a man of thirty-three years seeking counsel of a child.

His attempt to engage their interest in physical work had thus far been for naught. They seemed strangely content to sit and watch him move about as if he were performing for their amusement. He was reminded of the moving-picture cabinet in Shannon's house that thus far held little appeal for him.

"Where are your safety glasses?" asked Charlie, the oldest. "That guy on TV says you gotta wear them all the time."

"That guy don't know nothing," said blond-haired Angela. "My cousin's got a power saw in his basement and I never seen him wear glasses."

"That's 'cause he's stupid."

"Is not."

"Is."

"Is n—"

"Sweet Jesus!" Andrew roared. "Lend some assistance where it is needed and cease that infernal racket *now!*" Four young faces stared up at him, mouths agape, but nobody moved. Andrew pointed toward Charlie. "You will hold the ladder while I climb.

And you—" he singled out Angela "—will fetch nails for me. And the rest of you will stack the wood."

"I don't know how to stack wood," said Derek.

"'Tis a simple enough task," he said.

The boy frowned. "D'ya think there are any spiders in the wood?"

"I cannot say with certainty but the wood is freshly cut. I do not believe spiders have found it yet."

"Okay," said Derek. "Then I'll do it."

"Good decision," said Andrew, biting back a smile. He did not hold a great deal of affection for spiders either.

He felt naught but affection for Derek. His black skin mattered not at all.

But Derek is still a boy, a voice inside him spoke. *How will you feel when he is a man and vying with you for a place in the world?*

He thought of his reaction to Shannon's friend Karen. Had he responded solely to her race and gender, or had there been something else at work, a sense that in this world he might not measure up to their standards of success? The idea was one he did not wish to pursue.

The children set to work with speed if not enthusiasm. The boys were dressed in a most peculiar fashion—baggy pants rolled up to midcalf, shoes the size of rowboats with the laces untied, strange caps with the bill worn in back. The girl wore short pants in a bright green color and a half-sleeved shirt that was many sizes too large for her small body.

They looked strange to his eyes, yet in many ways little had changed in two hundred years. Children still reacted to a strong leader and to discipline.

"Is this right?" Derek called out. He was lugging a good-sized log to the stack already begun near the back door.

"'Tis most right," Andrew said, climbing the ladder.

"You talk funny," said Charlie, holding the ladder. "Are you English?"

"I was born in Boston." He could not remember being as comfortable in the company of adults as these children seemed to be. To speak so freely to a man old enough to be your father—he could not imagine doing so as a child.

"They talk strange in Boston."

He reached down for a handful of nails. "They talk strange in New Jersey."

"Nah," said Charlie. "We talk normal."

"'Tis a matter of perspective."

Angela squinted up at him. "What's that?"

"Perspective is how you look at things." Across the yard Derek struggled to lift a second log.

"Take a smaller one," Andrew called out. "Better two trips than to overtax yourself."

Derek nodded then did as Andrew suggested, and Andrew found himself sharply reminded of his son. David had been much like that boy, eager for direction. Eager for guidance.

Eager for approval.

Aye, there is the rub. There had been so little time for them to spend together—six short years—and most of those six years Andrew had squandered in the pursuit of his career. Ofttimes weeks would pass when he did not see his son, weeks in which the boy changed in ways Andrew could but wonder at when he returned home.

His eyes swam with tears. He blinked rapidly and willed them to stop. He had done the impossible and traveled through time to a world two hundred years in the future, but he had never found the way to tell his son that he'd loved him and been proud of him.

"'Tis a fine job you're doing," he said to the children. "All of you."

"Thanks," said the one holding the ladder, "but now the gutter's crooked. You gotta do it over again."

Andrew looked, then looked again. "You are right."

"Yeah," said the boy, grinning. "I figured you'd wanna know."

"'Tis always better to know," he said, using the back of the hammer to remove the nails.

"Not everything," said the boy. "My mom says what you don't know can't hurt you."

"Your mother is wrong," Andrew said with conviction, thinking of a little boy who lived on only in his heart.

It was what a man didn't know that had the power to hurt most deeply.

Chapter Fifteen

15

Dakota rounded up the kids and took them back to the shelters a little before five o'clock. Shannon had always marveled at her friend's ability to relate to children without talking down to them, a particularly tricky proposition when you were dealing with children from families torn apart by abuse. Before the night was over Dakota would have not only determined their reading levels, but she would have won their hearts, as well.

Shannon wandered about the house for a while. She flipped on the news, watched a bit of it, then turned off the television. She couldn't concentrate on a magazine, didn't feel like listening to music. Actually she found it impossible to do anything but think about the book she had hidden in the library. How could she think of anything else with the battle raging between her heart and her conscience?

She sank onto the bottom step in the foyer and rested her head in her hands. The vision of him, shirtless in the fierce sunshine, burned against her eyelids. *Is this what you want for him, Shannon? Is he going to spend the rest of his days fixing loose gutters and splitting firewood?*

He'd been there only a handful of days, she reasoned with herself. You couldn't expect him to leap into a new life with career and future intact. Those things took time, even under more normal circumstances. Granted, he couldn't return to practicing law but there had to be something he could do, something important and fulfilling. Something that would keep him by her side forever.

There's nothing wrong with manual labor. Some people would say it's more honorable than practicing law.

But there was a limit to how many repairs he could do on her house. She had a brief, ridiculous vision of herself as Penelope, the wife of Odysseus, but instead of unraveling a tapestry each night, she broke windows and pulled down gutters—all so Andrew would have work to do the next morning.

You're a rich woman. You could start a business and make Andrew the CEO. He'd have a job and self-respect and—

"You idiot," she muttered, dragging her hands through her tangled hair. Who was she kidding? He was a proud man. A situation like that would be a sure recipe for disaster somewhere down the line.

He had no identification—good grief, the only driver's license he was likely to ever have belonged to Emilie Crosse, and she was alive and well and living in 1776. Any records pertaining to his existence were centuries old.

Think, Shannon. There has to be a solution. She'd created a new life for herself, albeit with a little help from the Feds. She'd overcome the horror of her marriage and found a way for other women to benefit from her experience. Surely she could find a place in her world for an extraordinary man like Andrew McVie.

But whatever she found, whether it was a position as a CEO or day work as a laborer, was there anything in her world that could compare to being a hero in the world he'd left behind?

"Dakota's wrong," she said, rising to her feet. Andrew had told her that according to Emilie and Zane there was no further mention of him in history books after the summer of 1776. What Dakota had found had to be a mistake…or maybe a coincidence.

For all Shannon knew someone had appropriated the name Andrew McVie and performed one lone act of heroism that managed to get itself reported in one lone history book. Big deal. It didn't prove anything.

The only thing she knew with certainty was that Andrew McVie was in her world and part of her life and she intended to do everything in her power to keep him there.

Shannon went outside around six o'clock.

"I'm going to fire up the barbecue and cook up juicy, politically incorrect steak," she called up to Andrew. "Do you like yours rare, medium or well?"

"'Tis still daylight," he said, wiping his arm across his forehead. "I will continue to work until dark."

"Those eaves can wait another day," she said lightly, watching him replace a board.

"They cannot," said Andrew. The pounding of the hammer provided a counterpoint to his words.

"Is something wrong, Andrew?"

"A strange question." He pounded in another nail. "'Tis nothing wrong."

"You don't seem like yourself." *Is that your guilty conscience speaking, Shannon?*

"Nightfall approaches," he said, "and I have much to do."

"If you change your mind, all I have to do is toss another steak on the grill."

But he didn't change his mind. Not that she really thought he would. The set of his jaw told her that more clearly than any words he could have spoken.

Something has changed, she thought later as she ate her steak on the patio and watched him work. For the past two days he had shadowed her movements, been part and parcel of her every waking moment. And now everything was different and she couldn't say why. It wasn't as if he knew about the book Dakota had found, for that was still safely hidden in the library, far away from curious eyes.

She speared a lettuce leaf from her salad plate and considered him. There was a barrier between them now, a sense of separateness that hadn't been there before.

She sat straight up in her chair, fork poised halfway to her mouth. She no longer heard his voice within her heart. That was the difference. The almost mystical connection between them that had swept away her sense of caution had been replaced by the sense that this interlude was only temporary.

Damn Dakota and her psychic nonsense. She pushed her plate away and sat staring out toward the pool. If Dakota's fortune-telling skills were half as good as she claimed, the woman would be picking lotto numbers, not working three jobs and wearing thrift-shop clothing.

Wonderful, Shannon. Now you're turning into a bitch as well as a liar.

She loved Dakota dearly and knew there was nothing phony or self-serving about her otherworldly talents. Shannon had seen too many of her friend's predictions come true to consign her to a nine hundred number on late-night TV.

But Dakota couldn't be right this time. Shannon was willing to fight the gods to keep this one chance at happiness from slipping through her fingers. Fate had brought Andrew to her and she wasn't about to let fate take him away.

Not in this lifetime or any other.

Andrew ceased work at dusk. He collected the hand tools scattered about the ground and was carrying them into the garage when Shannon appeared in the gathering darkness. She wore white pants that left her legs bare and a yellow bodice that revealed her midriff to his eyes. Her feet were bare, and even in the blue light of dusk he could see the pale pink color gleaming up at him.

He caught the scent of her perfumed skin on the soft night air, and a fierce hunger came to life deep inside his body.

"You must be hungry," she said, following him into the garage.

"Aye," he said. "The smell of beef on the fire has that effect."

"There's salad and corn ready now." She watched him as he placed the hand tools in the receptacle. "The steak'll be ready by the time you're finished."

He looked at her sharply. "You are a rich woman," he said. "How is it you do your own chores?"

"I don't always," she said. "Mildred usually cooks for me. Didn't I tell you about Mildred and Karl?"

"Aye," he said. "Still, I cannot imagine another woman of your wealth performing menial chores for a stranger."

Her sigh floated toward him and he wished he could reach out and capture it and hold it close to his heart. "I enjoy cooking, Andrew. Especially when there's somebody around to appreciate it."

They had turned to leave the garage when Shannon stopped abruptly.

"Sweet Jesus," Andrew said.

"The balloon." Her voice was little more than a whisper. "What on earth—?"

The covering he had placed over the balloon and basket had slipped off, revealing a most disturbing sight. The silk fabric of the balloon was faded almost white, while the basket appeared to be disintegrating before his very eyes. They looked as if they had traveled through the centuries and scarcely survived the journey.

The thought came to him that what had been done could not be undone, for without the balloon and its magic fire he was destined to live out the remainder of his days in Shannon's world.

"Poor Andrew." She placed a hand against his arm, and he felt her touch move through his body like a brushfire. "We'll find a way to make this work."

"Aye," he said. "I made my choice when I climbed into the basket, and I do not regret it."

"I hope you never will."

Will you still feel thusly in a month, lass, or will you wish me gone when I wish with all my heart to stay?

She met his eyes and he watched as a look of pure joy lit her lovely face from within. He did not know what had caused her to look at him with such wonder, but he knew that he would carry the memory with him to his grave.

Andrew ate as he did most things, with appetite and enthusiasm. After he finished, Shannon cleared the table then suggested they watch television in the den while they shared coffee and dessert.

"You still don't seem very enthusiastic about television," Shannon observed as they clicked past a "Cheers" rerun.

"'Tis like reading a book but without the challenge," he said. "There is no room for the imagination."

"Imagination is in short supply these days," Shannon said. "Most people want their entertainment as simple and easy to digest as possible." She channel-surfed until she landed on "I Love Lucy." "Now this is required viewing if you want to understand American culture."

It was a classic Lucy episode. Ricky was putting on a show at the Tropicana and Lucy wanted to be part of it.

"I do not understand his reluctance," Andrew said. "Why does he not grant her wish?"

Shannon grinned. "You've heard her sing. Lucy has no talent, that's why."

Andrew considered her statement for a moment. "I have seen no evidence of singing ability from Ricky Ricardo."

Her grin widened. "I think 'Babalu' is a masterpiece."

"Lucy is a comely lass," Andrew went on, a gleam of amusement in his hazel eyes. "She would be an asset to her husband."

"Another sexist statement! You must stop seeing women as adjuncts to men. We're free and independent and we don't need men to provide for us."

"I am a product of my time. I make no apologies for it."

"If you're going to make a life in the twentieth century, you have to adjust." She watched as he devoured a chocolate chip cookie in an exceedingly male fashion, and felt a delicious tingle of excitement. *You're in bad shape, Shannon. Getting turned on by a man eating cookies.*

"Turned on?" Andrew asked.

"Turned on?" she echoed.

"You do not know the meaning of the phrase, either?"

"I mean— It's just—" She stopped and took a deep breath. "We turn on lights and televisions and radios."

"That is not what you meant."

"How do you know what I meant? I don't recall saying anything like that."

"You did," he persisted. "I heard the words most clearly."

"I don't think so."

"Aye, Shannon." His voice grew lower, his tone caressing. "They were your words and I heard them inside my heart."

"I don't think we should talk about this." Talking might make it go away and that was the last thing she wanted to happen. Just a few hours ago she'd thought that magical connection was lost to her forever. But then, in the dim light of her garage, she had heard his thoughts as clearly as she heard her own and it seemed as if someone had handed her back her heart.

How could there be any doubt that she'd made the right decision when she hid the book Dakota had found?

He wanted to stay with her.

In her time. In her world.

When two people were so attuned that their thoughts were one, it had to mean their destinies were one, as well.

"You have experienced it also," Andrew said. "I know by the way you look at me, the things you say."

"It happened that very first night." She glanced away. "Yesterday your thoughts were closed to me until—"

"I know," he said. "It was thus for me, as well."

She met his eyes again, seeing beyond his physical self to some place deeper, more complex, more wonderful. "I have never felt this way before."

"Not with your husband?"

She shook her head. "I loved Bryant, but it was different." The love she'd had for her first husband had been built upon a foundation of family expectation and naiveté, and when harsh reality showed its face she'd accepted the blame the way other women accepted compliments. "Surely you loved Elspeth."

"With my entire heart," he said simply. "But when she left this world she no longer loved me."

"You can't know that," Shannon said, wishing she could ease his pain as he had eased hers.

"Aye," he said. "I can. On the last day I saw her, she said the love she'd held for me had died and only duty remained." His voice broke and he cleared his throat. "She was a good woman. She deserved more than I had been able to provide."

"The world hasn't changed very much in two hundred years," Shannon said after a moment. "We still make the same mistakes." Their gazes met. "And we still hope for a happy ending."

"As in a child's story?" he asked, a slight smile playing at the corners of his mouth.

"Is that so awful? Where is it written that the things we wish for can't come true? You wished to travel to the future and you did it,

Andrew. And I—" She stopped abruptly as hot color flooded her cheeks.

He captured her hands in his. "What is it you wished for, Shannon?"

"You," she whispered. "I wished for you."

Chapter Sixteen

16

Words.

Plain words, simple in their meaning.

But with those words the world was his and everything in it.

Andrew's heart soared with joy as he drew Shannon into his arms. She was so small against him, her frame so delicate and womanly, that the need to protect her against the world battled his own fierce need to possess her right there on the floor as if she were a—

He pushed her away, struggling to douse the fires raging throughout his body.

"Andrew?" Her aqua eyes were wide, her lips soft and pink. Had she no knowledge what such a look could do to a man? "Is something wrong?"

"Aye," he managed with great difficulty. "You have an uncommon effect upon me."

"I'm glad."

Her words puzzled him. It was not the reaction he had expected. "That does not offend you?"

"It pleases me," she said in a voice that promised wonders beyond knowing, "for you have an uncommon effect upon me, as well."

"It is not my wish to cause you alarm."

"I know," she whispered, laying her hand against his cheek. "I think I've known that from the first moment."

"In my own time I would not hesitate, but here—" He shook his head. "I fear the rules of courtship are much changed."

"Court me, Andrew. Court me the way you would have if we'd met in your world."

He clasped her hand in his, marveling in the fragile bones that hid the strength of ten.

"'Twould be a slow and careful wooing." He bent his head forward and raised her hand to his lips. "There would be much time for walking together—" he pressed his lips against the palm of her hand "—and for social intercourse." He closed her fingers to hold the kiss. "And for watching the fire dance on a cold winter's night."

Her eyes seemed to grow darker as she watched him. "But it's summertime...what did you do in the summertime?"

"This."

She fit against him as if she'd been fashioned for his pleasure, and he knew that his pleasure had grown most apparent as she moved closer. His hands spanned her waist, that naked expanse of skin that had tantalized him the first time he saw her standing by the rectangular pond, and he feared his control would not withstand the temptation.

"A slow wooing," Shannon said in a dreamy voice. "Exactly how slow would that be?"

"Many months," he said as she linked her arms behind his neck. "A man might court his lady a year or better before—"

"Too long." She kissed the side of his neck. "We move a lot faster today."

"'Tis true," he said, blood rushing southward. "I have seen the speed at which you move."

"Life is short," she said. "That's one of the things we've learned."

"If my life ended at this moment, Shannon, I would die a happy man because I would be with you."

She pressed a kiss to the line of his jaw. "I'll bet you say that to all the girls you drop in on."

"I am not a flatterer. I speak what is on my mind and in my heart."

"I know," she said, placing her index finger against his lips. "I have heard all you have to say but now I want you to be quiet and kiss me."

Her words were powerful and they had a most amazing effect upon his person. He blazed to life, hungry for her yet painfully aware of his own strength.

"I am a...passionate man," he said bluntly. "I have no desire to cause you any discomfort." He would rather die celibate than hurt her in any way.

"I know you won't hurt me." She sounded surprised that he would say such a thing.

He thought of the pain she had suffered at her husband's hands, and persisted. "There are times when I do not know my own strength."

"I'll be the first one to remind you."

He cupped her face in his hands and met her eyes. "I have not been with a woman in a long while. I may be less than you expect."

"Never," she said, her voice fierce. "You are already more than I've ever dreamed."

He claimed her mouth with his, but in truth he knew that it was Shannon who was claiming him, heart and soul and body.

Somewhere in the background Lucy and Ethel were cooking up another harebrained scheme, but Shannon didn't hear a word.

Andrew swept her up into his powerful arms and, not breaking their kiss, carried her upstairs to her bedroom on the second floor. The door was ajar and he kicked it the rest of the way open with the tip of his boot and a thrill of recognition rocketed through her body. Without breaking stride he crossed the room toward the four-poster bed beneath the window and an instant later they were tangled together on the feather mattress.

He kissed her hungrily, as if he couldn't get his fill of the taste and smell of her. His naked hunger brought her to a fever pitch and she moved against him, running her hands along his back, down to his waistband, sliding her fingers beneath his shirt until she found his smooth, warm skin.

Was it possible to get drunk on the feel of a man's body beneath your palms? That powerful swell of muscle, the heat, the knowledge that you were playing with fire and looking to burn.

He spanned her waist with his hands, intoxicated by her smell, the satiny feel of her skin, the knowledge that all that separated him from paradise were a few thin layers of fabric and a supreme act of will.

They lay together on their sides, legs entwined, breaths mingling, hearts pounding wildly. She ran her hands up the length of his back and he feared he would lose all control.

"Nay," he muttered, moving away from her on the soft and welcoming mattress. "I am in danger of reaching the end before we have the chance to begin."

She reached for him, urging him closer by the look in her eyes, the soft smile on her beautiful mouth. With a groan he pushed her back against the mattress and straddled her hips. He found the closure of her short trousers but his fingers could not work it open.

"It's called a snap." Her voice was husky, different. He watched as she pulled the two pieces of fabric apart.

He fingered a tiny metal tab that waved just beneath the snap. "And this?"

"A zipper." She sounded unbearably alluring to his ears. "You pull down on it."

He did as she instructed, easing the tab over the gentle curve of her belly, lower, then lower still until he could feel her heat. "A zipper," he said as the garment fell open, exposing a small band of cream-colored lace to his gaze. "A new invention?"

"Not that new."

"'Tis amazing." He bent lower over her body, breathing deeply of her scent, then pressed his mouth against her belly.

She made a sound deep in her throat as he traced a design with his tongue. He tugged at the scrap of lace with his teeth. "A world of wondrous inventions."

She moved restlessly beneath him as he stripped her of her outer garment. His breath caught sharply in his throat as he gazed upon her shapely legs and hips, clad in naught save that wisp of lace so sheer he could see the thick, dark curls covering her mound. He cupped her with his hand, felt her wet heat against his palm, imagined burying his length deep inside her body and hearing her cry out as she found her release.

Shannon reached again for him, tugging at his shirt, fumbling with the buttons, baring his chest to her hands and mouth. She pressed her face against him at the point where his arm met his torso and drew in a deep, shuddering breath that he felt in all parts of his body. She seemed to find great pleasure in the sight and touch of him, and his own pleasure multiplied in response.

Her blouse was fastened with ordinary buttons and he quickly slipped them through the buttonholes, only to discover more cream-colored lace, this time hiding her breasts from view. But not entirely. He saw the dusky shadow of her nipples beneath the filmy barrier and with trembling hand he drew a finger across curve, then valley, then curve again.

"What is this called?" he asked, hooking a finger under a strap.

"A bra," she said. "Actually, a brassiere. The purpose is—"

"The purpose is plain," he said, "even to me."

Less plain, however, was how to remove the brassiere from her person.

"Having trouble?" she asked.

"'Tis a devilishly puzzling garment." He ran his hands beneath the stretchy fabric.

"Most boys can open a bra before they're fifteen," she said with an innocent smile.

"Are you implying I am less skilled than a child?" he asked, growing most annoyed with his lack of ability.

"You're a resourceful man," she said. "I have no doubt you'll figure this out."

And when he did she laughed, a soft, throaty, woman's laugh that pleased him beyond measure.

"See? I told you that you were a resourceful man," she said with obvious delight.

"Aye." His own delight was obvious, as well. The brassiere was still warm from her body. Indeed, it seemed to retain her shape with its own. He gazed down at her, his blood heating with a need that went beyond desire. She was small but beautifully made, as if an artist had created her from a dream of splendor. A dream he'd never dared dream before now.

He rose from the bed and removed shoes and stockings, then unfastened his trousers. The undergarments—briefs, she had called them—were an embarrassment and he felt more himself when he was naked on the bed with her.

"Come to me, mistress," he said, opening his arms.

She smiled, recognizing the endearment, and did as he bid her to do. There was nothing hesitant about her demeanor, nor anything coy. She seemed as eager for what was to come as he, without artifice or apology. He had never before known a woman with such a capacity for joy, and the sensation brought him close to the edge.

She lay at an angle across his body, her breasts flattened against the hard wall of his chest. He held her by the hips, moving her slowly—wonderfully, deliciously—against his arousal until she thought she would faint with longing.

But it was more than longing. It was hunger, a hunger that went so deep, cut so close to the bone, that she couldn't hide from it even if she wanted to. The hunger slashed through her defenses and exposed her beating heart, the heart she'd thought locked away forever.

I can take no more, Andrew. His cadence had somehow become her own. *Now...please, now....*

He slid his hand inside the leg band of her panties and stroked her. "You are certain?" he asked.

She was beyond speech, beyond thought, beyond everything but the moment—and the man.

He inched her panties down over her hips, her thighs, then slid them off and tossed them to the floor. "Nothing will happen that you do not wish to happen," he said as he poised himself over her body. "It is for you to say."

"Yes," she whispered, opening her arms wide. "I say yes."

With a groan he covered her body with his own. His powerful erection pressed hard and fiery and magnificent against her belly. She cupped his face with her hands and willed him to know that she belonged to him alone, that traveling through time was nothing compared to the miracle of finding love when you'd given up hope.

He fit himself between her legs. She felt him press against her wet heat. She arched upward. He thrust forward. She opened for him, surrounded him, met his passion with more love and joy and wonder than she'd ever believed one woman could hold inside her heart.

She gave him her body, but more than that she gave him back his soul. He knew the precise moment it happened. When he entered her, her aqua eyes opened wide and she looked at him, watched his face as he sank deeper into her willing softness, and she smiled. Smiled as if he'd somehow managed to gather up the moon and the stars and place them at her feet.

He had been with many women in his life. He knew that the moment of euphoria he found in a woman's arms never lasted the night. With the cold light of dawn came the realization that he was alone, had always been alone, would be alone until he drew his last breath.

But this time it was different. He pleasured her through the darkest hours of the night, and with the approach of dawn he took his own pleasure in the sight of Shannon, asleep in his arms.

Her thick tangle of lashes cast shadows across her cheeks. Her tousled hair lay soft against his shoulder. She stirred, turning onto her other side, and he felt a sharp pain in his heart as he saw the shiny white curve of the scar that her husband's knife had left behind.

He came from a rougher world than the one in which he found himself. Men ofttimes spoke with their fists, even within the four walls of their home. Somehow he had imagined better of the twentieth century. They had been blessed with riches beyond knowing and yet the same problems that had beset the men and women of his time still existed today.

Leaning forward he pressed his lips against the pale scar tissue, breathing in her scent. Not even those dark thoughts were enough to dim the joy she'd awakened inside his heart simply by virtue of her existence. The fact that she had lain with him, offered him the wonders of her body—was there a man in this world or any other who had ever been granted a greater honor?

She slept deeply, her bosoms rising and falling with the rhythm of her breathing. After a while he slept, as well. He did not dream, for nothing he could dream could compare to the wonder of lying there next to a woman such as Shannon.

In truth, he did not know what it was that awakened him, but he found himself drawn from the warmth of the bed he shared with Shannon. He crossed the room swiftly and went straight to the window, where he pulled the curtains and looked out on a landscape oddly dark for that hour of the morning.

The yard was shrouded in shadows. An unnamed dread filled him as he lifted his gaze to the tops of the trees and saw a most peculiar cloud cover towering up toward the heavens. He knew the striations of dark and light, the low whistle of the wind, the way it called to him like one of the sirens who lured sailors from the sea.

"The lighthouse," he murmured as the sense of dread grew stronger. That same cloud cover had enveloped the lighthouse on the day Andrew had left his old life behind.

He stood there as the cloud cover lingered then passed, feeling as if something had been asked of him and he had failed to answer.

"Andrew?" Shannon's soft murmur curled itself inside his ear. "Come back to bed."

"Aye," he said, turning away from the window. "'Tis the one place I wish to be."

Chapter Seventeen

17

Dakota was halfway out the door when the telephone rang.

"I can't talk to you now, Ma," she said, cradling the receiver against her shoulder. "If I'm late for the library one more time, Forsythe'll have my head."

"I had a dream," Ginny Wylie said in the tone of voice she reserved for major announcements.

"So what else is new?" Dakota mumbled, eyeing the clock over the refrigerator.

"Dakota? What did you say?"

"I really have to go, Ma. Why don't I call you at lunch—"

"This will only take a minute," Ginny said with the blithe confidence of a woman whose place in the world was secure. "You're going on a trip."

"To work," Dakota said, "if you'd let me hang up the blasted phone."

"I don't have to tell you any of this," Ginny said, sounding aggrieved. "I'm just trying to give you food for thought."

A car phone, Dakota thought eyeing her old Mustang in the driveway. *Give me a car phone so I can get to work on time.*

"You've met a man," Ginny continued, "and he's going to change your life forever."

The hairs on the back of Dakota's neck rose and she sank onto a kitchen chair. "A man?" She forced a laugh. "The only man in my life is Dr. Forsythe, and we both know how much he loves me."

"He's not handsome, but he's...compelling." Ginny drew in a long, noisy breath. "And he's not from around here—Dakota? Are you still there?"

"I'm here, Ma." *With my head between my knees.* She felt the blood rushing to her brain but didn't dare sit up straight for fear she'd pass right out on the floor. "Does this guy have a name?"

"Adam," said Ginny. "Andrew, maybe?"

The room swam in front of her eyes. "He's a friend of Shannon's," she whispered.

"There's more to it than that, isn't there?"

"I really can't talk about this now, Ma."

"Your future is tied up with his."

"I don't think so."

"Yes, it is," said Ginny, "and when he goes home, you're going to go with him."

She sat straight up and burst into laughter. "I don't know how to break it to you, Ma, but this time your dream radar is way, *way* off base."

"So where's he from?" Ginny asked. "Chicago? I know you hate Chicago."

"It's worse than Chicago."

"Denver?"

"Worse than Denver."

There was a long silence, then, "I'm not picking anything up on this, Dakota. Why is that?"

"Good grief," said Dakota, leaping to her feet, "will you look at the time! Gotta go, Ma. Talk to you later." She hung up the phone and raced for the door before Ginny had the chance to redial her number. Right on cue, it began to ring as she locked the door behind her.

Ginny was nothing if not persistent.

And accurate?

She closed her eyes and tried to imagine herself with Andrew McVie, but her mind was a blank screen. He and Shannon belonged together and nothing would change that.

But you know your future is linked with Shannon and Andrew's.

"Of course I do," she said out loud—never a good sign, even in the best of times. "That doesn't mean I'm going to be their shadow." As the only single Wylie sibling, she'd had more than her share of being the fifth wheel. She couldn't imagine spending her life in that position.

Andrew's stay here was only temporary. Of that Dakota was sure. And, God knew, she'd never seen two fates more intertwined than his and Shannon's.

So where does that leave you?

"I don't know," she said, starting toward her beat-up Mustang, which was parked at the end of her driveway. She supposed that left her where it always left her, playing the good friend, or the witty psychic sidekick.

Or maybe the catalyst.

She stopped dead in her tracks as she considered the notion. A catalyst? It didn't make sense. She hadn't brought Andrew and Shannon together, and she certainly would never do anything to keep them apart. Other than swoon every time she saw him, the only thing she'd done was dig up a dusty old history book that had turned Shannon into a crazy person.

Still, the feeling persisted that there was more to it than that. All her life she'd had the feeling she was meant for more than the mundane reality of everyday existence. Was it possible there was a grand adventure waiting for her, right around the corner?

Like maybe in the next hot-air balloon that floats by.

"Yeah," she said as she climbed into her car and started up the engine. "Right."

The only grand adventure in store for her was a trip to the unemployment office if she didn't get to the library before Dr. Forsythe.

"Three billion sold," Andrew read from the sign beneath McDonald's golden arches on Route 206 a few miles north of Princeton. He turned toward Shannon. "Three billion what?"

Shannon pulled into the parking lot. "Hamburgers."

Andrew looked at her with a blank expression on his face.

"Chopped beef that you form into patties and fry on a grill then serve on little round pieces of bread."

"To what purpose?"

"Your dining enjoyment. It's the same as the hamburgers we had at the restaurant before." She laughed and got in line behind a Chevy Blazer loaded with little kids. "Did I forget to tell you about the pickles, lettuce, onions, ketchup and special sauce?"

"Aye," he said. "You forgot."

A minute later she stopped in front of the menu board and a voice crackled through the speaker, "Welcome to McDonald's. Can I take your order, please?"

"Sweet Jesus!" Andrew leaned across Shannon to take a closer look. "Is there a machine to replace each one of us?"

"Just about," said Shannon.

"Your order, please," repeated the speaker voice.

"Big Mac, chef's salad, large fries and two iced teas."

"Drive up to window one."

"Real food will be found at window one?" Andrew asked.

Shannon grinned. "American classic cuisine at its best."

"'Tis a most amazing thing."

No, she thought a few minutes later as they sat together in the car and ate lunch. *The only amazing thing in this big wide world is that you're sitting here beside me.*

"So, what do you think?" she asked as he swallowed a bite of his first Big Mac.

He popped a fry into his mouth while he considered the question. "I think I should like another one."

"A junk food junkie," she said with a rueful grin. "Who would've thought it?"

He looked at the burger with suspicion. "Mayhap I will reconsider. 'Tis not a good thing to eat junk."

"You're so literal minded, Andrew. Junk food means quick food, fast food, anything that's not your regular sit-down dinner."

He attacked the burger again with gusto and she found herself shivering with delight. Last night he had brought that same exuberant appetite for pleasure to her bed. She had lived almost thirty years and had never known her body was capable of such transcendent delight until Andrew McVie took her in his arms.

She had gone to her ex-husband a virgin, both emotionally and physically, and Bryant had taken that naiveté and destroyed it. From the start she'd believed she wasn't good enough, pretty enough, sexy enough to satisfy him, and it had taken a very long time for her to understand that none of it was her fault.

She'd regained her self-respect but she'd never believed that sensuality would be part of her life. She told herself it was okay, that you couldn't miss what you'd never known, but there was a hollowness inside her heart that wouldn't go away.

Until last night.

She felt her cheeks redden and she looked away, a smile playing at the corners of her mouth. All it took was the thought of his strong hands stroking her inner thighs, the sound of his voice as he said her name over and over and over again to bring her once again to life.

So this was the secret, the force that made rational people into fools and fools into poets. She glanced toward Andrew and found him watching her. The sunlight brought out the golden flecks in his hazel eyes and she thought she'd never seen a man more magnificent—or glimpsed a heart so true.

Andrew remembered Princeton as a small town situated in the midst of heavy woods and lush farmland. For the most part, to his amazement, it still was.

In truth, the farmlands were diminished and the heavy woods were confined, but the character of the place was unchanged. Princeton was a small town blessed with intellectual and artistic energy, both of which were blended with a rural take on life that had survived the years.

When Shannon turned the car to the left and drove down Nassau Street, he found himself engulfed in memory of a time just a few weeks past—and many worlds away.

"A tavern once stood here." He pointed to the corner of Nassau and University Place. "'Twas a common meeting place for the spy ring."

"I hear your words," Shannon said, "but it's so hard to believe you're seeing Princeton from across two centuries."

"Emilie and Zane stood on that corner. It was there that she told me in her time women ruled countries and went to university and did all that men do, but I did not believe her." And now, with the truth in front of his eyes, he still ofttimes found it difficult to fathom. "She took great offense at my disbelief."

Shannon abruptly pulled the car off to the side and stopped.

"'Tis something wrong?"

"You loved her," she said flatly. "Didn't you?"

"Nay, Shannon, 'twas not love but infatuation."

"But you thought it was love at the time."

He would not deceive her, not even to make things between them go more easily. She deserved better from him than that. "Emilie was unlike any woman I had ever seen before. She spoke of wonders beyond knowing. 'Twas easy to mistake that for something more."

"And what about me? Would you have felt— Are you with me because I am the first woman you met or because you want to be?"

"I am with you because there is nowhere else in this world or any other that I wish to be."

An odd look drifted across her face, a look he had never before seen. "What if you could go back to your own time?" she asked.

"That question is not relevant, for the opportunity to do so does not exist."

"But what if?" she persisted, resting her hand on his wrist. "Now that you've seen this world, what would you do? Would you go back?"

"I would stay with you," he said, feeling the truth of his words deep inside his heart. "Whatever the time or place." He leaned across the small barrier she called an armrest and touched the soft skin of her cheek. He wished he could reach inside her head and banish all memory of the husband who had treated her so badly.

Mayhap then she could believe happiness was theirs for the taking.

Shannon parked the car in the U-Store lot, then she and Andrew walked over to Nassau Hall. Except for Dakota's involvement with the historical society, she'd never given much thought to the wealth of history that surrounded them in central New Jersey. But when you were walking with a man who'd been around when the history was being made, you couldn't help but gain a new perspective on things.

Some of the houses on Alexander and University boasted plaques that commemorated their dates of construction: 1752, 1768, 1772. Once Andrew placed his palm flat against the door knocker of a stately three-story house and said, "William Strawbridge was a terrible merchant but a true patriot. He passed along many a message at great risk to his own family."

Stockton and Witherspoon weren't streets to Andrew; they

were people. Richard Stockton and his wife, Annis, who buried the family's silver—much as Andrew's friend Rebekah Blakelee had—to keep it safe from the marauding British soldiers. And John Witherspoon, who came from Scotland to be president of the College of New Jersey, only to become the lone man of God to sign the Declaration of Independence. People who had lived and breathed and fought in Andrew's own time. People who were remembered still.

As Andrew would be if he'd stayed in his own world.

No. She refused to think like that. She wasn't responsible for him climbing into a hot-air balloon and taking off for the twentieth century. He'd come here of his own free will and he was staying here for the same reason.

"We could drive over to Morven or Drumthwacket," she said as they started walking down University Place near the Princeton railroad station, where commuters caught the shuttle known as the "dinky" that connected them to the main line. "I believe Morven was built before the war started."

"Nay," he said, "but there is one thing more I would like to see before we leave this place."

"Anything," she said, summoning up a carefree smile that hid her guilty conscience.

"The Blakelee farm."

"I never heard of a Blakelee farm anywhere around here. Was it close by?"

"Aye," he said. "Naught but a short walk from the center of town."

"I doubt if it still exists, Andrew. You can see what's happened. Much of the farmland has been turned over to developers for housing."

"Your friend Dakota," he said. "Does she not work for an historical society?"

Dakota couldn't believe her eyes.

She'd just come back from a quick lunch at the pancake shop

near the movie theater when she saw Andrew McVie and a grim-faced Shannon walking toward the reference desk. McVie was dressed in jeans and a plain white cotton shirt that strained against his powerful shoulders. He still didn't do much for her, but she had to admit he looked wonderful today. Especially with that ponytail. She'd always been a sucker for men with ponytails, and he looked exceptionally good with it.

Shannon, however, looked as if she was about to jump out of her skin.

I know you don't want to be here, Dakota thought, trying to send the vibes directly to her friend, *but can't you see what's happening?* Fate had the three of them all tied up together in one unwieldy package and there was nothing any of them could do to change that.

Wasn't this proof positive of that? Shannon would rather chew ground glass than visit the museum. And she certainly didn't want Dakota anywhere near Andrew.

But there they were, coming toward Dakota like a pair of intrepid bloodhounds in search of quarry. She looked from Shannon to Andrew, then back again. No, she was certain Shannon hadn't told him about the history text hidden behind Plutarch's *Lives,* which meant they wanted something else—something Shannon obviously wasn't too thrilled about. But what?

"Hi," she said, leaning across the reference desk. "Fancy meeting you guys here."

"Good day, mis—Dakota." Andrew favored her with a pleasant smile. "You are looking well."

"And you have wonderful taste." She glanced down at her Mexican peasant blouse and grinned. "Fifty cents at the thrift shop in Somerville." *I haven't swooned yet,* she thought. *It's a miracle!*

"This isn't a social call," Shannon said, a warning look apparent in her eyes. "We need some information about a revolutionary-war-era farm outside of town."

"Then you've come to the right place," Dakota said easily. "Whose farm?"

"The name was Blakelee," said Andrew. "Josiah and Rebekah."

"We have records in the archives," Dakota said, "but a master list on microfiche." She spun her chair around and turned on the machine. "Let's see what I can find out." She mechanically flipped through the pages. "There was a Blakelee farm between here and Griggstown but, according to the records, it passed into the creditor's hands in 1778." She spun back around to face Andrew and Shannon. "Much of the property was sold in the 1950s to a land developer but part of it was reserved under the Green Acres provision."

Andrew looked so distressed that her heart went out to him. "Are they—" He cleared his throat and began again. "What happened to the family?"

"It doesn't say here but, if you like, I can check some of our other records."

"I would be in your debt," said Andrew.

She shot a look in Shannon's direction. *You have to do something about his speech patterns,* that look said. This was 1993. Nobody was polite anymore, not unless they were displaced time travelers who hadn't learned the ropes yet.

"Give me a minute," she said. "Archived material is kept downstairs." She gestured toward the leather sofas lining the window. "Make yourselves comfortable." She glanced down and noted that they were holding hands. Apparently they were already more comfortable than she'd realized.

Oh, Shannon, she thought as she raced past the leaded windows that looked out on Dr. Forsythe's colonial-era knot garden. *Do you really think this is going to last?*

Hiding behind a pillar she looked back at the two of them, seated together on the sofa with the light spilling over them like a benediction. She closed her eyes for an instant, praying she'd been wrong, praying things would be different, but when she opened her eyes and looked—really looked—at Andrew, she found nothing had changed.

The man had no aura. The light around him was from the sun streaming through the windows and nothing else. He was as irrelevant and temporary in this world as a good hair day was to Lyle Lovett.

The wonder was that nobody else saw the things she saw when they looked at him. A chain of history followed him wherever he went. Thousands of lives were somehow tangled up with the fate of this one solitary man from another time.

Would those lives vanish into the mists if he remained here? Would it be as if they never existed, never had the chance to live and love and walk this earth? A wave of dizziness crashed over Dakota and she clung to the pillar for support. She rested her hands on her thighs and bent her head, struggling to regain her equilibrium for the second time that day.

Shannon loved him. You had only to see the two of them together to know that for a fact. And, God knew, she deserved the best life had to offer. But nothing good could come of flying in the face of history.

Unless that book was wrong.

The thought caught her attention and she straightened up, her head clearing. How many texts had she thumbed through that were filled with errors, both minor and major? Hundreds, that's how many. Scholars were not infallible, no matter what they might like the hoi polloi to believe. One book did not a destiny make.

Love was a powerful force, she thought as she continued on her way to the basement. She prayed it would prove to be more powerful than the sense of farewell that was growing stronger by the minute.

Chapter Eighteen

18

"She is gone a considerable time," Andrew observed as he and Shannon sat on the couch and waited.

"I know," said Shannon, tapping her finger against the armrest. "Maybe she ran into Dr. Forsythe and he sent her to do something else."

"Dr. Forsythe?"

"Her boss. They have, shall we say, a confrontational relationship."

"She watches us as if she knows what we are about. 'Tis a most disconcerting notion."

"That's one of the problems with having a psychic for a friend. Keeping a secret is harder than it should be."

"She does not know how it was I came to be here, does she?"

"She knows about the balloon," said Shannon, shifting uncomfortably on the leather cushion. Hiding the history book was one thing; lying to Andrew was something else. "She—she seems to suspect there's more to it than that."

"Aye," said Andrew. "'Tis as I thought. It is in her eyes each time she looks at me."

But it wasn't anything like he thought. Dakota knew everything except for the fact that Shannon and Andrew were lovers, and considering Dakota's psychic antennae she probably knew that, too.

Shannon stood and smoothed the front of her walking shorts. "You know, it's beginning to look like Dakota's going to be stuck for a while. Why don't we just leave her a note and she can drop off whatever information she finds when she comes by to teach the kids?"

Great idea, but about thirty seconds too late.

Shannon and Andrew were halfway out the door when Dakota came racing across the room waving a sheaf of papers.

"Sorry I took so long," she called out, "but some idiot filed these with survey maps instead of death records."

Andrew recoiled noticeably, startling Shannon. *These are his friends,* she reminded herself. *A few days ago they were alive and well and celebrating their daughter's wedding.*

"It was a bit hard to find," Dakota went on, acting as if there was nothing unusual going on, "but apparently the Blakelees moved back to Princeton in 1785 and lived here until their deaths. Josiah died in 1799. Rebekah followed in 1801."

Andrew nodded, a muscle on the right side of his jaw jerking spasmodically.

"There is another couple," Shannon said, knowing he would not ask, "who once lived in Princeton with the Blakelees. I heard about them once—Zane and Emilie Rutledge."

"Where did I hear those names before?" Dakota wondered. She looked at Shannon, then her cheeks reddened. "Give me five minutes and I'll see what I can do."

Andrew reached for Shannon's hand as Dakota hurried away. "'Twas a generous thing you did."

"I must be crazy," Shannon said with a quick laugh. "Finding out about my own competition."

"There is no other," Andrew said. "No woman could compare to you."

His words touched Shannon's heart and she pressed a quick kiss against his lips. "I knew you wouldn't ask for yourself, so I figured I would." *Generosity, Shannon, or just your guilty conscience?*

Dakota was unable to find any information pertaining to Emilie and Zane Rutledge, but when Andrew mentioned that Emilie's maiden name was Crosse, the floodgates opened.

"Crosse Harbor," said Dakota as she handed Andrew a sheaf of papers. "It looks like Emilie and Zane had a mansion near Philadelphia and a summer house on the Jersey shore. Since this is a New Jersey museum, that's how it was referenced."

"How did Crosse Harbor come to be known by her maiden name?" Shannon asked.

"Who knows?" Dakota shrugged her shoulders. "Maybe she was emancipated before her time. It's not that unusual for a woman of the era to wish to perpetuate her family's name in some way."

'Tis Emilie as I knew her, Andrew thought. He looked toward Shannon and felt a wash of emotion that warmed him, body and soul. *A woman unlike any other until you.* She met his eyes and he knew by the expression in their aqua depths that she'd somehow heard his thoughts and understood his meaning.

His eyes burned with unshed tears as he looked down at the top page. "The Rutledge family, one of the foremost families in the Commonwealth of Pennsylvania, was founded by Zane Rutledge and his wife, Emilie Crosse. Their five children, Sara Jane, Andrew—"

"I cannot read this," he said, folding the papers and stuffing them into the breast pocket of his shirt. *A child,* he thought. *A boy who carries my name...*

He could feel the eyes of the two women boring into him with iron-hot intensity but he could not find the words to explain his actions.

"We should go," Shannon said. "You know what rush hour on 287 is like."

Dakota seemed reluctant to let them leave. "If you wait a little bit longer, I might be able to find more information on the Rutledges of Pennsylvania."

"Nay," said Andrew a bit more gruffly than he intended. "'Tisn't necessary. I know all I need to about them."

Dakota walked with them to the door. "So I'll see you guys later. I'm bringing over a pile of 'Sesame Street' books my mother found at a yard sale."

"'Sesame Street'?" Shannon asked. "Aren't the kids a little old for that?"

"When you can't read it doesn't much matter if you begin with Ernie and Big Bird or Shakespeare. All that matters is that you learn to read."

It occurred to Andrew that Dakota was as extraordinary in her own way as his Shannon was. These women felt commitment to a cause beyond themselves, as he once had, and he wondered if they knew how fortunate they were.

Dakota stood in the doorway and watched as Shannon and Andrew walked hand in hand down the street.

"Coward," she whispered to herself. Maybe Shannon didn't have the heart to tell him the truth about his destiny, but there was no excuse for Dakota. She wasn't in love with him. In fact, except for the way he looked at Shannon as if she was the best thing since sliced bread, she wasn't entirely certain she even liked him. What kind of man would leave a time where everyone's effort counted, where one person could bring about changes that would affect a nation's destiny?

He had no business abandoning his true fate. So what if life was not what he had wished it to be? Maybe if he'd stayed put instead of leaping into the first hot-air balloon to come along, he might be carving a place for himself in history, a place reserved for heroes.

Down in the archives she had uncovered two more documents with mention of Andrew McVie's heroism during the winter of 1779-1780 featured prominently in the text. *You don't understand,* Shannon had said. *He left in August 1776.*

And you don't understand, Dakota thought. *He's going back again.*

Shannon was quiet on the drive home. She blamed it on the rush-hour traffic, which was true enough, but that was far from being the entire reason.

You're getting good at this, Shannon. Bet you never thought you were such a skillful liar.

Lying? She hadn't lied to Andrew about anything. She'd side-stepped, underplayed and concealed, but she hadn't lied.

Can you look him in the eye and say that, Shannon?

"Oh, shut up," she muttered, exiting the highway.

He looked toward her. "Lass?"

"Nothing," she said. "I was just talking to myself."

"'Tis a bad sign," he said with a playful grin. "When I practiced law in Boston, that was cause for arrest."

"We're not in Boston," she replied.

"Aye," he said, rubbing his chin, "and this is not 1776."

She looked at him sharply. "You sound disappointed."

"That was not my intention. I am but stating a fact."

"I know what year it is, Andrew. I don't need you to point it out to me."

"You are unwell?"

"What makes you ask that?" Her tone of voice was cool enough to frost a margarita glass.

"'Twould seem the best explanation."

"I'm not entitled to a bad mood?"

"You do not wish an answer to that question."

She glared at him. "Wimp."

"I do not know that word."

"Good," she said. "It's an insult. Not particularly apt, but an insult."

"You are behaving in a most uncharacteristic fashion, lass. In truth, it appears each time you and your friend Dakota are in each other's company."

"You're imagining things."

"Nay," he said. "I know what I see and hear."

"Maybe time travel damages the gray cells."

"I do not understand the meaning but I believe it to be another insult."

What in hell are you doing, Shannon? This is the man you've waited your entire life to find and now you're pushing him away with cheap wisecracks a cut-rate comic in Las Vegas wouldn't touch.

She turned onto the long, winding driveway that led up to the house. She wanted to tell him she was sorry, but the words wouldn't come. She felt brittle as glass, as if the slightest movement would shatter her heart into a thousand pieces.

She suspected Dakota had found something more about Andrew, probably more proof that he had saved the world or something equally grand and heroic...and impossible if he didn't go back where he came from. Shannon could feel the truth of her suspicions deep inside, in the place where her guilt was growing bigger by the minute. She'd thought her heart would stop beating when Dakota handed over those pages about Emilie and Zane.

She glanced over at Andrew and saw the bulge of photocopied papers in his breast pocket. God only knew what information they contained.

The question, of course, was why reading about people who were two hundred years dead should bother her as much as it did. Those people were no more real to her than Julius Caesar or Napoleon or Genghis Khan. How was it Andrew's friends exerted an influence over her across the centuries?

Maybe it's because you don't believe it's over.

She glanced over at Andrew, who was looking straight ahead, his jaw set in granite.

Maybe it's because I love you.

He turned to meet her eyes.

Neither said a word as she pulled the car into the garage.

The moment lengthened, shimmered, wrapped itself around their hearts and drew them closer together.

"I'm sorry," she whispered. "I've been hateful."

"And I have been a fool." From his pocket he pulled the sheaf of papers Dakota had given to him and ripped them in half. "The past is done."

Shannon watched as the pieces of paper drifted to the ground near the hot-air balloon and prayed Andrew would never regret his decision.

They lay together that night in a spill of moonlight. Their lovemaking had been sacramental, a joyous celebration of the miracle that had brought them to this time and place. If there was anything more to ask of life, any blessing she'd been denied, Shannon couldn't imagine what it was. Lying there in Andrew's arms she felt a sense of wonder that filled her with delight and made her feelings of guilt seem insignificant.

"Are you happy?" she murmured, her lips brushing against his chest. "Is this everything you thought it would be?"

"A strange question, lass, considering the events of the past two hours."

She laughed softly and circled his nipple with her tongue. "I want you to be happy," she said fiercely. "I don't ever want you to wish you'd stayed in your own time. We can make this work, Andrew. I know we can."

Her words caught him by surprise. He'd never understood a woman's need for constant reassurance. Apparently it was one trait that had survived throughout the centuries.

He grabbed her by the waist and pulled her up the length of his body until her mouth was but a kiss away from his. "Have I expressed dissatisfaction?"

"No, but—"

"Am I here with you, in your bed?"

"Yes, but—"

"Then say no more, for we have other business to conduct between us."

"You couldn't possibly… I mean, we just—" A low, throaty laugh. "How positively amazing!"

"Aye," he said, reaching between them until he cupped the hot wetness between her legs. "Amazing."

She was slick with their spent passion. He slipped one finger into her willing body and felt his shaft grow hard as her muscles tightened around him. With his thumb he toyed with the lush curls that covered her mound, then gently rubbed the source of her greatest pleasure. She arched against him and her soft moan of delight brought him close again to madness.

He wanted more. He wanted to worship her, glory in her, brand himself with the smell and taste and heat of her.

"I will not hurt you," he said as he moved her to the edge of the bed. "You believe that, do you not?"

"Yes," she whispered. "I believe that."

He knelt on the floor next to her and spread her thighs, burying his face at her most secret, woman spot. He found her with his mouth. She smelled of sex and of life…hot…sweet…as ripe and juicy as a fresh peach on a summer's day.

She arched against him, presenting herself for his lips and mouth and tongue, and he took all that was offered and demanded more. She spent herself again, her cry of ecstasy ringing out in the quiet room, and he found himself close to ecstasy at the sight and sound of her passion.

He lay with her on the mattress and held her close as her heartbeat slowed.

"No one," she whispered, kissing his mouth...tasting herself upon him. "No one but you. Not ever."

He understood the meaning of her words and they filled him with a sense of triumph. "Only me, Shannon," he said, his voice fierce with pride. "From this day forward, there is only me."

She leaned up on one elbow and even in the darkness he could see the shimmer of emotion in her beautiful eyes. "Lie back down," she said in a tone that brooked no argument. "Now it is your turn."

He had never before known a woman who so firmly took control of the act of love. Even the whores with whom he'd taken his ease were paid to do a man's bidding. Such enthusiasm and invention were beyond his ken. He did not know whether to protest or go willingly.

In truth, he had not time to make that decision, for his beautiful Shannon made it for him. She trailed kisses down his torso, his belly, until she reached his manhood. He ached for her touch but she was coy, fingering him lightly with teasing strokes along the inner muscles of his thigh, cupping him, then withdrawing her touch until he felt he would explode with need.

"You play a dangerous game, lass," he said as she drew her tongue upward from the base of his shaft. "A man can be contained for only so—"

His moan was wrenched from the depths of his being as she took him in her mouth. Her movements were tentative at first, as if such an act was alien to her, but her eagerness and desire to pleasure him were so intense that she quickly discovered how to bring him to a fever pitch. She suckled him, she teased him with her lips and tongue and teeth, she fondled him as if the weight in her palm brought her pleasure.

Indeed, she seemed by her demeanor as if the act of bringing him pleasure brought her such, as well. He would not have thought it possible that a woman could derive physical satisfaction from pleasuring her man, but the proof was undeniable.

"No more, lass," he said, grabbing her by the shoulders and drawing her up the length of his body. "'Tis a release we will find together."

She smiled at him, a smile of dark pleasure and understanding, then straddled him in much the same way she had straddled him the night they met. But this time it was different. She was naked, in both body and soul, hungry for the act of completion that could only come with the joining of a man and a woman in sexual congress.

He lowered her onto his hard shaft, slowly, gently, until with a sigh of pleasure she took his full length. She moved to an inner rhythm, one he swiftly made his own, and moments later they found paradise together.

I love you, lass, he thought as he fell back to earth.

He heard her voice in the darkness. "Aye," she said.

Chapter Nineteen

19

"Remember," said Shannon the next morning as she moved her hip closer to his, "this was your idea."

"I know that, lass."

"It might hurt."

"Aye."

She shifted her weight and set herself. "On the count of three. One…two…three!" Andrew went flying over her right shoulder and landed with a thud on the grass at her feet.

"See?" she asked, crouching next to him. "A woman *can* best a man."

Andrew lay there on his back and stared at her without moving.

She bent over him. "Andrew?" She placed a hand on his chest. "Are you okay?" There was no response. Her heart beat faster. "Andrew! Don't do this to me…. Say something, please."

With a roar he gathered her to him and rolled her onto her back, covering her with his body. "'Tis a parlor trick you play, lass," he said while she laughed. "Naught but a strange sleight of hand."

"It's called karate. Anyone can do it." She grinned. "After many years of practice, of course."

He kissed her soundly. "A most unusual skill for a woman to possess."

"A necessary skill for a woman to possess if she's smart. I wish I'd known how to do this when I was married. Things might have been very different." At the very least, she would have left Bryant at the first sign of violence.

"And this is what you teach the women who come through your shelters?"

"Among other things, yes." She took his hand and he helped her to her feet. "Mostly we teach women self-respect. Learning to defend yourself is a great way to start."

He was quiet for a moment. "The girl Angela has need of such knowledge, as well."

"Damn," Shannon whispered. Children were so vulnerable. To suffer at the hands of a parent was unthinkable. "It starts so early."

"Is there something you can teach the children that would give them this self-respect you talk about?"

"There are all sorts of role-playing games that the social workers—" She stopped. "That sounds ridiculous, doesn't it? Those kids need something more than role-playing to give them confidence. They need someone to teach them how to find their place in the world."

"Aye," said Andrew, "and they need someone to teach them how to find their way through the woods." He shook his head. "Within shouting distance of the house and they could not find the path back again. 'Twas a sorry thing to see."

"That's it!" Shannon grabbed his arm. "We could do a kind of mini Outward Bound program."

"I have no knowledge of Outward Bound."

Enthusiasm bubbled through her. "One of the things we've lost in my world is the ability to live without modern conveniences. Outward Bound takes people into the wilderness and forces them to develop survival skills."

"'Tis something those children would be well served by."

"Would you?" she asked, excitement building.

"I do not follow, lass."

"You could take them camping for a night, Andrew! I know they'd have a wonderful time and, best of all, you could pass on what you know about living with nature."

"My knowledge is of another time."

"Some things don't change. Basic survival skills, for example. Technology can't help you when you're alone in the woods with only your wits."

"'Tis something to consider."

"It could be great fun, Andrew," she said. She smiled at him. "Besides, I could use a refresher course myself."

"You should have been a lawyer, lass, for you plead your case with great skill."

She wound her arms around his neck. "We need to do it soon. It's Thursday already and I doubt if any of them will still be here this time next week."

"Then we will do it tonight."

She kissed him hard. "Not tonight. I'm not ready to share you with anyone tonight."

His beautiful hazel eyes twinkled with delight. "When will you share me, lass?"

"I've been meaning to talk to you about that, Andrew. How would you feel about escorting me to a charity ball on Saturday night?"

"What is the alternative?"

"I attend alone."

He bristled and she loved him for it. "Then I will escort you."

She grinned up at him. "You'll need a tuxedo."

"Tell me what it is, lass, and I will decide if I do."

"It's a type of formal apparel."

His sandy brows slanted downward. "Would it require another visit to the tailor?"

"Of course."

"Then I will not go. That man measures more than the length of a seam."

Shannon started to laugh. "They have your measurements on file. I'll go to the mall and you can stay here."

"'Tis fine with me. I noted that the garage needs repair," he said. "I will tend to it while you are away."

She glanced up at the sky. "Looks like a storm is brewing. I'd better get out and back before those black clouds open up."

She kissed him, then ran back to the house to change her clothes. Andrew's smile vanished when she disappeared inside.

Those are not storm clouds, lass, he thought, looking up at the sky. Once again it was the same cloud cover he'd seen the day he climbed into the hot-air balloon...and the same cloud cover he'd seen at dawn yesterday.

Mayhap there was nothing so peculiar about those clouds after all, he reasoned as he crossed the wide expanse of lawn and headed toward the garage. They seemed to occur in this world with some frequency, if the past few days were any indication.

The garage was open and he stepped inside. His intention was solely to gather up the hand tools and set to work, but he found himself drawn to the corner of the structure where he'd stored the basket and balloon.

"'Tis a mistake to look," he said aloud as he approached. What did it matter if the silk of the balloon had faded even more or if the basket looked as if it had traveled through a nor'easter? He did not seek a way back to his own time.

Still, his curiosity could not be denied. He pulled the cover from the odd contraption and stared in disbelief. This time it was not the fading of the fabric that gave him pause; it was the nature of the fabric itself. The color had remained constant since last he viewed it but the silk was thinner, almost transparent in nature, so sheer it looked as if it could not sustain a puff of smoke, much less the magic fire that had transported him there. The torn pages Dakota had given to him were scattered about and he pushed down the stirrings of curiosity.

"No matter," he said, turning away. Emilie and Zane... Josiah and Rebekah...they were gone, all of them. Their lives had been played out long ago. It was his turn now. His turn to choose the life he deserved.

He was not looking to leave this place. Not so long as Shannon loved him.

"You look awful, honey."

Dakota looked up from the stack of papers she was cataloging. "Mom! What are you doing here?"

Ginny Wylie was the mirror image of her daughter, except twenty years older. They shared the same short-cropped black curls, dark eyes, funky clothes sense and psychic abilities. Over the years the latter had made the mother-daughter relationship rocky at times and sublime at others. The one thing it never was, was boring.

"I had another dream," Ginny announced. "I had to come see for myself."

Dakota removed her glasses and rubbed her eyes. "Well, now you've seen, Mom. I'm still here, still single. I haven't run off with some mystery man. Satisfied?"

Of course, Ginny wasn't. She sat on the edge of the desk and considered Dakota. "You've gained weight."

"Thanks, Mom. Have you noticed the bags under my eyes, too?"

"I'm not being critical, honey. I'm worried about you."

"There's nothing to worry about," Dakota said, wondering where this was leading. "I'm fine."

"No, you're not."

"Is this a psychic assessment or a maternal judgment?"

"A little of both." Ginny leaned forward and grabbed Dakota's hands in hers. "You've been having dizzy spells, haven't you?"

"I'm not pregnant, if that's what you're asking."

Ginny made a face. "Of course you're not pregnant. You need a man to get pregnant."

"Thanks again, Mom," Dakota said dryly. "I'm fat, light-headed and manless. And people wonder why I'm considering therapy."

"They've been here, haven't they?" Ginny lifted her head and practically sniffed the air like a bloodhound.

Why waste time denying it? This was as bad as when Dakota was sixteen and praying Ginny's ESP wouldn't come up with the fact that she was dating the town bad boy. Unfortunately that sounded more exciting than it actually was. In her day, the Princeton High School bad boy was a rich kid with an overbite and five overdue library books.

"Yes," Dakota said at last. "They were here yesterday."

"You can feel it in your bones," Ginny said. "The man has quite a force field around him."

"Tell me about it," Dakota muttered.

"That's why you've been fainting, isn't it?"

"I haven't been fainting. I've been swooning. There's a difference."

"Is it only when he's around?"

You're good, Mom. I have to grant you that. "He doesn't have an aura, Mom. Standing next to him is like standing at the edge of a black hole in space." *Great going, Dakota. As if she doesn't know enough already.*

"So when's he going back?" Ginny asked with the same matter-of-fact tone she used to ask if you wanted more mashed potatoes.

"Back where?"

"Wherever he came from." Ginny waved her hand in the air. "To 1588, 1776, 1812. It's somewhere around there."

"What makes you think he's from another time?"

"I have no idea," said Ginny. "I just know it's true."

Dakota tried to sidestep the issue. "He's living with Shannon."

"Not for long," said Ginny. "He has an opportunity to go back right now but he isn't paying attention to the signs."

Dakota swallowed. "You feel that, too?"

"Who wouldn't?" countered Ginny. "It's clear as the nose on your face."

"What if he doesn't go right now? Will he get another chance?"

"The window is shrinking," Ginny said with conviction. "Sooner or later he'll lose his opportunity."

"And then what? He won't die or anything, will he?"

"I don't know," said Ginny. "But there will be far-reaching repercussions. His future is tied in with the futures of many others. That's one thing I'm sure of."

Dakota thought of the papers she'd given to Andrew. She wondered how he felt reading about the struggles his friends had endured during the war, the dangers they'd faced. "I wish I could make Shannon see that."

"She's in love with him, isn't she?"

Dakota nodded, wishing she had some Oreos. "I'm afraid so."

"Tell her not to worry," Ginny said with breezy assurance. "She can go with him."

Dakota had to laugh out loud. "You make it sound so easy."

"It is easy," Ginny said. "Just follow your heart."

"Most people don't have to follow their hearts across the centuries."

"Life's an adventure, honey. Most people are scared to death of living out their dreams."

Dakota was reminded of the time fifteen or sixteen years ago when her parents had taken the family to see *Close Encounters of the Third Kind.* They'd all been mesmerized by the story of ordinary people handpicked by extraterrestrials to experience life on another planet. After the movie Ginny had asked the kids what they thought about the movie, and Dakota's siblings had all agreed they'd like to see the inside of a spaceship but they wouldn't like to live there.

"I would," Dakota had piped up. "I'd go to outer space in a minute."

Her brothers and sister had laughed and teased her mercilessly but Ginny had met her eyes, and in her mother's look Dakota had seen understanding and admiration.

"I really should get back to work, Mom," Dakota said. "Dr. Forsythe's been on my case lately."

Ginny made a face. "Oh, who cares about him. You're not going to be here forever, honey."

"You're a regular ray of sunshine," Dakota said. "First you tell me I'm fat, then you tell me I'm heading toward unemployment. What's next, Mom? Gonna tell me there's no Santa Claus?"

"Very funny." Ginny leaned across the desk and kissed her daughter's cheek. "Don't forget what I said, honey—life's an adventure."

"What exactly does that mean?"

"You'll know when the time comes." Her mother's aura was a sunny lemon yellow, probably just like Mother Teresa's.

Dakota let out a sigh of exasperation. "This is how psychics get a bad name," she said, feeling irritable and out of sorts. "If just one of us could answer a question in plain English, we'd all be a lot better off."

"I'll ignore that," said Ginny. "Your aura's looking a little off today." She patted Dakota's hand and stood. "The Fountain of Vitality has a sale on ginseng. You might want to stock up."

With that her mother swept out of the library in a cloud of patchouli, leaving Dakota staring after her.

Of course, Dr. Forsythe chose that moment to pop out of his office.

"You know how I feel about visiting with friends on work time, Miss Wylie."

Dakota looked up at him blandly. "You've mentioned it a time or two."

"Friends visited you yesterday." He made it sound like a crime against humanity.

"With a legitimate question of an historical nature." *Don't look at me like I graduated from Romper Room. I went to college, too, Forsythe.*

"And what about that oddly dressed lady who was sitting on your desk?"

Dakota grinned. "That was no 'oddly dressed lady' sitting on my desk, Dr. Forsythe. That was my mother."

His cheeks reddened. "Well, keep her off your desk."

"I'll do my best," said Dakota.

"See that you do."

"Puce," said Dakota.

He looked at her. "What was that?"

"I said puce. Your aura's puce. You really should do something about that, Dr. Forsythe."

Dr. Forsythe stormed off, muttering something about insubordination, but Dakota just smiled. *You're right, Mom,* she thought. *I won't be here forever.*

She wondered how she would like unemployment.

Chapter Twenty

20

The salesclerk at the men's store at Bridgewater Commons had turned fawning into an art form. Shannon, never a fan of groveling adults, found it difficult to mask her distaste.

"You're certain you can deliver the tuxedo by tomorrow afternoon?"

"You have our word, Ms. Whitney," he said with a slight bow of his head. "The End of Summer Masked Gala is a most important event here in Somerset county. We would never let any of our illustrious patrons down." He bared his teeth in an approximation of a smile. "Your friend is a lucky man to be so well taken care of."

Of all the nerve, Shannon fumed as she headed across the sunny corridor toward Lord & Taylor. The salesman made it sound as if Andrew was a gigolo or something. A kept man, if there really was such a thing. Women picked out suits and shirts and all sorts of things for their husbands. Entire sitcoms had been created around that premise. For all that cretin knew, Shannon was Andrew's wife, out to do some more clothes shopping for her husband.

Feeling a little touchy, are you? an annoying voice asked.

She marched through the cosmetics department, scarcely noticing the squirt girls with their loaded perfume bottles, ready to assault unsuspecting customers. Of course she wasn't feeling touchy. The only thing she was feeling was annoyed that she'd let an obsequious salesman get away with that untoward remark.

Right, that annoying voice continued. *And this has nothing to do with what you saw in the garage, does it?*

She wheeled past the DKNY display of lush autumn knits and headed for the down escalator. She'd been doing her best to push it from her mind but apparently her best wasn't good enough. The image of Andrew, standing before the hot-air balloon and basket, was as vivid in memory as it had been in reality. She'd noted the faded silk, the crumbling basket, but more than that she'd noted the look in Andrew's eyes.

He hadn't seen her standing in the shadows as he ran his hand along the rim of the gondola, an odd expression on his face. You didn't have to be clairvoyant to know that he had been thinking about the life he'd left behind. There must be something he missed about his old life, something he longed for.

I'll make you forget all of it, she thought as she headed for the men's department. *Whatever it is, I'll find a way to make it all up to you.*

She was flipping through a display of white dress shirts when she had the uncomfortable sensation that someone was watching her. She glanced over her right shoulder and noted a well-dressed man in a business suit peering at her from behind a rack of silk ties.

She went back to looking at the shirts. If he was looking to strike up a conversation with her, certainly he'd get the message that she wasn't interested.

"Excuse me," he called out.

She turned with studied reluctance. "Yes?"

"Don't I know you?"

"I don't think so."

"I'm sure we've met before," he said, walking toward her.

"I don't believe so."

He extended his hand in greeting. "Linc," he said. "Linc Stewart."

"I'm sorry, Mr. Stewart," she said, moving away, "but you must have me mistaken with somebody else." The man was nothing if not persistent.

"Now, wait," said Linc Stewart. "Don't tell me. I'll remember your name in a second."

"Really, Mr. Stewart," she said, starting for the up escalator, "I'm in a hurry. I'm sure I'd remember if we'd met."

"Kitty...Katie...Katharine! That's it. Katharine Morgan."

The shock of hearing her old name on his lips sent the blood rushing from her head and she feared she would pass out at his feet.

"You okay?" he asked, his voice deep with concern. "Let me get you some water."

"I'm fine. It's just—" She searched frantically for a workable lie. "I'm pregnant and I tend to get dizzy at the drop of a hat. John—my husband—told me to slow down but you know how it is...." She favored him with the most dazzling smile at her command. "I'm afraid I'm not your friend Katharine Morgan," she said easily. "Sorry."

He considered her for a moment while her life passed before her eyes. "No," he said, "I guess you're not, but let me tell you, you could be her twin."

"I must go," she said, stepping onto the escalator. "It's been lovely talking with you."

She didn't draw a deep breath again until she was safely behind the wheel of her car and back on the highway headed for home. The odds against bumping into someone who knew her from her old life must be a million to one. Whoever this Linc Stewart was, he couldn't have been an important part of either her or Bryant's daily existence. And she hadn't been an important part of his. It was one of those random meetings that made for three minutes of conversation over dinner and then were forgotten.

"That's what you should do," she told herself as she turned up the road that led to her estate. "Forget about him." It was a fluke, one of those bizarre occurrences that happen every now and again and amount to nothing. Bryant had been on parole for over six months now and there hadn't been so much as a whisper of trouble. He was somewhere in California and, please God and the judicial system, destined to stay there.

She longed to see Andrew, to feel his arms around her, to push the whole strange incident from her mind. She left the car at the top of the driveway, then ran into the garage. Andrew wasn't there. She turned to leave, but that damn balloon stared at her from the corner. Then the flutter of torn papers on the ground caught her eye.

It was obvious Andrew hadn't looked at them. Shannon, however, found herself compelled to gather them up and see what was important enough for Dakota to photocopy and press into Andrew's hands when she knew how Shannon felt. She brushed off some dirt and flipped through the half pages. Much of the information was boring detail about the Blakelee farm, the crops they'd grown, the dimensions of the original house. But buried in that minutiae was a paragraph that made her blood run cold.

She stuffed the torn pages into her purse, then ran outside. She didn't see Andrew anywhere. She tore around the side of the garage toward the backyard. He wasn't there, either.

"Andrew!" Her voice sounded shaky, not at all like herself. "Andrew, where are you?"

"Here, lass."

She spun around.

"Look up."

He was perched on the top rung of the ladder, working on the roof of the sun room.

"Oh, Andrew. . . ." With that she burst into tears.

He had never seen her cry before. The sight tore at his gut, and he jumped the ten feet to the ground, landing hard, then raced to her side.

"Shannon, lass. . ." he murmured, gathering her into his arms. "There, now. . .don't cry. . . ."

"I never cry," she said, sniffling as she struggled to regain her control. "I can't believe I'm doing this."

"'Tis nothing unnatural. Crying soothes the soul."

"M-my soul doesn't need soothing."

"Something caused this, lass. Tell me what it is."

"I don't know." She buried her face against his shoulder. "Nothing. . .everything." She looked up at him, face streaked with tears. "I'm not making any sense, am I?"

"None at all," he said, holding her close. He pulled away slightly so that he could look deep into her eyes.

"I couldn't find you, Andrew," she said after a moment. "You weren't in the garage, then I didn't see you in the yard. I don't know what came over me. I thought you'd gone away."

"Where would I go, lass, when I have all I could ask for here in my arms."

She reached up and took his face in her hands. "We don't have to stay here, Andrew. There's a whole big world out there for you to learn about, and we can go and see it all."

"You have a life here," he said, uncertain where this was leading. There was an edge to her voice, a touch of something akin to desperation. "People who rely upon you."

"The foundation runs itself. I signed the papers the other day. I could run off to Borneo and live on coconuts and the foundation would be just fine." Her eyes flashed with a fire unlike any he had seen before. "Anything I do for them is extra, more for me than for anyone else. By this time next week there will be a twenty-four-hour-a-day staff to keep things running."

"You sound unhappy."

"I'm not unhappy. I'm glad things are going well. Don't you see? I'm rich, Andrew! I have enough money to take us anywhere we want to go. We won't live long enough to spend all the money. I'll take you on a jet plane, in a helicopter, on the Concorde, buy you a car—"

"Enough!" His tone was harsh but that could not be helped. "What in bloody hell has brought this about, Shannon? I am not a man who takes from a woman. I make my own way in this world."

"Oh, don't be ridiculous," she said, brushing away his words. "First you have to experience this world before you can make your way in it. And trust me, Andrew, there's more to the world than New Jersey."

"We will see the world when I can afford that privilege."

"I can afford it now, Andrew. Why should we wait?"

"I am an educated man. I will find a way to secure a living in your world."

"Oh, God, Andrew...you just don't understand. You have no identification, no birth certificate, no résumé, no driver's license. For all practical purposes, you don't even exist."

"In my time a man's presence was enough to prove his existence."

"Life is more complicated now."

"There are records of my birth and marriage in Boston."

"I'm sure there are," said Shannon with a sigh, "but they're from the eighteenth century. We're going to have to get you some fake identification, and soon."

"That can be done?"

"Yes," she said, "but it will take me some time to ask around and find out where we can do it."

"It was done for you," he observed, "when you created this new life for yourself."

"I had some help," she reminded him. "I had the government behind me."

"We will ask the government to help me."

"It doesn't work that way, Andrew."

"The government is in contact with you, to see that you are safe."

"Actually, nobody is in contact with me. The government created my new identity and then they bowed out."

"Did the government provide your wealth?"

She shook her head. "The wealth was mine. My trust fund came through when I turned twenty-one."

"So what you are saying is that although I exist, I do not really exist until I have papers to prove that existence."

"Well, yes," Shannon said. "I suppose I am. But don't you see? None of that really matters. I'll buy you some papers some place, you'll get a passport, then we're off to see the world."

"When I am able to pay for the experience."

"We'll talk about that," Shannon said, her jaw set in a stubborn line.

"Aye," said Andrew. "We will talk about that."

Shannon brightened. "The masked ball on Saturday night! Why didn't I think of it before? You'll meet every important person in the state. We're bound to connect with someone who can help us."

"You put great store in an evening of entertainment."

"Oh, the ball is a lot of things, Andrew, but entertainment isn't one of them. Charity events are work, same as going to the office."

"And you believe some profit might be gained from attending?"

"I can almost guarantee it."

And because she was so beautiful and so kind—and because he was so much in love with her—Andrew almost believed it.

Four women from the shelter sat on the grass Friday morning and looked up at Andrew as he painted the front door of the cottage. Shannon was sitting on the step next to him, just out of reach of his paintbrush. They had brought the women together to outline their plans for the mini Outward Bound camping trip, and so far the response had been less than overwhelming.

"I don't know about any of you," said Pat, "but I'm not letting my kids spend the night in the woods unless I'm with them."

"Wouldn't catch me in the woods in the middle of the night," said her mother, Terri, shuddering. "Too many creepy-crawly things all over the place."

Derek's mother, Rita, laughed. "That's the point, isn't it? Getting used to bugs and strange animals and no bathrooms." She looked at Shannon. "I've heard about this kind of thing. It's a confidence builder, right?"

"Exactly. It's been used by breast cancer patients, business executives—" Shannon gestured toward the women "—people like you and me."

"You?" said Pat with a short laugh. "I know you said you went through it, too, but—" She gestured toward the house and the estate grounds. "Kinda hard to figure what your problem was. If I had your money, I'd have left a long time ago."

"It's not always a question of money," Shannon said, not wanting to minimize the importance of being financially secure. "Yes, I had money but I didn't have something else that was a lot more important."

"Keys to the safety deposit box?" Pat asked.

"Guts," said Shannon. "And self-respect. If you don't have those two things, you don't have anything at all."

"And you think a night in the woods will give us guts and self-respect?" Pat asked with obvious skepticism.

"I think it's a damn good place to start."

There was a long silence. Shannon wondered if she'd gone too far and alienated the lot of them, but they needed to hear the truth.

"I don't know about the rest of you," said Rita, breaking the silence, "but I could use a night out. Count my kids and me in, Shannon."

"Not me," said Terri. "I'm going to stay in and watch a movie."

Pat looked at her mother, then at Shannon. "I'll go, but if I see one spider I'm out of there."

"And your kids?" Shannon asked.

"They love spiders." Pat smiled for the first time in days and Shannon felt a burst of elation.

"My kids are older than yours," said Sara, "but if we're still here Sunday, I'll try to convince them to tag along."

The women joked among themselves about the problems inherent in trying to convince teenagers to do anything at all.

Shannon looked up at Andrew. "Looks like we'll have our work cut out for us."

"Aye," he said, "we will, at that."

Their eyes met and held, and for a moment she remembered another man, other promises, and she thanked God for bringing Andrew McVie into her life.

Chapter Twenty-One

21

"You look magnificent," said Shannon on Saturday night as she gave a final adjustment to the cloth about his neck.

"I look the fool." Andrew grimaced at his reflection in the mirror. "No man, save a Virginia plantation owner, should wear so many ornaments upon his person."

She considered him, her eyes twinkling with delight. "A bow tie, a cummerbund, cuff links, your basic tuxedo…that's not very much, Andrew."

"'Tis more than I like."

"You're a hunk," she said.

"I take offense, mistress."

"Don't," she said, starting to laugh. "That's the highest compliment for a man these days."

"Has the sound of an insult about it."

"Well, it isn't. The women are going to be falling all over themselves, Andrew. I hope they won't turn your head."

"Would you be feeling proprietary, lass?"

"Aye," she said, kissing his mouth. "Very proprietary."

"'Tis a higher compliment to me than any other."

In truth, the highest compliment of all was that a woman of such beauty and splendor should desire his company. The sight of Shannon in her floor-length white silk gown shot through with shimmering threads of gold put him in mind of celestial beings. Diamonds glittered at her throat and dangled from her ears. A narrow gold bracelet, also studded with diamonds, graced her right wrist.

"'Tis a king's ransom, Shannon." It struck him most forcefully that in his entire lifetime he would not be able to provide even one of the gemstones she wore with such ease, and that realization was not a happy one. "A man could live forever in my world with the money from one of your earbobs."

"I'll remember that next time I buy a plane ticket to 1776," she said with a saucy toss of her head.

He smiled at her jest, but for an instant found himself wondering how it would be to return to his own world with such a woman by his side.

"The limousine will be here any moment," she said, fetching a small beaded bag from the table near the door.

"I do not understand the need for another person to drive when you are most capable."

She gestured toward her slim-fitting dress. "You-can't work a clutch in a Versace gown."

"This limousine, how does it differ from a car?"

"It's bigger," she said, adjusting her earbobs. "And it's terribly impressive."

"You wish to impress others?" That did not sound like the Shannon he had come to know.

"At events like this I do. The more impressive you are to others, the more likely they are to support your charity. It's a game, Andrew. Like playing chess but with real, live pieces." She met his eyes. "Karen Naylor and her date will be sharing the limo with us."

"The Negress lawyer?"

"Must you label her that way?" Shannon countered.

"I am not here long, lass. How else am I to remember the various players?"

Her dark brows drew together in a frown. "I have the feeling you remember Karen quite well."

"Because she is a Negress?"

"Because she's African-American."

"A cumbersome phrase."

"But accurate," she shot back. "A problem that might not have had such tragic consequences had the men of your time seen fit to prohibit slavery."

"You speak as if I had the power to change the course of events. I was not privy to the discussions at Carpenters' Hall, mistress. My opinion on the keeping of slaves mattered little in the scheme of things."

"You're wrong," said his beautiful warrior woman. "How can you, of all people, say that the opinion of the common man doesn't matter? The revolution was based upon the opinion of the common man."

"And that rebellion had not enjoyed much success when I took my leave."

"Maybe if—" Shannon stopped abruptly, horrified by what she had been about to say. *Maybe if you hadn't left...*

"Finish your sentence, Shannon. I am eager to hear your words."

"Forget it," she said. "There's no point to this discussion." Certainly not if she was going to say something as idiotic as that. She'd been on edge since Thursday morning and that odd encounter in Lord & Taylor. It had been so long since she'd heard her old name, much less met anyone who associated her with it, that she'd found herself looking over her shoulder more than once, almost as if Bryant somehow was going to find her again.

Ridiculous, she thought. She had a new home and a new identity. The odds of Bryant ever finding her were a million to one.

About like the odds of meeting Andrew McVie?

Fortunately the doorbell sounded, signaling the arrival of the limousine and putting an end to further conjecture.

"The masks," she said, looking around.

Andrew moved next to her, blocking her way. "They are in my keeping."

She nodded, then waited, but he didn't move. "We should go, Andrew. We don't want to keep Karen waiting."

"Aye," he said. "We would not wish to do that."

"Make an effort," she said in a soft voice. "Please don't make this difficult for everyone." If they were going to share their lives, it would have to begin now.

"I am not the ogre you paint me to be, lass. I am in new circumstances and doing my utmost to bend my will to the greater will of the times in which I find myself."

Unexpected tears filled her eyes. "I know you're not an ogre. It's just—"

"You wish me to see your friends in a favorable light."

"And I wish my friends to see you in a favorable light, as well."

"I had not thought of it in such terms."

"I know," she said, reaching for his hand. He was so strong within himself, so sure that his way was the right way, that the opinions of others were of little consequence. *This isn't the world you knew, Andrew. This is my world and you must learn to live by its rules.* Why was it that thought suddenly filled her with great sadness?

"I will make an effort," he said, "although those rules are ofttimes difficult to understand."

She smiled, feeling once again connected to him in the deepest way possible between two people, deeper even than the act of love. "I can't ask for more than that, can I?"

"Nay," he said, "you cannot." He shot her a bemused glance. "But I am of the opinion you will try."

Shannon had told him to avoid the topics of politics, religion and sex, but it appeared to Andrew as if he alone refrained from discourse on those subjects. He heard odd bits of talk about such things as test tube babies, gay rights and born-again Christians, and found he could understand little.

"You're very quiet, Mr. McVie," said one of the women at their table. "Surely you must have an opinion on abortion."

"Aye," he said, "and that opinion is as personal as the topic itself."

"Right to life," said the woman with a knowing nod of her head. "Typical evasive answer."

He felt Shannon's concerned gaze from across the table but this stranger's barb made him wish to deal with the matter directly.

"I stated no preference in the matter," he told the woman, "only that my opinion is of a personal nature."

"You're among friends, Mr. McVie," she continued. "Why not share your views with us?"

"Because my views are of no consequence in what is a private matter between a man and his wife."

Her painted blond eyebrows lifted above her mask and she laughed. "'Man and his wife.' What a quaint notion." She turned toward her companion, dismissing Andrew in a most obvious fashion.

He felt a hand on his arm. "Great job," said a familiar voice.

He looked to his right and saw Karen standing next to him. She wore the same bejeweled mask everyone but Andrew sported. "There was much left unsaid."

"She'd never hear you, Andrew. The woman's head is filled with cement."

"You heard the conversation?"

"Every last phrase. Not many people hold their own with Lydia. You deserve the croix de guerre."

He glanced toward Shannon, who was engaged in conversation with the silver-haired man who had accompanied Karen. He sensed, however, that she was fully aware that Karen was at his side.

"There is much intolerance of opinion at this party," he said.

"You noticed." Her tone was dry, but he heard the leavening note of humor.

They watched as Shannon rose from her chair to dance with the silver-haired man.

Karen smiled at him. "If you ask me to dance, I won't say no."

"If I ask you to dance, you will be most regretful, for I was cursed with lack of ability."

"So was I," Karen said. "That's why John is dancing with Shannon. Why don't we show them we're not lost causes?"

She was a woman of wit and charm and he was not unaware of the olive branch she extended toward him. They both shared a Harvard education, a dislike of fools and a strong affection and respect for Shannon. In truth, he could not think what else was required as a point from which to start.

He rose and inclined his head in her direction. "Lack of ability does not mean lack of the ability to *learn*. May I have the honor, Miss Naylor?"

She laughed and gave him her hand. "You may, Mr. McVie."

Together they took the floor.

"I thought you couldn't dance," Shannon said when they exchanged partners for the next song.

"And that is true," Andrew said, sweeping her into his arms.

They took a few steps and Shannon started to laugh. "You're right," she said. "You can't dance."

"And neither can Miss Naylor. We were a most agreeable combination."

"So I noticed." She forced them to a stop. "I'll lead, you follow." They began to move again on the beat. "See? You have potential."

"Aye," he said. "'Tis a miracle."

"Thank you, Andrew," she said softly. The sight of him dancing with Karen had given her hope.

"There is no reason for thanks, lass."

"I know it was hard for you."

"No harder than it was for Miss Naylor. She is a most intelligent woman and a true friend to you."

"I know," said Shannon. "I'm glad you realize that."

"It occurred to me that she is living my life, had I been born in your time."

"What an odd way to look at it, but I suppose that's true." They were about the same age, had the same educational background, the same drive.

"Now I am a lawyer without a practice and a farmer without land. It would seem my only claim upon this world is a result of your generosity. Every man in this room has a trade save for the man with whom you have cast your lot."

"Do you think I care about that, Andrew? You can't choose a profession before you learn all there is to learn about the world you're in. We'll travel. You'll get to learn all about the country...all about the world. Then you'll know what it is you were meant to do."

He fell silent and her heart went out to him. *You'll find your way, Andrew,* she thought. *Just give it time.*

The masks came off at midnight with great fanfare.

"As if we didn't know exactly who everybody was," Karen said with wry amusement. "The rich are *definitely* different." She grinned at Shannon. "Present company excepted, of course."

"Of course," said Shannon, grinning back.

Andrew and Karen's companion, John, were engrossed in conversation. Shannon couldn't imagine what they had in common but they seemed to be getting on well and for that she was grateful.

"Photos, everyone!" Madolyn Bancroft, coordinator of the gala, popped up at their table. "We have the *Star-Ledger, Philadelphia In-*

quirer, New York Times and *Town and Country* waiting for you. Smile pretty!"

"Smile pretty." Karen groaned. "That woman is so perky there are times I want to strangle her."

"I know what you mean," said Shannon. "But that's probably why she's so good at what she does."

They rose from the table and moved toward the fountain, where the photographers were gathered snapping pictures.

Shannon drew Andrew aside. "They're going to photograph us," she said sotto voce. "They'll aim the camera in our direction and you'll see a bright light flash."

"And that captures our image, does it not?"

She smiled. "Depends how good the photographer is."

They took their places.

"Great," said one of the photographers. "Good contrast. Now you, mister, put your hand at the lady's waist. Big smile...big smile...great! You'll see the results in the morning paper, folks."

"'Tis an amazing thing," Andrew said as they made room for Karen and John to be photographed. "Our image on paper for the world to see."

She thought of the man who'd recognized her at the mall, and a shiver of apprehension moved through her. All evening she'd found herself looking at the masked faces and wondering if Linc Stewart might be here, as well. Foolish thoughts. Ridiculous, idiotic nonsense. If only she could put it from her mind.

"Lass? Are you unwell?"

"I'm fine," she said, summoning up a smile. "Just tired."

"Aye," he said, his hazel eyes twinkling. "The thought of bed holds definite appeal."

You've had your photo in the paper before, she told herself as they left for home. *There's nothing to worry about.* It might be the best thing that could possibly happen. Linc Stewart would see the picture and discover that her name was Shannon Whitney, not Katharine Morgan, and the whole thing would be forgotten.

Karen suggested they stop at the Bridgewater Diner for coffee and conversation, but neither Shannon nor Andrew was much in the mood.

They rode home in silence, a silence that seemed different from any that had come before.

"We shouldn't have gone to the gala," Shannon said later as they lay in bed together. "You had a terrible time."

He didn't deny it. "They talk and talk and nothing comes of it. You say they were the best the state has to offer and I did not see a man or woman of true accomplishment among the lot of them."

She leaned up on one elbow. "Andrew, how can you say that? Philip Stallings is president of the biggest computer company short of Microsoft. Francesca Duval is CEO of Le Visage Cosmetics, a Fortune 500 company. Lee Prescott is—"

"Yet among them I did not see a happy face."

"Dinner was an hour late," she said with an uneasy laugh. "Nobody was very happy about that."

"There is more to it than that, Shannon. Those men and women have all that I came here to find, and still—"

"I know," she whispered. "I know."

They didn't make love. Instead they held each other close and waited for the dawn.

Chapter Twenty-Two

22

"'Tis not right to leave you alone," Andrew said the next afternoon. "This trip into the woods can be done another day."

"No, it can't," Shannon said firmly. "Most of these kids will be gone in a day or two." She smoothed the collar of his work shirt. He looked much the way he had the first day they met, and less like the man she had created. It was not a thought she wished to pursue. "Besides, I'm exhausted after last night. I don't think I have the energy to rough it with the rest of you explorers." She had dozed for a little while just before sunrise, only to awaken to find Andrew standing by the window, staring up at the towering cloud cover.

"Your fatigue does not worry me, lass. 'Tis the fact that you will be unprotected that causes me concern."

"I was unprotected, as you put it, for quite a few years before you dropped into my life, Andrew." She softened her words with a kiss. "I think I can manage one more night."

"The doors and windows have been repaired and you will use the mechanical alarms."

She saluted. "Yes, sir."

Apparently he didn't see the humor in the salute, for his expression remained serious. "I understand more now than on that first night. Your world is a place of violence and cunning. If the alarm can guarantee a measure of safety, you will use it."

She wrapped her arms around him, glorying in his strength and solidity. "Poor Andrew. I should never have told you to watch the news on television."

"'Twas more than that, lass. I left in the midst of a rebellion, only to find a war raging right here."

"I'll admit we have problems, but it isn't as bad as all that."

"Social anarchy," he said, warming to the topic. "Good men—" He paused, a sheepish smile spreading across his face. "Good men *and* women without a way in which to make a living, while the devil's own thrive."

She couldn't argue the point. "We have wonders that didn't exist in your time, modern medicine for one. People no longer die from smallpox and influenza. Certainly that makes up for at least some of our shortcomings."

"This world has you," he said. "That is wonder enough for me."

She walked outside with him and found Dakota waiting in the driveway, perched atop her beat-up Mustang.

"Need an ex-Girl Scout and former librarian on the camping trip?" Dakota asked.

"Former librarian?" Shannon countered while Andrew headed for the garage. "Forsythe fired you?"

"Fired. Sacked. Got the pink slip. I'm finished."

"We shouldn't have dropped by that day."

"It wasn't you, it was my mother. She sat on my desk and told me about her dreams."

"He fired you for that? The man's a beast."

"Yeah," said Dakota. "And cheap, too. So far, no severance pay."

"Isn't that against the law?"

"Try telling that to an academic despot. You won't get very far."

Shannon lowered her voice. "You're not serious about the camping trip, are you?"

"Actually, I am. Two of the kids, Derek and Angela, told me about it and asked me to tag along." She grinned ruefully. "And since I don't have anything else to do, I said I would."

"I don't think it's a very good idea."

"If you're afraid I'm going to swoon every time I brush elbows with Balloon Boy, I promise you I won't."

Shannon laughed despite herself. "Don't call him Balloon Boy, please! That's our secret. Besides, how do you know you won't swoon?"

"Because I've had a long talk with myself, that's why. If I'm ever going to figure out why he doesn't have an aura, I'd better stay conscious."

"That's the second time you've brought up that aura. What do you mean, he doesn't have one? I thought even inanimate objects have auras." She'd seen Kirlian photography in some magazine once, where scientists claimed to have caught the aura of both a carrot and a garden rock.

Dakota's eyes darted toward the garage, the swimming pool, everywhere but Shannon. "Well, yeah," she said, finally meeting her eyes. "Most objects have an aura, but he doesn't."

"Of course he does."

Dakota brightened. "You've seen it?"

"Well, of course I haven't seen it. You're the one who sees things like that. I'm just saying, he's here, he's real, he must have an aura."

"You'd think so, wouldn't you?"

"Maybe I'd better go on this camping trip with you, after all."

"I didn't know you'd decided against it."

Shannon shrugged. "I'm tired, headachy and PMS-ing up a storm. I figured I'd stay home and give the rest of you a break. You won't—"

"Tell him I know he's from the past?" Dakota broke in. "Not if you don't want me to."

"I don't want you to," Shannon said.

"Thank you for making that clear."

She took Dakota's hands, desperate to make her friend understand her position. "It's not you," she said. "It's me. It's Andrew. It's the two of us together. The best thing for both of us is for him to cut ties with the past and make a life for himself here. You can't live in two worlds forever."

Dakota was silent, but the expression in her dark brown eyes spoke volumes.

"You're not going to start that 'this is only temporary' routine again, are you?"

"I guess not."

"I can give him a life like he never dreamed, Dakota. He'll never want for anything. How can his world offer him anything to compare?"

Dakota didn't say anything.

She didn't have to.

That passage in *Forgotten Heroes* had said it all.

Andrew and Dakota left an hour later to meet the others at the shelter and begin the great camping expedition.

Shannon waved goodbye, then opened the French doors and stepped into the sun room. It was a beautiful house but it had never seemed like a home until Andrew. Of course, it wasn't the house. She'd lived in enough different places to know that. It was being with him that made her feel connected to the world, safe and cherished and filled with hope for the future. *Their* future.

Don't say anything, Dakota, she prayed silently. *Let us make our own decisions.*

She'd been tempted to join them, but she was so bone-deep

weary that the thought of trekking through the woods—even if they were *her* woods—was more than she could contemplate. At least she knew why she was tired. Typical PMS exhaustion.

And maybe a touch of regret?

She leaned back on the chaise and closed her eyes.

"Yes," she said to the empty room. "Regret."

Regret that there wouldn't be a child of her union with Andrew McVie. The emotion was so primal, it cut so deep that it stole her breath. She hadn't thought about children in years. It was as if that part of her heart had been sealed away and forgotten. But loving Andrew had thrown open the doors and windows and made her want things she'd thought beyond her reach.

Husband. Home. Children. The entire American dream, no matter the century.

She settled down on the sofa and tried to imagine herself back in Andrew's world. There would be no central air-conditioning, no big-screen TV or VCR. A war raged as the nation struggled to be born, while men and women of character sought to carve a place for themselves and their families.

She closed her eyes, letting the images come to life. So much could be done, she thought. So many mistakes could be avoided. *You're a born crusader,* Dakota always said, looking to save the world from its own excesses. What would it be like to go back to the beginning and have a chance to do it right?

Their children and their children's children would go forward with knowledge that would make them leaders, and all of it would happen simply because Shannon Whitney and Andrew McVie met and fell in love one warm summer's night in central New Jersey.

Central air was a small price to pay for such riches.

But, of course, it was ridiculous to even think about it. It wasn't as if she could drive over to the hardware store, buy a propane tank and fire up the hot-air balloon. There was no explanation for what had brought Andrew into her life, and she could only pray that same mysterious force would not see fit to take him from her.

She tried to read but couldn't concentrate. She scanned the latest copy of *People,* then tossed it aside. *Newsweek* and *Time* quickly followed suit. Television held no appeal. She'd already leafed through the Sunday papers and had been relieved to note that the picture of her and Andrew was a grainy shot, buried on page three of the Living section. She couldn't resist, however, and clipped the photo and article and set it aside.

The good thing about PMS was the fact that it explained more than her sudden exhaustion. It put a lot of other things into perspective. The way she'd overreacted to that man in Lord & Taylor the other day. And the jolt of apprehension she'd experienced last night at the ball when faced with the photographers.

Life was good, she thought, closing her eyes as fatigue washed over her. Each day Andrew adapted to another quirk of twentieth-century life...and the shadow of his old life grew fainter. Less threatening. He no longer tried to wind quartz timepieces or talk back to the answering machine, although last night when he'd pounded the table while the others applauded the singer, they'd locked eyes and burst into delighted laughter.

"Yes, life is good," she murmured, drifting toward sleep. And, as long as they were together, it would only get better.

"Straight to the matter," Andrew said, plunging deeper into the woods.

"I thought you were gonna show us how to find our way around," Charlie said.

"That is what we're about."

"I don't see us doin' nothing special," said Angela. "We're just walking."

"We're doing more than walking," Dakota said. "Right, Andrew?"

"In truth, there was much to be learned if you had looked with open eyes."

"A bunch of trees and plants," said Derek. "Big deal."

"Aye," Andrew said, "'tis a big deal, indeed. Skunk, raccoon and deer are nearby."

"No way," said Charlie. "I didn't see anything."

Andrew squatted near a fallen tree and pushed aside a handful of dead leaves. He gestured toward a series of depressions in the soft earth. "See the shape of the hooves clearly rendered, the way they overlap? The sign of a deer walking at a normal pace." He then gestured toward scrapes on the bark of the fallen tree. "'Twas a fine supper for a doe or buck."

They crowded around him, disbelief turning slowly to wonder as he showed them the five-toed mark of a skunk and the distinctive impression of rabbit. "A young rabbit can be taken by hand," he said in a most ordinary tone, "but many a man has starved on a diet of rabbit alone. 'Tis not enough fat to—"

With that little Angela burst into loud sobs. "Mommy! He says we have to eat bunnies."

Angela's mother stepped forward to hug her daughter while the other mothers gathered around.

"I have no wish to make the child unhappy," he said, patting the girl on the head, "but 'tis a fact of life that to survive we must ofttimes perform unpleasant tasks."

A look passed between the women and then Angela's mother met his eyes.

"Go ahead, Mr. McVie," she said. "I think it's time we all learned how to survive."

Jules, the shelter's driver, called a little after five o'clock.

"I didn't wake you, did I, Ms. Whitney?"

"No, of course not," Shannon lied, stifling a yawn. "New arrivals?"

"Looks like," said Jules. "We're taking this one to the house you rented in Morristown, but I don't have the key."

"I don't think I—" Shannon thought for a second. "Karen has it." Now that the papers had been signed, sealed and delivered, Karen and the foundation would be handling the day-to-day running of the shelters. "Wait a minute," she said. "I forgot to give her the key. It's right here."

Jules was silent for a moment. "I gotta be at the police station in Flemington in twenty minutes to pick 'em up, but I could swing by and get the key after."

"Whenever you can, Jules. I'm not going anywhere."

"Don't want to be a bother, Ms. Whitney. Just leave the key in your mailbox and I won't have to disturb you."

"You're good at this," Dakota said to Andrew as he struck a spark from a rock with the blade of his knife. "You don't meet too many lawyers who can start a fire without a match."

"You were to gather tinder," he said, meeting her eyes. "I see no contribution from you."

"I gave at the office," she said, then stopped. Of course he wouldn't understand the reference.

"You are a good friend to Shannon," he said, watching her.

"I like to think I am."

"You are," he said. "I know that for a fact, but what I do not understand is why you dislike me as you do."

"I don't dislike you," Dakota said carefully.

"Aye," he said. "You do."

Dakota took a deep breath. "I'm worried, that's all."

"I will not hurt Shannon. You have my oath."

"I know you won't hurt her intentionally." She touched his forearm. "But—"

She felt as if she was falling end over end through space, tumbling toward the earth, faster and faster and—

Her eyes opened and she found Andrew kneeling over her, extending his cupped hands.

"Drink this," he said.

She looked at the brackish water.

"Where did you get that?" she asked.

"From the stream."

She shuddered. "Not on your life. I'm not a fan of toxic waste."

"Each time we meet, mistress, you swoon." He crouched closer to her. "What would be the reason?"

"It's— I..." Her words faded.

"You know." Andrew's voice was low so that the others could not hear. "You have known from the start."

She looked away. "I promised Shannon I wouldn't talk about this."

"You have second sight. My mother did, as well."

Her eyes widened. "You believe in such things?"

"I believe there are things beyond understanding."

He smiled and she started to laugh. "All things considered, I suppose you would." After all, the man got there from an eighteenth-century hot-air balloon.

"But there is something else you see, isn't there?"

"Look, Andrew, I really can't talk about this. Shannon's my friend and I told her I wouldn't."

"God's oath, mistress, there are two things I swear—I will not hurt Shannon and I will never leave her."

Dakota's eyes welled with tears. "You will leave," she said. "That's one thing I'm sure of."

She could feel it in her bones.

Shannon awoke with a start. She'd dozed back to sleep after Jules called. The key, she thought, stretching lazily. The key to the Morristown house was still in her purse instead of in the mailbox where she'd promised Jules it would be.

Stifling a yawn, she stood, tightened the belt on her silk robe, then padded barefoot to the sun room. She switched off the alarm to the French doors, stepped outside, then hurried around the side of the house and down the driveway to the mailbox.

Clouds slid across the moon, obscuring it, while she walked back up the driveway. *Too dark for me,* she thought, wrapping her arms around her chest. Strange how eerie your own driveway could look at night when the house was empty...when you'd gotten used to it being not empty.

She would have laughed if anyone had told her it was possible to miss someone as much as she missed Andrew. The man had been gone only a few hours and it felt like days. *He's in the woods, not Wyoming. He'll be back tomorrow morning.* She was almost tempted to venture into the woods herself, flashlight and compass in hand, and look for him.

Almost, but not quite.

She heard a rustling sound from across the yard and shivered. It gave the old phrase "the night has a thousand eyes" a brand-new twist.

She reached for the handle on the French doors, then paused. Too many strange noises. This time it was a snapping twig to the left. Some enterprising bureaucrat should outlaw strange noises on dark nights when a woman was home alone.

The wind rustled the trees and she caught the scent of something unfamiliar mingled with the smell of pine and hot summer air. A fragment of memory danced just beyond reach but she couldn't bring it forward into the light.

She swung the door open and was about to step inside when something hit her hard from behind and sent her sprawling, face first, to the floor of the sun room. Her right knee struck the tiles first. She waited for the pain to start but it didn't.

Maybe you had to breathe to feel pain...but she couldn't breathe...or think...or feel anything. There was only terror and the deep certainty that her worst fears were about to come true. *Andrew.* His dear face flashed through her mind. *Dear God! Will I ever see you again?*

She closed her eyes, face pressed to the cool tile floor. She tried to make herself small, insignificant, invisible, but the world was narrowing down, growing smaller and smaller, until she was the center and there was no place left to hide.

"This is scary," Derek said. "Are we lost?"

Andrew smiled. "Far from it." He pointed up toward the sky. "See that band of stars arcing upward?"

Derek nodded. "You mean the Milky Way?"

"Aye," he said, although the term was unfamiliar to him. "Follow a straight line with your eye from the handle of the Plough to the brightly shining star. The polestar will always guide you."

"I don't get it," said Derek. "It's just a dumb star. Why don't we use a map?"

"Rambo's got night-vision goggles," said Charlie. "That's what I'd use."

"Sometimes you have naught save your God-given wits to guide you," said Andrew. "What would you do if—" He stopped abruptly. "Did you hear someone call my name?"

Derek shook his head. "Uh-uh."

"Not me," said Charlie.

Inexplicably the hairs on the back of Andrew's neck began to rise and he stood.

"Something is wrong," he said, turning to Dakota. "Do you feel it, too?"

Dakota tilted her head. "What do you mean? A storm or something?"

"'Tis Shannon," he said, the dread inside his chest growing. "You do not sense a darkness settling over her?"

Dakota shook her head. “But that doesn’t mean anything. Trust your gut. We’ll be fine.”

He gestured toward the others. “I do not wish to add to the women’s distress.”

“I was a Girl Scout,” Dakota said. “Not that you know what a Girl Scout is. This is survival training. We’ll manage.”

His brow furrowed. “I will not leave you unprotected.” He handed her his knife. “Use this well.”

“I hope I don’t use it at all.” A small smile tilted Dakota’s mouth as she accepted the weapon. “Go to Shannon. I promise everything else will fall into place.”

Chapter Twenty-Three

23

"Good to see you again, Katharine," her ex-husband said, yanking Shannon to her feet by her hair. It was the voice she'd heard every day of her marriage and in every nightmare since the divorce. "So where've you been hiding yourself?"

Bright waves of pain blurred her vision. She caught the image of a tall, handsome man in a hand-tailored suit. The kind of man you'd see in a corporate boardroom or a five-star restaurant. She tried to get into position to knock him off balance but her knee gave way and she staggered against him. His fingers were still threaded through her hair and he pulled again. She wondered how it was her scalp didn't separate from the rest of her.

Think, Shannon! You know how to deal with this. Just don't be afraid...think! His height gave him an advantage but she knew she could best him if she could just regain her footing.

"Surprised to see me?"

She wouldn't answer him. He could go to hell before she'd answer him.

He reared back and swung at her, holding her head still so she absorbed all of the blow and more. The iron taste of blood filled her mouth and she tried not to gag.

"Not talking, Katharine?" His fingers dug into her scalp. "You never used to be this quiet."

With his other hand he grabbed her face, forcing her to look into his eyes. Once, a long time ago, she'd thought those gray eyes were beautiful. How wrong she'd been...how pathetically, tragically wrong.

She thought of Andrew. His infinite tenderness, the strength that was as much a part of him as his hazel eyes. A rough man, from a rougher time, and yet he knew more about love—in all of its aspects—than Bryant could ever understand.

"You had a lot to say to the police, didn't you? And you didn't shut up when you talked to the lawyers and the judge. What's wrong, Katharine?" His laugh made her tremble. "Will you talk to me if I call you Shannon? That's your new name, isn't it? Shannon." He looked at her, long and slow, his gaze traveling up her legs, over her belly, lingering on her breasts. "You don't look much like a Shannon." His fingers pressed harder against her temples until she felt as if her head would explode. "Shannon puts out, doesn't she? The way I remember it, Katharine didn't much like it."

For a moment she was that other woman again, the girl who'd come to him in hope and joy, eager to build a life with him, a life they could share someday with children. She could feel her strength ebbing away, her hard-won self-esteem crumbling beneath her. *No,* she told herself. *Don't let him win. You've come so far....*

She wasn't that woman any longer. She was somebody new, somebody strong. She'd left Katharine Morgan behind and created a woman who would fight for the right to live life without fear.

You're not going to win, Bryant. Never again....

He pulled at her hair hard, snapping her head back with the force, making her bones rattle.

Let yourself go, she told herself. *Make him think he's winning, and you can take him by surprise....*

Her gun was useless, locked away in the coat closet in the foyer. Bryant would kill her before she made it into the hall. Her adrenaline was flowing fast, screaming for her to fight Bryant *now* and with every weapon at her disposal. But she couldn't. She had to control her need for revenge because the element of surprise was the best weapon of all.

Letting go was the toughest thing she'd ever done. She felt physically sick at the thought of the pleasure Bryant would take from her weakness.

It's the only way, Shannon. You can't get to the gun. Andrew isn't around. There's no one to hear you scream. The mailbox was at the far end of the driveway. Unless Jules walked up the path and rang the doorbell, he'd never know anything was wrong. And even if she could hit the alarm, she knew it would be over before the police arrived. Bryant had violated his parole, flying across the country for this confrontation, and Shannon wasn't naive enough to believe he'd risked his freedom for anything less than seeing her dead.

She had only herself and her wits to save her.

She sagged against Bryant, forcing her arms to hang loosely at her sides, her legs to go limp. He caught her roughly by the shoulders, his strong fingers digging into her flesh. She knew that the pain would come later, but it didn't matter.

Survival was all.

The house was ablaze with light. Andrew breathed a sigh of relief when he noted that Shannon's car was parked in the garage as it should be.

Still, apprehension tugged at him and he moved quickly around to the back of the house. Ofttimes in the evening they sat together by the swimming pool. He had no wish to cause her alarm, appearing like an apparition from the shadows, but he would not rest easy until he saw her lovely face and could reassure himself of her well-being.

The French doors were closed. His brows knit together as he stepped closer. The red light above was blinking. Was it not supposed to glow steadily to indicate the alarm system was guarding the door as it should? That she was alone inside the house and unprotected made his very blood run cold.

He climbed the steps and reached for the handle. Had the woman no sense? She would not like it, but he intended to speak harshly to her. This was a dangerous world. He would see her safe or know the reason why.

"I've been watching you, Katharine," Bryant said as he dragged her into the kitchen. "That guy you're shacking up with is gone for the night."

She nodded, trying to look submissive rather than terrified. Bryant's rage fed off terror.

"This isn't going to take long." He flung her aside and she fell against the kitchen table. The table skidded on the shiny tiles, sending two of the chairs crashing to the floor and taking Shannon with them. The pain in her right knee was intense. Balance and control were everything when it came to using karate. What if she couldn't stand up when the time came?

I don't feel the pain, she told herself. *There* is *no pain.*

He ran his hand along the countertop and grimaced. "Still not much of a housekeeper, are you, Katharine?"

"I'm sorry," she whispered, the dutiful ex-wife, while bile rose into her mouth. "Mildred and Karl are on vacation."

"You never did understand how to run a household. You held me back, Katharine. Another woman would have understood what I needed." He fingered a glass left in the sink. "That's why I had to explore other avenues."

"I understand." She cast her eyes down, praying he didn't realize she was calculating the distance between them and planning her move. "I'm sorry."

"I'm sorry," he mimicked, moving toward her.

Come on, Bryant...keep walking....

He was about twelve feet away from her. His Italian loafers barely made a sound against the tiles. "Is that all you can say...I'm sorry?"

Ten feet away. *Okay...okay...this is it.*

She shifted her weight to her right hip, leaned back on her arms. Her muscles contracted in preparation. It was all a question of leverage and angles. Balance on the right hip, lash out with the left leg. Simple, clean, powerfully effective.

Just a little closer, Bryant, just get in range.... She'd done it a hundred times in class. A kick to the groin would stop even a bastard like Bryant in his tracks, but she had to do it right the first time, because if she didn't, she would be dead.

The sun room looked much as it had hours ago. Andrew, his senses alert, moved carefully through the room and took its measure. The chaise longue was pushed slightly out of position and as he moved to right it, he noticed the belt to Shannon's robe under the glass-topped table.

He bent to retrieve it and as he did he heard the crash of furniture from the kitchen. *Sweet Jesus,* he thought. His premonition of danger had come to pass. Pressing himself flat against the wall, he moved slowly toward the hallway that led to the kitchen. Shannon's voice floated toward him. He could not distinguish her words but he recognized that her tone was both timid and uncertain, unlike any he had heard from her before.

The man's voice held the cultured tones of education and privilege but there was no mistaking the menace behind the words.

Her husband, Andrew thought with certainty. In his mind's eye he saw the pale curve of the scar on her shoulder blade and his gut twisted. The man who had committed that crime against her person was on the other side of the door. A red mist of rage clouded his vision and the need to spill the man's blood burned within his breast, yet he knew that to burst into the room without first knowing the situation could cost Shannon her life. Still, the taste for blood grew stronger with each second that passed and he wished he still had his knife.

"Come on, Shannon," Bryant said. "Let's go for a little walk upstairs."

He stepped into range.

Now! Do it now! Shannon centered herself, met his eyes, then lashed out with a vicious kick meant to tear straight through the bastard's groin and come out the other side. She caught him in the thigh but fell short of her goal.

"You bitch!" He lurched to the left then turned back toward her.

Panting, she tried to crawl away from him, struggling to ignore the stabbing pain in her right knee and the smell of fear that suddenly filled the air. He grabbed her by the hair and pulled her back across the floor.

"You feel like playing rough?" he asked. "I can play rough."

She watched as he pulled a small revolver from the waistband of his trousers where it had been concealed by his jacket. Grinning, he aimed it at her.

"How rough do you want to play, Shannon Whitney?" He pressed the gun against her temple. "We can do this fast or we can do this slow. Your choice."

She spat on the floor at his feet.

He jammed the gun deeper into her temple.

A buzzing sound started inside her head. It wasn't supposed to end this way. Not here. Not like this. She'd come so far, learned so much, found the one man on earth who was everything she'd dreamed a man could be. But none of it mattered any longer.

Her strength, her dreams, her future—everything was gone in the space of a heartbeat.

Bryant had won.

And she had lost.

Andrew, she thought. *If only*…

She called to him. No words were spoken aloud but still they reached Andrew's mind and heart as clearly and truly as if they had been.

The connection between them defied space and time and he somehow knew not even death could break the bond that drew them together.

But she would not die. Not that gallant, beautiful woman who had captured his heart. He would lay down his life if it meant that she would live.

He propelled himself across the room with power born of love. The other man was tall and broad but Andrew held the element of surprise. He used his entire body as a battering ram, knocking the bastard to the floor. They crashed into the tumbled kitchen chairs, then slammed into the stove.

"Andrew!" Shannon screamed. "He's got a gun!"

Her warning came an instant too late. Andrew found himself pinned on his back with a pistol jammed into his mouth and the face of evil looking down upon him. He leveled his gaze upon his enemy. *Kill me if you must, but spare her. She has suffered enough by your hand.*

He knew the truth of what would happen. The man would not leave before he had sent them both to their Maker.

From the corner of his eye he saw Shannon crawling toward them.

Run, damn you, lass! I am of no consequence in this world. You must survive!

Run? She wouldn't run. There was nothing on the face of the earth that would make her leave Andrew.

"This is it, pal," Bryant said, setting himself. "Say your prayers."

In that instant Shannon didn't feel the pain. She didn't feel the fear. All she knew was that the man she loved was in danger and she was the only one on earth who could save him.

Few people were given a second chance. She wasn't about to waste it.

Grabbing hold of the legs of a kitchen chair, she leapt to her feet and swung that damn chair at Bryant with every ounce of power, every day of helpless anger. She swung that chair for herself and for every woman who'd ever passed through a shelter—and for every woman for whom it was too late. The chair caught him between the shoulder blades and it caught him hard.

He dropped to the floor, body held at an odd angle, then, with a cry of pain, went unconscious. The gun fell from his hand and skittered across the floor.

Andrew scrambled to his feet and reached for the weapon.

"Don't!" Shannon said. She grabbed the pistol from the floor and aimed it at her ex-husband. It would be so easy to pull that trigger.... "Get rope from the pantry and tie his arms and legs before he comes to."

Andrew looked sharply at her—and at the gun in her hand—then did as she asked.

"He probably has a broken shoulder," Shannon said dispassionately. "I should put him out of his misery."

"Nay, lass," said Andrew, covering her hand with his own. "He is not worth the price you'd pay." The bloody bastard deserved to die, but Shannon would carry the mark on her soul forever. He knew he could do the deed and suffer not a moment of remorse. "Give me the weapon. I will do it for you."

"Don't touch the gun!" She took a step back. He feared she would shoot her husband then and there, but she did not. "We can't let anyone know you were involved, Andrew. How could we explain your existence to the police?"

"The police will understand once I explain the facts to them clearly."

"You have no identification, no way to prove who you are. They'd take you away. Please," she said urgently, "go back into the woods and don't come back until the police are gone. Protect yourself, Andrew."

"I care not about my own well-being. 'Tis you I care for, lass. You alone."

"Then do as I say," she pleaded. "It's our only hope."

"I will not leave you again."

A look of sadness shadowed her face. It was unlike any look he had seen thus far and he knew a different taste of fear. "Yes, you will," she said softly and then she said no more.

He left the house through the French doors and lingered in the backyard long enough to see her set the alarm then trigger it with the muzzle of the gun to alert the authorities. Swiftly he headed into the woods to make certain all was well with Dakota and the others.

Their trail was easy to follow, even in the darkness. He counted the sleeping forms, reassuring himself that each was accounted for, then looked toward Dakota, who was awake and sitting by the dying fire. She brushed at her cheeks as he approached.

"It was Bryant, wasn't it?" Her voice was low.

"Aye," said Andrew, squatting by the fire.

"Is he dead?"

"I regret to say he is not. I wished to accomplish that with my own hands but failed."

"Is Shannon all right?"

"To the eye, yes. Beneath the surface, I cannot tell. Something troubles her."

"Bryant's return, probably."

"Nay," said Andrew, "'tis not that. She wishes to speak of it later and I—" He stopped and shook his head. He would not give voice to his fears. He had failed Shannon as he had failed Elspeth, as he had failed everything and everyone in his life. Regret lay bitter on his tongue.

Emilie had come to his time believing him a hero who saved General Washington, only to discover it was her own husband who did so.

And now, with Shannon, when he had wished to save her with his courage and gallantry, he had instead found himself with the barrel of a pistol shoved into his mouth—as trapped and useless a figure of a man as ever he had been.

He had believed this world of the future was where he would find riches and success beyond his wildest imaginings. In truth, he was but a babe in the woods, destined to rely upon Shannon's generosity for his daily bread.

You deserve better, lass, he thought, staring into the dying fire.

She deserved the hero he could never be.

Chapter Twenty-Four

24

Shannon watched as the blinking lights of the last police car disappeared down the road that led to her house. The sound of the vehicle crunching along the gravel seemed very loud in the predawn stillness.

It felt strange to be alone in the house again. She stepped in through the French doors and stood in the middle of the sun room. She'd always loved the sun room, with its polished oak floor and the pale yellow chaise. Now she could never look at it again without seeing Bryant.

She wrapped her arms across her chest and took a deep, calming breath.

The fact that Bryant had found her surprised her less than the way it had happened. He'd known her whereabouts for weeks now and it had nothing to do with the man she'd met in Lord & Taylor.

Bryant was a lot more clever than that. He'd put people on her trail while he was still in prison, and this midnight visit had been the climax of a carefully constructed plan. He'd checked in with his parole officer that morning, then boarded a friend's private jet for the flight east. If his plan had gone as he'd believed it would,

Bryant would have been asleep in his west-coast bed when the authorities came looking for him.

And she and Andrew would be dead.

Prison didn't seem half good enough for him.

She walked slowly into the kitchen, then bent to right the chairs, feeling the sharp edges of pain in her knee and rib cage. But that pain was nothing compared to the deep longing she felt for the life she'd been denied. They couldn't stay here any longer. Bryant had seen to that. She had to move on, find a new home, build a new life, same as she had done before. Had any place ever felt like home? She couldn't remember. Not with her parents. Not with Bryant. This house had come close to being home, but that special sense of belonging hadn't happened until the moment Andrew McVie had walked into her life.

How ironic that the one man on earth who had made her believe in the future was the one man she could never have.

She sat at the table and rested her head on the cool surface. She was tired of fighting the inevitable. He didn't belong here. This world didn't deserve a man like Andrew McVie.

And maybe neither did she.

Tears sprang to her eyes and she didn't try to wipe them away. She had the right to cry. Damn it, she'd earned that right. And it wasn't because her entire life had been turned inside out tonight or because her head ached or her knee throbbed. It was because there was a sorrow inside her heart, in a place so deep she hadn't known it existed until Andrew.

She'd believed it could work, that somehow she could offer him something so wonderful, so lasting, so overwhelmingly *right* that he would never again want for the things his old life could provide. She couldn't pinpoint the change, couldn't put a name to the forces that were at work, but when he risked all to save her from Bryant's rage, she knew beyond doubt that he deserved so much more than a life in the shadows.

"You are more than I deserve, lass."

Her entire body was galvanized by the sound of his voice. She lifted her head and saw him standing in the doorway.

He opened his arms wide.

The distance between them vanished and she went into his arms, glorying in the touch and smell and sight of him. He was everything good and strong and decent the world had to offer and in that instant she knew she loved him enough to let him go.

He sensed the change in her immediately. Her body stiffened and he felt as if a wall of glass had been placed between their souls.

"I am not the woman you think I am, Andrew."

He considered her carefully, his own soul aching at the sight of the bruises blossoming along the side of her delicate jaw. "Aye, lass. I know that your identity is not that with which you were born."

"That is not what I mean."

Despair hovered in the shadows but he refused to acknowledge it. "Then say it plainly, Shannon, for I have no wish to guess at the meaning of your words."

She pulled away from his embrace. "Come with me," she said. "There is something you need to know."

He followed her through the hallway and into the library. She pointed to the top shelf of the middle bookcase. "Behind Plutarch's *Lives,*" she said, her voice taut. "There's a book that I want you to have."

He reached up, pushed Plutarch aside, then removed a slim volume from the shelf. *"Forgotten Heroes,"* he said, reading the title on the spine. The irony was not lost on him.

"Page 127," said Shannon quietly.

"There is nothing for me in this book." He pushed it toward her.

"Page 127," she repeated.

He found the page in question. "'Tis half torn," he observed, scanning the paragraphs. "What value can this—" He stopped abruptly. Blood pounded in his ears like the roar of the ocean as the words seemed to leap up at him from the printed page.

In an act of courage unequaled at that time in the War for Independence, Boston lawyer-turned-spy Andrew McVie staged a daring raid on British troops near Jockey Hollow during the winter of 1779-1780 and single-handedly saved two of the most important members of the Spy Ring from certain death—

"I lived," he said, dumbstruck. "I do not know how it is possible, but my life was lived out in my own time."

"I know," she whispered. "It's your destiny."

High color darkened his craggy face and he began to pace the room. "This cannot be. This is not what Emilie told me of my fate."

"Emilie was wrong."

"You cannot say that with certainty. That page was torn."

"Yes," she said sadly. "I can say it with certainty."

He ignored her. "Where did this bloody book come from?"

"The library."

"Dakota's library?"

"Yes."

"The woman does not hold me in esteem." He glared at the book as if it were a viper, coiled and ready to strike. "'Tis a joke of some kind, made to tear us apart. You should have burned it in the hearth."

"And what if I had? That wouldn't change anything, Andrew. Your fate is there in black and white."

"How did it come to be hidden on your library shelf?"

"I put it there."

"You kept it from me?"

"I didn't want to lose you." She met his eyes. "You gave me back my heart, Andrew. I'll never forget you—" Her voice broke and she could say no more.

"Do you think so little of me, lass, that you believe words in a book could make me turn from you? Magic brought me here and I see no magic awaiting to take me back." He reached for her hand and headed for the sun room and the French doors. "I will prove it to you."

The sky was growing light as she followed him across the backyard and into the garage where the balloon rested.

"See this," he said, pulling the cover from the balloon and gondola. "The fabric turns to dust, while the basket could no longer carry a child." He grabbed the lip of the gondola and began to drag it from the garage, not stopping until it rested in the middle of her curving driveway. "No magic fire, Shannon. No strange clouds come to carry me back. 'Tis a lie, that book, and nothing more."

"There is something more," she said.

"I do not wish to see it."

"You must."

He gripped her hands tightly in his. "Why is it you push me away, lass, when I have no wish to leave?"

"It is not up to either of us, Andrew. It was decided a long time ago."

"Aye, and this country is the proof of that. My existence played no part in her growth."

"What about the men you saved?"

He looked away. She saw a muscle in his jaw twitch. "They have no meaning to me when compared to all that I have found with you."

"Oh, Andrew," she whispered. "There is so much you don't know." She reached into the pocket of her robe and withdrew a wrinkled sheaf of papers.

"Dakota again," he said with an impatient shake of his head. "I grow tired of the woman's nonsense."

She pushed the papers toward him. “I did my best to piece them together.”

“There is no purpose to this, lass. It changes naught.”

“The spies you saved—”

“I do not want to hear this.”

“Andrew, listen to me! You saved Zane Rutledge and Josiah Blakelee.”

“That cannot be.”

She fanned the patched pages out and waved them beneath his nose. “Three separate sources and each says the same thing. You saved their lives, Andrew. The children we read about, the farms, the families they founded—none of it will happen unless you return.”

“You are my destiny,” he said to Shannon. “You are all that I want.”

“You must go.”

“There is nothing else in life beyond you.”

“You would never be happy. You need so much more than that. You deserve so much more.”

“No,” he said, his voice fierce. “You are all that I need.”

He kissed her with a hunger that left her breathless.

“Andrew, look!” She pointed toward the sky. “Those clouds! I’ve seen them before.”

He said nothing, but made to kiss her again.

“Last week,” she said in a voice of wonder. “When you landed in the woods.”

“Aye,” he said, “and twice since.” He turned away from the balloon and he had no need to see the clouds.

“That’s it, isn’t it? That’s how it happened.”

“Still, it cannot be,” Andrew said forcefully. “There was a magic fire propelling the balloon and that fire does not exist any longer.”

"What if the fire appeared," she pressed, her aqua eyes alight with a dangerous glow. "What would you do?"

"I would turn away," he said, "for I have no wish to leave you—not in this life or any other."

She rose on tiptoe and peered over his shoulder. "Oh, God! Andrew, look!"

"Nay," he said. "I will not."

"It's happening.... My God, Andrew!"

Slowly he turned and saw a sight that was beyond reason. The basket appeared to his eyes as perfect as it had on the day he climbed aboard. And the balloon—Sweet Jesus! The balloon was a vivid crimson red and it was growing larger with each second. Had the clouds somehow rejuvenated the balloon?

"The magic fire," he whispered, staring in wonder at the flames rising up from the basket to inflate the balloon. "This cannot be."

"Maybe not," said Shannon, grabbing the lip of the gondola, "but it's happening right here in front of us, Andrew, and we both know why."

He thought of Zane and Emilie and their hopes for the future...of Rebekah and Josiah and their children. Did their futures rest on his shoulders alone? Was he meant to be a hero, after all, the kind of man Shannon deserved?

But what did any of it matter if they were separated by time, destined to live out their lives in loneliness?

"I love you, Shannon Whitney," he said. "I would mark myself a liar if I said the past does not call to me but, in truth, I cannot envision a world without you."

"Then ask me, you fool! Ask me to come with you."

"I cannot," he said, his heart at war with his head. His gesture encompassed the house, the land, the rectangular pond. "How can

I ask you to abandon all that you have for love of me when I can offer you naught save a life of hardship and uncertainty?"

"Wealth doesn't guarantee happiness, Andrew," she said quietly. "I know that firsthand."

"You do not know what you are saying, lass."

"I know exactly what I'm saying. I know what it's like to be rich, but I don't know how it feels to be happy. You can show me, Andrew. Only you can do that."

"I have no home, no prospects, not even the guarantee that we will end up in the same world I left behind."

"I don't care," she said as joy filled her heart. "I have enough faith for both of us. Don't you see? This is why you came, Andrew. You came to find me."

He looked at her hard and then his hazel eyes crinkled and his mouth curved upward and laughter—joyous laughter—rose up from the depths of his lonely soul. "Aye," he said, gathering her into his arms. "And I will never let you go."

"There are things I expect from you," she said sternly. "I want to love and be loved in return. I want us to be partners. I want us to be kind and tolerant of each other's faults. And I want your children." A smile played at the corners of her mouth. "Did you hear me, Andrew? I want to bear your children."

"Aye," he said, his voice gruff with emotion. "'Tis great good fortune that we wish the same things from life, mistress."

"And about that 'mistress' business, Andrew." She poked him in the chest with her forefinger. "I think we'd better make it legal."

"You are proposing marriage?"

She looked up at him, then started to laugh. "Will you marry me, Andrew McVie? Will you carry me off into the sunrise in your hot-air balloon and make an honest woman of me? Will you love me forever and ever?"

"I would gladly take you as my wife, lass, but know that I do not believe in divorce. When we say our vows before God, we will be wed into eternity."

"Eternity," she said, her voice a whisper. "I can't imagine anything that could please me more than sharing eternity with you."

They turned to look at the balloon, which bobbed high above the gondola now.

"'Tis almost ready," Andrew said. "Soon it will begin to rise."

"We can't go yet," she said, reality sinking in. "I have to pack my belongings."

"There is no time, lass. It will leave with us or without."

"One minute, Andrew! I'll be back in time. I promise."

She was as good as her word. She returned moments later, carrying a large satchel.

"You will turn my hair gray, lass," he said, swinging her into the basket as the balloon shuddered, eager to rise. He tossed in her bag then leapt in after her. "What was of such importance that you risked our future?"

"Patience, Mr. McVie." Her smile was one of mystery and promise. "You'll find out in good time."

He reached for the satchel and she pushed him away, laughing, but not before he saw a most familiar item tucked among the assortment. "'Tis the picture of us from the newspaper."

"For our children, Andrew." The look she gave him was one of such love that it filled his heart with joy. "It will help us explain a miracle."

He thought of a girl with her beauty and generosity of spirit, of a boy with her courage and wit. Once he had thought himself destined to walk this world alone, but then he found Shannon and suddenly the future glittered before him, more precious than gold.

"'Twas an adventure," he said, holding her close as the balloon shuddered again then began to rise.

"I know," Shannon whispered, resting her head against his shoulder. "But now it's time for us to go home."

"Aye," he said, as the sun pierced the clouds. "'Tis time we did, at that."

Epilogue

"You don't look so good," the little girl said as she peered up at Dakota.

"Thanks a lot," said Dakota, ruffling the child's hair. "I'm getting too old for these late nights." She glanced around the front yard of the shelter. "Everyone accounted for?"

One of the mothers flashed her the thumbs-up sign.

They had arrived back at the shelter as the sun rose over the tops of the trees. If it hadn't been for the strange clouds towering overhead, it would have been a beautiful morning. As it was, the kids were ready for breakfast. Their mothers looked pleased to have made it through the night.

And Dakota felt as if she'd been run over by an eighteen wheeler.

"I make great scrambled eggs," said one of the mothers. "You're welcome to stay."

"I'd probably fall asleep with my face in the toast." She grabbed her purse and car keys. "I'm going to head for home."

"Take some doughnuts with you," the woman said. "You're too thin."

"God bless you and your children and your children's children," said Dakota while the woman filled a bag with jelly doughnuts. "I don't know who decided double-digit dress sizes were against the law but the man should be shot."

Her car was covered with a light mist and she ran the wipers for a few seconds to clear the windshield. She wondered how Shannon and Andrew were getting on but decided against stopping by. God knew, they'd been through enough for one night. Besides, she wasn't feeling all that well. She was not only tired but weak, as if she'd been sick in bed for weeks and this was her first day on her feet.

Bed, she thought, backing down the driveway and turning right on the road. Bed and a good twelve or eighteen hours' sleep should do it.

A flash of something red caught her eye and she braked slightly. It wasn't anything much, just the tiniest hint of something barely peeking over the trees by Shannon's house. An odd fluttering began deep inside her chest. It reminded her of the way she'd felt each time she'd swooned over Andrew McVie. Strange that she'd be feeling that way now when he was nowhere in sight.

She looked toward the red spot over the treetops and the fluttering intensified.

"The balloon!" The words tore from her throat. It was happening right this very minute and she suddenly knew this was Andrew's last chance to go back where he belonged.

Minutes later the Mustang skidded to a stop in Shannon's driveway, and Dakota found herself staring at the balloon and gondola as they drifted a few inches above the driveway.

Her heart did a little leap as she saw Shannon and Andrew waving to her from the basket. *They're together,* she thought with elation. *And they're going home.* Her eyes swam with tears as she noticed the shimmer of gold all around them, bathing the two travelers in its benevolent glow. And they even had matching auras....

The balloon began to rise higher. Already the gondola was a foot off the ground.

"Wait!" she yelled. "I have something for you."

"Hurry!" Shannon called out. "We haven't much time."

She tried to race, but her legs felt leaden and she had scarcely enough energy to put one foot in front of the other.

The gondola rose another foot.

"It's jelly doughnuts!" Dakota yelled, tossing the bag to them. "Don't squish them, whatever you do." They might need a snack. After all, their next meal was a century or two away.

The bottom of the basket was at waist level. The crimson silk was growing more vivid in color; the gondola, even more substantial. She looked down at her hands...her arms. Her aura was gone. She touched the basket. Her aura returned. She released the basket, then watched in horror as her physical self seemed to grow transparent, almost as if she were about to disappear.

Fatigue made her head swim, and she struggled to hang on to her equilibrium. She felt so weak, so temporary, as if her soul and her body were parting company. Dear God in heaven, she was dying! The only thing anchoring her to the mortal world was that hot-air balloon, and in another second it would be gone and she—

Shannon stared at her in obvious horror. "Andrew, my God! We have to do something."

"What's the matter?" Dakota managed to say. "I finally found a diet that worked...." *Always leave 'em laughing, Wylie. Can't you even be serious when you're about to kick the bucket?*

Andrew leaned forward until he was half out of the gondola. "Give me your hand."

"Absolutely not. If I swoon again, I'm a goner."

"As I see it, mistress, you have but one choice."

He leaned over the basket and grabbed Dakota by the arms, swinging her into the gondola with them as the balloon rose toward the clouds.

"A fifth wheel in two centuries," Dakota said as her heartbeat slowly returned to normal. "It's not too late if you want to back out. Tell me to leave, why don't you? I could jump. I'd probably only break a leg or two but what's a fractured limb between friends?" She waited. "Guys, I was just kidding. If you want me to leave, I'll—"

But Andrew and Shannon hadn't heard a word. Wrapped in each other's arms they were already in a world of their own.

A big fat lump formed in Dakota's throat and she blinked back tears. There was something about destiny being served that brought out the romantic in her.

"A fifth wheel," Dakota said, turning away. But somehow the words no longer stung.

They sailed up into the clouds and her fears vanished like the morning mist. It was a beautiful late-summer day. The sun was shining. The air was sweet. There was an adventure waiting for her out there and she was glad she was her mother's daughter, eager to take that first step into the unknown.

She heard the sound of soft laughter and turned toward Shannon and Andrew. The golden glow still surrounded them, but there was something more, something that had nothing to do with auras, and everything to do with the power of love. Her eyes grew misty as she shamelessly watched them. Andrew looked at Shannon as if he held the secret to life in his arms. And Shannon! Shannon looked up at Andrew with such pure joy that Dakota found herself struck once again by the miracle of love.

You never knew when it would happen to you. You never knew where. He could be a doctor, lawyer, Indian chief, or a renegade patriot spy. The only thing that mattered was that you'd found the other half of your heart.

She smiled and turned away once again as Shannon rose up on tiptoe for Andrew's kiss. Sometimes you even had to travel across the centuries to find it.

Her stomach growled and she plucked a jelly doughnut from the bag. *Raspberry,* she thought as she took a bite.

It was a good omen.

She could feel it in her bones.

DESTINY'S CHILD

For The Graduate,
best husband in this world or any other

Prologue

Dakota Wylie had spent every summer of her youth in the back seat of her parents' van, wedged between her younger sister, Janis, who existed on mascara and diet soda, and her twin brothers, Conan and Tige, whose joint claim to fame was the ability to play "Disco Inferno" with their armpits.

Frederick and Ginny Wylie believed that the best education they could give their children was to be found at sixty miles per hour on Interstate 80 as they crisscrossed the country paying homage to every national monument and rest stop they encountered. Other kids went to Camp Winnemukluk and learned how to braid lanyards and smoke cigarettes without inhaling; Dakota learned the location of every Stuckey's between Princeton and the Grand Canyon.

Her father, a professor of physics, spent the dreary winter months with his desk littered with road maps and notebooks while he planned every step of the summer's journey. He approached the project with mathematical precision and an engineer's sense of efficiency. Getting there wasn't half the fun for Dr. Wylie; it was everything.

Her mother, a bona fide, card-carrying psychic, indulged her husband's love of ritual and technology but she despaired when she saw those careful traits rearing their heads in her children. Ginny knew life's greatest adventures were the ones that were unplanned, and of her four children only her oldest seemed to understand.

Which was how Dakota Wylie—unmarried, unemployed and overweight—found herself that fine late summer morning in the gondola of a hot-air balloon bound for the eighteenth century.

At least, that's where Dakota thought they were headed. It suddenly occurred to her that, considering the circumstances, she was taking a great deal on faith.

When you were about to challenge the laws of nature, you'd think there would be trumpets and fanfare, some kind of celestial send-off that acknowledged the enormity of what was about to happen.

It wasn't every day a woman went leaping through time. Except for Einstein, most rational human beings put time travel up there on a par with the existence of the Loch Ness Monster and the Easter Bunny. Fun to think about, but not bloody likely.

For weeks Ginny had told her something was on the horizon, an adventure more amazing than anything either woman could imagine, but Dakota had been so busy trying to figure out what Andrew McVie was all about that the signs had passed her right by until it was almost too late. Every time she'd seen Andrew she'd passed out at his feet, overwhelmed by the force field his presence generated.

It hadn't taken her long to realize he wasn't part of the twentieth century, and even less time to discover that he and Shannon Whitney, the woman he'd traveled across the centuries to find, had to go back through time to the place where they both now belonged.

Still, she hadn't figured they'd be taking her with them.

The basket shuddered as an air current buffeted it from the

east, and Dakota glanced around. She was all in favor of adventure—but why couldn't it take place at ground level? Shannon and Andrew were wrapped in each other's arms, oblivious to the fact that the only thing between them and instant death was that puny fire that kept the bright red balloon aloft.

"Sure," she mumbled. "What do you care if I'm a fifth wheel in two centuries?" This was their destiny, after all. As far as Dakota could tell, she was just along for the ride, comic relief to keep them laughing as the decades whizzed by.

"You won't be here forever," Ginny had said a few days ago. Dakota had thought she meant the library where she worked. Why was it her psychic abilities were able to zero in on everybody else in the western hemisphere with laserlike precision but when it came to her own life, she invariably came up empty?

For instance, it would have been nice to have had some advance warning. If they were really traveling through time, she was going to need a make-over from Martha Washington as soon as they landed, because her dusty jeans, worn running shoes, and Jurassic Park T-shirt weren't going to win any fashion awards. Then again, neither was her coiffure. She reached up and touched the close-cropped mop of jet black curls that had probably never been in fashion, no matter the century.

Next to the beautiful Shannon with her elegant bone structure and glossy tresses, she probably looked like a boy with a severe water retention problem.

"I have a question," she said to the embracing couple who shared the basket with her. "How do we know if we're going the right way? I mean, this thing doesn't come with a road map. What if we end up back in the seventies or something?" A lifetime sentence of leisure suits and disco. It was enough to make her leap overboard.

"You are the one gifted with second sight, Mistress Dakota. Do you not know the outcome?" Andrew wasn't a handsome man by any account, but even Dakota had to admit he was quite something when he smiled.

"That's right," said Shannon. "You're psychic. You should know these things. We were counting on you to keep us on course."

"Just because I'm psychic doesn't mean I have a sense of direction," Dakota retorted. "You'd think there'd be some way to steer this thing." An odd prickle of apprehension twitched its way up her spine as she had a sudden and clear vision of thick woods and a child too young to find her way home.

"Dakota?" Shannon's voice reached her as if from far away. "Is something wrong?"

"I don't know," Dakota said. She shivered as a glimpse of tear-stained cheeks and tangled hair spun past. "I must be flashing on last night." She'd spent the night in the woods with some residents of the battered women's shelter in an Outward Bound experiment, meant to enhance self-esteem and independence. Dakota had spent most of the hours after dark worried that one of the kids would wander away and get lost and she'd have to venture deeper into the bug-infested woods to look for the child.

"Mistress Dakota has no fondness for nature's wonders," said Andrew. "She was most distressed when a spider took up residence on her arm."

"You would've screamed, too, if you'd seen the sucker," Dakota said to Shannon. "The darn thing was the size of a blue jay."

Andrew held his thumb and forefinger an inch apart and Shannon laughed out loud. "Now you know everything you need to about Dakota. She hates spiders and loves jelly doughnuts."

"Raspberry jelly doughnuts," Dakota said. "If you're going to spill my secrets, at least be accurate." She patted her hips. "I've worked hard for each one of these pounds."

Shannon executed a curtsy in her direction. "I stand corrected, Mistress Dakota."

Andrew's head snapped around. "I have not heard you speak thusly."

"'Tis time," Shannon said. "I must learn to fit into your world, Andrew."

Dakota watched, a huge lump throbbing in her throat, as the lovers took each other's measure and were well satisfied. Their auras shimmered like molten gold and Dakota found herself blinking back tears of joy...and envy. They said there was someone for every man and woman on the earth but at times it seemed to Dakota as if she were meant to go through life alone.

She'd been born with a wisecrack on her lips and cellulite on her thighs and that wasn't a combination destined to bring men to their knees. No, most men liked their women straight out of a Victoria's Secret catalog, demure and airbrushed to within an inch of their perfect lives.

She forced a saucy grin. "You're our time-traveling resident expert, Andrew. How long is this going to take?"

"You are wrong, mistress. I am no expert in such matters. 'Twill take as long as it takes."

"That's what my father used to say when we were halfway to Walt Disney World and had run out of comic books and candy bars."

Andrew met Shannon's eyes. "Walt Disney World?"

"You didn't tell him about Walt Disney World?" Dakota stared at her friend in disbelief.

Shannon shrugged gracefully, the way she did everything. You'd never believe her life had been anything but blessed. "We covered all major wars, important scientific advances and why Dick Clark still looks twenty-five when we all know he's one hundred and seven. I had to forget something."

"An unforgivable gap in your education," Dakota declared to Andrew. "Walt Disney World is a theme park."

Andrew looked at her blankly.

"A place where adults and children go to have fun," she explained, "and it all centers around a mouse named Mickey."

"'Tis a good thing I am leaving your time," Andrew said, shaking his head in amazement, "for your world is a place of uncommon strangeness."

Shannon went on in great detail about mice in short pants who always had a date for Saturday night, ducks with attitude problems and amusement-park rides whose sole purpose was to make grown men and women lose their lunches.

"Andrew is right," Dakota said, wiping away tears of laughter. "When you put it that way, it *does* sound strange. Maybe—" She stopped. "Did you hear that?"

Andrew and Shannon exchanged looks. It was obvious they had no idea what she was talking about.

"The magic fire," said Andrew, pointing toward the flame that kept the balloon inflated. "'Tis a distinctive sound."

"Not that," Dakota said with an impatient wave of her hand. "It's softer…more like a cry."

Shannon tilted her head to listen. "I don't hear anything, either, Dakota."

Dakota wrapped her arms around her chest as a blast of wind rocked the fragile gondola. The little girl knelt in front of her, crying brokenly over a tattered rag doll. The child's brown hair was tangled about her shoulders and was badly in need of a good shampoo and conditioning, while her cotton dress was woefully inadequate against the cold. The image was so clear, so real that Dakota wanted to reach out and wipe away the tears streaking down the girl's dirty face.

She hated it when the visions came at her like this, swift and hard as a punch to the gut, knocking the wind from her lungs and toppling her defenses. No matter how many times it happened, she never quite got used to this sudden stripping away of the shadowy barriers between the different levels of reality.

Most of the time she accepted her abilities the same way other people accepted a gift for music or a talent for drawing. They were part and parcel of the way she viewed the world and the way she viewed herself. But there were times, like now, when she devoutly wished she could be like everyone else and see life in only one dimension at a time.

The child's cries tore at her heart. "She's lost...she'll never find her way out of the woods." *It's too late, Dakota. You can't help her. Her time is spinning past....*

A stiff wind blew in from the west, rocking the basket as if it were made of tissue paper. The hairs on the back of her neck rose in response. *This isn't the way it's supposed to happen. Something's terribly wrong!*

"Dakota?" Shannon placed a hand on her arm. "Maybe you should sit down."

"I don't belong here," she whispered. "This is a mistake. I have to go back."

"Nay, mistress, 'twas no mistake." The basket lurched to the right and Andrew steadied her. "You are here because it was meant to be thus."

"We saw you, Dakota," Shannon said. "You were fading away right before our eyes. It was this or—"

Another gust of wind buffeted the balloon, to the left this time, sending the three of them smashing into the side of the basket.

"Andrew?" Shannon's voice sounded high and tight. "Is something wrong?"

"I do not know. My own journey to your time was most enjoyable. Indeed, I did not believe I had traveled anywhere at all until I found you and saw the newspaper."

I'm the reason things are going wrong. This trip should be as easy as the last. I'm the problem....

Dakota swallowed hard. Another blast of wind like that and they would all be tossed overboard like excess baggage. She closed her eyes, struggling to capture an image, a whisper, some indication of what was to come, but her thoughts were filled with the sight and sound of a little girl's tears.

"Look sharp!" Andrew's cry pierced through the roar of the wind. "To the left."

The cloud, an angular black mass, towered upward like a caricature of a twister. She didn't need second sight to know what it meant.

"Hang together!" Andrew called out. "We will—"

His words were torn apart by another vicious gust of wind that grabbed hold of the basket and threatened to flip it end over end. Her granny glasses slipped off her nose and blew away.

This is wrong, Dakota thought, clinging to the lip of the basket as the child's cries grew louder inside her head. Shannon and Andrew were meant to journey safely back to his time. The lives of Zane Rutledge and Josiah Blakelee, and the lives of their descendants, depended upon it. Wasn't she the one who'd found the proof in black and white on page 127 of *Forgotten Heroes?* The name Dakota Wylie didn't appear anywhere. She was the wild card, the X factor that changed the equation and threatened their future and she wanted to go home where she belonged right now.

The fire sputtered as the basket withstood another pummeling gust of wind. Shannon crouched on the floor, gripping the ropes that connected the gondola to the balloon itself, while Andrew reached out to Dakota.

"Grab my hand, mistress!" His voice rang out.

The basket tilted wildly to the right and she let out a scream as she fell to one knee.

"Now!" Andrew commanded. "We are dropping fast."

A few years ago she'd gone to the World Trade Center for dinner at Windows on the World when the elevator malfunctioned, dropping the car three stories in the blink of an eye. This was the same stomach-turning sensation, magnified a hundredfold. Was she dropping only through space or hurtling down through time, as well?

The towering black cloud enveloped them in a tunnel of darkness. She could hear Shannon's and Andrew's voices rising above the roar of the wind but it was impossible to see them.

The bottom of the basket made a sickening noise as it scraped the tops of the trees. Her nostrils twitched at the smell of pine and rich earth coming closer, closer.

"I hate you!" The child's voice trembled with pain. "I *hate* you!"

Dakota felt the little girl's pain in the center of her heart, in that place reserved for the children she would never have. *Go with it. You have no other choice.*

Whispering a swift prayer, Dakota climbed to the top of the basket railing and jumped.

Chapter One

1

It was said by the good people of Franklin Ridge, in the Colony of New Jersey, that Patrick Devane was the angriest man in four counties, and on that December afternoon he did nothing to dispel the notion.

His housekeeper, Mrs. O'Gorman, dabbed at her rheumy eyes with a wrinkled handkerchief. "'Tain't my fault, sir," she said through loud sniffles. "The child's willful as her mother and there wouldn't be a thing I could do to stop her."

"The child is six years old," Patrick snapped. "She requires a firm hand and a watchful eye, two things you are unwilling or unable to provide."

Mrs. O'Gorman's expression shifted from lugubrious to sly. "And a child needs a father, if I may be so bold, and it seems to me you been one in name only."

"Enough!" His roar rattled the walls. "You'll be out of my house by nightfall."

"And I'll be thanking the Almighty for that," Mrs. O'Gorman said, thrusting her chins at him. "I'd rather be workin' for Fat George in London than spend another day in this terrible place."

"Take care, woman, or I'll see that you get your wish."

Mrs. O'Gorman, no longer concerned with employment, was a woman unleashed. "'Tain't my wish that's comin' true, mister. 'Tis yours. The child is gone—just the way you wanted it—and if she has the sense of a mayfly, she won't be back here where she ain't wanted."

With that the woman stormed from the library.

He swore softly at her retreating back. The truth ofttimes carried with it a scorpion's sting.

He'd heard them whispering belowstairs. How his cold heart had driven his warm-blooded wife into the arms of another man. And the way he treated the child was cause for scandal. He kept her clothed, fed and sheltered as was his duty as a Christian man. And now he would see to her education, as well. More than that he could not be asked to provide.

"'Tisn't natural to treat your own flesh and blood this way," Mrs. O'Gorman had said to her cronies the other day when she thought he could not hear. "All that money and not an ounce of warmth in his black heart."

"My papa is the best man in the world," Abigail had declared, biting Mrs. O'Gorman in her plump forearm.

Mrs. O'Gorman had tried to shake her off but the child had clung to her like a hound to a fox and it had taken three servants to finally pull her away.

"Poor little thing," Rosie, the scullery maid, had whispered loud enough to be heard in Trenton. "Him always treatin' her like a poor relation when it's his fault she's the way she is."

Abigail had rewarded the girl with a kick in the shins that had sent Rosie packing. If he did not put a stop to it, the child would drive every member of the staff from the house, nursing bite marks and bruises.

His hand had been forced and he was not ungrateful.

"This cannot go on, Abigail. Arrangements will be made for you to attend school in Boston."

"No!" Her gray eyes had darkened like the sky before a storm. She had spirit, this child. He would grant her that. It would serve her well in the future, since she had not been granted beauty. "You cannot make me!"

He'd chosen to ignore the challenge. "The Girls' School of the Sacred Heart is a fine place. They will teach you the things a young lady must know to make her way in the world." The things a mother would teach her daughter, if the mother had seen fit to stay.

Her plain little face had crumpled beneath his gaze. So much power to have over one so small and defenseless. Better to break the cord between them cleanly and be done with it.

"I hate you!" she'd cried when he informed her that the matter was closed to further discussion. "I hate you!"

"I don't doubt that," he'd said, turning away. "There is little reason for you to feel otherwise."

She lacked her mother's beauty, but she had her mother's spirit, that fiery temper and pigheaded stubbornness, and for a moment he'd felt a stab of dark emotion in the center of his chest. How many nights had he stood over her cradle, watching the way her tiny fists pumped the air as she slept? *She's fighting the world,* he'd thought as pride filled his heart. Same as he'd fought the world as he struggled his way out of poverty. The notion of life renewing itself suddenly made sense to him in a way he'd never imagined.

What a fool he'd been.

He had loved once and deeply and he would never love that way again. Few who knew him today would believe him capable of so tender a sentiment, but there had been a time when his bitter heart had known how sweet life could be. A time when all things had seemed possible, if only because he knew how to make dreams come true.

"I'll build you the grandest house in the thirteen colonies," he had promised Susannah in the throes of new love. "You'll have servants and fine gowns from Paris, everything your heart desires."

His dreams were as big and untamed as the country that had given him birth, and with a woman like Susannah VanDorn by his side, there was nothing he couldn't do, no dream he couldn't make come true.

He'd built the house. He'd filled it with servants. He'd showered her with silk gowns and satin slippers and more love than any woman had ever known. For every dream he fulfilled, a new dream sprang to life, eager to take its place.

But those dreams were now long gone. Susannah had destroyed them the day she walked out the door and into the arms of another man.

The child. There is the child to consider. The child he had once believed the reason he had been put upon this earth. The sad-eyed little girl who looked to him to explain something even he didn't understand.

The truth was Abigail wasn't his child at all but the offspring of another man. Living proof that he'd been cuckolded, not just once but a multitude of times, by a wife as faithless as a stray cat.

"My parting gift," Susannah had called the revelation as she'd rolled her rings and earbobs in a long strip of velvet and tucked it into her satchel. "I had been with three other men the month she was conceived." Her full red lips curved upward in a smile. "The odds are not in your favor, my sweet."

He came close to murder that night. Blood lust flooded his brain, forcing out reason and sanity. With one blow he could snap her fragile neck and put an end to the pain and misery she'd caused him. Salvage what remained of his pride.

"Do it," she'd dared him, her eyes blazing. "Do it and pay for the action the rest of your pathetic life."

He'd let her live and regretted that decision every hour of every day since.

Not even Susannah's death one year later in a carriage accident had lessened his rage.

He saw their looks each time her name was mentioned. He heard the whispers when they talked about the child. Pious, sanctimonious bastards, the lot of them, feigning concern when all they cared about was lively gossip for their parties. Martha Washington's latest haircomb or his miserable plight—it was all the same to the good people of Franklin Ridge.

He knew more about the lot of them than they could ever imagine. He knew the spies and the traitors, knew how many guineas it took to sway a man's devotion to a cause. Every man had his price, whether it be silver coins or the golden glow of a woman's hair. He made it his business to know what that price was.

"Sir?"

He turned at the sound of Cook's voice in the doorway. Her full face was still flushed from the heat of the hearth fire. Her fingers, knuckles swollen with arthritis, twisted the coarse tan fabric of her apron.

"You wish something?" he asked. He saw to it that his tone did not betray his chaotic thoughts.

"The child," Cook said, meeting his eyes. "She missed the midday meal. My boy, William, from the stables and Joseph are willin' to lead a search for the wee one."

"This is not the first time she has done this and it will not be the last."

"But the sun will set within the hour and—"

"I know when the blasted sun sets, woman! Do you take me for a fool?"

She was wise enough to keep her own counsel. "Begging your

pardon, sir. 'Tis dangerous times and many's the innocent who comes to a bad end. We love her like she's one of our own."

And for all he knew, she just might be.

"Have William saddle my horse," he roared, tired of the censure in their voices. "I'll search for the blasted child myself."

And when he found her he would see that she was on her way to the Girls' School of the Sacred Heart in Boston before the sun rose in the morning.

"I hate you!" Abigail Elizabeth Devane cried as she lashed out at Lucy with the toe of her leather boot. Her six-year-old heart was set upon murder. The doll's soft rag body tore at the seam beneath the right arm and a strip of pale green cotton poked through. Lucy was stupid, a baby's plaything, and Abby wasn't a baby any longer. That's what her father had told her that morning when he had said that she was to be sent away to school near a place called Boston.

She reared back and kicked the doll again, harder this time. A rip opened up on Lucy's left leg. Wads of yellow checkered cloth bunched through the opening. Good! That was better than blood, better than big pieces of broken bone. She wanted to throw Lucy into the river and watch her sink. She wanted to toss the doll into the cooking fire in the kitchen of the big house and smell the stink of burning cloth.

Grabbing Lucy by the right arm, she made to fling her against one of the big pine trees when she noticed that Lucy's head was hanging by a piece of yarn no thicker than a cat's whisker.

"Lucy!" All thoughts of violence forgotten, Abby clutched the doll to her breast and began to sob. The tears came all the way from the soles of her feet, big ugly gulps that would have embarrassed her had there been anyone around to hear. Big fat tears rolled down her dirty cheeks and she was glad there was no one there to see her wipe them away with the back of her arm.

The only person on earth who loved her was Lucy, and see what she had done to her. Everything Abby had suspected about herself was true, every terrible thing she'd heard whispered when they thought she wasn't listening. She was as ugly of spirit as she was of face, and even Papa was counting the days until she left for the Girls' School of the Sacred Heart.

"If only the little one was pretty," Cook had said the other night as she stirred the stew pot bubbling in the grate. "Pretty makes up for a multitude of sins. That might warm his cold heart some."

But Abby knew she wasn't pretty. Her hair wasn't shiny like gold coins or red as the leaves that had fallen from the trees. It was mud brown, as ordinary as the day was long. And instead of eyes as blue as the sky, hers were round blots as gray and ugly as winter rain. Was it any wonder Papa always looked away and frowned whenever she entered a room?

"I'm sorry, Lucy," she wailed, clutching the doll even tighter. She had a mean, wicked temper and now Lucy would be the one to pay the piper. It wasn't fair, it just wasn't—

She tilted her head to the left, listening. What a strange sound that was, a sputtering hiss that made her think of a big tomcat with his back arched, ready to fight. She knew by the strange clouds towering overhead that a big snowstorm was on its way, but not even the winds that howled down from the hills made such a horrid noise. Heart thudding inside her chest, she peered into the surrounding woods, afraid she might see a giant peering back at her with fire in his eyes.

Cook had told her a story about a ferocious mean giant who feasted on the bones of wicked Englishmen. Abby had the feeling a small girl from the Colony of New Jersey would make a tasty morsel.

She waited, but the woods remained still and silent. The noise sounded again, louder this time, and Abby wished she'd stayed closer to home. Hunters trapped bear in these very woods. She tried to imagine what she would do if a snarling, furry beast leapt out from behind a tree, ready to pounce. Maybe if she ran really fast she'd be able to make it back home before anything terrible happened to her.

She tucked Lucy inside the front of her cotton dress and was about to hike up her skirts and run when she saw the most amazing, the most splendid sight in the world! There, dancing across the tops of the trees, was a big red ball, so big that it blotted out the sky. It moved slowly, hissing as it did, swinging a funny-looking basket beneath it.

She watched, awestruck, as the bright red ball seemed to dip toward her in salute, then suddenly caught a breeze and rose higher and higher until it didn't seem big at all anymore.

"Oh, Lucy," she whispered, her temper and the frigid weather forgotten. "Did you ever see anything so beautiful?" It had hovered over the stand of pines just to the left of the clearing, as if beckoning her to jump into the basket and go off on a grand adventure. And she would have, too, if it hadn't floated away before she could run over and grab hold.

Short legs pumping fast beneath her skirt, she ran toward the trees. If the big red ball returned, she and Lucy would be there waiting and they wouldn't think twice before leaping aboard.

Papa would feel so bad that he'd forget all about that school in Boston and let her stay with him forever. And Mama would hear about her wondrous adventure and she would come back from heaven to stay and the big white house would be filled with laughter the way it used to be.

It wasn't as if Dakota had never been in a ridiculous situation before.

Just two months ago she'd accepted a blind date with the son of her mother's favorite tarot card reader from south Jersey, a guy named Brick who sold vinyl siding for a living and had all the creative imagination of his namesake. They'd spent a terrific hour and a half discussing the relative merits of faux cedar shakes before Dakota developed a sudden headache and had to cut the evening short.

"You didn't give him a chance," her mother had said in an exasperated tone of voice. "Elly read his palm a week ago Thursday and she swears she saw your name scrawled across his life line."

Which didn't surprise Dakota. Her name was scrawled across the life line of every loser on the Eastern seaboard. As bad as that blind date had been, nothing—not even the time she'd trailed toilet paper from the ladies' room at the swanky Palmer Inn—was worse than this.

You didn't need psychic powers to know nothing good ever happened when you threw fate a curveball.

Anyone with a brain knew her destiny was clearly tied up with Andrew and Shannon's. She'd been fading away like a ghost in an old B movie and she had no doubt she would have vanished into thin air in another moment if she hadn't managed to scramble aboard with Andrew's help. Climbing into that gondola had been the equivalent of psychic CPR.

She glanced at her hands. At least she couldn't see through them. That had to be a good sign. Wherever she was, she was solidly connected. But where was she? Where were Andrew and Shannon? And, even more important, *when* were they?

Her stomach lurched as she remembered the sickening sound the basket had made as it scraped the tops of the trees, and the look of fear in Shannon's eyes.

"They're fine," she mumbled. Their destiny had never been in doubt. She was the one who'd been heading home with a bag of jelly doughnuts, only to find herself propelled headlong through time.

You panicked, kiddo. The second that balloon tilted, you were ready to bail out.

"Ridiculous!" She'd heard that little girl as clearly as she'd heard her own voice and something, some suppressed maternal instinct, had taken over and forced her to leap from the basket.

You leapt just before it went down, Wylie. You'd have been something on the Titanic.

So she was an idiot. Big deal. A few crossed neurons and she'd conjured up a lost little girl that only Dakota Wylie, Super Librarian, could rescue.

Now there she was, a good twenty feet off the ground, clinging to the branch of a naked maple tree that didn't look strong enough to support a blue jay, much less a plump American woman who believed in physical exertion only at gunpoint.

Of course, there was always the remote possibility that some kind soul with a reinforced aluminum ladder would come strolling through the woods in search of a damsel in distress.

Why on earth had she eaten that last raspberry-jelly doughnut anyway? Those few ounces of fat and sugar might be enough to send her crashing to the ground. She shifted her weight over to what she prayed was a sturdier limb.

The branch creaked loudly in protest but it held, and she breathed a huge sigh of relief. Somebody should invent a way to determine these things without offering yourself up as a human sacrifice.

As it was, if the fall didn't kill her, the weather might. The dark, jagged cloud cover that had rocked the gondola was gone now, replaced by heavy ivory-colored skies that promised snow. Lots of it. Goose bumps marched up and down her arms and her teeth chattered from the cold. Her-T-shirt and jeans weren't going to cut it for very long.

Now you've done it, Wylie. Leave it to you to screw up the forces of destiny.

She clung to the branch as a furious blast of wind shook the maple. Maybe she wouldn't have to worry about climbing down from the tree. Another icy gust like that and she'd drop to the ground like an overripe peach. She longed for a down-filled jacket and fur-lined boots. Hard to believe last night she'd been praying for central air-conditioning and something cool to drink.

So now what, hotshot? How are you going to get out of this one?

She hadn't a clue. A lot depended on where—and when—she'd ended up. What if she really had jumped out during the seventies? She'd need a shoehorn to get her hips into one of those slinky polyester dance dresses, the kind that required lots of attitude and breasts that saluted the sun.

Well, there was no hope for it. She couldn't hang there like a bat for the rest of her natural life. Those snow clouds lowering overhead meant business, and if she was going to find shelter before nightfall, she'd better get to it.

In a nearby tree a woodpecker tapped relentlessly against the hard wood. The machine-gun rat-a-tat-tat provided a counterpoint to the din of two jays squabbling overhead. Another, sweeter sound floated up toward her.

"Oh, Lucy...it was so beautiful!" A child's voice, high and clear.

"Hello!" she called out. "Is somebody there?"

She waited, listening to the quality of the silence. Was she crazy, or was it different than it had been a few moments ago?

"I heard you," she continued, trying to sound as friendly as the circumstances would allow. "Don't be shy. I need your help." *And I need it now.*

She waited, scarcely breathing, as the branch she clung to creaked ominously. Finally she heard the crunch of frozen leaves underfoot as a little girl of no more than five or six stepped into the clearing.

Her brown hair was plaited into two uneven braids that drooped over narrow shoulders. She wore a heavy woolen cloak that brushed her ankles and leather slippers that had seen better days. The cloak was unfastened and Dakota spied a plain cotton dress, faded from many washings. There was nothing of the twentieth century about the child.

Was this the little girl she'd heard just before she leapt from the gondola? She waited for the stirring of her blood, the rush of excitement that always accompanied a leap into another person's mind, but there was none.

The girl's narrow face was pale, her nose unremarkable; the last time Dakota had seen eyes that wide and round was at a revival of *Annie.* The child was a little slip of a thing with an air of sadness about her that Dakota could feel in her very bones without benefit of psychic help.

A coincidence, she thought, looking away. The woods were probably lousy with kids. Just because the Little Match Girl down there had popped up right on cue didn't mean she had anything to do with Dakota.

This couldn't be her destiny. Kids weren't part of her karma. She'd known that since she was fourteen years old, and she'd be willing to bet that not even the fact that she'd barreled through time like a human cannonball could change that fact.

Chapter Two

2

"I'm up here," an unseen monster called out to Abby. "In the maple tree."

The monster could see her! It made Abby feel shivery inside, the way she did after Cook told her an Irish ghost story. Even though she knew she shouldn't, she turned toward the voice.

"The *maple* tree, little girl, not the chestnut."

"But the leaves are not—" Abby pressed her lips together to stop the flow of words. She didn't want the monster to know she couldn't tell a maple from a chestnut without their brightly colored leaves.

"Look right, then up! Believe me when I say you can't miss me."

Don't listen to the monster, Abby. You'll be gobbled up like one of Cook's apple pies.

Terrible things happened when you listened to monsters but she didn't know how to say no. Slowly, carefully, she peered up as ordered. "I still cannot see you."

"Don't you watch 'Sesame Street,' kid? I said look right." The monster didn't sound quite so friendly this time.

Abby popped her thumb into her mouth, the way she always did when she was afraid of something. Cook always said a little lady didn't—

"That's it!" the monster bellowed. "The hand you just used…that's your right. Turn that way."

Cautiously Abby did. Her eyeballs all but popped from their sockets at the sight of the creature with the black curls and white shoes. The monster wasn't so terribly large but it seemed to Abby she'd never seen feet so big in her entire life. Why, the soles of the monster's shoes were thicker than the feather mattress on her bed!

"So you finally found me."

"Ohh," Abby said as her breath locked deep inside her chest. The monster sounded like a girl but no one, not even a boy, would have such short and peculiar hair. "Oh, my!"

"Look," said the monster, just as pleasant as can be, "this isn't the most comfortable spot in town. Bring me a ladder and then we'll talk."

Abby took a step backward. "No."

"Help me get down from this tree and I'll give you something special."

"You are a monster," Abby said. "I want you to go away."

"Hey, I may not be a *Vogue* model, but isn't that monster business getting kind of personal?"

Abby clutched Lucy more tightly. She didn't understand everything the monster said but she had to pretend she did. You had to be clever to best them. "If you are not a monster, then what are you?"

Somewhere between "Hello," and "Bring me a ladder," Dakota had lost total control of the situation. The sky was growing darker, the wind was howling and, unless she missed her guess, those were snowflakes drifting past her nose.

"Listen, kid, think of me as your fairy godmother. Now, will you please find somebody to help me down from this tree?" Historically, fairy godmothers got good press, and from the look of interest in the kid's eyes she'd said the right thing.

"Are you a fairy godmother like in Cook's stories?"

"Absolutely."

Now all she had to do was provide some physical evidence. Whispering a silent prayer to the goddess of women stuck in maple trees, Dakota unloosed her death grip and waved her left hand in the air.

Her six silver rings reflected the fading light and she milked the effect for all it was worth, moving her hand in a wide arc like a crazed traffic cop. Her crystal bracelets proved even better. The kid seemed downright spellbound as the stones refracted what light there was into arrows of pure color. Too bad her granny glasses had disappeared. The lavender-tinted lenses—more fashion than function—would have blown the kid away.

For once she was glad good taste had never marred her talent for overstatement.

"Are they magic?" The child's tone was downright reverential.

In for a penny, in for a pound. "Yes, and if you help me get down from this tree, I'll prove it to you." How hard could it be to dazzle a little girl with an eye for gaudy costume jewelry?

"If they are magic, why can't they get you down from the tree?"

"They're a different kind of magic," she hedged. A logical kid. Just her luck. "They don't do tree magic."

"You are not a *real* fairy godmother."

Dakota tried to look demure. "Why do you say that?"

"Fairy godmothers are pretty."

"Like you're another Shirley Temple?" she muttered under her breath. She forced herself to bestow her best smile on the little darling. "Maybe I'm a different kind of fairy godmother."

"No." The child shook her head. "There is only one kind."

"Listen, kid, I'm trying real hard, but you're making it awfully tough to like you."

"I do not like you, either." The little girl's trembling chin punctuated the words.

Dakota cautiously shifted her weight over to a lower branch and pretended the creaking noise wasn't a portent of disaster. "You're not going to cry, are you?"

On cue the kid's eyes flooded with tears.

Dakota wrapped her legs around the trunk of the tree and eased herself down a good eighteen inches to another miserably scrawny branch. "There's nothing to cry about." *At least nobody called you a monster.*

The kid's mouth opened wide and she let loose a wail loud enough to be heard in the next county.

"Jeez." Dakota grabbed for the next branch down and breathed a sigh of relief when it didn't crack beneath her weight. "Crying never solved anything," she said. "Why don't you tell me what's wrong?"

The child clutched her pathetic excuse for a doll and mumbled something.

Dakota leaned forward. "What was that?"

"Papa does not..." The rest of the sentence was whispered into the doll's head and punctuated by noisy sobs.

Stay out of it, Dakota. Whatever it is, keep your nose out of it. Kids weren't her strong suit. Most people found their honesty charming; it scared the hell out of Dakota.

The branch creaked loudly. "What about your papa?" *Does he have a nice ladder I could borrow?*

The plain little girl fixed her with an unnervingly adult gaze. "Papa wishes I had never been born."

That was quite a non sequitur. It took Dakota a moment to get her bearings. "I'm sure you're wrong."

"Mrs. O'Gorman says it is so. And so does Rosie and William and Cook—"

"What does your father say?"

"He says, 'Abigail, you are incor—'"

"Incorrigible?"

The kid nodded. "And that I must leave tomorrow for the Girls' School of the Sacred Heart in Boston."

Dakota sighed. It was straight out of a segment on *Oprah*. "And you were running away?"

"I will not go away to Boston. Mama ran away and that is when Papa stopped loving me."

The bastard. Dakota's heart lurched. *I don't want to hear this.* She had her own thwarted destiny to worry about. She didn't need the child's problems, too. Kids got annoyed with their parents every day of the week, then forgot their annoyance by bedtime. "Your mother ran away?"

"To Philadelphia."

Dakota took a deep breath. Now they were getting somewhere. "And where do you live?"

The child pointed beyond the clearing to the west. "The big white house."

"And where is the big white house?"

"It is—" The child froze and tilted her head.

"What's the matter?" Fear rippled up Dakota's spine. She'd heard the noise, too. "That's only the wind in the trees." She winced as the branch trembled. "Hey, wait a minute! Where are you going? Don't—"

Too late. The little girl vanished back into the woods as the branch Dakota was clutching groaned, cracked in two, then sent her crashing the rest of the way to the ground.

"I am sorry, Mr. Devane, but I fear we have not seen Abigail in weeks. Perhaps you did not know we have sent our dear Jonathan to his grandmother's in—"

Patrick cared little for the whereabouts of Mary Whitton's brat. "I regret the inconvenience, madam. I bid you good day." He inclined his head in the stiff and formal manner for which he was known, then turned sharply on his heel and headed for the door. The sun was dropping low in the sky and he intended to find the child before nightfall.

"Mr. Devane!" She stepped forward and placed a hand on his arm. "Have you spoken with Mistress Williams? Abigail oft spends time with Margaret's youngest...now, what is her name? Lily? Daisy? Rose! That is it. You must speak to Mistress Williams. I am sure that she—"

He neither slowed his pace nor met her eyes. "Thank you, madam. I will give your words the consideration they deserve."

With that he bounded down the porch stairs, mounted his chestnut stallion and was gone before the addlebrained woman could draw another breath.

It struck him how little he knew about the child's daily life, with whom she spent her time. He had assumed she passed her days alone, amusing herself either in the house or frolicking on the wide expanse of yard that was to have been Susannah's English garden. That she had companions was a revelation to him.

He was familiar with the Williams's house, a ramshackle bedevilment of wood and brick, situated on the other side of town near the encampment. That the child had managed to find it amazed him. She would need to traverse not only considerable open fields but a densely wooded area that many a learned man found challenging.

And there was the matter of twelve thousand troops, scattered from Morristown to Jockey Hollow to Franklin Ridge. They had felled trees, commandeered property and generally brought bedlam to the area. The men were ill-fed, ill-clothed and ill-tempered and he feared for the child's safety should she cross their path.

Still, she was a bright child with a talent for geography, unusual in one so young. He enjoyed a similar understanding of place, a knowledge of terrain that had stood him in good stead during his brief alliance with the Continental army. He wondered what other traits they shared, then laughed bitterly as he remembered that a shared bloodline was not among them.

Dakota lay facedown in a pile of leaves that smelled like wet squirrel. Not that she'd smelled many wet squirrels in her day but, like skunk, it was one of those things a woman never forgot. Her knee throbbed where she'd hit the ground, and she was reasonably sure her ankle was either broken or badly sprained.

Lifting her head, she looked up at the darkening sky. Fat white snowflakes landed on her cheeks and lashes and, if possible, it was even colder than it had been a few minutes ago. If she hadn't been so foolhardy, she'd be with Shannon and Andrew right now, facing their combined destiny like three time-traveling musketeers. She refused to believe her own destiny was to be found nose-deep in dead leaves.

Her psychic antennae were still all out of whack. Somehow she'd picked up on that little girl's temper tantrum and twisted it around until it became a plea for help. Pretty easy to see which one of them needed help. At least the kid knew what century she was living in.

"Damn," she whispered. If only she could home in on Shannon and Andrew's whereabouts. For weeks she'd felt as if they were Siamese triplets, attached at the psyche. But now there wasn't so much as a blip on her internal radar screen. The balloon had been in trouble when she bailed out. Were they in the same century? The same country? Dear God, were Shannon and Andrew even still alive?

She closed her eyes and emptied her mind of all but the image of her two friends. If they were anywhere nearby, certainly she'd pick up something. A vibration, a sound, a deep sense memory that could lead her to them.

The silence within was profound.

Her hands began to shake and she dragged them through her short, curly hair. *Calm down. This isn't the end of the world.* She'd just fallen out of a tree. That would be enough to shake up anybody's neurons. She'd try again in a few minutes. All she had to do was give her aura a chance to settle down and she'd be back in business.

Besides, she had more pressing problems to deal with. Survival, for one. If she lay there much longer she'd be a prime candidate for hypothermia. She had no intention of ending her days as a bear's Tastee-Freez.

She sat up, trying to pretend her ankle wasn't throbbing like crazy. Her immediate wish list wasn't that difficult. She needed shelter; she needed clothing; she needed to find a bathroom.

When she'd asked where the child lived, the girl had pointed beyond the clearing, toward the west. That was as good a place to start as any. She didn't know what she would say once she got there, but time was running out. Her earlobes ached from the cold; her fingers and toes were numb from it. Her brain would be the next to go.

She tried to stand, but her ankle gave way. "Damn," she whispered. "Damn, damn, damn." *Are you going to let a little thing like a broken ankle slow you down?* The snow was beginning to stick, both to the ground and to her person. *Think past the pain. The pain doesn't exist. Just get moving!*

She scrambled to her knees and was about to go for broke when she realized that wasn't a woodpecker she heard in the distance but a horse's hooves, and they were coming closer.

Dakota Wylie's First Rule of Survival: when in doubt, run for cover.

She dived into a huge pile of leaves and began to pray.

Patrick's chestnut hated the snow. The stallion was skittish at the best of times, and the accumulating snow made him almost impossible to manage. Patrick breathed a sigh of relief when they left the town proper and plunged into the woods. The multitude of evergreens formed a natural shield from the worst of the storm. The nervous beast quickly calmed.

Moments later, to Patrick's dismay, a white-tailed deer leapt from the bushes and bounded across the path, directly in front of them.

The chestnut whinnied and reared; Patrick fell backward and landed in a huge pile of leaves.

The chestnut, unperturbed by his predicament, stood a few yards away, rooting through another mound of leaves in search of something edible.

"Watch it!"

Patrick tilted his head. The voice sounded to be that of a female, but there was something sharp about the tone that was most unattractive. A young man, perhaps. One too youthful to grow whiskers but too old for the nursery. The chestnut rooted more deeply into the leaves, tail twitching with interest.

"Cut that out!" The accent was reminiscent of his own, yet different. A Marylander, perhaps.

Spies abounded everywhere. They worshiped at the First Presbyterian Church; they lifted a glass to General Washington's health at Arnold's Tavern; more than one had dined at his own table.

And unless the chestnut had developed the power of speech, one was hiding in the leaves.

Dakota held her nose as warm equine breath gusted toward her. *Haven't you ever heard of dental hygiene?* And the breath was nothing compared with the thought of big yellow horse teeth poking at her ribs. Did horses bite? Except for the appendix, nature rarely gave creatures body parts they didn't need. Those teeth were probably huge for a reason, and she'd bet it wasn't just to eat carrots.

And that wasn't the worst of it. Unless she'd dropped down onto the Ponderosa, horses didn't wander around without riders, and she'd bet her last jelly doughnut that this horse's rider was somewhere close by.

She lay there scarcely breathing, listening to the sound of her heart beating in her ear…and footsteps crunching through the snow, heading straight toward her. A nervous laugh struggled to escape.

The footsteps sounded angry and male. Brimming with testosterone. She tried to focus in on those footsteps and conjure up a picture of the man responsible for them, but her mind screen was still blank.

For the first time in her life, she was on her own.

Patrick Devane was no man's fool. These were dangerous times. A body did not hide himself in a pile of leaves unless he wished to escape notice. He cursed the fact that he'd left his pistol in his study. The Colony of New Jersey was a hotbed of infidels and opportunists and the best way to deal with any and all of them was from the right side of a weapon.

He stepped between the chestnut and the coward who lay quaking beneath a pile of brittle maple leaves.

"Show yourself, man!" His voice filled the clearing. No boy still wet behind the ears would best him, no matter the situation.

The leaves fluttered, but there was no response. A wry smile twisted his lips. The sorry bastard was trembling, more likely than not. An unworthy opponent, but he would see it through. He dug the toe of his riding boots beneath the leaves and nudged the coward.

"My patience grows thin," he warned, thinking of the encroaching darkness and the missing child.

He nudged harder.

"Once more and you lose the foot," came the voice from the leaf pile.

He watched, openmouthed, as a person of indeterminate age and gender sat up in the fallen leaves and stared at him.

"Sweet Jesus!" He stepped back. His eyes darted from one indescribable part of the stranger's body to another. Black hair shorter than a newborn babe's. Trousers of faded blue material. A thin shirt with odd words embroidered across the breast. The stranger wore enormous silver earbobs that dangled on its shoulders, their lacy pattern looking for all the world like tracings of ice on a windowpane.

He narrowed his eyes. The breasts seemed too full to belong to a boy but not full enough to belong to a grown woman. Still, he was reasonably sure the stranger was female.

"You're staring," the stranger said.

"I am," he said, not seeking to avoid the truth, "for I have not seen the likes of you in this or any other life."

Chapter Three

3

"Thanks a lot," Dakota said, sitting in the leaves like a toadstool. "I'm going to take that as a compliment."

"It was not meant thus."

"You don't do irony," she noted. "I'll have to remember that."

He was the kind of man who'd gone out of fashion about two hundred years ago and somehow continued to thrive in the romantic imagination of women on every continent.

Take a good look at him, Dakota. This is the stuff dreams are made of. Tall, lean and harboring major attitude. He wore tight, tobacco brown breeches that were tucked into high boots, an ivory-colored shirt and a flowing black wool cape that fell from shoulders as wide as an NFL linebacker's. His dark brown hair was pulled straight back and tied in a ponytail. He should come with a warning label attached: Danger! Foolish Women Proceed At Your Own Risk.

Late eighteenth century, she thought, heart pounding. Both the clothes and the man. And, dear God, what a man he was.

Unfortunately he was staring at her breasts and it was painfully clear he wasn't sure if he should be attracted or concerned.

"Stop it!" she ordered, attempting to take control of the situation as romantic conjecture swiftly gave way to reality. "You're being rude."

"Explain your meaning."

"Tell me which word you didn't understand and I will."

His jaw tightened. "Your words are not the problem, madam. Your appearance is." He stripped off the cloak and tossed it to her. "Cover yourself."

A man of few words and all of them were orders. She considered tossing the cloak back to him, but death seemed too high a price to pay for the pleasure. "One size fits all," she remarked, pulling the cloak around her shivering body.

"Madam?"

"Private joke."

Somehow he didn't look like the type who cared for jokes, private or otherwise.

"How do you call yourself?" he asked.

She'd never seen anyone bristle with menace before, but darned if the guy wasn't doing exactly that.

"Who's asking?"

The look of surprise on his gorgeous face was priceless. It was obvious the man was accustomed to being obeyed. "Patrick Devane." He executed a curt bow, more a knee-jerk response than a display of polite behavior. "And I am addressing—?"

Great posture, she thought as he straightened. You didn't often see posture like that on anything but a department-store mannequin. "Dakota Wylie."

His frown deepened. "What manner of name is that?"

"What manner of question is that?" she parried, cursing herself for not inventing a nice normal name like Mary or Sarah. "It's a...family name."

He nodded. "Stand up, madam."

"I don't think so."

"I am not a patient man."

"So I've gathered." She rubbed her hip. "Those boots of yours are lethal weapons."

"Stand," he repeated, "or I will not be held responsible for my actions."

His hands were huge. Big, workman's hands that were at odds with his elegant dress and carriage. She wondered how those hands would feel against the bare skin of her back...or wrapped around her throat.

"Now, madam!" he roared.

So much for fantasy. "I can't."

He moved toward her, those big hands clenched into fists.

He means business, Dakota. She'd better curb her tongue or he'd curb it for her permanently. This wasn't the nineties. She glanced at his attire. At least, not the 1990s. Historically, smart-mouthed women earned themselves a one-way ticket to oblivion and she wasn't about to let that happen. Not with Andrew and Shannon's destiny at stake.

"M-my ankle," she said with a pathetic attempt at female vulnerability. She wondered if she should bat her eyelashes at him, then thought better of it. She might have traveled through time but she still had her scruples. "I—I fear I've sprained it."

A ruse, Patrick thought, and a most unconvincing one. This odd-looking female must take him for a fool.

"And how did you sprain your ankle, madam?" He wondered if she concealed a weapon in the pile of leaves in which she sat. Surely she did not intend to defend herself using only her wits.

Still, there was something about her countenance that made him wonder if she did not intend exactly that. She was no coy miss, deferring to a man for the very air she breathed. Both wit and intelligence were evident in the dark eyes that dominated her pale moon of a face. Her skin was smooth and unblemished, an unusual sight in a woman beyond childhood. No scars from smallpox. No ruddy cheeks or broken veins from hours spent tending a hearth. Perhaps with a more womanly toilette she would appeal to a man, but Patrick found himself unmoved by the dimple that appeared in her left cheek as she offered up an uncertain smile.

"I—I fell from a tree."

He said nothing. Her smile faltered, then faded to memory.

"The maple tree," she said, pointing.

"And why is it you were in the maple tree?" he asked, not knowing why it was he chose to indulge this particular flight of imaginative fancy. The women of his acquaintance did not make a habit of climbing trees.

"A bear," she said, then nodded as if pleased by her words. "I feared for my safety."

He took stock of the immediate vicinity. Only human footprints were visible in the thin crust of yesterday's snow. "I see no tracks."

"Well, I didn't actually *see* a bear. I heard one."

"And you sought shelter in the maple tree."

"Exactly." Her smile reappeared. Her teeth were remarkably white and even. He wondered where she had purchased them. "Better safe than sorry."

"And where is the bear now?"

"Beats me."

"Madam?"

"I don't know where the bear is."

"Mayhap there was no bear."

"Look," she said, dark eyes flashing with sudden anger, "if you're going to do something awful, then just do it. The suspense is killing me. If falling from a tree is a capital offense around here, then do what you have to and get it over with." She struggled to her feet, then, with a yelp, sat back down again. "I think it's broken."

He bent down next to her. "Show me."

"You don't believe me?"

"I do not believe you."

She pulled up the leg of her peculiar garment and exposed a badly swollen ankle. "Do you believe me now?"

"The evidence seems irrefutable." In truth, her action surprised him. Displaying her limbs to all and sundry as if doing so were an everyday occurrence. Another woman would have swooned at the thought. Had the woman no modesty?

Indeed, it was a most pleasing ankle and that surprised him most of all. There was little else about her person that spoke of femininity.

"Do you think it's broken?" she asked, her tone subdued.

"I cannot tell through observation alone."

She pulled up the other leg of her garment. "Look at the difference."

He did. The uninjured ankle was delicate, almost fragile. The skin was pale and smooth, and a most unexpected feeling heated his blood. Leaning forward, he encircled the uninjured ankle with his hand, then attempted the same with the other.

A hiss of pain issued forth.

"I meant no harm, madam."

"I know," she said. Nothing more than that. Again he was struck by the differences between this stranger and other women of his acquaintance.

"A nasty sprain," he said at last, rocking back upon his heels. "One that will require attention."

She scowled at him. "Why don't you just climb on your horse and get lost? I was doing fine before you showed up."

"You have an uncommon sharp tongue, madam, for one in so

precarious a position." A plain woman with the fiery spirit of a beauty and the speech patterns of a learned man. It was a combination Patrick did not happen upon every day of the week. He was intrigued despite himself.

"It will be dark in a matter of minutes," he stated. "You will not make it through the night out here."

"I have no intention of staying here all night," she retorted.

"And where is it you intend to stay?"

She pointed across the clearing in the direction of his house. "I plan to stay with friends. They're expecting me."

He arched a brow. The situation grew more strange with each revelation. "I am not familiar with this town," he said blandly. "Where do your friends reside?"

"They live in a big white house," she said. "Darling little Abigail said—"

One second Dakota was seated in a pile of leaves, the next she was dangling in the air, nose-to-nose with the angriest man on the planet.

"What on earth—"

"Abigail." You could actually growl a word. She wouldn't have believed it if she hadn't heard it with her very own ears. "If you know anything of her whereabouts, speak now, madam, or speak to your Maker before the moon rises."

"Too late." The words popped out before she could stop them. Talk about a death wish. "The moon's probably already up." Though you couldn't see it for the storm.

He pulled her close to him until she could feel the horn buttons on his coffee brown waistcoat pressing against her belly. He held her fast with just one arm—a remarkable feat considering the fact that her bathroom scale issued daily warnings. She felt downright petite and delicate, the way she had when he'd encircled her ankle with his hand. She'd always daydreamed about having a man span her waist with his hands, and this was about as close as she was likely to get unless she met a guy with hands the size of a cherry picker.

Too bad he had to go and ruin the moment by wrapping one of those big hands around her throat and squeezing.

"I will continue to apply pressure, madam, until you tell me what you know about the child."

His fingers pressed harder on her windpipe. Good thing she'd had her tonsils removed when she was three years old, otherwise they'd be popping out the top of her head.

Your smart mouth's going to get you in trouble one day. If she'd heard it once, she'd heard it a thousand times. Looked as if her mother was right. She was about to give her life for a one-liner.

"You are moments away from unconsciousness," he said calmly. "Consider your options swiftly."

"C-can't talk." She pointed to her throat. "C-can't breathe, either."

"Be quick, madam, or face my wrath."

Who does your dialogue? she thought. *Rafael Sabatini?*

"Where is the child?" he repeated.

The pressure eased and she gulped in a deep breath. "I don't know." The pressure returned briefly, a subtle reminder of who was in charge. "She ran off when she heard you approaching." *And now I know why.*

"Where did she run?"

"Into the woods." She watched, astonished, as the expression in his dark blue eyes changed from anger to fear. He was the kid's father. "What on earth did you do to that child?" she berated him, hanging from his arm like an overcoat. "She said you wished she'd never been born."

He met her eyes. "The child is right."

The son of a bitch. What a way to build a kid's self-esteem. "No wonder she ran away."

"Abigail does not wish to attend school in Boston. That is the reason she fled."

"So you're blind as well as obnoxious. What a marvelous combination."

"Madam, we have yet to explore your own virtues."

He threw her over his shoulder and started toward his horse. Damn the luck. He had her cellulite in a death grip.

"Put me down!"

He ignored her.

"If you don't put me down I'll scream loud enough to wake the entire town."

"We are at war, madam," he retorted, not breaking stride. "A scream in the night is a frequent occurrence."

Her breath caught inside her chest. At war! Dear God, could it be? Had she somehow tumbled into the very place she needed to be? She struggled to stay calm. "How goes the fighting? I have had no news in days." Not bad. She sounded like a cross between "Masterpiece Theatre" and *Poor Richard's Almanack.*

"Clever, madam. A simple request for information." She felt his chest rumble with laughter. "These are dangerous times. Spies come in many guises, some more memorable than others."

"You think I'm a spy?"

"I have yet to make that judgment."

"Trust me," she said. "I'm no spy. You have nothing to worry about on that account."

They reached the horse. He swung her up onto the saddle as if she was a child, then took his position behind her.

"You're making a mistake," she said. "There's nothing I can do for you."

"You will help me find the child, Mistress Dakota Wylie." He grabbed the reins and they were off in a swirl of snow and leaves.

Twenty-four hours ago she'd been camped in the woods with a

bunch of women and kids, wondering if she was doomed to spend the rest of her life with people who couldn't remember her name. They'd called her Utah, Nevada and Montana and she supposed she should have been grateful they'd restricted themselves to states west of the Mississippi.

Now there she was, galloping through the woods with a man who not only remembered her name but was able to carry her in his arms without turning red in the face or gasping for air.

Too bad it would probably end up with her in the town jail before sunrise.

She smelled better than a woman so strangely attired had any right to smell. There was about her person the scent of something floral and sweet, a scent at direct odds with her masculine attire and unusual haircomb. It rose up from her hair and skin, discernible even through the cold, wet smell of snow. Indeed, he could remember few women who smelled as enticing, especially when not fresh from bathing.

Susannah. The way the sun played off her lustrous golden hair. The laughter like a carillon of bells.

The heart of stone.

And you, madam? he thought, glancing down at the woman cradled against his chest. *What manner of treachery are you about?*

She could be a spy, sent by the British in New York to acquire information to help them in their cause. She could be a patriot, determined to discover where his own loyalties rested. She could be a good wife who had followed her husband into battle, only to find herself lost and alone as a storm approached.

Good wife. The words sounded false to his ears. There was something most peculiar about the woman and he would be damned if he let her out of his sight until he determined exactly what it was.

"Stop!" Her voice sounded urgent.

He did as requested. "You are in pain, madam?"

"Over there." She pointed down and to her right. "That's Abigail's doll. Or at least part of it."

He turned to look. "I see naught but rags."

"I know that striped cloth," she persisted. "It was poking out from the doll's shoulder."

He had not realized Abigail possessed a rag doll. "This is no revelation, madam. No doubt both Abigail and her doll have traversed these woods with great regularity."

"She's here now."

"You cannot know that with certainty."

"Yes, I can."

"You are uncommonly stubborn, madam, or blessed with second sight."

"Do you want to argue with me or find your daughter?"

He dismounted. "I wish to put an end to this encounter as swiftly as possible."

She lowered her voice to a whisper. "Then listen to me. Abigail is behind the holly bushes about fifty yards from here. The hem of her cloak is showing."

He grabbed the peculiar woman by the waist and swung her down from the saddle.

"You can't expect me to walk with this ankle. Put me back on the horse."

"That would be most unwise."

"Don't be ridiculous," she said. "Where am I going to go?"

Grimly he tossed her over his shoulder like a sack of flour.

"You didn't really think I was going to run away?" Her voice was muffled by his back.

"Draw your own conclusions, madam, from the evidence at hand."

"Trust me, you didn't have to worry. Horses and I don't get along. When I was a child I never..."

She talked more than any three women of his acquaintance, but it was she who had spotted the hem of Abigail's cloak. That truth rankled as he strode toward the bushes with bleak determination.

Of course, Dakota had lied to him when she said she had no intention of escaping. She'd had every intention of digging her heels into the horse's flanks and galloping hell-bent for leather as far away as she could possibly get.

Which, all things considered, would have been a mistake. Maybe all the blood rushing to her head as he carried her was helping to clarify the situation.

Dakota supposed any woman in her right mind would be royally insulted at being draped over a man's shoulder like a mailbag. An hour from now she would probably be furious, too, but right now she was enjoying the whole thing immensely. There was something to be said for feeling like a fragile flower of femininity. She wouldn't be surprised if her T-shirt and jeans were morphing into a satin ballgown. Even her hair felt longer and straighter.

Still she refused to believe her destiny was tied up with Devane and his daughter. This whole adventure was nothing more than the equivalent of taking the wrong exit on the highway. You mutter a pungent phrase or two, then get back on the highway and try again. Of course, it would help if you had someone to give you directions.

Too bad Patrick Devane didn't seem the helpful type.

You're a smart one, she thought. *I'll give you that. You're not going to make this easy on me.*

He might be smart but she was smarter. She had two hundred years of additional evolution on her side and she had the feeling she would need every one of them.

Chapter Four

4

Abigail peered out from behind the holly bush at the astonishing sight. Papa had killed the monster and was carrying the body home so everyone would know how brave he was. The monster didn't look half so fierce draped over Papa's shoulder. It looked little and weak, and Abby felt sad that it had come to such a terrible end.

"Abigail!" Papa's voice rang out. He sounded angry, the way he had when Mama left with the soldier.

She ducked deeper in the bushes, holding back a sneeze as icy snowflakes tickled her nose.

"Now, Abigail!"

Maybe if she crouched down low and didn't so much as breathe he wouldn't realize she was there.

"This is stupid!"

Abby's head popped up at the second voice.

"The poor kid's scared to death of you."

The monster was alive! How could that be?

Papa stepped forward until the toes of his black leather boots were close enough to touch. Her nose twitched from the smell of polish and earth.

Her teeth were chattering like marbles on a tin roof and all she could think of was Cook's tasty mutton stew, all piping hot from the hearth. *Don't be a baby, Abby! If you go home Papa will send you away to Boston.*

She had to stay there in the woods even if she was afraid the bears would find her and grind her up for dinner.

"Abigail!"

He grabbed for her sleeve, but she was too fast for him. Clutching Lucy, she darted out from the bushes and ran deeper into the woods. She wasn't afraid of anything, not wolves or bears or monsters. If Papa was going to send her off to school in Boston, first he'd have to catch her.

The kid ran as if the hounds of hell were at her heels. Those short legs managed to eat up an incredible amount of ground, and in an instant she vanished into the woods with her father close behind.

She had to hand it to the man. He somehow managed to run as if he weren't lugging a full-grown woman for ballast. Maybe cross-training had started a lot earlier than she'd first thought.

"Whither thou goest," Dakota muttered as Devane leapt a fallen tree like an Olympic hurdler. Too bad his boots hadn't been fitted with shock absorbers. Her teeth rattled with every step he took and her midriff smarted from banging against his rock-hard shoulder. It was pretty obvious he was going to catch his daughter or kill himself in the attempt.

Her psychic antennae might be down but her imagination was up and running, and every scenario she came up with cast Patrick Devane as the villain. Not that the kid wasn't showing a marked tendency toward villainy herself—apparently tantrums had been invented long before child psychologists.

Father and daughter had some pretty strange family dynamics going on between them, and if this were the twentieth century she'd say they were prime candidates for therapy.

They must have been halfway to the next state by the time they caught up with the kid. Abigail had stumbled over a rotted log and was scrambling to her feet when Devane found her.

"No!" the girl shrieked as he scooped her up with his free arm. "I will not go! I will not! You cannot make me!"

He strode toward his horse with Dakota tucked under his right arm like a football and Abigail under his left.

"Not a word," he said, "from either one of you. We ride in silence."

He swung Dakota up onto the horse.

"About this horse stuff," she began.

"Silence."

His look was almost enough to do the trick. "I came close to falling off before. Maybe—"

There it was again. The Look. Okay, so maybe silence wasn't such a bad idea.

Was she imagining it or did a smile flicker briefly across his handsome face?

No matter. It was gone before she could be certain.

"No!" Abigail shrieked, clutching her father tightly about the neck as he swung her onto the saddle in front of Dakota. "I will not! You cannot make me!"

"Enough!" he ordered in a voice that brooked no argument. "Isn't it enough that you waste my time with your foolish tantrums?"

"She's only a child," Dakota piped up. "Why don't you—"

"Your opinion is unwelcome, madam."

"Are you joining us?" she asked sweetly as she patted the saddle in invitation.

By way of answer, he took up the reins and started walking toward the clearing.

Abigail cast a series of worried glances over her shoulder, as if she were calculating her odds of survival.

"Enough with the dirty looks," Dakota said. "We're both freezing to death. Why don't you sit back and share this cape with me?"

"N-no!" The kid's lips were turning blue from the cold but she had her righteous indignation to keep her warm.

"I don't like this any more than you do, but I'm willing to share."

She could see the wheels turning inside the poor kid's head. Freeze to death or cuddle up with a monster? Talk about a tough choice. Against her better judgment her heart went out to the kid once again.

"I promise I won't bite."

Obviously that was the wrong thing to say because the kid opened her mouth wider than Dakota would have thought humanly possible without a submarine sandwich in the vicinity and screamed.

"Damnation!" Devane roared. "What in the name of God is going on?"

Dakota fixed him with an evil look. "She thinks I'm a monster."

He stared at her, uncomprehending.

"You heard me," she snapped. "Your daughter thinks I'm a monster right out of a fairy tale."

Abigail bristled with indignation. "*You* said you were my fairy godmother."

"I was being sarcastic. As you pointed out, fairy godmothers are pretty."

"Great God in heaven, cease your infernal racket!" Devane bellowed. "Is it not enough that a blizzard is unleashing its fury upon us?"

"A blizzard?" Dakota looked up toward the sky. "What do you mean, a blizzard?"

"You are unfamiliar with the word?"

"Get real."

"Madam?" How he managed to put such a disagreeable spin on a lone word was beyond her.

"This is a minor snowstorm, not a blizzard." She couldn't contain her snicker of amusement. "I just can't believe you'd call a few snow flurries a blizzard."

Her words were innocent but Patrick knew her meaning was not. Had no one ever told her that a pleasant temperament was a most agreeable quality in a plain woman?

"The signs are inarguable, madam."

"*Un*arguable," she said. "Trust me on this one."

She infuriated him beyond endurance. "I graduated William and Mary," he said through clenched teeth.

"Did you see *1776,* too? That's exactly what Thomas Jefferson said."

It was not the response he expected. First she asked about the year of our Lord 1776, then she compared him to the farmer from Virginia. At no time did she express regard for William and Mary. The mere mention of the illustrious center of classical education should render a normal man or woman speechless with admiration.

"You have heard of William and Mary, have you not, madam?" Mayhap she was from the country and ignorant of such things.

"Of course I have," she said, as if astonished he could think otherwise. "I graduated—" She stopped abruptly, pressing her lips together until they formed a thin line.

"Do not stop, madam," he urged as they reached the edge of his property. "From which esteemed academy of learning did you graduate?"

She glanced toward Abigail, who was wide-eyed at the exchange, then back again at him. "It's a good thing your daughter is here, Mr. Devane, or I'd give you a piece of my mind."

"I do not doubt that," he drawled. "But have a care, madam, for soon you will have given all away."

Pompous dimwit.

As if graduating from William and Mary made him master of the universe. She'd come this close to telling him she'd graduated Harvard. The words had been burning a hole in her tongue and it had taken every single ounce of self-control she possessed to hold them back.

Oh, what she would have given to see his smug and perfect face go slack with disbelief. Too bad it would be another two hundred years until women would be admitted to the university's hallowed, lousy-with-Y-chromosome halls.

He was a disagreeable, argumentative sort without a sense of humor. She couldn't imagine going through life without, at the very least, a healthy sense of the absurd. But not Patrick Devane. He was humorless, literal to the extreme and quite obviously heartless, as well.

Still, his daughter loved him. She supposed that was a point in his favor, even if he treated the child as if she was so much excess baggage. *Don't you know what you have?* she wondered. *Don't you know how lucky you are?* A child's love was a precious gift. He should be down on his knees thanking God that he was lucky enough to be Abigail's father. She was a brat, but she was *his* brat. They were so much alike that Dakota felt sorry for the kid.

"Papa!" Abigail cried out. "Look!"

Dakota twisted around in the saddle and looked in the direction the child was pointing. Two men on horseback galloped toward them. The combination of darkness and driving snow made it difficult for her to see more than that.

Devane swore under his breath and abruptly stopped walking.

"What's wrong?" Dakota asked. "Are we in danger?"

He ignored her question.

"Soldiers," said Abigail, casting a look in her direction.

"Our side?" Dakota asked, not sure she wanted to know the answer.

"Papa hates soldiers," the little girl confided. "He says…"

The child's words faded as a buzzing sounded in Dakota's head. Squinting, she tried to focus through the snow on the approaching riders, but without her glasses it was all but impossible. *Contact lenses,* she thought. Now she understood why people loved them. At least contacts might have survived the trip. Even though her glasses were more for fashion than function, she would have welcomed the edge they provided.

Men in uniform had never done much for her on a personal level, but she had to admit the sight was pretty darned impressive. They sat tall in their saddles, which made her wonder if perfect posture was the norm around there rather than the exception it was in her own time. Both wore buff-colored breeches and waistcoats, high boots and a navy coat with turnings at collar and lapels of the same buff-colored material as the breeches.

She knew those uniforms. Just last month she'd helped put together a new display at the museum. She'd dressed three aging Princetonians in reproductions that had been authentic right down to the worked buttonholes.

"Halt!" The soldier on the right angled his horse across the roadway some ten feet in front of them, blocking their way. "Who goes there?"

Devane dropped the reins and stepped forward. "You trespass, sir. State your business."

The soldier's hand hovered near the hilt of his sword. Dakota tensed, drawing the cloak more tightly around herself and Abigail in a gesture more instinctual than practical.

This isn't a re-creation, she told herself as the two men faced off. The two soldiers were patriots. Every freedom she took for granted had been hard won by men and women just like them. And, unless she missed her guess, it was all happening right now before her very eyes.

Devane's voice pierced the cold. The man really was good at growling his dialogue. "...will not allow my home to be turned into a Continental circus!"

Abigail started to speak but Dakota placed a hand over the child's mouth to stop her. She couldn't afford to miss a word of this.

The second soldier dismounted. Dakota spotted a green ribbon pinned to his waistcoat. She was fairly sure that meant he was an aide-de-camp but wished she'd paid more attention to detail when she'd had the chance.

The soldier nodded at Devane. "You will ask your family to dismount."

Family? She swallowed hard. If Devane turned her over to the army she'd probably end up hanged for treason, sold into indentured servitude or enlisted. The thought of trying to explain her attire—not to mention her haircut—was enough to make her weep.

Why shouldn't he turn you over to the army? He can't wait to get rid of his own daughter. He'll be ecstatic to get rid of you.

"I will not inconvenience them."

"We must insist."

Abigail squirmed and the cape shifted. Dakota managed to pull it back into position a millisecond before the words *Jurassic Park* were exposed to one and all. She met Devane's eyes and he held her glance. His eyes were beautiful, a dark and wondrous shade of blue, but she could read nothing in them.

Time slowed around them.

One of the horses whinnied with impatience.

Say something, Wylie. This is your chance. At least she knew which side the soldiers were on, which was more than she could say about Devane.

His expression gave away nothing. Would he hand her over to the soldiers? Leave her alone in the woods to fend for herself? Take her home and lock her in the attic like the mad wife in *Jane Eyre?*

Drawing in a deep breath, she willed herself into his head, but all she could hear was the sound of her heart beating and her own jumbled thoughts. Nothing in his expression betrayed his thoughts and she found herself longing for the abilities she'd taken for granted.

The second soldier dismounted and started toward Dakota and Abigail.

"No." One word. A single syllable. But the power in Devane's voice stopped the man in his tracks.

"My wife and child are tired and cold. You will not inconvenience them with your nonsense."

My wife?

We've hit the jackpot, Ma, she thought. *And I only had to travel two hundred years to do it.*

The second soldier bowed low to Dakota and the child, then held out his hand. "Madam, I will assist you and your daughter as you dismount."

Abigail, as if on cue, burst into noisy, shrieking tears that made both soldiers wince.

You're good, kid. Shirley Temple couldn't have done better herself.

Dakota whispered a silent prayer, then plunged in. "It has been a difficult journey," she said with the proper amount of deference, "and I have an injured foot. I beg your indulgence, sir, just this once."

The two soldiers looked at each other.

"A terribly difficult journey," she repeated, wishing she had her sister's talent for crying on command. To think she used to believe speaking French was more important.

"We will grant your request," the first soldier said with a neck bow.

"Move," Devane commanded. "You have wasted enough of my time already."

"There is still the matter of housing to be considered," said the first soldier. "His Excellency regrets any inconvenience to you and your—" he cast a peculiar look in Dakota's direction "—family, but the housing problem in Morristown—"

"Hang Morristown and hang the lot of you! You will leave my property now."

The original alpha male, Dakota thought. Defending turf, protecting women and children, acting like a horse's ass.

"His Excellency's orders are clear." The second soldier met Devane's eyes. "You have no choice in this, sir."

"I'll torch the damned place before I'll have the vermin-infested lot of you beneath my roof again."

Pretty clear on which side of the war his loyalties rested. Wasn't it just her luck to whiz through the centuries only to land in the lap of a Tory sympathizer?

The first soldier reached inside his cloak, then removed an envelope. He handed it to Devane, who regarded the seal with something close to disgust.

Dakota craned her neck to get a better look at it. The wax was thick, a deep shade of cranberry that approached maroon. It made a satisfying crack when Devane lifted the flap. He unfolded the letter, read swiftly, then crumpled it in his hand.

"Stop!" she cried out. "That's a letter from George Washington!" *Father of our country. Slayer of cherry trees. The guy on the dollar bill!*

"And a most unusual event," Devane said, his deep voice rich with sarcasm. "If the man spent as much time with the sword as he does with the pen, his cause against the British would be greatly advanced."

He tossed the crumpled letter to the ground the way another man would toss a cigarette butt. She considered leaping from the horse and making a grab for it, but the way her ankle was throbbing she'd probably end up in an ungraceful heap on the ground.

The soldiers looked at each other, then back at Devane. Dakota held her breath. The male ego was a force to behold.

"His Excellency's most esteemed colleague General McDowell requires two front rooms and the second-floor bedrooms for his use. You and your family may enjoy the remainder."

"Hang General McDowell!"

"Papa's angry," Abigail whispered.

"I know," Dakota whispered back.

It was an awesome sight.

His jaw was set in stone. His thick dark brows met in a square knot over his nose. His blue eyes burned with a fury she was glad was not directed at her.

"May you and General Washington rot in hell."

Grabbing the reins of the horse, he headed up the hill the rest of the way to the house.

A small farm south of Franklin Ridge

Emilie Crosse Rutledge watched as her husband buttoned the heavy black wool cape at his throat.

"Look at you," she said, reaching up to tuck his shirt collar inside the cape. "Can't even manage to get dressed on your own."

"Everything's going to be fine, Em," he said, drawing her into his arms. "Josiah and I will be back by morning."

She tried to smile but failed. "I don't know what's the matter with me," she said, pressing her forehead against his shoulder. "All day long I've had the strangest feeling that something terrible is going to happen."

He inclined his head toward the staircase. "Something terrible's going to happen, all right. In about ten minutes Andrew and Sara are going to wake up from their naps and all hell will break loose."

Not even the thought of her beloved children could wipe the fear from Emilie's mind. "Be careful," she said, cupping his face between her hands. "Nothing is worth losing you."

"It's a simple drop," Zane said. "We ride to the White Horse Tavern near Jockey Hollow and leave the blankets with the owner. What can go wrong?"

"I don't know," Emilie said, "but I'm afraid something will."

"You didn't embroider the wrong codes in the binding, did you?"

She shook her head. "Of course I didn't. I'm the one who originated the idea, remember?"

"Then there's no problem."

"That inn is dangerous," she said, trying desperately to shake off the feeling of dread building inside her heart. "What if the Tories figure out you're really a counterspy? They hanged three men last week, Zane. How do you know Patrick isn't part of it?" She'd heard the gossip about him, how his loyalties had shifted to the British when his late wife ran off with a Continental army officer. They said he had a heart of stone and that not even his little daughter could make him smile.

"Remember Philadelphia," she warned. The Tories had stolen their farm away from them, but not before they'd seen Devane in the company of Benedict Arnold and his young wife, Peggy Shippen, on more than a few occasions. You didn't have to be a rocket scientist to know what that meant.

"They won't figure out a damn thing," Zane said, his jaw set in lines of granite. "Patrick's a good man. He wouldn't put us in any danger."

This time it was Emilie's jaw that turned to cement. "I don't like him."

Her husband laughed. "You don't really know him."

"I don't care," she said, waving a hand in dismissal. "I didn't like him when we lived in Philly and I don't like him now. He's a cold-hearted rat and I'll bet you my last packet of pins that he's working for the British."

"He's a patriot."

"I wish I could be as sure of that as you are."

"Trust me, Em. The guy's on our side."

Josiah Blakelee, a huge bear of a man, appeared in the doorway to the parlor. "The horses are saddled and ready," he said.

Zane nodded while Emilie struggled to compose herself. She looked up at Josiah. "Where is Rebekah?"

"She will not come down to bid me farewell."

"I know exactly how she feels," said Emilie. When they first joined the spy ring three years ago, it had seemed exciting, but now that she was the mother of twins she knew only terror.

The war was everywhere. It sat at your kitchen table while you drank hot cider instead of tea; it climbed your stairs as you searched for an extra blanket to give to a freezing soldier asleep on your porch; it crawled into your bed at night and colored your dreams.

The war was fought in front yards and village greens. Mothers brought buckets of water to sons as those sons battled to hold on to the hill where they had played as children. Even knowing that the war would soon end and that their side would be victorious, Emilie experienced moments of fear so powerful, so deeply visceral, that it made her wonder if her heart would stop beating.

All day long she'd been filled with profound dread, and now that it was time to say goodbye to her husband, she wanted to throw her arms around him and beg him to stay home where he was safe.

"Godspeed," she whispered, touching Zane's cheek with her hand.

"I love you, Em," he said quietly. "I'll be home before dawn."

She stood by the window and watched as the two men trudged through the snow to the stables where their horses waited.

Be careful what you wish for, she thought with a bittersweet laugh. She had wanted a husband who understood the meaning of commitment to something greater than himself, and in this second marriage to Zane she had been granted everything she'd ever wanted.

The man she'd loved then divorced all those years ago no longer existed. He had been replaced by a man of vision and commitment, a man whose loyalty to country was second only to his loyalty to the woman he loved and the children they shared.

They both belonged to this time and place. Their children were the children of two centuries, conceived in the twentieth and delivered in the eighteenth, and she marveled at the miracle fate had wrought from nothing more than a man and woman in love.

She'd fallen in love with a rogue only to have him turn into a rebel hero, and there were times late at night, when her fears ran free, that she would trade the hero for the rogue in an instant if it meant she could keep him safe.

She waved farewell as Zane and Josiah rode off down the lane. Snow had begun falling an hour ago, gentle flakes that softened the edges of everything they touched, even the ugly reality of war. She turned to leave the window when something caught her eye in the sky above the stables.

"Oh, God," she whispered. Her pulse beat hard at the base of her throat. A jagged tower of black clouds rose up in the distance toward Franklin Ridge, obscured by the snow. Three years ago she'd seen a cloud formation just like that and it had changed their lives forever.

"No," she said, stepping back as if she could put distance between herself and her fears. It couldn't be. Not again.

Not now. Not when victory would soon be within reach.

She knew all about that cloud formation, knew exactly what it meant. The first time it had appeared, it had carried her and Zane back through time in a crimson hot-air balloon to this place where they'd found happiness. The second time it had appeared, Andrew McVie had flown off in the same bright red balloon to meet his destiny.

She peered into the gathering darkness, straining for a glimpse of crimson silk against the snowy sky, praying she wouldn't see it. The clouds were nothing without the balloon, nothing but a lot of bad weather.

As long as there was no balloon, she had nothing to worry about.

Nothing at all.

Chapter Five

5

The house rose up through the snow like a mirage. Two stories of beautiful Georgian architecture, untouched by time. The Colonial era's love of symmetry was apparent in the way the house grew outward from the center, with an equal number of windows to either side of the front door. The building boasted a fresh coat of whitewash. The shutters that framed each of the twelve windows were painted a dark forest green. Snow blanketed the shingled roof, while four tall chimneys puffed white smoke into the evening sky.

I know this place, Dakota thought. Everything about it seemed familiar, from its front door with the brass knocker to the huge expanse of land on which it had been built. The area was too hilly to be Princeton, too wooded to be the Shore, but she knew it was New Jersey because it felt like home.

In many ways the place reminded her of the Ford Mansion in Morristown. She'd worked there as a docent during summer vacations, handing out brochures and keeping her eyes on squabbling kids determined to bounce on the bed where George and Martha had slept during the infamous winter of 1779-1780.

Most people thought the Valley Forge winter was the worst of the war, but 1779 had it beaten. The snows started early and came often, twenty-eight blizzards by the coming of spring.

"Abigail," she said, "has it been snowing a lot lately?"

The little girl, who apparently had decided Dakota wasn't a monster after all, twisted around to look at her. "Don't you know?"

Dakota shook her head. "I am new to the area."

"It snowed for my birthday," Abigail said. "Cook says she cannot ever remember such an early snowfall."

"Your birthday," Dakota persisted. "When would that be?"

The little girl's forehead puckered in a frown much like her father's. "In September," she said, then held up ten fingers twice.

Good grief, Dakota thought. The twentieth of September. That was an early snowfall for Nome.

A young boy rounded the side of the house and raced toward them.

"William!" Abigail cried out. "We saw soldiers in the woods!"

William skidded to a halt next to Devane. "They said they had the right to take over the house, but Ma turned them out on their ears." His jaw dropped open when he spied Dakota. Splotches of bright red spread across his cheeks.

"This is my fairy godmother," said Abigail. "I thought she was a monster but she isn't."

If possible, William looked even more astonished. Devane's patience snapped.

"Look sharp, boy!" He handed the reins to William then wheeled and started up the stairs to the house. "Do not move until you're told to."

"Hey!" Dakota called out. "Aren't you forgetting something?"

He didn't break stride. "I will send Joseph to help you."

She wished she had a tomato to lob at his fat head.

"Who's Joseph?" she asked the boy.

"M-my pa."

"Where is he?"

"I don't know," said William.

"It's freezing out here."

"Yes'm."

"Maybe you should go look for your father. We don't want Abigail to get sick, do we?"

"No'm."

"So why don't you go get him?" she asked sweetly.

"Cannot. The mister said he would do it."

"Mr. Devane will understand. I'll explain it to him."

"Papa will be real mad if you do that, William," Abigail piped up.

Score another one for the kid. William maintained his tight grip on the reins while Dakota struggled to keep a tight grip on her sanity. More than anything she wanted to kick William, then the horse, and gallop off into the storm.

But even Dakota knew better than that. You don't run away from hot food, warm clothing and shelter on a cold winter's night. She must have been crazy to even think about it.

Patrick flung open the front door, then strode into the main hallway. "Mrs. O'Gorman! Damnation, where are you, woman?"

Cook bustled into the room, face flushed as always from the hearth fire. "Begging your pardon, sir, but you let Mrs. O'Gorman go this afternoon. Right after the wee one disappeared."

He'd put it from his mind in the uproar surrounding the child. "And Rosie?"

"She'd be gone, too. Said she wouldn't be working with a child what bites. I been expectin' my niece Molly to lend a hand, but what with the storm blowin' in, I don't think—"

"Then it falls to you." He had no time for her domestic intrigues.

Cook eyed him with some suspicion. "Begging your pardon, but a lot be falling to me of late. I'm not as young as I used to be and getting older every day."

"As are we all. A guest will be staying with us overnight. You'll see to it that the rear bedroom is ready."

"The rear bedroom? Nobody's been in that bedroom since—" She looked away.

They both knew what she had been about to say. *Since the missus ran off with the soldier.* Susannah's paramour had stayed in that room.

"She is outside," he said, striding toward the library with the housekeeper hard on his heels. "Her ankle is sprained. Send Joseph to assist her."

Cook was a good, hardworking woman. As a rule she did as told with little by way of complaint or question. This time she stood her ground. "And who will fetch wood for the bedroom fire? A body can do just so much, sir."

"William is a strong young man."

"Yes, sir." Her round features clearly expressed her displeasure.

The rum on the sideboard beckoned to him. "Is there anything else, Cook?" He doubted there was enough rum in the Colony of New Jersey to slake his thirst.

"Your visitor," she said, aquiver with curiosity. "Would this be the next Mrs. Devane?"

His pithy response sent the poor woman scurrying for the safety of her kitchen.

There would never be another Mrs. Devane, of that he was certain. He poured himself some rum, then filled his belly with the potent liquid. One attempt at matrimony had forever rid him of the desire to take a woman to wife. There was more honor among thieves than had existed between himself and Susannah. And, he was certain, a great deal more respect.

At least there was no danger of matrimony with Mistress Wylie.

No, he thought as he poured himself another rum, he could not imagine a more unlikely prospect. Her manner of dress was most peculiar: she wore leggings like a man, a printed undergarment over her breasts, and shoes the likes of which he had never imagined. They were constructed of heavy white cloth with soles thick as a feather pillow. He wondered if her feet were outsize or in some way malformed, for certainly no woman would choose to wear such enormous footwear.

And then there was the matter of her hair. Cut short and close to her head, the dark curls were uncommonly shiny and lustrous and, in their own way, quite suitable to her face. He found that last fact most disconcerting. A luxurious mane of hair was a woman's most visible asset, yet Mistress Wylie did not seem to require such bounty. Susannah had prided herself on her spill of golden waves. He remembered the way she'd sit before the glass each night, drawing her brush through the silky mass over and over again until she'd accomplished one hundred strokes. In their bed, he had—

He swallowed the last of the rum, eager to burn the image from his brain.

Yes, there was no denying the powerful beauty of a woman's hair. No woman would willingly sacrifice so wondrous an asset unless she had good reason. He'd heard tales of wives who, driven by the need to be with their husbands, had disguised themselves as men in order to fight the enemy at their beloved's side.

He paced the library, his boots leaving wet stains on the dark rose-and-green rug. Such a thing would explain her mannish attire, as well as her combative demeanor. It took a most unusual woman to garb herself as a man and take up arms against the enemy, all in the name of love.

Of course, there also was the possibility that she had been afflicted with head lice and had had to shear off her tresses in the name of good health.

"Damnation," he muttered, wishing he had more rum. Her attire and haircomb were of no consequence. There was something most peculiar about the woman, something that went beyond the way she looked. Spies abounded in the Colony of New Jersey and he had best look sharp lest he find himself dangling from the hangman's noose in the town square.

"Can't we go in the front door?" Dakota asked as Joseph led her around the side of the mansion. The throbbing pain in her ankle had subsided, replaced by a dull ache. She thanked God it wasn't broken.

"Begging your pardon, mistress, but those wouldn't be the clothes most of our guests be wearing when they come calling."

"So where are you taking me?"

"Servants' entrance, right near to the kitchen."

A round-faced woman with a sweet smile and a mobcap on her head waited in the open door. "Have a care, Joseph," she chided the man. "The poor thing looks half-frozen."

She leaned on Joseph as he helped her up the three stone steps and into the kitchen.

"Now out with you, Joseph," said the woman named Cook. "Fetch some wood for the bedroom while I see to our visitor." She turned her attention to Dakota. "Don't you worry. I promise you'll be all toasty in two shakes of a lamb's tail."

"It's so warm in here!" Dakota exclaimed as soon as the door closed behind Joseph.

"That it is," said Cook, hanging her cloak on the wooden peg by the door. "We tend the fires day and night."

Dakota stood before the hearth and rubbed her hands together. The blast of heat from the fire was almost painful against her skin. The kitchen was all stone and heavy wood saved from depressing darkness by the blaze of fire and candles everywhere. The ceiling was constructed of exposed dark pine beams with bunches of dried herbs and flowers hung at random intervals. The air was fragrant with wood smoke, roasting meat and the pungent smells of rosemary and thyme.

"Hot cider if you'd be of a mind," Cook said.

Dakota offered the woman a shivery smile. "I'd be of a mind, thank you."

"And some clothes, missy. Makes a body cold just to be lookin' at you."

Dakota waited, fully expecting a question or two about her strange attire, but there was none. Cook plucked a ladle from the rack hanging above the massive stone hearth. Bending forward, the older woman dipped the ladle into a metal pot that rested on the ledge, then poured the contents into a pewter tankard.

"Drink up and warm your bones."

"My bones could use it, I assure you." Dakota accepted the tankard gratefully. "How wonderful! I can't remember the last time I had hot cider."

Cook's eyebrows disappeared up into her mobcap. "Like mother's milk to me." *And to everyone else in the world,* her look all but screamed.

Details, Dakota reminded herself. Wasn't it always the tiny details that tripped a person up? She cast around for a safer subject. "It's so quiet in here. How many people work for De—Mr. Devane?"

"Not half enough," said Cook. "Not that he'd be asking me my opinion."

"This is an enormous house. I would think you'd have considerable staff."

"Getting and keeping are two different things, missy."

Dakota nodded. "He must be a difficult man to work for." She'd known him less than an hour and she would've bet the farm on that fact.

"Oh, he is that," Cook agreed, "but it's the wee one what's driving them away."

"Abigail?"

"Four housekeepers in as many months. Mrs. O'Gorman packed her bags and left this very day, with Rosie right behind her."

"All because of Abigail?"

The woman nodded. "Now me, I have a soft spot for the poor little thing, but not all have my way with the children." Cook lowered her voice and leaned toward Dakota. "Needs a mother's touch, that's what I say."

A mother's touch. A wave of sadness broke over Dakota, surprising her with its force. *Oh, Ma,* she thought. *You knew this was going to happen to me, didn't you?* Her mother's ESP had zeroed in on her daughter's future, the same way it had zeroed in on her weight problem and lack of male companionship. Dakota and her mother had spent the better part of Dakota's life getting on each other's nerves, and lately it had escalated to a particularly annoying battle of wills.

For the past few weeks Ginny had taken to popping up unannounced at the library, making bizarre pronouncements about Dakota's future. She'd all but told her daughter to pack her bags and say goodbye. Dakota had been ready to declare herself an orphan.

Strange how it took a little thing like a two-hundred-year separation to make a daughter realize that it had all been part and parcel of the mother-daughter bond. The criticizing. The bitching. The endless search for approval. All of it tangled up with love Dakota had somehow never found time to express.

Cook placed a hand on her forearm. "Look at me, talking like an old fool, and you standing here all cold and wet. Come with me, missy, and we'll find you some warm clothes."

Dakota was so pathetically grateful that her eyes filled with tears. There had to be a catch somewhere, but damned if she could find it. If the woman had questions about Dakota's appearance, she was keeping them to herself.

Which was more than Patrick Devane was likely to do.

Cook showed her to a bedroom on the second floor. It was a small room by late-twentieth-century suburban standards, but quite pleasant. The bed dominated the room with its thick feather mattress and canopy, complete with bed hangings to ward off the cold.

"Joseph will be up directly to light the fire," Cook said, smoothing a hand over the heavily embroidered spread. A tree of life, worked in shades of earth and berry and moss, spread its branches from one side to the other. "Won't take but a few minutes to take the chill out. Himself is many things but he sees to it we're warm."

"Does he have guests often?"

Cook's laugh held the bite of sarcasm. "No, he's a solitary one since the missus—" Her words stopped abruptly and she busied herself picking imaginary pieces of fluff from the spread.

"Since the missus what?"

Cook glanced toward the door. "Begging your pardon, missy, but it ain't like me to speak out of turn. I've already said more than I should."

Dakota feigned interest in the dark pine armoire in the corner. "Abigail mentioned that her mother lives in Philadelphia." *Perfect.* The statement was so casual that Cook would never suspect that she was bursting with curiosity.

There was no mistaking the look of disgust on the woman's face. "A fine how-do-you-do that was. Sneaking out in the dead of night like a thief and all the time they'd been carrying on in this very room while her husband slept—"

Cook stopped abruptly. Dakota nearly wept with disappointment.

Don't stop now. This is better than "Hard Copy."

"'Tain't Christian to speak ill of people," Cook said.

Sure it is, Dakota thought. *Gossip transcends religion.*

"Let the dead rest in peace, I always say."

"Dead?" Dakota's voice rose in surprise.

"Well, sure she's dead, missus, otherwise you wouldn't be here, now, would you?" Cook said with a bawdy laugh.

Divorce had yet to become the national pastime it was in the latter part of the twentieth century. She'd have to remember that.

Cook flung open the wardrobe doors. "She left her things behind. Now, I couldn't be squeezing myself into any of her gowns, but you're a slip of a thing. You'll do fine."

God bless you and your poor eyesight, Dakota thought as she gaped at the array of outfits. She'd been called many things in her life, but a "slip of a thing" wasn't one of them.

The gowns were utterly magnificent. Dakota had been around many reproductions of eighteenth century garb, but even the fine work done by the Princeton Historical Society left her unprepared for the splendor of the real thing. The absent Mrs. Devane might have had questionable taste in men, but her fashion sense was beyond reproach. Gowns of vivid scarlet, sky blue, lemon yellow the color of sunshine on an April morning—the beauty stole Dakota's breath away.

"Six ballgowns," she said, turning toward the older woman. "Did she do anything besides dance?"

Cook's round face crinkled with laughter. "One other thing," she said, eyes twinkling, "but I'd be too much the lady to tell you what it was."

To her surprise, Dakota felt a twinge of sympathy for Devane, but Cook's next words dispelled that emotion.

"You can't be leavin' a young and beautiful girl alone like that," the woman said as she supplied Dakota with a pitcher of water, a basin and soft cloths. "Flowers need tending, plain and simple, or else they find some place else to bloom."

It was as good a rationalization for infidelity as Dakota had ever heard. Still, whatever had happened between Devane and his wife, it must have been volcanic because no woman in her right mind would leave these treasures behind.

Cook excused herself and went back downstairs to tend to supper, leaving Dakota alone with six gowns, eight day dresses and the slim hope that one of them might actually fit.

She rummaged behind two exceptionally gorgeous satin numbers with bodices cut down to there and settled on a flower-sprigged muslin in shades of butter yellow and antique gold that would probably look like hell on her but was too spectacular to ignore.

She kicked off her running shoes, unzipped her jeans, then pulled her T-shirt over her head. Clad in cotton bra and panties, she stared at herself in the cheval glass then sighed. She was glad she didn't have her glasses. She doubted there were enough whalebone stays in the world to cinch in her waist tightly enough to fit into Mrs. Devane's clothing, but she'd give it her best shot.

"Easier said than done," she muttered a few minutes later. The full skirt did hide a multitude of sins but the bodice revealed her lack of assets. She ended up ripping the sleeves off her T-shirt and using them to provide what nature had forgotten.

The waistline was too snug for comfort but as long as she didn't breathe too deeply she'd survive. Besides, what was one popped button when there were four hundred more where that came from? As far as she could tell, the average woman had to get up three hours early just to be dressed in time for breakfast. She peered into the mirror. But maybe it was worth it. The bodice laced up the front and did a spectacular job of making very little look like a lot.

"So who needs a WonderBra?" She vamped in front of the mirror, enjoying the illusion of cleavage, when she noticed Abigail standing in the doorway.

"How long have you been there?" she asked in what she hoped was a pleasant tone of voice.

Abigail pointed toward Dakota's shoulder. "What's that?"

The tattoo. "You don't like the dress?" When your back is against the wall, play dumb.

Abigail shook her head. She stepped into the room, a tiny commando on a search-and-destroy mission. "I saw a picture on your shoulder."

"You must mean my birthmark."

"It looked like a heart."

"It's a family trait."

Abigail looked at her with those sad gray eyes but she didn't pursue the issue. Still, Dakota felt as if the child had her dead to rights.

"Papa wants to see you in the library. Cook said to tell you because she's only one woman and can't do everything." The last was delivered with Cook's intonation, right down to the vaguely Irish lilt to the voice.

"Thank you." Dakota wished the kid would stop looking at her as if she expected Dakota to sprout fangs and breathe fire. "I'll be down shortly."

"Papa doesn't like to be kept waiting."

And I don't like being ordered around. "I won't keep him waiting long."

Abigail wandered into the room and sat on the foot of the bed. "I know how you came here."

Dakota's spine stiffened. "Sure you do," she said easily. "We shared a saddle on your papa's horse."

"No," said Abigail, fixing her with a look. "It was that big red ball in the sky."

Oh, my God! "I—I don't know what you're talking about."

"That big red ball floating over the trees. I saw it."

"And you think that's how I came here?" Her heart was beating so hard that her ribs hurt.

Abigail nodded her head. "When I saw it, I wanted to fly away in it."

"What a funny idea." She hated herself for lying to the child, but there was no alternative.

"It was not funny," Abigail said, eyes narrowing. "'Twas real."

"I'm sure it looked real."

"It made a funny sound." She mimicked the intermittent hiss of the propane tanks.

Dakota almost choked on her own saliva. How was she going to convince the kid she'd been hallucinating?

"Were you scared up there in the sky?" Abigail persisted.

"I'd love to talk to you, Abigail, but your papa is waiting for me downstairs and you know he doesn't like to be kept waiting."

"My mama had a dress like that," the child said in her serious way.

"I, uh…" Dakota's voice trailed off. This was even more dangerous territory than hot-air balloons.

"You look pretty."

Definitely a day for surprises. "You called me a monster before, remember?" *Good going, Dakota. You can't even take a compliment from a six-year-old.*

The kid's lower lip trembled. "*You* said you were a fairy godmother."

Dakota sighed, then caught herself. Another sigh could cost her five or six buttons. *I really don't want to like you, kid, but you're starting to get to me.* "So we both made mistakes," she said after a moment. "Maybe we should start all over again."

Abigail's forehead puckered in a frown. She really was the image of her father. "I do not understand."

Dakota extended her right hand in greeting. "My name is Dakota."

"M-my name is Abigail Elizabeth Devane and I'm six years old." Cautiously the child extended her hand until their fingertips touched.

"I'm happy to meet you."

Abigail removed her hand from Dakota's. "That's Mama's dress, isn't it?"

"I needed something to wear."

"Where are your shoes?"

"I took them off." Running shoes didn't make quite the fashion statement she was looking for.

"You have to wear shoes."

"I'll find something."

"Mama's shoes are still here."

"I know, but your mama had smaller feet than I do."

"Cook has shoes."

"I'll see if she has an extra pair."

Abigail nodded as if satisfied. Dakota was about to congratulate herself on surviving questions about tattoos, shoes and transportation, but Abigail wasn't quite finished.

"When will the big red ball come back?" she asked in a matter-of-fact tone of voice.

"Honey," she lied, "I just don't know what you're talking about."

"Yes, you do," Abigail said sagely, "and when it does, I'm going to fly away."

Chapter Six

6

Abigail's words lingered with Dakota as she hurried downstairs to the library. The last thing she needed was for the child to tell anyone else about the hot-air balloon. How could you possibly explain something that hadn't been invented yet?

Still, Abigail was on to something, no doubt about it. She was only six years old, but she held Dakota's eyes with her own in a way that was almost eerily adult. *As if she knows what I'm thinking…*

"Ridiculous," she murmured as she limped her way, barefoot, through the long hallway to the library in the front of the house. If the girl knew what she was thinking, she'd know that Dakota had been lying through her teeth.

Just as she intended to do with her father.

"You wanted to speak with me?"

Patrick turned from the window where he'd been looking out at the drifting snow. Dakota Wylie stood in the doorway, clad in one of Susannah's dresses. The skirt was too long for her, as were the sleeves, but on the whole it was a most pleasing sight. A fact that annoyed him immeasurably.

"Come in." He motioned for her to take a seat in front of the fire. "You have eaten, I assume."

"No, actually, I haven't." She sat on the chair then leapt back up to rearrange her skirts. She mumbled something under her breath but he couldn't make out the words. Then she sat down again.

"I will ask Cook to prepare a plate."

"Don't go to any trouble on my account. I'll help myself."

"That is her job. She will see to it."

"Doesn't she have enough to do? Your housekeeper's gone, half of the maids have quit—"

"Damnation, woman! You have been under my roof for one hour and you presume to tell me how to run my house?"

There was nothing deferential in the way she looked at him, nothing feminine or ladylike. Her gaze held both challenge and reproach and he found himself oddly stirred by it.

Her bosoms rose and fell as she drew in a deep breath. Odd, he thought. The right one seemed larger than the left.

She was a most unusual woman.

"All I'm saying is that Cook has enough to do without making her wait on me. I'll take care of myself."

Words he had never heard Susannah utter.

He looked down at her feet, then looked again. They were bare. Her toenails were painted a vivid shade of red. He had never seen a more astonishing sight. "Your shoes, madam?"

"I didn't want to make Mr. Blackwell's list."

He did not know who this Mr. Blackwell was but did not wish to reveal his ignorance. "You require shoes, madam."

She glanced down at her bare feet. "I'll find something."

"I will see what I can do."

It would not be an easy task. Much of George Washington's army went barefoot these days. There were those who said you could observe their progress by following the trail in the snow left by their bloody feet. Shoes for a mere woman would be difficult to find, for few would condone the waste of good leather when there were valiant soldiers in need of boots.

She rose from the chair. "Well, if that's it, I think I'll see about dinner."

"Sit down."

She did not. "I'm tired and I'm hungry," she said in an even tone of voice. "I appreciate your giving me a place to sleep and I promise that I will be gone by daybreak tomorrow."

"You are going nowhere, mistress."

Fire flashed in her dark brown eyes. She truly did have the spirit of a beauty. "I do not appreciate orders, sir."

"You are in my house. You will do as I say."

"So this is how it is? You fight British tyranny only to inflict your own form of tyranny on your household." The fire flashed brighter. "Or is it you find no problem with tyrants?"

"Angry words, madam. Watch what you say lest you find yourself cast out into the snow."

And you'd do it, too, Dakota thought.

One look at that stubborn jawline and she could imagine him dragging her through the hallway, then booting her butt out into the night.

You're blowing it, Wylie. Get a grip on your temper and think *before you shoot off your mouth!*

She was two hundred years away from home and smack in the middle of a revolution. This was no time to congratulate herself on her snappy comebacks. A little humility. A touch of vulnerability. That was the secret to success.

Even if she choked on it.

"My apologies, sir," she said, gazing up at him through lowered lashes. "It has been a most difficult day."

Is that humble enough for you, Devane? That granite jaw softened the slightest bit as she sat back down. *See? We can get along. All I have to do is turn into a mindless twit.*

"You were on my property," he said without preamble. "I demand an explanation."

She gave him her best wide-eyed and innocent look, the one that had never worked on her boss at the library. "You own the woods?"

"I own the town."

"An overstatement, I'm sure."

"An understatement, madam. I am a wealthy and powerful man."

"Don't forget modest," she murmured.

"Say again."

Not on your life. "If I trespassed, I apologize." If he lived in the twentieth century he'd probably install a surveillance camera in the highest pine tree and monitor the deer.

She watched his face, waiting for a reaction to her apology. If there was one, she couldn't see it. *Remind me never to play poker with you, Devane.*

"What is it you sought in the woods, madam?"

The sixty-four-thousand-dollar question. Now all she had to do was come up with an answer. "It was a difficult journey," she said carefully. "I lost my way."

"Where is it you wished to go?"

"I—I do not know."

"You try my patience, madam. Do not play the fool, for I will not allow it."

"I tell the truth. I do not know my destination."

If possible, his glower grew even more threatening. *Go ahead,* she thought. *Hook me up to a lie detector. I'm giving it to you straight.*

"You are in the habit of wandering the woods, half-dressed, in a blizzard?"

"That's about the size of it."

"An unusual expression, madam. Where did you come by it?"

She ignored the question and plunged ahead. "I have lost the people near to me." The quaver in her voice surprised her; it was the real thing.

"You have lost them to death?"

She looked away. "I do not know." The balloon had been in dire trouble. Although it terrified her to think about it, anything was possible. "My family is gone. My friends are lost to me. I do not know where I am, only that I am probably in New Jersey."

"Franklin Ridge," he elaborated. "In the house of Patrick Devane."

"I have traveled long and far. I do not even know the day of the month."

"The first of December, madam." A hint of a smile flickered across his face. "The year of our Lord seventeen hundred and seventy-nine."

The thundering in her head drowned out everything else. 1779...the worst winter of the war. Before the month was out, snow would drift past the first-floor windows, choking the roads, killing the soldiers, making her escape impossible.

"Madam?" Devane stepped closer to where she sat. "Are you unwell?"

"Yes—I mean, no."

"You are trembling."

"The cold." She leaned back into the chair.

"This room is warm."

"I'm cold," she repeated.

"That is a trait we share in common."

"I was speaking of the temperature."

"As was I, madam." His expression betrayed nothing, but she had the oddest sense that he had revealed himself to her in an intimate, if puzzling, way.

They fell quiet as Cook's husband, Joseph, entered the room, bearing an armful of wood. Working swiftly, the gray-haired man added the logs to the fire, pumped the bellows a half-dozen times, then bowed and left the room. Her mind raced, leaping between possibilities, dodging probable land mines, searching for something—anything—to say that this suspicious man might believe.

Devane waited until Joseph's footsteps faded down the hallway, then he turned to Dakota. "Your story, madam," he said without preamble.

"My husband was a simple man. . . ."

She lies, Patrick thought, watching the play of light and shadow on the woman's face as she wove a story of sorrow and loss. He was not a man who put much stock in second sight, but there was no denying the strong feeling inside him that all was not as it seemed.

Not that her story wasn't most believable. The woman wove a canny tale, designed to bring a hard-hearted man to tears. A loving husband whom she had joined in battle, only to lose to a Lobsterback's bayonet. Faithful friends had opened their heart and home to her and she had found a measure of contentment under their roof until they were routed by British General Gage's men.

She spoke with animation. At times her voice shook with emotion. From another woman, at another time, he would have had no reason to doubt her veracity. When she told him about the stagecoach accident along the Millstone River and the blow to the head that had rendered her unconscious, he had felt her pain.

At least, he had felt her pain until he remembered that the stagecoach had not run along the Millstone River in many months.

You are a liar, madam, he thought, watching as her dark eyes shimmered with tears. *And a most accomplished one.*

Dakota Wylie was a spy. Of that he was certain.

The question now remained—to which side did she belong?

He's buying it, Dakota thought gleefully. *Hook, line and sinker.*

The more outrageous the story got, the more certain she became that he believed every single word. So far, she'd created a martyred husband, saintly parents in New Hampshire and wonderful friends whose sole purpose in life was to see to her comfort and happiness. She was even pretty darned certain she'd noticed a single tear forming at the inner corner of his right eye as she described her loneliness at being separated from people who meant so much to her.

For a woman who'd never told a lie in her entire life, she was showing an appalling talent for tall tales. She hoped the fact that it was a life-or-death situation would make up for it later on.

And it *was* a life-or-death situation.

If Devane found out she was lying, she had no doubt he'd kill her.

The guy simmered with rage. It was in the look in his eyes, the way he carried himself, that low growl of a voice. No wonder his wife had run off to Philadelphia. Being married to Patrick Devane had to be like sleepwalking through a minefield.

"Begging your pardon." They both turned toward the doorway, to find Cook standing there. "I fixed a nice plate for the lady. Fresh bread right from the oven and my own cider to wash it down."

"That sounds wonderful." Dakota rose from her chair. "I'm on my way."

She made to leave the room but Devane blocked her way. "We have not finished our conversation."

"I think we have," she said.

"There is still the question of your future plans."

She looked up and met his eyes. "I don't see why my plans should be any concern of yours."

"You are in my house and that makes you my responsibility."

"Sorry," she said lightly. "I'm not buying that."

"Madam?"

"I don't believe you. Be honest with me, Mr. Devane—you do not care what happens to me, any more than I care what happens to you. You offered me your hospitality for the night and I accepted. Beyond that, you owe me nothing at all."

"Look." He strode toward the window. How he managed to pack such a testosterone punch into such a simple gesture was beyond her. He drew the drapes back. "A blizzard, Mistress Wylie. You will not be going anywhere tomorrow or the day after."

"Oh, God," she said, peering through the frosty glass at the Currier & Ives scene in front of her. "I may not be going anywhere until spring."

Their eyes met. If possible, he was even more devastating by firelight, with the angles and planes of his gorgeous face chiseled to perfection by light and shadow and one damn fine set of genes. It was one of those Kodak moments diehard romantics celebrated in greeting cards and sappy love songs.

A magnificent man.

A lonely woman.

A roaring fireplace.

Anything seemed possible.

The tight waistband of her gown must be cutting off circulation to her brain. This wasn't the "Love Connection." For one thing, there wasn't the slightest hint of attraction between them. Suspicion, yes. Curiosity, definitely. But attraction? Not on your life.

Still, there was no denying that everything about the man had been designed to get a woman's attention. What was it about bad-tempered macho types that set a good woman's blood racing?

"Excuse me," she said, turning away from the window—and from temptation. "Cook must be wondering where I am."

He didn't move aside. Somehow she wasn't surprised. Crowds probably parted for him like the Red Sea for Moses.

"I will have my answer," he said. "Make no mistake about it."

"I have told you all there is to tell."

"I fear I do not believe you, madam."

"And I fear that is your problem, Mr. Devane."

Getting out of here is mine.

Chapter Seven

7

No matter how hard Abby tried, she couldn't fall asleep.

Papa had sent her to her room without dinner—punishment, he'd told her, for running away from home. "Disobedience will not be tolerated," he'd said in his angriest voice. "If I cannot teach you, the good sisters will."

Her stomach rumbled and she shifted position, drawing her knees up close. Papa thought that being hungry would teach her to behave, but so far all it had done was make her even angrier. Papa still thought she was a baby. He didn't realize she knew exactly where Cook stored wondrous things like leftover stew and bread, and as soon as the house fell quiet, she would sneak down the back stairs and eat to her heart's content.

She wondered when Papa and the lady from the maple tree would stop talking and say good-night. Abby would give anything to know what they were saying. She couldn't remember the last time a stranger had spent the night in the big white house, especially not a stranger as peculiar as Dakota Wylie.

She pulled the coverlet up over her shoulders and made sure

Lucy was tucked in safe and snug. She had said terrible things to the lady, calling her a monster and saying she wasn't pretty when in truth she was. Abby's cheeks burned as she remembered her words. It was just that she had never seen a grown woman sitting in a maple tree before. And she surely had never seen one wearing breeches or with hair so short that it made her look like a child.

In truth, Dakota didn't look anything like a monster, but Abby knew that monsters came in many guises and she was smart enough to be careful.

It seemed as if Papa and Dakota had been talking for hours. She wondered if they were talking about her. Maybe Papa was telling Dakota about the Girls' School of the Sacred Heart in Boston and Dakota was telling Papa why he shouldn't send his little girl so far away.

Sometimes when she closed her eyes and made her mind go all dark and empty, she could see what was going on in other parts of the house, really see them, same as if she were standing right there in the room. But tonight she just couldn't make the pictures appear inside her head. She squeezed her eyes shut as tightly as she could and waited, but she didn't see or hear a thing.

A very long time ago she'd asked her governess why it was she heard people talking when they didn't even move their lips. The governess, a sour-faced young woman from New Hampshire, had given her a peculiar look then laughed and said that Abby had something called an imagination. But when Abby told the governess that she really shouldn't think such peculiar things about the way Cook's son looked without his breeches on, the governess had let out a shriek, then rushed up to her room to pack her bags.

Abby never talked about it again with anybody.

Abby wasn't like the others. Mama had known it and that was why she'd left. Papa knew it, as well, and that was why he was sending her far away to school. Other boys and girls laughed and played and had parents who loved them more than anything.

She threw off the covers and shivered as a cold draft ruffled the hem of her nightdress. When she'd seen that bright red ball dancing over the tops of the trees she'd been possessed of a feeling that something wonderful was right around the corner, something so splendid and unexpected that all the sad things that had come before it would be forgotten.

But then she'd found Dakota in the maple tree and thoughts of the big red ball had been pushed aside by silly talk of monsters and fairy godmothers.

She wrapped her arms about her knees and sighed. She wasn't entirely sure about monsters, but she knew fairy godmothers were only in stories. If fairy godmothers really existed, she wouldn't be forced to leave her home and everything she loved in order to go to some dreadful school in faraway Boston. If fairy godmothers really existed, Mama would still live in the big white house and Papa would be happy again and Abby wouldn't be sitting there in the darkness, feeling cold and hungry and lonely.

Gently she plucked Lucy from under the covers and cradled the battered rag doll against her chest. She guessed it must be near to midnight. Surely Papa and Dakota had finished talking by now and it would be safe to sneak down the back stairs to the kitchen.

She tiptoed across the room, making sure to avoid the squeaky floorboards near the rocking chair. Easing open the door, she stepped into the hallway. There wasn't a sound to be heard. If she was very quiet and very careful, she could sneak downstairs, find some bread or stew to fill her belly, then be back in her bed before anyone knew she was missing.

She crept past Papa's room, then was about to slip past Dakota's when a sound caught her attention. She held her breath and listened. *Oh, Lucy! She's crying.* Abby could scarcely believe her ears.

Grown people didn't cry. Sometimes their eyes got all watery, but they never cried the way she did when she was sad.

Her heart ached as if someone had grabbed it with a giant fist. *She's lonely,* Abby thought, then wondered how it was she could know such a thing about a stranger. The woman missed her mother same as Abby did and was afraid she would never see her again. *Don't be sad,* Abby thought. Dakota's mother loved her and held her close to her heart and one day they would be together again—something Abby knew would never, ever happen for her.

"Oh, Mama," she whispered, her lips pressed against the soft top of Lucy's head. "I miss you so."

Patrick muttered a curse, then stepped deeper into the shadows at the top of the stairs.

Damn Susannah. Damn her cheating soul. The child deserved better than either one of them had been able to provide.

It is for the best, he told himself as the child wiped her eyes with the sleeve of her nightdress. Sending her away was the only solution. There was nothing for her here but loneliness and pain and even danger. To keep her here with him was to do her a disservice. The child was the only true innocent in the situation, and he prayed the good sisters of the Sacred Heart would keep her that way.

Hardening his heart once again, he moved toward her.

"Abigail."

She started in surprise, her gray eyes wide and fearful in her tiny face.

"To bed, Abigail," he said, pushing away the memory of how she'd lain in his arms as a newborn. So deeply wanted. So well loved.

"Papa," she whispered, "the lady is crying."

He started to say he thought that prospect highly unlikely but then, in the brittle silence of his house, he heard the sound of a woman's tears. He found it difficult to imagine Mistress Dakota with her sharp tongue and peculiar ways indulging in something as soft and vulnerable as tears.

"To bed," he repeated, placing a hand on her shoulder. "The hour is late."

"She is sad," the child said softly. "She misses her mother."

Her words startled him. "You and Mistress Dakota have talked of such things?"

Abigail shook her head.

"Then how is it you know this?"

Her brows slid together into a knot over the bridge of her upturned nose. He waited as she struggled to find the words to explain her flight of imaginative fancy.

"She comes from far away," Abigail said at last, sounding suddenly far older than her half dozen years. "And she can never go back."

A changeling, he thought. The child was unlike anyone he had ever known. Certainly nothing like himself.

She shivered and he noticed her feet were bare. "To bed with you," he said, his voice gruff. "You cannot travel to Boston if you are sick."

"Good," she said, lifting her chin in defiance.

Did she have to look at him like that, as if he were sentencing her to a life of indentured servitude? "I was sent to school at your age, Abigail. It is a good thing, not a punishment."

Her gray eyes flashed. "Mama wouldn't have sent me to Boston."

He felt his temper rise. "Your mother is not here, Abigail."

"I hate you!" Abigail kicked his ankle with her small bare foot.

He watched her run down the hall to her room. There were no dark secrets hiding in the corners of his loneliness. Nothing to rear up, stare him in the eye and force him to see things the way they really were. He knew the breadth and depth of it and somehow the knowledge sustained him.

It was the unexpected that had the power to destroy.

The child's tears were no business of his.

Nor were the tears of the woman on the other side of the closed door.

Turning, he headed for the stairs and the other life that awaited him miles away from this house of pain.

Dakota's breath caught in her throat at the sound of his retreating footsteps.

She leaned back against the door and closed her eyes, waiting for her heartbeat to return to normal. "Ridiculous," she said aloud, her voice breaking the quiet of her room. As if it mattered, what he thought of her.

When she'd first heard Devane and Abigail whispering in the hallway, she'd been too caught up in her own woes to pay much attention. But that was before she realized they were talking about her.

Scarcely breathing, she'd pressed her ear to the closed door and tried to make out their words. The sounds were hushed, almost inaudible, but she'd caught enough of it to know that Devane was a hard-hearted bastard and that one day Abigail would thank her lucky stars that she had lived with him for only six years.

She'd had a good mind to fling open the door and tell him that, too. The man needed to have his butt recalibrated and she was in the mood to do it for him. At least then she'd be doing something, not staying cooped up in a strange room, crying from fatigue and frustration.

Her fingers had curled around the latch and she had been about to swing open the door and surprise the living hell out of him when Abigail's clear, sweet voice had floated through the heavy wood.

She could still hear the words. *She is sad...she misses her mother.*

That was impossible. Dakota hadn't been gone twenty-four hours yet. Ginny's last "You've gained weight and you're still single" remark was still fresh in her mind. Sometimes a week or two went by when she didn't talk to Ginny at all, and she enjoyed every day of it.

No, the kid was wrong. Right now the only things she missed were indoor plumbing, Letterman and possibly her sofa bed with the fluky spring and the tendency to open itself up without human assistance.

She was a firm believer in destiny, confident that nothing in life happened without a reason, but darned if she could figure this one out. No one had ever accused her of being a closet Mary Poppins. And, even if she was dying to be someone's nanny, the kid was being shipped up to Boston tomorrow, so she'd end up being unemployed in two centuries without even trying. That alone could win her a spot on "Nightline" when she got back to where she belonged.

She comes from far away and she can never go back.

Dakota shivered and wrapped her arms across her chest.

Maybe you're right, Abigail, she thought as she moved away from her own door. Maybe the plain little girl with the big gray eyes had zeroed in on the truth that Dakota wanted to avoid.

Suddenly it seemed so clear to her that it took her breath away.

The spider plant in her bathroom would probably die from neglect. Her mail would pile up and everybody would know she didn't just read the *National Enquirer* in line at the supermarket, she actually subscribed to it. Her landlord would call the sheriff to break down her door and instead of her dead body propped up in a chair with a container of Häagen-Dazs clutched in her rigor-mortised hand, they'd find a couple of centuries' worth of dust balls.

Tears welled and she didn't bother to blink them back. What if she couldn't go back? Just because Andrew had been able to get back home didn't mean she'd be that lucky. The tears flowed more freely and she made one attempt to stem the tide, then realized it made no difference at all. There was no one there to see her. No one to give a damn if she never watched the home shopping channel again or ate a Big Mac or sat with her family over Thanksgiving dinner and explained why she still wasn't married.

She used to believe she thrived on adventure, that she'd be the first to leap aboard a UFO and fly off to parts unknown. "Footloose and fancy-free," she'd called herself. Ready to kick over the traces of her everyday life at a moment's notice.

So much for what she used to believe. She was turning out to be a gutless wonder, one of those passive people she despised who waited for life to do its worst.

Instead of sniveling alone in her bedroom, she should be downstairs searching for a map, a newspaper, anything that would help her pinpoint her location. Once she figured out exactly where she was, how hard could it be to find Andrew and Shannon?

Andrew and Shannon were the key to everything. This was their destiny, after all, not Dakota's. As close as she could tell, her only purpose had been to return Abby to her father. Beyond that, she was as useful as a VCR in a world without television. If she could find Andrew and Shannon, she could find the balloon that had brought them there and once she found that balloon, she'd be halfway home.

So what're you waiting for, Wylie? There was no "Nick at Nite" to keep people up late. They went to bed early and they stayed there, mainly because there was nowhere else to go.

She wiped her eyes with the back of her hand and straightened her spine. Why wait for tomorrow and have to worry about dodging Devane? He was probably tucked away in bed like a good little dictator. This was the perfect time to do some sleuthing.

It was at least seven hours until dawn. You didn't have to be a budding Jessica Fletcher to be able to get the goods on someone in that amount of time.

Chapter Eight

8

They met in the shadows behind Arnold's Tavern in Morristown, shielded from the snow and cold by naught save the bare branches of dormant oaks and maples.

"Victory is at hand," said the youngest of the three, "but at what cost? Six lives lost and maybe more and now our two best are at the mercy of the British."

"The cause is all," said the peacemaker of the trio. "'Twas understood by each before the campaign was engaged. Sacrifice is both honorable and necessary."

Their words reached Patrick through the dark cloud of despair that had enveloped him since learning Blakelee and Rutledge had been taken prisoner by the British. They had supped at the White Horse Tavern and made to leave the embroidered blanket with the tavern owner when a pair of British soldiers had arrested them on charges unspecified. And they wondered how it was the Americans fought so hard for their rights....

"Aye," the peacemaker was saying, "but still the goal remains elusive."

"Always the goal," said the youngest. "What of the cause which brings us here?"

"We have no time for philosophy," Patrick said over the howling of the wind. "We will meet again tomorrow, for there is still much to do."

He turned to leave, but the peacemaker stopped him. "There is another matter. A most peculiar sighting to the west."

He thought of the towering cloud formations he'd noted upon leaving Mrs. Whitton's home. "The storm," he said, dismissing the man's words. "'Tis nothing but a strange new pattern."

"Not the clouds," the man persisted. "Something far more strange than that."

Patrick listened to the story, then threw back his head and laughed. His colleagues looked at him, openmouthed, for he had never laughed before in their presence. This story, however, merited little else.

"A large red ball seen bouncing over the treetops?" he asked for once forgetting the anger in his belly. "Mayhap our good soldiers should reconsider their love of rum and the grape."

The peacemaker shook his head. "'Twould seem so, but 'twas not the case. All were teetotal."

"A trick of those clouds and the setting sun," Patrick said, determined to find a reasonable explanation. Nonsensical stories such as this one ofttimes destroyed the most carefully wrought plans. Better to stop it now.

"His Excellency himself laid claim to the sight," said the peacemaker.

Patrick arched his brow. "This story stops now," he ordered. "It serves no purpose, save to foster unrest."

The youngest of the three opened his mouth to speak, then closed it again.

"Say your piece, man," Patrick ordered, noticing the man's unease. He wondered if the innocent face hid the heart of a traitor. "Have done with it now, then get on with the business at hand."

"There are those who say a man and two women floated from a basket suspended below the big red ball and that the man was Andrew McVie."

"Yes," said Patrick, ruing the day he'd thrown in his lot with beggars and fools. "A most likely occurrence." McVie had vanished three summers ago and Patrick had every reason to believe him dead and buried.

"A farmer near to King's Crossing claims to have seen them sail off behind the hills then disappear. A shopkeeper in Morristown says the Lobsterbacks brung them to the ground and threw them in jail."

The peacemaker laughed. "Next we'll hear that King George was with them, drinking tea."

Could the gentle-voiced man be the one who sold their secrets to the enemy?

"Nonsense, all of it," Patrick stated in a tone that brooked no argument. If Andrew McVie was alive and anywhere in the thirteen colonies, he would know about it. "Put an end to conjecture and concentrate on the job at hand."

He turned once again to leave.

This time no one stopped him.

Dakota quickly discovered that the man of the house was pathologically tidy.

His desk top was a testament to anal-retentive decorating. The blotter was perfectly centered. A chunky glass inkpot was situated at the upper right-hand corner. Two quills rested next to it, points aimed toward the door.

If he had any personal effects, he kept them well hidden. No miniatures of the wife and kid. No busts of either of the Georges,

Washington or king. It wasn't as if she'd been expecting to find a framed eight-by-ten glossy or manila folder filled with carbon copies of his correspondence, but she'd certainly figured to uncover more than this.

She tried the top drawer but it was locked. So were the other three. Devane didn't strike her as the kind of guy who would take the time to lock his desk, then hide the key under the blotter. He probably slept with the damn thing under his pillow.

The thought made her laugh out loud, and she stifled the sound with her hand. She could just imagine herself slipping back upstairs, sneaking down the hallway to his room, then trying to inch her hand under his pillow. He'd probably shoot her dead before she made it back out the door.

So that left the books themselves. Maybe he had a map or a copy of some incriminating correspondence tucked between the pages of Aristotle or Shakespeare's sonnets.

She paused, waiting for that tingle of energy that she knew so well, but nothing came. It had been so easy with Andrew McVie. The image of the book *Forgotten Heroes* had come to her so clearly that she'd never doubted its existence—or that she would find the passage that spoke of Andrew's destiny, saving the lives of his friends Rutledge and Blakelee.

But it was different this time. Her mind was empty of everything but the terrifying notion that her world had suddenly gone from Technicolor to black and white. If this was how the rest of the world went through life, she wasn't impressed. Instead of relying on those mysterious inner voices, she was reduced to using logic.

"No use whining about it, Wylie," she said with a sigh. The clock was ticking and if she didn't want Devane to catch her in flagrante delicto, she'd better get cracking.

She thanked her years of library science classes as she climbed the ladder and reached for the copy of *Aesop's Fables*. Librarians knew how to handle books. She could make her way through Devane's entire library in a few hours and he'd never even know she'd been there.

The first thing Patrick noticed as he approached the house was the light burning in the library window.

"Bloody hell," he swore under his breath. The dark-haired wench was up and about. He should have realized she would not miss an opportunity to pry into his affairs. He was grateful he had remembered to lock his desk drawers and secret the key upon his person.

He reined in the black stallion that had been Susannah's favorite and dismounted. The beast was high-strung and possessed of a foul disposition, yet he feared nothing. Patrick's own chestnut had patently refused to venture into the storm.

Quietly he led the horse back toward the stable and settled the animal in for the night. He had given William permission to sleep in the main house during the winter months, as much for his own convenience as for the boy's comfort.

Of late he and his companions had enjoyed much luck in their endeavors, despite the traitor among them who oft fed information to the other side. They moved swiftly and secretly about the countryside, gathering information, freeing innocent men held against their will. And with every day, every raid, he came closer to his goal.

He slipped into the kitchen and shut the door behind him. The hearth fire was banked, but warmth still rose up from the embers. His body registered the heat, but he took no pleasure from it. He allowed himself to think of naught save stopping the short-haired wench before she stumbled upon the truth.

The library door was closed. The yellow glow of candlelight spilled through the cracks and out into the darkened hallway. Mistress Wylie had a great deal to learn. A more experienced member of a spy ring would have known to block the escape of light with cushions or books.

Grim faced, he reached for the latch.

"The man's a sociopath," Dakota muttered as she slid a heavy leather-bound tome back onto the shelf. It was bad enough that Devane didn't have any fascinating knickknacks scattered about his library, but she'd at least hoped his choice of books would shed some light on the man.

You'd have to check into the morgue to find a more deadly dull collection of books. Where were the hand-drawn maps? The letters from family and friends? The telephone wouldn't be invented for another hundred years, for heaven's sake. If you wanted to get in touch with someone, you wrote a letter, but so far Dakota hadn't found one single shred of information that would give her even the slightest idea of where she was or what was going on around her.

If she didn't come up with some answers soon, she'd be forced to do the unthinkable and ask him.

She knew that asking questions made you vulnerable; it provided your enemy with a road map of all your weaknesses. But when you came down to it, what choice did she have? It wasn't as if she could turn on CNN to catch up on things.

If nothing else, she finally understood why the heroines of the Gothic novels she'd devoured as a teenager never asked questions. She couldn't count the number of times she'd flung a poor unsuspecting book against the wall and snarled, "Why didn't you just *ask?*" at the hapless heroine. Now she knew. If the heroine had uttered so much as "Where am I?" the antihero would have known she was ripe for the taking.

No, she'd have to find a more subtle way to get at the truth.

She was considering that when something caught her eye near the corner of the room. A piece of paper stuck out from beneath the lush Persian carpet. Quickly she crossed the room and grabbed for it.

Pay dirt!

It was a list of some kind. Two columns of names written in a strong, masculine hand. She scanned the long left-hand column and saw the names McDowell, Grant and Arnold. Her eyes shifted to the right-hand column, where the names Rutledge and Blakelee leapt out at her. Her heart pounded wildly and she had started to zero in on the others when she heard footsteps in the hallway. She barely had time to stash the slip of paper back underneath the carpet when the door swung open and Devane loomed in the doorway.

"What in bloody hell are you doing in my library?" he roared.

"Trying to figure out where in bloody hell I am," she roared back.

The room fell silent.

It was the *hell* that did it, she thought. The look of utter amazement on his face was priceless. It was almost enough to make up for the fatal error she'd made. Now he probably thought she was a fallen woman on top of everything else.

She took a deep breath and squared her shoulders. "So where am I?" she asked.

"Franklin Ridge," he said after a pause. "You asked that question before, madam."

"Are we near Princeton?"

"You do not know?"

"If I knew, I wouldn't be asking you."

"Is it that you have no sense of geography or are you not from this colony?"

"A little of both."

He stepped into the room and closed the door behind him.

The library suddenly got a lot smaller.

Her dark eyes held a fierce glitter within their depths, but was it the glitter of madness or commitment? He needed to find out.

"We are a half day's ride from Princeton to the north," he said.

"Near Morristown?"

"A stone's throw."

"And where's the closest jail?"

"Sweet Jesus, madam, but you try a man's patience beyond endurance."

"You're not a walk in the park yourself."

Again the words were recognizable but the pattern was not.

He closed the distance between them. "It is now my turn to ask the questions and, by all that is holy, you are to answer with the truth."

"And I've told you the truth. My name is Dakota Wylie. I have no sense of direction and, believe me, I'm not from around here."

"And where are you from?"

"I told you before, sir, or were you not listening?"

She was a canny wench, one not easily bested, but he was not a man easily deterred by a challenge.

"New Hampshire, did you say?"

She hesitated. It was clear she did not remember what lie she had perpetrated upon him.

"Or was it Boston?" he prodded.

"It is none of your business, Mr. Devane."

"But I think it *is* my business." He moved closer. "I find you on my property. I find you in my library. If not mine, then whose business is it?"

"This is getting ridiculous." She stepped backward.

He stepped forward.

"If you're trying to intimidate me, it won't work."

"I am trying to obtain an answer to my question, madam, and if intimidation is the means by which I will succeed, then we will soon find out who the victor is."

"Move out of my way," she ordered. "It's late. I wish to sleep."

He blocked her passage. "You had your chance to sleep and it has passed."

"No wonder your wife left you," the woman snapped. "The only thing that surprises me is the fact that she made it past the honeymoon."

Uh-oh, Dakota thought as she watched a human face turn to granite before her very eyes. *Wrong thing to say.*

She gauged the distance between herself and the door and considered making a run for it. *Right, Wylie. Like you have a chance in hell of outrunning the guy.* The last time she'd done any running it was to grab the last bag of chips at the supermarket. As it was, he looked as if he wanted to wrap his enormous hands around her throat again and throttle her.

"You will not talk of my wife or my marriage again." His voice was low, menacing. "Not in this house. Not with anyone."

She lifted her chin and met his eyes. "Why?" she asked, sounding braver than she felt. "Got something to hide?"

"That is not your concern."

"I'm not the one who goes sneaking around at night during a snowstorm." She grinned as he glanced down at his snow-covered cape and the pool of water forming at his booted feet. "Didn't think I'd notice, did you?" she asked, reveling in his surprise. "Details, Mr. Devane. It always comes down to the details."

She had to hand it to him, however. He dissembled faster than a speeding bullet. "What did you seek to find in my library, madam?"

"A map," she said, opting for the truth. "I needed to know my location."

"And what will you do now that you have found your location?"

"I'll leave tomorrow at dawn."

"To find your husband?"

She nodded. "Yes. And to find my friends."

"Tell me their names," he persisted, stepping into her space. "Mayhap I have some knowledge of their whereabouts."

"You wouldn't know them." *Trust me on that one.*

"Their names," he persisted.

No way, Devane. That's the last thing I'm about to tell you. She was unimportant in the scheme of things but Andrew and Shannon had a destiny to fulfill. "I don't see what—"

"Their names."

"Ronald and Nancy Reagan."

He considered her words. "I do not know them."

She bit the inside of her cheek. "I didn't think so."

He studied her carefully. The last man to study her so carefully had the initials OB-GYN after his name. "And you last saw them—"

"In the snow," she said, feigning a look of deep sadness. "In the woods."

He took another step toward her. She took another step backward. The edge of his cherrywood desk bit into the back of her thighs. "And what of your husband, madam? When last did you see him?"

"The same time," she said, her heart thudding painfully inside her chest. "I—"

He pinned her hands behind her back and pulled her against him. If he hadn't looked bent on murder, it might have been exciting. "You lie, madam." His voice was low with menace.

"N-no," she stammered. "I'm telling you the truth."

"The grieving widow had best get her story straight."

Widow? Oh, God... She'd totally forgotten the glib story she'd spun for him in this same library a few hours ago. She tried to look suitably mournful. "I—I am terribly tired, sir. A slip of the tongue, that's all." *Think, Wylie, think! What tall tale did you foist on the man?* "We were walking—"

"You were in a stagecoach."

"Near Princeton—"

"Millstone."

"And we had an accident."

"At last," said Devane. "You have stumbled upon the truth."

"Okay," she said, utterly exasperated. "So I lied to you. Can you blame me?"

"And what else have you lied about, madam?"

"Nothing," she lied. She summoned up a weak and guilty smile. "You are a stranger to me. These are, as you have said, dangerous times. Would you have bared your soul to the first person to come along?" She was on a roll. "I think not. I think you would—"

Chapter Nine

9

Her mouth was full and inviting and, had the situation been different, he might have taken advantage of that fact.

"Say nothing," Patrick murmured, almost brushing her lips with his. "We are being observed."

She lashed out with her foot. He angled his body away from her and pulled her even closer.

"Careful, madam." He cupped her face with his hands and met her eyes. She looked flushed and ruffled, eminently desirable. "You may yet sign your own death warrant."

"Don't tell me what to do. I'll—"

"Soldiers," he said in a low voice as he brought one hand to her throat as a warning. "At the window."

She threw back her head to scream but he quickly moved his hand to her mouth.

"Sweet Jesus!" he muttered as she kicked him then darted toward the door. He tackled her about the waist and lifted her off the floor. "You will regret this."

"Let me go! If you think I'm going to let you bully me into—"

The pounding at the front door drowned out her words.

"Choose sides carefully, madam," he warned as he dragged her across the hall. "Your situation is most unusual and few would be so tolerant."

They reached the door as the Continental soldiers kicked it open.

"The list grows," Patrick said, eyeing the damage with some disgust.

The young officer, in full uniform despite the hour and the weather, bowed curtly to Patrick and more cordially to Dakota, who stood behind him.

Patrick recognized the man as one of the soldiers they'd met earlier.

"We heard a...commotion," said the soldier, his expression bland. "I wish to inquire of your safety."

"How kind of you," Dakota said, stepping forward. "As it happens, I need—"

"Privacy," Patrick interrupted. He gestured toward the door. "If you would take your leave, sir, we will retire once again."

The soldier made no move to leave. "While it was my wish to express concern for your well-being, sir, I fear that 'twas not the sole reason for this visit."

"Out with it, man," Patrick ordered. "The hour is late."

"'Twas our hope you would experience a change of heart, sir, but it becomes imperative that we take such matters into our own hands."

"What's he talking about?" Dakota's voice rose in question.

He shot a quelling look at the short-haired woman, but doubted it would have the desired effect. Was she the only citizen of the thirteen colonies who did not understand the gravity of the situation?

"This house remains private property, sir," Patrick said to the soldier. "I wish you godspeed in securing another property for your needs."

"Your good wishes are unnecessary, sir." The officer reached inside his coat and withdrew a letter, complete with that all-too-familiar seal. "We have secured that which we require right here."

"George Washington again," Dakota whispered as the soldier extended the letter toward him. "This place is a gold mine."

Ignoring her, he folded his arms across his chest and glared at the young officer. "You are not welcome here."

"That may be, Mr. Devane, but still we are come to stay." He nodded toward Dakota, who now stood next to him. "We shall not inconvenience you and your wife."

"I'm not—"

He drew Dakota to his side. It would not go well for either of them if she chose this moment to inform the officer that they were strangers to each other.

Patrick placed a hand at her waist. "We are just wed, sir. This is not a time for company, even of a patriotic sort."

The officer's expression remained carefully blank. "The matter is beyond my power, sir. I offer you most humble apologies, but beg your indulgence as we prepare for the general's arrival."

"The general!" Dakota's heart was beating so fast she thought she'd pass out. What red-blooded American woman wouldn't be thrilled by the thought of actually meeting the father of her country? Certainly her excitement had nothing to do with the fact that Devane had almost kissed her. "Is George Washington coming *here?*"

The young officer looked at her and smiled, the first real smile he'd offered since noticing her hair. "An honor it would be, Mrs. Devane, but His Excellency enjoys fine accommodations with the Widow Ford and her children."

She could barely contain her disappointment. "What general, then?"

"General McDowell, madam, His Excellency's most trusted colleague and friend."

"A braggart and a coward," Devane said. "Unworthy of the command given him."

The officer's jaw tightened visibly. "An untoward comment, sir, from one who has chosen not to serve."

"Let General McDowell stay with the Widow Ford and her brood if the accommodations there are to everyone's liking."

"Would that it were possible, sir, but with Lady Washington's arrival imminent, there is no room for General McDowell."

"You bleed me like a stone with your taxes, then take what you want from my home. Is there no end to the Continental treachery?"

"Take care, man," the soldier warned, "for your reputation precedes you. 'Tis a short leap from debate to treason."

Treason? Had she missed something? She thought they'd been having a discussion about closet space. She bit back a sigh. What she wouldn't give for five seconds inside Devane's head, just five measly little seconds and she'd at least have a handle on what was going on.

"Are you calling me out, sir?" Devane's voice rippled with menace.

The soldier took a step forward, his gloved hands clenched into fists. "If that is what you—"

The thought of physical violence made her go weak in the knees and she allowed herself to tumble in a heap at Devane's booted feet. She would have two-stepped to a chorus of "Disco Duck" if she'd thought it would break the tension but, given when and where she was, swooning seemed a safer bet.

The fact that she'd managed to stay upright this long was more of a miracle than she dared to contemplate. His touch had unraveled her defenses. Maybe if she'd been touched more often—and more recently—she wouldn't have reacted so strongly to the feel of his fingers against the skin of her throat.

He stared down at her.

She fluttered her eyelashes in a pathetic attempt at wielding her feminine wiles, praying he didn't leave her curled at his feet like a stray cat.

After what seemed to be an eternity, a grim-faced Devane swept her up into his arms. A bizarre feeling of relief washed over her and she almost laughed at the absurdity of it all.

He didn't owe her anything at all. In fact, she wouldn't blame him if he handed her over to the soldiers and washed his hands of her.

"The hour is late," Devane said in that deadly tone she was coming to know. "My wife is exhausted."

Dakota stifled a yawn. Some might call it overacting but it seemed like a nice touch.

After what seemed an eternity, the officer nodded. "We will limit ourselves to the main floor for the night."

"You will limit yourselves to the main floor for the duration of your stay," Devane said.

"The general's wife will be joining him by week's end. Her requirements are quite specific."

"Hang the general's wife!" Devane roared.

Dakota laid a hand against his stubbly cheek. "Darling, you're tired," she said, praying he wouldn't stare at her in openmouthed astonishment. "You can see to this tomorrow."

He started to erupt again, but she increased the pressure on his cheek.

"The matter is not resolved," he said instead to the officer. "We will continue this discussion in the morning."

"As you wish, sir." The young officer bowed deeply from the waist. "But our position will not change."

"Shut up," Dakota whispered in Devane's shell-like ear. "Two guys with really big muskets are standing near the library and they don't look friendly."

She could almost feel the adrenaline flowing through his body as she spoke. The guy really liked a challenge, she had to grant him that.

I could get used to this, she thought as he carried her up the staircase in a major display of machismo. This was Rhett and Scarlett and her big wide smile the morning after. Of course, she didn't exactly have Scarlett's eighteen-inch waist, but she could cop an attitude with the best of them.

"Wait a minute!" she protested. "That's my room you just zoomed past."

"You forget, madam," he said through gritted teeth. "We are on our honeymoon."

"That was your idea, not mine. The soldiers are downstairs. They'll never know the difference."

"You believe that to be true?"

"Absolutely."

"Then you are a fool, madam, and all the more reason to keep a close eye upon your activities."

"My activities are none of your business."

He pushed open the bedroom door with the tip of his boot. "As long as we are husband and wife, they are most definitely my business."

Her pulses leapt. "I think you've lost your mind, Devane. We're strangers."

He kicked the bedroom door shut after them. "That no longer matters."

He strode toward the bed. It was big, wide and too darned inviting.

"Don't even think about it," she warned.

"Trust me, madam." He continued through a side door and into an anteroom that was outfitted as a small bedroom, then deposited her in the middle of the feather mattress. "It is the last thing on my mind."

She scrambled to her knees, sinking into the softness. "If you think I'm sleeping in here with you, you're crazy."

"I will be in my own bed, madam, and of no danger to you."

"I want my own room."

"You cannot have it."

"Then I'll sleep downstairs with Cook."

"Where a score of suspicious soldiers in need of a woman rest, as well."

"Then let me go back to the room you gave me in the first place."

"Most married couples do not sleep in separate rooms."

"But we're not married."

"They believe so."

"Look, I appreciate what you did before, pretending I was your wife and everything, but enough's enough. This joke is getting out of hand."

He gripped her by the shoulders. "You have thrown in your lot with a dangerous man, madam. They will be watching us closely."

"What do you mean, dangerous? I know you're not the friendliest guy in town, but..." Her words trailed off.

"I will spend the night in the main bedroom. Your virtue will remain unassailed, madam."

That's a good *thing,* Dakota reminded herself as he bowed and left her alone.

For a split second she'd been ready to toss reason aside and fling herself at him the way she'd previously only flung herself at Mrs. Fields's chocolate chip cookies, but twenty-six years of caution washed over her like a cold shower, bringing her back to reality.

He was a hunk. That much was a given, assuming you liked them tall, dark and dangerous, which she did. Thank God he found her about as appealing as a kid sister or some other annoying relative you couldn't wait to get rid of.

This wasn't a romantic encounter. She was only using his house as a colonial Motel 6, a place to crash until the snow stopped falling and she could set out to find Shannon and Andrew and the hot-air balloon that had carried them across the centuries.

Nothing about the experience felt right. She couldn't shake that sense of going from a Technicolor world to a black-and-white landscape. Her thoughts were chaotic and one-dimensional, her emotions were out of control, even her skin seemed as if it belonged to someone else. Shannon and Andrew had an eighteenth-century destiny to fulfill. All Dakota had was the feeling that she'd overstayed her welcome.

She'd crammed more excitement into the past twenty-four hours than the law allowed and, while she didn't regret a moment of it, she was ready to go back where she came from, back to the twentieth century with all of its problems. Back to her chaotic but loving family.

Back home where she belonged.

The farm

The evening seemed endless to Emilie. The twins were in a rambunctious mood, not that unusual for a pair of two-year-olds, and she breathed a sigh of relief when she finally got them put down for the night in the trundle bed by the fire.

"I know, I know," she said to Rebekah, who sat in the rocking chair, nursing her newest child. "They will not be two years old forever."

"Nay," said Rebekah, adjusting the light blanket draped across her shoulder, "they will not. By the time they have attained five or six years, you will find yourself longing for these days when they belonged to you and you alone."

Tears burned behind Emilie's eyelids and she made a pretense of yawning. "It has been a long day."

"And 'twill be a longer night," Rebekah said. "I fear I do not rest well when Josiah is away."

"It is the same for me when Zane is away."

She curled up on the hearth rug near her friend and prayed the warmth would seep through to her bones and burn away the terrible sense of dread that had taken hold. "How did you manage, Rebekah?" she asked. "When Josiah was in prison, how on earth did you get through the days?"

The babe in her arms whimpered as Rebekah moved him to her other breast. "I had the children," she said after a long silence. "They gave meaning to my days."

"But the nights," Emilie whispered. "Not knowing where he was or if he was even alive—" She shivered violently and drew her shawl more tightly about her shoulders.

"I always knew," Rebekah said fiercely in a tone of voice Emilie had never before heard her use. "His heart beat within mine, and as long as it did, I knew we still shared the same world as before. The Almighty would not take him before his time."

Emilie arched a brow. "You believe that?"

Rebekah met her eyes. "I believe that."

"Oh, 'Bekah..." Emilie buried her face in her hands. "I'm so scared."

Rebekah murmured soothing words of comfort, much as she would for one of her many children, but Emilie was beyond their reach. Her friend thought she worried about the mission Zane and Josiah were on, but that was the least of it.

I'm afraid it's going to happen again, Rebekah. I'm afraid that bright red balloon is going to swoop down on Zane and he won't be able to resist.

It wasn't as if it hadn't happened before. She and Zane hadn't planned to make their life together in the eighteenth century. They didn't wake up one morning and say, "Hey, we're tired of the old neighborhood. Let's try something around 1776 on for size." The moment she had climbed into the basket of that hot-air balloon and Zane had leapt in after her, their future had rested in the hands of destiny.

And destiny had been kind to them. Theirs was not an easy life, but it was a good one. They had a home of their own, two healthy children and the Blakelees, dear friends with whom to share it all. She thought of Andrew McVie and his longing for the world she'd left behind and wondered if destiny had been as kind to him, as well.

One of the twins sighed softly and Emilie rose to her feet to see if all was well. She touched her lips to her daughter's soft pink cheek, kissed the top of her son's fair head and told herself everything would be all right.

There was nothing dangerous about clouds, not even when they towered overhead like dark and forbidding cliffs. In a few hours the clouds would drift away. Zane would come home and he would climb into bed beside her and her fears would be forgotten.

Chapter Ten

10

Abby woke at first light.

Shivering in the morning chill, she ran to the window, pushed aside the heavy curtains and peered through the heavily frosted glass. She whooped with delight at the splendid sight below.

"Oh, Lucy!" She leapt back into her warm bed and pulled the quilts up to her chin. In her whole life she'd never seen so much snow. "Now we don't have to go to Boston."

The snow was piled higher than the front steps, higher than the bare rosebushes lining the walk. Papa would never send her away in such a terrible storm.

Oh, yes, she thought, burrowing deeper under the covers. She had the feeling it would snow all winter long.

"Don't mind tellin' you I've never seen a storm like this in all my born days." Cook set a bowl of oatmeal in front of Dakota and pushed a pitcher of molasses toward her. "Will said he fair to disappeared in a drift out by the stable this morning. Looks like my sister's girl Molly won't be around here to lend a hand until the thaw."

Dakota stared at the older woman in dismay. "It's stopped, hasn't it? I mean, the storm *is* over."

"Over?" Cook threw back her head and laughed. "Missy, it's like to snow till Christmas."

Dakota tilted the jar of molasses over her oatmeal and watched as a stream of brown goo rained down. "I don't suppose you have any Oreo cookies, do you?"

Cook looked at her, obviously puzzled. "If you give me the recipe, I'd be pleased to make them for you."

Dakota smiled up at the woman. "That's okay. I don't know what made me think of them, anyway." Other than the fact she felt like going on a twelve-day chocolate bender.

"Ahh," said Cook with a wink. "How long will it be?"

Dakota swallowed a spoonful of cereal-flavored molasses and grimaced. "How long will what be?" she asked.

"The baby," said Cook. "The signs are plain as the nose on your face."

Dakota did a spit take Robin Williams would have envied. "Baby? What baby?" *I'm fat, lady, not pregnant!*

"You and the mister." Her round face beamed with delight. "He's a sly fox, he is, keepin' the good news of your wedding from those of us few what care for him."

Dakota suppressed a groan. Word certainly traveled fast around Happy House. "We, um, we were going to make an announcement tonight at dinner but I guess…I suppose—" She looked up at Cook. "How *did* you find out, anyway?"

"Soldiers talk, missy."

"Oh, God." Who would have figured that whey-faced soldier would have such a big mouth?

"Don't be shy with me," Cook admonished. "Joseph and I been married twenty-five years. There's nothing new under the sun to me."

Dakota buried her face in her hands. *Quiet, Cook! Please don't tell me that you and Joseph swing from the chandeliers.*

"Wouldn't have figured you for a shy one, but the world's full of surprises."

"Oh, yes," said Dakota, choking back a laugh. "The world's definitely full of surprises."

"So when is the little one due?"

"I don't...I mean..." She struggled to find the right words.

"There, there." Cook patted her on the shoulder. "An early baby's something to celebrate."

Dakota took a deep breath and plunged ahead. "I'm not with child, Cook."

The woman's face fell. "Don't you be worryin', missy. 'Twill happen before you know it."

No, it won't, Dakota thought. She could travel through time, but she couldn't do the one thing that every woman on earth took for granted. It seemed such a simple thing. A man and woman come together and from their love a child is conceived. Rich or poor, smart or slow. It didn't matter. The miracle was there for the asking.

But not for Dakota.

Each time she thought she had moved beyond the pain, it rose up from deep inside her soul and stole her breath away. Such a small thing to ask from life. And so impossible.

"I hope you wouldn't be holding it against me," Cook was saying. "All that talk about the other missus."

"Of course not," Dakota said, cheeks flaming. "You were only answering my questions."

She pushed her chair back from the table and rose to her feet. Her ankle still throbbed and she wished she had some Advil. She thought about Shannon and the bulging tote bag she'd brought with her on the hot-air balloon and wondered what latter-day miracles she'd managed to pack.

"Have you seen Abigail?" she asked, pushing away thoughts of her friend.

Cook nodded. "She gobbled up her breakfast and went outside to watch the soldiers set up camp."

"We have not told her yet about our...marriage. We think it best to wait until she gets to know me a bit better."

Cook winked at her. "Don't you be waitin' too long, missy. Better she hears it from you and the mister."

Better I throw myself into a snowdrift, Dakota thought as she made her way down the hall toward the library. This was a terrible thing to do to a kid, even one as feisty as Abigail. Her mother was a bolter. Her father was as demonstrative as a hollow log. The best thing that could happen to the kid would be to go off to school and bond with a group of other lonely kids who'd provide the family she needed.

Not that it was any of her business. Abigail could go off and join the circus for all she cared. Devane could declare himself the next king of England. She didn't belong there and she wasn't going to stay one moment longer than necessary.

You didn't feel that way when you thought he was about to kiss you.

"Baloney," she muttered. She knew a business kiss when she got one. He'd been trying to shut her up so she didn't tell the soldiers they really weren't married. Although why he'd told them that in the first place was beyond her. Saving her sorry fanny wasn't his first priority.

Which meant that he had another, more personal reason.

Don't flatter yourself, Wylie. He's just never seen anything quite like you before.

Short-haired, tattooed women weren't exactly a dime a dozen around there. She was bound to make an impression. A pair of lips. An almost-kiss. Just because it had made her downright dizzy with excitement was no reason to think it had rocked his world.

You're an idiot,Wylie. Maybe if she had a few more kisses under her belt and a few less jelly doughnuts she wouldn't find her head turned by the first bad-tempered Colonial landowner to come along.

The hallway was littered with military gear—everything from rolled-up blankets to muskets to dispatch boxes lined her path. Uniformed soldiers with ramrod-straight posture carted firewood and odd pieces of furniture. The beautiful entrance hall had been reduced to an eighteenth-century version of Grand Central Station.

A young soldier nodded at her as she approached the front door. A wicked-looking bayonet rested near him. She noted a slight twitch in his left cheek. He probably didn't like that bayonet any more than she did.

"So," said Dakota, smiling, "is it cold enough for you?"

He didn't so much as blink. "Yes, ma'am."

She sighed. Poor guy didn't get the joke. Give him another couple of hundred years and he'd be as sick of it as she was.

Still smiling, she swung open the door. *I have to get out of here,* she thought as she stepped past the guard. Another bad joke and she'd end up on the business end of one of those bayonets. Maybe Cook had been exaggerating. One woman's blizzard was another woman's flurries. Weather didn't faze her. It would take more than a lousy storm to stop Dakota Wylie.

Still smiling, she stepped out onto the front porch. Her smile quickly faded.

The snow was level with the top step and still falling.

The worst winter of the century was under way.

Patrick swore as he paced the length of the library. The bloody beggars were everywhere. General McDowell's men had taken over the two front rooms, plus the servants' quarters on the first floor, and plans were afoot to build an additional kitchen before the arrival of the general's lady. Cook and Joseph had been forced to move their belongings up to a tiny attic room, while William was once again relegated to the barn. The other servants slept crowded together in the kitchen and pantry.

He had refused to allow the interlopers access to his library or to the room he now shared with Dakota Wylie, but he knew that when the general arrived, the argument would resume.

And then there was the issue of Abigail. Her room afforded a splendid view of the yard and the road beyond it. The general's aide-de-camp had earmarked it for the general's use, but once again Patrick refused to yield. As long as the snow made her departure for Boston impossible, he would not have Abigail banished from her room.

Quite the altruist, Devane. Such concern for the welfare of a child.

The truth was an uncomfortable fit. He wished the child well. He prayed her life would be a long and happy one, but no longer would he allow emotion to determine his fate.

In truth, it served his purpose to allow the child to stay. The child's presence would distract the soldiers from what he was about. There was still much to be accomplished and time was growing short.

Dakota Wylie presented a problem of a different sort. She said she was a widow, who once had disguised herself as a man in order to fight side by side with the man she loved. A noble sentiment, to be sure, and one that would explain the odd manner in which she wore her hair. Torn by grief at her husband's death, routed from her home, she was traveling with friends toward some unknown safe harbor when she was separated from them and thrust into her current circumstances.

He might have believed her story had she not contradicted herself last night upon questioning.

His eye was caught by movement outside the library window. Soldiers, some young enough to be his sons, struggled against the fierce snow and wind as they dragged newly felled trees across the yard. Their uniforms were a pathetic mix of tattered breeches, worn coats and anything else they could find to protect them from the cold. Half went shoeless. The footprints in the snow were tinged red with blood.

All morning he'd heard the muffled thuds of falling trees as the soldiers systematically cut down the finest pines and maples to turn into makeshift shelters while the officers slept peacefully in feather beds. Many of those young men would be dead before the winter was over.

Patrick didn't give a tinker's damn what happened to the fat and happy officers, but he cared a great deal what happened to the young boys and old men they sent into battle.

He turned away from the window and thought again of the woman. Would her heart break at the sight of those hapless young men or did she conspire to send them to their deaths?

"Stop it!" Dakota said as she stared out the front door at the steady fall of snow. "Enough's enough."

She turned at the sound of a childish giggle.

"Think it's funny, do you?" she asked Abigail, who was sitting near the hearth, her bedraggled rag doll firmly in hand. "I'll bet you never had to shovel the stuff."

"Who were you talking to?" Abigail asked, those big eyes of hers wide with curiosity.

"Myself."

Abigail considered her for a moment. "I talk to Lucy."

"Lucy? Who—" She stopped, then nodded. "Your doll?"

Abigail hugged the doll close to her narrow chest. "Mama gave her to me."

Dakota's interest was piqued. It was hard to imagine the kind of woman Devane had been married to.

"Better be careful," she said, crossing the stone floor to where the girl sat. "Her stuffing's coming out."

Abigail shied away from Dakota.

"I'm not going to hurt her. I want to help."

The child gave her a sidelong look that seemed terribly adult coming from someone so young. "Lucy has a hurt shoulder."

"I know," said Dakota. "I think she needs a Band-Aid."

Abby's brow puckered. "A Band-Aid?"

Uh-oh, thought Dakota. *Culture shock.* "She needs to be repaired."

"You can do that?" Abby asked.

"If you find me a needle and thread I can."

"Mama had a sewing kit in her room. I can show you where."

"Sounds good to me." She followed the kid to the back staircase, wondering if she'd lost what was left of her mind. She sewed about as well as she sang coloratura. But, damn it, there was something about the look in the kid's eyes that made her want to help. It felt strangely like a maternal instinct and Dakota didn't like it one bit.

They passed three perfectly uniformed officers in the upstairs hallway. The men stepped aside to make way for them, which seemed a polite enough gesture, but Dakota was aware of their intense scrutiny burning a hole in her back. *Take a good look, fellows,* she thought as Abby pushed open the door to Devane's suite of rooms. *You've seen the future and I'm it.*

Not that they'd believe her. In truth, she didn't totally believe the whole thing herself. She'd half expected to wake up this morning in her lumpy sofa bed with the bad spring, serenaded by her mother's voice floating through the answering machine.

"Mama's sewing box is in here," Abby said, snapping Dakota from her reverie. "She forgot it when she left."

"Smart woman," said Dakota, without thinking. "Why sew if you can buy retail?"

"What's ree-tail?" asked Abby.

"A new kind of cloth," she said after a moment. These cultural references were going to trip her up sooner or later.

Abby nodded as if it all made perfect sense and Dakota felt like the rat that she was.

"I know," said Abby.

Dakota frowned. "Know what?"

"That you feel bad because you're not telling the truth."

Chapter Eleven

11

If Dakota had had dentures, they would have dropped to the floor. "I—I mean, you don't..." She came to a rolling stop. "How did you know?"

The child shrugged her shoulders. "I just did."

Dakota chose her words with care. Her thoughts, however, were beyond her control. "I'm sorry I didn't tell you the truth, Abby. I should have."

"Yes," said Abby solemnly, "but grown people never do. I hear them in my head and I know that."

"Of course you hear them," Dakota said easily. "Most grown people talk too loud."

"No." Abby tapped her temple with a forefinger. "I hear them up here."

"Are their lips moving?" A basic question, but important, given the circumstances.

Abby shook her head. "No, but I hear them anyway."

Oh, God, Dakota thought. Was it possible she and the kid had more in common than gender? "Can you hear me that way?"

Abby considered her for a moment. "Sometimes."

"Can you hear me now?" *Row, row, row your boat…*

"No," said Abby. "I can't hear you at all today."

"So how did you know I wasn't telling the truth?"

"I felt it."

"In your bones," Dakota whispered as a shiver rippled up her spine.

"Yes!" The sorrowful expression in Abby's eyes vanished, replaced by something close to joy. "Way down deep inside."

Dakota had been called crazy, high-strung, a compulsive liar—and that was on the eve of the millennium. She could only imagine how Abby would be treated less than one hundred years after they'd burned witches at the stake in Salem. "Have you told anyone?"

"Mama," she said, her gaze never leaving Dakota's face.

"And what did she say?"

"That I was a wicked girl and I should never talk of such things again."

Considering what she'd heard about Mrs. Devane, it was about what Dakota had expected. "And your papa?"

Abby shook her head. "Not Papa, but I told a governess once and then she screamed and ran away."

"My aunt did that." Impulsively she smoothed the girl's plain brown hair. "Screamed so loud her wig fell off and scared the cat."

Abby giggled. "You hear things, too?"

"Yes," she said. "At least, I used to."

"You don't hear them anymore?"

"Not in a while."

"Why don't you hear them?"

"I don't know, Abby."

"Will I stop hearing them?"

She sighed. "I'm afraid I don't know the answer to that, either."

The child thought about that for a moment. "I know lots of

things," Abigail said, with a kid's leapfrog logic that never failed to disorient Dakota. "I know where Papa hides special treasures."

This is none of your business, Wylie. You'll only end up getting the kid in trouble. Devane seemed to think little enough of his daughter as it was. If he found her leading Dakota on a scavenger hunt, he'd hit the roof. She opted to change the subject.

"Lucy is looking pretty sad," Dakota said, pointing toward the doll clutched in Abby's arms. "I think you should get the sewing basket so I can fix her up."

"Here," said Abby, handing the doll to Dakota. "You hold Lucy."

The doll was as scruffy as her owner, a skinny little thing stuffed with rags and dressed in them, as well. It was painfully obvious that Abby loved the toy, and Dakota wondered if anyone had ever loved Abby half as much.

Abby fixed her with a look. "You're crying."

"No, I'm not."

"Your eyes are red."

"I didn't get much sleep."

"I know that," said Abby. "You and Papa were talking until very late."

Dakota looked toward the window. She was only two floors up. If she jumped, the snow would cushion her fall. "How do you know that?"

"I could hear you."

"Did you really hear us or did you just feel like you heard us?"

"I—"

"Abigail!" Cook's clarion call rang out from the downstairs hallway. "I'm givin' you the count of ten, missy, before I toss your stew to the pigs."

"Cook gave William's supper to the dogs last week," Abby said in a horrified tone of voice as she turned toward the door.

"Wait a minute!" Dakota said. "What about the sewing basket?"

"In there," Abby said, pointing toward a large cherrywood armoire.

She ran from the room in a flutter of pigtails, leaving Dakota alone in Devane's bedroom.

Talk about temptation.

"No," she said out loud. Talking to herself was getting to be a habit. "I don't need to know if he wears boxers or briefs."

No, she didn't *need* to have that bit of information, but that didn't mean she wouldn't give ten IQ points to know the answer. But at least she knew her limitations. If she so much as touched a knob on that armoire she'd be sunk.

What she should do is walk through the adjoining door to her room and lock it after her and forget all about that armoire and whatever secrets he had hidden inside.

What about Lucy? The doll's lucky if it makes it to the end of the week.

"What about her?" she muttered. It's not as if the doll was entered in a beauty pageant. It wouldn't kill Lucy if she waited a while longer for cosmetic surgery.

But think about poor little Abby. Wouldn't she just love to come back and find Lucy as good as new?

Sooner or later Devane was going to pack Abby off to that boarding school in Boston, and the only thing the kid would have to remind her of home was this sorry-looking hunk of rag and wool.

She eyed the armoire. Who said she couldn't open the doors, remove the sewing basket, then close the doors again without taking a peek at whatever else was stowed away in there?

It wasn't exactly a Herculean task.

All it called for was a little self-control. Certainly she could muster up enough to grab a sewing basket.

"Okay," she told herself. "In and out."

She opened the doors and was greeted with an array of drawers and cubbyholes that reminded her of a rabbit warren. The first drawer she tried was empty. So was the second one and the third. And the fourth. Every single drawer was empty.

What on earth was with the man? Didn't he believe in personal possessions?

She peered inside the cubbyholes at eye level and below, then reached up and stuck her hand into the cubbyhole on the upper right-hand side. The flimsy interior of the armoire surprised her. She'd always believed shoddy construction was a product of the age of indifference.

Her fingers closed around a cold piece of metal that felt like a drawer pull or latch of some kind. She tugged, but met with considerable resistance. Curious, she raised up on tiptoe, changed her grip and—

"What in bloody hell do you think you're doing?"

Devane! Her heart almost burst through her chest. "Don't you know better than to sneak up on people? You almost gave me a heart attack!" She sounded amazingly defiant, considering the fact she was up to her guilty elbows in his stuff.

She withdrew her hand from the cubbyhole, then pointed toward the rag doll resting on the foot of his bed. "I'm looking for the sewing basket. Lucy needs some repair work."

"Take care what you say, madam. You are not speaking to a fool."

She marched toward the bed and grabbed the rag doll. "Look for yourself. Her head's falling off, her shoulder's ripped."

"And how is this your concern?"

"It isn't," she retorted, "but it should be your concern. This doll is your daughter's favorite thing in the entire world and it's falling apart."

"You are a seamstress then, madam?"

"No, I'm not a seamstress, you—" She stopped. Calling him a supercilious jerk didn't seem a wise thing to do.

"Finish your sentence," he ordered, arms folded across his muscular chest. "I am sure I have been called worse."

"Don't bet on it."

The wench had a marked affinity for danger.

Patrick wondered how it was she had managed to live so long.

The last time he had encountered such ferocity, his opponent had topped six feet in height and carried a loaded musket. In truth, he considered himself lucky that Mistress Dakota did not have access to arms, for he had no doubt she would use them against his person.

He met her fury with anger of his own.

"Explain yourself, madam, if you can."

"I did explain myself." Her words were clipped. "Perhaps if you paid more attention to your daughter and less to yourself, you'd understand how important Lucy is to her."

"The child is no concern of yours."

"And apparently she is no concern of yours, either."

"Tread softly, madam, for you are on dangerous ground."

She poked him in the chest with a beringed forefinger. "I don't care what you think of me, Mr. Devane. I'm going to be out of your life as soon as the snow stops. But Abigail is your child and you owe her better than this."

"Abigail is not—" He stopped. What was it about the woman that brought his emotions so quickly to the surface?

Her gaze never left his and he had the unsettling feeling that she saw into his black soul.

Still, there was something strangely appealing about the woman who stood before him, prepared to do battle. Her soft dark eyes were lit from within, burning with the fires of righteous anger. She was a woman of passion, this short-haired wench with the sharp tongue and quick wit. A man would be well-served to have such a partner at his side.

Susannah had cared for little but her own immediate pleasures. French perfumes. Fancy dresses made of satin and lace. Endless hours spent primping before the glass in her dressing room. The sweetness of her disposition had been directly related to the number of compliments he saw fit to bestow upon her. The thought of the beauteous Susannah trudging through mud and snow to follow him into battle was as laughable as it was unlikely—for many reasons.

He had oft heard stories of women whose courage matched or surpassed the courage of men in Continental uniform. Women who donned masculine garb and followed their beloveds into the fray. Until this moment he had not believed such a woman existed.

There was much about Dakota Wylie to make him believe.

She had known Abigail for less than twenty-four hours, and already she'd risked his considerable wrath in defense of the child. Abigail's own mother had not seen fit to do that.

An elaborate ruse, a voice inside him cautioned. *She seeks to insinuate herself into your household for her own nefarious purposes.*

Her story had been rife with inconsistency. At one point she had seemed to forget the very husband she'd claimed to have loved and lost. Yet the one thing that never varied was her desire to find her friends—and the passionate determination with which she said it.

Her arrival was well-timed, the voice continued. *She appeared with the storm that keeps her captive in your home.*

A coincidence or the carefully laid plan of a woman more cunning than any he had ever known?

Grimly, he determined to uncover the truth.

"Don't you dare walk out on me!" Dakota snapped as the louse turned away.

If that arrogant stinker actually thought they were through talking, he had another think coming. She hadn't traveled two hundred years to be insulted by a man who didn't even know the name of his daughter's favorite doll.

He continued toward the door with the stride of a man who knew what he was about. The nerve of him. She might not be a raving beauty who brought men to their feet, but she was a human being and she deserved at least a modicum of respect.

"Devane! You can't leave before I—"

"Once again you speak too soon, madam." He slammed shut the door to the bedroom, then turned back toward her.

Life as she knew it ground to a sudden stop. "Wh-what do you think you're doing?"

"I am doing as you ordered me to do, madam." He strode toward her, all menace and—to her dismay—devastating sensuality.

"You haven't heard a word I've said."

"I have heard all of the words, Dakota Wylie, and the time has come for silence."

"I don't believe in silence," she said as pulse points sprang to life all over her body. "Silence is vastly overrated."

"And how would you know that, madam, when you practice it so rarely?"

"I'm a talker," she agreed, taking a step back. "Talking's good. Talking bonds people together."

He moved closer still. "There are other ways to bind a man and woman together."

"What?" She tried to take another step backward but found herself pressed up against his bed.

The expression in his eyes was nothing short of dangerous. "You play the innocent," he observed. "An interesting diversion, but unnecessary given the circumstances."

She scrambled onto the mattress and scooted toward the other side. "I'm in mourning," she reminded him.

"Are you, madam?"

"Of course I am." She summoned up a suitably mournful expression. "I would appreciate it if you left me alone now."

He arched a dark brow. "Moments ago you wished me to remain."

"I've changed my mind," she said. "Feel free to go."

"Your company intrigues me. I choose to stay."

"I want to be alone." It had worked for Greta Garbo. Too bad she didn't have as much success. She reached the other side of the mattress, only to find herself wedged between the bed and the window.

He rounded the foot of the bed. "A husband should know certain things about his wife."

"I'm not your wife." Talk about stating the obvious.

"To the soldiers you are."

"Fine," she said. "I'll remember to look subservient when I'm downstairs."

"Your late husband," he said, moving closer. "Did he find your sharp tongue an obstacle to happiness?"

"My husband loved me as I am." Or he would have if she'd ever managed to find herself one.

"And how long were you married to this patient man?"

"Your own tongue is sharp as well, Mr. Devane."

"You have not answered my question."

"My marriage is none of your business." Her back was pressed against icy-cold panes of window glass. Talk about a metaphor.

"*You,* madam, are my business."

Not in this lifetime, she thought. "Don't be absurd. As soon as the snow stops, I'll be out of your hair."

"You have an unusual manner of speaking, but your meaning is clear."

"Good," she said. "Then we have no problem."

"No problem at all," he said smoothly. "You will leave when I say it is time for you to leave and not before."

"Excuse me, but you don't have any rights over me."

"This is my house. That gives me the right."

"No wonder you hate those soldiers downstairs," she snapped. "If they win the war, you won't be able to pretend you're king anymore."

"A man will always be king in his own house."

She choked back her laughter. "Oh, Mr. Devane, how I wish I could see your face when you find out."

"Explain your meaning, madam."

Once again she'd taken things a step too far. Women's liberation was still a long way off— "I'm tired," she announced with as much haughty disdain as she could manage. "I wish to rest."

His gaze drifted toward the bed. "Your idea has much to recommend it."

She watched, astonished, as he stretched out across the bed, his huge leather boots stark against the embroidered spread, and patted the spot next to him. She had a quick vision of herself arranged amid the bedcovers, looking all soft and feminine and artfully backlit, while he dropped to his knees in speechless adoration.

"Join me, madam. This is a most comfortable bed. You will rest easy here."

"I'd rest easier on a bed of nails," she muttered.

"You are alone," he continued, "as am I. We should take our comfort where we can."

This isn't funny, Devane. I'm not a charity case. Unexpected tears burned behind her lids and she prayed she wouldn't start to cry. Crying would show him she was vulnerable, and that was the last thing she wanted him to know. "I will find all the comfort I desire when I rejoin my friends."

"These friends of yours," he said slowly, arms crossed behind his head. "Could it be they do not exist?"

"Believe what you will," she managed to say with as much dignity as she could muster. "It is of no concern to me."

He met her eyes. "A man and woman were found dead this morning," he said in a tone of voice much softer than any he had used before.

The room began to spin and she clutched the bedpost for support.

"They were near to Morristown," he said, watching her closely. "A man of some two score and ten and a woman of the same years. Are they the pair for whom you search?"

She lowered her head as a powerful wave of relief rocked through her body. "They are not my friends," she said after a moment, "but I thank you for the information."

He inclined his head, an absurdly formal response from a man stretched out on a feather mattress like a *Playgirl* centerfold. A few less-than-innocent fantasies played themselves out as heat gathered inside her chest. She was shocked that desire was so close to the surface.

"Abigail is waiting for me to repair Lucy," Dakota said, aware that she was suddenly babbling like a fool. "She must be wondering what is taking me so long."

"Cook called the child to her midday meal."

"Unless it's a ten-course feast, she must be finished by now." His eyes narrowed, and instantly she regretted her flip tone and sharp-edged words. If she ever made it back to her own time, she was going to write a handbook on how to hook a man, and the first rule would be "Smart-mouthed dames need not apply."

She started toward the door as fast as her dainty size eights would carry her.

Before she knew what he was about, Patrick reached out and encircled her narrow wrist with his fingers. Again he was struck by the softness of her skin, and he willed himself to ignore the perfumed sweetness that rose up from her person to ensnare him. He had known women far more beautiful than this odd, dark-tressed creature, but something about the woman reached deep into his black soul and touched his heart in a way he did not understand and, most assuredly, did not want.

She met his eyes. Another woman would have recognized the moment and used her feminine charms to dissuade him from his purpose. At the very least, he would have seen a spark of recognition that they were a man and a woman alone together with all the possibilities such a combination entailed.

Not Dakota Wylie. He saw fear in the ebony depths of her eyes, and he saw something else, as well: a strength of character—a sense of resolve—that he had believed to be solely the province of men. For a moment he hesitated. He had lived so long amidst liars that perhaps he had lost the ability to recognize truth when he heard it spoken. Was it possible she was indeed the grieving widow of her story, a good wife with a heart that yearned for the husband she had lost to the capricious whims of fate?

Or had he finally lost his mind?

Chapter Twelve

12

They said position in life was everything, and for the first time in her life Dakota agreed. The world looked entirely different from her position underneath Patrick Devane.

One minute she'd been striding toward the door, Lucy in her hand, and the next she was on the feather bed and Lucy was lying near the door. It occurred to her that maybe she should have put up some kind of struggle, that surrender really wasn't a viable option for a twentieth-century woman, not even one who'd found herself living and breathing in 1779. She was smart enough to know better, but there was something deeply pleasurable about the idea, something dark and dangerous and so compelling that twenty-six years of independent thought were in danger of going up in a haze of erotic smoke.

He cupped her face in his hands. "How long has it been, Dakota Wylie, since a man held you like this?"

All my life, she thought. No one had ever looked at her with such intensity before, as if he could see her heart beating beneath her skin. Drawing in a breath became a supreme act of will.

He stroked her cheek with the pad of his thumb. His fingers

were callused from riding. The roughened skin sent a thrill of excitement rippling up her spine and she shivered involuntarily. She met his eyes but could read nothing in his expression.

"Don't," she whispered, sounding painfully vulnerable to her own ears. She heard the loneliness beneath the words, the aching need, and she closed her eyes, praying he wouldn't know the effect his touch was having upon her.

"Be still," he said, spreading his hands along the base of her throat, her collarbones. "You are a woman. You need the touch of a man."

Inflammatory sexist claptrap, she thought, but sadly—painfully—true. His touch made her feel dizzy, as if she'd climbed to the top of the tallest tree and was falling, falling through sweet green leaves.

"Beautiful eyes," he murmured, caressing her shoulders, her upper arms. "I have never seen a color such as that before."

"It's called brown," she said, trying to remember that this wasn't real. He wasn't her friend and he wasn't her lover. He wasn't anything to her but the man who stood between her and the world she'd left behind. If she believed it was real for even a moment, she would be lost.

"Midnight black," he said. "Dark as ebony."

"Ebony?" She had to be dreaming. Didn't he know she wasn't the kind of woman a man whispered insincere compliments to?

"It is as if you hear the words for the first time," he mused, cupping her elbows in a way that was illegal, or should be. "Your husband must have told you these things."

She struggled to remember her fictional husband, old what's-his-name. "H-he was a man of few words."

Those few words had barely escaped her lips when he lowered his head, bringing his mouth closer to hers, then closer still. He had a beautiful mouth, full and perfectly formed. She couldn't believe that mouth was only inches away from hers.

"No more words," he said, eyes glittering dangerously.

"But—"

He claimed her mouth as if she'd given him the right, as if everything that had ever happened in her life had given him that right. His touch was gentle at first, his lips moving against hers with a subtle, coaxing motion that weakened what remained of her defenses. She exhaled on a long sigh and as her lips parted, he deepened the kiss.

Nothing mattered but the feel of his mouth on hers. He tasted of oranges and cherry tobacco and some sweet, sweet narcotic that was slipping into her bloodstream in a flood of heat, making her forget how she had come to be there in his arms.

She yielded to him with an eagerness that was almost his undoing. He grew hard and he made no attempt to disguise the desire he felt for her. Everything about her person pleased him. Her soft skin. The scent of flowers that surrounded her. The gentle curves of her woman's body as she lay beneath him. He could imagine her naked, skin gleaming in the firelight, as she welcomed him into the haven of her arms.

Were she not a liar and a spy sent to thwart his cause, he might have pressed his advantage, but Patrick Devane had had enough prevarication to last him his lifetime. He had made a costly mistake with Susannah. He would not make another one now when there was so much to lose.

"The grieving widow," he murmured, breaking the kiss. "I think it is not for your husband that you grieve, madam. I think it is for your freedom."

Her ebony eyes fluttered open and she met his gaze with a forthrightness that once again surprised him. "I—I don't know what you're talking about."

He kissed her again, hard and long, and she arched against him.

"That is not the response of a good wife who mourns the passing of her husband."

"You know nothing of my response," she snapped in a voice of surprising vigor. "A man who must entrap a woman for his own amusement is not one to judge the quality of a kiss."

Had he imagined the heat of her response? There was nothing of the supplicant in either her voice or manner.

Irritated, he gathered her wrists in one hand and pinned them over her head. He placed his other hand at her throat where her pulse beat heavily against his palm.

"There is no dead husband, is there, *Mistress* Wylie? No beloved companions whose loss you mourn."

"I have told you my intentions," she said, neither flinching nor looking away. "As soon as the storm ends, I will be on my way to find my friends."

"And I will find the truth," he warned, his grip on her wrists tightening. "Better to unburden yourself now than to risk my anger later on."

"How courageous," she said, her tone heavy with irony. "You threaten a *mere* woman but refuse to take up arms against the enemy." Her eyes narrowed as she looked ever deeper into his soul. "Or is it that you're having trouble deciding which side you're on?"

So that's *a glower,* Dakota thought as his expression darkened. She'd always wanted to see one somewhere besides a comic strip. The man had a quicksilver temper. Sooner or later he was going to explode like Mount St. Helens, and she didn't want to be around when it happened.

He straddled her, knees pressing against her hips. She wondered if he'd believe she padded her petticoats the same way she boosted her bodice. She didn't know whether to laugh or cry. To think she'd believed for even one second that they had some chemistry going between them. He was about as attracted to her as she was to "Beavis and Butthead," and it was time she remembered that.

"Get off me!" she ordered.

"Tell me the names of the friends for whom you search and I'll do as you ask."

"I already told you their names."

"I grow forgetful. Tell me again."

She could do what she did the last time, toss out the names Ronald and Nancy Reagan and be done with it, but she no longer felt either flip or funny. Andrew and Shannon were out there somewhere in that storm and she knew if she didn't find them soon, she'd be trapped there forever.

She could be walking straight into the jaws of a trap, but it was a risk she had to take.

"Whitney," she said after a moment. "Shannon Whitney."

"'Tis an odd name."

Not where I come from. "She is traveling with a man named Andrew." If Devane's dubious loyalties lay with the British, betraying Andrew McVie's identity could compromise his safety, and Shannon's, as well. "I do not know his family name."

"He is your friend and yet you do not know his full name?"

"Shannon is my friend. Andrew is her companion." She struggled for the properly archaic way to express herself. "I have only recently made his acquaintanceship."

"Andrew." He seemed thoughtful, almost pensive. "No," he said, more to himself than to her. "It is not possible."

"What is not possible?" she asked, almost afraid to hear the answer.

He parried with a question of his own. "This Andrew you speak of—what is his association with Shannon Whitney?"

"They're lovers, not that it's any of your business."

To her amazement, his cheeks reddened and she was reminded

once again of the differences between her world and his. *So you're human after all,* she thought. Who would have imagined a man like Patrick Devane had sensibilities? Her innocent words must have sounded shockingly blunt to him, and she couldn't quite hide her smile.

"You find humor in the situation?" he asked.

"Yes," she said, meeting his eyes. "I'm afraid I do."

Their gazes held while the room did a slow fade until there was nothing but the big feather bed and the ragged sound of their breathing.

"You are a puzzle to me, madam. I know beyond doubt that you weave a fabric of lies, but still I find myself unable to determine clearly if you are friend or foe."

"I am neither," she said, her voice husky. She tried to ignore the way his big strong body felt covering hers. "I'm nothing to you at all. Once I leave here, you'll never see me again."

His expression softened and he touched her cheek in a spontaneous gesture unlike the calculated kisses and caresses of moments ago. She felt as if he'd somehow reached into her heart and discovered a place no one knew existed, the secret place where she kept her dreams. His hold on her wrists loosened, until it was more caress than bondage and she wondered if—

"Papa, is it true?" Abigail's voice shattered the spell.

They both jumped, startled to find the little girl standing in the open doorway with a tattered Lucy clutched to her chest. Her eyes were huge in her narrow face as she stared at the sight of her father and Dakota entwined on the feather bed.

Devane rose easily from the bed as if his daughter found him lying on top of a woman every day of the week. No doubt about it, the man was one cool customer. Dakota, on the other hand, felt as if she'd been caught swinging naked from a chandelier. She couldn't have felt guiltier if they'd actually been doing something—

which they hadn't been, but that fact somehow seemed beside the point.

She sat up and tugged at the bodice of her gown, praying the rolled-up sleeves of her dinosaur T-shirt didn't choose that moment to make an appearance. That would really put a lid on what was turning out to be the weirdest day of her life.

Devane stood in front of his daughter. His back was ramrod straight, in marked contrast to the rumpled look of his shirt and waistcoat.

"How long have you been standing there, Abigail?" he asked the child.

If Dakota hadn't known better, she'd have thought he was talking to a stranger rather than his own flesh and blood.

"I saw you kissing her," Abigail said with the alarming directness most kids lost around puberty. The child approached the bed where Dakota sat with her feet on the floor and her hands primly folded on her lap. "Cook says you're my new mama."

Dakota felt as if she'd been hit in the stomach with a two-by-four. She looked toward Devane, whose face had gone ashen. His spur-of-the-moment statement to the young soldier had come back to haunt them both. Why hadn't Devane realized the impact it would have upon his daughter?

"You can answer this one," she said to him, thankful for the opportunity to pass the buck.

"Did Cook say anything else to you, Abigail?" he asked in that same maddeningly bland tone of voice.

"She said it was time that a woman warmed your bed. But I told her grandmama's quilt was in the—"

"Oh, God..." Dakota sank back onto the mattress and wished she could disappear beneath the covers.

Abigail's steady gaze pierced her heart. "Is that why you and Papa were lying here together, to warm the bed?"

Dakota could count on the fingers of one hand the times she'd been struck speechless. The glib remarks that usually flowed from her lips like mineral water at a trendy restaurant dried up and disappeared. She wasn't given to saccharine displays of affection toward children, but there was something about the little girl that inspired the oddest emotions. She didn't particularly like kids, but she wanted to gather this one into her arms and make her smile. Go figure.

Abigail climbed up onto the bed and looked Dakota in the eye. "Tell me!" she demanded in her childish voice. "Are you my new mama?"

Dakota met Devane's eyes. The warm fire she'd noticed before in their indigo depths had been extinguished. His expression was as cold as the bitter winter winds that rattled the windows and whistled down the chimneys.

What do I do? she pleaded silently. *How can we lie to her about this?*

He nodded curtly, a quick dip of the head, and her heart sank. He actually expected her to say something to Abigail. But what?

She tried to speak but the words wouldn't come. They were trapped behind a wall of regret so high and wide she wondered if she would ever be able to break through.

She cleared her throat, praying that whatever she said wouldn't hurt the child any more than life had already hurt her.

"Your papa and I—"

"Yes," Devane broke in, reaching for Dakota's hand and clasping it in his. "Dakota is your new mother." He paused, meeting Dakota's eyes with a glance that warned her not to disagree.

Abigail's light brown brows slanted toward the bridge of her tiny nose.

Smart kid, thought Dakota, squirming beneath the weight of the child's scrutiny. *I wouldn't believe this bilge water, either.*

The child spoke up again. "Cook says she'll make a wedding dinner or know the reason why."

"No!" Dakota suddenly found her voice. Both Devane and his daughter looked at her in surprise. No wonder. She probably sounded as horrified as she felt. "These are difficult times," she explained swiftly. "Certainly a big party would not be proper in light of the hardships we are all facing from the enemy."

Abigail's braids bobbed as she shook her head vigorously. "Cook says all the best houses have parties." She lowered her voice to a mock whisper. "Cook says it will be scand'lous if you do not."

"Maybe Cook should mind her own business," Dakota muttered sourly. "This place is worse than 'Knots Landing.'"

Patrick's attention was snared by her words. Knots Landing. He wondered if that was near to Philadelphia. It was the first true nugget of information Dakota had provided for him, although he was certain she did not realize he had heard her words. He would peruse his maps of the colonies later on and see if he could find the town.

"Go downstairs, Abigail," he said, dismissing the child.

"No." Her lower lip protruded much as Susannah's had when she didn't get her way.

"You will do as I say."

"I want to stay here." A dangerous glint flickered in her eyes, as if a storm were gathering in the gray depths.

"Abigail, you will—"

Dakota reached for the child's hand. "Why don't you go downstairs and ask Cook for needle and thread," she suggested in an even tone of voice. "I have figured out the perfect way to repair Lucy and I can't find your mama's sewing basket anywhere."

"But I told you where it is," Abigail protested. "In Papa's cabinet."

Dakota shot him a fierce look of triumph. "I looked where you told me to look, Abby, but it wasn't there."

"It is!" Abigail started toward the chest of drawers, but Patrick placed a hand on the child's fragile shoulder.

"Go downstairs," he said, aware of Dakota's steady gaze upon him. "I will find the bloody sewing basket myself."

Still the child stood there, tiny feet planted like the roots of an oak tree. *I was stubborn like that once, as well,* he mused, then banished the thought for the foolishness it was.

Dakota turned from him and spoke to the child. Abigail nodded, then, with nary a look in his direction, ran from the room.

"Children respond to kindness," Dakota said. "It's probably an alien concept to you, but you might want to try it some time."

"Refrain from giving advice on child-rearing, madam," he said, "until you have attempted such yourself."

Her cheeks reddened at his words. "I don't need to be a parent to know what a child needs to be happy."

"And where did you acquire such profound knowledge?"

"I have a brain." Her implication was quite clear.

"Speak your mind, madam," he invited dryly. "Do you mean to say I lack the same?"

"No," she said, "you have a brain. What you don't have is a heart."

"And upon what do you base your observations," he asked, "when you have known me less than one full day?"

"Have you looked at your daughter's face?" she asked, her anger a third presence in the room. "She adores you and you cannot give her the time of day."

"She is well cared for," he said, wondering why he found it necessary to explain himself to a stranger. "When the storm ends, she will leave for Boston—"

"Where she will be somebody else's problem."

"Where she will receive an education."

"You can lie to me all you want, Mr. Devane—I really don't give a damn—but don't lie to yourself. You're too smart for that and she's too important."

He grabbed her by the shoulders and pulled her up until she was kneeling on the soft feather mattress. She used the language of a man to make her point, with little regard either for his sensibilities or her own. It should not have excited him—but it did.

"What business is it of yours, madam?" he demanded, his fingers pressing deep into the soft flesh of her shoulders. "What care you if I love the child or curse her existence, so long as she is not ill-used?"

Tears pooled in her dark eyes, then spilled down her smooth cheeks. "She loves you so. Doesn't that matter to you?"

"No," he said, remembering how it had been in the days before he'd learned the truth of the child's paternity. "It no longer matters at all."

Chapter Thirteen

13

"What a terrible—" Dakota stopped in midsentence as the vision rose up before her, clear as the view outside the window.

The room was in shadows. Muslin curtains had been drawn across the wide, leaded-glass windows, but the faintest rays of dawn were beginning to seep through the loosely woven material. From the kitchen came the spicy, sweet smell of apples cooking for breakfast. The pine cradle rested next to the big feather bed, piled high with quilts and knitted coverlets in soft whites and blues.

Inside the cradle the baby slept, her eyes pressed tightly closed against the coming of morn. She had a thick head of silky light brown hair and fingers that were surprisingly long and graceful for someone less than one month old.

But it was the man who drew Dakota's eye. He was bent over the cradle, his tall, strong form looking absurdly masculine in the gentle room as he looked down upon the sleeping child.

How he loved her!

Emotion flooded the darkest corners of his heart with golden light. He would fight lions with his bare hands to keep her safe from harm. Lasso the stars and hang them from the ceiling to make her laugh.

She was every good thing he'd ever done, every dream he'd ever dreamed but didn't believe would come true. She was his miracle.

She was his daughter....

Dakota opened her eyes and found herself cradled against Devane's strong chest. He was looking down at her, an expression of concern on his normally unreadable face.

She felt disoriented and strangely sad, as if she'd awakened from a dream she couldn't quite remember. "Wh-what happened?" she asked, pushing away from him as she struggled to regain her composure.

"I hoped you would tell me, madam."

"I didn't faint, did I?" She'd fainted all the time around Andrew McVie; his force field had been that strong.

"You swooned," he said in a careful voice. "Is that a common occurrence?"

She snapped her fingers in a nonchalant gesture that was at odds with the turbulent emotions raging inside her chest. "I do it all the time."

"There is no cause for alarm?"

"Not the slightest."

"You are not with child?"

She almost choked on her own saliva. "Absolutely not!"

He arched a brow. "You are a married woman," he noted.

"I'm a widow," she corrected him.

"Mayhap your stays are too tightly laced."

"Mayhap you should mind your own business." She glared at him. "Are you implying that I'm fat?" she asked, paranoid to the end.

"I did not say those words."

"Maybe not, but you thought them."

A damnable twinkle appeared in his deep blue eyes. "And you are privy to my innermost thoughts, madam?"

"Wouldn't you love to know," she muttered darkly.

"Is it so unusual for a lady to overzealously tighten her stays in the interest of vanity?"

She hesitated, once again reminded how different this world was from the one where she belonged. Back home they did it with Lycra spandex and step aerobics.

"Strange, madam." He moved closer to her. "There are times it seems as if you see the world for the first time."

"It's part of my charm."

"I had not thought of it thusly."

She gathered the tatters of her dignity around her and stood. "This interlude has been charming, Mr. Devane, but I'm afraid it's time I went back downstairs to help Abigail repair her doll."

"You are a kind and generous woman."

"Yes," she said, favoring him with a quick smile. "I'm glad you noticed."

His dark-eyed gaze swept over her body, igniting small fires everywhere it lingered...and a few places where it didn't. "There are other things I have noticed, as well."

"Your daughter isn't one of them." The words were out before she could stop them.

"Confine yourself to mending, madam. I will care for the child."

"Did you hear what Abby said?" Dakota demanded, meeting his eyes. She hadn't intended to broach the topic, but now that she had there was no stopping her. "The whole town is talking about us and I haven't even been here a full day."

"Amazing," he said dryly. "I would have ventured it had been much longer."

"Insult me all you want," she said, stung by his words, "but that doesn't change things. You've put your daughter in the middle of a mess and I want to know what you're going to do about it."

She didn't give a damn for herself—as soon as she found Andrew and Shannon and the hot-air balloon she would be on her way home again—but for some reason she cared greatly for Abigail. There were few enough ways in which a girl could make her mark in the eighteenth century. She didn't want scandal to be the way that was thrust upon Abby.

"'Tis of little consequence," Devane said in a voice that betrayed nothing of what he was feeling. "I have seen most of the Commandments broken by the good people of Franklin Ridge. Their opinions carry no weight in this house."

"Apparently they carry a great deal of weight with some people in this house."

"Cook has a marked affinity for the grape," Devane said, dismissing her concerns. "She speaks when she should be tending her fires."

"And she speaks to your daughter," Dakota snapped. "This ridiculous charade has gone entirely too far. If you don't tell her we're really not married, so help me, I'll do it myself."

"Do so, madam, and I will see to it you spend this night in jail."

"For telling the truth?"

"For being a spy."

Her breath left her body in a sibilant whoosh. "You're joking, aren't you?" she demanded when she could breathe again. "Me? A *spy?*" A bark of hysterical laughter echoed in the high-ceilinged room. "I'm the one who didn't even know what town she was in."

"A clever ruse," he said. "Like the sorrowful story of your widowhood."

"You're a cruel man," she observed, "delighting in the misfortunes of others."

"And you, madam, are a liar."

Patrick watched as she swept from the room as quickly as her full skirts would allow. It was obvious she wished to put as much distance as possible between them, and he was relieved.

The wench was willful, argumentative and ungrateful, and still she had managed to awaken inside his breast emotions he had thought long dead. He had believed himself long past tenderness and compassion but when she had lain unconscious in his arms he had experienced a surge of fear that lingered with him still.

Why he should care about the well-being of a woman he had known for less than twenty-four hours was a question for which he had no answer, and he vowed to waste no time pondering such things. He was a man and it had been a long time since he had held a woman close. That was reason enough.

The child, however, was another matter. Dakota Wylie was right to be concerned for Abigail's standing in the town. He did not love her for she was not his own and never could be, but he understood the ways in which scandal could mark her future, and he wished better for the chit.

She was the only true innocent in the whole unfortunate matter of his marriage to Susannah. Even if he could not find it in his heart to love her, he owed Abigail a future of promise as befitted a man of his position, which was all the more reason to see to it she reached the Girls' School of the Sacred Heart as soon as possible.

He had little respect for the convenient morals of the good people of Franklin Ridge.

How they loved to cluck their tongues in righteous disapproval over an eight months' baby...or the affairs of a wayward wife. He had suffered the smug glances dripping with amusement and pity and vowed that the opinion of others would never matter to him again.

But her opinion matters, a voice inside his head mocked. *You desire her approval more than is wise.*

The thought was laughable. Patrick Devane didn't give a damn about anyone's approval. Certainly not the approval of a woman whose lies were as blatant and poorly conceived as Dakota Wylie's. Each time he pressed her for the details of her situation, she grew flustered, then angry, and the centerpiece of her story shifted position like a willow tree in a windstorm.

Why that should endear her to him was a question Patrick did not wish to pursue. He had no patience with liars and no faith in women and she was both. Yet each time he looked into her onyx black eyes he felt something deep inside his soul stir with recognition, as if he had been searching for her his whole life long.

Damn nonsense, he thought as he caught the faintest scent of her perfume in the air. He wanted naught from her save answers to his questions. The mythical dead husband. The friends she longed to find. Where in bloody hell Knots Landing was situated and why the women of that town had strange names like Dakota and Shannon—

Andrew.

His gut tightened. She had said one of her companions' names was Andrew and that she did not know his surname.

Some say 'twas Andrew McVie dangling from the basket of the bright red ball in the sky....

And all of this had happened on the day he found Dakota Wylie under a pile of leaves.

"Damn nonsense," he said again as his heartbeat accelerated. McVie was dead. Why else would the risk-taking patriot have vanished so completely? Besides, the notion of a basket propelled through the air by a huge red ball was too laughable to countenance. There had been rumors of such monstrosities being constructed by the French, but all such attempts had ended in disaster.

Still, the coincidence of events made him uneasy and he vowed to keep a sharp eye upon Dakota Wylie while she was under his roof.

Which should be an easy task, since she was living there as his wife.

As the afternoon wore on, Dakota had the distinct feeling that time as she knew it had slowed and she was living many lifetimes in the space of a day. It was an odd feeling, as if time were trying to help her grow accustomed to her new way of life. She found herself acutely aware of her surroundings, senses heightened to the point of pain, as she drank in the details of eighteenth-century daily living.

And the fact that Abby thought she was her new mother.

They sat together near the fireplace in the front room while Dakota struggled with needle and floss. It had taken her a full five minutes to thread the damn needle. She wondered if they had a colonial Lenscrafter nearby. At the moment poor Lucy's chances for a full recovery were looking as grim as any guest-wife for the Cartwright boys on "Bonanza" reruns.

Great analogy, she thought, stabbing the doll's innards with the needle. Too bad there wasn't anyone around who'd know what she was talking about.

"Do you love Papa?" Abigail asked out of the blue.

Dakota stabbed her finger with the needle. A tiny drop of blood pooled on the tip and she popped it into her mouth. "What a question!" she said, forcing a small chuckle.

"Yesterday in the woods you didn't like him at all."

"Well," said Dakota slowly, "things have a way of changing, don't they?"

"I thought Papa lied when he told the soldiers we were a family."

Dakota swallowed hard. "I—I do not think he meant to share that fact with them, but the circumstances were such that—"

"Did you know I was your daughter when you first saw me?" the child interrupted, eager to move on to a more important topic.

Her heart lurched. She blamed it on major jet lag. "No, Abby, I didn't."

"You didn't like me."

"I didn't know you."

"I didn't like you."

Dakota grinned. She couldn't help it. The kid was so damned honest it was either grin or throttle her. "I didn't much like you, either," she admitted.

Abby nodded solemnly. "I know. You thought I was plain."

"I never said—" She stopped, cheeks turning red with embarrassment. "You heard it in here, didn't you?" she asked, placing her hand over her heart.

"Yes," said Abby. "And you thought Papa was going to kill you."

"He was very angry."

"Why would you be afraid of Papa if he was your husband?"

The kid would be a whiz at Twenty Questions. "Because even married people have arguments."

Abby considered her statement with all the gravity it deserved. "Papa doesn't like you."

"We had a disagreement," Dakota went on, stung by the innocent words. "It will end soon." *Like the moment I walk out the door.*

"You can't walk out the door," Abby said in a prim and singsong voice. "'Tis snowing harder even than before. Papa won't be able to send me to Boston for a very long time."

The child looked smug and proud of herself, as if she had called down the storm to suit her own needs. Who knows? Dakota thought. Maybe she had. Anything seemed possible.

She carefully placed two stitches along Lucy's right underarm seam. She couldn't control her thoughts, but she could control what came out of her mouth. It occurred to her that this was as good a time as any to begin laying the groundwork for the dissolution of her faux marriage.

"You know, Abby," she began as she tied off the end of the floss, "sometimes a marriage does not last forever."

"Mama and Papa were going to get a divorce," the child said sagely, "but Mama died."

Dakota couldn't hide her surprise. She was sorry the little girl knew so much. "Sometimes men and women believe they can live together but find it to be much harder than they thought."

"Reverend Wilcox says marriages are made in heaven and that God says they are forever."

Dakota thought of a number of things to say but they were all too blasphemous for the child's ears. She settled for a simple, "Nothing is forever, honey."

"You are," said the child. "You and Papa will be together forever and ever."

She's right, Dakota. Her mother Ginny's voice seemed to fill her chest with sound. *You finally met Mr. Right.*

Dakota almost laughed out loud. They had nothing in common, not even the century in which they lived. This place, this man's house wasn't where she was meant to be. It was no more than the paranormal equivalent of changing planes at O'Hare: complicated, a little dangerous and forgotten as soon as you got home.

But you'll never forget this, her heart whispered. Not that sad-eyed little girl with a head full of dreams she couldn't quite understand. And not the angry man who had held Dakota in his arms and kissed her the way no man had ever kissed her before or ever would again.

The farm

The sun rose and still Zane and Josiah did not return.

Neither Emilie nor Rebekah said anything about that fact as

they fed their children steaming bowls of oatmeal and tended to the hearth fire and did the thousand other chores necessary to keep a home in proper running order.

They are safe, Emilie, Rebekah's look said across the bustling kitchen. *Put your trust in the Almighty and you will not be disappointed.*

But Emilie didn't have Rebekah's faith. All she had was a dark sense of foreboding that settled across her shoulders like a mantle of lead. There was so much Rebekah didn't know, so much Emilie had never told her.

So many times she had wanted to tell her friend the truth, but the words always died in her throat. How could she expect Rebekah to believe that the couple she had taken under her wing in the summer of 1776 had traveled across the centuries to be there?

Besides, the twentieth century was nothing but a distant dream to Emilie now. There was nothing there she wanted, nothing there she missed. Everything she valued in the world existed in this time and place.

But what if there was a way to go back? a small voice asked as she cleaned oatmeal from her daughter's chubby hands. *Think of how much more you could give them in the twentieth century.*

"No," she whispered fiercely. "Never!"

Sara Jane looked up at her, bright blue eyes wide with question. Emilie kissed the child's fingers as her heart thundered inside her chest.

She wouldn't go back, not even if the balloon landed right there on the front porch and promised she could pick up her life exactly where she'd left off, but this time with her husband and family by her side. She was part of something important here. Not only did she contribute to the cause of freedom with her work for the spy ring, she was part of a real community of people who understood the importance of liberty in a way her world of the twentieth century had long forgotten. She wanted this world for her children.

She wanted them to grow up without drive-by shootings and crack dealers and the bone-deep pessimism that permeated every corner of life in the 1990s.

But what about Zane? that small voice continued. *Are you sure he'd feel the same way?*

It was one thing to make the best of an odd situation. It was another thing to embrace it, knowing there was a means of escape. He'd wanted to leave from the very beginning. She remembered the morning the balloon had appeared by the lighthouse, how she'd believed that he would leave her and return to the world they'd left behind. Did he ever regret his decision? she wondered. What would he do if he had a second chance?

The cloud formation was fainter than yesterday, but it was still there. She thanked God there was no sign of the hot-air balloon, but she knew in her heart that it was only a matter of time before it appeared. She had to find Zane before it was too late, before fate made the choice for both of them.

"Papa!" Andy pointed toward the hallway. "Papa home."

"Listen," said Rebekah, a bright smile wreathing her tired face. "Footsteps! They're back."

Emilie leapt to her feet and ran into the hallway.

"G'mornin', Emilie." Timothy Crosse, Rebekah's son-in-law, stood in the hallway knocking snow from the soles of his boots. "Got that flour you ladies been askin' for, and at a fair price, too. Hope that means you'll be makin' some of your biscuits."

"Zane and Josiah," she said, grabbing him by the lapels of his jacket. "They went out last night and haven't come back yet. Have you seen them?" She didn't care if Timothy thought they'd gone out whoring. She just wanted an answer.

"Ain't seen either one," Timothy said, "not since t'other day near the church. Lots of snow out there, Em. Reckon they're findin' it real hard to get home." His cheeks reddened as he obviously thought of another reason that two men wouldn't make it home at night. "Wouldn't be any real cause t' worry."

She drew in a deep breath and brushed snow from the young man's hair. "You must be freezing," she said. "Why don't you have some hot cider? Rebekah made corn bread this morning and it was grand."

"Don't mind if I do," Timothy said, obviously glad the topic of conversation had shifted to corn bread. "Big commotion north of Franklin Ridge," he said as he followed her into the kitchen. "Say the Redcoats caught themselves a big red ball that floated over the trees."

The blood pounded so hard in Emilie's ears that she could barely make out Timothy's words. *No! Please, God, no!*

"A big red ball floating over the treetops?" Rebekah laughed as she poured a cup of cider for her son-in-law. "Sounds to me like the stores of rum are fast being depleted in Franklin Ridge."

"They swear up and down 'tis true," Timothy went on, taking the cider from Rebekah with a nod of acknowledgment. "Even went so far as to say there were people floating with it."

"People?" Emilie couldn't keep the sharp note of fear from her voice. "Who?"

Timothy eyed her curiously. So did Rebekah. Emilie refused to meet her friend's eyes.

"Some say a man and a woman," Timothy ventured, obviously uncomfortable. "Some say two women."

Rebekah threw back her head and laughed. "The day we fly like birds over the trees is the day you can bury me six feet deep. Such nonsense!"

Timothy laughed as well, but Emilie didn't. It wasn't nonsense, not even close, but how could she expect her eighteenth-century counterparts to understand that? The advent of hot-air ballooning wouldn't dawn for another few years, and then it would be in France.

Not New Jersey.

Not today.

"Would you excuse me?" Emilie said, struggling to sound matter-of-fact. "I have to fetch my knitting."

"Emilie?" Rebekah forced Emilie to meet her eyes. "Is something wrong?"

"Just tired, 'Bekah. I don't sleep well when Zane isn't home."

Rebekah nodded, but Emilie knew her friend suspected something. *I'd tell you if I could, 'Bekah,* she thought as she hurried from the kitchen, *but you'd never believe me.*

Emilie grabbed her cloak and gloves from the peg near the front door. Her boots waited on the front porch. Quietly she slid open the drawer to the secretary she shared with Rebekah and removed a sheet of parchment. She dipped the quill into the inkwell and penned a note to her dearest friend.

Rebekah was the finest woman Emilie had ever known. If something happened to her and Zane, the children would be left in kind and loving hands.

She rested the note on top of Rebekah's sewing basket, then retrieved the small felt pouch of gold coins from her own basket, beneath her embroidery tools. Her heart ached with longing to kiss her children, but that would feel too much like goodbye.

And this *wasn't* goodbye. She refused to even consider that possibility.

She slipped from the house and, minutes later, guided Timothy's horse-drawn cart down the snowy lane toward Franklin Ridge.

Chapter Fourteen

14

It seemed to Patrick as he rode toward the meeting place near Jockey Hollow that the Almighty had conspired to test him to the very limits of his endurance.

Snow fell with unceasing fury, blinding his vision and making it difficult for his horse to gain purchase on the slippery ground. His heavy woolen coat did little to shield him from the bitter winds or from the harsh bite of his conscience. He told himself that it was for the greater good that he stayed safe and well-fed while others fought the enemy, but on days like this he found it difficult to live within his own skin.

Rutledge and Blakelee had been taken prisoner by the British, and it was Patrick who bore the blame in the eyes of the world.

Word of Patrick's treachery had already reached Franklin Ridge, and the chilly smiles of the townspeople he passed had frozen solid as the icy ponds. The Continental army teetered on the verge of collapse, and he sensed deep in the black emptiness of his soul that the worst was yet to come.

The thought was horrific enough to almost make him laugh. Indeed, how much worse could matters get? Already a new pair of boots commanded more than many farmers earned in a year. The cost of a new horse would support ten families. Did no one else see the excess that threatened the framework of the Revolution? Did no one else care?

He found the righteous anger of the townspeople amusing. How many of them were willing to risk their own comfort to aid the patriots about whom they wept? Quick to weep false tears and condemn all and sundry for imagined misdeeds, nary a citizen of Franklin Ridge saw fit to step forward and offer assistance.

His anger increased with each mile he traveled. The thick woods north of town were being chopped down, the logs dragged to the encampments to be used to build huts that would house the enlisted men. He wondered how it was that General Washington had managed to keep them from breaking rank and fleeing back to their farms and families in the face of almost certain annihilation at the hands of the Redcoats. And he wondered if it would ultimately be worth the sacrifice.

Death was everywhere. He saw it every day in the tearstained faces of the men and women left behind. He smelled it in the air, heard it in the crack of rifle shots echoing through the dark night.

And all for a cause that might already be lost.

"What are we going to do?" Cook demanded of Dakota as General McDowell's men set up cots in the parlor and the dining room.

"I don't know," Dakota said. "Do they have the right to take over like this?" Of course, she knew the answer to that. They had every right in the world. This was war and the normal rules of society didn't matter.

"The mister is going to be mad as a hatter." Cook poked the rising lump of bread dough with an angry forefinger. "Joseph heard one of them say the general wants the library for a meeting room."

"Not the library!" Dakota exclaimed. How could she get her hands on that list of names if the place was knee-deep in soldiers?

"That's what I told him," Cook said, high color staining her cheeks, "but he wouldn't listen to the likes of me." She tilted her head in the direction of the library. "But he'd listen to you."

"Me?" Dakota made a face. "Why on earth would the general listen to me?"

"You're the lady of the house," Cook said, eyebrows raised all the way up to her mobcap.

"I'm the lady of the house?" Dakota muttered as she strode toward the library. She didn't feel like the lady of the house. She felt like exactly what she was: a woman looking for a way out.

She prayed General McDowell was a trusting sort, because she wasn't sure she could pull it off.

The general turned out to be charming, attentive and understanding—all the things Devane was not—but, unfortunately, he also had a will of iron.

"I understand your concerns, madam," he said in a lazy voice that had more than a touch of London nibbling around the edges, "and I would like to address them with your husband, if I may. Patrick and I are friends of long standing." He made a show of glancing about the room. "And where might the good fellow be?"

Beats me, she thought, offering him a demure, poor-little-me smile. The last time she'd seen Devane, he'd been stomping his way down the hall, looking ready to do battle with the world. "Cook informed me that my husband has gone for a ride."

"Madam, there is a full foot of snow in the hills and more coming. Now, I know Patrick is a most physical fellow—I can remember him riding to hounds on the most ungodly day—but you must admit that, even for so hale a fellow as your dear new husband, this is hardly riding weather."

Look, bozo, what do you want from me? All I know is that he's gone. She deepened her dimple, praying she wouldn't burst out laughing at the absurdity of the whole situation. "My husband cares not about the weather."

"And what pressing engagement tears him from the side of his new bride?" It was said with a wink, but Dakota sensed more than passing curiosity behind the question. Who could blame him? Few grooms would prefer a blizzard to their bride.

She lowered her eyes, the demure and blushing new wife plotting her next lie. "My husband has his concerns," she said sweetly, "as I have mine—to make him happy."

McDowell nodded, a benevolent smile on his face. "The way it should be, madam. The issue of the library will wait awhile longer."

Unbelievable, she thought in amazement. Either men had gotten a lot smarter by the twentieth century or she'd missed out on something big time. Were they all this easy to manipulate, or had she stumbled across a particularly malleable bunch?

She realized he was still talking.

"…to celebrate your marriage."

Her smile widened. "How wonderful!" She hadn't the foggiest idea what he was talking about but unless someone had just suggested a trip to the guillotine, "how wonderful" usually did the trick. Maybe a career in diplomacy wasn't that farfetched after all.

She floated back to the kitchen on a wave of self-congratulations.

"Praise be!" Cook turned away from the hearth and beamed at Dakota. "He'll let the mister keep his library."

"He didn't actually promise anything," she said, peering into the soup pot, then back at Cook, "but he did say he'll postpone moving his gear into it. At least until he talks to Dev—I mean, to my husband."

"And a fine mood the mister will be in when he comes home," Cook said with a shake of her head. "We'll be thinkin' the war is being fought right here in the house."

"Yes," Dakota said, recognizing an opening when she heard one. "My husband is certainly very…particular about his home, isn't he?"

Cook tossed some cubes of turnip into the soup pot, then wiped her hands on the rough fabric of her apron. "Won't let a body into that library unless he's standin' there like St. Peter at the gates of heaven, watchin' everything that goes on."

"He does love his books." Dakota snatched a piece of warm bread from the pine table where it had been cooling.

"Books!" Cook pursed her lips as if she'd been sucking on a lemon. "If you ask me, it's not the books he's worryin' about."

"Hmm," said Dakota, feigning uninterest as she chewed her bread.

"Rosie said she thought he had gold hidden away in there, but I don't think it's gold. I think he's a sp—" The woman stopped mid-word.

Spy, Dakota thought. *You think he's a spy, too!*

"Beggin' your pardon, ma'am." Cook's ruddy cheeks burned hotter. "Joseph always says I talk before I think."

"You need not apologize to me," Dakota said. Of all times for the woman to have a crisis of conscience. "You have a right to your own opinion." *And I wish you'd share it with me.*

"You won't tell Mr. Devane what I said, will you?"

"Not a word," she promised as she left the kitchen.

McDowell and his men were closeted in the library, probably exchanging wallpaper samples and planning how to redecorate. She had to admit she understood what Devane must be feeling. She was enough of a loner herself to shudder at the thought of a platoon of strangers barging into her home and getting intimate with her things.

But it was more than empathy that had her lingering near the closed door, ear pressed up against the well-polished wood. She hadn't imagined the names Rutledge and Blakelee scrawled across that piece of paper and she wasn't going to rest until she figured out what it was all about.

A buzz began in her fingertips, gentle at first then growing stronger, more insistent as it moved its way up through her hands, wrapped itself around her wrists, slid up her arms until it vibrated behind her rib cage.

Let down your defenses, honey...soften that sharp tongue...this is what you've been looking for...this is the place.

The voice drifted away and, with it, the buzzing sensation inside her chest.

"Mom?" she whispered, leaning against the closed door for support. She waited, but there was nothing except the low rumble of male voices coming from Devane's library and the sudden, inexplicable sense that she was running out of time.

The meeting place was two miles southwest of the jail where Rutledge and Blakelee had been taken, a clearing behind a farmhouse owned by a member of their spy ring.

The man who had watched Rutledge and Blakelee taken away waited for him there.

"Son of a bitch!" Patrick's fist crashed into the man's chin with a resounding crack. "What in bloody hell have you done?"

"'Twasn't my fault," the man whimpered, spitting blood onto the snow. "The Lobsterbacks come and took 'em away and there weren't a thing I could do to stop 'em, not and live to tell the tale."

"Is there more?" he demanded, shaking the man by his shoulders. "Did the soldiers say anything that might help us find Rutledge and Blakelee?"

"They said—" The man gulped as if struggling to draw air into his lungs. "They laughed when they took them, said now it be too late."

"Too late?" Patrick snapped. "Too late for what?"

"I don't know nothin'," the man wailed like a frightened child. "They wouldn't be tellin' the likes of me about a hanging."

"A hanging? Sweet Jesus, man, tell me what you know or, mark me well, you will have breathed your last."

"There's a hanging in the wind and ain't nothing going to stop it now. Not even you."

He threw the man aside, as angry with himself as with the fool.

"Surprised you care," the man went on, rubbing his elbow where it had struck the ground. "Seems like you're the one everyone be talkin' about, you and your new wife that come to town with Andrew McVie."

McVie! Once again the man's name was mentioned after years of silence. How quickly news spread in times of war. What strange events were conspiring to bring his name to everyone's lips?

"Need I remind you that McVie is dead?" he asked in a voice of deadly calm. "Or that my wife never knew the man."

"Don't know what she been tellin' you, but a score of folk near to King's Crossing say they saw two women with McVie in a flying basket and one of those women sounded like she be your new wife."

"You're daft, man," Patrick said despite the doubts that suddenly plagued him. "You partake too much of the grape."

"Ask her," the man said, meeting Patrick's eyes. "Ask her where she be t'other afternoon." The man's expression shifted from anger to pity. "Maybe you went and picked yourself the wrong gal again."

By the time Cook served supper to Dakota and Abigail in the kitchen, General McDowell and his men had taken over most of the house from cellar to attic.

"An outrage!" Cook complained as she placed a bowl of soup in front of Dakota. "You'd think they were the king's men, and not our very own soldiers, the way they've taken over. After the last time, I swore I'd be finding a new place to work rather than serve the likes of them again."

"I like the soldiers," Abigail said as she chewed a piece of buttered bread.

Dakota glanced across the table at the child. "You do?"

Abigail nodded her head vigorously. "The house doesn't seem so big with them here."

Cook snorted. "Fine for you to say, missy. It don't fall to you to keep them all fed."

In truth, it didn't fall to Cook, either. General McDowell's private chef was en route from Philadelphia and was expected to arrive by midafternoon the next day. The general had already set into motion his plans to construct the additional kitchen off the west side of the house, one that would be off-limits to Cook.

"If the mister was here, he'd tell that general a thing or two."

Dakota swallowed a sigh. "He can tell them anything he wants, but it won't change a thing. They're here and they're not going to leave." They might be fighting a war for independence but that independence didn't preclude the Continental army's right to take what it needed...and what it liked.

Still, it annoyed her that Devane had removed himself from the situation. He had known that General McDowell's arrival would throw the entire household into an uproar and that Cook would be unable to cope. And, to make matters worse, Cook had adopted the annoying habit of deferring all decisions to the "mistress of the house," as the woman now referred to Dakota.

They ate the rest of their meal in silence, listening to the laughter of General McDowell and his cronies as they played cards in the front room. Outside the snow continued to fall, light and relentless, and Dakota found herself wondering if Devane was out there somewhere, stranded in the storm, or if he'd decided to bail out on the lot of them and head for Tahiti.

Abigail finished the last of her apple betty, then yawned. Her eyes were heavy, and Dakota's heart did one of those funny little lurches with which she was rapidly becoming familiar. The kid was crawling under her skin and she didn't like it one bit.

"To bed," Cook said in a stern but maternal tone of voice, "and no fancy talk."

Abigail's expression shifted instantly from sleepy innocence to hot-headed anger. She tipped over the rest of her apple cider and was about to lob Dakota's leftover piece of bread at the back of Cook's head when Dakota pushed back her chair and stood. Cook was frazzled to the point of mayhem. The house was in utter chaos. The last thing any of them needed was a full-fledged temper tantrum from a six-year-old expert.

She took one of the candles that rested on the sideboard and made sure it was securely placed in its holder.

"Come on," she said, extending a hand to the child. "Let's go upstairs together."

"No!" Abigail's lower lip protruded dangerously.

"Bring Lucy with you."

Abby threw Lucy to the ground and kicked her with the toe of her leather slipper.

Cook muttered something dark and threatening, but Dakota ignored her. She bent and picked up Lucy, then placed the doll on a ledge near the door.

She held out her hand to Abigail and waited.

The little girl hesitated for a long moment, then tossed the bread down onto her plate and put her hand in Dakota's. A lump the size of eight of the thirteen colonies formed in her throat.

"What about Lucy?" Abigail asked, casting a glance toward her companion.

"Tomorrow morning," Dakota said. "You can play with her again at breakfast but tonight she stays down here." Maybe when she returned home she could do a prime-time special on alternative child care.

"Cook doesn't like me," Abigail observed as they climbed the stairs to the second floor.

"No, she doesn't today," Dakota admitted, making sure she held the candle away from her voluminous skirts, "but you didn't give her much reason to like you, did you?"

Abigail's soft brows knit together in a scowl. "What does that mean?"

They reached the landing and turned right toward Abigail's room.

"It means that you can't treat people badly and expect them to treat you with kindness."

"Like Lucy?"

Dakota suppressed a smile. "Exactly like Lucy."

Abigail was quiet until they stepped inside her room and Dakota closed the door behind them. She touched the flame from her candle to the candle resting atop Abigail's small dresser. The soft light spilled across the yellow pine.

"Cook is unkind to people," Abigail said.

Dakota sat down on the edge of the child's small bed. "Why do you say that?"

Abigail shifted her weight from one foot to the other. "She's mean to Joseph. She yells at him and makes him sleep on the floor when he has too much rum and stays out real late."

"Married people often fight." *Not that I have any personal experience, but...*

"She hit Will with her cooking spoon when he did something bad."

"Why are you telling me this?" she asked the child gently. "Is there something you want me to know?"

Abigail shrugged her narrow shoulders, so fragile beneath her cotton dress. "My head hurts," she said suddenly. "I want to go to sleep."

Dakota stood and smoothed the front of her skirt with a surprisingly natural gesture. It frightened her how natural it was *all* starting to seem.

"Sleep well," Dakota said, moving toward the door. "Don't let the bedbugs bite."

A funny little giggle broke through Abigail's solemn demeanor. "I don't have bedbugs."

"I'm very glad to hear that," Dakota said with mock gravity. "I hope I'm just as fortunate."

The only thing she had to worry about in her bed was Devane.

Dakota couldn't sleep.

She'd tossed and turned for at least two hours, trying everything from counting sheep to counting calories, but no dice. She lay there, fully clothed, on top of the feather bed in the small room adjoining Devane's, waiting for the sound of his boots on the staircase. How could she possibly fall asleep when she knew he could turn up at any moment and climb in next to her? Not that she expected him to, but still…

Her pulse leapt into overdrive just thinking about it. She'd made a fool of herself this morning, going all feminine and vulnerable when he held her, and she was determined not to make that mistake again.

And it *was* a mistake. Not even a woman of limited experience like Dakota could possibly believe it was anything else. He was a gorgeous eighteenth-century misogynist and she was a chubby twentieth-century liberal. Opposites might attract, but sooner or later they'd end up trying to kill each other. Who needed the hassle?

That's what she told herself over and over as the minutes ticked by and then the hours with no sign of Devane.

Maybe he really has *gone over the wall,* she thought as the tall clock in the downstairs hall tolled midnight. He'd made no bones about wanting to get Abigail out of the house and up to school in Boston. His wife was dead and buried. His house had been taken over by the soldiers he hated. He had a fake wife he couldn't stand and, at least according to Cook, he was the most hated man in town.

He'd have to be crazy to hang around. He had enough money to go anywhere he wanted and no reason to stay in Franklin Ridge. Why was she wasting one moment of her precious time thinking about any of this when she should be worrying how she was going to get back home?

She climbed from the bed and went to light the candle on the nightstand, then quickly realized she had no idea how to go about it. No lighter. No matches. She considered rubbing her thighs together to make a fire but that would only encourage her cellulite and it wouldn't do a darn thing for the candle.

She thought for a moment then pulled open the drapes, and the room was flooded with moonlight bouncing off the snow. Just enough light to invade someone's privacy.

"So sue me," she muttered as she walked into Devane's room and headed for the massive armoire. She'd never claimed to be perfect. She'd been born with a slow metabolism and a hyperactive sense of curiosity about things that were absolutely none of her business.

But it is your business. How else are you going to find a way to get back home?

Not a great rationalization, but not half-bad, either.

His room was exactly the way she'd hoped it would be: vacant. The armoire was there and Devane wasn't. Maybe she'd finally get some answers.

If only Abigail hadn't chosen that moment to scream as if the hounds of hell had leapt onto her bed and were demanding kibble or her life. Dakota fought off the urge to run to the kid's side to see what was wrong.

She's not your problem, Wylie. Let someone else take care of it.

Surely Cook would come to the rescue, or one of the handful of parlormaids still in Devane's employ. She listened at the door for the sound of footsteps on the stairs, but heard nothing except Abigail's shrieks. Not even one of the soldiers peered out into the hallway to see if there was something amiss.

What was the matter with those people? Were they deaf? Couldn't they hear the terror in Abby's voice? Worse, didn't they give a damn?

Dakota glanced longingly at the armoire, then, with a sigh of resignation, ran straight to Abigail's side.

Chapter Fifteen

15

The White Horse Tavern

"Be happy to get you more stew if you have a mind for it, ma'am." The serving girl hovered by Emilie's seat, obviously intrigued to find a woman traveling alone.

"No, thank you," Emilie said in a quiet voice. "I would like some more cider."

"Pleased to oblige." The girl lingered, fiddling with the pewter knife that rested near Emilie's plate.

"Is there something else?" Emilie asked.

The girl started to say something but a burly man in the far corner of the room called out, "Molly! I ain't payin' you to talk, now, am I?"

Emilie's shoulders sagged as the girl hurried off. She forced herself to sit straight, then decided it wasn't worth the effort. She was exhausted to the point of lunacy and frozen straight through to the marrow. She'd been on the road for hours and she still didn't know where her husband was, and it didn't look as if she was going to find out any time soon. This was the tavern where Zane and Josiah were to have made the drop, and so far she hadn't seen or heard anything that would help her unravel the mystery.

She'd tried to find some of the members of the spy ring by visiting their usual haunts, but the storm had kept most people close to home. She'd stopped at churches and apothecaries and taverns in search of her husband and their friend, but had been met with nothing but blank looks and uninterest.

The townspeople had more fascinating things to think about. Everywhere she went, she'd heard about the bright red ball that had floated over the trees yesterday afternoon, and with each telling, Emilie lost another piece of her heart to fear.

"Who was in the basket?" she'd asked a farmer she'd spoken to a little while ago, right outside the inn. "Two men? Three? Men? Women?" She'd heard every combination.

"Too much snow to see real clear," the man said, eyeing her with great suspicion. "Shouldn't you be home where you belong, missy?"

Of course I should be home, she thought as Molly deposited another tankard of cider beside her plate. She should be bundled under a pile of quilts with her husband, safe and well-loved in his arms, while their children slept soundly in the next room.

A wild laugh erupted and she covered her mouth with both hands to muffle the sound. Too bad Zane didn't have a beeper or a cellular phone, then all she'd have to do was dial him up and see if he was okay. Or maybe she could fax the farm and ask Rebekah if the guys had shown up in time for supper.

It was all so absurd that you had to laugh or go crazy.

That was when she started to cry.

Dakota found Abigail crouched at the foot of her bed, eyes wide open in terror, small hands clutching her throat.

"Honey?" Dakota knelt at her side, frightened by the look on the child's face. "Did you have a bad dream?"

Abigail clawed at her throat while she gasped frantically for breath. Tiny veins on her forehead and neck pulsed fiercely while her legs stuck straight out in front of her like legs on a cartoon character. Was she choking on something? Dakota was about to wrap her arms around the child's slender body and perform the Heimlich maneuver when she realized Abigail was speaking.

"...rope...the big tree..."

She was dreaming, but dreaming with her eyes wide open. Dakota tried to remember what you were supposed to do in that situation, but the only thing she could think of was an old episode of "The Honeymooners" where Ed Norton became a sleepwalker and Ralph turned into a baby-sitter.

"You're okay, Abigail," she said softly, sitting down on the bed next to the child. Cautiously she rested an arm on the delicate shoulders. "You're only dreaming."

"No!" Abigail's cry rang out. "The hangman! The hangman is coming!"

"Wake up, honey," Dakota said gently, touching the child on the shoulder. "You're safe."

"The hangman!" Abigail cried out again. "He's coming! He's coming!"

Suddenly Dakota saw herself twenty years ago, sobbing in her father's arms because she was sure the bogeyman had her name and address in his hip pocket and was on his way.

She gathered the little girl to her and hugged her close, stroking the fine brown hair with gentle fingers, whispering words of comfort in her ear, words that Abigail probably wouldn't remember in the morning but words that made all the difference now.

Patrick watched from the shadows as the woman cradled the child. They did not know he stood there in the darkness, and he wished it to remain so.

He was not a man easily moved by displays of emotion or sentiment. He had been trained to hold such displays suspect, and his brief interlude with Susannah had proved the folly of revealing your heart to another.

But there was something about the scene in the darkened bedroom that moved him beyond words on a day in which he needed to be reminded that life was not always a thing of darkness.

The child was curled against Dakota's chest, her head resting beneath the woman's chin. The woman's arms were wrapped about Abigail, holding her close while she talked to her in a low, soft voice that evoked memories of dreams he'd spent a lifetime struggling to forget.

All is not as it seems. The warning sounded in his head, but he turned a deaf ear to it. The sight before him was so powerful, so deeply compelling that all else faded into nothingness before it.

But it wasn't for him. Not the warmth or the promise of something that went deeper even than blood. Those things belonged to other men.

Two good men, men with faithful wives who loved them, with children who looked toward them for guidance—two brave men were marked to die, and all because Patrick Devane had failed as a patriot as he had failed as a husband...as he had failed as a father.

One hour ago he had learned the truth from the owner of the White Horse Tavern, a man known for being sympathetic to whoever held the purse strings. The British planned to hang Rutledge and Blakelee one week hence in Elizabethtown.

He looked at the child nestled in the arms of a stranger, a woman who had already provided more warmth and affection than he had given the child in years. For all he knew, Dakota Wylie was the one who had conspired to send Rutledge and Blakelee to the gallows.

Muttering a curse, he drew back into the shadows and turned away from the light.

The White Horse Tavern

Thanks to the storm, the inn was filled to overflowing with travelers. In the best of times, private rooms were the exception rather than the rule, and tonight it would be six to a room.

Emilie surveyed her possible roommates. She'd sleep in the stables with Timothy's horse before she shared a bed with any of them.

"Missus." The serving girl named Molly stopped her at the door. "You can have my bed upstairs, if you'd be of a mind."

"That's very kind of you." The girl was clean and neatly groomed, which was more than could be said for most people in the establishment. "There's a gold piece for your trouble."

Molly's green eyes widened but she shook her head. "Nay, missus. I'm just looking to help."

"Why?" Emilie asked, too tired to be polite.

Molly lowered her voice to a whisper. "I heard you askin' about your friends and I—"

"Molly!" the tavern owner bellowed over the noise of laughter and clinking glasses. "To work, lass, or out into the snow with you!"

She raised her voice. "Be there directly!"

"Wait," said Emilie, placing her hand on the girl's arm. "Do you know something? You must tell me—"

"The last room on the third floor," Molly said. "I'll find out what I can."

Dakota stayed with Abigail until the child fell back into a peaceful sleep.

She settled the quilts around Abby's shoulders, then smoothed a strand of silky hair from her cheek with a gesture that felt strangely familiar to her, as if she had done the same thing in just that way many times before.

Of course, that was impossible. Except for her volunteer work teaching children to read, she had little to do with kids. She'd never felt particularly comfortable with children, not even when she'd qualified as one of them. Even with her sister Janis's sons she'd felt that sense of not quite clicking—as if they spoke a language she'd never understand. Actually, it was pretty much the same way she'd felt around most of the men she'd dated.

Abigail was a hardheaded, hot-tempered brat and her father was about as dangerous as they came. A woman would have to have a few screws loose to even consider setting up housekeeping with a pair like that.

So why did this feel so right? Why did she feel as if the last puzzle piece of her life had settled into place?

Because you're a sucker for hard luck cases, she thought as Abby's breathing settled into a slow, even rhythm. *And because you know it's safe...that one day soon you're going to walk away from all of this and step back into your own life....*

She was tired and lonely and far from home in every way she could imagine, but she'd have to be subhuman to not feel something for a terrified little girl who was crying her eyes out. It didn't mean she wanted to play a game of let's pretend and try on stepmotherhood for size. This whole thing was only temporary. If she knew nothing else, she knew that for a fact.

She closed the door quietly behind her and started down the hall. It was almost unnaturally quiet, as if the house were holding its collective breath, and she shook off an odd feeling of anticipation.

Halfway between Abby's room and Devane's suite she noticed small pools of water on the polished wooden floor, each one a man's stride away from the next. She bent and touched her finger to the liquid. It was cold and slushy, obviously melting snow.

Soldiers, maybe? She looked toward the top of the staircase but didn't see any footprints on the steps or the landing. "Weird," she muttered. How had they managed that trick? Did they carry their boots up the stairs then slip them back on, or walk on their hands like acrobats in Cirque du Soleil?

Even more unnerving, the trail of melting snow led straight to Devane's rooms. The door was closed. She was certain she hadn't left it that way. Cautiously she pushed it open and stepped inside.

The curtains were open. The candles were extinguished. Devane's bed was untouched. Everything was as she'd left it except for the trail of melting snow that led straight to the armoire.

Don't even think it,Wylie! This isn't the time to turn into Nancy Drew.

Hidden staircases and mysterious messages hidden in old clocks were fine in the pages of a book, but they had nothing whatsoever to do with reality.

Reality? Like time travel happens every day?

She had no answer for that. All she knew was that Devane had watched her comfort his daughter, probably even heard the child's cries, and chosen to do nothing about it. He had stood in the doorway to his daughter's room then turned and walked away.

He wasn't going to get away with it. Not if she could help it.

A towering sense of rage filled her and she swung open the door to the armoire, practically vibrating with the certainty that Devane's secrets were within her reach. She'd find him even if she had to track him through the centuries.

His treatment of Abigail was unconscionable. The thought that he could watch the child cry and do nothing, *feel* nothing, defied reason. He was the lowest type of slime crawling on the earth, and she intended to tell him so as soon as possible.

She peered inside empty drawers, felt around for secret compartments, would have settled for a pair of linsey-woolsey Jockey shorts with hearts embroidered on them, but no luck. The armoire was still as empty as her bank account back home, but the sense of certainty inside her didn't lessen.

She ran her fingers across the smooth wood of one of the inner drawers. The armoire was a strange piece of furniture. The drawers were flimsy and cheaply made, while the wardrobe itself was almost a work of art. Each piece of pine fit into the next piece seamlessly, as if the entire thing had been wrought from one enormous tree. The only board that didn't seem quite a part of the whole was the one in back, but that could be a trick of the dim light and not a blemish on the craftsmanship.

Or maybe it was something else. Her fingertips tingled as she ran them up the vertical grain and her pulse rate leapt exponentially. She'd experienced that kind of thing often enough in her life to know exactly what it meant, and she thanked God for it.

She slid the drawers out and stacked them on the floor by her feet. Her hands had a life of their own as she lifted out the runners and laid them next to the drawers. Then *bingo!*

Her palm found a slight depression near the seam on the right-hand side of the board and the metal latch she'd discovered earlier. She gave a tug and then a push, and as it swung open it was all she could do to hold back a whoop of exhilaration.

The passageway was dark and narrow, but she felt no fear. She was meant to be there. Every cell and neuron in her body told her so. Her extrasensory abilities were beginning to flex their muscles once again, and she felt more like her old self than she had since climbing into the hot-air balloon a thousand lifetimes ago.

She stumbled twice on the uneven stone floor but continued to move forward. Boards creaked overhead and she heard a scurrying noise that sounded awfully mouselike, but she tried not to think about it.

She'd read about secret passageways that snaked their way through old houses, and knew they invariably led outside. She didn't have a terrific sense of direction, but if her guess was right, she was heading toward the stables.

Why would Devane feel he needed to use a secret passageway when he owned the house in question and dominated everyone in it with his iron will and bad attitude? You'd think a man like that could come and go when he wanted without having to answer to another living soul.

A man who worried about his reputation would use a passageway like this to conduct a love affair away from prying eyes, but in Devane's case that didn't make sense because he was no longer a married man and could conduct a love affair in broad daylight in the center of town if that was what he wanted to do.

No, the only reason a man like Devane would go to such lengths to conceal his movements was if there was something greater at stake, something of such importance that it had to be kept secret at all costs.

Something like spying.

The explanation she'd been circling since she'd dropped out of the tree at Devane's feet was inescapable now. Everything he did, everything she'd seen and heard, all pointed toward the obvious conclusion. His hatred of the Continental army had been hot enough to blister paint. She'd sensed that he was a Tory sympathizer when they first met; now she was certain.

She consoled herself with the fact that when she found him she could berate him not just for being a lousy parent but for being a traitor, as well.

The passageway took a sharp left, narrowing until she wondered whether she'd be able to wedge her well-padded hips through. She could imagine some archaeologist finding her bones in the passageway a few hundred years from now and branding her demise as "death by cellulite."

She smothered a laugh. At least her sense of the absurd was still intact. Her courage, however, was another story. It seemed to be waning fast. Her ankle throbbed and she did her best to ignore it. A loud scratching noise sounded overhead and she cringed, convinced that one of Mickey Mouse's less affable cousins was going to make an unwelcome entrance.

Carefully she made her way down a steep staircase, navigated a series of sharp turns, then descended another set of steps that apparently led into the bowels of the earth.

Where on earth was she going to end up? The possibilities were not too pleasant. What if Devane had a guard posted, some bayonet-happy traitor who'd turn her into a human shish kebab? She hadn't thought to bring a weapon of any kind with her.

No matter. It was too late to turn back. That sense of destiny, of rightness, was gathering force with each step she took. Somehow it was all tied together—Patrick Devane and Abigail and this house and the sense that where she was at that moment was where she was meant to be, the path that would lead her home.

The White Horse Tavern

Molly Cutter's third-floor room boasted a thin feather mattress that rested atop a narrow iron bed. The ceiling angled sharply down to a waist-high window that overlooked the stables.

It reminded Emilie of her dorm room in art school, a sad little closet that was Dante's Inferno in the summer and a meat locker the rest of the year.

The girl's meager belongings were lined up neatly on the shelf that served as a dresser: a wooden comb, a length of black ribbon, a skein of indigo blue yarn and bone knitting needles.

That's all she has in the world, Emilie thought as tears stung her eyes. In the time she had left behind, even the poorest soul had more.

She turned away and looked out the window. Snow continued to fall. The wind had picked up some since she had arrived, and drifts were forming against the side of the stables. She thought about Timothy's horse and hoped that the stable boy had understood the coin she gave him came with the expectation of services rendered. If she wasn't so tired, she would go back downstairs and make sure, but a sickening lassitude had taken hold and it was all she could do to make it to the narrow iron bed and lie down.

She lay there for a long time, dozing fitfully, awakening herself each time a crimson hot-air balloon floated into her dreams.

At a little after midnight she heard Molly climbing the twisting staircase, and she sat up as the girl entered the room.

"What did you find out?" she asked as the door closed behind Molly. "Where is my—where are Rutledge and Blakelee?"

The expression in Molly's green eyes was serious. Too serious for Emilie's taste. Blood hammered in her ears, making it hard to hear the girl's words.

"...or she'd take the strap to me."

"What was that?" Emilie stared at her. "Someone said she'd take a *strap* to you?"

"Yes'm," said Molly. "Said to stop asking questions that weren't my business or I'd be sorry."

"Did you ask about the red ball that everyone's talking about?"

"No'm, never got the chance. Soon as I mentioned your two friends it got quiet as church on Monday morning."

"So you didn't find out anything?" Emilie asked, on the verge of tears. "Nothing at all?"

There was a slight pause, so slight that under normal circumstances Emilie never would have noticed it.

"The Redcoats," said Molly sadly. "I'm sorry, missus, but the Redcoats are goin' to hang them."

Chapter Sixteen

16

Rum had never failed Patrick before, not even during the darkest days after Susannah left him. Rum had filled the coldness in the center of his soul where Abigail had been. Rum had warmed the bed where his wife had lain beside him.

But this time rum couldn't begin to soothe the ache inside his chest as he thought of the comrades he had condemned to death. There wasn't enough rum in the world to help him forget what he had done. To forget that two men would die because he had not recognized danger when she appeared before him.

He'd suspected it from the beginning, but something inside him, some weakness of the soul, had kept him from accepting the truth that he could no longer deny.

He heard the soft sound of her footsteps as she made her way through the dark and narrow passageway, and he felt a grudging admiration for her courage. He knew few men who would venture alone into that passageway and fewer still who would not turn back long before reaching their destination.

But still she came, moving closer to him with every beat of his heart. He found it hard to reconcile his suspicions with the inexplicable sense of joy he had felt as he watched her hold Abigail to her breast in the darkened bedroom.

"Bloody fool!" He gulped down more rum. The quickest road to disaster was to trust a woman. He would not make that mistake again.

"What has kept you so long, Dakota Wylie?"

She jumped at the sound of his voice. Squinting, she made out his shadowy figure near the end of the passageway.

"What are you doing here?" she demanded, as if she were Our Lady of the Passageway.

"Waiting for you, my dear wife. The night is long and cold without you."

"Stick a sock in it." Her aura was shooting sparks. She was surprised he couldn't see them arcing over her head, making her brave and powerful and impossible to deny.

"I am pleased you have decided to join me," he drawled. He was close enough for her to smell the faint scent of rum on his breath and she moved back, but she needn't have bothered. He made no move to touch her.

"You should be back in that house, taking care of your daughter."

"You served her well, madam. There was nothing more that I could do."

"Nothing more you could do?" She laughed out loud. "You did nothing at all."

"Nothing was required."

"She had a nightmare."

"All children have nightmares."

"And their parents comfort them until the bad dream passes."

"Who will comfort her in school, madam? It is time she learned the difference between dreams and life."

"You treat her like a stranger. Cook would be a better parent to her than you have been."

"You overstep your bounds." He loomed over her and she knew the only thing between herself and death was the extent of his self-control. "Even if it were your concern, this is not the place for serious discussion."

"The hell it isn't."

There was just enough light for her to see the surprise in his deep blue eyes. "Your language offends me, madam."

"Your treatment of Abigail offends *me.*"

"She wants for nothing."

"Except for your attention."

"She is a child."

"She is your *daughter,* your own flesh and blood."

He turned and strode away, but she wasn't about to let him get off that easily.

"You don't want to hear it, do you?" she demanded as the passageway opened into a small room dominated by a large wooden table and a narrow bed. "Why do you hate Abigail so much? What on earth could she have done to deserve—"

"Be warned, madam."

"You owe it to her." She pressed on, the memory of the child's tears still fresh in her mind. "You're her father."

"Bloody hell, concern yourself with your own predicament, because it is considerable."

"My predicament?" She poked him in the chest with her forefinger. It was like poking Mount Rushmore. "You're the one with a predicament."

He pushed her down onto the bed. The mattress felt like a soggy matzo, but she didn't think this was a good time to lodge a complaint with the management.

"Mark my words well, madam, for they have great meaning for

you. Today we lost two of our best men because I sheltered a traitor in my midst."

"Lost?" she asked. "What do you mean, *lost?*"

"Captured and condemned to death. Lost to all who care for them."

"Not to worry." She waved his words away like flies at a picnic. "I know all about that. They're in jail near Jockey Hollow."

"And how is it you know that, madam?"

"You just told me."

"I did not mention Jockey Hollow."

"I, um, I must've heard it somewhere else."

"Where?"

"I don't know…somewhere."

"That answer will not serve. Tell me the name of your spymaster or I will end your worthless life in this very room."

"Wait a minute!" she said, her face growing pale. "I can take a joke with the best of them, but this isn't funny anymore. I don't have a spymaster, Devane. I don't even know what a spymaster is."

"Two good men are sentenced to die, Dakota Wylie, and you are to blame. Why should you be spared?"

"Look," she said, "I know all about Rutledge and Blakelee. You don't have anything to worry about. Everything's going to be okay."

He grabbed her by the upper arms and lifted her off the bed. "Where are they?"

She neither blinked nor looked away, not discomfited in the slightest by the indignity of her position. Her courage was greater than the courage of a dozen men of his acquaintance. He would give all he had and more to have such a woman by his side.

"Put me down!" she ordered.

"Answer me first."

Her knee banged against his hip and he thanked the Almighty that her aim was left of center.

"Where are they?" he asked again as he lowered her to the ground.

"I don't know," she said honestly, "but I can make a guess."

"That is not good enough."

"Jockey Hollow," she said. "They're supposed to be in a jail near Jockey Hollow."

"A fine statement, madam, but I fear 'tis inaccurate. There is no jail near Jockey Hollow."

"There has to be."

"A law has not been passed to that effect," he said dryly. "I grow tired of this charade. Mayhap a night in the Franklin Ridge jail will bring out the truth."

She met his eyes. He wasn't kidding. *Go to jail. Go directly to jail. Do not pass Go. Forget about your two hundred dollars.* She'd read enough about those jails to know she'd never last twenty-four hours under such terrible conditions. *So what are you going to do, Wylie? Offer him your lily white body like Mata Hari would?*

Maybe she'd do something even more dangerous, like telling the truth. "You were right about Andrew McVie," she said. "He *is* a friend of mine."

The joy in his eyes was unmistakable and her heart soared. The lousy rat might be a spy, but at least he was on the right side.

Of course, he quickly masked his joy with a veneer of mild curiosity. "It is said he floated over the treetops in a basket suspended from a bright red ball."

"It's called a hot-air balloon."

"You floated over the treetops with him?" He tried, but he couldn't conceal his disbelief.

"Yes, I did."

"How came you to be separated from your friends?"

"The balloon was in trouble. We were falling from the sky and I—I guess you could say I bailed out."

"You abandoned your friends."

"We were going to crash."

"And so you chose to save your own life."

"No," she retorted angrily, "I chose to save your daughter's life instead."

"I fail to see how Abigail enters into this story."

"I heard her crying. I thought she was in danger."

"You leapt from the basket to save Abigail?"

"I didn't seem to have much choice in the matter."

"You would have me believe you risked your life for one you did not know."

She sighed. "I wouldn't have you believe anything, Devane. I'm just telling you what happened."

He considered her for a moment. "You say you are a friend of Andrew McVie. If that is so, where has he been these three years past?"

"I can't answer that."

"Cannot or will not?"

It was a little of each but she didn't dare tell him that. "I met Andrew only a few weeks ago. I have no idea what he was doing before then, but I *can* tell you that he's going to rescue Rutledge and Blakelee."

"That is naught but conjecture."

"No," she said carefully. "It's a fact."

"You would have me throw in my lot with a woman who claims to foretell the future?" If the look on his face was any indication, she'd better never tell him she could see auras, read tarot cards and chat with her mother long-distance.

"At least you know on which side my loyalties rest. Why don't you show me something to prove you're not a Tory? A letter of protection from George Washington, for starters." The man had written to everyone else in the thirteen colonies; he must have written at least a billet-doux to Devane.

"A letter of protection would render me useless," Devane said coolly. "The suspicion under which I am held is my most valuable tool."

"That leaves us in the same position we were before. I still don't know exactly where you stand."

"I am a patriot," he said after a moment. "I have no love for the officers of the Continental army, but a great deal of love for what this country can be."

"You can hate the army that fights for your independence and still call yourself a patriot?"

"The Colony of New Jersey has been cruelly used. Farms have been destroyed, houses confiscated by generals who ought to spend more time in battle. Women have been raped and murdered, all in the name of the Continental army. It is possible, madam, to support the cause but hate the way in which that cause is pursued."

"Would you feel that way if your wife hadn't run away with an officer from the army?"

A muscle in his left cheek twitched but he ignored the question. "I am perceived as sympathetic to the British and that allows me access to places and people closed tight to my brothers in the spy ring."

He was a smart man. He had to know he was handing her a sure way to betray him, but that still didn't mean he was telling her the truth. "Maybe you shouldn't be telling me this after all."

He met her eyes. "I have already done so."

She waited, but there was no flash of psychic energy, no buzzing vibrations along her nerve endings to tell her what to believe. In the end there was only her heart, and her heart could no longer be denied.

"I know," she whispered. "And I'm glad."

Reason told Patrick that only a madman who had taken leave of his senses would have done such a thing, but unfortunately his sense of reason had abandoned him the first moment she came into his life.

He had lost hope that she would find him. He had waited years for her, thought Susannah was the woman who would unlock his secrets, but it had been Dakota Wylie all the time. This uncommon woman with the strange name and unusual manner had performed a miracle he would have deemed impossible: she made him feel alive.

He hated her for the way she looked at him, as if she could see inside his soul, for the way she stood her ground, forcing him to see her as a person and not just a woman. He hated her for making him want things he knew could never be.

It was more than the soft dark curls that framed her face, more than the sweet scent of her skin, more even than the fact that her nearness roused in him a silken web of emotions that wrapped themselves about his heart and drew him closer to her. Not even Susannah with her great beauty had called to him in the same way as this uncommon woman with the uncommon name.

His entire world had been turned upside down since Dakota Wylie's arrival. His life seemed different with her in it, as if he had come to the end of a long journey to find that home lay at the end of the road. In truth, he feared for his sanity. Such changes in his heart and soul were not possible. He would not allow them to be thus.

Still, how else could he explain that even time itself no longer moved at the accustomed pace? Such intensity of feeling came with the passage of weeks and months. It was not possible in mere days. There was the sense that forces he knew nothing about controlled his destiny.

"I should not believe you," he said at last, "but I do. I should not trust you, yet I do. 'Tis a considerable problem, madam, one for which I see no solution."

"That's not surprising," she said. "We barely know each other."

"'Tis true, and yet I feel as if I have known you for a very long time indeed."

"Oh, God," she whispered. "You feel it, too."

"It is as if the nature of time has somehow changed."

"As if we're living an entire lifetime in the blink of an eye."

"I do not believe in magic, Dakota Wylie, but what I feel for you is unlike anything in my experience."

"I know." Her voice was low, almost inaudible. "It is the same for me."

"Why am I bedeviled as never before? Is it love, then, that we feel?"

Her eyes swam with tears. To hear those words from such a man. To be able to spend a lifetime as his partner, his lover. *His wife.* "I don't know. I'm not even certain that I like you very much."

"We are connected in some way that I do not understand."

Now's your chance, Dakota. Tell him the truth! Tell him how you really got here. "We share a friend in common."

"It is more than that, madam."

"We are both on the side of the patriots." How could she tell him she'd traveled two hundred years to be there? There was nothing in his frame of reference to help him believe something so bizarre. There were times when she wasn't sure that *she* believed it.

"This goes deeper, Dakota Wylie, to a place I have never been."

His words resonated deep inside her soul. Suddenly she wasn't longing for something she'd once had or dreaming of what she hoped to find somewhere else. The easy jokes, the layers of protective armor she'd built up around her heart had all been created to protect her from this moment, from the first wild stirrings of impossible love.

The room faded away and all she saw was the man standing before her.

"There was no husband," she said.

"No husband?" He cupped her chin in his hand. "No man to whom you have given your heart?"

"No one," she whispered, leaning into his touch. "No one in this world or any other."

A strange sensation filled his chest as he remembered the sweetness of her kisses. Was it possible he was the only man to have known them? The thought filled him with a towering sense of joy.

Her hair was soft against his hand, like fine silk. He found himself mesmerized by the gentle curls that entwined themselves about his fingers. He met her eyes.

"You are free to go if you choose." From this point forward they would meet on level ground.

Her eyes glittered with tears. She understood his meaning and she knew there was only one answer.

"I'm not going anywhere," she said, then stepped into his embrace.

For the longest time they stood together in the middle of the room, not kissing or speaking. Her head rested against his chest, the horn buttons of his jacket pressing into her cheek. She loved the smell of wool and soap, loved the sound of his heart beating beneath her ear, loved the fact that sometimes the unexpected happened and your life would never be the same again.

She ran her hands up his arms, relishing the way the wool tickled her palms as she felt the contours of his forearms, his biceps, his shoulders. She let her fingers trace the proud curve of his jaw, the straight nose, the swell of his sensual mouth. The lines that creased his eyes and cut into his cheek, lines so deep and sorrowful that she wondered how it was she hadn't seen them before. *A river of pain,* she thought. *An ocean.*

He said nothing as she touched him, but his pulse beat visibly at the base of his throat. That pleased her more than any words possibly could.

She trailed her hands back down over his shoulders, and he reached up and took her hands in his. Looking into her eyes, he raised her hands to his mouth and slowly, deliberately, kissed her wrists, her palms, each finger in turn, until she moaned deep in her throat.

He swept her up into his arms and carried her to the bed. Emotion filled every corner of her mind, it twisted through her rib cage and shot sparks of light from her eyelashes and fingertips and toes.

He laid her down on the mattress and somehow it seemed softer than before, more inviting. Candles flickered on the tabletop behind him, making it seem as if he were surrounded by a golden aura. It seemed like a lifetime since she'd been able to see anyone's aura, and the illusion somehow made her feel more sure of herself. More like the woman she had left behind.

"Is this your choice, Dakota?" His voice rolled over her like clover honey warmed by the sun. She'd never liked the sound of her name before, but the way he said it, it was a love song. "Yes," she said softly. "Oh, yes..."

He stripped off his coat and shirt with swift, sure motions, then sat on the edge of the bed to pull off his boots. His back was smoothly muscled, like the back of Michelangelo's *David.* A thing of unutterable beauty. Was this desire, then? she wondered. This sense of hunger and worship, this longing to both surrender and conquer?

He rose from the bed and looked down upon her. His breeches hugged his narrow hips and strong legs. Smiling, she glanced away, secretly delighted that she hadn't imagined his desire for her.

"Madam?" His voice was husky, urgent. He extended his hand toward her and she reached for it, then rose to her feet.

Puzzled, she frowned. "I thought—?"

"In due course, madam." His hands found the top buttons of her bodice. "First this." He kissed the base of her throat, then undid the first two buttons. "Then this." His lips moved down her breastbone. Two more buttons. "So sweet you are, madam. So finely made."

He trailed a line of fire between her breasts. Heat gathered low in her belly and it occurred to her that if she died right then, at that very moment, she would have known more than her share of pleasure.

"You tremble," he said as he unfastened the final button and eased the bodice over her shoulders. "You have nothing to fear."

She knew he spoke the truth, but the enormity of what she was about to do overwhelmed her. This was the man she'd dreamed about, the one who had captured her heart. She hadn't been looking for him. How could she, when she hadn't even believed he existed? He was hardheaded and difficult, complicated and more than likely dangerous, yet giving herself to him seemed the wisest decision she'd ever made.

Whatever happened, wherever the future led, she would always have this memory, and if it wasn't enough, it was more than she'd dreamed.

"I'm not afraid," she said, cupping his face with her hands. "I just don't know what's expected of me."

"Nothing is expected of you." He dipped his head toward her. "It is enough that you are here."

He nipped the side of her neck and she shivered with delight. His enormous workman's hands clasped her by the waist and she felt both fragile and powerful, exultantly, wildly female. Everything she'd thought possible for other women but never for her.

He kissed her collarbone, tracing his tongue across to her right shoulder. She was hallucinating. She had to be. Didn't he know she was just an out-of-work librarian from Princeton, New Jersey? The kind of woman men forgot the moment they met. The kind of woman name tags were invented for.

"Dakota Wylie." He kissed her shoulder, and the heat in her belly grew more demanding. "You are unlike anyone I have ever known."

She moaned low in her throat as his hands cupped her breasts. "You told me that once before," she murmured. "I didn't think it was a compliment."

He hooked a finger under the strap of her bra. "A strange device. A new invention, perhaps?"

"It's from Paris," she managed to say. "You'll be seeing a lot more of them in the future."

"And this?" he asked, his mouth against her tattoo. "'Tis a strange sight upon a woman's body."

She wanted to tell him it was a birthmark but couldn't manage the lie. "Are you offended?" she asked.

"Nay, madam." He worked the hooks on the bra easily. Apparently some men just had the knack. "I am intrigued."

"Not everyone likes tattoos," she went on, trying to pretend he wasn't unfastening her skirt. "Some people say they're—ohh." Her breath left her body in a sibilant rush of air. She was naked except for a pair of white cotton panties she'd washed and dried by the fire the night before.

He knelt before her and slid his hand beneath the waistband. "From Paris?" he asked, a devilish gleam in his dark blue eyes.

Actually, they were from the U.S. of A. via Macy's, but she didn't suppose he wanted that level of detail. He was on his knees before her, hands clasping her buttocks, his face dangerously close to where every degree of heat in the universe was gathering at the juncture of her thighs. His gaze never left hers as he slid her panties over her hips and down her thighs. She stepped out of them, thankful she didn't fall over. The way her legs were shaking anything was possible. Instinctively her hands went to cover herself, but he shook his head.

Tears of embarrassment welled up. "I'm too fat," she said, wishing they were lying on the bed. Or that she had a bathrobe. Or that the candle would extinguish itself. "I've been meaning to lose those last fifteen pounds but—"

"'Tis something I do not understand, Dakota." He rose to his feet and gathered her against his chest. "Is it possible you do not know the effect you have upon my person?"

"If you want to stop, it's okay," she babbled on, feeling more gauche and uncertain by the second. "I've waited twenty-six years for this. It won't kill me to wait another twenty-six."

He took her hand and placed it flat against his groin.

"For you," he said simply, "and for you alone."

It was the greatest gift anyone had ever given her. With those words he erased the last of her fears and freed her to give in to the dazzling sway of sensuality that had lain dormant inside her for so long. Twentieth-century worries about cellulite and single-digit dress sizes didn't matter any longer. This was about reveling in the feel of someone's body against yours, about skin against skin, about the fact that he was laying her down on the bed and stripping off his breeches.

About the fact that she'd never guessed, never imagined, never dreamed that it could be like this, that two people could ignite sparks more beautiful than a Fourth of July fireworks display.

He found her mouth with his and she opened for him. Their tongues met and she tasted the faint sweetness of rum. He kissed her as if kissing was an end in itself, as if he wanted nothing more than this from her, but his heart-stopping erection told her otherwise. She'd seen enough *Playgirl* centerfolds in her day to know fate had dealt him a generous hand.

It didn't seem possible, what they were about to do, but she knew that it was. Still, the logistics of the whole thing boggled the mind. She wondered if it was like this for every woman, her body responding wildly to sensation while her mind offered color commentary like one of those guys on Monday Night Football.

And then he found the center of her being with his gentle fingers and she finally understood what heaven was all about.

Patrick had never seen a woman more lovely than Dakota Wylie as she lay with him on the narrow bed. The fire crackled in the grate and the play of light against her smooth white skin was more beautiful than the most wondrous sunset. Her skin was the purest marble, so exquisitely perfect that he could be content to feast his soul upon it for the rest of his life.

The soft dark curls that covered her mound beckoned to him, and he found her with his hand. She arched against his palm, whimpering softly low in her throat, and he knew a moment of exultation that not even paradise could match. No other man had heard that sound. No other man had separated her petaled lips. No other man had felt the honeyed walls of her sheath close around his fingers as he made her ready for him.

But it was more than the simple fact of her virginity that excited Patrick: it was her self. Whatever mysterious forces that had come together to create such an uncommon woman. Her strength. Her loyalty. The sweetness of her person, the graceful line of her limbs. Her sharp intelligence and the wit that she wielded as a shield for her vulnerable heart.

She had said there had been no other man, not in this world or any other, and it occurred to Patrick that he could say the same thing. There was but one Dakota Wylie on this earth and he held her in his arms.

Dakota felt as if she were riding wave after wave of sensation, climbing to the top of a swell then sailing down the other side only to be buoyed up again by the fierce power of the sea. He had the hands of a magician, amazing, wonderful hands that found beauty wherever they touched. Her breasts turned golden when he cupped them. Rainbows arced above her hips. The rapid sound of their breathing was a love song.

She gasped when he positioned himself between her thighs, then thought she would die when he bent forward and curled his tongue around her moist, pink bud of flesh. Pleasure and pain were indistinguishable as intense shafts of sensation tore away her last hold on sanity. She cried out, as much from longing as fear, as he sought entrance, his incredible erection sliding between the slick folds of her vagina.

He didn't move at first and she began to relax, feeling her body mold itself to his in a most amazing fashion. A restlessness began to grow deep inside in a place she'd never known existed, a yawning emptiness that cried out to be filled. It was so simple, so elemental, that tears spilled down her cheeks at the wonder of it all.

He saw her tears and felt as if a dagger had been plunged deep inside his soul. "I have no wish to hurt you," he managed to say, even as his own body cried out for release. She was so small, so tight, that he knew pain to be inevitable.

"You'll only hurt me if you stop."

Her words lifted him above the bed, above the house, above the clouds. Reining in his power, he angled his hips then swiftly broke the sweet band of flesh and felt the warmth of her blood on his member.

"No more pain," he whispered against the fullness of her lips. "Never again."

He began to move slowly at first, then faster, and nearly growled with pleasure when she moved with him. The thrust and parry of their bodies, locked in a primal rhythm, carried him closer and closer to the edge of madness, that place where life and death met and became one.

Dakota was sure she'd died because nothing else could explain the way she felt. Bright lights exploded behind her eyelids. Pinwheels of fire and sparks of heat danced across her skin. The ocean roared in her ears, while the smell of a forest after a rainstorm filled her head. Only death or madness could explain the barrage of sensations that rippled from her head to her feet then back again...and always, always centering deep in the pit of her belly.

He filled her, filled every part of her until she cried out not from pain but from a hunger so fierce it knew no words. He looked different by the light of the fire, his naked body backlit by the glow. Stripped of clothing and the veneer of civilization, he was a powerful male animal in his prime. Sweat glistened on his shoulders like diamonds. It tasted salty and fine against her tongue. She wanted to know every part of him, to take him in her mouth and feel the surging power of desire, but that would have to wait.

This time it was about mating, the fierce, primitive urge to join together two separate beings and make them one. He moved above her in a seductive rhythm, urging her hips to lift up from the mattress to meet his thrusts. Her muscles clenched around him, drawing him more deeply inside her body. More deeply inside her heart.

An exquisite tension filled her limbs. She was waiting, striving, yearning toward something, some wonderful mysterious something that she'd only read about and never believed would happen for her. When it did, it was as if the power and beauty of the universe and everything in it belonged to her and her alone.

The world as they knew it disappeared and there was only that room, that bed, that moment in time.

Chapter Seventeen

17

They made love again, with greater urgency this time, as if they both were aware that what they'd shared was as fleeting and beautiful as moonlight on snow.

He was a tender, passionate lover who saw to it that she found one shuddering climax after another before he allowed himself to be pleasured by her. And pleasure him she did. With her hands and her mouth…with her heart and soul. There were no barriers between them, no inhibitions. In that secret room, with only the crackling fire for company, they discovered the secrets of each other's body, worshiping each other the way lovers had since the beginning of time.

He watched her as she slept, her lovely face in the crook of his arm. Her thick dark lashes cast a shadow on the smooth white skin of her cheek, and he was mesmerized by the sight. If he were an artist he would capture that shadow on canvas so that in some cold and distant future he could remind himself that once he had known how it felt to be truly happy, for somehow he knew it would not be forever.

Who are you, Dakota Wylie? he wondered as she slept. Nothing about her was as it should be. Her appearance, her actions, the freedom with which she expressed every thought that passed through her mind—was there another woman in that vast world like her? He could not imagine it to be so. There was something so individual about her, so set apart from the rest of the world, as to make him wonder if she was flesh and blood at all but an apparition sent to ease the endless pain in his heart.

I do not wish to feel this way, madam, but you inspire in me something perilously close to love.

Dakota murmured in her sleep as she sank more deeply into a dream. The nursery...the hand-wrought cradle...the beautiful infant who slept peacefully beneath her lace-trimmed quilt...the man whose heart seemed too small to contain the boundless love he felt for the innocent babe—

She awoke with a start, surprised to find herself still nestled in his arms. How easy it was to get used to being happy. How dangerous when you know it could never last.

She opened her eyes slowly. His face was the first thing she saw. He was looking down at her with something approaching adoration. She closed her eyes again. *Anytime you want me, God.* It couldn't possibly get any better than this.

"You were dreaming," he said, smoothing a dark curl back from her temple.

She pressed a kiss to the warm skin of his shoulder. "How did you know?"

"You smiled," he said, drawing the quilt up over her shoulders and pulling her closer. "Mayhap the dream was of me?"

"I dreamed about you and Abigail," she said softly. She saw the nursery and the cradle, saw the sunlight streaming through the windows, felt the love filling his heart until it hurt him to breathe.

He pulled away from her as if she had slapped him. "I will not discuss this."

"Patrick, she's your little girl—"

"Do not pursue this line of inquiry, Dakota."

"She's your daughter—"

"I will not talk about this with you."

"Your flesh and blood—"

"The child is not mine."

It took a moment for his words to penetrate. She sat up straight, clutching the quilt to her breasts like a shield. "What did you say?"

He met her eyes. "I said I am not Abigail's father."

"Of course you're her father," she said automatically. "She's just like you. Anyone can see that."

"My wife took a lover in the same room in which you slept your first night in my house."

Dakota felt as if he had reached inside her chest and grabbed her heart with his bare hands. Cook had told her the same thing and she had urged the woman to share all the juicy details. How different those details sounded from his lips. And how ashamed she was of herself for wanting to know.

His tone was emotionless, but she knew it was only a front. "It was not the first time Susannah had broken her marriage vows."

"I don't care about your wife," Dakota said as a vision played out inside her head. "She doesn't matter. You were standing over Abigail's cradle, the one with the embroidered curtains that had belonged to your grandmother, and—"

He stared at her as if she'd sprouted horns and a tail.

Oh, my God, Dakota thought. *What have I done?* Abby wasn't an infant any longer, she was a little girl. The cradle had long since been replaced by a small bed.

And she was in big trouble.

"How do you know these things?" he demanded, placing his hands on her shoulders and forcing her to meet his eyes. "How is it you know of things that happened before you came to this house?"

"I don't think you really want an answer to that," she whispered. *And I certainly don't want to tell you.*

"Were you a friend of Susannah's?"

She had been right about the name and she knew she was right about this, as well. "I never met your wife."

"My family is dead. You cannot have learned this from them."

"Do us both a favor and don't try to figure it out. Just consider it a lucky guess."

"Tell me how you know these things."

"Would you believe I'm just very, very smart?"

His jaw grew noticeably tighter.

"I guess you wouldn't believe that." She regrouped. "Okay, here's the truth—I'm psychic."

"Say again."

When had the word *psychic* come into common use? "I have second sight."

"You see the future?" He sounded the way most people sounded when she told them.

She nodded. "Sometimes I get a glimpse of the past, too, but not very often."

Patrick had known from the start that Dakota Wylie was unlike most women, but he had not suspected anything of this most incredible nature. "And that is how you came to know about the cradle and the curtains."

"Yes." Her voice was soft, almost sorrowful. There was a new expression in her dark eyes, a tenderness he did not wish to see, for it would be his undoing. "You love Abby very much."

A great shaft of pain pierced his heart. "I loved her once." He paused. "When she was my child."

He had said those words to no man or woman who walked the earth. They tore into his gut and twisted hard. The pain burned deep into his heart and then, when he thought he could stand it no longer, she reached out and placed her hand on his forearm and he felt as if she had somehow laid a healing balm against his tortured soul.

"She *is* your child."

"No, madam, I assure you she is not."

"How can you know that?"

"That revelation was my wife's last gift to me." Again he had never spoken these words to anyone, but he felt compelled to speak them to the dark-haired woman who watched him so closely. Who seemed to know the contours of his heart. "Susannah had lain with two other men the month she conceived, either of whom could claim the child as his own."

His rage and sorrow permeated her skin and filled her lungs until she could scarcely draw a breath. Dear God, how much it had cost him to tell her. "I'm so sorry."

"You offer me pity?" he challenged, his gaze never leaving hers.

"I would never do that to you. I offer you truth. Abigail is your daughter. Six years of loving her is proof of that."

"I have made my peace with the situation and moved forward."

"You haven't moved. All you've done is turn away from your child."

"Have you not heard my words? She is not my child. Another man's blood flows through her veins."

"And what if it does?" she countered. "Does that change the love you had for her? Does that make her love you any less?"

"There are those who say I drove Susannah from our bed."

"You are a difficult man. Living with you wouldn't be easy."

"How quickly you have learned that."

"Don't punish your daughter for something your wife did." Dakota grabbed his hands in hers with a gesture so unexpected that another layer of his defenses shattered. "Abby needs you so much."

"I have no wish to hurt her, but I cannot change what is."

"Do you have any idea how lucky you are to have Abby? I'd give anything to—" She stopped, appalled by what she had been about to say.

"You cannot know how it is for me," Patrick said. "Such things are not in your experience."

"You're wrong," she whispered. "I cannot have children, Patrick, but I can tell you that I would love Abby as much as if she had grown beneath my heart."

The moments ticked by silently, then the minutes. They lay together on the narrow bed, not touching or talking, as the barriers between their separate lives once again fell into place and the empty chill of loneliness recaptured their hearts.

Dakota supposed she should be relieved. There was something terrifying about being that vulnerable before a stranger. Not even with him cradled inside her body had she felt so open and exposed as she had these past few minutes.

He isn't the man for you, Wylie. He can't even love his child. What chance would you have? The wounds Susannah Devane had dealt him had been fatal. Whatever capacity to love he'd possessed was gone now, destroyed by her treachery, and not even Dakota Wylie, girl librarian and psychic, could bring it back.

She and Devane had been brought together to help Andrew McVie take his place in history, and nothing more. Once that happened they would go back to their separate worlds and life would go on as if paradise hadn't been right there for the asking.

"It must be nearly daybreak," she said when she could stand the silence no longer. "We should be getting back."

"I will see you to the room, then set forth to find McVie," he said reaching for their clothes, which were scattered on the floor next to the bed.

"Not without me you're not." This was her destiny he was messing with. If anyone was going to find Andrew, it had better be Dakota Wylie or she'd know the reason why. "Where do *we* plan on searching?"

"*I* will begin with my neighbors. Mayhap he has sought shelter with one of them."

"I'll come with you."

"Nay, madam. It is too dangerous for a woman."

"Too dangerous to visit the neighbors? I'll pretend I didn't hear that."

"You will go back to the house and wait."

"*You* go back to the house. I've spent more than enough time in your house." Didn't he realize the biggest danger she faced was in pretending she belonged in his life?

"Your company will make my job more difficult."

"You're taking your beloved new wife out to meet the neighbors. What better way to get into their houses so you can snoop?"

"I am not known for my affability. Their suspicions would be aroused if I came calling with my wife in tow."

"It's not like you have time to build secret passageways to every house in Franklin Ridge."

A smile tugged at the right corner of his mouth and her damnably vulnerable heart ached in response.

"You believe the good people of Franklin Ridge will take you to their bosoms and reveal their secrets?" he asked.

"It's either that or I'll be forced to look in their medicine cabinets."

"Madam?"

She sighed. *We couldn't have made it over the long haul even if we wanted to, Devane. You'll never get my jokes and I'll never be able to heal your broken heart.*

"You say nobody in town likes you, and from what I've heard, you're probably right. If you start popping up on their doorsteps for a cup of tea, they'll have you arrested." She paused to let him consider the vastness of his unpopularity. "If you take me along with you, they might give you another chance."

"I am not that good an actor, Dakota."

"But *I* am. I'll make them believe we're the most wonderful couple since George and Martha."

He had cut himself off from the daily fabric of life in Franklin Ridge. Susannah's treachery had plunged him into solitude and it was that very solitude that had made it possible for him to move between the worlds of home and war. But now he needed the information he could glean from the townspeople, and to obtain that information he needed the woman next to him. Needed her in ways he dared not contemplate.

"They will watch us closely to see if we are indeed the happily wed couple we claim to be."

"And they won't be disappointed."

"You will do this for me?"

Her smile was quicksilver. It was gone before he could capture it in his soul. "No, but I will do it for me."

Dakota was silent as she followed him back through the dark passageway to the house. This was the stuff of a Victoria Holt novel and all she could think about was how many spiders were lurking overhead, ready to pounce. She hadn't given a thought to spiders when she was angry and her adrenalin was pumping, but now she was convinced there was a platoon of black widows waiting for her.

"Mmmph," she said as she walked headlong into his shoulder. "Why did you stop? I want to get out of here."

"The door is locked."

"That's ridiculous." She ducked under his arm and pushed hard. "The door is locked."

"Precisely, madam. Did you do so?"

"Of course I didn't. In fact, I meant to ask you how you managed to reassemble the armoire from inside the passageway. That was a pretty neat trick."

"It requires patience," he said, "and a degree of strength. Nothing more."

"So who closed it after me?"

"It would appear that someone knows of the secret passageway and is revealing that knowledge to me."

"Not very subtle, if you ask me. Why didn't they just leave a note? Everyone around here seems to be into writing letters. Maybe—"

"Madam, would you refrain from that constant chatter while I ponder the situation."

She couldn't believe her ears. They were locked out of the house, stranded in a secret passageway that probably bred spiders the way picnics bred ants. "Ponder? I can't believe I'm standing here in the dark with a man who'd use a word like *ponder.* How about a nice active verb like *escape* or—"

He clapped a hand over her mouth and silenced her.

"You will remain here," he said. "The hidden room exits beneath the stables. I will walk up to the main house and unlock the wardrobe to release you."

She removed his hand. "How do I know you won't forget about me?"

"It is a matter of trust between us."

"That's what I was afraid of," she said. "That's why we're going to do it my way…."

Dakota and Patrick entered through the front door just as Cook finished stirring the breakfast porridge. Standing in the hallway, they brushed snow from each other's hair and shoulders, laughing just loudly enough to draw Cook from the kitchen. The idea was to make the household believe the two lovers had gone out for an early-morning stroll in the snow.

"She's watching us from the hallway," Dakota murmured as Patrick pressed a kiss to the nape of her neck. "I think she is about to faint."

"'Twill reach Morristown by the noon hour," Patrick said dryly as Dakota straightened the collar of his jacket. "News of the happy couple will be served with the midday meal.

The truth was it was frighteningly easy to play the happy couple. All Dakota had to do was think about how she had felt in his arms and she was awash with violent, spectacular emotions.

"G'morning, sir." A young soldier called out a greeting as he lugged a barrel of flour through the hallway. "And g'morning to you, too, ma'am."

Dakota favored him with a warm, wifely smile. "It's a wonderful morning, isn't it?" she asked, meaning every syllable. "The best morning ever!"

The soldier eyed her curiously, then shrugged his bony shoulders. "If you say so, ma'am, I s'pose it is."

"Do not overplay your hand," Patrick warned her as they strolled toward the kitchen for their morning meal. "Such exuberance might strain their ability to believe."

"Too bad," she retorted with a snap of her fingers. "We're newlyweds. Newlyweds are supposed to be exuberant."

He looked at her strangely but said nothing more.

"Good morning to you," said Cook as they took their seats at the table. "And a fine day it seems to be all around."

Patrick grunted a response, while Dakota beamed another megawatt smile in the woman's direction. "It's most definitely a fine day, Cook." She turned toward Abigail, who was seated across from her. "Morning, Abby."

"I waited and waited," Abigail said, looking from Dakota to Patrick then back again, "but Cook said I could eat my johnnycakes before you came down."

"Cook did exactly the right thing," Dakota said, leaning across the table to pat the child's tiny hand. "You're a growing girl. You need your food."

Cook served Dakota and Patrick each a plate of johnnycakes.

"And porridge afterward," said Cook, "if you have the appetite for it."

"These are wonderful, Cook," Dakota said with a smile as the woman served up some more of the pancakes. "Just what we needed to warm our bones."

Turning away from Patrick, Cook winked broadly at Dakota in a way that made Dakota want to giggle like a guilty teenager.

"Oh, I'm certain your bones are plenty warm, missus."

Patrick looked up from his steaming cup of chocolate. "Have you nothing better to do with your time, woman, save stand there simpering like a fool?"

"Begging your pardon, sir." Cook winked again at Dakota and turned back to stir the porridge.

Patrick muttered something dark about an unpardonable lack of privacy, but Dakota laughed and patted him on the hand in what she hoped seemed like a natural, wifely gesture. In truth, it was anything but. The simple touch of his hand beneath her fingertips sent ripples of sensation up her arm and straight to her heart. If this was what a wife felt every time she touched her husband, it was a miracle anyone made it to their first anniversary.

Abigail fidgeted with the bowl of porridge that followed the johnnycakes. Her eyes were heavily shadowed and she had none of her usual six-year-old sparkle.

"Abby?" Dakota asked. "You didn't sleep very well last night, did you?"

Abigail shook her head. Even her braids had lost their bounce. "My throat hurts," she said, placing her hand over her windpipe. "Like someone squeezed it real hard."

Dakota rose from her chair and rounded the table to the child's side. She placed the flat of her hand against Abby's forehead. "You feel cool enough. Are you sneezing?"

"No."

Something niggled at the back of Dakota's memory, like a forgotten phrase from an old song, but she couldn't quite grasp hold of it. "Maybe you should stay in today. It's just awful outside."

The room shook as another tree toppled in the woods behind the house. The solders were making short work of the thick woods as they raced to complete their huts before the next storm.

"Bloody fools," Patrick swore. "There will be naught but open fields remaining when they have done with it."

"You begrudge them their huts?" Dakota asked.

"I do, madame, and I begrudge the fact that my trees are used to construct a new kitchen for McDowell's chef."

Abby moved her spoon around in her bowl of porridge, then pushed the whole thing away from her.

"Why don't you go upstairs and get Lucy?" Dakota suggested. "I found a lovely piece of wool that would make a splendid dress for her."

Abby turned to her father. "May I, Papa?"

He nodded and the child ran from the room.

"What are they going to do about the foot soldiers?" Dakota asked, pouring herself some more hot chocolate. She was aware that Cook was hanging on every word. "Those poor men are sleeping in the snow."

"First the general's needs," Devane said, meeting her eyes across the table, "then the needs of his men. Neither of which are my concern nor should they be yours."

Behind her Cook sniffed, obviously distressed by Patrick's cavalier attitude toward the plight of the soldiers. Dakota had trouble suppressing the urge to defend him to all and sundry, but knew that would not help advance his cause. The suspicion under which he was held was his greatest asset.

He pushed back his chair and rose to his full height of over six feet. "We will ride out this afternoon to call on the Bradleys, the Vliets and the Atwaters. Be ready by two o'clock."

We're supposed to be newlyweds, her look admonished him. *If this is going to work, you'll have to play along.*

His glance held hers for a moment. A slow, lazy grin spread across his handsome face like daylight breaking after a stormy night. She could almost hear Cook swooning as she chopped vegetables for the soup pot.

"I will wait for you in the front hall."

He turned to leave, then apparently thought better of it. Dakota watched, mesmerized, as he closed the distance between them, then bent over her and kissed her.

Thoroughly.

If she'd been standing when he kissed her, she would have toppled over in a heap as bells, whistles and the Vienna Choir Boys exploded into full, exultant life inside her head the moment his mouth claimed hers.

"Two o'clock," he said, touching her chin with the tip of his forefinger.

"Two o'clock," she whispered.

Chapter Eighteen

18

After she recovered from Devane's unexpected kiss at the breakfast table, Dakota managed to compose herself long enough to ask Cook a few discreet questions. Within two minutes her worst fears had been confirmed. Probably the only thing between Patrick and the hangman's noose was the fact that he was not only the most disliked man in Franklin Ridge, he was also the wealthiest.

War had taken its toll on the small community, and without Devane's financial support they would be in even more trouble than they already were. Human nature being what it was, that made the good citizens hate him all the more. It wasn't going to be easy to get them to open their doors to Devane, but they would give it the old college try.

After the morning meal Abby ran off to watch the soldiers build their huts while Dakota went upstairs to tackle her main problem: What did a woman wear to visit neighbors who hated her husband's guts? She debated between the pale blue moiré she'd laid across the bed and the dark rose muslin with the flowered skirt that was draped over the back of the chaise longue. The blue moiré had a particularly low-cut neckline, which was terrific if you were built like one of the girls on "Baywatch," and not so terrific if you were actually human.

What about that nice yellow dress with the crocheted lace at the cuffs?

Ginny's voice was as clear and distinct as if she were standing in the room with her daughter. Dakota spun around and looked to make sure she wasn't.

"Ma!" she said out loud. "Is that you?"

Don't even think about that blue dress, not unless those falsies you made from the T-shirt will stay in place.

"Where are you?"

I'm at the kitchen table. Janis is coming over for a tarot reading in a little while and I thought I'd drop in and see how you were doing before things got too hectic.

"Drop in? You make it sound like I'm living in an apartment on the next block."

You're going to have to make a decision soon, honey. I hope you'll be ready for it.

"A decision? What kind of decision?"

I can't tell you that. But I can say that if you follow your heart, you won't be sorry.

"How are you, Ma? Is everyone all right?"

You've only been gone two days, honey. Everyone's just fine.

"I miss everyone so much," she said, blinking back tears.

You sound surprised.

"I am. Who would've thought I'd turn out to be such a wimp?"

He loves you, you know.

"Oh, my God!" Ginny Wylie, a Peeping Tom? "You didn't—?"

I'm insulted.

"Can't blame me for asking, Ma. You did read my diary when I was thirteen."

This is different.

Dakota laughed out loud. "You don't know the half of it. . . ."

Listen with your heart, honey, as well as your head, and everything will be just fine.

Dakota shivered as if a cold wind had moved across her skin. "What do you mean, he loves me?"

Silence.

"Ma?" Her voice rose in alarm. "I'm coming home as soon as I find Andrew and Shannon and the balloon. This was all some kind of cosmic mistake. I really wasn't meant to be here. Say something, Ma!"

Wouldn't you know it? The first time in her life that Dakota actually wanted romantic advice from her mother and Ginny vanished without a trace.

She fondled the silky skirt of the blue moiré between her fingers and sighed. She'd look like a flat-chested female impersonator in it. The rose made her look like a new red potato. She hated it when her mother was right.

"Yellow it is," she said, struggling to ease the garment over her head and not suffocate beneath the weight of the skirts. Dozens of tiny pearl buttons ran down her back and for the life of her she couldn't think of a way to fasten them other than throwing herself on the mercy of a parlormaid.

She was considering changing into the blue dress with the buttons in the front when Abigail's scream split the air.

"What on earth—?" She'd seen the child not more than twenty minutes ago and, except for that sore throat, everything had been fine.

Gown still undone, she hurried down the hallway to the child's bedroom, where she found Abby huddled near the window in the fetal position.

"Abby!" She ran to her side. "What's wrong?"

The child lifted her eyes to Dakota, but it was clear Abby saw something—or someone—else standing before her. The child clutched her throat, pulling at the collar of her plain cotton dress as if it were choking the very life from her.

Dakota unfastened the top two buttons, but it didn't help. Abby pushed Dakota's hands away and struggled for breath. She had the same look in her eyes she'd had last night when Dakota had comforted her after her bad dream.

"Abby, can you speak to me?" Dakota asked as she tried to hold the girl in her arms. "Can you say anything?"

A sheen of sweat broke out over the child's upper lip as she struggled to form a word.

"What was that?" Dakota leaned closer, straining to hear. "Say it again."

"An—Andrew."

The hairs on the back of her neck rose. "What about Andrew?"

"The hangman," she said, same as she had last night. "The tree by the gray house—"

"What house?" Her head was buzzing and the sound grew louder with each word Abby uttered. "Where is the tree, Abby?"

"The mountains," Abby said, erupting into noisy tears. "The big red ball can't save him!"

Abby's words seemed to be traveling toward her through a wind tunnel. "Abby, please, you have to tell me what you see! Where is the big red ball? Is anybody on it? What—"

"Papa!" Abby cried out, looking past Dakota. "Papa!"

Dakota turned toward the door in time to see Devane cross the threshold. Before he could say a word, the child hurled herself at him, crying as if her heart would break.

He pulled back, his spine stiffening noticeably, but Abby would not be denied. She hung on to him for dear life, her words lost amid the tears, but his hands remained resolutely at his sides.

His eyes met Dakota's. The world and everything in it seemed to come into sharp focus. His expression remained impassive but this time it was different. This time she could see beneath the surface, past his anger and his pain, to the part of his soul he hid from the world.

You have a heart, she thought, willing him to hear her plea. *Does it matter whose blood runs through her veins? She's only a little girl and she loves you so much.*

Devane looked down at Abby. The child's shoulders shook with her sobs. She was so tiny, so fragile despite the enormity of her spirit, and once upon a time she'd been the most important thing in the world to him.

Remember! Dakota pleaded silently. *Remember how much you loved her.*

Whether or not Susannah's parting words had been true, the fact remained that in all the ways that mattered Abby was Devane's daughter and always would be. He was the one who had held her when she cried. He was the one who had stood over her cradle and dreamed of her future. Nothing Susannah had done mattered compared to that.

Touch her, Patrick! Just reach out and touch her and it will all fall into place.

Dakota held her breath as he lifted his right hand, then slowly brought it to rest atop the child's head.

The child's hair was cool to the touch. The shiny brown strands were soft as the finest silk, and a powerful flood of memories, long buried, welled up deep inside Patrick's chest as he cupped her head with his hand.

Not that long ago he'd held her in his arms, terrified he might hurt her with his big clumsy hands. She'd been an infant then, a tiny slip of a thing, helpless as a baby bird fallen from the nest. He'd trembled when the nursemaid placed her in his arms, and had tried to hand the blanket-wrapped bundle back to the woman, but then the infant had looked up at him with her serious gray eyes and he'd felt the walls around his heart crumble and fall at his feet.

He cleared his throat, aware of the intensity of Dakota Wylie's gaze.

"What is the problem here?" His tone was gruff but he did not break the connection between himself and Abigail.

"The hangman!" Abigail cried out in a voice he'd never heard before. She sounded terrified, as if she'd witnessed something unspeakable.

"A bad dream?" he asked.

Dakota shook her head.

"I do not understand," he said cautiously, wondering what had become of the straight path his life had been. "What is this talk of the hangman?"

"The two men," Abby cried, tugging at his sleeve. He could see some of the terror giving way to a determination far beyond her years. "The tree by the gray house..." Her words drifted into soft sobs and he let his hand slip from her head to her shoulders and held her close.

"It's a premonition," Dakota said. "Your daughter also has second sight."

"I hardly think Abigail is a seer."

"Think again, Patrick. She has the gift."

It would explain so much about the child. How many times had Abigail surprised him with a bit of knowledge or information that seemed out of keeping with her tender years?

"You believe this to be the case?" he asked Dakota.

She nodded. "Absolutely."

He knelt in front of the child and, without thinking, brushed the tears from her cheeks with the tip of his forefinger. It was the first spontaneous gesture he had allowed himself toward her since Susannah had shattered his dreams.

Awkwardly he placed his arm about her fragile shoulders, and the child seemed to blossom before his eyes. A wave of guilt assailed him. It took so little to make her happy.

"The hangman is all ready," Abby said. "Now that the snow has stopped they can hang the rope from the big tree behind the house."

Patrick's eyes locked with Dakota's. Every house in the Colony of New Jersey had at least one big tree behind it.

Dakota crouched down in front of Abigail. "Honey, your papa and I are going to go for a carriage ride. Would you like to come with us?" And if she saw a gray house…

The elation on the child's face was painful to his eyes. "May I, Papa?"

He cleared his throat then said gruffly, "Yes, yes, of course you may. Two o'clock, Abigail. In the front parlor."

He turned toward the door but not before Dakota saw the glint of tears in his eyes.

Abby clutched Lucy to her chest as she sat on the edge of the top step and waited for the hall clock to toll two times. Her heart was beating so loudly inside her chest that it hurt her ears.

"Oh, Lucy!" she whispered. "Papa wants me to ride with him in the carriage." And even better than that, better than anything in the world, he had hugged her just like her friend Mary's papa hugged his children.

She leapt to her feet as the clock began to toll. Dakota had helped her put on her very best dress, a green-sprigged muslin that made her feel almost pretty. She smoothed the skirt and brushed a fleck of dust from her scuffed kid slippers, then flew down the stairs as if she had wings.

Papa stood near the door. He looked so handsome in his pale

breeches and dark brown wool cape, and his hair scraped back and tied with a strip of leather.

"Abigail." His mouth quirked up at the sides as he turned toward her. "You look very pretty in that dress."

She buried her face against Lucy's yarn hair. "Thank you, Papa."

"Your hair," he said, looking at her carefully. "Is it different somehow?"

"Dakota combed it smooth then tied it with a piece of velvet ribbon."

"It becomes you," he said, nodding. "You should comb it that way all the time."

She would! She would comb her hair and tie it with a velvet ribbon every single day of her life if it meant Papa would smile at her like that, as if he loved her and was glad she was his little girl.

Jacob Wentworth, one of the good citizens of Franklin Ridge, watched their departure from his front door, his face taut with silent disapproval. If he had a shotgun, Dakota had no doubt the three of them—Patrick, Abigail and herself—would resemble Swiss cheese by now.

"You were right," Dakota said as she accompanied Patrick and Abigail back to their waiting carriage. "Everybody *does* hate you."

Patrick gave her a sidelong glance in the gathering dusk. "'Tis as I thought it would be."

"Ten houses and nobody would open their door to us," she continued. "They wouldn't even invite us in when Abby asked."

"Will you now allow me to obtain information in my own way?"

"I can't believe people would be so rude," Dakota went on, ignoring him. "Whatever happened to hospitality? It's freezing out here. Wouldn't you think someone would at least offer us a cup of hot cider?"

"Mayhap if the cider were laced with poison."

She couldn't argue with that. The withering hatred they'd encountered had put a new spin on everything. *So, you're not the heartless monster you pretend to be with Abby,* she thought. There could be no future for the little girl as long as Patrick was ostracized by the townspeople. The only hope for Abby was to send her to the Girls' School of the Sacred Heart where she would be accepted into the fold in a way she could never be here in Franklin Ridge.

Abigail ran ahead through the snow to investigate a fallen bird's nest at the edge of the woods.

"Abigail!" Patrick's voice rang out as she disappeared into the shadows. "Do not venture too far."

He quickened his pace to keep up with the child. Dakota was about to quicken her own pace when something caught her eye. About ten feet to her left the pristine whiteness of the snow was marred by an odd, shadowy depression. Curious, she picked her way through the snow and bent to investigate.

She didn't know exactly what she'd expected to find, but she did know a loaded handgun wasn't on the short list of possibilities. She was no firearms expert, but she knew she'd seen this gun before and it hadn't been in a museum.

It was Shannon's, the one her friend had kept locked away in her desk drawer. A flood of possibilities rushed through her mind. Had the gun tumbled out of Shannon's bag or had she deliberately tossed it away, to keep the gun from falling into enemy hands? Instinct told Dakota it was the latter. While she'd come through time armed with jelly doughnuts, apparently Shannon had had the foresight to bring something equally lethal, albeit in a different way. She glanced toward the woods. Patrick's back was to her. She whispered a quick prayer of thanks. If he saw the gun, he'd ask questions and she'd be forced to tell him everything.

Quickly she reached under her skirts and tucked it into the top of her left cotton stocking, then continued on toward the carriage.

Approximately thirty minutes later Patrick guided the horses up the lane toward the house. To Dakota it seemed as if they'd been on the road for thirty days. The gun was wedged firmly between the carriage seat and her thigh and she'd shifted her position more often than a politician.

"'Tis the fifth time you have done so," Patrick observed. "What gives you such discomfort?"

She crossed her fingers beneath the lap robe. "My back hurts."

He nodded and she breathed a guilty sigh of relief.

Patrick brought the carriage to a stop at the front door. Abby, who had been napping beneath her lap robes, burrowed more closely against Dakota's side.

"It seems like a crime to wake her up," Dakota said innocently as Patrick climbed from the carriage and came around to help her. "She's sleeping like a log. Why don't you carry her upstairs to her room?"

He swung Dakota from the carriage, letting her slide slowly down his body until her feet touched the ground. As if they *could* touch the ground when she was this close to him.

"You try my patience, Dakota Wylie," he said as she met his eyes. "Can you not allow the future to proceed at its own pace?"

Oh, Devane, she thought wistfully as the gun slid down to the back of her knee. *If we only had the time....*

Chapter Nineteen

19

The house was in chaos when they returned. If possible, more soldiers than before were crowded into the front hallway and main rooms, and each one of them seemed to consider it his solemn duty to make as big a mess as possible.

"What in bloody hell is going on?" Patrick demanded as the door closed behind them.

Dakota glanced around at the confusion and noticed most of the furniture had been moved out. "Looks like McDowell meant what he said about throwing a party for us. I thought he was just talking to hear himself speak." She'd known lots of blowhards in her time and McDowell had seemed about as reliable as any of his kind. "He's probably moving the furniture to make room for dancing."

Devane's jaw tightened. "The house still belongs to me, whether or not McDowell wishes to acknowledge that fact. I will not have my possessions removed without my permission."

Abigail tugged on his sleeve. "Don't be angry, Papa. They'll be gone soon."

Dakota crouched down next to her and helped the child off with her cloak. "Not soon enough for your papa, honey. The soldiers will probably be here until spring."

Abigail's gray eyes took on the dreamy expression Dakota had come to recognize. "Not him," she said, tilting her head in the direction of the library where McDowell was sequestered. "He'll be far 'way by Christmas." Abby turned and ran toward the kitchen for a cup of cider.

Patrick stormed toward the library and Dakota seized the opportunity to flee upstairs with the gun.

There weren't a lot of hiding places to choose from, not with a child, an inquisitive male and a score of soldiers in the house. She slid it under the feather mattress in the anteroom, then smoothed the quilt and fluffed up the pillow. So what if it would be like sleeping on top of a hand grenade? The important thing was that nobody found it.

"Dakota! Where are you?"

"Be right there, Abby," she called out, thanking God the child hadn't popped up ten seconds earlier.

Abby stood near the armoire in Devane's room and, for a moment, Dakota was afraid the child had flashed on the hidden passageway, but Abby had something much more exciting on her mind.

"Papa found two more ladies!"

I'll bet he'd be dynamite on a treasure hunt. "Two more ladies?" she asked, tugging on one of Abby's braids. Probably new parlormaids to help Cook run the household. "Where did he find them?"

"They were standing right there at the kitchen door when I got there!" Abby's eyes were wide with excitement. "They're so pretty...."

Dakota's smile faltered. *I really don't want to hear this.*

"...And then she slapped Papa and called him a monster!"

She snapped to attention. "Somebody hit your father?"

Abby nodded vigorously. "The lady with the red hair. She said Papa had ruined her life."

A knot formed in the pit of Dakota's stomach. "Did she say how he'd managed to ruin her life?" *It's 1779, Wylie. Take a wild guess.*

Abby frowned as she thought. "She said her children would not have a father, and that's when Papa told me to leave."

"You stay here," she told Abby. "I'm going downstairs to see what's going on."

She went straight to the kitchen where she'd heard the commotion. Cook was kneading bread with large, angry motions. Will sat on a chair near the back door while a beautiful young blonde warmed her hands by the fire. Dakota winced. The girl was young enough to be Patrick's daughter, which meant she was probably exactly the right age to date him.

If that was the competition, she might as well fling herself into the stew pot and be done with it.

You're the mistress of the house, she told herself as they noticed her standing in the doorway. It might be a temporary role, but she was going to play it to the hilt while it lasted.

"My husband," she said to Cook, with a nod toward Will and the lovely young woman. "Where will I find him?"

"The front room, missus. But I don't think you want to be going in there, what with the commotion and all."

Let this one be homely, she prayed. *Thirty pounds overweight would be nice.* Just once in her life she'd love to nurse a healthy superiority complex about something other than the fact she could reshelve books faster than any librarian in the Western world.

Patrick sat in the wing chair near the window. He didn't look happy to see her. "Go back upstairs," he ordered. "Now!"

She resisted the urge to click her heels together and say, "Yes, *mein Führer.*"

The woman wasn't anywhere in sight. Obviously he hoped to

keep it that way. "Abby told me we had company," she said sweetly. "I thought you might like to introduce us."

"I said leave *now!*"

She stepped into the room. "Don't bother trying to hide her, Devane, because I know what's going on."

"Do you?"

Dakota spun to her right at the sound of the female voice. A gorgeous redhead stepped from behind the door. She was a good six inches taller than Dakota and twenty pounds lighter, and she had a pistol pointed straight at Patrick's heart.

"Come in," said the woman with a brittle smile. "Sit down next to your husband. You might want to hear about the kind of man you married."

"No, thank you," Dakota said with an equally brittle smile. Damn the luck. If she still had Shannon's gun tucked inside her stocking, she could give the woman a run for her money.

"My wife knows naught about the situation," Patrick said. "Do not bring her into this."

The red-haired woman dismissed him with a contemptuous glance. "Then it's time she learned, isn't it?" She gestured toward a wing chair opposite Patrick's. "Sit down."

Dakota considered making a run for it, but it was obvious the woman was at the end of her rope. She sat down opposite Patrick.

The woman was still talking, but suddenly Dakota couldn't make out what she was saying. She could see the woman's lips moving, but the words were garbled. As if they were coming at her fast and loud but in a foreign language.

"What was that?" she asked, leaning forward in her seat.

The buzzing inside Dakota's head drowned out all other sounds. Patrick touched her arm. She knew he did because she saw his hand upon her forearm, but it felt as if he were touching her through layers of cotton wool.

What was going on? She had the same drifting, otherworldly feeling she'd had that last day when the balloon was about to sail off. But the balloon wasn't anywhere around.

A lighthouse...a sense of danger everywhere...a tall, red-haired woman—

"Emilie?" Dakota asked.

The woman looked down at her, gun still aimed at Patrick. "We know each other?"

"In a way," she said.

Emilie moved closer to Patrick. "Been talking about me, have you, Devane? I'm surprised. I thought you kept your secrets close to your vest."

"Let my wife go," he ordered, his voice cool as ice. "Grant her safety and I will tell you all."

"Tell me all," Emilie countered, "and then maybe I'll let your wife go."

"You're making a mistake," Dakota said, unable to keep silent. "Don't you realize you're both on the same side?"

"So he has you fooled, too," Emilie said, glancing toward Dakota with pity in her eyes. "The man's a spy."

"So are you."

Next to her Patrick started in surprise.

"You're right," Emilie said to Dakota, "but the trouble is he's passing our secrets on to the British and now my husband is going to pay the price."

Tell her the whole story, Wylie. Tell her you know how it's all going to end up.

"Where is Zane?" Emilie demanded in a tone of voice bordering on hysteria. "Where did they take him?"

"I do not know, madam," said Patrick. "I wish with my entire heart that I could find those two brave men, but thus far I cannot."

Emilie spat at his feet. "Liar!"

Dakota leapt to her feet. "Patrick is telling you the truth."

"If you believe that, you're an even bigger fool than Zane and Josiah were."

"He *is* on their side."

"Madam," said Patrick dryly, "I can fight my own battles."

"Apparently not," Dakota observed. "Otherwise she wouldn't have that gun pointed at your head."

"I never trusted you," Emilie said to Patrick. Her entire body was trembling. "Not from the first. But even I didn't believe you would do something this terrible."

Once again Patrick explained the situation, that someone from within the spy ring had betrayed Rutledge and Blakelee. But Emilie was having none of it.

"I realize love must be an alien concept to you, Devane, but my husband is everything to me. We have gone through a great deal to be together…we have two beautiful children and another—" She paused for a moment then shook her head as if to clear her thoughts. "Family is the most important thing on earth, Devane, but—"

Emilie swayed on her feet. Patrick leapt from his chair to catch her before she fell, while Dakota grabbed for the pistol.

"Damn you!" Emilie dropped to the floor and buried her face in her hands. "I have looked everywhere for them…asked everybody I met…but no one will—"

"Dakota?"

The room fell silent. In unison the three of them turned toward the door to find Abigail standing there.

She looked curiously at Emilie and then at Dakota. "You're both the same!"

"Go back to your room, Abigail." Dakota couldn't control the fear in her voice.

Emilie turned toward Dakota, eyes blazing with curiosity. *"Dakota?"*

The vibes between the two women were almost painful. Dakota felt as if she'd been hooked up to an IV drip and they were shooting straight adrenalin into her veins.

"'Tis a family name," Dakota managed to say.

Abby sidled up to Emilie and, to Dakota's horror, that dreamy expression was on her face again. "One day I'm going to—"

"Abby," Dakota said, fear rising. "Go upstairs!"

The child ignored her. "Sail away over the treetops in a bright red ball—"

"Don't, Abby," Dakota whispered. "Please don't...."

"Just like you and Dakota did when you came here from the future."

"Oh, my God!" Emilie met Dakota's eyes as the child's words faded away. "You, too?"

Dakota nodded. She had a sudden, fleeting vision of a dinner table many years in the future and of families linked together through time. It vanished as quickly as it had come and she realized Patrick was staring at her. *I'm so sorry. I didn't want you to find out this way.*

"Explain, madam," he said, his voice tight. "I have heard much but understand little."

Abigail grabbed the sleeve of his jacket. "They rode in the big red ball, Papa. They came from very far away where people fly like birds with silver wings."

Emilie ruffled Abby's bangs with the easy grace of a woman comfortable with children. "ESP?"

Dakota nodded again. She couldn't find her voice.

"Beggin' your pardon, sir." Cook poked her head into the room. "Supper be ready in two shakes."

"Shepherd's pie?" Abigail asked, forgetting about silver birds for the moment.

"And a fine Indian pudding if you have the appetite, missy." If

Cook was curious about what was going on in there, she gave no sign.

"I have to find Lucy!" Abigail cried and raced from the room with Cook close behind.

The tension in the room made Dakota's nerves jangle like bad jazz. There was so much she wanted to ask Emilie, so much Emilie probably wanted to ask her, but all she cared about was Patrick.

"We have to talk," she said to him.

He inclined his head but did not speak.

Emilie looked from one to the other, then rose to her feet and smoothed her skirts. "That shepherd's pie sounded wonderful. Would you mind if I supped with Abigail? I have not eaten since last night at the inn."

Patrick turned away from her, while Dakota managed a weak smile.

"We'll talk later," Emilie whispered, then left the room.

Patrick waited until the woman's footsteps faded away.

"What is it you wish to talk about?" he asked Dakota, although he knew the answer. Last night he had given her his heart. Today she would give it back to him, torn asunder.

"I think you'd better sit down for this."

"I will stand."

"Trust me, Patrick." She pulled one of the chairs closer. "You'll be glad you listened to me."

He was the kind of man who gave orders, not obeyed them. Still, there was something about her tone of voice that made him bow to her wishes. She paced back and forth in front of the fire. Her cheeks were flushed with color.

Do not leave me, madam, he thought, *for I cannot live this life without you in it.*

Dakota stopped dead in her tracks. "What did you say?"

"I did not say a word, madam." Had she managed to hear the

thoughts inside his heart? "'Tis obvious you wish to deliver news of an unpleasant nature. It would benefit us both if you did so with no further delay."

"What's happened to you?" she demanded. "Did I imagine last night? I must have, because I seem to be the only one in the room who remembers what happened between us."

"I remember, madam," he said, his voice deadly calm. "I am reminded of it each time you speak of returning home. What we shared was a thing apart."

Dakota waited for him to say more, to declare his undying love, his eternal devotion, his unbridled passion, but he refused to cooperate. She sighed loudly.

"You're not going to make this easy on me, are you?"

"Nay, madam, I am not."

She sighed again.

"Louder, madam," he said dryly. "They have not heard you yet in London."

"Do you remember asking me where I came from?"

"Many times." He leaned back in the chair and rested his left leg on his right knee. His boots gleamed in the candlelight. "And I remember that your answer varied according to the story you chose to tell."

"There was a reason for that. I didn't think you would believe the truth."

He said nothing.

"I *am* from New Jersey, but not the New Jersey you know."

"I have not traveled south of Trenton, but have been told it is not unlike Franklin Ridge and the environs."

"That's not exactly what I mean." *Just do it, Wylie! He's not going to believe you no matter how nicely you phrase things.* "Damn it, Patrick, I'm from the future."

His jaw didn't sag open. His eyes didn't pop. He didn't leap to his feet and shout "Hallelujah!" The louse didn't do anything at all except continue to look at her impassively.

"Did you hear me, Patrick?" she demanded. "I'm from the future."

"I heard you clearly, madam." He brushed a speck of dust from the fine leather of his boot. "And from what distant world is it you come?"

"From 1993."

"The dawn of the twenty-first century?"

"Actually, we call it the millennium."

"And how did you find your way to this time?"

"Remember that bright red ball that flew over the treetops?"

"The one in which you rode with Andrew McVie and his woman."

"Her name is Shannon and yes, that's the one."

"You are saying you rode through the clouds from the future."

"I guess that's exactly what I'm saying." Even if it did sound like the biggest whopper ever told.

"And you are saying that Andrew McVie sailed with you from the future?"

"Exactly!" Finally they were getting somewhere. "You were wondering where he's been all this time and that's the answer."

Patrick leapt to his feet, toppling the chair with a crash. "You try my patience to the breaking point with these tales. Do you mark me for a fool who would believe such nonsense?"

"You're a smart man, Patrick. You know what I'm telling you is true."

"I know no such thing, madam, for what you tell me lies beyond the laws of nature and man."

But he was starting to believe her. She could see it in his eyes.

"Think about it. Andrew disappeared without a trace over three years ago. No one heard a word from him, no one saw him, no one buried him. And now here I am and suddenly everyone is talking about him. Doesn't it all make sense?"

"Such things are not possible. A man lives and dies within his own time. It can be no other way."

"That's what I thought, too, until it happened to me." She grabbed his sleeve and forced him to stop pacing and look at her. "You know I'm not like anybody else you've ever seen. My hair is too short." She lifted her skirts to the ankle, revealing her running shoes. "I *know* you wonder about those shoes." She let her skirts drop. "I don't think or speak or act like anyone you know."

"You are an individual with individual tastes."

"I'm weird."

"Your words, madam, not mine."

"Remember the shirt I was wearing when I arrived, the one with Jurassic Park written across my breasts? When did you ever see anything like that? Come on, Patrick, tell me!"

He was staring at her with eyes wide. "In truth, I have never heard a woman speak such words in my life."

"Jurassic Park?"

"Breasts."

She started to laugh. "There you go. Doesn't that tell you something?"

"You are plainspoken to a fault. That does not mean what you tell me is true."

She let out a shriek of frustration. "Wake up and smell the coffee, Devane! I'm from the future and that's all there is to it."

"Have you proof of your claim?"

"Shannon and Andrew could prove my claim."

"Shannon Whitney—she is from the future too?"

"She and Andrew met and fell in love in my time."

His brow furrowed. "And she chose to leave her own world to live in his?"

"She loves him, Patrick, and he was needed here."

"Do you love him as well, madam? Is that why you left your home?"

"I had no choice in it."

His eyes widened for the first time since she'd launched into the story. "They took you against your will?"

She described what had happened that last morning, the sensation of fading away into nothingness until the only thing anchoring her in the mortal world was the basket of the hot-air balloon. "You think I'm crazy, don't you? You don't believe one damn word I'm saying."

His silence told her she was right.

"Isn't this ridiculous? I've spent the past two days wondering how I was going to hide the truth from you and now that I'm baring my soul, you don't believe me." A wild laugh erupted. "Abby believes me! She knows it's true."

"Abigail also said she saw birds with silver wings."

Dakota grabbed him by the front of his waistcoat. His tension rippled through her skin. "She's right, Devane! Those birds with silver wings are called airplanes and they can fly hundreds of people anywhere in the world they want to go. China! Africa! Paris! And you can get there in just a few hours."

He pulled away from her. Anger and fear formed a shield around his heart that even she couldn't penetrate. "Madness! All of it. I will hear no more."

If only she had a newspaper or a photograph or a driver's license—anything to show him that what she said was true. She considered the gun, but in his frame of mind Patrick would probably chalk it up to one of Ben Franklin's inventions.

An idea popped into her head. It was ridiculous. Ludicrous. Embarrassing.

And it might work.

"Damn it, Devane, take a look at this!" She gathered up her outer skirt, her underskirts, her petticoat, then found the waistband of her panties. The manufacturer's label was still there. "Read this."

Patrick stared at the sight before him. Dakota Wylie's skirts frothed about her head in a profusion of yellow and lacy white. Her shapely, round legs were encased in pale stockings that, under other circumstances, would pique his curiosity. And covering her bottom and mound was that most intriguing bit of fabric that conformed to her lush body and left naught to the imagination.

"A tempting offer, madam, but one better extended in the privacy of my rooms."

She grasped a small tab of white fabric between her fingers and pulled. To his amazement the entire garment stretched like a lazy tabby after a long nap. "Just read it!"

"'One hundred percent cotton,'" he said slowly.

"Keep going."

"'Machine washable.'"

"There's more."

"'Made in the U.S.A.'" Blood pounded in his ears. He felt as if his heart would burst through his chest. "What is the meaning of this? What do these words represent?"

"U.S.A.," she said softly. "The United States of America."

Chapter Twenty

20

"Sweet Jesus!" He leapt back as her skirts settled back into place.

"You're going to win the war, Patrick," she said. "It won't be easy and it won't happen tomorrow, but you're going to win." She told him that the thirteen colonies would one day become fifty states, that the nation they were fighting to create would still thrive and grow more than two hundred years into the future.

His chest heaved with the impact of her words. She could not know such things. No one could.

And yet, what wonderful words they were....

"Think about what you said last night," she urged, "that time itself has seemed different to you since we met, as if we're living a lifetime in a matter of days. You're not imagining it, Patrick, it's *real,* and I'm the reason why."

Patrick did not want to believe her, but he could no longer deny the truth. "Sweet Jesus," he said again. He saw her as if for the first time and wondered how it was he had been so blind. There was a glow about her person, a golden light that set her apart from the rest. "'Tis a fantastic story, madam, one that goes beyond the bounds of my understanding."

"I wish I could explain it to you, but all I know is that it has something to do with the balloon—they call those bright red things hot-air balloons—and some very strange cloud cover."

Recognition hit him like a bolt of lightning. "I had seen naught like those clouds in my lifetime. They towered upward like a great dark mountain yet had no effect upon the air."

"Yes!" came a voice from the doorway. "That is how it was the morning I left. Those clouds are the key to it all." Emilie Crosse Rutledge glided into the room.

Patrick looked from Emilie to Dakota.

"I was just getting around to that part," Dakota said with an apologetic shrug. "Emilie and Zane are from the future, too."

Again his chest heaved as if struck a blow. Was there no end to this? He had worked with Zane for nearly three years and never noticed anything amiss.

Emilie considered him. "You look as if you'd seen a ghost."

"Nay, madam," said Patrick, slumping back into his chair. "'Twould be easier to understand if I had indeed seen an apparition." He gathered his thoughts into an untidy bundle. "Were you brought here against your will?" he asked Emilie.

"It was nothing I had looked for or expected," she said, meeting his eyes, "but I thank the Almighty every day for giving me the chance to live this life."

"And your husband," Patrick continued. "Was it his choice?"

Emilie nodded. "We had our chance to return a few summers ago but it was Andrew McVie who traveled through time in our stead."

"But he's back now," Dakota reminded them. "Andrew is the one who will rescue Zane and Josiah from the jail near Jockey Hollow." She groaned. "That is, he'd rescue them from the jail near Jockey

Hollow if there actually *was* a jail. We're going to have to work on that part of the equation."

Emilie's eyes lit up with joy. "Andrew is back?"

Dakota nodded. "I traveled with him and Shannon."

"Please tell me he's happy. When he left he was so lonely...so alone."

"He's in love," said Dakota. "He and Shannon plan to be married."

Emilie's brows lifted. "This Shannon...is she a friend of yours?"

"A good friend."

"She'd better treat him right," said Emilie, "or she'll be hearing from me."

Dakota grinned. "I was thinking the same thing about Andrew."

"Still, that doesn't explain where Zane is being kept. You started to tell me something before," Emilie said, warming her hands near the fire. "That Abby had seen a vision or had a dream?"

Dakota met Patrick's eyes.

"It is not a pleasant vision, madam," said Patrick. "Mayhap you do not wish to—"

"I already know about the hanging, if that's what you mean. Molly told me what she knew last night." Her voice was steady but her hands trembled.

"Molly?" Patrick and Dakota asked simultaneously.

"A serving girl I met at the White Horse Tavern. Turns out she is your cook's niece. It was quite a coincidence, actually, that we met. Cook has been expecting Molly, but with the snow and all, Molly couldn't find a carriage heading this way." Emilie shot them a bemused smile. "And since I was already coming here to confront you, Patrick, I invited her along to keep me company."

"The hanging," Patrick said. "There was talk of it at the tavern?"

"They talk of everything at the taverns," Emilie said. "All I kept hearing about was the bright red ball and that it had fallen into British hands. I was so afraid it meant that Zane would—"

Patrick leapt to his feet, the future forgotten for the moment. "That is what I was told the night Zane and Josiah were taken prisoner."

"Yes," said Emilie, appraising him with her eyes. "That's the night it happened. They said the Lobsterbacks brought down the balloon and took a man and woman captive."

"Oh, my God!" Dakota felt light-headed, as if she might faint. She bent forward, resting her forehead against her knees while she struggled to draw in a breath.

"Dakota?" Patrick was at her side, his great strong hands holding her by the shoulders.

"I'm fine," she said, shaking her head to banish the buzzing sound building inside her brain. "How did this Molly know about Zane and Josiah?"

"She said the tavern has been abuzz with talk these past few days. When I came asking questions, she put two and two together."

Something wasn't right, Dakota thought as the buzzing grew louder. But what?

"She's a sweet thing," Emilie was saying, "but she appears to be quite afraid of her aunt."

Dakota shook her head to banish the cobwebs. "Maybe it's Joseph and Will who should be afraid. Abby says that Cook makes her husband sleep on the floor when he's had too much rum."

Emilie looked over at Patrick. "How long has Cook worked for you?"

Patrick shrugged his shoulders. "I cannot say with precision, but she has outlasted anyone else in my employ by some years."

"I don't trust her," Emilie said. Her tone was apologetic; her words were anything but. "I can't put my finger on it, but something just isn't right with her."

Dakota disagreed. Except for her propensity for gossip, Cook seemed a harmless sort. "The only vibes I've picked up from Cook are curious ones. The woman's a born yenta."

"Yenta?" asked Patrick.

The two women laughed.

"That's a New Yorkism," said Dakota. "It means she's a real talker."

Emilie's expression turned wistful. "Somehow I never thought I'd hear the word *yenta* again as long as I lived. I miss our language."

"I miss raspberry-jelly doughnuts," said Dakota. "And toasted bagels with cream cheese."

"Pizza," said Emilie. "Pepperoni and onion."

"Big Mac, double cheese and large fries."

"You'll like it here," said Emilie. "They're big on cholesterol."

"Aren't you homesick?" Dakota asked, leaning toward the red-haired woman. "Look at all you left behind—electricity, indoor plumbing...Häagen-Dazs."

Emilie smiled the way she was supposed to but Dakota could see she didn't quite mean it.

"Häagen-Dazs?" she repeated. "The mantra of single women from coast to coast." Fat. Calories. Instant gratification.

"I miss all that," Emilie said, "but somehow none of it seems very important to me anymore." Both women were silent for a few moments. "I was meant to be here, Dakota. I never fit in that other world."

"That's what I thought, too," Dakota said, "until I landed here."

"The moment I got here I knew I'd finally come home."

"The moment I got here I started looking for a way to get out."

"Maybe the difference was Zane. When I realized I was pregnant with the twins, I knew this was where I was going to stay. I couldn't risk their lives, not even to go back with him."

Dakota's jaw dropped open. "He was going to leave you?"

"He came close. I'll admit I had a few bad moments when the balloon came back again. This has been a tough transition for him but I think we've managed to make it work."

"What made him stay?"

Color flooded Emilie's cheeks as she met Dakota's eyes. "Love."

"That's what I was afraid of," Dakota said. "That means I'm definitely on the next balloon out of here." The words were no sooner out of her mouth than she remembered Patrick was there, listening.

"Don't worry," said Emilie. "He left when we started talking Häagen-Dazs." Her tone made it clear how little she still thought of Patrick.

"He really *is* on our side," Dakota said. "He was distraught about Zane and Josiah."

"He should be. This was his fault. If anything happens to them, I'll—"

"But it wasn't his fault, Emilie, don't you see? This is history. Everything is unfolding the way it's meant to. This is Andrew's destiny. He's the one who saves your husband and Josiah, and it's going to happen very soon." The buzzing inside her head returned and she closed her eyes for a moment against a rising wave of dizziness. For a moment she imagined she could see the fabric of her skirt through the back of her hand, but then the image vanished. *Maybe even sooner than I thought.*

She told Emilie everything she knew, right down to the nonexistent jail in Jockey Hollow.

"I don't like the sound of this," said Emilie. Her eyes brimmed with tears. "How can Andrew save Zane and Josiah if there is no jail? How will he find them?"

"I don't know," Dakota admitted, "but I know it's going to happen." She took Emilie's hand in hers. "How else can you and Zane end up with five children and beachfront property?"

Emilie started to laugh through her tears. "Five?"

"Five kids, a mansion in Philadelphia, a summer place in Crosse Harbor and a mention in the history books."

Emilie squeezed her hand. "From your mouth to God's ear."

"Don't worry," Dakota said. "It's going to happen. I can feel it in my bones."

Now if only she could figure out how.

"Where did Papa go to?" Abigail asked as Dakota tucked her into bed a few hours later. "I looked for him right after supper but he was gone."

Dakota fluffed up the child's pillow and made sure Lucy was tucked in, too. "I don't know where your papa went to, Abby, but I intend to find out."

"Are you angry at Papa?"

"I'm not happy."

"Is it because of the lady with the red hair?"

I wish it was that simple. "Not exactly."

"Why do you want to go back in the big red ball?" Abigail asked.

No wonder she'd never been comfortable with kids. They asked the tough questions adults made sure to avoid. "Because that's where my home is."

Abby shook her head. "No," she said emphatically. "Your home is here with us."

"Coming here was a mistake, Abby. I'm meant to be back in the world where I came from."

"Your mama doesn't think so."

"How do you know what my mother thinks, honey?"

"She told me."

Ma, so help me... "She *told* you?"

"While I was eating Cook's shepherd's pie."

"What exactly did she say?"

Abby's face grew soft and dreamy. "Life's an adventure! Follow your heart!" She parroted Ginny's tone so exactly that Dakota could only stare at her in utter disbelief. "She says Papa loves you and that we can be a family."

Something inside Dakota's heart shifted like tectonic plates. "I wish that was true," she said softly.

"It is!"

She couldn't speak over the lump in her throat.

"Are you sorry you came here?"

Dakota shook her head. "I wouldn't have missed knowing you for the world."

"Then why do you want to go home again? Is it because you don't like me?"

"Oh, honey!" Dakota smoothed the girl's hair from her cheek. "I like you very much."

"You didn't like me when you first saw me."

"That's true," Dakota admitted. "And you didn't like me very much, either."

Abby buried her face against Lucy's yarn head. "I like you now."

"I know that. And I—" She cleared her throat. The words wouldn't kill her. She could say them and still walk out that door. "And I love you."

Abby lifted her head cautiously, then met Dakota's eyes. "You love me?"

Dakota nodded. When had it happened? Suddenly she couldn't remember when the sad-eyed little girl hadn't owned part of her heart. Dakota chucked her under the chin. "As it turns out, you're quite easy to love."

Abby's cheeks turned rosy with pleasure and her eyes once again got the dreamy expression Dakota knew meant the kid's ESP was kicking in. "You and Papa will be together for always."

To her horror, Dakota's eyes flooded with tears. "You said that once before, honey, but I don't think you're right this time."

"I am," said Abby, nodding her head. "I know it is true."

"I have to go home some day, Abby, and I don't think your father will want to go with me." Abby just gave her a Mona Lisa smile and said nothing, which undid what was left of Dakota's equilibrium. "There are things you don't understand, honey...things even I don't understand."

"I don't care," said Abby without missing a beat, "because I know you and Papa will be together always."

Dakota was overcome with a wave of maternal love and longing that was enough to send her racing toward the twentieth century without benefit of hot-air balloon. She could take just about anything life dished out, but she couldn't take this.

She ran from the room as fast as her shaky legs would carry her, then leaned against the closed bedroom door and let her tears fall. She didn't cry at sad movies or weddings, so why was she crying because a little girl with psychic abilities thought she saw a happy ending in her future?

You're wrong, Abby, she thought, wiping away her tears and straightening her shoulders. There could never be a future for her and Devane, not in a million years. She wasn't meant for the eighteenth century and she was damn sure Patrick wasn't cut out for the twentieth.

Quietly she walked down the hallway to the room she was sharing with Patrick and closed the door behind her. Emilie Rutledge was asleep in the room where Dakota had spent her first night, while Cook's niece Molly slept downstairs in the kitchen with the help.

A candle burned brightly in the window and she sat down on the bed, tired to her bones. Patrick had been gone for hours. He'd disappeared during her conversation with Emilie and he hadn't returned for supper. When she'd asked Joseph where Patrick had gone, Joseph had shrugged his shoulders. "He told me to saddle his horse and he left," Joseph said. "'Tain't my place to be askin' questions."

"'Tain't my place, either," Dakota said to the silent room. Whatever magic she and Patrick had shared was over. Finished. Vanished as if it had never happened. You couldn't drop a bombshell like the one she'd dropped on him and expect to escape the aftershocks.

Patrick lived in a world without electricity or flush toilets, and there she was telling him about time travel and jet planes. She must have been crazy to believe for one second they had a chance. Talk about being geographically undesirable: she and Patrick were off the scale.

She lay back on the feather mattress and pulled a quilt up over her shivering body. She was cold from the inside out. Ever since dinner she'd found it impossible to get warm and, even more frightening, twice more her hands had seemed to grow transparent.

She buried her face in his pillow. The scent of his skin still lingered in the silky cotton.

She could feel the forces of destiny at work, moving the players around on some cosmic game board until they were all in position for the final play.

Andrew would meet his destiny. Zane and Josiah would be saved, and Andrew would achieve the recognition he deserved. All three men would be reunited with the women who loved them and their families would be together down through the years.

But what about Patrick and Abby? What will happen to them?

She tried to see into their future but all she saw was darkness.

Patrick returned to the house in the hour after midnight. He had ridden far in search of answers and had not been disappointed. The simplicity of it all astounded him and he wondered how they had not realized it sooner. But therein lay the beauty of the enemy's plan.

As he crossed the yard between the stable and the main house he looked up at the night sky. Clouds were moving in from the east, an unusual occurrence in itself, but these were clouds unlike any of his experience. He had seen the dark, jagged tower but one other time, on the day Dakota had come into his life.

Those clouds were a precursor to the events Dakota spoke of, events that would happen on the morrow. He now knew where Josiah and Zane were being held prisoner. He knew that Andrew McVie and Shannon Whitney lived. Tomorrow he would throw in his lot with fate and pray that when it was over, Dakota Wylie would still be at his side.

The only sound inside the house was the ticking of the tall clock in the hallway as he climbed the stairs to his second-floor room. He stripped off his clothes, washed, then climbed into the big bed next to Dakota. Her plain cotton nightdress was bunched up around her hips and she had tossed the pillow to the floor. He fit his body to hers spoon-fashion, then gathered her close.

She murmured something soft and infinitely appealing and pressed her rump against him. His arousal was violently sudden, springing to powerful life against her soft, firm cheeks. She moved again, a sinuous fluid motion, and he slid his hand between her thighs, then cupped her against his palm. She was wet for him already, her juices hot and sweet on his fingers as he stroked her lower lips, feeling them swell with her eagerness for him.

And it was for him. He would not think otherwise. No matter what else happened, he had been the first man to know her body. The first man to love her. The first man to take her with his mouth....

Dakota had never had a dream like this before. Voluptuous waves of pleasure washed over her, almost drowning her senses in sheer bliss. She felt graceful...infinitely desirable...moving perfectly with the ebb and flow of the tides.

Her back arched and she opened her legs wider. Wave after wave of sensation...wetness...heat...a throbbing pressure that was building...building—

Her eyes flew open and she realized what was happening.

"Patrick!"

He looked up from between her thighs. His mouth gleamed wet and hot by moonlight. "Your honey is sweet," he said, sliding up the length of her body. "Taste yourself on me."

"Oh, my God—" Not even in her most detailed fantasies had she even come close to this.

His mouth found hers, his lips slick. He ran his tongue along the place where her lips met, urging her to open, to taste. A shudder of delight rippled through her body as he deepened the kiss. Just the thought of his mouth pressed between her legs was enough to send her tumbling into madness.

His erection throbbed against her thigh and suddenly she wanted to do for him all that he had done for her.

"I want to taste you," she whispered, wild and hungry for him. "I want to feel you in my mouth."

"Yes," he said, his voice almost a growl of delight. "Take me in your mouth."

The bedclothes rustled as they sought a new way to love. She knelt between his powerful thighs and cupped him in her palms. "I won't be able to—" She stopped, not sure how to phrase it.

"Just suckle me," he said, placing his hand behind her head, guiding her forward. "As much as you can take."

His erection was smooth to her tongue and hot. She could feel the blood pulsing in the blue vein that ran along the underside.

"For you," he said, his voice floating toward her in the darkness. "All of it, everything."

Instinct took over. She drew him more deeply into her mouth, bringing him closer to ecstasy with her hands and mouth and tongue while he writhed beneath her. She felt more womanly at that moment than she ever had before, as if the secret of a woman's power were hers for the taking.

Suddenly, when she was sure he was near a climax, he grabbed her by the shoulders and pulled her up the hard, muscled length of his body. She straddled his hips and lowered herself onto him, feeling her body open for him, envelop him, draw him deeply into her secret self until she could no longer tell where she ended and he began. She didn't need to know. They were one being, one heart, one life.

She cried when it was over. Loud, messy tears of pleasure and sadness and he held her close and stroked her hair until the storm passed.

"There is so much to tell you," she whispered, rubbing her damp cheek against his chest. "So much I want to share with you—"

He silenced her with a kiss of such tenderness and love that tears again filled her eyes.

"There will be time for that later," he said, rolling her onto her back and moving between her willing thighs. "Tonight there is only us." He found her entrance. "Only this pleasure." He slid inside her welcoming sheath. "Only this moment."

Chapter Twenty-One

21

"You look beautiful," Emilie said as Dakota twirled in front of her. "Nobody would ever guess you grew up wearing jeans and T-shirts."

Dakota took one last look in the cheval mirror in the corner of the room. The dress she had chosen for McDowell's party was a deep gold satin with intricate embroidery on the bodice and sleeves. The bodice was cut low in front and, thanks to clever corseting, she actually had cleavage. She didn't dare tell Emilie that when she looked into the mirror she saw a beautiful dress but the woman inside the dress was fading away.

"You might try smiling," Emilie suggested. "If you go downstairs looking like that, they'll think there's trouble in paradise."

Dakota turned and met Emilie's eyes. "*Trouble* doesn't begin to cover it." She gestured toward the window. "Did you see?"

Emilie nodded. "I've been trying to ignore it."

"I can't ignore it," Dakota said. "It's like that damn cloud is screaming my name." She looked into the mirror again, and could barely make out her own image.

"Funny," said Emilie. "I'm afraid it's screaming 'Zane Grey Rutledge! Here's your second chance!'"

"No," Dakota said. "Trust me. This one has my name on it."

She'd awakened early to find Patrick already gone. If it weren't for the rumpled sheets and the delicious ache between her legs, she would have thought she'd imagined their wondrous lovemaking. Cook said he'd saddled up early and ridden off toward town, but as the hours wore on, Dakota began to worry.

"I don't think he's coming home," Dakota said, twisting the silver bracelets she wore on her left wrist. "He was furious with McDowell about this party. It wouldn't surprise me if he boycotted."

"Zane and I met General McDowell two years ago in Philadelphia." Emilie shuddered. "The man redefines the word *sleaze.*"

"Patrick seems to think McDowell's loyalties are suspect."

"I know," said Emilie. "McDowell and his wife introduced Benedict Arnold to his bride, Peggy Shippen, and we both know where that's going to lead. Besides, he—" She stopped and looked out the window.

"He what?" Dakota prodded. "What were you about to say?"

"Just that McDowell was instrumental in bringing Patrick and Susannah together *and* in tearing them apart." Apparently Patrick and Susannah had met at one of McDowell's parties and, a few years later, it was at another of McDowell's parties that she'd met the young—and very wealthy—officer with whom she'd run off, back home to Philadelphia. She'd abandoned both her husband and child, humiliating before an entire colony the man she'd once loved.

"No wonder Patrick hates the man," Dakota said.

"There's more to it than that," Emilie said. "Everyone in the colony knows McDowell is dealing with the British. The problem is getting proof."

"How did Susannah die?"

"A carriage accident near the Delaware. She and her officer friend drowned."

Dakota tried to muster some sympathy for the dead woman but came up empty. Patrick and Abigail continued to suffer from her selfish choices every day, in ways only they understood.

"Are you sure you won't join the festivities?" she asked Emilie.

The red-haired woman shook her head. "I'm too tall to wear Susannah's dresses. I'll sit in the kitchen with Cook and Molly and listen to the local gossip."

An odd sensation washed over Dakota as she looked at her reflection in the mirror. The dress glittered in the candlelight but the woman wearing it seemed as transparent as window glass. As quickly as the vision appeared, it vanished again.

"Tonight," Dakota said. "I can feel it in my bones."

Emilie glanced toward the window. If anything, the clouds seemed darker, angrier, the edges more jagged and threatening. "God help me, so can I."

Abigail was curled on the window seat in Papa and Dakota's bedroom. Lucy was propped up on the sill, looking quite pretty in the new dress that Dakota and the red-haired woman had sewn for her that afternoon.

Abby had wanted to put on a pretty dress of her own and go to the party, too, but Dakota had promised to save her a piece of sugar cake and tell her all about the music and dancing in the morning. Abby's temper had heated up really fast when she heard the word no, but when she'd thought about how much she wanted Dakota to stay with them and be her new mama, she'd decided to mind her manners.

Fancy coaches and carriages wound their way up the snowy lane to the house and Abby pressed her nose against the windowpane as she watched the men and ladies step down. Many of the men wore powdered wigs tied at the napes of their necks with brightly colored ribbon. Abby giggled as a fat gentleman tugged at his ponytail, only to send his wig sliding down over one ear.

The ladies wore their hair in elaborate arrangements that puzzled Abby. How did they make their hair stand up that way? she wondered. Was it a secret you learned when you grew up? She hoped so, because she would so love to look beautiful.

It was great fun to sit there, so warm and cozy with Lucy, and watch the parade of guests as they arrived at the house, but it was the big ugly cloud that fascinated Abby most of all. She didn't know what it was, but the cloud made her feel funny inside, the way she felt when a lightning storm was coming, all jumpy and filled with excitement.

The bright red balloon was coming back and when it did, Abby and Lucy would be ready.

Abby grabbed her cloak, tucked Lucy under her arm and tiptoed toward the back stairs.

The blows came hard and fast but Patrick refused to sway. They would have to kill him before he bent a knee before the bloody traitors. The good people of Franklin Ridge, the same good people who had ostracized him, had cradled a viper to their bosoms. It should not surprise them when the viper bared its fangs.

McDowell. The very name was a blight upon the cause. *May you rot in hell for eternity.*

The crack of bone echoed inside his head. His bone? He waited for the pain but it never came. He was beyond pain, into another, more terrifying realm of sensation.

The butt of the musket slammed into his shoulder and he staggered but did not drop. One week ago he had lacked a reason to go on, but all had changed. His life had opened up before him, filled with promise, and he would not, could not, let it slip through his fingers.

Dakota. He saw her clearly in his mind's eye, saw the sweetness of her soul, the fire of her convictions. He saw her heart, the depth and breadth of everything she was...everything he could be.

He would not give up.

He would not die before he saw her face again.

General McDowell was outraged when he realized Patrick wasn't at the party.

"To leave you in such trying circumstances," he said, feigning sympathy for Dakota's plight. "A most ungentlemanly thing to do."

Dakota debated between defending her husband and siding with the enemy. She opted for the enemy. "Quite," she said, taking the arm the general offered. "I don't know what possessed him to do such a thing."

"Most thoughtless," McDowell went on. "I'm of a mind to have my men comb the area until they find the reprobate."

"Don't do that!" Dakota snapped, perhaps a shade too harshly. "I will not force my company upon anyone...especially not my husband."

"You have been ill-used, my dear," McDowell said as they entered the enormous front hall that tonight served as a ballroom. "Much as dear Susannah had been."

Dakota nearly choked on her own saliva.

"My plainspokenness surprises you," McDowell said, chuckling. "I do not mean to make you uncomfortable, my dear, only to remind you that you are not the first young woman Devane has mistreated nor, dare I say, will you be the last."

And thank you so much for sharing, you moron. If the situation had been different, if she hadn't learned what kind of man Patrick truly was, McDowell's comments might have been devastating. As it was, she regained her composure just in time to take her place in the receiving line to greet their guests.

Emilie was curled up by the hearth fire in the kitchen, pretending to doze. Neither Patrick nor Dakota put any stock in her suspicions about Cook, but the sense that all was not as it seemed had grown stronger as the day progressed.

One thing was certain: Cook was running poor Molly ragged. The young woman had kneaded a dozen loaves of bread, cut the vegetables for soup, plucked four chickens, then set out to lug an enormous bag of flour down to the basement.

"You can't do that," Emilie had said to the girl. "It's too heavy."

Molly wiped her forehead with the back of her hand. "Aunt says I must, ma'am, and she doesn't take kindly to slackers."

"Tell Will to come in here and do it."

"Will's off t' the stables, helping his father." Molly offered her a sunny smile. "'Tain't the worst thing I've done in my life."

"Still, it's too heavy for you. I would help you myself but I am two months with child and must be careful."

Molly's smile was maybe a shade too hearty and Emilie grew suspicious. "Like I said, 'tain't the worst thing I've done." With that, Molly set out to drag the sack out the back door then down the stone steps to the cellar.

All day long it had been that way in Cook's kitchen. Harsh voices. Even harsher tasks. Enough whispering to make the most trusting soul suspicious. Something was going on and Emilie was determined to get to the bottom of it. She didn't have Patrick's knowledge of the area or Dakota's extrasensory perception, but she did have the strong feeling that Cook was involved in something much bigger than what was in her stew pot.

"That's a lazy one," Emilie heard Cook say as she pretended to nap by the fire after supper.

"She's not a worker, Aunt," came Molly's sweet voice. "She's a guest."

"Hmmph," Cook snorted. "Guests sleep upstairs in a regular bed. They don't curl up by the fire like common folk."

You're a snob, Cook, thought Emilie. *But are you a traitor, too?*

Under different circumstances Dakota could imagine enjoying an eighteenth-century party in her honor. And there was certainly something to be said for men in uniform. Add to that the music and the rum punch and the laughter, and it made for a heady brew.

Too bad the *if onlys* made it impossible for her to enjoy.

If only she belonged.

If only the marriage they celebrated was a *real* marriage, not a sham.

If only Patrick had seen fit to be there with her.

What do you expect, Wylie? She thought as she twirled around the dance floor in the arms of a ruddy officer from Philadelphia. She'd turned Patrick's entire life upside down. She looked up at her dancing partner, who favored her with a huge smile. *What would you say if I told you I was born in 1967?*

She knew darn well what he'd say. He'd scream, "Witch!" and start a bonfire.

Patrick hadn't done that. He'd tried to understand and to believe, even when reason must have told him he was mad to consider it. Last night he'd made love to her, body and soul. It had been about so much more than sex, so much more than desire, that she'd felt as if their two hearts had become one.

He knew this wasn't her world. He knew she would be adrift in a sea of unfamiliar faces, unfamiliar ways. No matter how much he hated General McDowell, Patrick never would have left her alone at this party. Not unless—

"Madam?" The officer's brow creased with concern. "Are you unwell?"

"No—I mean, yes." She lowered her eyes and swayed. "I am feeling quite unwell. Will you excuse me?"

"Let me accompany you from the dance floor."

"No, no, you needn't do that. Please find another partner and continue dancing."

She hurried away before he had time to protest, and barely reached the back stairs before she ran into Emilie.

Emilie grabbed her by the arm and pulled her into the pantry.

"I was right!" Emilie's voice shook with triumph. "It's Cook!"

Dakota stared at her in the murky light. "What?"

"Cook is the missing link."

"That's crazy," Dakota said, even though the buzzing in her head and down her spine told her otherwise. "How could Cook possibly—"

"I don't have time to explain it all," Emilie said, "but Molly put the pieces together."

"You're talking too fast," Dakota protested. "Slow down. I don't know what you're—"

"Listen!" Emilie gripped Dakota's forearms and shook her hard. "Cook's sister Margaret works at the Ford house where General Washington is staying." Emilie paused for effect. "And Margaret is Molly's mother."

"So what? That doesn't make her a spy. My mother has a martyr complex but that doesn't make me Joan of Arc."

"Don't you understand? Cook and Margaret passed messages back and forth through poor Molly. The two women have had a rivalry going on since the cradle and finally Margaret had something to hold over Cook's head."

"General Washington?" Dakota breathed, suddenly beginning to understand.

"Exactly," said Emilie. "And the more detailed information Margaret passed on, the more jealous she believed Cook would get."

But Margaret didn't know her sister as well as she thought. Cook had bigger and better plans for the juicy information Margaret was relaying through poor Molly. No, Cook didn't get jealous; Cook was getting rich.

"...the White Horse Tavern where Molly worked..." Emilie's words penetrated the loud buzz inside her head.

She struggled to zero in on what the woman was saying, but she felt as if Emilie were a thousand light-years away.

"What about the White Horse Tavern?" she managed to say. "Isn't that where you met Molly?"

"And it's the place where Zane and Josiah were making the drop the night they were captured. The owner was a staunch patriot."

Dakota met her eyes. "Or so you thought?"

"Exactly," said Emilie. "The bastard betrayed us. Loyalists paid him in gold to alter his allegiance."

Dakota sagged against the cold stone wall of the pantry as dark images, shadows, danced at the outer reaches of her peripheral vision.

"Dakota?" Emilie kept her from falling. "Are you okay?"

"Patrick's in danger," she said, knowing the truth of her statement in every cell and fiber of her body. "I have to find him."

"It's dark out there. You don't know the area. You'll never be able to find him."

"I'll find him," Dakota said. It was her destiny, the reason she'd traveled through time.

"I'm coming with you," Emilie said.

"No!" Dakota was adamant. "You can do more here. Someone has to watch Abby and keep McDowell from getting suspicious." Her mouth curved in a quick smile. "Besides, you're pregnant. You can't take any chances."

Emilie sighed and placed her hands over her belly. "Godspeed," she said, hugging Dakota fiercely. "Come back safely."

Dakota hugged Emilie back but said nothing. It would be a miracle if she came back at all.

"Cook's coming!" Emilie said. "Give me two minutes to get her to the kitchen, then you can make a run for it."

It was the longest two minutes of Dakota's life. Finally she peered out from the pantry, saw nobody peering back in at her, then tore up the back stairs to the bedroom. She wasn't going anywhere without Shannon's gun. Abigail was sound asleep, sprawled across the enormous feather bed. Dakota resisted the urge to press a kiss to her forehead. Goodbyes were dangerous.

She slipped into the anteroom, slid her hand under the mattress and retrieved the gun. This time she didn't hide it in her stocking but tucked it in her bodice, fashion be damned, then grabbed her cloak and was off.

She bumped into Joseph near the top of the stairs.

"Don't go down there," he said, blocking her way. "Not if you're lookin' to get away."

Their eyes met. He was on her side.

"Use the passageway," Joseph said, glancing down toward the first floor. "I'll close up for you."

"Did you do that the other day?"

"Beggin' your pardon, ma'am, but I did. She snoops when she thinks no one's around," he said, meaning Cook. "If she'd be seein' that—"

"Don't apologize," she said with a gentle laugh. "Just don't lock it this time."

"'Twas that or you give the missus the surprise of her life."

Somehow Dakota didn't think there was much that could surprise Cook, but she let it pass. It was enough that Joseph was on their side.

"We'll have to be quiet," she said as he followed her into the bedroom. "Abby's asleep."

"Where?" Joseph asked as they stepped into the room.

Dakota turned around. The bed was empty.

"She was here a minute ago."

"Pardon me sayin' so, but you don't have time to be worryin' about the girl."

Joseph was right. Emilie would make sure Abby was safe. The time had come to leave and delaying it would only make it harder.

Joseph removed the last dresser drawer and Dakota swung open the doors to the armoire. With a whispered thank-you to the man, she vanished into the passageway. She was more surefooted this time. At least she knew what to expect at the other end.

Minutes later she reached the secret room. No candles or crackling fire awaited her. No Patrick with the raging heart she longed to soothe. She didn't linger but climbed the stone steps that led up to the stable, then quickly realized she had no idea how to attach the wagon to a horse.

She stepped outside into the cool night air. Maybe that wouldn't be a problem after all. The place was filled with wagons and carriages, all of which came with horses conveniently attached. No point getting too fancy, she thought as she surveyed some of the more elaborate rigs belonging to the party guests.

A small open wagon caught her eye. Especially the lumpy tangle of blankets in the back. For a second she thought she saw one of those blankets move, but it was her imagination playing tricks on her. Besides, who needed blankets when you had sheer adrenalin to keep you warm? The horse didn't seem too thrilled about being singled out but he didn't try to bite her. She took it as a good omen and climbed up onto the bench.

So far, so good. She had wheels. She had horsepower.

The horse gave her a snotty look over his shoulder, but she chalked it up to equine ego problems.

"You mind your business and I'll mind mine," she told him, grabbing the reins. "Now giddyap." To her amazement the horse did exactly that and the wagon bounced off down the snowy road.

Underneath the tangle of blankets in the back of the wagon, Abby clutched Lucy to her chest and smiled.

Chapter Twenty-Two

22

Rand McNally had nothing on Dakota. No wrong turns, no missed intersections, no false stops. Destiny held her in its arms and it wasn't about to let go.

A light snow was falling, just hard enough to lower visibility. She supposed she should be grateful for the snow. It illuminated the road almost as well as street lamps did in her time. Not that it mattered. Some other force was in charge here, guiding her to the place she needed to be.

Finally she crested a hill and the White Horse Tavern appeared, nestled snugly in a clearing. Her heart lurched. The place looked deserted. There wasn't a carriage or cart to be seen anywhere. A lone candle burned in an upstairs window.

Patrick's presence whispered in her ear. It reached into her heart and touched her soul. He was there and he was in trouble. She would do anything on earth to save him. Abigail needed him so much and—

And so do you.

"No," she said out loud. She refused to acknowledge the words.

She had no business needing him. She wasn't part of his life and she never would be.

She urged the horse down the slope, then brought both horse and cart to a stop just inside the woods. She looped the reins around a low-hanging branch, made sure the gun was tucked securely in her bodice and set out to search for Patrick.

If she were an eighteenth-century man, where would she stash a prisoner? The cellar was an obvious choice. Maybe too obvious?

She crept toward the cellar door. Her heart was pounding so hard it hurt. *Please be in there,* she prayed. *Please be safe.* Carefully she eased back the latch and opened the door.

A guard slept at the bottom of the stairs. The man sat on a rolled-up blanket, his back resting against the wall. He cradled an ugly musket in his arms and, as far as Dakota could tell, he hadn't bathed in months. She peered inside. She saw a dark form in the middle of the room and she moved closer.

Oh, God. She stifled a cry. Patrick was chained to the floor in the middle of the room. His beautiful face was badly bruised. A cut slashed diagonally across his right cheek and one eye was partially closed. Her stomach heaved and she was afraid she would vomit. She willed herself to be strong, to remember why she was there. She hadn't traveled more than two hundred years through time to blow it now.

I'm here, Patrick. She concentrated every ounce of strength and power. *Open your eyes. I'm here and I'm going to make sure you get back to Abby before it's time for me to go.*

He shifted position, muttered something, then opened his eyes.

The look of joy on his face would be with her until the day she died...and beyond. She placed her fingers to her mouth. *Keep quiet, Patrick, or we're in big trouble.* Not that he could say anything around the gag jammed into his mouth.

The first step was to get the key from the guard so she could free Patrick and then—

A rough hand grabbed her from behind and threw her to the ground. *Wrong again,Wylie,* she thought as her bad ankle twisted beneath her. The first step should have been to knock the guard unconscious.

"What have we here, missy?" The foul-smelling guard slipped his hand beneath her skirts. "Someone be sending ol' Harry a present to warm his nights?"

I'll give you something to warm your nights.... She brought her knee up sharply right between his legs, then landed a palm-strike to his jaw.

I owe you one, Shannon, she thought as the guard doubled over. Karate really did work. The sound of Patrick's rage seared her brain as he struggled against the metal chains that held him fast.

"It's okay," she said, scrambling to her feet. "The keys are hanging around his neck. I'll—"

All things considered, she wouldn't have believed the guard could move so fast. He threw himself on his musket and before she could take in what was happening, he had the clumsy weapon aimed straight at Patrick's heart.

"You don't much care what happens to yourself, missy, but seems like you care a whole lot what happens to your friend." He jammed the musket into Patrick's chest.

Patrick's fury echoed inside Dakota's head, pushing aside her own terror.

"He's not my friend," she said, looking directly at the guard. She lifted her chin and prayed she was making the right choice. "He's my lover."

Her plain words had the effect she'd been hoping for. The guard licked his lips. His rheumy eyes traveled the length of her body. "You spread your legs for him, do you, missy?"

She nodded. "For him and any other man who pleases me."

He cupped his crotch with one hand and winced. "'Tain't kind the way you treated ol' Harry."

"I decide who lays between my thighs," she said, arrogant and powerful and totally in control. "You should have waited until you were asked, Harry."

She had his attention. Slowly she unhooked the frog closure of her cloak and let it drop to the floor. The guard's breath hissed as he devoured the sight of her in the shimmery gold dress. The dress cost more than he would earn in a lifetime.

It was obvious she wasn't a tavern wench trading her favors for a half crown, or one of the whores who followed soldiers from camp to camp. She knew exactly what the dress represented to the guard and she knew how to use it.

She moved a few steps closer to where the guard stood, his musket still aimed at Patrick, just close enough for the guard to catch the sweet scent of her perfume. She wasn't Dakota Wylie anymore. She was somebody else, a woman who would do whatever she had to do to save the life of the man she loved.

"Do you want me, Harry?"

He grunted. She'd take that as a yes.

She cupped her breasts. Shannon's gun had settled between the neckline and her midriff. Swallowing hard, she recalled every bad line of B-movie dialogue she'd ever heard.

"Do you want to do this to me?"

She slid the first two buttons from their loops, deepening the décolletage.

Harry groaned and lowered the musket to half mast.

She slid her hand inside the bodice.

"How much do you want me, Harry?"

Harry moved toward her, musket forgotten, and she pulled out the gun from between her breasts and pointed it straight at his head.

Patrick's anguished wail ripped through her, but she couldn't let his fear—or her own—stop her.

Harry stared at the gun, then coughed out a laugh. "Never seen a pistol that small before, but it don't matter much." He aimed his musket at the center of Patrick's chest again. "You want him so bad you'll be havin' to pay a high price for him, missy."

"The hell I will." She pulled the trigger. The bullet whizzed past Harry's right ear and pinged off the wall behind him.

"Now you done it, missy. May as well toss down your toy and play with ol' Harry."

He threw the musket down, confident she'd fired her only available bullet, and started toward her.

She aimed the gun.

Harry laughed. "Empty guns wouldn't be scarin' me, missy. Now why don't you—"

She pulled the trigger again and this time she didn't miss.

Harry fell backward with a thud. She forced herself not to notice the blood or the blank expression in his eyes as she lifted his head and removed the rope with the key attached to it.

You did what you had to do, she told herself as she ran to Patrick's side. *He would have killed the both of you.*

She unlocked the chains and he ripped the gag from his mouth.

"Oh, Patrick." She gently cradled his face in her hands. "What did he do to you?"

He took her hands in his and kissed them. "There is another cellar on the north side. The guards talked of the red balloon and the spies they had captured. With luck we will find McVie and your friend."

"Hurry!" Dakota urged, helping him to his feet. "It's all happening, Patrick. Everything...just the way I saw it...the way Abby knew it would be."

There was so much Patrick wanted to tell her, so many things he longed to say. He prayed there would be time.

They hurried around to the other side of the inn.

"It's locked," Dakota said, trying the door to the cellar.

He tried the key, but it didn't fit.

"We can kick it in," she said.

He looked at her, his magnificent warrior, and nodded. "On the third count...one...two...three!"

The door broke open with a resounding crash. He could not remember a more welcome sound.

"Dakota!" A lovely, dark-haired woman flew across the room toward them. "My God, it's really you!"

The women embraced as if they had been separated for centuries, not days. Patrick looked over their heads and found himself eye-to-eye with Andrew McVie.

"Sweet Jesus!" he roared, clasping the man to his breast. "'Tis a wonder to lay eyes upon you again."

"And you are a welcome sight, Patrick Devane." McVie clapped him on the back, but the joy in his eyes was soon replaced by determination.

"Blakelee and Rutledge?" Devane asked.

"Aye," said McVie. "They took them not ten minutes ago to the hanging tree at the foot of Clover Hill."

"We can be there within the hour," Patrick said. "I will not lose two good men."

"No!" Dakota's voice rang out. "This is Andrew's destiny, Patrick, not yours. He must do this alone."

"'Tis too big an undertaking for one man. I will lend what assistance I can."

The dark-haired woman with the aqua eyes blocked his exit. "Let him go," she said, her tone pleasant but firm. "He *will* succeed." She lowered her voice so Patrick alone could hear. "You must let him do this alone or he will never believe in himself the way that I believe in him."

He could not argue in the face of so great a love.

McVie kissed Shannon Whitney and was gone.

"Was that your horse?" Dakota asked as they stood on the slope behind the house and watched Andrew gallop away.

"It was," said Patrick, "but he is welcome to it."

"I didn't even notice the stable."

"Mayhap you had other things to occupy your mind."

She started to say something but the words danced just beyond reach. She felt light-headed, as if she hadn't eaten in weeks, and suddenly her knees gave out and she sagged into Patrick's arms.

"I do not understand," he said. "I see you before me, yet I seem to see through you, as well."

"This is how it happened the other time, Patrick." Once again she told him of her last morning in 1993.

"You tell me you had no choice in the matter?" Patrick asked. "That your choice had been made for you by fate?"

Dakota's eyes glistened with tears. "Yes." *Say something, Patrick! Tell me you want me to stay. Tell me you can't live without me, that life would have no meaning if I left—*

"All that kept you from death was the touch of the balloon?"

She nodded. *You don't understand. I had no reason to stay there.... I didn't have Abby...I didn't have you.*

He said nothing more. She sensed that he was pulling away from her, that sometimes not even a miracle was enough to make a happy ending. *Like you expected anything else, Wylie? You came, you saw, you saved his life. Now it's time to go back where you belong.*

"Who is he?" Shannon whispered to Dakota as Patrick strode toward the wagon.

"Patrick Devane," Dakota whispered back.

"The traitor?"

"The patriot."

"I've heard nothing but terrible things about the guy."

"That'll teach you not to believe everything you hear."

"Looks like we have a lot to catch up on."

I know, thought Dakota, *but I'm afraid we're not going to have time.*

They crossed the snowy field to the edge of the woods where she'd left the wagon.

A familiar noise sounded in the distance, the deep hiss of flame beneath a hot-air balloon as it drifted closer to the clearing.

The ground seemed to lift and tilt beneath Dakota's feet. She breathed deeply and closed her eyes, willing herself to deny the inevitable. Patrick had given as much as it was in him to give, and it just wasn't enough. He'd been hurt too deeply for her love to make him whole, and if he couldn't give her his heart, then she wanted nothing at all.

"Maybe it's not for you," Shannon said. "Maybe it's meant for someone else."

"It's for me," Dakota whispered. There was nothing for her here. Not any longer.

She turned away from both Patrick and Shannon, her tears blinding her to everything but the crimson balloon as it moved slowly, inexorably, toward her. The buzzing sound filled her head, scraped against her nerve endings, scratched against her spine. *It's over,* she thought as her heart cracked in two. *All over.*

"Don't go." His voice pierced her heart.

She'd imagined the words. Conjured them up from dreams and sorrow.

"Don't go," he repeated, more loudly this time. "Is it possible you do not know what it is I feel for you?"

"How would I know how you feel?" she countered. "You haven't told me."

"Some things do not require words."

"This does," she said quietly. "I need some words right about now."

"Words are empty things. I have shown you what I feel for you."

"Tell me," she said. "I need to hear it, Patrick."

The crimson balloon appeared grayish in the moonlight, a ghostly apparition.

"It is you I need, madam. It is you who makes my world complete."

The hiss of the balloon grew louder as it moved closer.

Her dark eyes searched his face and in that moment he saw the future without her, saw the days of his life stretched out before him, as cold and lonely as the snowy ground on which they stood. How could he embrace the bleak and endless night when he had finally learned to love the sun?

"This isn't my world, Patrick." Her voice was filled with longing. "You are asking me to turn my back on everything and everybody I've ever known...a way of life that will not come again for two hundred years. Do you need me to warm your bed? Do you need me to be a mother to Abby?" Her tone grew fierce. "Tell me, Devane! Tell me now before it's too—"

"I love you!" Terrible words of power beyond measure. Words with the power to strike a man down or to give him wings. With Susannah he had believed a golden future was his for the taking. Now he knew it for the blessed miracle it was, knew that life without this uncommon woman wasn't a life at all. "Stay with me, Dakota Wylie." He laid his heart bare for her, offered her his soul. "Be my wife and my companion and my lover in this life and the next, for I want no other by my side."

The crimson balloon skimmed the tops of the trees.

"I love you, Dakota," he said again, in a voice rich with yearning. "Only you. For all time."

"Yes!" She threw back her head and shouted her joy to the stars.

"I love you, Patrick Devane. I love you! I love Abigail! I don't care if that balloon lands at my feet…nothing will make me leave you, Patrick, not as long as I—"

"Papa! Dakota! I'm flying!"

Abigail?

The balloon dipped low, dropping the basket to eye level.

"Oh, my God!" Dakota screamed. "Abby! No!"

The child was in the basket of the hot-air balloon. She clutched Lucy in one hand and waved madly with the other. "Look at us!"

"Sweet Jesus!" It took Patrick a full second to comprehend the astonishing sight before him. Abby's eyes were wide with excitement as the balloon dipped and swayed before them. The child was filled with wonder, alive to magic and possibilities…she was *his.* It had taken him so long to realize the truth, so long to understand all that Dakota had tried to tell him about love. He prayed God it was not too late to make amends.

Dakota raced past him, heading straight for the basket, but he stopped her.

"Nay, I will not risk your safety." He closed the distance between himself and his daughter.

"No!" Dakota screamed. "Don't touch that basket, Patrick!"

It was too late. He gripped the railing, then was thrown through the air with a mysterious power the likes of which he had never experienced. He hit the ground hard but wasn't hurt. He tried to stand, but some unseen force kept him on his knees.

Dakota heard Shannon screaming behind her, but she didn't take her eyes from Abigail. She felt as if she were running through wet cement. It was so hard to move…so hard to breathe. Her mind was tangled in knots. Abigail was the only thing that was important. She had to save her…had to…

The basket trembled, then tipped toward the ground. Dakota threw herself into the basket and grabbed Abigail by the child's upper arms. The child tried to wriggle away but Dakota held her fast.

"No!" Abby cried. "Where's Lucy? I can't go without Lucy!"

The balloon began to rise again. As it lifted above his head Patrick broke free of the invisible force that had held him captive.

Dakota met his eyes as the balloon began to rise again, and he nodded.

Summoning up the rest of her strength, Dakota lifted Abby over the edge of the basket and dropped her into her father's waiting arms. Dakota's legs buckled. She grabbed for the lip of the basket for support, but slipped and fell to the floor. Lucy lay in the far corner of the basket, just out of reach. The rough wicker cut into her palms as she tried to pull herself up again and again, falling back to the bottom of the basket each time, growing weaker...fading...fading....

Late afternoon sun spilled over the kitchen table as Ginny sat there, shuffling her tarot cards. A cup of spearmint tea rested at her right elbow, a lighted Marlboro at her left. She wore bright red toreador pants, a Princeton T-shirt and a pair of dangling silver earrings Dakota had long coveted.

"So what took you so long, honey? I was wondering when you'd come to your mother for help."

"You were right," Dakota said. "He loves me, Ma."

"I knew that all the time. So what are you going to do, honey—let that idiot balloon make the decision for you? Fight for what you want!"

"What choice do I have? Take a good look at me, Ma. I'm unconscious."

"No, you're not."

"I dropped like a rock. I'm out cold."

Ginny sighed. "You're faking it, just like you used to do when there was a Latin test at school."

"You knew about that?"

"Of course I knew, and this is the same thing. You were always good at ducking the tough questions."

"What's that supposed to mean? I love Patrick. I love Abby."

Ginny smiled. "And you love me and you're afraid to say goodbye."

"Oh, Ma—" Dakota choked on a sob. "You knew that, too?"

"I'm supposed to know, honey. I'm your mother."

"I love you and Dad and everyone. I can't imagine never seeing you again."

Ginny clucked her disapproval. "Linear thinking, honey. Time is fluid. This isn't goodbye. This is only the beginning."

"The beginning of what? I don't understand. My destiny's been decided. There's nothing I can do to change it. I'll probably be home in time for dinner."

"Take a stand! You've spent your whole life straddling the fence. Commit to your new family. Your old one will always be here for you any time you want us."

Always...always....

She was instantly, completely awake. Her hands were solid. Her aura was back where it belonged. She was trapped in the basket of a hot-air balloon and the ground was fifteen feet below.

"I don't suppose you have a ladder?" she called out to the three people waiting for her on the ground.

"Jump!" they yelled in unison. *"Now!"*

She looked at her friend Shannon and thought of the new life she was about to start with Andrew McVie. *You're going to be happy, kid. You made the right choice.*

She looked at Abigail. *My child,* she thought as her heart filled with love. She grabbed Lucy and tucked the doll under her arm.

And finally she looked at Patrick Devane, at the man she loved and had almost lost, and knew she'd finally come home. He was proud and hot tempered, stubborn and opinionated—but then again, so was she. They were destiny's children and not even time could tear them apart.

"You sure you can catch me?" she called out. "I'm not exactly a feather."

"Madam, cease your infernal talk and *jump!*" His tone was fierce, but the smile on his glorious face was anything but.

He loved her and she loved him back.

Life just didn't get any better than that.

She climbed to the top of the basket and jumped headlong into their future.

Epilogue

Christmas Day, three weeks later

Patrick Devane and Dakota Wylie paused at the top of the main staircase before joining their guests.

"The whole town is here," Dakota said, amazed by the crowd milling about. "I can't believe it."

"The news has spread, madam. They all wish to meet you."

"Funny how quickly things change. A few weeks ago they wouldn't let us in their houses."

"'Tis different now," he said, drawing her close to his side. "Your magic has worked wonders."

"It wasn't magic," she said, wrapping her arms about his waist. "It's you." News of the spy ring and Patrick's bravery had spread throughout the countryside. His ability to move with secrecy was gone, but he had gained the respect and admiration of the townspeople.

He arched a brow. "I am the same man I was, madam."

"You're a hero to them, Patrick. The stuff of legends." *The stuff of my dreams.*

He kissed her soundly. "'Tis you who made it happen."

She leaned her head against his shoulder and thought about the past three weeks. Cook had been marked as the traitor she was and carted off to jail. Ironically, Joseph and Will looked happier than ever, and their gratitude and loyalty to Patrick for keeping them in his employ knew no bounds. Dakota suspected that some of that gratitude had to do with the fact that Cook no longer ruled their lives with a wooden spoon.

Poor Molly had been so distraught over her part in her aunt's treachery that she had fled the area the night the balloon had returned for Dakota. Wherever she was, Dakota wished her Godspeed, for the young woman had been a pawn and not a willing participant.

His Excellency General Washington had personally arrested McDowell, and it was rumored McDowell would meet his Maker before a firing squad when the New Year dawned. The list Dakota had found her first night in Patrick's house had been a list Patrick had confiscated from the British. The names had represented men whose loyalty to the thirteen colonies was thought to be suspect. The Redcoats had planned to approach Patrick about winning the men over to the side of the king. Rutledge and Blakelee had been on that list; Benedict Arnold had not.

So much for the best-laid plans.

It warmed her heart to know Andrew McVie had indeed fulfilled his destiny as the history books had reported, especially since she had played a major part in revealing that destiny to him. Zane Rutledge and Josiah Blakelee had been seconds away from death at the end of a British rope when Andrew had managed to save them.

One week later Shannon and Andrew had been married at the First Presbyterian Church of Franklin Ridge. Dakota didn't need psychic abilities to know their future was as golden as their auras.

"Papa! Dakota!" Abigail appeared at the foot of the stairs. "Reverend Wilcox says it's time to start!"

Patrick lifted Dakota's chin with the tip of his index finger.

"You have sacrificed much to be with me, Dakota Wylie," he said, his eyes filled with love. "I will never give you reason to regret your decision."

"I know that," she whispered.

"Second sight?" he asked, kissing her mouth.

"No." She placed his hand over her heart. "Some things a woman just knows."

"Hurry!" Abby cried, rushing up the stairs to the landing. "Aunt Shannon and Aunt Emilie say they'll come up here and drag you, Mama, if you don't hurry."

Mama. Dakota's heart did a little tap dance.

"You're crying," Abby said, eyeing her.

Dakota bent and hugged her daughter. "Only because I'm happy."

"That's silly," Abby said, smoothing Lucy's yarn hair.

"Just you wait until you're grown up," Dakota said, chucking her under the chin. "I bet you'll cry on your wedding day, too."

And so it was time.

Harpsichord music drifted toward them from the front parlor. A line of Continental soldiers formed an honor guard in the hallway. People she didn't recognize swarmed about, eagerly vying for a glimpse of Patrick Devane and his bride-to-be. But there, at the foot of the stairs, were the friends who would share the adventure with her. Emilie and Zane. Shannon and Andrew. Rebekah and Josiah. The friends with whom she would share her life.

"Madam." Patrick sounded anxious, appealingly vulnerable. She had never loved him more than she did at that moment. "'Tis time we were wed."

"'Tis time," she said softly.

Abby stopped them. "These are for you." A pair of dangly silver earrings glittered in her small palm.

They were the earrings Ginny had been wearing the night Dakota made the decision to stay.

She slid the earring wires into her lobes and gave her head a shake. "Thanks, Ma," she whispered.

Next to her Patrick started with surprise and placed a hand against his left cheek.

"Patrick?"

"It is not possible," he said, eyes wide with surprise, "but I believe someone kissed my cheek."

Welcome to the family, Patrick.

"Did you hear that?" he asked Dakota.

Dakota and Abby looked at each other and laughed.

"That's Grandmama Ginny," Abby said.

"My mother," Dakota said. "You'll be hearing a lot from her."

Patrick nodded as if the explanation made perfect sense. "Whatever you say, madam." Life with Dakota Wylie would never be dull.

She had an eighteenth-century husband and daughter to love and cherish, and her twentieth century to make her crazy…and to keep her sane. And as if that weren't enough she had friends from both centuries to share the joys and sorrows that life sent her way. Somehow she'd stumbled into the best of both worlds and she wasn't about to let go.

Dakota slipped her left arm through Patrick's, then took Abby's hand in her right.

It was going to be a wonderful life.

She could feel it in her bones.